Heliotrope

Palmer Pickering

Published by Mythology Press

HELIOTROPE

Copyright © 2022 Barbara Palmer Pickering

ISBN 978-1-7325688-3-9 (Trade Paperback - Amazon)
ISBN 978-1-7325688-9-1 (Trade Paperback - Ingram)

FIC009000 **FICTION** / Fantasy / General
FIC009100 **FICTION** / Fantasy / Action & Adventure
FIC009020 **FICTION** / Fantasy / Epic

Cover art and design by Dusan Markovic at www.markovicdusan.com
Interior design and layout by Gretchen Dorris at www.inktobook.com
Maps by Melissa Stevens at www.theillustratedauthor.com
Coin art by Nathan Hansen at www.nathanhansenillustration.com
Title page art by Aksol. Part art by Skalapendra (horse), Luka (falcon), and Dusan Markovic (griffin). Epilogue art by Gurjigur.

MYTHOLOGY
→P R E S S←

Published by Mythology Press
www.mythologypress.com

Revised edition. This edition includes minor revisions to the Epilogue, as of the fourth printing.

10 9 8 7 6 5 4

Dedicated to my mother, Marjorie D. Palmer,
for teaching me the love of reading.

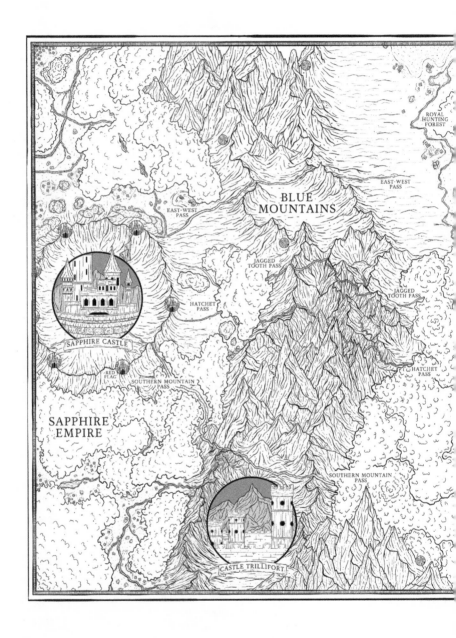

ROYAL
HUNTING
FOREST

EAST-WEST
PASS

BLUE
MOUNTAINS

EAST-WEST
PASS

JAGGED
TOOTH PASS

JAGGED
TOOTH PASS

HATCHET
PASS

HATCHET
PASS

SAPPHIRE CASTLE

RED
FLAG

SOUTHERN MOUNTAIN
PASS

SAPPHIRE
EMPIRE

SOUTHERN MOUNTAIN
PASS

CASTLE TRILLIFORT

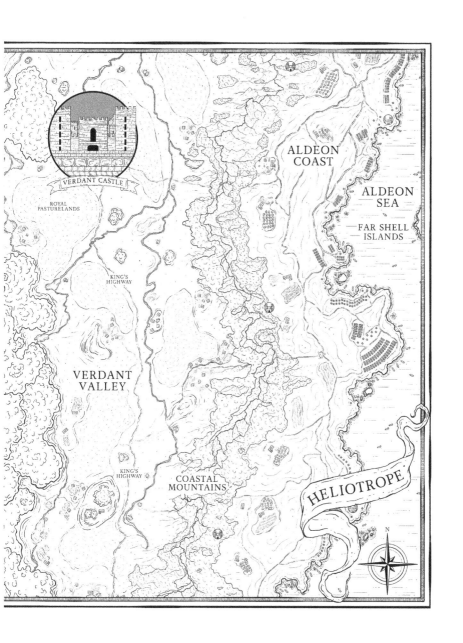

VERDANT CASTLE

ROYAL
PASTURELANDS

KING'S
HIGHWAY

VERDANT
VALLEY

KING'S
HIGHWAY

COASTAL
MOUNTAINS

ALDEON
COAST

ALDEON
SEA

FAR SHELL
ISLANDS

HELIOTROPE

N

Coin

- Gold Lion – 1,000 bits
- Silver Owl – 100 bits
- Silver Bit – 25 bits
- Bronze Bit – 5 bits
- Copper Bit – 1 bit

TABLE OF CONTENTS

PART ONE

VERDANT VALLEY

1

THE PEAR TREE

Teleo's knees hurt as he knelt on the queen's private balcony to set the tiles of his pear tree mosaic. Not even the square of saddle leather Teleo knelt on made his work comfortable, but kneeling was the only way he could properly lay the hundreds of tesserae that fit together like a puzzle. Perfectly carved jade leaves hung from tiger-eye branches, mirroring the living pear tree that hung over the second story marble railing.

Teleo had been hired for the job because he was a fine craftsman—and he kept to himself. He was too old to concern himself with court politics. He could feel his age in his back, or maybe he had gotten lazy with his sword practice. He vowed to himself that he would start practicing again with renewed vigor and dedication after the mosaic was finished. But for now he would enjoy his last days in the peaceful retreat of the Royal Garden, an enclosed courtyard where his ancestors, the Mages of long ago, had once meditated and conducted their spiritual practice. His father had told him that this compound had been their monastery, back in the olden days when Mages held a place in

3

the royal court, before magic was outlawed and the Mages were killed or driven off to the small villages and mountain kingdoms where people still believed in the ancient ways.

Teleo worked until dusk, laying the dozen pear-shaped tiles, each gold fruit as big as his hand and a quarter-inch thick. Teleo had fashioned them in the castle's masonry workshop, pounding together two hundred and fifty sheets of gold leaf per tile. Each tile was a fortune in itself. They had been the queen's idea. A king's squire had delivered the gold leaf, and a guard was posted at the workshop day and night. It had taken Teleo several days to make all the pears. The real tree hanging over the balcony was thick with branches filled with clusters of small green fruit, which Teleo would have thinned out by now. In late summer, the fruit would be heavy and copper-yellow, like those in his mosaic.

He sat back on his heels and asked into the air, "What do you think?"

The only reply was the chirping of finches as they flitted about and foraged down below. Otherwise, the courtyard was silent, as though holding its breath.

Teleo slowly scanned the shadows of the deepening dusk and soon found what he was looking for. Two unmistakable eyes glinted from above the terrace's white marble balustrade. The pear tree's branches hid most of the youngest prince, thirteen-year-old Kaspar, who had been secretly watching Teleo for the many days it had taken him to prepare the good-sized terrace and lay the mosaic. Teleo had not let on that he was aware of the prince's presence. He rather enjoyed the company, and having an audience made him work with precision and efficiency, which he needed more of in his life these days. He had grown sloppy during his years of retirement from the King's Army.

The younger men went to the borders now, leaving the old-sters behind to stir kettles of boar stew, train the young horses, and teach the boys to be soldiers. Teleo had retired to his small farm to raise his crops and animals and work his stonemason's craft, like his father before him. Teleo had employed his masonry trade over the years—to earn a living between war campaigns and during his quest to find his son—whenever he was short on coin. He liked working with stone. It was solid and quiet and soothed his mind.

His favorite thing was creating mosaics, immersing himself in the colors and textures of various stones, semi-precious gems, shells, or whatever materials his art called for. He enjoyed the meticulous work of chiseling and shaping pieces of stone into tesserae—tiles for his mosaics—a process that required focus and kept his wayward thoughts and worries at bay. The local Verdant Valley stone was granite: beige, red, and brown. White marble, including pale pink varieties, and various shades of blue argillite came from the Blue Mountains. Red, green, and purple granites were from the Aldeon Coast.

Teleo normally made the two-hour wagon ride from his farm to the castle market on Sundays to sell his creations. Some people paid handsomely for such things. One day, the queen had visited the market, creating a huge fuss with her entourage and causing the merchants to fall over themselves in a fawning effort to draw her attention. Teleo had stood behind his small table and watched. She had approached him, a glimmer of recognition lighting her eyes. She had examined his work and purchased a small tile depicting an owl. A week later, one of her assistants had approached him at the market with a request from the queen to commission a mosaic floor for her terrace.

But this young one—the prince who stared with unblinking eyes, knowing he had been detected—was never seen outside the confines of the Royal Palace or the king's private stables and hunting grounds, even on the rare occasions when the prince's two older brothers were allowed to compete in the tournaments with boys from high-ranking families. It was said the youngest prince was frail and sickly. Teleo did not think a frail and sickly boy could sneak his way nearly undetected every morning at dawn when Teleo arrived, climb a tree silently as a snake, and sit and watch Teleo, motionless for hours at a time. Every day, Teleo tracked the whispers of movement as the youth stealthily descended when the sun climbed high above the rooftops and the Royal Palace bustled with its daily routine. The prince returned again mid-afternoons when the palace quieted for tea, then stayed on his branch until the supper pots clanged from the kitchens, announcing that the evening meal was being served.

"What do you think?" Teleo repeated in a soft voice. "Is the tree done?"

The boy was not going to answer his question, although clearly it had been directed at him. Teleo would not have answered as a thirteen-year-old either. Perhaps by not moving, Prince Kaspar hoped he would blend into the branches and Teleo would think he had been imagining things.

Teleo rose stiffly to his feet, holding the small of his back. Sacks of dusty mortar sat stacked against the polished parapet, and a fine coating of dust covered the marble tiles that edged the terrace. The only thing remaining to be done was the base of the tree, where he had laid roots of tiger-eye. He had only to fill in the gaps between the roots with shaped bits of marble tile and replace the square tiles along the lower border of the mosaic to finish things off.

That was work for tomorrow. He dusted off his knees and climbed down the ladder they had set up for him so he would not have to tread through the queen's private chambers to access the terrace. He strode across the courtyard and through the stone tunnel archway to the north gate, where his friend Vigo, who had retired from the King's Army around the same time he had, greeted him from his guard post and wished him a good night.

———————◆———————

The dawn sky gleamed peach and gold as Teleo climbed the ladder to the queen's balcony. He was a little late this morning, having drunk one too many mugs of mead the night before. The prince was already on his perch. A fine jasmine scent gave him away—the queen's favorite soap, which the village women competed in making for the royal family, jealously trying to win the queen's business.

Teleo ignored Prince Kaspar, as usual, then took the straw broom and began to sweep the dust away from the tiger-eye roots in preparation for laying the filler pieces of marble. A glint among the roots made him stoop for a closer look. He picked up the chunk of stone and saw that it was a small mosaic of a bird, true to the size of the tiny finches that fed in the Royal Garden. It was a detailed mosaic made with several small pieces of gray slate, with smaller bits of mother-of-pearl to accent the wing feathers and two tiny bits of amber for eyes, all pressed carefully into a little block of white mortar. Teleo looked up at the tree, searching for the eyes of the prince. All he saw were leaves, but he could feel the boy's presence, watching him.

"Lovely," Teleo said, loud enough for the prince to hear. "I believe a flock of amber-eyed finches wants to feed at the roots of the jade and gold pear tree." Teleo could almost feel the delight of the prince vibrating through the air. Or perhaps it was Teleo's imagination. Nonetheless, Teleo climbed over the balustrade and down the ladder, startling a flock of the small birds as he picked through bits of mother-of-pearl mixed in with the blue pebbles that served as a pathway through the gardens, finding just the right pieces. Chips of gray slate formed the bed of the goldfish pond in a corner of the courtyard, and Teleo submerged his hand into the cold water and brought up a fistful of the small, flat stones, adding them to his stash.

He spent much of the day fashioning a dozen slate and mother-of-pearl finches, imitating the prince's design, and set them among the roots of the jade tree, as if they were foraging. He admired the lifelike finches, pleased with the spirit they added to the mosaic. The only things left were the birds' eyes—little white holes staring up at him—waiting for him to find bits of amber. He would buy some at the Sunday market from one of the bead and gem sellers. In the meantime, he filled the remaining gaps between the roots with marble. He still needed to replace the border tiles, but that could wait for tomorrow. The sun was setting and Prince Kaspar had already crept off for supper.

The following morning, Teleo knelt with delight at the lower border of the terrace. The mosaic finches all had eyes of amber gazing up at him, as though they had come to life overnight. Above the birds, two new diamond-shaped tiles shone blue in the dawn light. They each featured a thin blue shard of shell and four blue shell wings, perfectly depicting the dragonflies that zoomed through the courtyard during sunny afternoons. Teleo let out a low chuckle. The prince had outdone himself. Teleo peered into the tree. He could not see the prince nor smell the jasmine soap—he was a teenage boy after all, and it was awfully early for a bath—but Teleo was sure he would not miss observing his reaction.

Teleo rubbed his chin, scruffy with two days' growth. To properly place the dragonflies, he would need to chisel away two of the small diamond-shaped pieces of blue argillite he had laid to mimic a shimmering sky. He found two suitable spots in the stone sky and chipped away the mortar and argillite, impressed that the prince had thought to set the dragonflies into the same shape as the stones. Teleo mixed the mortar and laid them in, then stepped back to admire the prince's additions.

"Marvelous," Teleo said, giving the hidden prince a slight bow.

He finished laying the lower border tiles, smoothed on a final layer of grout, and then left the terrace to find some food for himself and allow the boy to slip away undetected.

***

The next day, Teleo checked the new tiles and grout. Everything had set properly. He let it cure for another day and then returned the following morning, spending the next few hours on his knees sanding the grout and giving the mosaic a final polish. Finally, he stood back and observed his work. The slate and shell finches were happily pecking among the pear tree's roots, and the shell dragonflies glinted in the sunlight. Teleo turned his attention to the real pear tree hanging over the balustrade but did not detect the prince. It was midday and Prince Kaspar was normally gone at this time—he must have slipped away while Teleo was preoccupied with his work.

Teleo shouldered the leftover sacks of mortar down the ladder and out to the wagon he had parked outside the north garden gate. He clicked his tongue at his horses, who nickered back at him. After loading his supplies, he meticulously swept the terrace and passed a polishing cloth over it one last time, leaving the new mosaic shining. The jade leaves glistened, the tiger-eye bark and roots shimmered, and the gold pears glowed warmly. But it was the finches and dragonflies that made him smile.

He turned to a rustle in the doorway. Queen Eleanor held her voluminous silk skirts off the floor and joined him on the terrace. She was a beautiful woman, a decade younger than his forty-five years, with hints of gray hair starting to streak through the golden-brown locks ornately twisted atop her head. He had been away at war during most of her years as a young woman, but he remembered her vividly as a child. His father had sent him to work at the castle as a teenager, hoping it would improve his social standing, and to train for war with other boys his age. One of his duties as a boy of lower birth had been to care for the horses of visiting nobility. He recalled several times taking hold of the future queen's father's horses as her family rolled up in their carriage for royal visits, no doubt planting the seeds of the marriage. He could still see the young girl with bouncy blond curls jumping down from the carriage and offering the horses bits of carrot and apple before scampering off to join her mother and sisters. Teleo was not sure if the queen remembered him from those days, but he liked to think that she did. Joy brightened her face as she regarded the mosaic.

She clasped her hands together and turned her golden-brown eyes to him. "Oh, Teleo Stonemason, it is indeed exquisite! Just as I knew it would be. And those birds and dragonflies—what a magical touch!"

He bowed his head in respect, wondering if he should reveal their true creator. He decided to keep the prince's secret safe. Or perhaps the queen had been in on it. "They do add welcome life to the scene," he said, returning her smile.

"You must do more masonry work on the grounds," she said, lacing her fingers together. "The place is falling into disrepair. I noticed the stones at the center of the training yard are loose and the young men trip over them. Not a good thing with a sword in their hands."

Teleo nodded. He had noticed the loose stones as well but did not point out that he thought they were good practice for the battlefield, which was always rough and messy. If a soldier did not have the agility to avoid a turned ankle on a stony field or bombarded castle, he would never survive.

"Say you will," she said. "And could you make it lovely as well? And can you start right away, while the weather is fine?" Her eyes shone hopefully, waiting for his response.

"Lovely?" he repeated. He wasn't sure how he could make cobblestones lovely, but he inclined his head dutifully. "As you wish. I shall begin tomorrow."

"Wonderful," she said with a little clap of her hands. "I will ask the castellan to inform the Master of Arms straight away."

Teleo tried to hide his displeasure at the mention of the Master of Arms. Gerik Stagga had assumed the role Teleo should have held, if skill and merit mattered more than who one's father was.

The queen disappeared inside and returned with a small purple velvet sack and placed it in his palm. "As we agreed for the pear tree mosaic," she said. "Plus half up front for the training yard work. I'll pay the rest when it is completed." The bag weighed heavily in his hand, and he bowed his head in thanks. She chatted with Teleo about the weather, then retreated to her chambers.

After she left, he opened the purple bag and bit his lip as gold glinted up at him. He quickly counted the coins. Six Gold Lions and ten Silver Owls. It was more coin than he normally made in an entire year. He pocketed the velvet bag, feeling giddy at his good fortune.

He gazed down at the jade and gold pear tree one last time, happy with the finished piece. It was time to leave its care in the hands of the queen. He climbed down the ladder, and as he cast a parting glance around the idyllic garden, he noted a thin layer of mortar dust coating the bushes below the balcony. He frowned and fetched his broom.

He shook the branches gently, wiping them off with a rag, and then swept under them. Grimy stonework emerged from where it had been hidden by sprawling undergrowth and dead leaves. He got on his knees and reached underneath the shrubs, wiping at the stones with the rag and revealing colored paving stones that formed the perimeter of a circle. He looked behind him. At the center of the courtyard stood a head-high bronze urn on a round, white stone. The stones framing the center circle formed a ten-pointed star. The long triangular rays were pure black, of a stone he did not recognize, whereas the rest of the complex pattern extending from the center was made of various shades of local and imported stone: white, tan, vermilion, brown, gray, cobalt, turquoise, and purple. Teleo had assumed the ten-pointed star had been set there to accentuate the urn. Now that he observed it more closely, the urn was a modern piece, probably commissioned by the queen, who loved such things. But the stone star was old. Very old.

Teleo's pulse raced as he began to suspect the nature of the stones he knelt upon. He got to his feet, trotted to the guardroom off the arched entryway where he had stored his weapons, and retrieved his short sword. It was more than adequate. He had used it to clear a path through tangled forests many times.

"Vigo," he said, stepping out into the dim tunnel. "I need to prune some bushes." He held out his stubby sword.

Vigo turned from his post at the outer gate and lowered his eyebrows, scowling at Teleo for making him decide between following strict protocol against weapons on the grounds and granting a request from his former brother-at-arms. Vigo sighed in resignation. "Go ahead."

Teleo returned to the dense undergrowth, cutting away dead lower branches and trimming vines that had crept out over the paving stones during the spring rains and warm days of early summer. The groundskeepers no doubt had been too busy tending the public yards for the endless string of tourneys and the recent Summer Solstice Festival to find time to manicure the royal family's private garden. Teleo trimmed around the edges of the large paved circle and brushed away leaves and dirt from the stonework radiating out from the central star. The polished stones, worn smooth with age, caught the sun and reflected a soft glow into the yard. The sweeping had revealed a complex, multi-colored mosaic made up of concentric rings of triangles, diamonds, and petals laid out in such a way as to create an optical illusion of a slowly spinning vortex. Goosebumps rose on his arms.

He had found a Heliotrope.

Teleo stared in wonder at the ancient stone circle where Mages of old had meditated and practiced the sword. His father had loved to speculate about Heliotropes, and the old tales of magic circles and battles with Mages flying through the air were Teleo's favorite bedtime stories. His father had given him an old scroll, passed down from his great-grandfather, which showed a Mage dancing the sword in the center of a star-patterned yard just like this one. But Teleo had never seen one in real life. He gazed, mesmerized, at the subtly undulating circle.

He longed to have lived in the days when Mages were free to pursue their practice. Wielding a sword back then was a high art and took decades of intense training to master. Teleo scanned the palace walls enclosing the courtyard and found the Focal Point for the sun. It was a round, glassless window set high atop the eastern wall. Clear blue sky formed a perfect circle through it. On the morning of the Summer Solstice, the rising sun would fit perfectly within the round window, framing a cylindrical shaft of sunlight that would fall upon the courtyard floor, illuminating the center stone. It was said that if you danced the sword in a Heliotrope while the shaft of Summer Solstice light shone upon you, you would be forever blessed in battle. Teleo had not known a Heliotrope existed on these grounds or he would have sought it out long ago.

He glanced around at the shadowed, pillar-lined porticos set along the interior walls of the ground floor of the palace, surrounding the courtyard and largely hidden behind fruit trees and a thick screen of flowering vines. Above the porticos stood evenly spaced balconies that marked the royal bedchambers, partially obscured by tree branches. All was quiet. It was mid-afternoon. Teatime. Most everyone was either lounging with family in sitting rooms or napping. Teleo grasped the tall urn and pushed on it, loosening it from where it stood in the center of the Heliotrope. Teleo carefully rolled it on its base and set it at the edge of the yard. The urn had left a ring of grime on the white, translucent disk at the center of the star pattern. He knelt and wiped it clean with a rag and ran his palms over the cool, smooth stone. He then stood up and stepped gingerly onto it. Generations of Mages had stood in this very spot, dancing with their swords, absorbing the sacred rays of the Summer Solstice sun, becoming infused with its magic.

Teleo held up his short sword. A clunky weapon—not a fine, thousand-fold blade of the Mages. He crouched into a practice form. It was not nearly as graceful a dance as he imagined the Mages must have done, but it was what he knew. Strike. Block. Thrust. Circle. Slash. He stopped the blade in mid-air. What was he doing, dancing around in the Royal Garden wielding a sword? He stashed the sword in the bushes and took his broom and held it with two hands, pretending it was his longsword. He couldn't get arrested for swinging a broomstick around. He strode to the center disk of the circle and swung the broomstick in figure eights, imagining he was dancing the sword, imagining he was a Mage of old, like his forebears. The magic ran in his blood, his father had told him, but Teleo suspected that magic was really only the mastery of something so difficult most people considered it impossible. Such mastery was gained by relentless will and stubborn repetition.

Teleo had never had the luxury of practicing the sword day and night like the Mages. When he was a youngster at the castle, he had done his daily drills with the other boys training for war and then headed over to the stables to tend the horses: mucking stalls, lugging sheaves of hay, and grooming the magnificent animals belonging to boys his age who had inherited a title and would not stoop so low as to brush a horse. Then he would stay up late into the night repairing harnesses or twisting fibers into rope.

He had accompanied the young lords on their hunts and was often called in after a long day of near misses and mounting frustration to deliver a crippling arrow to the prey—but not a deadly shot. His arrow would bring the prey to its knees so that the lords could deliver the final blow and claim the kill as their own. The lords rarely thanked or acknowledged him in any way, avoiding his eyes and bragging to the young women back at the castle how they had braved the ferocious animal, describing in gory detail how it had squealed and bled for them. Teleo would slip away to the kitchens and eat with the serving staff, preferring that to sitting at a table in the back of the hall and watching the prize animal be served to the lords while he was fed chicken or goat meat with the rest of the commoners.

He had often spent evenings in the kitchen playing cards with the servants and drinking ale. When the card games went very late, the older women and teenaged girls would shuffle in before the light of dawn, bleary-eyed, to bake the daily bread. Teleo would help them knead the mounds of dough with his toughened hands, gaining a limitless supply of fresh bread and sweetcakes for his efforts. He slipped into the kitchen between chores and helped carry barrels of ale, vats of pickled carrots and cucumbers, and goat and pig carcasses. He would help prepare the animals and impale them on spits, setting them over the hot coals for the thankful older women who ran the kitchens. He watched the cooks, learning which foods required which temperatures, what spices to use, how to preserve meats and vegetables—all the while being fed warm bread and butter or hot apple tarts and sausages, fresh from the stone ovens.

He reminisced about his youth while he pivoted on one foot, then the other, practicing his strokes with the broom handle, imagining it was a fine sword of folded steel glinting in the shaft of Summer Solstice sunlight. He left the center disk and danced several steps across the black rays and the outer rings of larger and larger tesserae to the edge of the ancient circle, where he danced along the Heliotrope's border, flushing a flock of finches that had been foraging. He held still, balancing on one foot, the broom handle raised. The finches dispersed in a flurry and several alighted on the pear tree. He switched feet and swung the broom in an arc in front of him and balanced again, holding his breath. A pair of finches fluttered into the air and one settled onto the tip of his broom handle. It was a tiny little bird, with gray and white feathers and amber eyes, reminding Teleo of how well the prince had captured its likeness with stones and shells.

The bird flitted away and perched on a pear tree branch. At that moment, Teleo spotted the gleam of two eyes watching him. The prince was crouched at the base of the tree, his brown tunic and cap blending in with its shadowed trunk. Their eyes locked. There was no avoiding the fact that he had been spotted this time. Prince Kaspar slowly rose to standing, his thin form taller than Teleo had expected. The young prince stretched out his arm and extended his index finger at him. Teleo was taken aback, afraid that the prince was upset with him for detecting his hiding place, when a blue dragonfly landed on the tip of the prince's finger. Teleo suppressed a laugh of relief and delight, meeting the prince's eyes again, which glittered at him for a moment before returning to the blue jewel perched on his fingertip. As quickly as it had alighted, the dragonfly flew away, darting back and forth in the sunshine above the sacred circle.

"Kaspari."

A woman's voice cut through the silence of the yard, and both Teleo and the prince turned to the servant who was bustling along the shell-and-pebble pathway. The youth stepped out from the shadows.

"What ... what ... what happened to the urn?" the servant asked Teleo crossly, her face flushing a deep red. "Kaspar, what are you doing out here? Come with me."

"I was ... sweeping," Teleo said.

"Oh. It's you, Teleo. I suppose you were trying to sneak into the kitchen to steal some sweetcakes," the Queen's Lady said with a smirk, reaching out her hand to the prince.

"Oh. Hi, Gwen," Teleo said, a smile spreading across his face. "I was just cleaning up. I finished the queen's mosaic." He glanced towards the queen's balcony and then back at his old friend who still wore the same childlike grin, even though time had aged her brown hair with sprinkles of gray. "I never had to steal sweetcakes. You always gave them to me."

"Funny how history rewrites itself," she said, laughing. "How have you been? The queen loves her terrace."

"I'm glad. I've been well, thanks. Growing older."

"Aren't we all? Come now, Kaspar. Your mother is looking for you." Gwen turned and herded the prince in front of her. The boy skipped down the pathway, and the Queen's Lady hurried after him.

Teleo stared after the prince. *Kaspari.* Gwen had called the youth Kaspari. A girl's name. He examined the prince's narrow hips and long legs, graceful wrists, and bouncing brown curls that had escaped the cap as the youngster skipped across the courtyard and disappeared into the dimness of the portico. The form that Teleo had assumed was the lanky body of an awkward thirteen-year-old boy was obviously the lithe, graceful form of a budding young woman.

Of course. It all made sense now. Why the prince was so rarely seen in public. Sheltered in the privacy of the royal chambers with the excuse of chronic illness. Leaving the castle grounds only to ride horses or practice archery with her family in their private fields and forest. But why did they hide her gender, telling the world *she* was a *he?* Was it because they wanted another prince in succession? She would be third in line, with two older brothers. Females had taken the throne before, but always by force. If there were no sons, the throne was given by tradition to the closest male relative from the king's side. Historically, daughters took over only when there were no living male relatives among the king's father's direct descendants, and only if the community rallied to a princess's defense against challengers. Kaspari had no uncles or male cousins on her father's side—but who would fight for her? No one even knew the princess existed.

The likelihood of both her older brothers dying was low. Even if Prince Kaspar did ascend to the throne at some point, the trick of keeping up the guise as a male for an entire lifetime while wearing the crown seemed nearly impossible. Teleo searched for another reason.

The Staggas.

Everyone knew the Stagga family desperately wanted one of their sons married into the royal family. The eldest son was Gerik. Teleo scowled. Gerik was forty-five years old, like Teleo.

But unlike Teleo, Gerik had never married. Gerik was a rough man—battle-hardened, but with a prestigious post at the castle as the Master of Arms. Gerik's father, Henrik, was the Royal Merchant, Senior Trade Advisor to King Elke. On top of that, the Staggas were very wealthy. They owned most of the best vineyards in the hills overlooking the northeastern coastlands, as well as vast sugar cane fields in the southeast, on the flatlands bordering the Aldeon Sea. The former Aldeon Coastal Kingdom had been absorbed into the Verdant Valley Kingdom generations ago, but the noble families there still had royal aspirations. The Stagga family also boasted a fleet of fast seafaring ships, which brought in fish and exotic goods from the Far Shell Islands and protected the coast from pirates and Far Shell marauders. Gerik would likely have been promised to a royal daughter, if there had been one.

Teleo knit his eyebrows together. It was a risky maneuver to lie about her gender. If Teleo were King, he would not want his daughter to wed such a mean-spirited man as Gerik but might be forced to by custom. Maybe King Elke and Queen Eleanor had dreamt up this ruse, waiting until Gerik got married off to some other noblewoman before revealing Kaspari's true nature. When Gerik had persisted in his bachelorhood, they had probably hoped he would get killed in battle—but no such luck. The next best option was to marry her off to someone else and suffer the political fallout afterwards. Teleo guessed that must be their plan, waiting until she turned fifteen, as tradition dictated. That would explain why the royal family was so private. No one was allowed into the residential wing of the palace or in the Royal Stables or Royal Hunting Forest without invitation. The royal family had a separate kitchen and a dedicated household staff. The children were tutored in their academic studies within the confines of the palace, and they were trained in weaponry and horsemanship by full-time instructors who did not teach anyone else. Still, there would be bad blood once her true identity and the slight to the Stagga family became known. It was a brazen move, and Teleo's respect for King Elke and Queen Eleanor heightened.

Teleo leaned on the broom and gazed at the stonework of the garden's Heliotrope. He would love to spend a couple of days giving the stones a proper polish to bring out their full luster, but decided it was best to let the circle's power remain obscured by neglect.

He stood transfixed by the optical illusion of movement and tried to determine how the pattern made the stones appear as though they were flowing in a vortex. Unable to decipher the secret of the design, he rolled the urn back to the center of the circle and gazed up at the Focal Point window. The Summer Solstice had come and gone several days ago. He had taken the holiday off and celebrated with his village at their small Solstice Festival, drinking mead and staying up all night, dancing and waiting for the dawn—followed by a day of feasting. It was a propitious day to be born or to seed a child. It was also thought to be a lucky day for battle. He had spent many a Summer Solstice creeping through pre-dawn forests to surprise the enemy, who were also on the prowl, leading to a long day of blood and regret. But those days were gone, thankfully.

It would be almost an entire year until the next Summer Solstice. He would need to find an excuse to visit this Mage's circle on that auspicious morning and dance in the blessed beam of light. In the meantime, his job was done and he had no further business in the Royal Garden.

He gave the Heliotrope one final sweep and brushed a few lingering specks of mortar dust from the undergrowth. Satisfied that the garden was in good order, he retrieved his short sword from the bushes and went to the guardroom, where he buckled on his weapons waist belt along with his masonry tool belt, strapped his short sword across his back, and took a drink from his leather waterskin. At the gate, he looked Vigo in the eye, trying to discern if his friend knew the royal family's secret of the princess in disguise. He could not read the man, who was too professional to let on about a thing of such huge import, even to his old friend Teleo. He nodded and wished Vigo a good day.

2

THE TRAINING YARD

Teleo watched from the shadow of the training yard gate as Gerik drilled the fourteen-year-olds. Teleo should have had that job, and they both knew it. Teleo was renowned on the battlefield, but Gerik had the family name. They avoided each other's eyes, but Gerik knew he was there—Teleo could tell from the way Gerik's shoulders hunched over in a knot of muscles and how he yelled louder at the boys.

Teleo was over the disappointment at being passed over for the prestigious post of Master of Arms. He liked his small farm—the peaceful fields, the simple life. He had no desire to be in the thick of court politics, living at the castle as employees needed to do. If he wasn't careful, the queen might get too dependent on his masonry skills, and he would need to live at the castle in order to start work early and end late as he had been doing during the terrace project. While he was there, he slept in the lower stables' lofts with the other temporary laborers and stable hands.

It had been pleasant spending time in the privacy of the queen's terrace and garden but laying stones in Gerik's yard was not where he wanted to be. He dreaded the prospect of encountering the man on a daily basis. Teleo would have to make the repairs quickly so that he could escape back home in time to harvest his apples and almonds.

Teleo watched Gerik demonstrate a block and thrust as he instructed the young men on the importance of offense as the best defense. Gerik was not a graceful creature but had a strong arm and had trained well in sword fighting—and he had killed his share of men in battle. Teleo observed four pairs of boys moving up and down the yard, forward and backward, facing off with heavy wooden swords. Gerik had taught them the basics, but like Gerik, they were depending too much on brute force and not enough on agility. After a few passes, Gerik demonstrated again, pairing up with the largest trainee in the group. He beat back the teenager with a bit more force than was necessary, knocking the boy's wooden sword to the ground. The boy bent over and held his forearm in pain. Gerik handed him his sword with a frown.

"You're not hurt," Gerik said gruffly. "Again!" he called to the group, and they sparred, one of each pair pressing forward while the other backed up.

Teleo waited until the training session was over and then approached Gerik as the boys shuffled out of the yard.

"Hey, Gerik."

"What're you doing here?" Gerik planted his feet in a wide stance and crossed his thick arms over his chest. His graying beard was neatly trimmed, but a straight gap in his facial hair betrayed the scar he'd gotten from the butt of an axe to the face. Teleo had been on the field that day and helped kill the man who'd attacked him. He had handed Gerik the axe as a battle prize. Gerik had been almost nice to Teleo afterwards, but that debt of gratitude had long since been forgotten. Gerik was now Master of Arms and looked the part, wearing a fine steel cuirass that had not seen a day of battle and knee-high boots polished to a shiny black. Teleo glanced down at his workman's clothing—roughspun linen, gray with mortar dust and patched in places.

"The queen wants me to fix the stones in the yard," Teleo said, forcing himself to give Gerik a small bow of respect.

"Oh, yeah, the castellan's squire told me about that," Gerik said. "We end around this time every day and start at nine in the morning. You can't interrupt our training."

"I understand. I'll stay out of your way," Teleo said, bowing again.

Gerik grunted and left the yard without a parting word. He had never been a friendly sort, particularly to those of a lower station. While Teleo had spent his days during the war out on the battlefield, Gerik had spent half the time hanging out with the noblemen, watching the skirmishes from the hillsides and only riding in for the large battles where they could claim glory, usually after the regular soldiers had assured victory. Teleo didn't blame them for wanting to save their own hides, but he resented them taking credit for battles won by others. But that's how it was in the Verdant Valley Kingdom, and Teleo had long since accepted that life was not fair—not by any measure.

The yard was empty now, and quiet. The flagstones were worn smooth with age, brought in from the granite quarries centuries ago. The stones around the perimeter of the yard were as wide as a man is tall, but closer to the center, the stones grew smaller and smaller. Teleo tried to discern what the original pattern had been so that he could match it.

He studied the yard, sketching the design into his workbook as best he could and then taking measurements of the various stones. There were more sizes and shapes than he had originally thought, particularly the intricate pattern at the center of the yard, which formed a large inner ring that measured several paces in diameter. That was the section the queen had described to him as needing repair. He slowly walked the perimeter of what remained of the inner circle, and the hairs on the back of his neck stood on end. Teleo stared, seeing it clearly for the first time. It was another Heliotrope. Old and broken, its magical order disturbed and neglected, but a Heliotrope nonetheless.

The round white center stone was fractured into several pieces, some of them missing. It measured an arm span across, twice as big as the smaller version in the Royal Garden, but was beyond repair. Only two of the star's ten black rays were intact, partially buried under years of dirt. Other rays were shattered or missing entirely. In the surrounding concentric rings, patches of dirt filled gaps where stones once had been. Expertly carved tesserae had been replaced by round river rocks, completely disrupting the energy flow of the original design. The Heliotrope pattern, or what was left of it, was identical to that in the queen's garden, only larger in scale—and the optical illusion of movement had been broken. He searched the eastern wall for the Focal Point and found the round glassless window in a raised arc of stone. How had he never recognized it as a Focal Point before? He had been in this yard hundreds of times. He had always assumed it was a hole for archers, or to dump vats of hot oil down onto the heads of unlucky attackers.

Teleo scaled the narrow stairs that led up to the top of the wall and stepped out onto the battlements. Warm summer air gusted up from the valley below as he surveyed the panorama. Cultivated fields spread out like a green-and-brown patchwork quilt to the east, forest and craggy rocks stretched to the north, more forest spanned the western flank and up into the foothills, and grazing land rolled in gentle folds to the south, fading into the distant hills and mountains in foggy hues of blues and grays.

He tried to detect his village beyond the grazing lands where fields and mixed forest dotted the southern landscape, but it was too far away. Turning back to the yard, he softened his gaze, trying to detect the pattern of the Mage's circle before age had marred it. The multitude of bad patch jobs, dirt gullies, and crumbled stone made Teleo shake his head, and he began to agree with the queen about the need to fix it.

Teleo gnawed at his lip. The prospect of repairing a Heliotrope both excited and intimidated him. Ancient stone masters had created these circles, and Teleo dared not claim to possess such skill. He would do his best, and no one but him would know the difference. Teleo sighed and rubbed his back, sore from bending over the queen's terrace. Now he would be dealing with heavier stone. Loading and unloading slabs would work his back muscles in a different way and he would be sore all over again. At least he would stay strong, even if he missed some of the summer farming season. His cousin's grown boys were happy for the extra work of tending his farm while he was away, as his cousin had done when Teleo had left on his quest to search for his son. Before that, he'd had his father to care for things. And his wife.

Teleo drew the fragrant valley air into his lungs and blew it out slowly, trying to release the memory of his wife, Bella-Mae. Her gray eyes. Her soft lips. He returned his attention to the training yard. From what was left of the Heliotrope, Teleo could make out portions of the diamonds and triangles that interlocked to form a complex star-like pattern—a star inside a star inside a star. Or was it rings of flower petals radiating out from the center? Form and order revealed itself and then shifted again as Teleo gazed at the stone mosaic. He tried ignoring its blemishes, straining to see it as it once had been. He rubbed the stubble on his chin. He wasn't sure he could exactly replicate the complicated design. It was a lot easier to create a work of art from scratch than it was to restore someone else's work. Particularly a work imbued with magic.

Such a large Heliotrope must have been a renowned power center in its day, its purpose long forgotten. The Mages of old had perished, their exploits left to legend. Still, it must impart some power to those practicing the sword on this once-sacred ground. The teenaged boys, they must get some benefit from it. Teleo must have gained something when he was a boy, practicing on the stones every day. Gerik must still be absorbing its power.

Teleo sneered. It was not right that such an arrogant man as Gerik should enjoy the power center of Teleo's ancestors, the Green Mages of the Verdant Valley. They were said to have been unbeatable in battle. Their swords were unbreakable. Their movements were like the wind; their swords struck like lightning. Teleo sighed. What he wouldn't do for one of the ancient swords.

The sun was dropping in the western sky by the time Teleo left the training yard. He would go to bed early and get up at dawn so he could spend the day at the stone yards. He returned to the stables and briefly exchanged pleasantries with the old groom, who was sitting out front in his wooden chair, enjoying the cool air of early evening. The man had been kind to him when Teleo had been a young lad working at the stables, teaching him how to keep the tack shiny as new for the noblemen and how to braid ivy and flowers into the horses' manes for when the noblewomen went out on their picnics. Now the groom was hard of hearing and hobbled around on stiff legs, but he kept the younger grooms on task and the horses healthy.

Teleo bid good night to the groom and took a lantern into the large stall that his two horses shared. They were his prized beauties. A matched pair of dapple grays, mother and son, as strong at pulling a wagon or plow as they were agile for hunting—able to clear felled trees and brooks with ease. When the horses were not pulling the wagon for him, he let them out behind the stables in the former moat, which now served as a long narrow paddock between the interior and exterior walls, separating the castle proper from the sprawling town that had built up around it. The groom had brought them inside, but Teleo was responsible for their feeding and grooming.

Teleo brought them fresh water and hay. "No oats till morning, Missy Daisy," he said, patting the mare's neck. She nuzzled at his shirt pocket. He took out the apple he had stashed for her, and she ate it from his palm.

The gelding preferred carrots and pushed his muzzle at Teleo's shoulder. "You are so spoiled," he said as he took the carrot from his other pocket and fed it to Benny. "Did you have a good day?"

Daisy tossed her head and Benny munched contentedly.

Teleo continued talking to the horses while he mucked their stall and brushed their coats. "I know, I need to exercise you more often. I'm sorry." They were such fine horses. Much too fine to be hauling wagonloads of hay and stone. Daisy was sired by Silver Moon, a great warhorse who had taken his uncle Brady into battle. His uncle, Teleo's mother's favorite little brother, had died from a sword to the gut, but the stallion had survived. Benny was Daisy's son, sired by another dapple-gray warhorse Teleo had found all the way down on the southern Aldeon Coast.

Teleo gave them each a parting pat and headed for the back corner of the stable where a ladder led to the small hayloft where he slept. The large black horse in the far stall snorted and shifted his hindquarters, flicking his tail. He was a mean horse, put out to pasture because no one could break him of biting and kicking. He had been given a stall because he had supposedly carried a cousin of the queen into battle during the war. The cousin had been killed. The horse had made it out alive, but had never been the same. No one wanted a crazy horse, but the old groom had taken pity on him and cared for him as much as the ornery gelding would allow.

The horse turned to face Teleo, giving him the stink eye. Teleo had always ignored him and the horse usually ignored him back, but today the beast was shifting in his stall and glaring at him.

"What's wrong with you, BlackJack?" Teleo asked. He was a massive warhorse, eighteen hands high and heavy around the girth. His coat was coarse and patchy, and his mane looked like it hadn't been brushed in months. He probably wouldn't let the groom near him and the old man had given up. Teleo peeked over the stall railing to see if maybe he had come up lame, but he was putting his weight on all four legs without favoring one. A patch of black in the hay caught Teleo's eye. His vision adjusted to the shadowy corner of the stall. Lying on the floor, partially covered in hay, was a raven-haired boy. The side of his face was swollen and purple.

"What did you do?" Teleo reprimanded the horse. He fetched a rope and quickly tied a loop and lassoed the horse around the neck, then tied the end of the rope to a hook on the facing wall outside the stall.

"There now, boy. Easy." The horse danced around nervously but deftly avoided stepping on the boy. Teleo took a switch that was leaning against the back wall, opened the stall door, and lightly tapped BlackJack's rear flank.

The horse left the stall, clomping his enormous hooves on the dirt floor and snorting.

"Stay there," he told the horse. Teleo slipped into the stall, closed the gate behind him, and knelt next to the boy. The lad was curled up on his side and his breathing was labored. The boy grunted and his eyes cracked open. He flinched at the sight of Teleo, then pushed himself back against the wooden wall and pulled his knees to his chest defensively.

"I'm not going to hurt you," Teleo said. He recognized the boy as the Hill orphan who lived behind the blacksmith's forge in an old tool shed. A boy brought back from the war: a common practice on both sides of the conflict, and one that pained Teleo's heart. Villages were often ransacked and the inhabitants killed. Young boys were sometimes kidnapped and taken back to be raised as slaves. His own son, Oren, had suffered such a fate, or so Teleo chose to believe. It was either that or Oren had been killed during the raids, along with his wife, Bella-Mae, and daughter, Abigail, even though no one had ever found his boy's remains. Teleo chose to believe he had been kidnapped and was still alive somewhere. Looking at the Hill boy brought up Teleo's guilt over abandoning his quest to find Oren. He would have been fourteen by now—about the same age as this boy. *Was* the same age. *Is.*

Teleo shook off his constant heartache and regarded the boy. Blood had matted his dark hair and dried on his ear and neck. "Let me take a look at that. Looks like you got a scalp wound," Teleo said. "They bleed a lot."

The boy eyed him warily as Teleo reached out and gently examined his head. He found the open gash, which was still seeping blood behind the right ear, even though the wound appeared to be several hours old. The orphan's skull did not seem to be injured, and judging by the way the boy moved, his spine was not injured, either. The bruises did not look to be from a horse's hooves, as Teleo had first thought. He suspected the boy had been beaten up. Probably by the young teenagers who trained under Gerik. They roamed around town in a pack, cocky and bellicose in their burgeoning adulthood.

He pressed on the boy's abdomen and kidney area. He was sore but not in excruciating pain. Teleo worked his way up the back of his ribcage, pressing gently on each rib, and then examined his chest. Based on the boy's reactions, two front ribs were cracked.

"You been coughing up blood?" Teleo asked.

"Only from my mouth," the boy mumbled.

"Let me see." Teleo gently pulled back the boy's swollen lips. The gums were bleeding and his two front teeth were chipped. Teleo pushed at them gently. They were loose, but Teleo did not think they would fall out. "They broke your teeth?"

The boy's eyes flashed with fear, and that was Teleo's answer. Teleo scowled. A fist would not have done that kind of damage. They must have used an implement, maybe the short wooden clubs the young men wore on their belts.

"What are you doing in here?" Teleo asked. "That horse will trample you. Did the boys throw you in here?"

The boy shook his head, avoiding looking Teleo in the face. "They're scared of him."

"Ah," Teleo said. "He protects you?"

The boy nodded and Teleo inspected him curiously. "You're good with horses, then?"

The boy tried to shrug but ended up clutching his ribcage and wincing instead. He had the shaggy black hair of the Hill people, large slanted brown eyes, honey-colored skin, and heavy bone structure.

Although the war was over between the Verdant Valley folk and the Sapphire Empire's Hill people, most Verdant Valley people still despised their longtime enemies. Teleo did not. This orphan was just a boy, the victim of a cruel practice that stabbed at Teleo's own heart. At least King Elke had brought an end to the violence and made a treaty with Cornwal, the latest emperor of the seven Hill Tribes and the fertile Sapphire Valley that lay beyond the Blue Mountains to the west. King Elke was opening up trade routes and his policies sparked bar brawls and created rifts between family members—those who hated the Hill people and loved war versus those who had had enough of hatred and bloodshed and just wanted to raise their crops and children in peace. The Royal Advisors were divided on the issue as well, if castle gossip could be believed. King Elke constantly had to defend his precarious peace plan while his soldiers continued to prepare for war as though they did not know how else to live. Young men were still going off to defend the border and practice their sword fighting skills in the small skirmishes that randomly flared up with bands of brigands or the independent mountain tribes, or the occasional Sapphire unit sent to harass the border outposts. Teleo was glad he didn't have to worry about fighting anymore.

Teleo left the stall and raised a bucket of water from the well out back, found a clean cloth and soap, and returned to the stall. The boy let him clean his face and scalp wound. "You need a couple of stitches," Teleo said. "I can do that for you if you want. Your hair will cover it up, so no one will see my sloppy work," he joked.

The boy gave him a half-smile, almost meeting his eyes. "Okay."

Teleo got a needle and a disinfecting ointment from the medical supply cabinet in the grooming yard. He snipped a tail hair from Daisy for the sutures and soaked it in a mug of boiling water he got from the old groom's teakettle, in order to make the stiff hair pliable. Finally, he brought the lantern closer and shaved clean a patch of scalp with his straight-edged razor. The boy took five stitches without a sound.

"Have you eaten?" he asked the boy when he was done.

The boy shook his head.

"I'll get you something. You can sleep upstairs with me if you want. No one will bother you up there."

The boy stared at his hands and did not respond.

Teleo had the small back loft to himself. The other workers stayed in the spacious front loft where Teleo had slept in his youth, where the roof was high enough that you could actually walk around and a window let in plenty of natural light and fresh air. These days, Teleo preferred privacy to comfort. The low-ceilinged back loft had not been used much in recent times, judging from the few burlap sacks partially filled with stale oats Teleo had found up there, and a large family of mice. Teleo had evicted them and moved in himself. Few people even seemed aware of the loft, with the ladder hidden in the shadows at the far corner of the large barn, back where the old horses lived and died.

"You want to come upstairs?" Teleo asked.

The boy considered his invitation, looking up from the stall, which was in need of a mucking, to the dark hole in the ceiling at the top of the wooden ladder. "Okay," he finally said.

Teleo helped him to his feet. The boy hobbled from the stall and out the back door to the outhouse while Teleo stood guard. The backyard was dark and vacant, a steady wind rustling the leaves in the ancient elm tree. The boy returned to the barn and headed for the back corner, stopping to open the stall door. BlackJack snorted and stomped his front hoof, showing the whites of his eyes.

"Watch out," Teleo warned.

The boy clicked his tongue, and the horse obediently shuffled into the stall, letting the boy stroke his flank and remove the rope from his neck.

The boy closed the gate, and Teleo waited down below as the Hill orphan pulled himself up the ladder with one arm, painfully holding each rung with his other hand as he reached for the next. Teleo climbed up after him and arranged a bed of straw for the boy. He then gave him his spare blanket and fetched two saddle blankets for the boy—one to lay over the straw, and the other to roll for a pillow. The sound of crickets drifted in through the small roof vents. The boy settled into the straw with a deep sigh and closed his eyes.

"I'll be back soon with food," Teleo said, but the boy was already asleep.

3

THE APPRENTICE

Teleo rose early, left some bread, boiled eggs, and a full waterskin for the sleeping boy, and then hitched Daisy and Benny to his wagon. They rolled over the cobblestone streets of Verdant City, which expanded south and east of the Royal Palace and Old Castle Town. The streets were already bustling with people rushing to work or lining up at tea stands. He passed the market, where the stalls were open and merchants were arranging their wares on tables or unloading produce and cages of squawking chickens from wagons. At other stalls, smoked fish and ham hocks already hung from lines, bushels of dry goods stood tilted towards the aisles to show off their contents, and oranges and lemons from the Aldeon Coast were stacked in neat pyramids. An old friend who sold hats waved to Teleo as he drove by.

He left the walled city through the East Tower Gate and headed out of town on the Aldeon Highway, which cut through the Guild Zone and then ran east over the coastal mountain range and ended at the sea. Even more than at the stables, Teleo felt comfortable in the Guild Zone, where tradesmen like himself worked and were treated with respect. Shops and yards flanked either side of the broad thoroughfare, and the hiss and tumble of the Copper River reached Teleo's ears from where it flowed behind the northern strip, powering the mills and armories.

Wagons trundled by, weighed down with heavy loads. Teleo passed the two largest lumberyards, run by families who had competed with each other for as long as Teleo could remember. One brought in pine, hickory, and oak from the Blue Mountain foothills. The other brought in redwood, olivewood, and madrone from the eastern seaboard. Freshly milled lumber was stacked in neat rows, and the buzz of saws and the scent of sawdust filled the air. Past the lumberyards stood the smaller shops of the wheelwrights, coopers, carpenters, and cabinet-makers. Next came the metal zone with smelters, armories, blacksmiths, copper and tin workers, and goldsmiths. Then came the potters, weavers, and tanners.

At the end of the strip lay the stone yards. There were four. Daisy and Benny turned into the largest—they knew the place well—and pulled the wagon into their usual spot against a large decorative slab of red granite that was mounted vertically and had a stream of water running down its face, splashing into a long granite trough. Teleo loosened their harnesses, and the horses plunged their noses into the cold water.

Teleo greeted the owner and wandered around the dusty yard. This yard supplied local granite from Verdant Valley. He picked out a few slabs of various earth tones, charged them to the king's account, and helped load them onto the wagon.

The second largest yard brought in rocks from the Blue Mountains and Sapphire Empire. The blue stone that gave the Blue Mountains their name was argillite, a high-grade rock that did not split easily and was good for carving. He bought some bright blue pieces, some of the more muted gray, and a slab of the darkest, nearly black variety. He also purchased a small slab of the highly prized lapis lazuli that had been used to build the Imperial Palace that stood in the center of Sapphire Castle. The deep indigo, gold-streaked stone was ridiculously expensive, but the Heliotropes had some of the polished stone—and it was the king's wallet, after all. Also quarried in the Blue Mountains were fine grades of marble. He purchased what he needed of the white and ivory stone. The white marble almost matched the central disk material of the Heliotrope, but it was not translucent enough and was riddled with veins. The owner of the yard did not know where to get the unblemished milky-white stone that Teleo described, nor the shiny black stone of the ten central rays.

The next yard was even smaller and specialized in exotic granites from the Aldeon Coast. Teleo purchased the remaining colors he needed to match the tesserae of the Heliotrope: cranberry red, peony purple, and feldspar green.

Lastly, he went to the smallest of the stone sellers, who carried semi-precious stones, the most expensive of which were from the Far Shell Islands. It was here he had purchased the leaves and bark for the queen's pear tree mosaic: jade and tiger-eye. There were also crates of quartz, amethyst, chalcedony, moonstone, feldspar, jasper, and the like. The seller did not know of the nearly translucent white stone, nor the black ray stone, so Teleo returned to the Blue Mountain dealer and purchased a slab of the shiniest, blackest argillite he could find for the star rays. He rejected the marble for the center stone because it had too many veins in it and chose instead a slab of white granite from the Verdant Valley yard—a piece that was heavy with quartz and had a gleam to it that reminded him of the round stone in the Royal Garden.

He spent the next several days in a corner of the Verdant Castle mason's workshop, rough-shaping the stones. He would finish them in the yard as he fit the puzzle pieces together. The center circle and black rays he finished at the shop, where he could easily carve the precise shapes. He was not happy with the replacement stones, but they would have to do until he found the proper sources.

When he had prepared enough stones to get started, he went back out to the Guild Zone for sand, gravel, and dirt, and dumped them in piles outside the training yard wall. The next morning at daybreak, Teleo went to the training yard and climbed up onto the ramparts where he could look down at the Heliotrope. The current stonework that filled the innermost section was in such disrepair that he was considering pulling up all the stones and laying out a new bed of sand and gravel, salvaging what he could of the original stones and replacing the rest with new ones. He didn't know how the magic circle really worked, though. Would he disrupt whatever power remained if he disturbed the original stones?

And who could have built such a circle? It did not look like the heavy and simple, albeit elegant, stonework of the Stone Guardians. The Heliotrope's stonework was much more complex, reminiscent of a fine-cut gem. Throughout Verdant Castle and the ancient fortresses scattered across Verdant Valley were remnants of stonework fashioned by Mages of old—ornate and decorative—versus the Stone Guardians' work, which was solid and organic as though sculpted from the ground itself. His grandfather had spoken of his father and his father before him. "Mage Stone Masters," he had called them. Maybe that name held more meaning than Teleo knew.

Assuming he could restore this Heliotrope to anywhere near its former glory, did he really want to create a power center for the likes of Gerik and a bunch of bullying teenagers? The queen had asked him to make it lovely—she had not asked him to reignite the magic of the Heliotrope. She probably did not even realize the treasures her own grounds held.

He sighed and descended the stairs. He would remove the mismatched stones and any that were broken or uneven, leaving the intact ones where they lay. He would work around the ancient stones and recreate the Heliotrope as best he could. The Mage's circle was a thing of beauty and deserved the best effort he could give it. Anything else felt wrong.

Daisy and Benny stood patiently outside the training yard, enjoying the warmth of the sun as it rose above the buildings. Teleo contemplated bringing the wagon all the way into the yard but did not want to suffer Gerik's complaints if the horses made a mess, even though Teleo would clean up after them. So he carted the stones one by one through the east gate and stacked them against the inside wall. A few of the stones were too heavy for Teleo to carry by himself, even using the hand cart he had brought. Getting them on and off the cart was the problem. He decided to wait for Gerik's trainees to arrive and ask for help.

He took his shovel and crowbar to the center of the yard and levered up the river rocks. They were easy. He loaded them onto the wagon and then used the hand cart to haul sand, red clay dirt, and gravel into the yard for temporary filler, then leveled the ground where the river rocks had been. He then pried up a few pieces of cracked granite from the outer ring of the circle and was able to get them onto the wagon and fill the worst holes before the morning training session began.

Gerik's assistant, Rickhart, arrived first, a squat man in his forties whom Teleo had fought beside more than once. Rickhart had been hit in the head a few too many times but could still swing a sword. Teleo started to cross the yard to ask him to help unload the rocks, but before he could take two steps, Gerik arrived and sent Rickhart out to the armory to get weapons. Gerik surveyed Teleo's work with a scowl. He looked hungover.

The trainees began straggling into the yard. The eight- to twelve-year-olds lined up against the northern wall, and the thirteen- to sixteen-year-olds gathered in the center of the yard.

Teleo took a deep breath and approached Gerik, wanting to catch him before he started drilling the boys.

Gerik watched him approach with bloodshot eyes.

"Can I get a couple of your older boys to help me carry some rocks?" Teleo asked.

Gerik cleared his throat loudly, spat on the ground, and gave him a foul look. "Do they look like laborers to you? These are sons of nobility."

Teleo held the man's ornery eyes. They both knew not all of them were sons of nobility, and they both also knew Gerik was reminding Teleo that he wasn't nobility either. Rickhart returned to the yard and pretended he wasn't listening as he walked over to the weapons rack with an armful of wooden swords and began hanging them from the brackets.

Teleo considered reminding Gerik he was doing stonework for the queen but didn't want to get into a pissing contest with him.

"Fine," Teleo said, and turned on his heel. He left the yard and went around the wagon to Daisy and Benny, trying to contain his annoyance. Benny snorted and tossed his head, and Daisy eyed him curiously. He brushed his fingertips along their soft, velvety muzzles. "He's always been a selfish bastard," he muttered. "I'll just find someone else to help."

He thought of the boy recovering in his loft. *Jessum.* He had been hiding out there while he healed. Teleo brought him food

every day and snuck him out back to the outhouse nights so
he could empty his slop bucket and relieve himself in a proper
latrine. No one seemed to notice or care that he was there. It
had been several days now since Teleo had found him curled up
in BlackJack's stall, and his ribs were healing nicely. He knew
the young man was going stir-crazy, and it wasn't good for
his health to be cooped up for too long. Every evening when
Teleo came home, he found Jessum in BlackJack's stall, either
sitting in a corner whittling chunks of wood into animals or
standing at the horse's head, stroking his neck. BlackJack was
calm under the boy's touch, and Teleo noted that the horse was
being groomed daily. His coat glistened and his mane fell in
long, flowing cascades. He was a beautiful horse, aside from the
puckered battle scars on his shoulders and hindquarters.

But Jessum couldn't hide out in the barn forever. He would
have to face his peers eventually. Perhaps Teleo could make him
his apprentice. That way, he'd start learning a trade, and Teleo
could watch over him. Maybe the other boys would leave him
alone if they knew he was working for Teleo. Teleo still had a
reputation as a fierce warrior, even if he was retired. Problem
was, Jessum had told him that he had been training with Gerik.
Jessum avoided Teleo's questions whenever he asked about it,
saying only that nobody would miss him and that they knew
he was hurt. In any case, if Teleo pulled Jessum out of Gerik's
training sessions to help with the stonework, a confrontation
was inevitable. The boy wasn't healed enough to lug stones,
anyway. Teleo would approach Gerik about the boy when the
time came.

Teleo went on foot to the mason's workshop, down the hill
past the Royal Forge. Two workers offered to help him, and
they went together to the training yard and unloaded the
heavy stones.

Gerik ignored them as they stacked the stones against the inside wall. Teleo observed the boys in the middle of the yard. They were the younger group, circling one another and sparring with staves. The sand, gravel, and clay mixture Teleo had laid down was solid under their feet. Gerik would have no cause to complain.

Teleo suffered Gerik's dark look as he dared fill two buckets with water for his horses from the training yard's cistern. He moved the horses into the shade, then walked with his helpers to the kitchen for the midday meal and ate out back at the picnic tables in the shade of the elm trees. After lunch, Teleo bid farewell to the workers and headed back to the training yard to get his wagon, after swiping an apple and carrots from the kitchen for the horses. He fed them their treats and they stood patiently while he put on their bridles, tightened their harnesses, and hitched them up. He climbed onto the driving bench, but his gloves were not there. He must have left them inside the training yard. He could hear the clack-clack of wooden swords.

Teleo climbed down and tried to slip unobserved into the yard. Gerik saw him right away. Teleo ignored him and walked to his pile of stones and found his leather gloves sitting on a stack of red granite. When he turned to leave, a shock of black hair drew his attention to a bench in the shadow of the southern wall. Jessum was sitting there, hunched dejectedly, and did not meet Teleo's questioning gaze.

Teleo tensed up with concern. What was Jessum doing there? His ribs were not healed yet. The eight older boys were in the center of the yard and focused on their swordplay, but as Gerik moved them into two groups of three against one, a few boys glanced gloatingly at Jessum. Teleo did not believe Jessum had come to the yard of his own free will.

Teleo simmered with anger and hovered at the east gate, considering his options. He could approach Gerik now and tell him he was taking Jessum as his apprentice and have it out right then and there. Or he could leave the boy to face the bullies and figure out how to deal with them on his own, as he must do at some point.

Teleo watched the two boys who were left solo turn and parry as they fended off their attackers, who were none too gentle. Gerik shouted encouragement to the aggressors, and Rickhart yelled instructions to the defenders. The boys were strong and Gerik was a good teacher, even if he was a jackass. The defenders ultimately were driven to their knees, and Gerik called off the attackers.

"Jessum!" Gerik yelled. "Get over here!"

Teleo's eyes darted to Jessum, who pushed himself up from the bench and shuffled across the yard, staring at the ground. Teleo's jaws clamped together.

Gerik grabbed Jessum roughly by the collar and pushed him into the center of the circle. The eight boys stood around him, wooden swords at the ready.

"Get 'em," Gerik called, and the boys started circling, eyeing their prey.

Rickhart tossed Jessum a wooden stave, and he caught it deftly. This did not appear to be the first time they'd done this drill. Jessum crouched and his eyes flicked from boy to boy, assessing his greatest threat. He responded quickly when the first boy lunged in with his wooden sword, and deflected it with the long, stout stave. The next attack came from behind but he saw it and caught it cleanly with his stave. Jessum was favoring his left side, trying to protect his ribs with his elbow. All the boys wore metal helmets, leather body armor, leather arm and thigh guards, and over-the-knee boots; all except Jessum, who wore his simple roughspun pants, tunic, and tattered leather shoes.

Teleo suppressed the urge to intervene and watched with growing rage as the boys took turns attacking Jessum. He was a strong boy but was already breathing quickly, needing to take shallow breaths because of his ribs, and sweat was beading on his brow. Even with sore ribs, he was adept at fending off one attacker at a time and then two as Gerik gave the command. Then three. Four.

Jessum was in a full crouch, spinning and using his feet and legs to kick away the boys and the wooden swords. His face was grim with determination. He had clearly been in this position before and was good at it, but at five attackers his eyes flashed with the wild terror of a trapped animal, and he growled and grunted as they struck him from all sides. They fell onto him like jackals on a rabbit, jabbing and kicking. Teleo watched painfully as Jessum lay curled in the fetal position to protect his ribs and shielded his head with his arms, taking the punishment in the back and legs as the younger boys jeered and cheered from the sidelines.

Gerik finally called them off. Jessum lay in the dirt, his back heaving with labored breaths. The young men looked proud of themselves, slapping each other on the back as they took off their helmets and wiped sweat from their brows. Gerik waved them away and dragged Jessum to his feet. Jessum stood, swaying, bright red blood dripping from his nose.

"Get out of here," Gerik said, pushing him roughly towards the west gate. Jessum tripped, falling to his hands and knees, then climbed to his feet and limped heavily out of the yard. The trainees gathered at the cistern, talking loudly and laughing among themselves as they dipped their cups into the water and drank. The younger boys took to the center of the yard, play-fighting as they waited for Gerik's command.

Teleo strode across the yard, unable to contain himself any longer. Gerik met him with a hard gaze.

"You trying to kill him?" Teleo asked gruffly.

Gerik flared his hairy nostrils. "He's just a Hill dog. The boys need real practice."

Teleo replied curtly, "He's still injured from the last time. His ribs are cracked."

Gerik shrugged, confirming Teleo's suspicions. "He was able to use the stave. I've fought injured lots of times. So have you."

Teleo narrowed his eyes at Gerik, who stood with his chest puffed out, daring Teleo to do something about it. Teleo did not want to have a physical confrontation with Gerik. Teleo would probably win the fight but would lose the battle in the end. The common people always lost against the nobility, one way or another, and Gerik was not one to forgive being publicly humiliated, especially in front of his students.

Teleo gave a slight bow of his head in acquiescence and backed away a step, then turned and left the yard.

———◆———

Teleo quickly drove the horses and wagon to the stables, stewing in anger. Gerik probably intended to let his trainees kill the Hill boy eventually. Maybe it would be a rite of passage. Their first kill before going off to defend the border.

Teleo unhitched the horses, removed their heavy harnesses, and led them into their stall, his hands trembling. They eyed him curiously. They could feel his agitation. He patted Benny's head, pushing his forelock away from his eyes. "Men are cruel," he said. "You're lucky you're a horse." Teleo quickly fetched them fresh water and hay, gave them a quick rubdown, and promised to return later to brush them properly.

He found Jessum lying on his back in the corner of BlackJack's stall, a bloody rag held to his nose. The horse's head was lowered over the boy. Teleo walked around and leaned over the side rail. "You okay?" he asked.

The horse cast Teleo a baleful look.

"Yeah," Jessum mumbled. He struggled to a sitting position. One eye was swollen shut and he dabbed the rag at his bloody nose. "They went easy on me this time. Probably because you were there."

"It's not right what they are doing," Teleo said. "I'm sorry."

"It's not your fault," Jessum said.

Teleo frowned. "Come upstairs and I'll look at that nose."

Jessum got slowly to his feet and edged his way around the horse, running his hand along his black coat. "It's okay, it's okay," Jessum said soothingly to BlackJack, watching his hindquarters as the big horse shifted his weight.

"Be careful," Teleo said.

"He won't kick me."

Jessum slipped through the gate as the big black turned around to follow him. Jessum closed the gate, murmuring, "No, BlackJack. Stay here."

"Here, give him this," Teleo said, handing Jessum half a carrot from his pocket. "How'd he get in from the paddock?"

"I called him." Jessum reached over the rail with the carrot in his open palm. BlackJack eyed it, then snatched it from his hand, baring his large yellowed teeth for a moment.

"You called him? Ha! You've really got him tamed," Teleo said. "Never thought I'd see the day."

Jessum watched BlackJack munch on the carrot. "I want to ride him."

Teleo laughed, glad the boy was not brooding over his injuries. "You're brave," Teleo said.

"I'll bet he's fast," Jessum said.

"I'll bet he is," Teleo agreed. "Come on."

The horse snorted and stomped his front hoof as they walked to the back corner of the stable. Jessum climbed the ladder slowly. Teleo followed him and lit a lantern, sending a spider scurrying behind a beam.

"Did they hurt your ribs again?" Teleo asked.

Jessum sat gingerly on his bedding and shook his head. "No, but they got me everywhere else." He let Teleo feel his ribcage.

Teleo helped him peel off his shirt and scowled, shaking his head at the fresh bruises that covered Jessum's back, legs, and arms.

"Let me look at your nose."

Jessum turned to face him and closed his eyes. Teleo gently felt the cartilage. It was crooked. Teleo's nose had been broken more than once. This was not a bad break, fortunately. "This might hurt for a second. Hold still," Teleo said, and before Jessum could object, Teleo had snapped the cartilage back into place.

"Ow!"

The boy's good eye teared up, and Teleo examined the nose again, gently holding the bloody cloth to Jessum's nostrils.

"There. Now you won't look like Rickhart," he said.

Jessum swallowed. "That's good," he said, trying to smile.

"Tilt your head back."

Jessum raised his chin and held the cloth to his nose.

"How did they find you? Did they come in here?" Teleo asked.

"No," Jessum mumbled through the cloth. "I was stupid and went to nab some food from the pig troughs."

Teleo raised an eyebrow. "The pig troughs ... I thought I was feeding you enough. Well, anyway, you can't stay holed up here forever. We need another solution." Teleo helped him lie down on his back.

"Like what?" Jessum asked. "Run away?"

Teleo frowned. "That wouldn't be safe for you, either." He didn't voice his fears—that a young Hill lad on the roads of the Verdant Valley Kingdom by himself wouldn't last more than a week before thugs, older and meaner than Gerik's bullies, took revenge on him for past raids or battles. "I'll think of something," Teleo said.

Jessum muttered, "I hate myself. I wish I wasn't from the Hills."

"Don't hate yourself. You're a good young man," Teleo laid his hand on the orphan's shoulder. "It's a big world. Not everyone is cruel. There are some good people out there."

The boy fixed his open eye on Teleo. "You're good."

"I try," Teleo said, smiling sadly. "The Hill people are a noble people. Proud and strong. Fierce adversaries, but they love their families. You come from good blood."

"You know some Hill people?" Jessum held Teleo's gaze, his eye glinting with hope and sadness.

Teleo could see the internal war the boy was waging against the shame of who he was. "Yes, I know some," Teleo said. He had killed some, but he had also met some on his quest whom he would consider friends. And he had wagered his sanity on the belief that good, loving people lived in the Sapphire Empire. People who would show a Verdant Valley orphan some kindness.

"Here, let me help you get cleaned up." Teleo climbed down the ladder and returned with clean rags, soap and salves, and a fresh bucket of water. He went to work cleaning Jessum's face and other minor lacerations. The boy would be sore for a few days but should heal up just fine. Teleo left him with a cold cloth compress on his eye and nose and two cloth plugs for his nostrils, then went out to the well. He washed up as best he could in the back courtyard, returned to the loft, and changed into his spare set of clean clothes. Jessum was lying on his bed staring bleakly at the ceiling beams. The horse was snorting down below and pawing at the gate.

"Can you let him back outside?" Jessum asked. "Please?"

Teleo raised his eyebrows. "I'll try."

Teleo descended the ladder and regarded the horse, who snorted at him and tossed his head.

"All right," Teleo said. "Don't bite me."

Teleo opened the gate and stood aside as BlackJack left the stall and walked directly towards the side door, snapping at Teleo's shoulder as he passed by. Teleo was ready for that, easily avoiding his teeth, and stood beyond reach of his hooves. "Move along, BlackJack. Move along."

The horse watched him from the corner of his eye and walked through the open doorway to the stone ramp and down to the dry-moat paddock. He broke into a trot down the gently sloping hill and joined the old horses and ponies who were gathered in the shade of an elm tree, pulling at what few tufts of grass hid among the rocky ground along the far wall. BlackJack's steps were light and his sleek mane and tail shimmered in the sunshine. He was a magnificent animal. Not only because of his glistening coat but because his spirits were good, probably from being treated with kindness. Teleo needed to tell Jessum to stop treating him so well or else someone like Gerik would notice him and put him back into service.

Teleo left the stables and walked along the cobblestone alleyways that led from the castle's service buildings to the Royal Palace. He approached the main palace gate.

"Back for more stonework?" the young guard asked.

"I'm repairing the training yard. The queen asked me to. I need to meet with her about it."

The guard wrinkled his forehead. "Does she know you're coming?"

"No."

The guard did not look happy but said gruffly, "Talk to the House Mistress," and swung open the wooden gate.

"Yes, sir." Teleo entered the outer bailey and headed for the garden gate that he always used. Vigo was on duty and stood up from his stool to greet his old friend.

"Teleo. How goes it?" The two men clasped forearms. "Repairing the training yard, I hear?"

"Yep. I got some of the new stones loaded in already and cleared away most of the worst broken pieces."

"That's good progress. How's your old friend, Gerik?" Vigo cocked an eyebrow.

Teleo laughed bitterly. "He's a fucking bastard."

Vigo chuckled with him. "So, nothing's changed."

The two men shook their heads.

"I need to speak with the queen," Teleo said. "Can you ask the House Mistress to see me?"

"She's at the market. I can ask Gwen."

"Perfect," Teleo said.

Vigo rang a bell for a page and sent the young girl to find the Queen's Lady.

Teleo walked down the dim entry tunnel to the guardroom and sat heavily on a bench. He leaned back against the stone wall and closed his eyes, suddenly exhausted.

After several minutes, Vigo poked his head inside the doorway, and Teleo followed him through the inner garden gate. Finches hopped along the edge of the Heliotrope and chirped from the pear tree's branches. Gwen bustled along the shaded portico, holding her long skirts off the marble walkway.

"Why, hello, Teleo," she said. "I didn't expect to see you back here so soon."

"I know. I have a question for the queen about the training yard stonework." He took a deep breath. He had come this far—it was too late to back out now. Someone had to stand up for the boy.

"What about?" Gwen asked, folding her arms across her chest.

"Um," he hesitated. "I need an extra pair of hands. The Hill orphan is doing nothing except sitting on the bench at the training yard."

She narrowed her eyes at him. "Why don't you ask Gerik?"

Teleo did not reply but held her eyes with a flat look.

After a long moment, she sighed and said, "Wait here." She bustled off and disappeared into the palace.

Teleo sat on a marble bench and waited, enjoying the peaceful garden and contemplating the pattern of the mystical Heliotrope.

Gwen returned a few minutes later. "Queen Eleanor will see you now," she said curtly, and led Teleo along the white marble arcade and into the palace. He had only been through this door once, for his interview to make the pear tree mosaic. Since then, he had always spoken to the queen on her terrace when she came out to inspect his work.

The two-story antechamber was cool, with a breeze wafting in through tall windows. The floors, pillars, and walls were white and pink marble. A fresco of white clouds on a blue sky decorated the ceiling. He followed Gwen down a wide hallway adorned with marble statues of dogs and horses and through the polished walnut doorway into the queen's audience chamber.

Queen Eleanor was sitting in her embroidered armchair, fanning her face with a delicate white wicker fan. Mounds of topaz-blue silk skirts draped to the floor around her slippered feet, and her thick golden-brown hair was elaborately coiled on top of her head, with a few perfectly coiled curls strategically hanging loose over her bare neck. Teleo bowed formally and took a seat in a straight-backed embroidered chair that a manservant pulled out for him.

"Thank you," the queen said to the manservant and Gwen. "That will be all." The manservant looked up and the queen nodded. "You may go."

The manservant lowered his head and backed out of the room with Gwen, shutting the great wooden door softly behind them.

The rhythmic swishing of the fan filled the empty space as the queen inspected Teleo. He waited for her to speak first, as protocol required.

"Teleo Stonemason," she said, after torturing him with silence for a full minute. "What can I do for you?"

He cleared his throat. "Thank you for agreeing to meet with me, Your Majesty," he said. It felt odd being so formal. They had chatted and laughed on her terrace several times. Once she had even brought him chilled tea on a hot afternoon and stood in her terrace doorway sipping hers while she told him about a journey she had taken across the Aldeon Sea to the Far Shell Islands.

"Um," he continued, his voice amplified in the wood-paneled room. "Some of the stones for the training yard are quite large. I could use a helper." He cleared his throat. "I was ... um ... I was thinking that maybe the Hill orphan would be good since he can't go to war and will need a trade. I can take him on as an apprentice." He could feel his face growing red as the queen gazed steadily at him over her motionless fan.

"I believe the Hill orphan assists at the training yard," she said, looking at him pointedly.

"Assists?" he asked, his face flushing further.

"Yes. Helps the boys in their training."

Teleo's pulse quickened and he swallowed. He could not read her. Did she approve of the treatment Gerik inflicted on Jessum, all in the name of training soldiers to kill? "I beg your pardon, Your Majesty?"

"Tell me why he would be a good apprentice," she said, resuming the rhythmic flapping of her fan.

Teleo took a breath. "He seems idle most of the time, sitting on the bench at the training yard. He is out of commission for days or weeks at a time after a particularly brutal session." He locked gazes with her. She held his gaze coolly, and dappled sunlight from a window glinted off her brown eyes. She was not stupid nor sheltered, as many of the gossips in town liked to say. She knew what was going on in her own castle. She was shrewd enough to protect her daughter from the same man.

"I cannot ask for any of the normal trainees," he continued, "and the village boys are all busy helping their families with the summer chores, and the farm lads are needed for the harvests."

Everyone knew Teleo did not have a family. That his only son had been stolen in a Hill raid. Or so the rumor went. So he believed. It would be a fair trade for him to have a Hill boy in exchange. He breathed evenly. He'd said what he had to say. Let her decide Jessum's fate.

She stared at him, unblinking. "What about the students of the Master of Arms?" she asked. "What will they do for their battle training?"

Teleo swallowed again, wondering how far he should take this. He chose his words carefully. "They already kill animals on the hunts. They will have an opportunity to kill another man in battle, if we ever return to war. It is not something that should be practiced for sport. In my opinion."

She stared at him, her fan stopping again. Perhaps he had crossed a line. What would she do to him? Send him home? Hire a different stonemason to repair the training yard and bar him from the castle? Worse? Send him to the dungeons for his brazenness? Hand him over to Gerik? Sweat broke out on his brow.

"I see," she said, waving the fan slowly. "So you believe it is a more fitting place for the Hill orphan to be carrying stones rather than learning how to fight from the most talented Master of Arms in the kingdom?"

He sat nervously, then began to understand where she was leading. "Yes," he agreed. "It is not fitting for someone of such a low station, a son of our enemies, to learn the fighting techniques of the Verdant Valley forces. It is more appropriate that he do manual labor for the kingdom."

She lowered her fan into her lap and rang a little bronze bell that sat on a side table. Shortly thereafter, the manservant and Gwen appeared in the doorway.

"Chilled tea for myself and the Stone Master, please. Bring the castellan."

The servants nodded and backed out of the doorway, leaving them in stiff silence.

"How is the stonework coming along?" she asked lightly, the formality suddenly gone from her voice.

"Oh. Well. Going well," he said, exhaling and folding his hands in his lap. "I've been to the stone yards and am doing my best to replicate the original design of the ancient masters that once graced the training yard. It was quite lovely at one time." He winced at his overly flowery language. He was not accustomed to sitting in a royal audience chamber perched on a chair embroidered with roses and butterflies.

"Wonderful," she said, riffling the fan closed with a snap and tapping it against her fingertips. "I trust with the boy's help you will be done before autumn?"

"Oh, yes, he will hasten my progress, most definitely," he said, bowing his head. "Thank you."

The door opened and Gwen appeared with a tray bearing two metal goblets, foggy with condensation. She served the queen and then placed a linen napkin in Teleo's hand, followed by a goblet.

"Thank you," he said, to her and the queen.

Gwen retreated to the back corner of the room, where she sat in an upright chair and went to work on a piece of embroidery stretched on a small hoop. Teleo and Queen Eleanor sipped their chilled lemon mint tea and discussed the forecasts for a hard winter. Teleo had nearly finished his tea when the manservant appeared with the castellan, a tall, narrow-chested man who ran the castle with rigid efficiency.

While the queen and the castellan greeted one another, Gwen disappeared and returned quickly with more chilled tea and a tray of almond sweetcakes. Teleo had only met the new castellan once, and the bony man examined Teleo with a frown, no doubt wondering why the queen's stonemason was in her audience chamber sipping tea. Teleo suddenly felt self-conscious in his brown roughspun pants and tunic, which marked him as a peasant, in contrast to the castellan's maroon silk brocade vest over a ruffled white shirt with puffy sleeves. The castellan's pants were tailored from fine black silk, tucked into shiny black leather boots. Teleo focused on the sweetcake. The only opinion that mattered here was the queen's, and she seemed to have no trouble with how Teleo presented himself.

Once the small talk was over with, the queen addressed the castellan directly. "I am giving the Hill orphan to the Stone Master as an apprentice."

The castellan swallowed his mouthful of sweetcake and took a gulp of tea. "Oh?" he asked, dabbing at his mouth with a napkin. "If I may point out, Your Majesty, the Master of Arms uses the orphan in the training yard."

She drew her lips into a thin line. "I am well aware of Gerik's use of the boy. It is a waste of resources. I need that training yard in good working condition. Gerik has let it fall into disrepair. We intend to host tourneys there at the Harvest Festival, and it is an embarrassment. In order to complete the work in time, I am giving the boy to the Stone Master. After that, the boy will continue as his apprentice. Hill orphans should be doing manual labor, not learning how to fight. Please inform the Master of Arms straight away. That will be all." Her eyes flashed, and the castellan rose awkwardly to his feet, brushing crumbs off his chest.

He dipped his head and shoulders in a low bow. "As you command, Your Majesty," he said, and left in a flurry of frills and puffy sleeves.

4

WAR ORPHANS

"I'm going to be your apprentice?" Jessum asked, propping himself up on his elbow on his straw bed. Relief washed over his bruised and swollen face.

"Yes," Teleo said, smiling. "You can start in few days. We need to let your nose heal a little first, and those ribs. How are you feeling?"

Jessum lay back down and rested his forearm across his forehead. "My head is killing me."

Teleo nodded. "It will for a while. Let me get you something."

Teleo went to his collection of tinctured herbs, chose a few to dull the pain and reduce swelling, and added several drops to water. Jessum sat up and drank, his face wrinkling from the bitter taste. "Yuck," he complained.

"It's good for you," Teleo said with a grin, and brought him some plain water to wash it down with.

Jessum lay back on the straw. "What will I have to do? Carry stones?"

"Yes, and I'll teach you how to carve and lay paving stones and build walls."

"Okay, good," Jessum said, his eye closing and his face relaxing.

Before long, the boy was asleep, his nose completely stuffed up and his mouth hanging open with a rhythmic snore. Teleo pulled the blanket up over him, tucking it around his shoulders so the chilly evening air wouldn't seep in. One of the herbs would also ensure the boy slept soundly, and Teleo did not want him to get cold.

Teleo got himself ready for bed and stretched out under his own blanket, wondering what Gerik's reaction had been when the castellan told him the queen's wishes. Gerik would know it had been Teleo's idea and would try to exact revenge somehow. The Master of Arms would not take kindly to his punching bag being taken from him, especially right under his nose, and then working the stone in his own training yard. Teleo had to make sure Jessum would not suffer because of it. Teleo sighed and rolled over. The sooner he could finish repairing the Heliotrope, the better, then he could get back to his farm with the boy.

Teleo pondered the flowing star pattern of the Heliotrope, reviewing the details of the intricate design in his head. What if he altered it a bit so that it still looked beautiful but would not confer magical powers upon those who danced on it? But the magical powers were only activated during the dawn of the Summer Solstice, right? By the time Gerik and the boys showed up in the yard, if they even trained on the holiday at all, the sun would have already passed above the Focal Point. Teleo tossed and turned and finally fell into a fitful sleep.

The next day, Teleo replaced the fragments of the center stone with the white granite disk he had shaped, rolling it on its edge across the yard and then lining it up in the exact position of the original slab. It marked the point from which the rest of the circular pattern emanated. He imagined how the Heliotrope would look after he fully restored it—ten black rays flowing into concentric rings of diamonds and petals that radiated outwards from the center for ten paces, where the colorful tesserae met a border of gray granite paving stones that filled the rest of the rectangular training yard. It was a magic circle large enough to accommodate two warring bands of seven Mages each. Teleo thought of the ancient scroll his great-aunt Bralla kept locked in a chest, depicting fourteen robed Mages flying in the air above such a circle, crossing swords.

Teleo walked the large circle, inspecting the stonework. A few sections were still intact and solid. He would leave those as they were. Over the next few mornings and evenings, he removed the rest of the broken stones and prepared the temporary yard surface with sand, clay, and gravel, raking it smooth, and then started laying the black rays.

Mornings, he left the training yard before Gerik arrived, then waited until supper was served to return, working by lantern light until midnight, when he left to check on the boy and steal a few hours of sleep before rising before daybreak to do it all again. One warm and humid night in the stuffy loft, Jessum said he felt better, and went with Teleo to the yard the next morning.

It would have been much more efficient to block off sections of the yard until they were completed, but he really did not want to hear about it from Gerik. So they prepared a small area, laid four of the larger tesserae in the outer circle, and then groomed the surrounding dirt for the trainees. Jessum was a bit slow and awkward, still suffering from sore ribs and a lingering headache. His nose was still puffy, and his black eye had faded to a sickly green. But he did not complain. They left well before nine, returned after supper and worked until one o'clock in the morning, and then were up at five the next morning to lay more stones.

They were just finishing raking the sand and gravel when Gerik clomped into the yard with an armful of swords, which he hung one by one on the rack. They were not wooden swords—they were steel—dulled for practice but a signal that the older boys had progressed to the next level. Teleo looked up at the sun. It was still relatively low in the sky and the eight o'clock bell had only rung a few minutes ago. Gerik was early.

The Master of Arms glanced over his shoulder and caught Teleo's eye. Teleo held his gaze for a moment, trying to read Gerik's mood, but the Master of Arms kept his expression stony and turned back to his swords, then left the yard without looking back.

"Let's go," Teleo said softly to Jessum, who was staring at the ground. They gave one final rake to the gravel and then left through the east gate. They paused in the morning sunshine outside the training yard's wall to drink from their waterskins, then propped the rakes and shovels on their shoulders. Teleo carried a collection of chisels, hammers, and knives on his belts, with his short sword strapped across his back. He wasn't taking any chances.

They crossed the outer cobblestone yard, passed through an archway, and traversed the castle compound through a maze of alleys. After meandering through the tightly spaced service buildings, they ended up at the back door of the kitchens, where the cooking staff prepared food for everyone at the castle except the royal household.

Teleo poked his head inside. An older woman saw him and motioned him inside. The air was redolent with bubbling stew. Teleo motioned for the boy to wait for him in the stone entryway, which served as a mudroom, furnished with two heavy wooden benches, a wall rack for coats, and a few wooden barrels. "Stay out of the way," he said. Jessum sat down and leaned the back of his head against the stone wall.

Teleo entered the warm kitchen. The primary cooking room was large, with two head-high fireplaces for roasting meat, two fireplaces for cauldrons, and several ovens built into the stone walls. A large wooden butcher block and an even larger stone countertop took up the center of the room, and two wooden tables stood against a wall, where the kitchen staff ate and where Teleo had played cards many nights in his youth. Several other smaller rooms branched off from the main kitchen: two prep kitchens, the well room, several storage rooms, and a ramp that led down to a cellar for cold storage.

"I still have some porridge," the woman said, poking a long wooden spoon into a cauldron set to the side of the cooking fire.

"Great. I need two bowls today," Teleo said, grinning. "I have an apprentice now." He had always pretended to get a second helping for himself when taking food to the loft for the boy, but he did not have to try and hide him anymore. Jessum was officially his apprentice by order of the queen.

The woman raised a gray eyebrow but served up two steaming bowls of porridge. Teleo brought them out to Jessum and returned for a basket of bread, a board of cheese and grapes, and two tankards of fresh cider.

"Here," the woman said, and tucked six hard-boiled eggs into the basket.

"Thank you kindly," Teleo said, and returned to the mudroom. He and Jessum carried their food to the backyard and over to the collection of wooden tables, all of which were empty except for one at the end occupied by the old man who tended the fowl and pigs. The elderly man looked up, his eyes resting on Jessum. The boy exchanged a brief glance with the old farmer, then lowered his eyes. Teleo and Jessum sat at another table and stuffed their mouths with hot porridge and bread. Teleo did not know what Jessum was accustomed to eating. Not much, by the looks of things. Even though Teleo had been feeding him for the past few weeks, he still gobbled down the hot porridge and fresh bread as though he had not eaten in days. Not being able to breathe well through his nose slowed him down today, but he finished his porridge before Teleo had eaten three mouthfuls. Jessum glanced up, catching Teleo watching him, and raised his brow in a question.

Teleo swallowed his food. "How's your head?" he asked.

Jessum shrugged and spoke through a mouthful of grapes. "Hurts."

The pace that Teleo had been keeping, working mornings and nights, was grueling. He was tired and the boy still needed to heal. Teleo had been trying to finish the training yard as fast as possible so that he could get back home in time to harvest the apples and almonds from his orchards, plus the root vegetables from his kitchen garden to tide him over for the winter. Now that he had Jessum, things would move faster.

"We'll just work nights from now on," Teleo said. Besides, there was less chance to run into Gerik that way, he considered silently.

Jessum nodded and stuffed his mouth full of bread.

They returned to the kitchens for a hearty midday dinner, then again for their evening supper, and at each meal, Jessum wolfed down his food as if he was starving. At sunset, they went to the training yard and worked into the wee hours of the morning, laboring by lantern light, the flickering flames making the yard move with ghostly shadows. The next morning, Teleo tried to sleep in but awoke to sounds of the old groom leading the ornery BlackJack out to the paddock, followed by Daisy and Benny. Teleo got up and went downstairs to the outhouse, then took a shovel and joined the old groom, who was mucking BlackJack's stall.

"You don't need to clean his stall," Teleo said. "The boy and I can do that."

"I know, but you worked all night," the old groom said.

"I guess you're not so hard of hearing after all," Teleo said, chuckling.

"I get up several times a night," the old groom said, raking wet straw out into the aisle. "One of the inconveniences of old age. I saw you shuffle in before dawn."

"Ah. Where are your stable hands?" Teleo asked.

"Some went home to help with the oat hay harvest, two are not feeling well, and the others are at the upper stables," the old groom said. "The royal family went hunting this morning and came back with a stag."

"Nice," Teleo said, nodding. Teleo fondly remembered his time as a teenager working occasionally in the upper stables, where the royal family stabled their personal mounts. The Elkes owned the finest horses in the land, and Teleo had felt honored just being allowed to brush them.

The upper stables stood outside the northern walls of the castle and were spotless, managed by the head groom. There was also a small trusted staff who exercised the horses, managed breeding, and maintained the royal family's private grazing paddocks, exercise rings, and an extensive jumping course, all situated on secluded, private lands.

But Teleo preferred the lower stables, which felt like a second home to him. He rested the shovel on the ground and regarded the long aisle of stalls, which was the last of four aisles. The lower stables accommodated the horses of visitors, temporary castle laborers, and a few favorite retired horses who lived out their days under the care of the old groom. The finest stalls, in the first aisle, were reserved for the horses of royal guests, and Teleo always enjoyed seeing the various horses come and go.

Teleo let Jessum sleep a few more hours before waking him. They ate their midday meal behind the kitchen at a table near the groundskeepers. Teleo knew some of the workers. They looked askance at the Hill boy, wondering with open scowls why he was sitting among them.

"The queen gave him to me as an apprentice," Teleo said, gesturing towards the boy. "We're fixing the stonework in the training yard. The queen wants it done before the Harvest Festival." Teleo's explanation seemed to satisfy them, and the groundskeepers returned to their food.

Jessum kept his head down, not registering any emotion, and gnawed on a chicken leg.

"Let's save these eggs and apples for a snack later," Teleo suggested, knowing that half the apples the cook had loaded into their basket today would go to his horses and BlackJack.

The boy nodded and kept eating.

After their meal, they went to the stables, stepping out into the dry-moat paddock to give Daisy and Benny their treats. The horses ate their apples while BlackJack eyed them jealously from across the yard. Jessum tossed him his apple, and the big horse picked it up off the ground with his teeth and ate it in one mouthful.

"Let's go for a ride," Teleo said to Jessum. "Benny and Daisy need some exercise."

Jessum stared down at his toes.

"What's wrong?" Teleo asked.

He hesitated before answering. "I haven't ridden a horse since ... since I left home."

"Oh," Teleo said. Of course. He hadn't been thinking. Who would have taught a Hill orphan to ride? Who would have let him ride their horse? He had no parents, no social standing, and no one watching out for him. He was like a stray dog who had been kicked all his life. "Come on, then, I'll show you," Teleo said. "It'll come right back to you. Missy Daisy is gentle. I'll ride Benny."

"Want to go for a ride?" he asked his horses. Their ears perked up and they trotted across the paddock and up the ramp. BlackJack stood under the elm tree, stomping his front hoof and blowing dust from his nostrils.

Teleo led the dapple grays through the stable and into the enclosed grooming yard where the boy hesitantly ran a bristle brush over Daisy's coat. Soon, Jessum lost his shyness and talked to Daisy as he brushed her. "That's a good girl," Jessum cooed softly. "You've got some pretty stars all over you," he said, grooming her side where her dappled pattern resembled stars more than spots.

"Jessum," Teleo said. Jessum stopped brushing and looked up. "I want you to stop brushing BlackJack." Jessum's face fell. Teleo continued, "And it's probably better if you're not so nice to him."

Jessum's mouth turned down. "Why?" he asked, his voice suddenly small like a child's.

A familiar pain wrenched Teleo's gut. Jessum could be his child, growing up somewhere in a hostile land. Neglected and lonely. Beat up for sport. And Teleo was taking away his one source of affection.

Teleo cleared his throat. "Well, he's a nice-looking horse. Even nicer since you started taking care of him. You're gentling him. Some lord will notice and take him for his own horse. The only reason he's been abandoned is because he's mean."

Jessum's mouth turned down even further, his discolored eye and swollen nose making him look truly wretched.

"Oh, I never thought of that," Jessum said weakly.

Teleo smiled kindly. "I know. Just let him get dusty. Let his mane and tail get matted again. And don't call for him."

Jessum was quiet as they brushed the horses with the hard brushes and then the soft brushes. Teleo watched with surprise as Jessum lifted Daisy's front foot, tucked it between his legs, and cleaned her foot with a hoof pick he took from a back pocket.

"What? How?" Teleo asked.

Jessum glanced up at him, then went back to the hoof as he answered, "I apprenticed with the blacksmith, Elias, before Gerik took me. Elias lent me to the farrier sometimes to help shoe the horses." Jessum moved to the other front hoof and talked as he worked. "I started with the blacksmith when I was eight. I can forge horseshoes and make some simple tools. I was supposed to start learning how to make blades next, but then Elias said I was to go to the training yard to learn how to use a sword, only Gerik never let me touch one. He only ever gave me a staff."

"When did you leave the blacksmith?" Teleo asked, examining Jessum's hands, arms, and shoulders, which were hard with the wiry muscles of a boy raised swinging a scythe or a sword, or in the Hill orphan's case, a hammer and staff.

"Last summer," Jessum said. "I still lived behind the forge before you took me in, so I helped him and the farrier sometimes when I wasn't at the training yard or hiding out."

"That's nice, that the blacksmith trained you," Teleo said.

"Nice?" Jessum asked, raising his eyes for a moment. "Lazy, more like. Elias's plan was to train me to do all the work so he could sit and drink all day. He used to tell me that all the time."

"How old were you when you were stolen from your people?" Teleo asked.

Jessum set down the hoof and stared at him, as though no one had ever asked him that question before. "I don't know. Six, maybe?"

"Elias the blacksmith raised you here, from the beginning?"

Jessum scoffed. He walked around Daisy, rested her rear leg on his bent thigh, and started cleaning the hoof. "No," he finally answered. "At first, they put me out back with the pigs and chickens. They were pretty nice to me. The animals, that is. They would share their slop with me. The old farmer used to throw me stale loaves of bread sometimes. He gave me straw and a blanket to sleep on. But no, nobody raised me."

Teleo tried not to show his horror. "Then you went to the blacksmith's when you were eight? Was he kind to you? Was his wife?"

Jessum laughed a bitter laugh. "Elias has no wife. He's drunk every night. He never cared for me. I had to steal food from the chickens and pigs to eat. The old farmer let me. I suppose you could say the farmer raised me. Though he never talked much."

"Did he beat you? The blacksmith?"

"Only when he was drunk."

Teleo couldn't bear to ask him anything more, and Jessum didn't offer. Teleo worked out the tangles in Benny's mane while the boy bent behind Daisy, gently lifting her other rear hoof onto his thigh and digging at it with the pick. Teleo stepped back to let Jessum clean Benny's hooves, noting that the gelding accepted Jessum's touch without flinching.

When the hooves were all cleaned, they took saddles and harnesses from the rack. Teleo helped Jessum put on Daisy's bridle, then Teleo saddled Benny, explaining what he was doing while Jessum imitated him and saddled the mare.

"Make sure it's tightened just right," Teleo said, and tugged at Daisy's girth strap that Jessum was cinching around her belly. "That's good."

Jessum's shaggy black hair fell over his eyes. He pushed it back. "I rode bareback a couple of times. On that old donkey who died last year. But never with a saddle."

"Okay, well, it's not too hard." Teleo demonstrated how to get into the saddle and how to dismount.

Jessum put his foot into a stirrup and reached up, gritting his teeth against the pain of his healing ribs. After two failed attempts and a boost from Teleo, Jessum climbed into the saddle and took the reins. Daisy stayed solid beneath him, sensing his inexperience. Teleo patted her shoulder. "Good girl." Teleo raised the stirrups a notch and showed Jessum how to hold the reins.

Teleo took the horses by their bridles and led them down the ramp to the paddock. A loud neigh echoed across the dirt yard. BlackJack stared at them from under the elm tree.

"He's jealous," Teleo said with a chuckle, and Jessum's face lit up with a rare smile.

Teleo got in his saddle and nudged Benny with his heels, and Daisy followed them. Jessum swung side to side in his saddle but relaxed down into it after a few paces. They walked the length of the yard to the old stone bridge that spanned the dry moat. The bridge was rarely used anymore. Everyone entered the castle through the new bridge that led directly to the grand entrance—a wide paved yard that offered sweeping views of the valley and featured a statue of King Elke's grandfather on a rearing horse, below the broad steps that led up to the royal compound and administrative buildings.

The old bridge's foundation arches were blocked off by steel grating and a locked gate, which led to more dry moat and a tall culvert that was used now as a shortcut to the Royal Pasturelands where sheep, goats, and cattle ranged south of the castle. They turned the horses and walked alongside the metal grating to the outer moat wall, then turned again to walk along its length. BlackJack stood under the elm with two old draft horses, two retired hunting mares, and three scruffy ponies. The small herd watched as they approached.

"Let's go around them," Teleo said as BlackJack and Benny eyed each other. Teleo squeezed his knees, directing Benny away from the big black, who pawed at the ground, tossing his head and whinnying.

Jessum clicked his tongue. "Quiet, boy," he said firmly. BlackJack tracked Jessum with his ears as they passed by, but he stayed under the tree. He was a warhorse, after all, and had known discipline at one time.

"Want to trot?" Teleo asked.

"Okay."

Teleo coaxed Benny into a small trot, and Daisy kept pace. Jessum bounced in the saddle.

"Stay light in the saddle," Teleo said. "Move with her. Loose knees, straight back."

Jessum bounced even more.

Teleo laughed. "You'll get it."

The poor boy was favoring his left side, and his head probably hurt with all the bouncing, but his eyes had a shine Teleo had not seen before. They slowed to a walk and went to the far end of the yard and back, transitioning in and out of a trot. They made a few more circuits, then dismounted. Teleo and Jessum led the horses through the barn and out into the grooming yard again, which was open to the sky and walled in by the tack and supply rooms. There, they took off the horses' saddles, groomed them once more, and let them back outside. The matched pair ambled over to the elm tree. BlackJack snorted and nipped at Benny's flank, his teeth flashing in empty air. Benny curled his lip at him but otherwise ignored the big black and joined the herd in the shade.

There were still several hours left in the day before it would be time to go to the training yard. They ate their snack of apples and eggs, then Teleo took Jessum out into the back courtyard where the outhouse was. They were alone. Teleo tugged at the wooden rails used to hang laundry and air out saddle blankets and leather tack, testing their sturdiness, then hung from one and did ten pull-ups.

Jessum watched him. "I don't know if I can do that with my ribs," the boy said.

"Maybe just hang and stretch," Teleo said.

Jessum did as he suggested, making a face. "That's not so bad," he said.

"Can you do one pull-up?" Teleo asked.

Jessum pulled himself up, wincing, then lowered himself. He tried once more but barely made it up and then dropped to his feet. "Hurts too much."

"That was good," Teleo said. "Try some push-ups."

Jessum got on the ground and was able to do ten. Teleo led him through more exercises. When the boy was winded, he let him rest and then made him do it all again. They drank cold water from the well and splashed the dust off. Jessum finally hobbled to the barn and up to the loft to nap until it was time to leave. Teleo stayed downstairs and chatted with the old groom, reminiscing about old times.

Every day, they rode the horses, exercised, ate, napped, and went to the training yard to continue their stonework. They did not run into Gerik again. They made slow progress—Teleo insisted that the stones fit perfectly with no more than a hair's width between each. Jessum was eager to learn and soon was shaping stones with a hammer and chisel. Teleo had decided to work from the outer rings inward, in order to teach Jessum on the larger stones before tackling the center, where the tesserae got smaller and smaller and the shaping more meticulous. The interlocking star and petal pattern was both simple and complex, forming different shapes depending on how you looked at it.

They did their best to match the colors so that the new stones did not stand out so starkly against the old. Of course, the original ones were worn smooth with age, and no matter how much they polished the new ones, they could not replicate the texture. Teleo did not think the difference was big enough for a casual observer to notice. Besides, the stones would be covered with boot scuffs and dust soon enough.

Jessum recovered from his injuries and was growing stronger from their workouts, which Teleo made more challenging every day. The boy was learning how to sit a horse, and Teleo set up small obstacles in the yard to practice jumping. The dapple grays loved it, and BlackJack continued to glare jealously from the shade of the elm tree, sometimes prancing out to greet them as though he wanted to play but then snapping at the other horses and rearing if they got too close. Jessum had stopped brushing him, and his dusty coat was slowly returning to its patchy, matted condition. But Teleo still caught Jessum talking softly to the horse in his stall when they came home from work in the pre-dawn hours and sneaking him snacks of carrots and apples.

Summer was quickly waning. The training yard was taking longer than Teleo had anticipated but he decided they could take one day off and still complete the yard by October.

They rose early and prepared for the ride to Teleo's farm. He hadn't been home in weeks and needed to make sure his cousins were tending his farm as they had promised, in exchange for half its output and all the perishables while he was away. The apples and almonds would be maturing, and he hadn't discussed their harvesting with them. They saddled up the horses and headed out. Daisy and Benny neighed excitedly when they came down off the hill of the sprawling city and left through the South Tower Gate, knowing where they were headed.

They emerged onto the King's Highway. The land flattened out and the road drew a straight line, bisecting the wide valley, which was built-up with modest stone houses and small plots of land just south of the city. The cobblestones gave way to a wide clay and gravel road with wagon ruts scoring both sides of the thoroughfare that brought in produce from the fertile valley. Each horse took a relatively flat section between the ruts. No wagons or riders were in sight.

"Ready to run?" Teleo asked Jessum and the horses.

They did not need any more encouragement. Although they had galloped in short spurts in the yard, the paddock was not big enough for a full-out, sustained run. The horses took off. Teleo watched Jessum. He kept his balance and moved with Daisy as the mare stretched out and flew over the ground. The boy's face beamed as the wind whipped his shoulder-length hair. Teleo finally reined in Benny and whistled to Daisy to slow to a canter. They had a long ride ahead of them.

The dwellings grew more sparse and soon gave way to vast grazing lands. The fields on the western flank were the Royal Pasturelands, owned by the king and enclosed by tall field-stone walls. Sheep dotted the king's land in the distance, and the walled Royal Hunting Forest painted a dark green swath running parallel to the road a couple of miles to the west, with the foothills and Blue Mountains looming beyond the private forest. To their left were open, public grasslands where a few brown-and-white cattle roamed, the fields stretching eastward for many miles to a misty horizon of low mountains.

They made good time and soon arrived at his farm. Teleo found things in decent condition—a few hens appeared to be gone and a few new chicks and ducklings were waddling around. His two young steers gazed at him from the back pasture. They were fattening up nicely.

They removed the saddles and bridles, watered the horses, rubbed them down, and put them out in a fenced pasture where Daisy and Benny immediately buried their noses in the deep grass. When Teleo could no longer avoid it, he took the long metal key from his pants pocket and slid it into his front door lock. The door swung open to the musty smell of a house that was not lived in.

The house was a vestige of a life he had once loved. He had thought more than a few times to burn it down. The grief that lingered there sometimes caught him in an unguarded moment and paralyzed him when he stumbled upon some little thing: a doll he had carved for Abigail hidden all these years in a dark corner behind a heavy cabinet; the little-boy overalls Bella-Mae had made for Oren that he found mixed in with a stack of his own forgotten work shirts; a polished shell comb of Bella-Mae's that he still kept where she'd left it by her mirror; the reflection of his haggard face that she'd once kissed.

But it was exactly those painful and precious memories that stopped him from setting fire to the place. Besides, he had built it too well. The floor was stone with a wooden floor laid over it, and the walls were thick granite blocks. The roof was made with heavy oak beams and boards he had milled himself from trees on his land and was shingled with oak shakes. He could maybe burn the roof and scar the floor, but the empty shell would remain.

"This is your house?" Jessum asked, turning in a circle in the middle of the main room, gazing around at the sparsely furnished space. "You built it?"

"Yeah. How could you tell?"

Jessum grinned. "Can't even fit a thin sheet of parchment between those stones." He pointed to the pale beige granite walls whose blocks met in nearly invisible lines.

Teleo grinned back. "My father taught me how to do that. He helped me build it."

Jessum nodded. "Does he live here with you?"

"No." Teleo shook his head. "He built his own house."

"Where does he live now?" Innocent curiosity lit the boy's eyes.

"He died during a raid. My aunt lives there now."

"Oh."

They stood in awkward silence, then Jessum piped up, changing the subject. "Who made the curtains?"

Teleo glanced at his wife's yellow gingham curtains, rippling from the air gusting through the open door.

"What, those don't look like something I'd make?" Teleo joked.

Jessum made a face and Teleo laughed, but his levity soon faded. The boy had lost his shyness with Teleo, which meant he was starting to trust him, and that made Teleo happy. On the other hand, Jessum was touching on tender topics and Teleo was tempted to shut down the conversation. The boy gazed at him with big brown eyes. He wanted to know. He deserved to know.

Teleo sighed. "My wife made them. She and our daughter were murdered in the same raid."

Jessum's face fell. His mouth worked, wanting to say something. Finally, he asked, "Was it the Hill people?" Horror and shame lined his face.

Teleo pressed his lips together and then spoke carefully. "Yes. It was the Hill people." His words bounced off the stone walls and died slowly in the stale air.

Jessum looked at the floor, and Teleo continued, "And my young son, Oren, was kidnapped. Or so I think."

The meaning of Teleo's words slowly sank in and Jessum looked up, his eyes round and glassy. "Like me?"

"Yes," he said softly. "Like you." Tears sprang suddenly to Teleo's eyes. He crossed the room and drew Jessum into his arms. They held on to each other, and the boy's heart beat against Teleo's chest.

5

STAGGAS

eleo and Jessum walked the land, inspecting Teleo's livestock, barns, fields, and orchards. His cousins Timmins and Tams Junior had done a good job tending the farm. The fences were intact, the recent cut of alfalfa was drying in mounds in the east field, and the two large haylofts were already filled. Finding everything in good order, he and Jessum picnicked in the apple orchard, sharing a simple dinner Teleo had packed, along with some tomatoes and cucumbers from his garden. They then spent some time polishing Teleo's two prized longswords, whose place was now over his fireplace instead of strapped across his back. One had been a gift from King Elke himself after Teleo had helped slay a dozen Hill raiders who had snuck into the valley one rainy winter. The other had been his uncle Brady's, who had received it as a gift for valiant service from the current king's father, King Elke the Fourth.

Timmins and Tams Junior showed up and eyed the Hill orphan curiously. Teleo introduced him as his masonry apprentice. They walked the land again and the boy trailed behind by a few paces, but Teleo could tell he was listening and watching as they inspected the orchard trees and tasted the apples. As Teleo had suspected, the apples needed a few more weeks.

"If I'm not back by then, go ahead and harvest them when they're ready. I can't really take the time off," Teleo told them. "Queen's got me working like crazy. The almonds should be ready a couple of weeks after the apples. Wait until most of the hulls are split. Harvest the potatoes, onions, beets, turnips, and carrots when the tops die back. You get half, as we agreed." The young men knew what to do—they had helped him for years—and they were happy with the assurance that they would have enough food to last them through the winter. Both their wives were pregnant.

Teleo and Jessum spent the rest of the day with his elderly aunt Bralla in the house where Teleo was born and had grown up, and where his father had died. She welcomed Jessum with a big hug and sat him at the table, serving him a mug of fresh milk. For a moment, the hardened teenager looked like a young child, contentedly drinking milk and basking in Aunt Bralla's love. It would be good for Jessum to live with Teleo and his extended family. Perhaps the boy would even recover and flourish here, after years of neglect and cruelty. Aunt Bralla shared her supper of ham hock and greens from the garden, then spoiled them with almond tarts with blackberries and whipped cream, and told them the village gossip.

Teleo and Jessum stopped by his farm again on their way back to the castle. Teleo grabbed another hammer from his workshop and a few items of clothing from the house. While Jessum was outside saddling the horses, Teleo dug around in the back of a drawer and found the yellowed scroll his father had given him. He unfurled it and examined the intricate indigo-ink drawing, studying the pattern of the Heliotrope and the image of the dancing Mage—a robed man leaping into the air with a sword raised in one hand and an orb of light cupped in the other. Teleo had believed his father's bedtime stories as a child, but as an adult he had dismissed them as fantastical fairy tales. Now he wondered ...

He rolled up the scroll and stashed it in his travel bag, then locked up the house.

The sun was setting when they finally left the farm. Halfway down the King's Highway, the last vestiges of daylight faded and a full moon rose, brightening the night sky and slashing the rutted road with dark shadows. They alternated between a slow canter and a brisk walk, and found Verdant City asleep except for a few noisy pubs.

The following day, they were back to their routine. They set stone at night, taking advantage of the moonlight, which gave the Heliotrope an eerie glow and made Teleo pause and admire the expanding star pattern as it came into being. It had been several weeks since he had started, and finally they had gotten to the inner sections. Teleo studied his drawings and compared them to the few original stones remaining between the black rays. Some of the pattern was completely missing, and he could not figure out exactly how the tesserae were supposed to fit together. He had inspected the scroll of the dancing Mage, but it did not provide enough detail to finish the complex, inter-locking puzzle. He decided that the only way to complete the yard was to go back to the Royal Garden and precisely measure and sketch the smaller Heliotrope's design.

The next day, Teleo rose before Jessum, gave his horses some oats and hay and waited for them to eat while he ate a quick breakfast of stale bread and boiled eggs, sitting on a stool outside their stall and enjoying their company. When they were done, he gave them a quick brushing and led them outside, mucked their stall, and then left for the Royal Palace.

It was mid-morning already, but the alleyways were oddly quiet. He glanced over his shoulder, wondering if it was wise to leave Jessum alone. Teleo squared his shoulders and continued on. He wouldn't be gone long, and the bullies would be busy training with Gerik. Teleo had considered teaching the boy how to use a sword, but he couldn't very well go against the advice he had given the queen as a pretext to pull Jessum out from under Gerik. Teleo shook off his worries and went to the Palace Gate, where the young guard nodded him through.

At the north entrance to the Royal Garden, the iron gate swung open. Vigo emerged from the shadows of the stone archway and greeted Teleo with friendly surprise. Teleo explained the purpose of his visit, and Vigo sent a young guard to find Gwen. Before long, the Queen's Lady came bustling through the entry tunnel and out into the sunlight.

They exchanged greetings and gossip, and Gwen gave her consent for Teleo to measure the stones in the yard. Teleo left his short sword, weapon belt, and tool belt in the guardroom and entered the private garden as Gwen disappeared into the shadows of the white marble portico.

Teleo breathed in the fragrant air. The serenity of the courtyard made him feel as though he had entered another world, and he wondered if the Heliotrope played some part in it. Birdsong rose from the pear tree, and the little finches fluttered through the branches. He walked to the center of the yard, rolled the man-sized urn to the edge of the Mage's circle, and took in the full mosaic. The white disk at the very center was glowing in the morning sunshine, and he returned to stand upon it. He had no idea what kind of stone it was, its origin as mysterious as the black rays that radiated from it to form the ten-pointed star. He rubbed his chin, wondering where in all the land he would find their source. Perhaps he should ask for the queen's help. She could ask Gerik's father, Henrik Stagga, the Royal Merchant, to find them. Maybe they came from the Far Shell Islands.

Diamond, triangular, and petal-shaped tesserae filled the spaces between and around the black rays, seamlessly merging with the outer rings of multi-colored stones and the flowing, undulating pattern, almost making him dizzy as he watched the pattern revolve around him. The perfection of the geometry inspired newfound respect for the stone masters who had designed the Heliotrope, no doubt Mages in their own right.

Teleo dropped to his hands and knees and got busy sketching, measuring, and counting the stones surrounding the translucent center circle. He was almost done when he heard the telltale whispering of the undergrowth around the pear tree. The prince. *Princess.* Teleo's back was to the tree, and he let himself smile. He had missed his little spy. He let the girl think he hadn't noticed her. Teleo finished his measurements and then checked them all again—he couldn't just come to the Royal Garden whenever he pleased.

When he was satisfied that he had everything he needed, he tucked his small sketchbook and charcoal pencil into his pocket. Wishing to delay his departure, he took a square of cloth from his pocket, polished the strange white stone in the center of the Heliotrope, then ran his fingers across its glossy surface. The bronze urn had left a faint, greenish ring. He rubbed at the stubborn mark with the cloth, wishing he had his polishing wax with him.

His reflection gazed back at him as he bent over the glimmering circle. Graying-brown hair that once had been straw-colored; gray eyes that some called blue; a smooth-shaven face and strong bone structure. His hand froze, clutching the cloth, as his eyes met his reflection. He looked different. The dark eyes in the reflection widened, startled, and the face leaned in. But Teleo had not moved. He blinked. The reflection did not. The brow in the reflection wrinkled, and a hand came up to touch the stone from down below, rubbing it with a bare palm as he had been rubbing it with the cloth. The hand was delicate, the fingers long, with a gold ring on one of them. Teleo held the air in his lungs, afraid to breathe lest the illusion disappear.

The feminine face backed away. Teleo stared as the palm of a hand was replaced by the soles of two bare feet. The image elongated before him. Then, through a clouded, distorted view, he realized that the person on the other side had stood up. It was a tall figure, thin and graceful, and clothed in a long red dress. Shiny black hair hung over the woman's shoulders. Teleo was mesmerized, his gaze transfixed on the wavering image that stood upside down as though it were a reflection in still water.

A shimmering sword came into view, held in both her hands as she crouched and turned, her eyes darting around, her nose raised as though sniffing the air. She spun and stared down at him in alarm, grasping the sword in one hand while the other hand gestured at him wildly. *Go. Run,* she mouthed. Teleo's heart caught in his throat and he sucked in his breath, his heart throbbing. She glared at him with wide eyes, as though wondering why he was not responding.

A loud crash came from the king's audience chamber. Yells and screams flooded the yard from the open windows of the ground level of the Royal Palace. The clanging of metal on metal. Men yelling. Women screaming. Banging and crying. Teleo hopped to his feet and crept backwards and then slipped behind the bronze urn. Grunting and thuds of hand-to-hand combat came from the garden's entry arch, and swords clashed in the covered portico across from where Teleo crouched. Vigo yelled and grunted as he fought at the gate, his cries ending in a gasp. Teleo reached for the sword at his shoulder but met empty air. The sound of many boots pounded through the entry tunnel where Teleo's weapons were stashed. A line of men ran along the portico, the aggressors running towards the reception chambers and flinging doors open. The fighting intensified indoors. Teleo identified the victims by their voices—commanding, yelling, pleading. *King Elke. His attendants. Serving women.*

Shrieks died to gurgles, announcing one death after another. The king's voice was silenced, and a hubbub of panicked yells and jubilant shouts announced his death. Teleo's mind raced and then slowed. He was in his battle brain, sensing with his entire body the threats and weaknesses of the attack that surrounded him. The skirmish at the entry arch was over. The tunnel was silent, as was the shadowed arcade lining the courtyard. The thunder of pounding footsteps floated through open windows. Thuds and scuffles from the tutoring room on the second floor. Crying. Begging. Small grunts and sharp yells. *The two princes. The Royal Tutors. Queen Eleanor.* Their death screams were followed by moments of silence and then more yelling men.

Commands echoed across the yard from an upper window. "Search the bedchambers. We need to kill them all." It was a familiar male voice. *Gerik.*

"The youngest prince is not here," responded a voice from the open doorway of a bedchamber balcony. A breeze fluttered the leaves of the pear tree.

"Find him!" Gerik yelled.

"Check the wardrobes and under the beds," another voice called out. Teleo recognized the gravelly voice. *Rickhart.*

Teleo peered over his shoulder. The balconies of the east wing behind him were empty, attached to guest chambers that were never used by the reclusive family. The loud crashes of furniture being overturned came from the royal bedchambers in the west wing, followed by shattering glass and a cascade of books hitting the floor from the library. Teleo crept to the undergrowth a pace behind him, crawled under the overhanging branches of exotic trees, and then squeezed between overgrown bushes until he was under the pear tree. The queen's chamber was quiet over-head. Banging and the sound of breaking furniture came from the study rooms in the second story of the south wing as the attackers moved methodically from room to room, searching for Kaspari, whom everyone knew as the sickly Prince Kaspar.

Teleo peered up into the branches. The princess was staring down at him, her face ashen. Her arms were wrapped around the tree trunk, her hands clutching the bark. She wore her brown cap with her hair tucked up inside, loose brown linen trousers and tunic that blended in with the bark, and boy's riding boots. She was beyond his reach, and he gestured frantically for her to come down to him. Teleo held his hands up, telling her with his eyes to hurry. She hesitated for a moment, then half-climbed, half-fell into his waiting arms. He helped her land on her feet and nudged her to go in front of him. They stole silently through the bushes, trying not to shake the branches. They froze as a half-dozen men ran along the portico and disappeared into the door that led to the king's audience chamber. When the arcade was silent again, they continued creeping until they were across from the arched entryway.

Teleo held his finger to his lips. She nodded, wide-eyed, and joined him as he pressed against the furry trunk of a tree whose long fern-like fronds draped over them.

There were four ways out of the Royal Palace: the grand staircase outside the king's audience chamber; the arched entry tunnel in front of them; the kitchen that was outside the dining room, below the library and across a small exterior courtyard;

or they could jump off the roofs onto hard cobblestones. Their best chance was through the garden gate. Teleo scanned the surroundings and pointed towards the archway, which stood four paces from their hiding spot at the edge of the portico.

The princess nodded, her mouth gaping in a wordless grimace. She was breathing in short little gasps but she was not crying; her big brown eyes shone with the wild, determined glaze of a fox trying to outwit a pack of baying hounds. Teleo took her hand, delicate and strong, and together they sprang across the portico and into the dim archway tunnel, then pressed their backs against the stone wall. The iron gate at the end of the shadowed tunnel was wide open. Framed against the light of the outer bailey stood two guards shifting restlessly on their feet, their backs to Teleo and Kaspari. Vigo was sprawled face up in a puddle of blood, and one of his young guards was lying on his side nearby, impaled by a spear, his mouth still leaking blood and his eyes staring lifelessly at the cobblestones. The door to the guardroom was set into the tunnel wall to Teleo's left, five paces away, and stood open. The guards were several paces beyond that. Teleo motioned towards the doorway, and Kaspari nodded. Taking advantage of more banging and yelling, they dashed to the guardroom and ducked inside.

The stone room was bare except for a cluttered wooden desk, two benches, and an empty sword rack. Teleo's weapons and tool belt sat on the bench where he had left them. He slid the short sword into its sheath across his back, then strapped on the belt with his collection of knives and clubs, and the tool belt with its chisels and hammers.

"Wait here and come when I call you," he whispered.

The princess clasped her hands together to stop them from shaking. They both knew they had only one chance to escape. He nodded at her and peered around the edge of the door frame.

Teleo crept stealthily through the shadows. He wanted to make the least commotion possible, and that meant catching the guards by surprise and dispatching them quickly. The guards were young and jittery, swords in hand. They wore standard armor: steel-plate cuirasses protecting their torsos, and simple steel dome helmets that covered the skull but left the face and throat open. Teleo wore no armor. He padded silently across the cobblestones and got a hand around the first soldier's mouth, put a knife to his throat, and pulled the blade across in one smooth motion. He always kept his knives sharp.

He pushed the dying man into his companion's arms and plunged the knife into the second soldier's neck, missing the artery. The soldier stumbled, dropping his sword, and Teleo ripped off the man's helmet and swung a hammer with all his strength sideways into his skull. The two soldiers fell against the wall in each other's arms as Teleo pulled his knife free, found the artery on the second try, and then backed away as the two men fell heavily into the archway. Teleo peeked around the corner, looking down both sides of the outer bailey. The way was clear—Gerik's forces were busy searching the interior of the palace.

"Come now," he called, his voice low but firm. Kaspari appeared and ran to him, hopping over the dying men, and clung to Teleo. Tears were streaming down her cheeks. He disentangled her hands from his shirt, gently squeezed her rigid fingers, and locked eyes with her. "Stay right behind me. If we meet anyone, stay behind my back where I can reach you. Do you understand?"

She nodded frantically.

"Stay strong," he said. "We're going to get out of here." She kept nodding, mucus running from her nose as she stared down at the man with the bashed skull whose limbs were still twitching. "Don't look." He took her chin and gently turned her head aside. "Let's go."

They left the archway and ran, staying in the narrow shadow that hugged the palace wall. As they reached the eastern end of the north wall, three soldiers rounded the corner. They all froze and stared at one another for a moment. Teleo reacted first and buried his dagger into one man's neck and jabbed his sword up into the second man's gut below the cuirass while the third man was still brandishing his weapon.

Teleo left his blades in the bodies of the two men who were staggering in a stunned dance, then dipped inside the circle of the third man's raised sword arm and squeezed his throat, taking him down to the ground and pinning his arms with his knees. The man was strong, and they rolled across the cobblestones. Teleo tucked his chin and squeezed his eyes shut against the man's scrabbling fingers, clasping his legs around the man's waist to keep him from drawing his belt knife. He kept his iron grip around the man's neck until he passed out. Teleo unsheathed his hunting knife and pierced the man's carotid artery, drawing a fountain of blood, then cut the artery on the other side of his neck to ensure he would not rise again.

He went back to the second man, who was on his knees, gasping, his hands wet with blood and clutching the hilt of Teleo's sword where it protruded from his belly. The Stagga sigil, a leaping stag, was molded into the soldier's metal chestplate. He stared up at Teleo, who grabbed his chin, pushed it back, and slit his throat like he would a sheep. The man stared at him as he fell slowly to the ground, grasping at his sliced neck, blood gushing out between his fingers. The boy couldn't have been more than eighteen. Teleo knelt down and slowly withdrew his sword blade, telling the young soldier, "It'll be all right. It'll be over in a minute." The soldier's mouth moved silently as he stared up at the sky. In the span of three of Teleo's labored breaths, the young man stopped moving, his eyes frozen open.

Teleo turned away and retrieved his dagger from the first man, who was already dead. Teleo quickly cleaned and sheathed his weapons, then wiped his bloody hands on the pant leg of a fallen soldier. He turned to Kaspari, who was huddled against the stone wall, staring at him. He grabbed her forearm and dragged her across the abandoned east bailey yard, through a servant's gate that stood open and unguarded, and into the maze of cobblestone streets.

They headed towards the stables, racing down narrow alley-ways. A group of laborers and cleaning women appeared around a corner, running towards the South Tower Gate. Teleo hid Kaspari behind him. The laborers and cleaning women slowed and stared at his blood-stained clothes.

"Leave the city," he told them. "Rebels took the palace." The group faltered for a moment and then continued running, and Teleo and Kaspari sprinted to the stables.

The old groom lay in a tangled heap in the doorway, his open eyes cloudy from cataracts. They must have broken his fragile neck. No other stable hands were to be seen. Teleo's heart hammered as he worried the attackers had found Jessum as well. But the princess was at his side, the lifeblood of the kingdom gazing up at him.

He and Kaspari stepped over the groom and entered the dim building. Only the buzzing of flies and shuffling of horses in their stalls disturbed the morbid silence. The Staggas' horses filled the front stalls, some of them pacing in tight circles in their box stalls and throwing their heads in agitation. Teleo thought to let them loose to deny the Staggas the use of their mounts, but they were too well-trained and wouldn't wander far, and Teleo couldn't bring himself to kill them.

They went to the last aisle and hurried down the line. Teleo poked his head out the paddock door and whistled softly. Daisy neighed and loped over, followed by Benny, both of them flicking their tails nervously.

"Yeah, I know," Teleo murmured. "The old groom is dead."

BlackJack pawed the ground and snorted from under the elm tree among the small herd of horses huddled against the back wall. BlackJack broke away from the herd, rearing and trotting around the yard, then stopped and glared at Teleo, his ears pinned back and his tail lashing back and forth.

"Don't look at me like that," Teleo said to him. "I didn't do it."

Teleo herded the dapple grays indoors and closed the gate behind him. His horses went directly into their open stall, expecting food. Daisy nosed his bloody shirt and gazed at him.

"It's okay," Teleo said soothingly, patting her neck. "We're getting out of here. But I need to check on something real quick." He glanced at Kaspari, who was silently looking on, her face pale.

He ran to the back corner and climbed the ladder. The loft was empty. He climbed back down, and Kaspari followed him out into the rear courtyard.

Jessum was sitting on the cobblestones, leaning back against the well. His hands were pressed over his abdomen, red with fresh blood. A swath of red crossed the yard where he had dragged himself several yards from the far corner.

"I tried calling for you," Jessum said weakly, his face contorted in pain.

"What happened?" Teleo asked, rushing to his side and feeling the pulse at his neck. His skin was cool and his pulse was weak.

"A couple of guys I'd never seen before. They were looking for you."

Jessum had another bloody gash on his thigh and one on his upper arm. The gashes were oozing blood, not spurting.

"Let me see," Teleo said, slowly lifting Jessum's trembling hands from the wound in his abdomen. It was a clean puncture wound, made by a sword.

"It went all the way through," Jessum rasped.

Teleo pressed the boy's hands over his abdomen. He frowned and went to the wash basin at the side of the yard, cleaning his hands as best he could, then returned to Jessum's side. He felt around his back and found the warm, wet exit wound with his fingers. Teleo had tended to many of his mates on the battlefield and assisted the field surgeons, and had seen this kind of wound before. At least the sword had been sharp, and the attacker had not twisted his weapon. Also, it was towards his side, and well below the ribs.

"How long ago did this happen?" Teleo asked as he took a linen fly sheet off a laundry rail and tore it into strips.

"I don't know." The boy was in pain, his voice hoarse. "Twenty minutes, maybe."

Teleo folded a piece of cloth for Jessum to press against his abdomen, pressed another to his back, and then tied a long length around his back and belly to help hold the bandages in place. He shook his head with concern. The boy needed surgery.

"Here, drink as much as you can," Teleo said, raising a bucket of water from the well and putting the drinking ladle to the boy's lips. Jessum took a few loud gulps, then turned his head away. Teleo quickly wrapped bandages around the boy's lacerated arm and leg, then looked up at the princess, who was standing to the side, frowning at him. Teleo took a deep breath and got to his feet, trying to decide what to do.

"Who's he?" Kaspari asked.

Teleo's throat tightened. "He's my apprentice."

"He's hurt badly," she said.

"I know," he said, forcing out the words. "But we have to go."

"You're not going to leave him here, are you?" Her voice was thin.

Jessum closed his eyes and moaned.

Teleo took a deep breath. "We don't have time."

A bell tolled frantically from the outskirts, urging them to run.

"We can't leave him here." Her voice was almost a wail.

"They'll be after you," he said, struggling between what he wanted to do and what duty demanded.

"We have to help him," she said firmly. Her suddenly commanding tone was that of her mother's.

"It will take time," he said.

"Then we must hurry," she said.

He shook his head, knowing he was making a mistake, but squatted and lifted Jessum into his arms. The boy was not light. "I'll do what I can, but you'll need to help me."

———◆———

Teleo carried Jessum through the barn and out into the grooming yard, with a string of instructions for Kaspari. "Get me a stack of those white horse fly sheets from the supply room, and the small wooden box on the counter. Get a block of brown soap and a clean grooming brush. Spread a sheet down here. Hurry."

She scrambled to obey his orders, spreading out the white cloth on the cobblestones by the inner wall of the grooming yard and then setting the stack of folded sheets down on it. The sheets were bright white linen, having been bleached and hung in the sun by the stable hands, and had the dead king's elk-head sigil embroidered on the flank panel in brown and gray.

"Buckets of water. I need as many as you can carry. From the well, in back," he said.

Kaspari ran off and he could hear the well crank working.

Teleo laid Jessum on his back with a rolled saddle blanket propping up his head, then went to the loft and grabbed his tin of herbs. Downstairs, he found the small coal brazier the old groom used to heat water for tea. The coals were still hot. Teleo carried the brazier into the grooming yard, stoked the coals quickly, and then set water to boil in the groom's teakettle. While it was heating up, he went into the supply room and searched frantically through the medicine cabinet, finally finding the tin he was looking for. He opened the lid. The tin was full of catgut sutures coiled in alcohol. Teleo silently thanked the old groom, then grabbed a jug of grain alcohol and a steel dish and went back out into the yard. He submerged his hands and forearms into a bucket of water, scrubbed them with the soap and brush, and then dried his hands on a white sheet.

"Wash your hands," he instructed Kaspari as she set another bucket down.

"Drink," Teleo said to the boy, filling his waterskin with clean water and putting the spout into Jessum's mouth, making him drink half of it. Then he took a dab of poppy paste and stuck his finger inside Jessum's cheek. "Swallow that," he ordered.

"Get me four strands of the dapple-gray mare's tail hairs. Hurry," he told Kaspari as she finished washing her hands. He gave her a knife and she ran into the barn, then returned, panting. He had her wash the long hairs and then coil them in the boiling water, then he found the sharp scalpels he would need from the wooden box, along with several needles, and dumped them all into the dish of grain alcohol.

He ran into the barn and slung two sacks of oats over his shoulders, then dropped them next to Jessum. Kaspari returned with a fourth bucket of water.

"Wash your hands again," he said as he washed his own. "Cut a sheet into small squares. This big," he said, outlining a foot-square piece. "Don't let them touch the ground. Stack them on the sheet." He took his knife and cut several long strips for bandages while she meticulously cut a square the size of a handkerchief.

"Faster," he said.

Her hands trembled as she quickly cut a second square.

Teleo cut away Jessum's pant leg, washed the deep and bloody cut, then wrapped Jessum's leg tightly with a bandage and propped it up on an oat sack.

"We'll come back to this later," he told Jessum, whose muscles were shaking. Teleo removed the bandage around Jessum's torso and quickly replaced the back compress with a clean one, wedging more cloth underneath his back to create pressure.

"Kaspari, take a white square and press down on his belly. Not too hard. Give me your arm," he said to Jessum. Kaspari glanced up sharply, then applied pressure to Jessum's abdomen while Teleo quickly cleaned and wrapped the arm wound and then raised the boy's arm onto the other sack of oats.

"Did you swallow that poppy? Here, chew on this," he said, putting a long stick into Jessum's mouth. It was an assortment of herbs wrapped around a sturdy oak dowel. His field surgeon friend, Filbert, called it the "soldier's best friend," a weave of white willow bark, cannabis bud, skullcap root, and mullein, which they habitually collected as they ranged the countryside, chewing on it on at night around the campfire. Everyone else called it the "happy stick."

Teleo ran back for two more sacks of oats and laid all one hundred pounds over Jessum's legs to hold them down. He lashed both of Jessum's wrists to horse hitches behind his head and moved the happy stick crosswise in Jessum's mouth like a bit. "Clamp down on that if it hurts. And it's gonna hurt. You ready?"

Jessum nodded, his eyes wide and his pupils already pinholes from the poppy.

Teleo dunked his arms into a fresh bucket of water, scrubbing quickly, and then dried his hands and knelt next to the boy. More bells tolled in the background.

"Cut away his shirt," he said as he washed the blood away from Jessum's abdomen while Kaspari peeled back the blood-soaked linen. If Jessum was lucky, the sword had only pierced the large intestine, not the nest of snakes, as Filbert liked to call the small intestines. If it had hit an artery, Jessum would have passed out already.

"I'm going to have to open you up more so I can get my hands in there and sew you up. Okay?"

Jessum's head lolled from side to side and he moaned.

Good. The poppy was working.

Teleo grabbed a sharp scalpel, took a deep breath, and carefully cut a big L into the boy's skin around the belly wound. A familiar growl of pain escaped Jessum's throat, just like every soldier who had withstood the knife.

"Soak up the blood as I go," Teleo said.

Kaspari obeyed, pressing a clean cloth to the incision.

Teleo cut through the next layers of tissue, separated the abdominal muscles, then cut through the membrane sealing the gut, careful not to go too deep. Jessum's legs were writhing under the oat sacks, and his arms strained at their restraints. "Bite the stick," Teleo commanded. Jessum grunted and clamped down on the stick.

Teleo gently peeled back the flap of flesh. "Hold this with a cloth," he said.

Kaspari hesitated, then grabbed onto the bloody flesh and held it back as Teleo took clean linen squares and packed them inside the abdominal cavity where blood had pooled, soaking it up. He found the pink fleshy tube of the large intestine. Half the tube was sliced cleanly, yellow-brown goo and blood leaking out. Teleo scowled and soaked up the mess.

"Get that fly out of here," he snapped, blowing at a fly that had landed on the bloody cloth in Kaspari's hand. "Keep them off him." She frantically swatted away the fly, and he realized vaguely that he was ordering around a princess.

The boy had fallen unconscious and was lying motionless. His pulse was steady. Teleo threaded a needle with catgut and went back inside Jessum's open abdomen. He cleaned the area and then placed several sutures to close the intestinal tube. Sweat was dripping from Teleo's brow, and Kaspari patted it dry with a cloth. There were nicks in two loops of the small intestine lying right next to the large intestine, and Teleo placed two sutures in each. He soaked up more blood, then checked again. Everything appeared intact. He hoped he hadn't missed anything.

"Soak a rag in clean water and give it to me," he said, and she scurried to comply.

Teleo cleaned things up in there as best he could and then applied honey-ointment and sewed up the interior of the exit wound. He sat back on his heels, taking deep breaths and resting for a moment. Kaspari waved away the flies buzzing madly overhead, attracted to Filbert's honey-ointment.

Teleo began again. He sewed up the layers of the L incision and sword entry wound, stitched closed the outer skin with horsehair, smeared the stitches with ointment, and finally laid a clean square over Jessum's belly.

The boy was sleeping. The happy stick had fallen to the side, and drool stretched from his mouth. Teleo pressed his ear to the boy's chest. He was breathing shallowly but evenly. His heartbeat was steady. He turned his gaze to Kaspari, who looked slightly nauseous.

"You are doing well," Teleo said gently. "Wash your hands and stretch your legs a bit. Then we will finish up. Okay?"

She nodded and draped a sheet over Jessum, then turned and sank her hands into a bucket, tinting the water pink as she scrubbed her hands. Teleo did the same.

Sounds drifted through the yard: bells tolling, distant yells, the snorting of horses. They had come this far—they would finish closing up the boy's wounds. If they died for their delay, so be it.

They pulled off the two oat sacks, unbound Jessum's wrists, and carefully rolled the boy onto his side. Teleo cleaned and sewed up the exit wound on his back, then took strips of cloth and wrapped clean bandages around his torso and laid him on his back again. Teleo took a deep breath and unwrapped Jessum's leg, forcing himself to concentrate for just a few more minutes. The boy stirred and moaned. The cut was deep but was in the fleshy part of the thigh and hadn't reached the bone. Teleo cleaned and stitched him up in layers, wrapped his thigh in a bandage, and then moved on to the arm.

He finally knotted the last suture and met Kaspari's eyes. "Good work," he said, and she answered with a weak smile. Filbert would be proud of him. Only time would tell if the boy had lost too much blood or would succumb to infection—if Teleo could get them out of Verdant City alive.

He washed the blood from his hands, then they carefully stripped Jessum of the remainder of his clothing and wiped him down. Teleo found a clean set of Jessum's clothes in the loft, and they dressed him, finally pulling on the new leather boots Teleo had bought for him. Teleo pushed a small hard candy down Jessum's throat—Filbert's recipe of honey, salt, licorice, cinnamon, and ginger root—followed by another dab of poppy paste and several spurts of water.

Teleo stood, his legs and back stiff. They wadded up the bloody sheets and stuffed them into an empty grain bin. He could hear Benny and Daisy nickering at him.

"Yes," he answered. "It's time to go."

———————————◆———————————

Teleo took a moment to think through his escape plan. The bells continued tolling—*dang dang dang*—and more yells rang out in the distance. He went up to the loft and quickly changed out of his bloody clothes and into his travel clothes: buckskin pants, a fresh linen shirt, his old leather cuirass and shoulder guards, and his riding boots. The leather body armor was from his soldiering days and bore a dented steel plate with King Elke's sigil molded into it: an elk's head with a massive set of antlers. He rolled up his and Jessum's blankets, stuffed their spare clothes and personal belongings into his two pairs of saddlebags, and passed it all down to Kaspari. He packed a few other important items into his travel bag, slung the leather sack over his shoulder, and climbed down the ladder.

Kaspari was waiting outside BlackJack's empty stall. Her clothes had some bloodstains, but nothing too noticeable. The shiny brown linen hid the dark splotches well. She still looked like royalty, however, with such finely woven fabric and the elk sigil embroidered on her tunic pocket. He ran to the front, rummaged through the stable boys' lockers, and found an old pair of overalls, a torn work shirt, and a tattered riding cap. He pushed them into Kaspari's arms. "See if these fit."

While she changed clothes in BlackJack's stall, Teleo went to the old groom's corpse and took a ring of iron keys off his belt, pilfered a small purse of coins from his pocket, and closed the man's eyes. "Rest well, my friend," Teleo said, a small, choking sob escaping his lips. He swallowed his sorrow and returned to BlackJack's stall.

Kaspari's new outfit made her look like a gawky stable boy, rumpled and dirty, like she had been mucking stalls all day.

"Perfect," he said. She still wore her expensive leather boots, but at least they were a dull brown and the toes were scuffed from kneeling over Jessum on the cobblestone yard.

"Come with me," he said. They ran to the tack room and he handed her Daisy's saddle. "You know how to saddle a horse?" he asked, grabbing Benny's saddle and their bridles.

"Of course," she said.

"They were just brushed this morning," he said, tossing her a saddle blanket.

They hurried back to the aisle and threw the saddle blankets over the backs of the dapple grays. Kaspari knew what she was doing and saddled Daisy nearly as fast as he did Benny.

She adjusted the girth strap, then looked up at Teleo, her eyes pooling with tears.

"I know it's hard, Kaspari," he said. "But you need to be strong."

"Can we get Marigold?" she asked.

"Marigold?" he asked.

"My horse." Tears trickled down her cheeks.

"Oh, Kaspari," he said. "Where is he?"

"She's out in the paddocks." Kaspari wiped at her cheeks.

Teleo sighed. "I'm afraid they will have secured the upper stables and Royal Paddocks already, Kaspari. It's too dangerous."

She sniffled and wiped at her nose.

"I'm sorry," Teleo said. "But we need to leave her behind. No one will hurt her."

Kaspari nodded and lowered her head.

Teleo strapped on the saddlebags, lashed his travel bag and bedroll behind Benny's saddle, and then rolled the princess's brown linen clothes in a blanket and secured the bundle behind Daisy's saddle. Finally, he fetched a bucket of clean water and handed Kaspari a ladleful.

"Drink," he said.

While she drank, he scooped up water for himself with his palms, then dunked his and Jessum's waterskins into the bucket, filling them quickly. He hung his across his shoulder and handed Jessum's to Kaspari. He then set aside a coil of rope and went into the grooming yard for Jessum, with Kaspari close on his heels.

Teleo tried to get more water down Jessum's throat, propping the boy's head up against his shoulder. The boy was still in a stupor, but Teleo managed to get some down without choking him. They wrapped Jessum's torso in a blanket, then Teleo hoisted the boy in his arms and carried him into the stable.

"Ready?" he asked Kaspari.

She nodded. Her eyes were fastened on him, and it struck him how completely dependent she was on him now. What responsibility had he assumed? He tried to give her a comforting smile, but her mouth only turned down further.

Teleo went to the mounting block and clicked his tongue for Benny. He climbed up onto the block and awkwardly lifted

Jessum onto Benny's saddle, hoping that the sutures would hold, and then climbed on behind him. Jessum slumped heavily against Teleo's chest.

"Hand me that rope," he said, and Kaspari scurried to comply. He uncoiled it and gave her one end. She helped lash Teleo and Jessum together under the armpits.

This was not at all how Teleo had envisioned their speedy escape. If they were attacked while he was burdened like this, they would all die. He was an idiot for putting the princess's life at risk for the sake of a Hill orphan. The thought was an empty echo inside his head. The boy had stolen Teleo's heart, and there was nothing he could do about it.

Teleo nudged Benny with his heels. The dapple gray went directly for the paddock door. Kaspari opened the door for the horses, closed it behind them, and then got in her saddle and followed Teleo down the stone ramp.

6

THE KING'S HIGHWAY

Benny and Daisy walked single file down the ramp to the dry-moat paddock. Teleo tried to hold Jessum steady as they headed towards the iron gate under the stone bridge. The moat was relatively isolated from view—the substantial walls shielded the castle and had been unmanned since the kingdom's borders had been secured after the Valley Wars.

Teleo wondered how many soldiers the Staggas had with them and how strong the resistance would be against their coup. Probably minimal. Gerik was the Master of Arms, and most active soldiers were away at the border outposts. Everyone else just wanted to live their lives and stay out of trouble. Even Teleo himself had not tried to stop the surprise attack. What could one man do against so many?

He regarded the princess, who sat confidently in the saddle and scanned the walls that hid her home and murdered family. Locks of hair had spilled out from under the stable boy's cap. Her curls were light brown, not the golden blond of her mother's, and cut short—barely covering her neck—but shiny and bouncy. Teleo did not know how he had ever seen her as a boy. Her skin was soft and rosy, her bone structure delicate, and her brown eyes large, with long dark lashes. The faster he could get her into female clothing, the better. They would be searching for a prince, after all, not a princess.

Teleo urged the horses into a brisk walk and wrapped his arm around Jessum's chest so that they moved together. BlackJack neighed at them from across the yard and trotted towards them, nostrils flaring.

"No, BlackJack," Teleo said as the fiery gelding approached.

The black horse pranced nervously behind them. They reached the gate and Teleo handed Kaspari the groom's key ring. She dismounted and after several panicked tries, found the right key and pushed the big gate open, the hinges creaking loudly. They passed through the gate, with BlackJack hovering nearby. The big black reared and landed on his front hooves, kicking up a cloud of dust. The gate was heavy, and Kaspari had to get behind it to push. Before she could close it, BlackJack leapt forward and dashed through the opening. He stopped a few paces away and circled, glowering at Teleo.

Teleo shook his head at the horse but let him be. Kaspari got in the saddle, and they walked several yards to the large culvert. An old rusted gate stood open, and the two dapple grays clomped through the dark tunnel and out into the sunshine on the other side. The trampling of hooves echoed behind them and BlackJack emerged, ears twitching and nostrils sensing the air. Benny and Daisy scrambled up the steep bank of the dry canal, over the lip, and down a short hill. BlackJack followed not far behind.

A grid of small homesteads came into view to the south, outside the city walls. Beyond the settlement were larger farms, then a rolling vista of grassland dotted with oaks stretching for miles into the distance. A large flock of the king's—former king's—sheep grazed a far-off field. The Royal Pasturelands were bordered on one side by the King's Highway and on the other by the Royal Hunting Forest, both sides hemmed in by walls of stacked gray fieldstones. Extending from the south gate in a straight line, the King's Highway was thick with people escaping the city.

They would intercept the road later. For now, he wanted to avoid the busy thoroughfare and the crush of fleeing families. At the moment, he and Kaspari were hidden from view of the castle, standing in the lee side of the canal bank—but meandering through the homesteads and then crossing the fields would leave them exposed. He wished they could simply take off at a gallop, but Jessum leaned heavily against his chest. He couldn't sprint with the boy in his arms. Besides, making a mad dash would draw too much attention.

He forced a few more squirts of water down Jessum's throat until water dribbled down his chin.

"Where are we going?" Kaspari asked.

"To my farm, south of here. Then we'll figure out where to go from there. But first we need to get out of sight of the castle. We'll have to take the long way around."

"There's a path that runs south, inside the Royal Hunting Forest," she said, pointing to the dense trees. "After several miles, there's a stream that cuts across the valley and joins the Silver River. We could follow the stream to the King's Highway."

"Okay," Teleo said. "Good idea."

He followed the princess down the bank and through a copse of ancient oaks. They made their way slowly, stepping over trunk-like tree limbs that grew along the ground, then around thickets of prickly holly bushes. Bells were tolling in distant villages, their discordant tones floating over the valley like a dirge.

Kaspari was silent, her face devoid of expression. The dapple grays plodded along, with BlackJack trailing behind.

They reached the stone wall and backtracked until they reached a gate.

"It'll be locked," Teleo said, doubting that the groom had a key on his ring for the king's private forest.

"I have a key," Kaspari said, and dismounted, pulling a set of long iron keys from her pocket. She tried a few, and one slid into the lock. Benny and Daisy stepped through, and Kaspari locked the gate behind them. BlackJack stomped angrily on the other side, his head swaying back and forth above the six-foot wall.

"Come on," Teleo said to Kaspari, shifting Jessum's head to his other shoulder.

They followed the dirt path and turned left onto a well-maintained grassy lane that cut straight through the forest, parallel to the wall. Smaller paths angled off into the woods to their right. They kept on in a southerly direction. Teleo exchanged glances with the princess at the sound of BlackJack crashing through the undergrowth on the other side of the wall, tracking along with them.

"He's persistent," Teleo said, smiling with her.

They transitioned into a smooth canter. Teleo held Jessum steady, worried that his stitches might get torn open, but more worried that they might be caught by Gerik's men. The boy groaned a few times, which Teleo decided to take as a good sign.

Benny was happy to be running on the perfectly groomed path, regardless of the two men on his back. At least Jessum wasn't quite full-grown, and they were certainly lighter than a wagonload of granite. Kaspari was a skilled horsewoman and Daisy was comfortable with her. All was quiet on the other side of the wall. They must have lost BlackJack, which was just as well.

Teleo clung to Jessum, focusing on keeping them both balanced. If they hadn't been running for their lives, Teleo would be enjoying himself, riding in the king's forest. But it was only a matter of time before the Staggas broadened their search for the prince. Teleo's absence might not cause alarm—from the looks of the King's Highway, the whole of Verdant City was clearing out. He wondered why the soldiers had been at the stables looking for him. Perhaps Gerik was afraid he would cause them problems—which he had. But the Staggas would be focused on finding the prince. Teleo would be an afterthought.

The sun was well past its zenith by the time they reached the stream. They left the path at the small stone bridge and followed alongside the rushing creek until they reached a land bridge with a small culvert flowing underneath it. The stone wall was built across the land bridge, blocking their way. The princess's brow furrowed. "There's a gate farther up."

They went back to the main path and walked the horses until an overgrown path cut off to the left. An old gate stood closed at the end, and Kaspari found its key, forcing the iron gate open. They exited into a grove of oak trees and locked the gate behind them. The trees thinned out quickly, and soon they emerged onto rolling grasslands. They stopped walking and peered northward.

Verdant City was a distant beacon on a hill. The pale granite of the Old Castle Town reflected the afternoon sunlight, and the city's mass of red tile roofs formed terraces down the gently sloping hillside. The white marble palace poked up from the top with its blue stone roofs reflecting the sky. It was beautiful from here, but tears streamed down Kaspari's face.

"No one will detect us at this distance," Teleo said gently. "We must go. Your parents would want you to make it out alive."

She sniffed loudly, wiping at her nose with the back of her hand, and then nodded. He felt bad for her, but they could not delay. There would be plenty of time to grieve later. The search would be on for her, and the young man in his arms was getting cold. He put his fingers to Jessum's neck. He still had a pulse.

"We have to go." He urged the horses forward, and they picked their way across the field. It was slow going, with rocks and holes hiding among the long grass. The King's Highway would be risky, but faster. They moved towards it, paralleling the stream and letting the horses find their way.

Halfway across the wide expanse of grassland, a high-pitched whinny rang out. BlackJack galloped towards them, leaping and zigzagging across the uneven ground, dodging hidden obstacles. He could break a leg at that speed, Teleo worried, but the gelding soon was upon them, breathing heavily, his coat shiny with sweat. They drew to a stop as the huffing horse came right up to them and stood a horse-length away.

"BlackJack," Kaspari said happily. "What a good boy."

The large horse stepped gingerly towards them. Teleo remained motionless and held Benny still with his knees. To his surprise, BlackJack stretched out his neck and nuzzled Jessum's cheek, his hot breath bathing Teleo's face. The boy turned his head and grunted.

Teleo held his breath until the horse backed away. The big black tossed his head and snorted, as though impatient for them to move on.

"I agree, BlackJack," Teleo said. "We must make haste."

They continued forward, with BlackJack flanking them, and made it to the fieldstone wall, which formed a five-foot-tall barrier between them and the King's Highway.

"There are no gates along this stretch," Teleo said. He looked out over the wall. Several wagons trundled north and south of them, but the road in front of them was clear.

"We can jump," she said.

"Easy for you to say," he said, holding Jessum tighter. He sighed. "There's only one way to do this."

Teleo untied the knot at Jessum's chest. Kaspari saw what he was doing and climbed from her saddle onto the wall, then dropped down to the other side. He removed the ropes, guided Benny to stand beside the wall, rolled Jessum from the saddle onto the top of the stones, and then dangled him by the armpits over the edge into Kaspari's arms. The weight of Jessum dropped her to her knees, and the boy rolled onto the grass, but at least she had cushioned his fall. She turned Jessum onto his back and started checking his bandages.

"Wait there," Teleo said.

He decided to ride Daisy. She was the braver of the two horses, and Benny would follow her anywhere. He secured Benny's reins, then mounted Daisy. "Let's go home," he said, and found a solid stretch of ground to give her running room.

"Yah," he said, kicking Daisy's flanks. She had hunted with him and knew what he wanted. The mare backed up a step, then charged the wall and cleared it gracefully, landing cleanly on the flat, grassy shoulder of the road. She tossed her head and pranced in a circle, proud of herself. Teleo called for Benny. Hooves pounded in response, and Benny's gray chest and forelegs appeared over the wall. He cleared the wall, landing heavily and running a few paces before snorting and turning back to them.

Loud neighing and stomping came from BlackJack, whose head hung over the wall.

"Jump, boy," Teleo said. "You remember how." He had been a warhorse. He knew how to jump. The horse paced back and forth on the other side of the wall.

"Chicken," Kaspari teased, but the big horse would not jump.

They took a short break and let the horses pick at the grass. A pair of wagons trundled by and Teleo exchanged greetings with the drivers. The families riding in the back were perched atop mounds of belongings and held wicker baskets of chickens, and stared at them as they rolled by.

Teleo waited for them to pass and then knelt next to Jessum. He was out cold. The boy's pants were soaked in urine, and Teleo quickly changed him into his one remaining pair of clean pants. While he was at it, he checked Jessum's bandages. They were bloody, but not overly so. The boy's skin was cold and clammy, his pulse erratic, and his breathing faint. Maybe Teleo had overdone it with the poppy. Or maybe Jessum had lost too much blood. Or perhaps he was in shock. Or all three. Teleo pushed two more honey drops down Jessum's throat and gave him water. The boy swallowed by reflex but did not awaken.

Teleo checked the dapple grays' hooves, digging a pebble out of Daisy's front left foot. They had to go. Teleo slung Jessum leg-first over Benny's saddle, and with Kaspari's help climbed up after him and maneuvered into position. Kaspari helped him lash the two of them together, and Teleo tied a quick-release knot. BlackJack snorted and stomped from beyond the wall.

The road's hardened clay surface was a relief after the uneven field. They proceeded at an easy canter. BlackJack followed along on the other side of the wall, his head appearing over the stone barrier, only to disappear again as he navigated the rough terrain of the pastureland. They passed a wagon heading in the other direction. It was filled with turnips and driven by an old farmer who stared straight ahead. A short while later, they passed the same pair of wagons filled with families and chickens. The drivers followed them with their eyes as they cantered past.

They continued on, eating up the miles as they alternated between a canter and a brisk walk, passing more families who were fleeing to their home villages. The traffic thinned out as riders and wagons turned onto side roads and headed east into

the fields, disappearing behind distant barns and stands of trees.
They were only a few miles from the turnoff to Teleo's village
when the pounding of hooves from the north made them pull
to the side of the road.

Four soldiers on tall bay horses thundered to a stop with
flying clods of clay, loud snorts, and creaking bridles as the soldiers reined in their sweaty mounts.

"Ho, there, off your horses," the leader commanded, waving
a sword tip at Kaspari and Teleo. "What have you got there?" the
soldier yelled, pointing the sword at Jessum, who was sagging
in Teleo's arms.

"Injured. Got thrown off his horse, then that crazy thing
jumped into the king's pasture," Teleo said in his soldier's
drawl, pointing to BlackJack, who was pacing nervously and
watching from the other side of the stone wall. Never mind
that BlackJack had no saddle ... Teleo was trying to distract
the soldiers long enough to see if he was going to have to
fight them off. He held the rope that bound him to Jessum,
fingering the end of the release knot, contemplating how
best to drop Jessum from the saddle without hurting him or
unseating himself.

"You, boy," the soldier barked at Kaspari. "What's your
family? Are you their father?" the soldier asked, turning a suspicious eye on Teleo. The soldier's gaze shifted back to Kaspari,
taking in the dirty stable boy's clothing and fancy boots.

"How old are you, boy?"

Kaspari stared at the soldier. Daisy danced nervously beneath
her while Kaspari kept her seat and firmly reined in the dapple
gray. "Thirteen, sir," she said.

Teleo bit his tongue.

"All teenaged males must report to the castle," the soldier
barked, gesturing to Kaspari and Jessum.

The soldier and two of his companions surrounded them, while the other tried to cut off Teleo from Kaspari. Teleo maneuvered Benny forward and took hold of Daisy's bridle.

"Not so fast. Their mother is expecting them," Teleo said, elbowing the nose of the young soldier's horse who was trying to force his way between Benny and Daisy. Benny backed his hindquarters forcefully against the soldier's mount, and the horses jostled, vying for position.

"All teenaged boys must report to the castle," the second soldier said as he took the other side of Daisy's bridle. The soldier at Teleo's flank drew his sword and pressed its tip to Teleo's shoulder blade against the thick leather armor. Teleo sidled away, still holding Daisy's bridle with one hand and hanging onto Jessum and the reins with the other.

"What business have you with the boys?" Teleo demanded.

The men's eyes flitted over Teleo's short sword strapped across his back, and his leather cuirass and spaulders that were beat up from years of fighting. Teleo's back was broad, his hands and arms were strong from stonework, and he knew the scars on his cheek and above his eye made him look mean. But he held a half-dead boy in his arms.

Teleo noted the Stagga sigil on their chest armor. "What jurisdiction do Henrik Stagga's men have in the King's Valley?" Teleo challenged, sizing up the men. Two seemed to be seasoned soldiers. The other two were awkward and nervous and looked like they'd never been in a real sword fight. The horses pushed at one another, their hooves striking the clay, leather saddles creaking.

A sharp neigh from Daisy drowned out the soldier's response as she reared and backed up, breaking the grips of Teleo and the soldier. Kaspari wheeled the mare away and turned to face them, balancing confidently in her saddle, her chin held high.

"I will go to the castle," Kaspari said, her voice ringing out.

"After we deliver my brother to my mother. As you can see, he is not well."

"He is a teenaged boy," the fourth soldier said, pointing at Jessum and narrowing his eyes. "He looks like a Hill lad. He your slave? No matter, he needs to come as well. You, old man, you bring them both." The soldier motioned for them to turn around and head northward to the castle. "Don't cause any trouble," the man warned, drawing his sword. The third soldier waved his sword blade at them threateningly.

"But he'll die," Kaspari complained.

"Didn't say nothin' about how alive they had to be." The soldier struck Benny's rear with the flat of his blade. "Get along," he ordered.

Benny shied away a pace. Teleo held on with his knees and steadied Jessum with one arm while he steered Benny to Daisy's side. Kaspari sat straight in her saddle and took everything in with flashing eyes. They faced off against the soldiers, whose four bays pranced and jostled as the soldiers tried to position them as a barrier across the road. The two seasoned soldiers had control of their mounts, while the young soldiers' horses neighed and nipped at one another.

Teleo pulled at the knot and the rope went slack, loosening and falling to his hips. He pulled the rope from around him and Jessum, tossing it to Kaspari, and drew up next to her until their boots and stirrups were touching.

"Switch horses," Teleo said softly. Kaspari hesitated for a second, then reached out and grabbed Jessum's shoulder as Teleo let go and climbed from Benny's saddle onto Daisy behind Kaspari while she scrambled over onto Benny's saddle, hanging onto Jessum as the boy's limp body tottered and fell to the side. Teleo saw Jessum and Kaspari slide from the saddle together. He did not wait for them to hit the ground before he charged Daisy forward, brandishing his sword at the four men.

"I can kill at least one of you," Teleo said menacingly, eyeing the leader. Daisy responded to his knees and stepped smartly side to side. "You first." He leered at the scowling leader. "Then maybe I'll take down one or two more. And the last suckling pig can run crying back to the Staggas with these two boys while we oldsters bleed to death on the King's Highway. Is that how you want to die?" He kept his gaze locked on the leader, whose resolve was visibly wavering.

The second soldier charged Teleo, sword out. Teleo met him steel on steel. Daisy was solid beneath him as he pushed at the sword. The soldier backed off and the leader came at Teleo with a heavy swing at his head. Teleo ducked as the sword blade whizzed overhead. He had no helmet on. That could have killed him. Anger flared up and he struck back, sinking the edge of his blade into the man's upper arm in the gap between his leather elbow guard and steel spaulder. The man swayed in his saddle, holding onto his arm as blood seeped through his fingers.

"I warned you," Teleo yelled, parrying another attack from the second soldier while the two rookies hovered on their nervous mounts. "Leave us be!" Teleo said sternly.

The leader charged again, his face contorted in rage. He was one-handed, swinging wildly at Teleo's shoulder. Daisy reared and kicked him in the chest, sending the man to the ground with a crunch of steel armor. Benny was suddenly at Teleo's flank, his saddle empty. He lunged at the second soldier, driving him back. The soldier's mount bit at Benny's neck, and the two horses reared, the tall bay throwing the soldier from his saddle, where he landed with a thud and rolled in the dirt.

Teleo leapt to the ground and killed the leader with a boot on his chest and a sword through the eye. It was a gruesome move—one Teleo had perfected. The second man crab-crawled away from Teleo as he went at him next.

The two young soldiers got brave, or scared, and charged Kaspari and Jessum, where Kaspari knelt protectively over the unconscious boy. A shrill shriek turned everyone's head.

BlackJack was airborne, leaping over the stone wall, and landed heavily on the grass border. In three strides, he was at Jessum's side. One more stride and he was up on his hind legs, slashing at one of the mounted rookies with sharp hooves. The soldier leapt off his horse with a startled cry. BlackJack turned on the last horse and bit its ear, blood flying and squeals splitting the air as the soldier was thrown off and his horse backed up, trampling him underfoot and rolling heavily to the ground before struggling to its feet and loping off into the field.

Teleo turned to the second seasoned soldier, who was flat on his back. The man held up his hands, pleading.

"Sorry," Teleo said. "I gave you a chance. I can't let you go back now." Teleo sank his sword into the man's lower abdomen in the gap below his chest armor, then took his knife and buried the blade up under his chin. The man's eyes rolled up in his head and blood gurgled out of his mouth.

BlackJack was screeching behind him as the big black and two bays slashed at one another with their front hooves. Teleo backed out of the way as their battle moved towards him. One young soldier was sprawled on the ground behind them, and the other had dropped his sword and was holding his face, stumbling towards the wall, blood dripping. Teleo ran up behind him, grabbed his helmet, and slashed his throat. The young man collapsed, but before he could hit the ground, Teleo crouched and lifted him overhead and tossed him over the wall, warm blood bathing his arm. A thump followed as the body hit the ground. The other young soldier was dazed and struggling to raise himself onto his elbow, one leg twisted grotesquely underneath him. Teleo finished him off with a knife to the throat. The clay road was splashed red with blood.

The soldiers' horses, two of them bloody, had retreated into the open field across the road and watched Teleo as he disposed of their masters, dumping them one after another over the wall, after taking whatever useful weapons he could find. One helmet fit him, and he pushed it onto his head and quickly strapped it under his chin. It did not bear the Stagga sigil, and Teleo needed a helmet badly.

When all the soldiers were out of sight, he turned his attention to Kaspari, who had dragged Jessum to the side of the road and was watching Teleo with huge eyes.

"They would have taken you back," he said gruffly, not liking the horrified look on her face. "And the boy." He couldn't let that happen. But now they really had to run. He had bought them a few hours, at best.

The four bays were several paces from the road. BlackJack ranged back and forth aggressively, pressing them further out into the field. One seemed badly hurt, his head hanging low and blood dripping from shredded skin. Another was injured but not as badly, and the other two were simply confused. They would probably make it back to the castle eventually. In any case, Gerik would send out a search party when his scouts did not return.

"Come on, we have to go," Teleo said to Kaspari. A farmer's wagon would arrive at some point, and he did not need any witnesses. He rolled the pilfered swords and knives in the blanket with Kaspari's linen clothes and secured the heavy bundle behind Daisy's saddle.

Teleo knelt next to Jessum. No bones appeared to be broken from his fall. "Help me get him back in the saddle," he said to

Kaspari, and called Benny over. They struggled with Jessum's limp body. Soon they were on the road again, cantering towards Teleo's village. They had put some distance between themselves and the four bays and dead soldiers when BlackJack came galloping up on the grassy shoulder alongside them.

"Good boy," Teleo called out.

The wind whipped at BlackJack's mane and tail, the long jet-black hair fanning out as he stretched his legs and passed the dapple grays, hooves pounding. He was a warhorse once more, having tasted the blood of combat and reveling in the pure joy of victory.

◆

The Royal Pasturelands ended with a stone wall that veered west and was replaced by open grasslands. BlackJack ranged out into the field, grazing and falling behind. They lost sight of him until he came thundering by—only to wander off again to graze.

As they approached the turnoff that led east towards Teleo's village, he considered the past and the future. He had left a trail a mile wide and plenty of clues as to what had happened. He had left two bodies in the palace archway. Three more soldiers were sprawled on the bailey cobblestones in another bloody mess. And he had left four scouts dead along the King's Highway, tossed in a heap behind the Royal Pasturelands' wall, and their bloodied mounts wandering riderless. The prince was missing and so were Teleo's two horses. It would not take a genius to put two and two together.

Teleo was positive Gerik's father, Henrik, was behind the coup. The trading magnate had probably already declared himself king, leaving Gerik with the title of prince. Nothing would matter more to the Staggas than finding "Prince Kaspar" and killing him.

Gerik would send a force to Teleo's home for sure. But Teleo would not be there to meet them. He had a princess to protect and an apprentice who was dying. Teleo needed to warn his cousins. He bit his lip, struggling with his decision.

When they arrived at his turnoff, the dapple grays' noses turned east, as was their habit, but Teleo steered Benny south to continue on the King's Highway. Daisy looked wistfully in the direction of the farm but followed Benny, and BlackJack shadowed them in the fields.

"Where are we going?" Kaspari asked, reading the horses' behavior.

"I don't think it's wise to show up at my farm right now after all. Besides, I know a healer over the ridge who can help Jessum." He nodded towards the southwest, where forested foothills rose from the valley floor and the Blue Mountains shimmered ghost-like in the distance.

"Is that his name? Jessum?"

"Yeah. You didn't know?"

The girl pushed loose curls away from her eyes. "No, you always just called him 'boy.'"

"Oh. He's the Hill orphan your uncle brought back from the war." Teleo had never liked the queen's brother, Osborn. But he was dead now, so there was some justice in the world.

"You mean the slave?"

Teleo didn't answer. Slavery wasn't a thing in the Verdant Valley Kingdom. They believed in the rights of people. But everyone called the Hill orphans "slaves."

"Well?" The princess asked. "Is he the slave?"

He met her curious gaze and answered stiffly, "He's my apprentice. There is no slavery in the Verdant Valley. You of all people should know that." She blinked in surprise. "Orphan boys are spoils of war, I suppose," he continued. "Or casualties, more like. But they are not to be abused. They should be trained in a trade and then freed. Or traded back to the Sapphire Empire for Verdant Valley orphans, of which there are many." He realized his voice had risen to a disrespectful pitch. The princess was staring at him open-mouthed. Even BlackJack was watching him.

"Come on," he said gruffly, and kicked Benny into a canter, the boy heavy in his arms.

They rode silently and the miles passed by. The pasturelands rose and fell and became hills, and trees began to replace grass. Teleo led them off the road onto no more than a sheep's path, which led over a grassy hill and descended towards a forest of tall pines, thick with blue needles and laden with clusters of small golden pinecones. BlackJack appeared over the crest of the hill behind them and came trotting down the slope. They reached the pines and BlackJack paced behind them, snorting and stomping.

"You coming?" Teleo asked. The big horse tossed his head and then followed them onto the narrow path that led into the shadows under the dark lattice of branches. The bed of needles muffled the horses' steps, and the air was suddenly moist and fragrant. Teleo breathed in deeply, letting the silence of the forest settle into him. The boy stirred and moaned.

The horses walked single file, Benny in the lead and BlackJack taking up the rear a few paces behind Daisy. The forest path forked several times, and Teleo had to close his eyes at each fork to determine the proper direction by feel. If he tried to navigate with his eyes or thought too hard about which way to go, he would get lost, as he had many times when he had first tried to find his cousin's hideaway. He would find himself wandering in circles and end up back at the grassy hill, as though spit out by the strange forest and told to go home.

They forded a small stream and began the long, steady climb into the foothills. The forest became denser and darker as they climbed, and the forks were ever harder to navigate. It was approaching evening by the time they came to a wide and rushing stream, which tumbled down cascades of boulders in a series of small waterfalls and was spanned by a rope bridge. There, they let the horses drink, and Kaspari regarded the bridge, which had a floor of hand-hewn pine planks wide enough for a wagon, which Teleo and his cousins had helped build for Dinsmora.

"Is it sturdy?" Kaspari asked, dismounting and walking out onto it. It did not even sway.

She got back on Daisy, and Teleo led them over the bridge, which creaked under their weight. BlackJack hesitated, then trotted after them. They came to a three-way fork in the road. Teleo always got confused here, wanting to take the center fork that led straight ahead. No, it was the right-hand fork—his cousin lived upstream. He closed his eyes and calmed his breathing. Finally, he opened his eyes and led them onto the left fork, and they marched away from the stream and deeper into the darkness.

They crested a rise and the terrain flattened out. The dense pine forest opened up into a mixed pine and deciduous forest, the floor carpeted with undergrowth and the late afternoon sun casting oblique rays through the branches. He exhaled with relief. They were definitely in his cousin's domain now. Birds twittered and their song followed them as they trod along the grassy path.

7

DINSMORA

Teleo's cousin, Dinsmora the Healer, came out to greet them from her collection of huts. Her hidden homestead was nestled in a meadow at the edge of a small tributary, which eventually made its way to the valley floor and fed into the Silver River. Dinsmora twisted her brick-red hair up into a bun and secured it with a long piece of carved bone as she walked across the clearing.

"Well, if it isn't the queen's personal stonemason," she said. Her dimpled smile fell as she drew closer and saw that Jessum was not moving.

"What happened?"

"Stabbed. Sword in the gut." Teleo untied Jessum and lowered him into Dinsmora's waiting arms and hopped down to help her, his legs and back stiff. They carried Jessum into her round healing hut while Kaspari tended to the horses. They laid him on his back on a straw mattress on the floor, cushioned with a sheepskin rug, and covered him with a woven flax blanket.

"I stitched him up as best I could," Teleo said. He described what he had done as she felt Jessum's pulse and lifted his eyelids. "I hope nothing tore open," he continued. "The journey was hard on him. He should be awake by now," he said with concern. "I gave him some poppy but not too much, I hope."

"His body needs rest," Dinsmora said. "You shouldn't have moved him."

"Well, I couldn't leave him there."

"You could have used a wagon."

Teleo held his tongue as they peeled off Jessum's clothes and unwrapped his bandages, silently bemoaning the fact that his best wagon and harnesses were still at Verdant Castle and he might never get them back.

Teleo lit a lantern, and Dinsmora inspected Jessum's stitches. The wounds were red and puffy, but the sutures were holding. She felt the boy's abdomen and put her ear to his belly. "Sounds good in there. Feels good," she said, watching his abdomen bounce back after she pressed on it. She washed the L-shaped incision and inspected the wounds on his back, leg, and arm.

"I'm mostly worried about his gut," Teleo said. "I hope it doesn't get infected."

"I don't want to open him back up again," Dinsmora said. "Not if you did it right the first time."

Teleo shrugged. "I tried. It was a clean cut. A little messy in there, but I've seen much worse. I'm just glad he survived the ride."

She cleaned the wounds and put ointment on them, then cradled Jessum's head and dribbled an herbal brew down his throat. He coughed and moved his head from side to side. His eyes fluttered open and rested foggily on Teleo.

"What happened?" Jessum muttered.

"You're okay," Teleo said, relieved that he was conscious. "We left the castle. We're at my cousin's house."

"Mmm," Jessum grunted softly, closing his eyes again.

Teleo and Dinsmora washed his body, dressed his wounds with clean bandages, and then wrapped him in blankets. While they worked, Teleo told Dinsmora of the coup by the Stagga traitors. He lied and said he had been at the stables at the time and had heard the attack over the palace walls, and had taken the two youngsters with him as he'd fled.

Teleo went to the stream to wash Jessum's clothes as the sun disappeared behind the hilltops. Kaspari was sitting on a boulder, which stood like a small island in the middle of the rushing water. Her legs were pulled up, her chin resting on her knees, and she was staring vacantly at the water as it flowed over submerged rocks, tear tracks lining her dusty cheeks. He left her to her grieving while he scrubbed the clothes, wrung them out, and hung them over a line.

Daisy and Benny were grazing in the meadow with Dinsmora's two blood bay draft horses, Cinnamon and Nutmeg, along with two white goats. A flock of chickens were filing into their pen and climbing the ramp into their coop. Teleo said hello to Cinnamon and Nutmeg and slipped them each a piece of carrot. They were another fine pair fit for battle—large and strong but agile and easy-going. Reddish brown with black manes, tails, and fetlocks, the brothers were a perfectly matched pair. Much as their other cousins tried to buy the geldings from Dinsmora, she would not part with them. They were her pets, as far as Teleo could tell. She had set up jumps along a flat trail where she exercised them. She was quite a horsewoman herself. But mostly they just pulled her wagon when she went to town to sell her herbs, fabric, and leatherwork, and to tend to the sick.

When Teleo returned to the hut, his way was blocked by BlackJack, who stood at the entrance with his head inside the round structure and his withers filling the open doorway. His long, tangled tail flicked back and forth. Teleo stopped a few paces away and listened to Dinsmora's soothing voice.

"He is fine, for now. He needs to rest. He will probably sleep for a while yet, but don't you worry." BlackJack stomped a front hoof. "No, you can't come inside. You're too big, and you're dirty. Go outside and rest. Looks like you've had a long day yourself. Go drink some water at the stream."

BlackJack backed away from the doorway and turned, keeping one eye on Teleo as he strode past on lanky legs, his rough coat dusty and his long fetlocks studded with small brown burrs.

"I ought to trim those for you, as well as your hooves," Teleo said. "If you'd ever let me near you."

BlackJack tossed his head and blew air loudly from his large nostrils, then went to the stream and sank his muzzle into the water. Kaspari watched from the boulder, her form a graying silhouette as twilight deepened. Teleo left them there and ducked inside the hut.

He sat cross-legged on the wood floor, at Jessum's side opposite Dinsmora, who held the sleeping boy's hand. Teleo took Jessum's other hand and pressed his fingers to the boy's wrist, finding a feathery pulse. He kept his fingers there, letting his own strong pulse lend support to Jessum's.

"Who are they?" Dinsmora asked, lifting her gaze to meet his.

"He's a Hill orphan."

She already would have guessed that from his thick black hair and slanted eyes, but Teleo did not explain further. Dinsmora's hazel eyes were somber. She had delivered both his children. She was the one he had run to for comfort after finding that

Bella-Mae and Abigail had been murdered and Oren had gone missing. She had held Teleo while he wailed with grief and wanted to drown himself in the stream.

"And the other one? The girl?"

Teleo chuckled. "Is it that obvious?"

Dinsmora made a face, her freckles brown against her sun-weathered skin, and replied, "Is the day long and the night dark?"

"Haha. Yeah. Well, we need some girl's clothes."

Dinsmora raised an eyebrow. "To disguise the girl as a girl?"

Teleo nodded. "You got it. Don't ask me anything more."

"Oh, I wouldn't dare. Her skin looks softer than a flower petal, and she rides a horse like she was born on one. I bet she knows how to handle a sword, too."

Teleo hadn't thought about that, but Dinsmora was probably right. Kaspari's parents had raised their daughter to survive. "Probably she does. We can't stay here long. We are endangering you."

"No one can find this place," she reminded him. "No one from the castle, that is." She raised her eyebrow again. "And unless you intend to leave the boy with me, taking him on the road again so soon will kill him. You'll need to stay here for a few weeks, at least."

"Okay," he said, not bothering to hide his relief. "As long as you're okay with it."

She pursed her lips at him. "Do you think you're the first one who has brought me trouble?" She laughed warmly. "Teleo, Teleo. I only wish I had the power to make our entire village invisible, then I would be able to run my healing practice from my family home." Her eyes grew distant. "Although I do love the forest, and the stream, and the wild animals. And my privacy."

"We need to warn the villagers," Teleo said. "Gerik Stagga's men will come looking for us."

"Oh?" she asked, frowning at him. "Trouble, indeed."

She stepped out of the hut and whistled a long, lilting tune towards the stream. Teleo stood in the doorway. An ancient pine stood as a skeletal sentinel against the darkening sky. A branch swayed high atop the tree and an owl soared down into the clearing, landing on a tall wooden pole that secured the laundry line. The owl was no bigger than a pigeon, with a white face and chest. Two large yellow eyes stared at them.

"Loyal friend, go warn Bralla. *Hide hide. Danger danger.*" Dinsmora said the last words in a screech that pierced Teleo's ears.

The bird screeched back. "*Wheeeee Wheeeee. Khreeeee Khreeeee.*" The owl lifted off in a swoop and disappeared into the night with a faint shushing of wings.

Dinsmora secured the chicken coop, then went into her cottage to prepare dinner while Teleo herded the dapple grays and Dinsmora's bays into a small wooden barn. The goats were already asleep in a corner. Outside, Teleo called for BlackJack. He could hear the big black tramping slowly through the undergrowth not far beyond the grass surrounding the buildings. He was happily foraging and ignored Teleo.

"Don't wander too far or get eaten," Teleo warned. Though it would take a pack of wolves to fell such a horse, and wolves did not roam east of the Blue Mountains.

Teleo stood outside in the quiet evening, enjoying the cool air of the forest and the melody of the mountain stream. A breeze drifted up from the valley, making the branches sing and leaves whisper to one another.

Teleo called across the water, "Kaspari. Time to come inside."

Nothing but the rushing of water answered him.

"It's getting dark out. You need to eat," Teleo said, pitching his voice to travel over the hiss and gurgle of the tumbling stream.

Teleo sighed, then removed his boots and rolled up his pants to his knees. He made his way gingerly over the slippery rocks, the icy-cold water biting into his bones. He climbed up onto the boulder and sat next to her.

Kaspari rested her chin on one knee and stared into the murky water. Her silence spoke of the gaping hole in her heart.

The darkness thickened and a clatter of dishes came from Dinsmora's cottage.

"You must stay strong," Teleo said. "You must eat."

"I'm not hungry," Kaspari mumbled.

"I know you're not," Teleo said. "But you need to eat anyway."

She did not respond. Her thin form hunched over her knees, still as the rock.

"I know how much it hurts," Teleo said.

"How would you know?" she asked bitterly.

He swallowed and stared up at the feathery treetops, black against a dusky sky. Stars were popping out one by one as the last hints of daylight faded. Crickets took up their song, chanting back and forth across the stream.

"My family was killed in a raid," he said. "I had a daughter. She would have been your age by now. I know it's not the same thing," he said, tears stinging his eyes. "But it's close."

A loud sniffle came from Kaspari, followed by shaking sobs. He reached over and rested his hand on her back. She leaned into him and cried in his arms.

They forded the stream together, the bracing cold chasing grief away for a welcome moment. They left the shrouded night outside and entered Dinsmora's cottage, bright with candles and lanterns casting golden halos.

Dinsmora fed them a stew of wild hare and carrots, hard white cheese with slices of brown bread and sweet butter, and a salad of tender baby lettuce, ripe tomatoes, and fresh fennel root, followed by bread pudding with stewed plums and a sweet cream sauce. After supper, Dinsmora gave Kaspari a clean linen shift and made a bed for her in a quiet corner of the great-room on a pile of sheepskins covered with linen sheets. She brought out an armful of patchwork quilts and feather pillows, with pillowcases embroidered with purple and yellow flowers.

Kaspari arranged her bedding, moving slowly and stiffly, as if forcing her muscles to move. Dinsmora brewed her a dark, fragrant tea and added dollops of cream and honey, cloves, and a stick of cinnamon. The girl took the earthen mug with a polite, "Thank you," and settled into her nest.

Teleo checked on Jessum in the healing hut. He was sleeping soundly. Sleep was the best medicine, and so Teleo crept outside and returned to the cottage.

Teleo joined Dinsmora at the table and sipped at the mug of sweet and spicy tea she had prepared for him.

"I found a Heliotrope," he said quietly, so as not to reach Kaspari's ears.

Dinsmora's eyes fastened onto his. "Where?" she whispered. "I didn't know any still existed."

"I didn't either," Teleo said. "I found two, actually. At the castle. Right under my nose this entire time."

He described the intact Heliotrope in the Royal Garden and the partially finished one in the training yard. He was suddenly glad he had not completed the larger one—he did not want Gerik anywhere near a source of magical power. As for the

Heliotrope in the Royal Garden, he hoped it was too small and decorative to be noticed for what it really was.

"I didn't recognize some of the stones, though," he said. "The center circle was a white, translucent stone. And a shiny black stone was used for the rays."

The illusion he'd seen in the center stone flashed across his mind. "And I saw someone in the white stone," he said in a hoarse whisper. "A woman."

He had not had a chance to consider the strangeness of the vision. It had seemed so real at the time.

Dinsmora's eyes narrowed and she tucked a loose strand of hair behind her ear. Anyone else would have thought he was crazy, but she listened intently while he described how the apparition had tried to warn him about the attack.

He went to his travel bag and returned with the scroll of the dancing Mage. They examined it together and traded stories they had been told by their elders—stories of Mages and Stone Guardians, Heliotropes and white crystalline swords, and battles of magic that had torn the kingdom apart.

"You probably shouldn't be carrying that around with you on the road," Dinsmora said.

"No, probably not," Teleo agreed.

"I have a place you can hide it, if you want," Dinsmora said, rising from the table. She took a lantern, and Teleo rolled up the scroll and followed her into the back pantry. She closed the door to the storage room, which was lined with shelves filled with various containers of spices, baskets of desiccated mushrooms, and crocks of pickled vegetables, honeyed fruits, and brined fish. From the ceiling hung strings of garlic and an assortment of dried herbs and cured meats. She stuck her hand in between two ceramic crocks, and the wall of shelves creaked open to reveal a hidden closet.

Teleo shook his head and grinned. "You are full of surprises," he said, and followed her into the small room.

It was a cool, windowless chamber with walls of stone. One wall was lined with shelves, upon which sat several vials with names of poisons carefully inscribed on their labels. In a corner stood a form with a long hooded cloak draped over it. Teleo approached the cloak and felt the brittle fabric. A puff of dust rose from his fingers as fibers disintegrated under his touch, but the remaining fibers were soft. Moth-eaten holes dotted the cloak, which looked to have been dyed purple at one time but was badly faded.

"Don't touch it," Dinsmora said, stepping to his side. "It's falling apart."

"Why are you displaying a moth-eaten cloak?" Teleo asked.

"It's a Mage's cloak," she said. "Great-Grandmother Edaline gave it to my mother, who gave it to me."

"What makes it a Mage's cloak?" Teleo asked. "It looks like a simple peasant's cloak, made of wool and ..."

"Flax," Dinsmora said, slapping his hand lightly as he went to touch it again. "I don't know what makes it a Mage's cloak," she said, shrugging. She turned and opened a chest filled with scrolls. "Here," she said. "You can stash yours here for now."

He handed her the scroll of the dancing Mage, and she tucked it away with the others. She rummaged around and pulled out a large, faded-yellow roll of parchment. "I wanted to show you this," she said.

"What is it?" he asked.

"A map."

They went back out into the pantry, closed the secret door, and returned to the table. Dinsmora unrolled the map and flattened it, weighing down the corners with ceramic mugs. "These are ancient Mages' temples," she said, and Teleo leaned in closer, his pulse quickening.

Dinsmora and Teleo inspected the faded, colored illustration. The mountain terrain was dark green for forests and deep blue for the forbidding, rocky peaks. The valleys were a yellowish green. The long, fertile Verdant Valley stretched north to south between the Blue Mountains and the Aldeon coastal mountain range. On the other side of the Blue Mountains lay the land where Teleo had searched in vain for his son. The Sapphire Valley was roughly circular and about fifty miles across. At its center stood Sapphire City, capital of the Sapphire Empire. The ancient empire was comprised of seven Hill Tribes, and the valley was defended on all sides by rugged low-lying mountains and a ring of seven tribal fortresses perched on high stony outcroppings, guarding the passages in and out of the Sapphire Valley.

"Look," Dinsmora said, pointing to one of the fortresses perched on a rocky crag. A little symbol like a sun was drawn above the castle. The symbol had a white center circle, yellowed with age, surrounded by ten black rays, faded to a dark indigo.

A Heliotrope.

Teleo looked more closely. Every fortress in the Sapphire Ring had one.

Teleo's blood rushed through his veins. At the center of the valley was the depiction of a large walled city surrounding the sprawling Sapphire Castle. At the very center, where the Imperial Palace perched, was a large sunray symbol. "The Sapphire Palace's Heliotrope," Teleo whispered breathlessly.

"You think?" Dinsmora asked. "My grandmother said those symbols denoted Mages' temples."

"My father told me that the Verdant Valley Palace used to be a Mages' monastery," Teleo said, shivers running up his spine. He hadn't thought much about it, but if the palace had been the Royal Mages' temple, then where did the king and queen live back in the olden days? How much power did the Mages actually have?

His skin prickled, but he brushed off his musings. It was the stuff of legends. Stories told around campfires late at night about magic tourneys at Verdant Valley Castle and the Sapphire Palace. Seven Mages facing off against seven Stone Guardians. Rivalries became more fierce, and battles were sometimes fought to the death, igniting a full-blown conflict known as the Magic Wars. The Mages usually won when they were in a Heliotrope. Anywhere else, the Stone Guardians usually won.

All of that knowledge had been lost after the kings had banded together, outlawed magic, and banished both the Mages and the Stone Guardians, killing them or chasing them into the mountains to work out their differences away from civilization. If they wanted to kill each other, so much the better. Everyone else wanted to raise oats and grapes, eat bread and drink wine, make fat healthy babies, and sleep safely next to their hearths.

And so came the Time of Peace. It lasted until those generations grew old and died and new ones were born and raised with no memory of the Mages and Stone Guardians except in stories. The Verdant Valley people and the Sapphire Empire's Hill people started to venture into the Blue Mountains again to explore and to trade, forgetting that the mountains separating the valley kingdoms were where the Mages and Stone Guardians had fled to. The Blue Mountain range was a strange, brutal land, and when wagon trains and merchants were butchered crossing the passes, the Hill people and Verdant Valley people blamed each other, and the Valley Wars began.

Teleo shook his head thoughtfully and said, "That symbol looks just like the center of the Heliotrope, with a circle and ten triangular rays. It must denote a Heliotrope. Or maybe all Heliotropes were built inside temples. I don't know."

On the map, a half-dozen additional castles with the sunray symbol were depicted, deep in the Blue Mountain passes. Another half-dozen were scattered across the Verdant Valley and the Aldeon Coast, in the old tribal castles. Teleo examined Verdant City. Sure enough, a Heliotrope symbol was drawn above the sector where the training yard would be. He searched for the symbol for a Heliotrope near the Royal Palace. Instead of a sunray symbol, he found a small white dot with ten black dots surrounding it, like a flower. He figured it must symbolize the smaller Heliotrope. He pointed it out to Dinsmora, and they searched other castles for the small floral design and found only four more: one at a Hill fortress guarding the Sapphire Valley, one within the Sapphire Palace, and not one, but two, at a castle in a Blue Mountain pass. Whereas the two Sapphire Valley castles had both a large and a small Heliotrope, like Verdant Castle, the Blue Mountain castle had only two small Heliotropes, if he was interpreting the symbols correctly.

There was no other information that they could glean from the map, so they took shifts sitting with Jessum in the healing hut while the other slept. Teleo had made a bed for himself at the back of the great-room on the floor outside Dinsmora's curtained sleeping area, next to a large loom with a half-finished length of linen on it. Kaspari was quiet as a mouse in her nest of quilts in the corner, and Teleo hoped she had fallen into a deep, dreamless sleep.

At dawn, Teleo forced himself out of bed to let Dinsmora get some rest, and stepped outside into the cool morning air, stretching and yawning. Dew covered the grass in a blanket of heavy droplets. The owl was perched on the laundry post, staring down at him. Dinsmora poked her head out of the healing hut, and the owl screeched at her. She screeched back. The bird cocked its head, then launched from the pole and flew into its tree.

"The message has been delivered," Dinsmora said, and shuffled sleepily to the cottage.

At noon, two ravens appeared in the yard, making a horrible racket.

Teleo stepped out of the healing hut as Dinsmora and Kaspari came out of the kitchen. Dinsmora clucked at the birds, then turned to Teleo.

"Soldiers are in the village," Dinsmora said.

Teleo held her eyes for a long moment. They broke their fraught gaze and returned to their respective duties. There was nothing Teleo could do for the villagers now. Hopefully, they had understood the message and were prepared. But for what, Teleo did not know. Would the Stagga soldiers kill his cousins if they found them at Teleo's farm? Or would his cousins face them with open hands and rational words, hoping to send the soldiers away peacefully? If his family had gotten word and the soldiers found the farm with no one there, would they grow angry, or greedy, and ransack his farm? Kill the chickens and livestock? Burn the fields? Then raid the village, tearing it apart, searching for Prince Kaspar? Teleo did not want to imagine what was happening.

He sat by Jessum's side and squeezed the sleeping boy's hand. "We had to save the princess," Teleo said, squeezing harder.

Teleo was dozing off while seated at Jessum's side, his chin hanging down to his chest.

"BlackJack! BlackJack!"

Jessum's yell startled Teleo out of a muddled nightmare. The boy rolled onto an elbow and tried to sit up.

"Easy, easy," Teleo said, pushing Jessum's shoulder back down onto the bedding.

"Where are we?" Jessum's pupils were dilated and sweat bathed his brow. He propped himself up again and looked wildly around the small hut.

"We fled the castle. We're hiding out at my cousin's. You're hurt."

Jessum pushed Teleo's arm away and tried to sit up. Teleo propped up the boy's back as Jessum grimaced and pressed his hand to his abdomen. "Where's BlackJack?" Jessum's voice was high-pitched with panic.

A loud snort answered him, and BlackJack's long nose appeared in the open doorway. Jessum crawled to his feet and stumbled the short distance to the horse and hugged the big black's neck, stroking his dusty coat. Teleo watched in wonder as the boy and horse embraced, the horse nuzzling his chin against Jessum's back.

"I thought I lost you," Jessum said, his mouth muffled by the horse's mane. He patted the big black's neck. "I thought I lost you." After a long moment of tenderness, Jessum limped past the horse, and Teleo could hear him urinating into the bushes. Teleo grimaced, wondering which of Dinsmora's medicinal herbs the boy was watering. The horse followed Jessum, and Teleo followed the horse. "There is an outhouse, you know," Teleo said, pointing to the little whitewashed shack with a star-and-moon cut-out high on the door.

"Oh. I didn't know," Jessum said, closing up his pants. "Sorry." He limped across the yard, leaning with his hand on BlackJack's flank as he passed, and went into the outhouse. The horse wandered to the side of the clearing and pulled a large tuft of grass into his mouth, munching contentedly.

Jessum eventually emerged, washed his hands and face in a washbasin on the little table beside the outhouse, and made his way back to the hut. He asked about his injuries and examined his bandages, then drank a large tankard of water. He followed that by slurping down some soup Dinsmora brought him before pushing it away and drinking a small cup of a dark green—almost black—herbal concoction. His face screwed up into a sour knot. "Yuck, what did I just drink?" he asked, coughing and holding his abdomen. "Ow."

"Don't cough," Dinsmora scolded. "You've got a fever. You need to sleep."

Jessum didn't argue but washed down the medicine with more water, crawled into his bedding, and relaxed immediately into deep, rhythmic breathing.

"Is he going to be okay?" Teleo asked, feeling the boy's hot forehead.

"We shall see," Dinsmora said. She disappeared and returned with a dripping wet sheet. She and Teleo woke Jessum while they were undressing him. He complained all the while but let them remove his sweat-soaked clothes and wrap the cold sheet around his burning body.

Jessum closed his eyes and soon he was breathing evenly again, his hand relaxing in Teleo's. The wet sheet quickly grew warm.

Kaspari poked her head inside the doorway. "Is he okay?"

"For now," Dinsmora said. "Fever's common after an abdominal wound."

Dinsmora met Teleo's worried eyes but neither voiced what they were both thinking. That swords to the gut were often fatal, if not from blood loss, then from infection. Teleo thought of his uncle Brady. Teleo held the boy's hand and reviewed in his mind the rushed surgery in the grooming yard. Had he found all the lacerations? Had he cleaned everything well enough?

Teleo got up to dip another sheet into the cold stream, and

Kaspari took his spot, sitting at Jessum's side and holding his hand in both of hers.

Teleo stepped out of the hut into the clearing. It was midday and sunny, and Daisy and Benny were grazing at the stream's edge with Cinnamon and Nutmeg. BlackJack was not far away, lowering his nose into the water and playing with it more than drinking. Teleo dunked the sheet into the stream and took it, dripping wet, to the hut and handed it to Dinsmora.

Teleo went back to the stream, removed his boots, and waded across the green and gold streamed to Kaspari's boulder. He sat by himself on the hot gray rock and stared at the water coursing around him.

———————◆———————

Simson, a cousin of Teleo's and Dinsmora's, appeared in the clearing four days later. Simson held Teleo's steady gaze as he told him that the village had been visited by the Staggas' men. They had been looking for Teleo.

"Did Aunt Bralla get the message?" Teleo asked.

"Yes. The owl came. The nephews stayed away from your place for two days. But the chickens needed to be fed and watered and the vegetable rows needed tending. Soldiers were camped out in your house, waiting for you. They killed Tams Junior and beat up Timmins pretty bad."

Teleo sank his head in his hands.

"Said they thought Tams Junior was you," Simson said grimly.

Teleo swallowed back angry tears, fury and guilt swirling in his head.

"His wife's almost due," Simson continued. "She's going back to her mother's village to have the baby."

If Simson had twisted a knife in his gut, it would not have hurt any worse. It was his fault for abandoning his farm in the first place and chasing fantasies of a life at court, with secret hopes of gaining respect and recognition. He should have just stayed on the farm and been happy with his hay and apples, his cattle and horses, chickens and ducks. It was a good life. A simple life. A life every soldier longed for.

"Don't blame yourself," Simson said.

"Who am I supposed to blame? Tams Junior is dead now because of me."

"You didn't kill him."

"Might as well have."

Simson patted his back. "I know. It feels terrible."

"I hate the Staggas," Teleo said.

"Me too," Simson said.

"I should have gone home and faced the soldiers myself," Teleo said. "How many were there?"

"A dozen."

Teleo whistled. "Wow."

"They said they'd be back. What did you do?" Simson asked. "Why are they after you?"

Teleo glanced over his shoulder. Dinsmora was keeping Kaspari out of sight, and the boy was sleeping quietly in the hut—the door was open, but the interior was shadowed. Even BlackJack was hiding somewhere out amongst the trees. Teleo walked with Simson to the stream bank, gazing out over the burbling water, and finally answered, "I killed a bunch of Stagga soldiers getting out of the city after the coup."

Simson examined Teleo's face, knowing there was more to it than that. Teleo would normally have run home to defend the village; he would never have let their young cousin die defending Teleo's home unless there was a good reason. Teleo was not going to tell him the real story—it was safer for Simson if he did not know.

Teleo met Simson's curious gaze and pressed his lips firmly together.

Simson nodded his head in tacit acquiescence.

"So we have a new king," Simson said, breaking the awkward silence. "King Henrik. How convenient that the Master of Arms sent all the troops to the border this summer."

"Yeah, not a fighting man over sixteen or under fifty in Verdant City, except Gerik's cronies and the Palace Guard," Teleo said. "They must have brought in their own men from the coast. I didn't recognize any of the ones I killed. Some were wearing the Stagga sigil."

"Were you at the castle?" Simson asked.

Instead of answering the question directly, he said, "I heard the Staggas murdered everybody. The royal family. All the palace guards. Housekeeping staff." Simson's scowl deepened and he held Teleo's measured gaze. He would understand by Teleo's non-answer that he had been at the castle but did not want to discuss it, even with his own family. Teleo returned to the safer topic. "So Henrik declared himself King already, eh?"

"Yep." Simson let out a bitter laugh. "Taxes will be going up, you can bet on that. And more young men taken from their farms and sent to the border to keep the Hill traders out, so he can expand his monopoly on imported goods beyond just the Far Shell Islands. Now he'll be able to control all trade with the Sapphire Empire too. How a man can desire so much riches I'll never understand. The guy already has four castles and a fleet of ships, and the best vineyards in all the land."

Teleo shook his head, missing the dead king already. "King Elke was a good man," he said. After the elder King Elke the Fourth had finally died, Kaspari's father had inherited the throne and led the charge himself to chase the Sapphire marauders out of their valley. King Elke the Fifth had followed them all the way over the Blue Mountains and commanded the assaults against Sapphire City. Teleo had been there, leading missions to try and scale the Sapphire City Wall, crazed over the murder of his family. The Hill warriors were fierce foes, though. Cunning and relentless. And the city was well fortified.

King Elke had finally pulled back, admitting defeat and abandoning his campaign to capture the Sapphire Valley. But their assault had weakened the Imperial Army enough to allow the Verdant Valley forces to hold their border and bring the Valley Wars to an end. The king then began negotiating peace treaties and trade agreements with the latest Sapphire emperor, Cornwal, which had dragged on ever since.

During the war, Henrik Stagga had stayed safely on the coast the entire time, except during the Sapphire City offensive when he had lived at Verdant Palace to "help govern" in the king's absence. It was all too clear in retrospect—how the Staggas coveted the crown, then finally just took it.

Teleo and Simson stood silently, watching the stream flow by. His aunt Ada and uncle Tams would be beside themselves with grief from the death of their son. Young Tams was such a good boy. A man. About to have a child of his own—a child who would never know its father. Timmins would be a wreck as well—he and Tams Junior had been inseparable.

They stared at the water. There was nothing more to say.

Dinsmora did not offer Simson a meal, and he did not invite himself inside. He understood the pointed, silent looks of Teleo and Dinsmora as veiled warnings to ask no more questions. He accepted a bundle of herbs and liniments for Timmins, and Dinsmora promised she'd be out to check on Timmins's pregnant wife before long.

Simson gave Teleo a rough hug. "You take care of yourself, you old goat."

Teleo nodded silently, holding onto the man he had grown up with. "When Timmins is up and about, ask him to gather a group of men and take the animals and the hay to old man Tams' farm," Teleo said. "Once the apples and nuts and root vegetables are harvested and the last cut of hay is brought in, there'll be no more reason for him to go back to my farm. It'll weather the winter just fine, as long as those bastards didn't damage the place. Well, they must have busted down the door. Not an easy task—I used four-inch-thick beams on that door. Or maybe they climbed in through the kitchen window. In any case, I'll fix it when I get back."

Simson promised he'd deliver the message to Timmins and check on Teleo's house himself, taking along a band of village men for protection. Teleo was embarrassed and grateful for the help of his family and friends, and he inclined his head in thanks. Simson rode off before the sun got too low in the sky, leaving time to navigate Dinsmora's strange forest and get off the King's Highway before nightfall.

❖

Jessum's fever broke and his appetite returned. Dinsmora kept him on a diet of soup and pudding. He hobbled outside a few times a day to go to the outhouse and visit with BlackJack, who stood quietly while Jessum hugged him and stroked his neck. The rest of the time he slept.

One day merged into the next. Rains came, then wind, then clear crisp days portending a cold winter.

Kaspari and Teleo helped Dinsmora process her latest batch of herbs: separating stems, roots, stalks, flowers, and seeds; preparing tinctures; expressing essential oils.

After a few more days, Jessum was up and about and eating normal food again. During the day, he mostly sat on a bench on Dinsmora's front porch, carving wood. His creations were lined up on Dinsmora's porch railing: squirrels, owls, horses, chickens, pigs, goats. They were crude carvings but captured the nature of each beast. Kaspari clapped with delight every time he finished a new figurine, admiring it from every angle and then displaying it with the others.

Dinsmora and Kaspari exercised the horses daily, taking them over the jumping course and through the wooded trails. First the pair of bays, then the dapple grays. Jessum watched them come and go from the porch. It had been over three weeks since his surgery, and Dinsmora finally allowed him to fish from the bank of the stream. Even then, she cautioned him to call someone to pull in the fish if he caught a big one.

The following week, Dinsmora found an old bridle and saddle in her tack room for BlackJack. Teleo oiled the leather, and Jessum spent time stroking the big black's head and was soon able to get the bridle on him. From that day forward, he walked the big horse around the perimeter of the meadow on a lead rope and BlackJack followed dutifully at his shoulder. Jessum resumed grooming the big horse and threw a saddle blanket over his back every day, getting him ready to wear a saddle again.

Evenings, Jessum sat inside by the fire with Kaspari. He carved animals and she drew the same animals with pen and ink on sheets of linen paper, adding details of feathers and fangs and placing them in magical forests of talking trees and poison flowers. One night, she told Jessum what she had learned about the Hill Tribes and the Sapphire Empire from her father.

"Back in the olden days," she said, "the region was ruled by seven tribes who competed for the fertile Sapphire Valley, sometimes living in peace and sharing the fields, sometimes fighting for territory. At one time, they were united under the ancient

Bedon tribe, who ruled from the valley and built the first castle in the center of the flatlands, where the current Sapphire Castle now sits." Jessum listened intently, the orange flames reflecting in his eyes.

Kaspari continued, "Battles between the Mages and Stone Guardians weakened the alliance, and the Bedons were killed off. The seven tribes retreated back into the hills and fought for the imperial crown. Rulership passed from one tribe to another, alliances forming and dissolving. The current emperor, Cornwal, cannot trace his lineage to any particular tribal leader. He climbed his way up the ladder as a wealthy merchant and royal advisor. The previous emperor, Arnbjorg, was murdered after the Valley Wars ended by someone within the palace. Cornwal took the crown and is in power still."

Her voice had thinned to barely a whisper. Jessum was hanging onto her every word, but she excused herself and went to bed.

Teleo could hear her blowing her nose and knew she was crying. He wished he could do something for her, but he had never discovered the cure for grief.

———————◆———————

Jessum's strength returned day by day. Teleo gave him the task of copying Dinsmora's Heliotrope map onto a smaller piece of parchment. Dinsmora provided Jessum with a quill and inks of various colors, and he set to work meticulously replicating the original while Kaspari drew sketches of birds and horses.

One afternoon, Teleo sat with the youngsters on the front porch, inspecting the weapons he had taken from the Stagga soldiers. There was a longsword, four standard-issue war swords, a lighter blade, and various knives and bludgeons. He chose a dagger and the longsword for himself, wishing he had his two longswords that were mounted uselessly on the wall of his farmhouse—or perhaps Gerik's soldiers had stolen them. He set aside the infuriating thought and returned to the steel in his hand. This longsword was to his liking—forged by a master, it seemed, and the right weight for him. It had been the leader's sword and was probably the man's family heirloom, with a breached whale scrimshawed into the whale-tooth pommel and the grip wrapped in sharkskin.

The Aldeon Sea craftsmen were known for their steel, made from meteorites found in abundance on a particular stretch of rugged land bordering the northern coast. The shoulder strap was sturdy leather, with ocean waves embossed on the indigo-blue scabbard. It would do nicely. He fastened it on his back, crosswise over his short sword, with a sword handle within easy reach over each shoulder. He adjusted the longsword's position so he could unsheathe it in one motion, with a nice ringing sound, and practiced sheathing it one-handed. He practiced drawing it together with his short sword, then went through a flow of two-handed forms, getting accustomed to its weight and length.

Kaspari and Jessum were watching him. He invited them to inspect the remaining collection of weapons laid out on the porch floor. They handled the various swords and knives.

"I need a sword," Kaspari said matter-of-factly. She checked the balance of the most finely crafted one. It was a relatively lightweight double-edged blade of medium length, with folded steel that rippled blue in the sunlight, and both edges keenly sharp. The handle had a straight cross guard and a simple round metal pommel, and the grip was green-dyed pigskin, spiral-wrapped with silver wire. She held the hilt with two hands, and Teleo watched as she went into a flow of sword forms. She had been trained by a perfectionist, that much was clear. What she lacked in strength, she compensated for with technique and agility.

He faced off against her on the grass and parried her gentle strikes with his short sword.

"Harder," he said.

"They're real blades," she said. "I don't want to hurt you."

He laughed out loud and lunged at her, stopping an inch from her belly. She stared at the tip of the blade. "You didn't stop me," he scolded. "Again!"

He lunged at her and she angled his blade off hers, hopping lightly to the side and landing in a practiced defensive pose. He tested her defensive and offensive moves. She knew the repertoire, but her teachers had been too gentle with her. "I will carve some practice swords," he promised her, "and teach you how to really fight."

"Okay," she said, breathing heavily and wiping sweat from her brow. She went to return the blade to the porch.

"It's yours," Teleo said.

She smiled happily and retrieved the sword's matching forest-green scabbard and slid it onto her belt, then wiped down the blade and slipped it into the sheath.

"Thank you," she said.

"You're welcome," he said. "Now choose a knife and a club."

She chose a small hunting knife with a tiger-eye handle, and a wooden club with a carved fish-head handle, both of which she strapped onto her belt.

"Now for you," Teleo said, turning to Jessum.

"Me?" Jessum asked, pressing his hands to his chest in surprise.

Teleo tilted his head at the lad. "Yes, you. Which sword do you like?"

"They're all the same," Jessum said, standing over the four standard-issue swords.

"No two swords are the same," Teleo said. "Each one is hand forged. You know that. Test them out. Choose the one that feels the best."

"These weren't forged by Elias," Jessum said of the Verdant Castle blacksmith he had apprenticed under.

"True," Teleo said. "The Staggas are from the former Coastal Kingdom. Those four men we fought off must have been members of some sort of Aldeon militia and carried their own weapons. They look to be of good quality." Teleo stole a glance at Kaspari, who was frowning down at the blades.

Jessum tried them all out and chose a sword, a knife, and a club.

Over the next few evenings, Teleo shaped four blunt practice swords from hickory. He then spent a few hours every day training Kaspari, pressing her hard. Sometimes Dinsmora joined in and taught Kaspari more devious methods of killing, using knives. Jessum watched jealously and practiced slow-motion sword forms, but Dinsmora prohibited him from sparring until she judged him to be completely healed. He was fascinated with the knives. Dinsmora worked with him on knife-fighting techniques at half-speed while Teleo and Kaspari were busy with sword drills.

* * *

"Are we going to stay here forever?" Kaspari asked Teleo one day while they were polishing their swords on the front porch and Jessum had gone inside to nap.

"No. We will leave as soon as Jessum is fit to travel," Teleo answered. He did not know exactly where he wanted to go, but they were a burden to Dinsmora and needed to leave before the snows came. He was hatching a plan, but he did not know if it was a good one. "I think it would be best if you dressed as a girl," he said, broaching a topic he'd been wanting to bring up.

She frowned at him. "How was it that you knew my name and that I was a girl?"

"Gwen called you by your true name in the garden that day," Teleo said.

"Oh, yeah," Kaspari said. "She was worried she had revealed our secret. But she said she trusted you." Kaspari met his eyes, and a shared pain passed between the two of them at the mention of Gwen.

"In any case," Teleo said, clearing his throat. "You should stop disguising yourself as a boy. Everyone still thinks that young Prince Kaspar has escaped. The Staggas are looking for him. I don't want them to find you. You are the rightful heir."

"Girls don't inherit the crown," she said.

"Some do. Some have in the past," he said.

"I know that," she said, lifting her chin. "Queen Liliana. Queen Robinelle."

"Yeah. See?"

"But that was in the olden days," she said, her chin lowering.

Teleo shrugged. "It could happen again. Queen Kaspari. That sounds nice."

She fought back a grin and shrugged. "I don't know," she said. "But I'm not wearing a dress. I hate dresses. You can't ride a horse in a dress."

"True," he said. He nodded towards Dinsmora, who was cutting back a blackberry bramble at the edge of the small meadow. "You could dress like her."

Kaspari silently examined the healer's attire. Dinsmora wore buckskin pants that he knew for a fact she had made with the hide from a deer she had killed for her winter meat two years before—he had been on the hunt with her. It had been a young six-point buck. In addition, she wore a beige linen shirt and her usual knee-length, sleeveless buckskin tunic, with back and side slits for riding. The tunic was heavily embroidered with leaves and swirls in shades of browns and greens that blended in with the forest and fields so perfectly that Teleo sometimes lost sight of her.

"I could," Kaspari said.

They said no more about it, but the next day, Kaspari and Dinsmora measured and cut lengths of buckskin for a tunic for Kaspari. The princess spent the evening with an embroidery needle and a basket of thread, stitching a leaf pattern along the hem by candlelight.

"Don't look at me like that," Kaspari said, glancing up at Jessum, who was sitting across the table from her, working on the map.

"Look at you like how?" he asked.

She scowled and laid down another stitch.

"I already knew you were a girl," Jessum said.

She pulled the thread through and glared up at him. "How did you know?" she asked.

"Well," he said, shrugging. "It's not hard to tell. You look like a girl. And you talk like a girl. And you act like a girl."

"Do not," she said.

"And you smell like a girl."

"What's that supposed to mean?" she asked, standing up and swatting him over the head with a length of buckskin.

"Ow," Jessum said, covering his head and laughing. "And your name is Kaspari. That's a girl's name. Obviously. Ow, stop that."

She continued swatting him over the head and giggling, and he stood up and ran from the room. She chased after him, their squealing and laughter drifting in through the open doorway along with a cool, night breeze.

———◆———

Dinsmora spent evenings sewing while Kaspari embroidered her tunic. Jessum put the finishing touches on the map and carved more animals, and Teleo sat in front of the fire, polishing his blades or studying the map and plotting their next move. Dinsmora made Kaspari and Jessum each a pair of buckskin pants, just like the pair Teleo wore, which she had made for him the previous season—soft but sturdy, with plenty of pockets. Then she made Jessum a simple brown buckskin shirt that went on over his head with lacing up the chest. It fell to his hips and had long sleeves for the winter. For Kaspari, she made a doe-hide shirt, cut for a woman's shape, the hide soft as velvet and the color of butter. Then she made the teenagers and Teleo each a pair of pants and a shirt made from her roughspun flax-and-wool weave. The fabric was durable and warm, but not too warm. Dinsmora offered to make them each quilted gambesons, if they would help her quilt the fabric.

She pulled out folded stacks of her natural flax-and-wool cloth and several lengths of dyed cloth for them to choose from for the outer layer. Dinsmora's own gambeson was dark beige from a pinecone dye, blending in naturally with her wooded surroundings. Teleo chose a rich brown fabric, colored with a dye Dinsmora had made from black walnuts. Jessum chose a deep madder-root red. Kaspari chose a purplish-brown fabric, from a dye made with lichen.

They made Teleo's gambeson first. Dinsmora measured his chest and arms, then layered a dozen lengths of her undyed flax-and-wool cloth with a layer of horsehair to form a thick, padded material that they quilted together, sitting around the table. When the quilted fabric was ready, Dinsmora fashioned a long-sleeved, high-necked coat that fit snugly over Teleo's chest. It reached to his knees, with a slit in the back for riding. It was as good as any gambeson the soldiers had worn under their armor during the war. For some of the foot soldiers, it was the only armor they wore, aside from helmets.

"This is armor, you know," he told her as he tried it on.

"I know, and I charge a pretty penny for these, too," she said, tugging on the shoulders. "Does it fit?"

"It's perfect," he said, strapping his leather cuirass and shoulder guards over the dark-brown gambeson.

They made Kaspari's and Jessum's next. The dusky mauve of Kaspari's gave the sturdy fabric a subtly feminine touch, whereas Jessum's dark red matched the flush of his cheeks.

Teleo compensated Dinsmora for the materials with a war sword and a knife from his plunder. He told her to go see Timmins and get herself a few bushels of apples and almonds from Teleo's orchards, as well as a wagonload of hay and a few chickens and ducks to help her through the winter, and anything else she needed from his farm. They were both happy with the trade. He asked her to see to it that the remainder of Teleo's half of the harvest went to Tams Junior's widow. "And tell Timmins to slaughter the steers. He can divide up the meat with everybody or sell some at the market, and he can sell the extra hay."

One morning a few days later, Teleo came back from hunting in Dinsmora's forest with a brace of rabbits and found Jessum bent over with one of BlackJack's hind legs resting on his thigh, cleaning the big black's hoof.

Teleo raised his eyebrows in surprise. "Wow, he really trusts you."

Jessum kept his focus on the hoof, going at it with a brush. The horse was freshly groomed, his coat gleaming and fetlocks trimmed. He set down the hoof and moved to the next one. "He'll need shoes if we're going out on the road again," Jessum said. "And your horses are outgrowing theirs. We're leaving soon, right?"

"Yes," Teleo said. "We'll leave before the snows come. Dinsmora said you're healing up just fine." It had been over six weeks since they'd arrived, and they had awoken to a frost that morning. "BlackJack will need shoes," Teleo agreed. "We'll be riding over some rough terrain. Daisy and Benny got new shoes not long before we left Verdant Castle, but they're due to be reset. I normally shoe Daisy and Benny myself when I'm on the farm, but I don't know if BlackJack will hold still for me," Teleo said. "We don't have shoes for him, anyway."

"I could make them, if we had steel and a forge," Jessum said as he patted the hoof and set it down.

"Dinsmora's got a small forge in her shop," Teleo said. "My father and I built it for her."

"Really?" Jessum asked. "I can make the shoes. But the farrier never let me nail them on."

"If you make the shoes, I can put them on. If BlackJack will let me, that is," Teleo said.

"I think he will. Right, boy?" Jessum asked, patting BlackJack's flank. The big horse shifted his weight but did not complain.

After lunch, Dinsmora took them inside one of her out-buildings. Under a stack of tree limbs she was seasoning, stood a hip-high, square stone hearth with an air hole and a brick chimney. They moved the wood outside, and Dinsmora opened a wooden bin filled with chunks of shiny black coal.

"Do you make your own horseshoes?" Jessum asked, dusting off a large anvil bolted onto a stump.

She laughed. "No. I try to repair my tools sometimes. I tried my hand at alchemy for a few years. I have no talent for that art,

I must confess. Come. Let me show you my collection of tools. I have some steel I was going to use as apron rods for my looms, but I never got around to it. I think they should work just fine for horseshoes."

They went to another outbuilding, which was a combination tool shed and junk room, where they found two hammers, a small curved knife, pliers, snippers, a metal rasp, and a handful of nails. A few steel rods were leaning up against a corner, and Jessum grabbed them.

They sharpened the tools and prepared a blacksmith's fire, blowing air into the hole with a hand bellows and using a bucket of water for quenching. When the fire was ready, Jessum heated and rolled the tip of the knife over into a blunt edge to use as a hoof knife, then tapered the nails. He then went outside and called for BlackJack and hitched him outside the doorway.

Jessum stood at BlackJack's head and talked to the horse while Teleo managed to lift his hooves without getting kicked. Teleo trimmed and shaped the hooves, then Jessum examined them to design the shoes.

Teleo assisted while Jessum forged the horseshoes. Teleo tracked Jessum's deft movements as he heated a length of metal rod and hammered it on the anvil—he had clearly done this many times before. Kaspari sat outside sketching and Dinsmora looked on with a frown as Jessum hammered the metal. She was probably thinking about his gut wound, but Jessum looked comfortable and happy and she didn't stop him. Jessum forged himself a pritchel and then used it to punch holes into the horseshoes.

When the shoes were finally done and shaped to BlackJack's hooves, Teleo nailed them on. Jessum finished by rasping the hooves.

The next day, they reset Daisy's and Benny's shoes. The following day, Dinsmora offered to let Jessum keep some tools in exchange for helping reset Cinnamon's and Nutmeg's shoes. He reset them and then chose a hammer, the hoof knife, a rasp, a pair of pincers, the pritchel he had made, and some nails. The boy looked happier than when Teleo had given him the sword.

Dinsmora gave Jessum permission to practice with the wooden swords, and Teleo resumed Jessum's workout routine, starting gently at first and then increasing the intensity over the next several days.

Jessum started riding Nutmeg, and the four of them took the horses out together on the trails. Dinsmora and Kaspari coached Jessum on how to take the low jumps, and Dinsmora had Jessum put the big bay through his paces in a large circle around the meadow every day while she helped him with his riding form.

On a crisp, sunny autumn morning, Teleo watched Jessum saddle the big black. BlackJack did not even flinch as Jessum tightened the girth and swung into the saddle.

"Good boy," Jessum said, patting the gelding's neck.

BlackJack's ears were cocked backwards, listening, but straightened right out when they started walking. The horse was relaxed and ready to go. The rest of them followed BlackJack onto the hunting trails, keeping their distance from the ornery gelding.

It was as though Jessum and BlackJack had been riding together for years. Jessum took him through his gaits, and one would never know the horse had been put out to pasture for bad behavior or that Jessum was relatively new to riding. The two of them were a striking pair. Jessum's jet-black hair had grown past his shoulders. He refused Dinsmora's offers to cut it, saying that the Hill people wore it long, which Teleo confirmed. "The men keep it in a ponytail, though," Teleo said, but Jessum liked it loose. It was thick and straight, and caught the wind like BlackJack's mane and tail as they cantered through the forest. Jessum heeled BlackJack's flanks, and he broke into a gallop. The horse was a thundering beast and took off down the straightaway. The other horses strained to catch up, but soon BlackJack and Jessum disappeared over a gentle rise.

Teleo clamped his jaws together and urged Benny forward. They crested the rise, and BlackJack was already trotting back towards them. Jessum had kept his seat and was grinning ear to ear. Even BlackJack appeared to be smiling.

———————◆———————

"We will spend the winter there," Teleo announced on a cold windy evening, his finger planted on the center of the map Jessum had completed. The others gathered around the table.

Teleo had chosen the castle the same way he navigated through Dinsmora's domain. He had closed his eyes and slowly moved his fingers across the vellum, following a subtle but unmistakable feeling that led his finger to rest directly on top of a castle nestled in the Blue Mountains. The castle was situated at the end of a spur off the Southern Mountain Pass, and when he saw that it was the castle with the two small Heliotropes, the hair on the nape of his neck stood on end.

Teleo had traversed the mountain passes many times but had never been to any of the castles in the upper reaches. The mountains were still a strange and lawless place. Both Hill and Verdant Valley people were afraid of the mysterious land of stone and snow, and even soldiers crossed the passes as quickly as possible. The Blue Mountains were shrouded in legend: fireside stories about Mages and Stone Guardians battling with magic in treacherous mountain canyons, and unlucky travelers disappearing forever in dark forests.

The mountain kingdoms remained independent principalities, their kings and queens descendants of ... no one knew ... and it didn't matter. The mountain fortresses were where people went to hide and try to fashion some sort of life after fleeing Verdant Valley or the Sapphire Empire for whatever reason. The three of them would fit right in.

———————◆———————

"We are leaving tomorrow morning," Teleo announced one evening over supper.

"But ... but ... we're not ready," Kaspari said, her eyes round.

"What is there to get ready?" Teleo asked. "We can only take as much as can fit in our saddlebags and on our backs. Swords. Tool belts. A change of clothing. Our new gambesons. Food and water for the road. We need to make good time."

They went to bed early and Teleo rose before dawn, but Dinsmora must have gotten up earlier. She had left a note on the dining table that simply said, WAIT FOR ME.

Teleo went outside. Her wagon, horses, goats, and chickens were all gone. How she had managed to gather them all and leave without awakening him was a mystery—but lots of things about Dinsmora were mysterious.

He ground his teeth together and stood with Benny's saddlebags in his hands. He had wanted to depart before the sun rose over the hills. Dinsmora never asked him for anything, and after all she had done for them, he had no choice but to honor her request. He took his saddlebags to the barn, then went back to the cottage for the new saddlebags they had made for BlackJack. They had packed them all with travel food and spare clothing the night before. He went about his final preparations, filling leather water sacks from the stream, then fetching the collapsible five-gallon canvas bucket he had made for their trip and which Dinsmora had sealed with beeswax. He then filled three burlap sacks with oats. Each horse would carry its own feed for those days when there was little forage in rocky terrain. Dinsmora had made three waxed canvas tarps that they would use to cover the loads if it rained or snowed, and which would also serve as makeshift tents. He tightly rolled the tarps and wool blankets she had provided in three separate bundles and added them to the pile. He stood with his hands on his hips.

The horses had been thoroughly groomed the night before, but Teleo grabbed a brush and called Benny over. A sleepy-eyed Jessum appeared in the barn doorway. He wordlessly took a brush and began grooming BlackJack.

Kaspari appeared a few minutes later, dressed in her travel leathers and embroidered tunic. "When are we leaving? Where's Dinsmora? Should I cook some eggs? Where are the chickens?"

"I don't know. We have to wait for her," Teleo replied crabbily. "I assume she went to our village. I have no idea why. Go ahead and groom Daisy. We can get breakfast after."

Kaspari took a brush and worked over Daisy's coat. After they were done, they went inside and cooked up eggs, sausage, onions, peppers, and mushrooms. Dinsmora had still not returned when the sun was well above the tree line, so they let the horses loose to forage.

Teleo and the kids waded out to the bank on the other side of the stream and threw fishing lines into the dark pools and eddies sheltered behind rocks and submerged branches. "If I'd have known we were going to waste another day, I would have fished at dawn," he said crossly. He reset the worm on the hook and threw it out again.

They fished all morning and caught several small trout, then cooked them up for their midday meal, saving two for Dinsmora. They harvested greens from Dinsmora's garden and ate oat cakes, blackberries, and goat yogurt for dessert. Teleo could not enjoy the meal. He had decided to begin their journey this morning and did not like it when his plans were disrupted for no apparent reason. *Dinsmora had her reasons,* he told himself.

He sat on the bench on the front porch and listened to the wind sweep in from the north. Branches clattered together, dry leaves whispered, and the feathery needles of the evergreens hummed a low, mournful song. The air had a cold bite to it, and Teleo worried that he had waited too long to depart. The boy was nearly back to normal and would have been fine on the road days ago.

Teleo watched Jessum practice his sword forms while Kaspari shot arrows into a log. Jessum's shoulders were filling out, and his arm and leg that had suffered the sword wounds were starting to regain their full range of motion. He was young—he would be good as new after a few more weeks.

The boy's face hardened with intensity as he lunged at a phantom enemy and slashed his sword. His skin had returned to its healthy, ruddy complexion, and his dark brown eyes were bright and glinting. Teleo's mind went to his own son, trying to imagine Oren as he would be now. Would he be hardy and resilient like Jessum? Would he manage to retain a positive outlook even if he were beaten down by his captors? And Kaspari—she had light brown hair like his own little girl. Abigail would have been fourteen by now. The familiar knot in his stomach twisted. The fact that he knew Abigail was dead made her absence almost easier to take than not knowing the fate of his son. Imagining Oren's life could easily drive him into a fit of despair. Teleo walked to the stream, where he knelt and splashed cold water on his face and then climbed to his feet, his face dripping.

———————◆———————

Teleo passed the time by bathing in the cold stream, shaving, and then pacing back and forth on the porch. He and the kids were splitting firewood for Dinsmora when the clomping of hooves and creaking of wagon wheels announced her arrival.

"It's about time, dear cousin," he greeted her, trying to sound patient and friendly.

"Oh, Teleo, I'm so sorry. You must be furious with me." She reined in the horses and climbed down from the driving bench. "I should have made up my mind sooner."

"Made up your mind about what?" he asked warily.

"Why, about coming with you, of course."

Teleo sputtered but could not speak. The wagon was loaded high with sheaves of hay and bushels of apples, almonds, carrots, turnips, and potatoes. The bushel baskets were his own, fashioned from slats he had milled himself from applewood.

"How's the farm?" he asked, hiding his displeasure by inspecting the apples.

"It misses you," she said, and walked around to unhitch the horses.

Kaspari and Jessum strode across the grass to join them.

"Where are the chickens and goats?" Kaspari asked as she moved aside some hay in a basket, exposing a layer of brown eggs.

"I gave them to Aunt Bralla," Dinsmora said.

"You're not coming," Teleo blurted out. "We are going on horseback."

"Oh, the wagon will be no bother," she said, loosening Cinnamon's harness and lifting off the collar.

"And we're leaving now," Teleo said, blood rising to his face. "We waited for you. Now we're going."

"Tomorrow will be just as good as today," she said, with a steely edge to her cheerful voice. She turned and faced him.

"We are leaving today. Now," he said sternly. He glared at her, not about to be dominated by his headstrong cousin. He stepped back a pace as the distinct sensation of sharp little daggers pierced his face.

"Ouch," he said crossly, pressing his fingers to his cheeks. "What was that for?" She gave him a gloating half smile. "You are a witch," he grumbled.

The young teenagers stood by, gawking as the two adults bickered. They had never seen Teleo and Dinsmora argue, but the two cousins had grown up together, and for a moment, Teleo felt ten years old again. "You might have evil little tricks up your sleeve," he said, "but the flat of my sword blade will knock you to your rump."

Dinsmora threw back her head and laughed. Her dimples deepened and curly locks of auburn hair fell from the bun that was twisted on top of her head, making her look like a child herself. "You just try it, Mister Stone Guardian."

He glowered at the insult. In the olden days, stonemasons were traditionally from the Stone Guardian clan—the despised enemies of the Mages. Their skilled stonework had built the Sapphire and Verdant Valley castles, back before the Stone Guardians and Mages had nearly killed each other off in the Magic Wars—before magic was declared punishable by death and the warrior and merchant classes took over.

"Very funny, cousin," Teleo said. Her dimples softened his temper, even if she was mocking him.

Dinsmora won, as usual. The next morning before first light, they saddled and harnessed the horses, loaded up the horses and wagon, closed up the cottage and outbuildings, and left Dinsmora's hidden glade.

8

THE SHEPHERDS

Teleo's head was pounding as they climbed to higher elevations. He was short on sleep and had not envisioned a farm wagon slowing them to a walk. After leaving Dinsmora's domain and heading northwest, the foothills rose steeply, transitioning to a pine forest of straight, tall trunks and a dense canopy that made mid-morning feel like twilight. The narrow wagon road was covered in a thick carpet of needles, and the only sound was the creaking of the wagon and BlackJack's occasional snort.

Teleo ranged ahead while Dinsmora held up the rear. The teenagers rode single file between them. Daisy and BlackJack had arrived at some sort of truce. Daisy did not look back at BlackJack, and the gelding did not dare bite the tough mare, who had shown him her hind hooves more than once.

By afternoon, the forest path intersected Jagged Tooth Pass. They turned west onto the well-worn dirt and gravel road. There were no signs of other travelers. A lone hawk keened and circled overhead. The trees quickly thinned out, replaced by rocky terrain and scrubland. As they made their ascent, jagged rock formations rose like fangs of a monstrous beast, giving the pass its name.

Indigo peaks of the Blue Mountains towered in the distance, and a cool steady breeze was at their backs. They took a break to let the horses forage in the brush, then continued on for a few more miles at Teleo's urging.

They did not encounter anyone until early evening, when they came upon a small cluster of huts flanking the roadway. They were private dwellings by all appearances, except for a small shop with a wooden sign mounted on a pole: *Jagged Tooth Mountaineering Supplies.* A second building was a small grocery with empty wooden shelves and barrels lining the front porch. Both shops were closed. They rode slowly through the little village. An old woman swept the front stoop of her humble home. She did not look up.

They left the village behind and made camp in a small clearing behind a group of boulders, which sheltered them from the wind and hid them from the road. The large rocks loomed like hulking beasts in the moonlit night. Teleo could not tell if they were benevolent or threatening, but the horses were calm and Dinsmora tended a small campfire without concern. They cooked half of a wild turkey Dinsmora had felled on the trail with a single arrow. The other half Dinsmora marinated in honey, salt, and spices.

Dinsmora took the first watch. Teleo and the teenagers wrapped themselves in blankets under a lean-to of waxed canvas set up against a rock. The night was chilly but not freezing. Dinsmora had brought two large sheepskins, and the three of them huddled together on the soft, fluffy rugs. As a soldier, Teleo had been thankful for a blanket on flat dirt, but did not complain as the soft hide cushioned his aging hip joints. He told Dinsmora to wake him up later and sank into a dreamless sleep.

When Teleo rose for his watch, strips of turkey meat were laid out on a rack of thin green pine branches that Dinsmora had woven together and propped above the red and gray coals. Occasional drippings made the fire flare up, and the smell of the sweet, seared meat was mouth-watering. He resisted the temptation to steal a strip. They would need the food for tomorrow. Teleo went behind another large rock to relieve himself and gazed up at the sky. The moon had set and stars blinked down at him. The rocks seemed larger than they had before, standing around him, gray and ghoulish. The night was eerily quiet and a chill ran up Teleo's spine. He returned to the sheltered camp where the campfire glowed orange and crackled comfortingly.

Teleo went to the wagon and found the barrel of hard cider Dinsmora had brought from his farm, made with apples from his own orchard the previous season, and filled a wooden mug she had packed in a crate that also contained wooden plates, forks, and spoons. He shook his head. *Women.* Fingers and a knife worked just fine for eating on the road. At least she had thought to bring the cider. It was crisp, tart, and potent. He sat on a small rock and watched the coals glimmer. By dawn, the strips of meat were shriveled into jerky and ready for traveling.

It was another cloudless day, and the weather was mild. It was likely the last warm spell before the days waned towards winter. Gray-green and rust-red shrubs and grasses blanketed the rocky hillsides. Stunted, twisted pines clung to outcroppings, and scraggly madrones with gnarled red trunks and waxy green leaves favored the lee side of ledges, their branches heavy with clumps of yellow berries. The hills rose and fell as they made the long, gradual ascent towards the Blue Mountains.

"Do you have a plan?" Dinsmora asked during a break. "They'll likely try to take Jessum at the border."

Teleo glanced over at the Hill boy and the princess, who were at a small brook filling the waterskins. They were laughing and splashing water at each other, happy in the moment as only young people could be while danger pressed in from every side.

"No." Teleo rubbed the stubble on his chin. "But the mountains are calling me. Every other direction feels like a trap."

Dinsmora nodded and lifted her nose, closing her eyes and sniffing the air. "The wind off the mountains is fresh. There is an opening there. We will follow this road west and trust in the Light of the Mages to show us the way."

He peered at her with narrowed eyes. The Mages believed one could tap into the energy of nature to detect the larger pattern and work within it to navigate through life. All one had to do was look for signs and follow the natural order of things.

"The river is flowing," she said, the corners of her eyes crinkling into a smile. It was an expression the oldsters used. The river was time, which flowed with everything that came into being and passed from this life.

Many of Teleo's hopes had drowned in life's relentless flow, and his jaw tightened stubbornly. "We may need to fight our way across the border," he said grimly.

"Or we will pass through like a shadow," she replied. Her smile deepened, her dimples reminding him of when they were children and used to practice creeping past the adults undetected. Dinsmora had always been better at it than he was.

He realized his hand was wrapped tightly around the knife hilt at his side. He relaxed his grip and let his eyes follow the rugged trail.

They spent two more days climbing Jagged Tooth Pass, encountering no travelers and no more villages. They were on the vacant stretch of scrubland between the thickly wooded foothills and the desolate border towns, which were little more than army outposts set up at the edge of Verdant Valley territory to guard against raids.

During the time when Teleo was a soldier during the Valley Wars, frequent raiding parties from the Sapphire Empire came down into the Verdant Valley through these hills, venturing over the peaks from their lands west of the Blue Mountains.

Since the truce, raids and skirmishes were generally contained to the upper mountain passes and border outposts, and consisted mostly of young men from both sides wanting to show off their fighting skills. Skirmishes were normally broken up by the commanders before too much blood was shed. The troops would retreat to try again another day. After the clashes, the Verdant Valley soldiers would drink potent mountain berry wine and fight amongst themselves with fists, then wake up the next morning with black eyes and hangovers, bragging of their heroics.

Teleo had spent a few months at such an outpost after King Elke brokered a truce, but quickly grew tired of the juvenile behavior, grief having aged him overnight. He had turned in his army-issued longsword and took the retirement he was due, keeping his cuirass and short sword, which he was given for his service. The longsword had been garbage, he recalled, rusting every dewy dawn. Teleo had kept it wrapped in an oily rag with his extra gear, preferring his own longswords that were made of well-wrought meteorite steel. His short sword, on the other hand—now that was a fine weapon, having been crafted by a blacksmith he knew out in the Guild Zone, who, when he had gotten the order from the old Master of Arms for a new batch of swords, had forged that one for Teleo special. Teleo had wrapped the handle with rayskin and kept the double-edged blade sharp and polished.

After he retired from the King's Army, Teleo had crossed the border one night during a heavy rain, when the Verdant Valley soldiers at the outpost were hunkered down in their barracks. The next night, he had snuck past the outfit of Hill soldiers who had been harassing their border outpost, passed out drunk in their not very well-concealed camp. From there, he'd ventured into the lawless wildlands, made it over the Blue Mountains to the Sapphire Empire, and begun the fruitless quest to find his son. Teleo pulled himself out of his reverie before sliding into a familiar melancholy. He did not have the luxury of self-pity right now. He had two young people to protect.

The brush grew more sparse and the land more rugged as they entered the borderlands, a slowly rising terrain of red rock formations, slopes of scree, and small hidden valleys that lay at the outer reaches of the Verdant Valley territory. After another day or two of climbing, they would encounter the Jagged Tooth Pass border outpost. Beyond that, the hostile blue argillite peaks would take over, with vast stretches completely devoid of plant life and the highest peaks covered in snow nine months out of the year. Teleo kept his swords at the ready, prepared at any moment to encounter raiders or Gerik's henchmen. If they were ambushed by brigands in the rocky passes, it would be the end of them. The women would probably be raped before they were killed. If Gerik's men found them, Teleo would have to kill them like he had the others. But he might not be so lucky next time around and could end up with his own throat slit. Jessum would be killed or enslaved again, and the women left to the whims of a band of soldiers far from the proprieties of Verdant City. He ground his teeth together and sat his horse impatiently, wishing he had not succumbed to Dinsmora's charm and her stupid wagon. They would have been deep in the mountains by now if he'd had his way.

He glanced over his shoulder, and Dinsmora waved at him cheerfully. She acted like nothing was wrong, as though they were taking a leisurely trip to the Verdant City market on a Sunday. Not fleeing a kingdom that had just changed hands in a violent coup—and sheltering the lone surviving heir.

The teenagers did not talk as they rode but scanned the landscape attentively. They knew how vulnerable they were.

Ten miles short of the border outpost, the sun fell towards the horizon and Teleo searched the surrounding terrain for a suitable place to camp.

Dinsmora stopped and lifted her nose to the wind.

"What is it?" he asked.

"Something. Someone," she said, her eyes unfocused. She turned her head to the left and squinted, peering at the hills. "Ah, there," she said. "Follow me." Her team of horses and the wagon trundled off the road.

There was nothing but dried grasses and rocky scrubland, but he and the teenagers followed her. A narrow wagon path appeared under Benny's hooves, and Teleo saw that it stretched south. They plodded along and Teleo searched for a camping spot hidden from the road. When they crested the rise of a low hill, a homestead spread out before them.

A small cluster of huts stood behind a fieldstone wall and a wooden gate. It was a shepherd's compound. A humble stone dwelling stood on the lee side of a hill, with three larger outbuildings nearby. Two dozen sheep dotted the rocky slopes, picking at tufts of prickly grasses. A hawk perched atop a lone stunted pine, hunting. A stooped man looked up from where he was sharpening a knife on a stone, the blade glinting orange from the setting sun. He straightened up and squinted at them.

Teleo raised his hand in greeting, and the man returned the gesture. The wiry shepherd kept his knife in his hand and walked over to the gate to meet them.

"What are you doing all the way out in these parts?" the shepherd asked from behind the locked gate, his gaze passing over the wagonload and the teenagers.

"The new king is rounding up all the teenaged boys," Teleo said. "Didn't want them to take mine." Teleo glanced at Jessum, who kept his eyes lowered.

The man raised his chin, a long brown and gray beard reaching to his chest. "They took my son several weeks ago," he said. "Our only child. I was heading to Verdant City with my boy for our winter supplies when soldiers took him."

Teleo could hear the pain in the man's voice and his heart went out to him. At the same time, he was selfishly relieved that Gerik's soldiers had already come and gone from Jagged Tooth Pass.

A woman appeared at the hut's doorway and walked over to stand with the shepherd. "What do they want with my son?" the woman asked, tears pooling in her dark brown eyes.

Teleo shrugged helplessly. The Staggas would not announce the real reason for the roundup—that a legitimate heir to the throne had escaped. It would only weaken their position. Teleo was not about to spread that rumor and encourage enterprising men to haul in every teenaged boy in hopes of a reward. He cast an eye towards Jessum and Kaspari, who sat nervously on their mounts.

"Your son should be fine," Teleo reassured the couple. "They'll just train him to fight. They're drafting boys younger and younger these days. I fought in the King's Army, under King Elke. Your son will come home to you in a couple of years a full-grown man."

Hope flashed in the woman's eyes, but her husband scowled. "I didn't like those men. They were none too gentle with my Flinn," the shepherd said, his leathery face sagging with worry.

"Why don't you let them take your son, then, if it's just to train in the King's Army?" the man asked, and fear returned to his wife's eyes.

Teleo answered, "His mother was of the Hill people, as you can see. They don't treat Hill boys too kindly."

The shepherds openly examined Kaspari and Dinsmora, trying to figure out how they were all related.

"Not many travelers notice our turnoff from the pass," the woman said, squinting at Teleo suspiciously.

Dinsmora answered, "Not many shepherds know how to blend into their surroundings so skillfully." She lifted an eyebrow.

The couple exchanged glances. "Where are you headed?" the husband asked, not unkindly.

"A castle up yonder," Teleo said, gesturing to the southern mountains. "We'll winter there, then cross into Hill country and look for the boy's grandparents. He needs to learn about his own people."

The lie rolled easily off Teleo's tongue, probably because there was some truth to it. He had been thinking about trying to find Jessum's relatives, though he had never said so to the boy. Jessum glanced at him from under dark locks of hair.

"Castle Trillifort?" the shepherd asked. "You're on the wrong road. Jagged Tooth Pass does not take you there."

"I know. I was hoping to find a way there from here and avoid the border outposts. It looks from my map like there are some paths that-a-way."

"Your map shows paths that-a-way, you say?" the man asked, his eyebrows knitting together. "Sheep paths, mostly. I know them all. I grew up in these parts."

Teleo met Dinsmora's eyes, and dimples deepened on her cheeks. "The wind is fresh off the mountains," she said, her eyes glinting. "And the river is flowing."

"Yes," Teleo agreed. He returned her smile and ignored the quizzical looks of the others. "I imagine the Jagged Tooth border crossing is well-guarded these days?" he asked the man.

"It is. The main traffic through here is to supply the soldiers. There are a lot of them. They probably will try to take your boy."

"Yes, that's what I'm worried about," Teleo said.

BlackJack shifted under Jessum, who patted the big black's neck.

"Do your horses need water?" the woman asked, opening the gate. "We have a well."

"Yes. Thank you kindly," Teleo said, and dismounted. His legs were stiff and sore. He was not accustomed to riding horseback all day anymore. They led the horses to a sheep's trough and let them drink, while Teleo, Dinsmora, and the youngsters filled their waterskins from the well pump and washed their faces and hands. The couple offered to stable the horses in the sheep barn and let their "family" spend the night in the hay barn. They promised to help them map out a route in the morning.

Teleo and Dinsmora readily accepted the offer and settled in as the sky turned from dusky lilac to slate gray. The small barn was clean and dry, and Teleo had a solid night's sleep for the first time since they'd left Dinsmora's.

In the morning, the couple invited them into their home for hot oatmeal and mutton sausages. It was cold outside, and they donned their gambesons and hurried to the warm cottage. They ate around a rough-hewn wooden table with long benches on either side. Dinsmora offered the shepherds herbal tea, which the woman steeped in a large ceramic pot.

"Have you ever lived up in the Blue Mountains?" the man asked Teleo, eyeing the scars on his face.

"I passed through a few times, during the war," Teleo said.

"It gets frightfully cold up there. Trillifort is on a high mountain pass."

Teleo nodded thoughtfully. "We hope to find shelter somewhere there. Get some work doing something. Hopefully, they will need skilled laborers."

The shepherd wrinkled his forehead. "Maybe," he said. "Queen Valona of Trillifort is a fair bit odd."

"Oh?" Teleo asked. "How so?"

The man looked at his wife, who pursed her lips and hesitated before answering, "The castle is haunted. It's driven the queen mad, some say."

"If she likes you, you'll be fine," the man said. "If she doesn't, well ..." His voice trailed off and nervous prickles crept up Teleo's back.

"You'll need real coats," the woman said. "Those quilted coats might be okay for the foothills but not the Blue Mountains." She eyed their new gambesons hanging on hooks by the door. "We can make you shearling coats in trade for some of those apples," she said. "They won't survive the freezing temperatures up higher anyway. There's snow on the northern peaks already. We could also use some hay if you have more than you need," she said hopefully, "and whatever else you have to spare."

Teleo traded glances with Dinsmora.

"We have raw eggs that won't freeze well," Dinsmora said. "If you could use some, you're welcome to them." The woman's eyes lit up. "If you would kindly boil some for us to take on the road, you can keep the rest," Dinsmora suggested.

Dinsmora invited the shepherds out to the wagon to inspect the load. In the end, the shepherds took six bushels of apples, the bushel of eggs, a bushel of almonds, two bushels of root vegetables, a bundle of medicinal herbs, and half their hay, in exchange for four coats, eight pounds of mutton jerky, and a barrel of water.

They spent the day cutting hides and assembling four long shearling coats with riding slits. All of them helped sew, under the direction of the shepherds and Dinsmora. They spent the night in the barn again and finished up the coats the next day. The following day, they sewed on pockets and bone buttons to secure the fronts, and made shearling hats with ear flaps. That night, Teleo was awoken by rain pounding on the roof. He pulled the blanket up over his head and went back to sleep.

The following morning, they wore their new shearling coats fleece side out and ran through the cold rain to the shepherd's hut. The shepherds convinced them they needed shearling boots too, and so they spent two more days making those in exchange for a sword and knife from Teleo's remaining loot. The rain passed, leaving the ground soggy and the air clear.

"You know, Verdant Valley troops patrol the border," the husband, Mazu, said as they sat around the hearth the night before they were to leave. "They don't just man the crossing."

"I know," Teleo said, polishing a knife that was already shiny as a mirror.

The shepherd knit his bushy eyebrows together and sipped on a mug of Teleo's cider. Jessum and Kaspari were sitting at the table, sewing shearling mittens.

"You said you would show us a sheep's path," Teleo reminded the shepherd.

"Those are known trails. I know another way," Mazu said slowly. "But it's dangerous."

Teleo set aside the knife and sipped at his own mug of cider. "How dangerous?"

The shepherd cast an ominous eye at Teleo. "Stone Guardians control that pass. Nobody else uses it."

Teleo gulped down a mouthful of cider. "Stone Guardians? I thought they were all dead."

Mazu wrinkled his lips and stared into the fire. "They're not dead. They just keep to themselves."

A shiver ran up Teleo's spine. Before he could respond, Kaspari piped up, "Does that mean Mages survive, too?"

Teleo glanced at the princess. Her posture was erect and proper, her chin raised inquisitively—far from the bearing of a humble peasant girl.

Teleo cleared his throat. "She loves the legends about the Mages," he said awkwardly.

"Oh, they're not legends," Mazu's wife, Tintin, said from where she and Dinsmora were washing the earthenware at the water basin.

"There are no Mages in these parts," Mazu said. "They live higher up. Some still control the mountain castles. Or so they say."

"Trillifort?" Dinsmora asked, appearing not at all surprised that the shepherds were discussing Stone Guardians and Mages as though they still existed.

Mazu and Tintin traded glances. "Like we said," Tintin said. "Queen Valona of Trillifort is a bit odd."

Teleo had heard rumors about mountain Mages but had always swept them aside as drunken talk. Now he had goose-bumps on his arms. He locked eyes with Dinsmora. No one knew the fate of their Mage ancestors. Some said they had been killed. Some said they fled to the mountains. Others said they escaped to the Far Shell Islands. Still others said they gave up magic and became craftsmen and farmers and settled in the Verdant Valley.

"Tell me more about the Stone Guardians' pass," Teleo said. Legend or not, they did not have much choice.

Mazu went into the back and came out with a hand-drawn map on sheepskin. The kids moved the mittens, and everyone leaned over the map. Mazu traced a line with his finger.

"This is a hidden gorge. A slot canyon called Rock River Gorge. A walking path is carved into the wall above the waterline. The path is wide enough for horses, single file, but not wagons. I followed it only once, when I was a stupid young man. I thought the stories about the Stone Guardians were myths, too." His wizened eyes peered up at them from below bushy eyebrows.

"How did you get out alive?" Dinsmora asked, inspecting Mazu curiously.

"I was leading my horse at the time. The path was too narrow for me to mount him, so I butchered him as an offering, then ran like hell."

The room filled with horrified silence.

"An offering?" Jessum said, his deep voice breaking into a higher register. "I'm not killing BlackJack."

Mazu peered at Dinsmora. "You have an extra horse."

"No," Dinsmora said curtly, twisting a dish towel in her hands. "Not my Cinnamon or Nutmeg."

"You have sheep," Teleo said. "We'll buy one. Two."

The shepherd raised an eyebrow. "Might need one for each of you."

Teleo wondered if the man was being greedy and had made up the tale to get more supplies out of them, or if he was genuinely concerned for their safety. He had been nothing but generous so far, but desperate people did desperate things, and his land was not much more than a field of rocks.

"How much?" Teleo asked, trying to keep the suspicion from his voice.

"You got gold?" Mazu asked, his eyes brightening.

"A little," Teleo said. He had a few Gold Lions, but he was not going to part with them. He pulled out the money pouch he had taken from the old groom, probably the man's life savings. Teleo dumped the coins into his palm and sorted through them. There were three Gold Lions, five Silver Owls, and an assortment of Silver, Bronze, and Copper Bits. He picked out an Owl and held it up to Mazu and Tintin.

Mazu licked his lip. "An Owl? Per sheep? That's not fair," he said, peering at Teleo with a shameful gaze. "Three each," he said stubbornly.

"One per sheep," Teleo said, not relenting. "We need four. I'll give you five Owls total."

Mazu's brows lowered and he looked at his wife. She drew her mouth down.

"Three Owls each," Mazu said firmly. "Twelve total."

"That's fair," Dinsmora said, ruining Teleo's negotiation. He cast her a dour gaze and she returned an innocent smile.

That equaled one Lion and two Owls. Lions were hard to come by, but so were fat, healthy sheep on the windswept slopes of Jagged Tooth Pass. "One Lion," he said, taking a Gold Lion and handing it to the shepherd, who accepted it with a satisfied look.

⸻ ◆ ⸻

They studied Mazu's map, and Teleo took out the map Jessum had drawn. Mazu marked Teleo's map with the path they were to follow using a sliver of charcoal.

"You'll start at Lamb's Bowl, which is a small secluded valley not far from here. Follow Lamb's Bowl southwest until you encounter the gorge," Mazu said, drawing a small oval circle for the Lamb's Bowl valley. He then drew a line that zigzagged north-south to represent the slot canyon. "The entrance to Rock River Gorge is hidden among the rocks. Watch your footing there, it's steep. Go into the gorge and follow it south for three days. At the end of the gorge, the river disappears underground and you will emerge into a long, grassy valley." Mazu took his charcoal and drew an X at the spot where the jagged line ended. "Follow the valley south until you come upon a crossroads marked with a pile of skulls."

"Skulls?" Kaspari asked. "A whole pile?"

"Yes," Mazu said. "A small mountain of skulls and bones. Entire skeletons."

Kaspari's eyes grew bigger. "Human skeletons?" she asked, her face growing pale.

"Yes. Human skeletons," Mazu said gravely. "They say the Stone Guardians pile the bones of their victims there as a warning not to enter their territory."

The four of them were quiet and exchanged nervous glances.

Mazu turned back to the map and marked the turnoff with a skull and crossbones. "At the pile of skulls, you will turn west onto Demon's Bones Trail." He drew a snaking line. "The trail is steep and hard to follow. It's a series of tight switchbacks that your horses should be able to navigate if you're careful. Just keep going up and keep an eye out for Stone Guardian hunting parties."

Mazu lifted his gaze to make sure Teleo was paying attention. Teleo nodded and Mazu continued. "After a day of climbing, you will go down a sharp incline and meet Hatchet Pass." Mazu drew a small hatchet marker next to a line that was already on Teleo's map. Teleo was familiar with Hatchet Pass. "That is where the Stone Guardian territory ends," Mazu said. "If you make it that far, you will have already left Verdant Valley territory and bypassed the Hatchet Pass border outpost, which is a day's ride east." He drew a small sword to represent the outpost. "The Verdant Valley patrols rarely venture very far up that pass," Mazu said, "and the Sapphire forces avoid it because of frequent ambushes. So be careful. Cross Hatchet Pass and continue southwest on Demon's Bones Trail. It's a well-marked path at that point." Indeed, the trail already existed on Teleo's map. "Two days later," Mazu continued, "Demon's Bones will intersect Southern Mountain Pass." He pointed to a thick green line on Teleo's map. "Follow Southern Mountain Pass west a couple of days until the white marble obelisk marks the turnoff south to Trillifort."

The obelisk was already marked on Teleo's map. The boy had done a good job. Teleo smiled and patted Jessum's back. Teleo had passed that obelisk many times. He and his fellow soldiers had always thought it marked the end of civilization and the beginning of the tribal mountain lands. They always hurried when they saw it, and no one had been brave or curious enough to see where the turnoff led. They had heard of an abandoned quarry and a fortress back there where mountain men went to die. No one wanted to find out what that meant.

Mazu continued, "Trillifort Trail hugs a white marble cliff, and after a day's ride, it ends at the pillar-lined approach to Castle Trillifort. You can't miss it." The illustration of a castle with two small Heliotrope symbols disappeared under Mazu's calloused thumb.

"Where exactly did you encounter the Stone Guardians?" Teleo asked.

"Here." Mazu pointed to a spot midway along Rock River Gorge. He marked the spot with a star.

The shepherd offered to take them as far as the entrance to Lamb's Bowl the next morning.

"The Stone Guardians will appear in the Rock River Gorge without warning," Mazu cautioned.

"An ambush? From above?" Teleo asked.

"No." Mazu shook his head. "From the rock. They will appear. Like stone."

"From hidden entrances?" Teleo asked. "Caves?"

Mazu shook his head again. "No. From the rock. I can't explain it."

Teleo swallowed and Dinsmora shifted uncomfortably. Jessum and Kaspari stared at the shepherd.

Teleo sighed. "We don't have much choice, do we? If we stay in Verdant Valley, the king's men will ..." His voice trailed off and he glanced at Kaspari.

"Take Jessum," Dinsmora finished for him. "We could go back to my place," she suggested.

"No," he said, shaking his head. "That's just a temporary solution. We can't stay there forever." Dinsmora's secret forest was nice, but it was relatively small. He could traverse its length in an afternoon. Dinsmora came and went as she pleased: on house calls; to gather herbs; to visit the small villages that dotted the countryside. Teleo and the teenagers would be trapped there. "We've come this far," he said. "If we can make it into the mountains, we'll be safe from Stagga's men."

They rose before dawn the next day and ate a farewell breakfast of fried eggs, lamb-and-potato pie, fresh sheep's-milk yogurt, stewed apples, and hot tea. They left the wagon, most of the hay, the cider barrel, water barrel, and other non-essential supplies with the shepherds, and packed as many sacks of oats, apples, almonds, and vegetables as they could carry. Dinsmora had brought a saddle for each of her horses and saddled both, but loaded up Nutmeg like a pack mule, with her sheepskin rugs, bundles of medicinal herbs, sewing supplies, coils of rope, a cooking pot, and other sundries that Teleo scowled at, with sacks of food and a few sheaves of hay balanced on top. Nutmeg didn't seem to mind.

They loaded up the other horses with more sacks of food and horse feed, and leather sacks filled with water, brewed tea, and hard apple cider. Their saddlebags were stuffed with spare clothing and personal items, and each was topped with a bedroll wrapped in waxed canvas, plus a pair of winter boots, mittens, and a hat rolled up in their shearling coats. Teleo strapped both his swords across his back and wore a collection of knives and hammers on his waist belts.

Mazu and Tintin separated four sheep from the flock. Tintin tied a halter on one of them and handed the lead rope to Dinsmora. "The others will follow her," Tintin said. "After a few days, she will follow the horses and you won't need the rope."

Mazu and Tintin went into a barn and emerged bearing a shepherd's crook in each hand. "You might need these," Tintin said as she handed one to Kaspari and the other to Teleo. Mazu handed one each to Jessum and Dinsmora.

Teleo's was of solid hickory, as long as a man was tall, with a carved hook on the end. It was old and polished with use, its handle worn smooth. Teleo thanked the shepherds and slid it through a loop on his saddle where he had sometimes carried a stave into battle. Jessum swung his around like a weapon, looking pleased.

Tintin waved from the doorstep as Mazu got on his shaggy gray mule and led their band of five horses, four humans, and four sheep up a hillside towards the rocky crags of the Blue Mountains.

PART TWO

BLUE MOUNTAINS

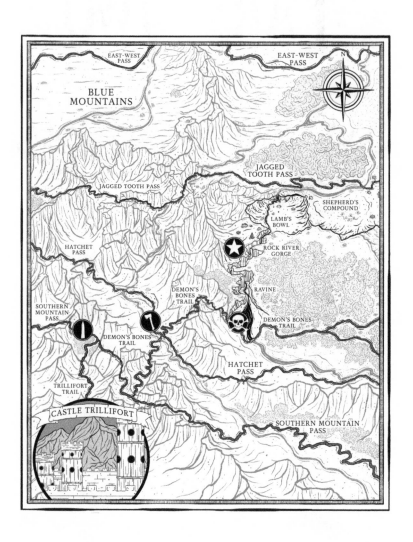

9

ROCK RIVER GORGE

It was mid-afternoon when they dismounted at the base of a red rock cliff. Mazu led Teleo between the cliff face and a dense grove of prickly holly trees and showed him a narrow cleft in the rock.

"Pass through here and you will emerge into the Lamb's Bowl valley," Mazu said.

Teleo peered into the fissure. It was a vertical split in the rock, wide enough for a horse to pass through. "I would never have found this," Teleo said. "Thanks for showing us."

Mazu nodded. They went back to join the others, and Teleo took out his map and spread it on the ground. Mazu knelt next to him and they reviewed the turnoffs Mazu had marked the night before.

"Remember, the Rock River Gorge path is treacherous. It is very narrow in places, with a sheer drop down to the river."

Teleo nodded. "We will be fine," he said, smiling reassuringly at the kids. They did not smile back.

"I'm sure you will," Mazu said. "Just keep your eyes open."

"We will," Teleo promised. Teleo rolled up the map and thanked the shepherd. The sun-weathered man patted his sheep goodbye, then lumbered down the path on his mule without looking back.

Teleo led his party behind the holly trees, and they walked single file into the rock fissure. The sheep hurried through the long narrow cleft, bleating happily as if they recognized the place.

They emerged on the other side, and a breathtaking green and gold valley opened up before them. The hidden valley was large and bowl-shaped, hemmed in by jagged red rock hills and stands of trees, and carpeted with lush grass. Teleo filled his lungs, enjoying the musky scent of autumn.

They stepped onto the soft ground, and the sheep and horses immediately buried their noses in the grass. They removed the horses' bridles and let them graze for a short while, and Teleo better understood how the sheep were so fat and healthy.

Everyone was jittery and anxious, so they bridled the horses and moved along. It was easy riding, and the late afternoon sunlight shimmered through stands of aspen trees bordering the green meadow, their leaves a burnished copper and exuding a warm glow. They made an early camp at the far end of the Lamb's Bowl valley and staked the animals nearby to graze. No one wanted to enter Rock River Gorge at nightfall. They decided not to make a fire and attract attention to themselves—Teleo was already looking over his shoulder and flinching at shadows. Using the shepherd's crooks as poles to hold up the waxed canvas tarps, they erected a small lean-to, spreading out Dinsmora's sheepskin rugs on the ground. They went to bed after a cold meal of dried mutton, hardbread, raw carrots, and apples.

Teleo took the first watch and as the moon traveled across the sky, shadows from the surrounding hills grew longer, forming shapes that looked to Teleo like monsters. Dinsmora rose for her watch halfway through the night and laughed at his reluctance to sleep.

"When the Stone Guardians appear from the rocks, you will face them bravely," she said. "So why are you afraid of shadows?"

He did not answer but spread out his shearling coat for an added cushion, rolled himself in his blanket, and promptly fell asleep.

———————◆———————

The next morning, they hadn't gone very far when the Lamb's Bowl valley narrowed at its end and tall pointed rocks closed in around them, Teleo wondered if the shepherd had led them into a trap. The grass had given way to rocky, uneven ground, and the horses stepped carefully. Teleo regarded the strange rock formations—hulking monoliths that could have been Stone Guardian giants wearing crimson cloaks with hoods pulled down over their heads. He shivered and guided Benny between the natural pillars, looking for the hidden entrance.

"Teleo. Here," Jessum called out, and the others joined him.

A steep path snaked down between monoliths towards a shadowy cleft. The path was dirt and gravel broken by a series of ledges, forming wide, shallow steps. Teleo dismounted, tied up the reins to his saddle, and clicked his tongue for Benny to follow him. Teleo led the way on foot, hopping and sliding from ledge to ledge and letting Benny choose his footing down the series of inclines and shallow drops. The others followed suit. Taking up the rear, Nutmeg balanced carefully with his load, nearly sitting and sliding down the steepest slopes.

When they had all safely reached the foot of the hill, they stood before the towering cliff and its dark, yawning fissure, which sliced through the rock in such a perfectly straight line that Teleo imagined an angry god had split the rock face with a great hammer.

Dinsmora closed her eyes and sniffed the air. "This is it," she said. "This is the way forward."

Teleo untied Benny's reins and led the horse on foot to the gap, but the gelding straightened his forelegs and would not budge, his ears pinned back.

"I don't blame you, Benny," Teleo said, dropping the reins. "I'll take a look myself. Wait here."

He stepped into the crevice. The chasm was cold and damp, cast in dark shadow. A faint breeze wafted up the narrow slot canyon, shushing along the red rock faces, and the whisper of flowing water reached Teleo's ears. He looked up at the ribbon of blue sky overhead. He continued forward until the cleft opened into a sandy gully with a spring bubbling up out of a jumble of rocks. The spring formed a small river of pale green water, which flowed into a long, silent gorge. Teleo took in a deep breath. The steep-walled canyon widened out from the narrow entrance, with sandy banks on either side of the jade-green river.

Teleo went back for his companions and coaxed Benny through the narrow fissure with slices of apple. The others followed.

They gathered at the spring and drank the icy water. Jessum splashed playfully at BlackJack, whose small, pointy ears stood erect, and wide nostrils puffed in and out. The big black ranged downstream, then stepped gingerly into the river where it broadened and rippled over a shallow, sandy ford. It was only ankle deep, and he crossed easily to the other side, where he paced back and forth, tossing his head and stomping loudly.

"We're supposed to be on the other side," Dinsmora said. "Thank you, BlackJack."

They gathered the horses and sheep, and Jessum lured BlackJack back over the water with a handful of oats. They mounted the horses and crossed the ford single file. Cinnamon drove the reluctant sheep through the cold water, and the band headed south along the sandy bank into the dark red shadows.

The further they ventured into Rock River Gorge, the colder it got. They wore their gambesons—it was chilly out but not nearly cold enough for the winter-weight shearlings. The red rock cliffs pressed in on both sides. The sandy bank grew narrower, and the river deepened and flowed with a quiet force. Benny's ears flattened but Teleo encouraged him forward, and the horse reluctantly obeyed. Teleo was apprehensive as well, but there was no good alternative.

Teleo hesitated when the gorge took a jagged turn. He peered around the rock wall before leading everyone forward. The water splashed and churned angrily against the stone outcropping, ending the path on the other side of the river. They followed the curve of the river, which widened and slowed in swirls and cross currents. Teleo led his party across a small beach bathed in sunlight and strewn with debris where the water must have risen in the spring rains. The gorge straightened out and grew dark again and the river deepened in a narrow channel.

The riverbank on the opposite side had completely disappeared, leaving a wall of stone for the water to rush against. Teleo silently thanked BlackJack, who plodded along the path behind him, occasionally nipping at Benny's haunches. Benny ignored him, flicking his tail as though pestered by a fly, and Jessum pulled on BlackJack's reins, scolding him. The river grew deeper and darker, and stray ripples revealed a strong current that ran beneath the deceptively glassy surface. Teleo did not want to test the river's force.

A cold wind hit him in the face and sent a shudder through

him. He pulled up on the reins and Benny stopped short. Teleo's heart pounded. They were easy prey—hemmed in by the towering rock wall to their right rising straight up from the narrow bank, and the river to their left rushing against the facing cliff. Stone Guardians could emerge from the shadows straight ahead of them, or ambush them beyond the next blind turn. Or they could surprise them at the rear, or attack from above. Teleo took a deep breath and urged Benny forward. The horse picked up the pace, his ears alert.

The day passed without incident. They set up camp on another small beach, and Teleo and Dinsmora portioned out oats and hay for the animals. They hadn't considered that there would be nothing for the animals to eat in the rocky gorge, nor had they packed extra feed for the sheep. Teleo watched with concern as the horses and sheep ate hungrily, and hoped that the path to Trillifort cut through lush mountain meadows.

Dinsmora passed out dried mutton, hardbread, cheese, and apples for their own dinner. When they were done eating, they huddled together in a curved hollow at the base of the cliff. The wind grew stronger and colder as the night darkened. By the time stars studded the narrow strip of sky overhead, the wind was howling through the canyon. Dinsmora and Teleo split the night into two guard shifts while the teenagers slept. At first light, they were on their way again, the horses snorting and blowing clouds of warm breath into the chill air.

The sun was high in the sky when the distant roar of rushing water first became audible. Teleo knew they were in trouble even before they saw the waterfall. Sure enough, the narrow river fell off a sudden cliff in a thunderous, misty cloud.

Teleo dismounted, walked to the overhang, and peered over its edge into the dark pool some twenty feet below. The river flowed away from the pool into a dark chasm up ahead, walled in by cliffs on either side. The shepherd had neglected to warn them about a waterfall. The riverbank of sand and pebbles they'd been following all morning dwindled away to a narrow shelf of stone that rose in four natural, knee-high steps to a rock ledge. The ledge was not much more than an arm span wide, forming a treacherous path along the towering cliff face. Teleo turned and glanced at the others, who were regarding the cliff with deep frowns.

"We're supposed to go on *that?*" Kaspari asked, eyeing the ledge warily. "Are we going to die?"

Teleo chuckled. "Well, we haven't died yet, and I don't plan to start now." He raised his eyebrows. "How about you?"

She pursed her lips and shook her head. "Not today." A small grin quirked up one side of her mouth.

"That's the spirit," he said, letting a full smile spread across his face. "We get to see a hidden waterfall and ride through an enchanted canyon. What could be more fun than that?"

Jessum rolled his eyes and BlackJack snorted.

Teleo turned away and let his smile fade. He inspected the stone ledge and could see that it quickly narrowed. Very shortly, the horses would be unable to turn around, and they would be unable to access the river to drink. Maybe they were making a big mistake. He reminded himself that the shepherd had made it across this same passage, although he had not been stupid enough to attempt it twice.

Dinsmora stood next to him, surveying their path forward, her usual cheerfulness gone.

She met his gaze, then closed her eyes and sniffed the air.

"What do you think?" he asked.

She opened her eyes. "The river flows," she said, gazing down into the water as it spilled over the edge.

"So it does," he said, inhaling deeply. "Let's water the animals and get going."

Teleo patted Benny's neck, removed his bit and bridle, and led the dapple gray to the river's edge. They let the horses and sheep drink and rest for a bit, topped off their leather water bags, and then approached the stone steps.

One by one, he and his companions led the horses and sheep up the incline. When they were all on the ledge, they mounted the horses and marched single file along the cliff face. Teleo was in front, followed by Jessum, then Kaspari, the sheep, Dinsmora, and finally Nutmeg taking up the rear. It was a sheer drop down to the river. Teleo and Benny hugged the wall on their right.

The ledge narrowed and then narrowed some more until Teleo's knee brushed the rock wall and Benny tossed his head nervously. Teleo clicked his tongue, encouraging the gelding forward. There was no turning back now. The river narrowed as well, rushing and hissing around clusters of jagged boulders and gurgling against the facing walls of the canyon. The sky was growing paler overhead, and the towering, reddish-brown cliffs closed in on them, leaving Teleo with a stifling claustrophobia.

"Ho," Dinsmora called out.

Teleo pulled up on the reins and looked behind him to see what was wrong. The sheep bleated in front of Dinsmora, their cries amplified in the rock chasm. Dinsmora slid off Cinnamon and edged around behind the horse. Teleo saw the issue. Nutmeg's bulky load was too wide. The horse's outer hooves were at the edge of the rock shelf. Dinsmora reached around Nutmeg's broad chest, then wedged herself between the draft horse's neck and the stone wall, then crept underneath bulging burlap sacks and the towering load. Teleo held his breath as the horse stood his ground. Kaspari and Jessum watched nervously, and the sheep bleated as Dinsmora cut loose sheaves of hay and one bulging sack after another, pushing them onto the stone trail behind Nutmeg. Their first offerings to the Stone Guardians.

Teleo clamped his jaws shut, wishing he could climb over the horses and help, but he was stuck up at the front. She cut loose two inner sacks and heaved them over Nutmeg's back and over the edge. They landed in the river with two distinct splashes. Teleo caught glimpses of the burlap sacks bobbing in the rough current before they were dragged down a narrow chute between two boulders and disappeared in the green froth.

Dinsmora left one layer of sacks, her cooking pot, and two sheaves of hay strapped to the big bay, then slid out from behind him. Nutmeg sidled closer to the wall, snorting loudly. Teleo exhaled with him. Dinsmora stood between her two horses and waved at Teleo to proceed. She would continue on foot. Teleo nudged Benny forward at a slow walk.

◆

The cliff path ran straight and unbroken for miles. The rushing flow of the river below threatened to lull Teleo to sleep in his saddle, but random patches of darkness in the stone faces jarred him back to full alertness. As far as Teleo could tell, they were alone in the river gorge. The path occasionally widened, allowing them to dismount and rest. They spread out hay for the animals to eat, but the river was beyond their reach.

"I hope we get out of here by tonight," Teleo said to Dinsmora, and she returned his worried look—the shepherd had said it would take them three days to traverse the gorge, and this was only day two.

During a break, Dinsmora stared into space, uncharacteristically sober.

"What's wrong?" Teleo asked softly while the teenagers were trying to hide in opposite corners of the sheltered area, relieving themselves.

"I'm trying to hold an invisibility barrier around us," Dinsmora whispered back. "But it keeps disintegrating. This place has a spell on it already, much stronger than anything I can create."

Teleo nodded thoughtfully, then concern creased his brow. "What if they can sense your magic?"

Dinsmora's mouth turned down. "Good point. It's not working anyway, and it's exhausting. It's like trudging through mud here." She ran fingers through her long auburn hair and then twisted it up into a bun and stuck a carved bone hairpiece through it. "Do you think they know we're here?"

"Probably," Teleo said. "The sheep have made sure of that with their incessant bleating. That and we're leaving a trail of piss and shit."

She nodded morosely. "Maybe they'll let us pass."

"We can only hope."

Time seemed to stretch out here, and Teleo had no sense of how far they had come. He made a rough calculation of the length of a day and their slow speed, and the approximation of distance he could derive from the rough map. By his best estimation, they would come upon the starred spot along the trail tomorrow morning. They could turn around now and go back the way they'd come. That might make the most sense—but Teleo hadn't survived this long by choosing the wisest options.

The kids returned and everyone mounted up. The sheep dutifully followed the horses by now, so they let them trail at the end of the line behind Nutmeg so that the humans could talk without raising their voices. They trudged on until the gorge was covered in twilight's shroud. At the next turnout they came to, they set up camp along the base of the cliff, leaving the animals in a group around an open sack of oats and the remainder of the hay.

Teleo and Jessum rigged a rope sling for the canvas bucket and lowered it into the river below, then hoisted it up again.

The bag arrived at the top only half full, but it was better than nothing. The animals made short work of the water as they nosed each other out of the way. They lowered the bucket several times until the animals seemed satiated.

If they did not reach the end of the canyon the following day, the animals' feed would be gone. Teleo considered that perhaps they should leave the sheep behind, but the prospect of needing to sacrifice one of the horses to the Stone Guardians made him dismiss the idea.

Teleo took the first watch and stared into the darkness. The humans and animals shifted until they found comfortable positions, then quieted down into a soft chorus of breathing. Teleo tried to detect the stealthy, creeping sounds of attacking Stone Guardians, but all he heard was the constant rushing of water amidst an otherwise cavernous silence. They were cornered. It would be a quick and bloody massacre. Or maybe the Stone Guardians would toss them down into the river alive, just for the sport of it.

Teleo unsheathed his longsword, propped it across his knees, and waited.

◆

The next morning, they rode along with a regular cadence of *clip-clop clip-clop*. Leather saddles creaked. BlackJack snorted. The susurrus of the river sounded like blood rushing through Teleo's veins. The sheep were quiet—perhaps the gentle beasts knew their fate hung in the balance and were on their best behavior.

Jessum's garbled yell jerked Teleo out of his reverie. *"Stone ...! Men ...! Teleo ...!"* Jessum gestured frantically across the chasm. A shelf of rock had appeared on the facing cliff where there had been none. It took a moment to discern the shapes of men. A line of warriors stood on the ledge and appeared to blend into the rock. Or to be rock. Stone-still statues wearing gray-and-brown textured armor. Teleo forced himself not to freeze and kept a firm hand on Benny's reins, continuing at their regular pace. Teleo wondered if the murky apparitions were real until one moved.

The Stone Guardian thrust a staff into the air and shot a bolt of white lightning across the chasm. Benny shrieked and reared, then lunged forward. BlackJack and the others clattered behind him in a frantic canter along the narrow path. Lightning crackled and fizzled around them in a blue net but soon sputtered and died. The sheep bleated and Dinsmora moaned. The air stank of sulfur.

Teleo slowed Benny to a jerky trot and glanced over his shoulder. Dinsmora was coughing and clinging to her saddle with one hand. The shepherd's crook was clasped in her other hand, smoking. She raised it and met another bolt that shot across the chasm. The lightning hit Dinsmora's crook with a loud pop and crackled across a defensive net, which emanated from her crook and surrounded their party. The blue net was smaller and weaker this time. Teleo pulled his shepherd's crook from its strap, and Jessum and Kaspari imitated him, raising their hickory staffs overhead. Teleo kicked Benny into a run. The horses needed no more encouragement and raced across the stone path.

Teleo raised his crook as another bolt shot across the ravine. It struck his crook with bone-shuddering force, sending a shooting pain down his arm and spreading a blue web of light overhead. He held on and glanced behind him. Jessum and Kaspari's crooks were raised and their heads were down while their horses ran as fast as they dared along the narrow ledge, with the sheep running behind them. The Stone Guardians sprinted on foot on a parallel path that ran along the opposite cliff. New warriors emerged from the rock wall and another bolt struck the center of their party. Kaspari yelped and Teleo glanced over his shoulder in time to see her shepherd's crook fall into the chasm. He did not wait to watch it splash into the river but spurred Benny forward. The horse responded and stretched his legs, more afraid of the lightning bolts than of making a misstep and plunging to their deaths.

The Stone Guardians continued their attack, white bolts crackling across the drooping web of blue light held by the three remaining shepherd's crooks. A Stone Guardian appeared in front of Teleo, barring his path. Teleo drew Benny up short, then changed his mind and dug his heels into Benny's flanks. The horse obeyed and shot forward. The Stone Guardian faded into the rock as Teleo rode straight through the flickering mirage. He had no time to figure out what had just happened but urged Benny forward, glancing behind to make sure everyone was still with him.

They ran until the lightning bolts stopped and the stone shelf on the other side of the ravine returned to sheer cliff. The path was clear in front of them, and Teleo pushed on at a fast trot until Benny was covered in sweat and puffing loudly. Teleo finally slowed him to a walk and looked over his shoulder. His party was strung out behind him but were all accounted for, including the sheep who trailed in the rear, heads hanging from exhaustion.

They came upon a sheltered nook and gathered together. Teleo dismounted and checked on everyone. Dinsmora was the worst off. He helped her from her saddle and she collapsed in his arms.

"I can't go on," she said, trembling. Tangled strands of red hair were plastered across her sweaty forehead and neck.

"It's okay, it's okay," Teleo said, letting her sink to her knees. He untied one of her sheepskin rugs from Cinnamon's bundle and spread it out next to the stone wall. She crawled onto it and stretched out with a quivering sigh. Kaspari brought a waterskin and encouraged her to drink while Teleo covered her with a blanket.

"I just need to rest for a minute," Dinsmora said, closing her eyes.

Jessum and Kaspari tended to the animals while Teleo stood at the edge of the cliff and scanned the rock walls for Stone Guardians. The gorge was still and peaceful. Even the river was free of rocks and flowed with a gentle murmur.

Kaspari and Jessum spread a blanket on the ground and laid out a meal of dried mutton, hard cheese, apples, and carrots. Kaspari brought some to Dinsmora, who roused herself enough to eat a few mouthfuls before pulling the blanket over her head and going back to sleep.

They spent the rest of the day in the hollowed-out nook, and Teleo resigned himself to spending the night there. If the Stone Guardians wanted them dead, there was nothing Teleo could do about it. If they only wanted them to leave their territory, then they shouldn't have attacked them. They were moving as fast as they could, and Teleo was not about to leave Dinsmora behind.

They hoisted up water for the horses and sheep and opened the last two fifty-pound sacks of oats. It was not enough feed for the big draft horses and so many sheep, but it was all they had. Teleo tossed them several apples and carrots, hoping for the best. He stood watch all night, stealing a couple of hours of sleep as dawn crept across the sky. Jessum stood watch for him, promising to wake him at the slightest shadow.

When Teleo awoke, Dinsmora was sitting upright, leaning against the rock wall and drinking water. She smiled weakly. "What do you think of my magic?" she asked.

"I think you are a wonder," he said, sitting next to her and meeting her glinting eyes. "Where did you learn how to make a shield like that?"

"My mother taught me, but I never tried a moving one before. I always wove it out of the branches of trees. I never tried weaving one out of thin air, but it works."

"So it seems," Teleo said. "Nearly killed you, too."

"No," she scoffed. "Just wore me out a bit."

"It didn't affect us like it did you," Teleo said. "I'm not sure we helped."

"You did. With your help, I was able to keep the shield propped up over all of you. I had felt it collapsing around me until you all raised your crooks."

"What do you make of those shepherd's crooks?" he asked.

"I think those shepherds were more than they appeared," she said, the corners of her eyes crinkling.

Teleo nodded. "They knew the way to a secret Stone Guardian canyon, after all."

"Yes," Dinsmora agreed. "And they've managed to survive all these years alone in the forbidding hills of Jagged Tooth Pass."

"But they couldn't protect their son," Jessum cut in, spitting apple seeds over the edge of the crevasse.

Teleo did not have an answer for that, and neither did Dinsmora. That brought the conversation to an end until Kaspari broke the silence.

"I dropped my crook," she said despondently.

More silence.

The shepherd's crooks had proven to be powerful beyond all reason, but there was no retrieving the lost crook. It was probably broken or snagged under a river rock by now.

"If Stone Guardians hate Mages," Kaspari said, "then they'll hate us. Right?"

More truth that the adults had no response to. Dinsmora had revealed her nature, but Teleo did not know the extent of his cousin's powers. She probably did not know, herself. Dinsmora had gathered scraps of ancient knowledge and cultivated the old ways as best she could, all the while risking being discovered by the kingdom and put to death for breaking the prohibition against magic. Teleo stole a glance at the princess. If Kaspari somehow came into power, would she continue enforcing the laws against magic? Teleo sighed. That was a worry for another time. First, they had to make it out of this gorge alive.

"We need to go," Teleo said, climbing to his feet. He held out his hand for Dinsmora and helped her up.

They ate a quick breakfast of hardbread, cheese, and hard-boiled eggs, hoisted up more water for the animals, and fed them a small snack of carrots and apples. They brushed and saddled the horses, then lashed on their supplies and made ready to leave.

"Are we going to butcher the sheep for an offering?" Jessum asked.

Teleo regarded the sheep, who were waiting patiently. They had kept pace without a fuss and were good-natured creatures. The end of the rocky gorge should be near, leading them into another valley thick with autumn grasses, he hoped, so he saw no immediate reason to slash their throats. Besides, Dinsmora was lovingly scratching one under the chin and peering side-ways at Teleo with a stern frown.

"No," Teleo said. "They've made it this far. No sense killing them needlessly."

The four sheep bleated at him, as though they understood his words.

"Let's go," he said. Teleo patted Cinnamon and formed a step for Dinsmora with his hands, giving her a leg up into the saddle. He mounted Benny and they took to the stone trail at a brisk walk.

Teleo spent the day watching for shadowy men and lightning bolts that never came. Late that afternoon, Rock River Gorge ended abruptly in a tumble of giant stone blocks and a dark emerald pool whose center was a swirling black vortex, which made a disturbing sucking sound. They emerged from the tight clutches of the slot canyon, and the blue sky opened up above them. The animals lined up side by side on the rocky bank and sank their noses into the pool while Teleo and the others filled their waterskins and larger water sacks.

When they were ready, they climbed up a dirt path that ran beside the rockfall, scrambled over a steep rise, and emerged into a grassy valley. Teleo breathed a sigh of relief and examined their surroundings. The long narrow valley was bordered by sloping hillsides thick with a mixed forest of short stubby pines bearing tufts of long needles and heavy pinecones, and deciduous trees that had nearly lost all their leaves, carpeting the ground with a patchwork of red, yellow, and brown.

Teleo did not want to stop, but the animals were hungry, and riding at night through an unknown valley was a bad idea. They set up camp next to a large boulder while the animals grazed. Dinsmora fell promptly asleep, and Kaspari sorted through their dwindling food supplies. Teleo took the opportunity to sharpen his swords while Jessum sat on top of the boulder, keeping watch. Night fell, and the air was alive with the distant howling of wolves and a pair of owls hooting back and forth in the nearby forest.

Morning broke with a heavy frost on the grass, transforming the autumn scruff into a carpet of sparkling colors as the sun rose over the horizon and reflected off the ice crystals.

They ate a quick breakfast and got on their way, hooves crunching through the melting frost and the sheep romping in bouncing leaps behind Nutmeg.

Teleo did not know how far it was to Demon's Bones Trail, but the valley stretched between the hills as far as the eye could see before disappearing behind a distant rise. The path was no more than a faint indentation where the grass was shorter than everywhere else. The valley was peaceful, but Teleo was not fooled—the woods to either side hid shadows behind shadows. He held his shepherd's crook and rode forward.

As the sun rose higher in the sky, the sparkling grass turned limp and sodden and the shadows melted away. Still, they rode silently and held their crooks. The horses pulled on their reins to steal mouthfuls of shaggy grass and the sheep kept wandering from the trail to eat, so they decided to dismount and let the animals graze. Teleo removed Benny's bridle and surveilled the edges of the fields for movement but saw nothing more than the fluttering of leaves and the low flight of a hunting hawk.

After a time, nervousness tugged at Teleo, and he and his party mounted their horses and continued on. Benny scanned the bordering forests along with Teleo. Periodically, his ears would flatten and Teleo would tense up. BlackJack danced behind him, wanting to run, but Teleo wanted to save their energy in case they needed to sprint away from an attack.

Teleo's stomach was growling and his bladder urged him to stop for a break when Benny's ears flattened again.

"Whoa, Black," Jessum said behind him. BlackJack reared and lunged forward, passing Benny and breaking into a full gallop.

Benny took off after him, and Teleo grabbed a fistful of mane with his crook hand, the hickory shaft banging against his thigh. "Benny, steady!" Teleo yelled, tugging at the reins, but Benny's ears were back and his nose was in the wind. Hooves pounded behind him and he stole a glance over his shoulder. Daisy, Cinnamon, and Nutmeg ran in a pack, and the sheep raced in a line not far behind. Kaspari leaned forward and Dinsmora shook her crook in the air as her hair came loose and streamed out behind her with her embroidered tunic fanning out like wings.

A low buzz cut through the pounding of hooves. The sound assaulted them from the woods, flanking them left and right. The grating buzz pulsated Teleo's eardrums, making him want to cover his ears. Shadows flitted behind trees, pacing their panicked band on either side. He leaned over Benny's neck, urging him to run faster. The horse leapt forward and Teleo's stirrup jostled Jessum's as Benny raced BlackJack, vying for the lead, legs outstretched and hooves skimming the grass.

Teleo held on with his knees and thrust his shepherd's crook into the air. His hand caught the buzz, vibrating his arm bones and radiating ripples of blue light from his hand. He jerked his hand down and the air fell quiet. The grid of blue closed over his head and faded, and the buzz grew louder.

"Teleo, the shield!" Dinsmora cried sharply.

Teleo pushed his shepherd's crook back up into the charged field. It stung his hand but he held on tight. The blue grid hissed and brightened. Dinsmora's net draped over their heads, forming a protective cocoon. BlackJack fell back and Benny surged ahead. Teleo and his crook held the point of the shield. Teleo glanced behind him as Jessum pushed his crook upward, connecting with the blue grid of light and propping it up over him and Kaspari.

They rode like that for what seemed like miles at a rolling canter. Teleo's arm ached from holding it up. The forest closed in on them, and still they rode. The horses were huffing and laboring in a jerky trot by the time a towering stack of bleached-white human skulls and bones glinted in the sun ahead of them. The mound stood at a crossroads of two dirt paths in a large clearing, taking up most of a grassy corner. He drew Benny to a stop, both of them gasping for air. Teleo held his breath and listened. His arm was numb. He lowered it, letting go of the shield. He could feel it disperse in a wave of prickles against his skin.

The buzzing was gone. Birds whistled a rollicking tune to one another, and a hardy cricket chirped from a nearby branch. A light breeze bathed Teleo's sweaty forehead. He circled Benny around and the five horses gathered in a huddle.

"You okay?" he asked everyone.

Jessum's hair was wet and stringy. "Yeah," he said breathlessly.

Dinsmora's head was bowed and she leaned over Cinnamon's neck, clutching her crook and Cinnamon's tangled mane for support. She nodded.

"Where are the sheep?" Kaspari asked.

Teleo peered behind them. The trail was empty.

"Offerings," Jessum said.

Teleo cocked his head, listening, and surveyed the forest.

"The Stone Guardians are gone," Dinsmora said, wiping at her nose. Her hand was trembling. "For now. Thanks for helping." She looked up. Her eyes were tired but gleaming.

"That was incredible," Jessum said, grinning.

Kaspari pursed her lips and said nothing, then turned and peered at the mound of bones.

The pile was so high that the skulls at the top must have been tossed up there. Some skeletons were completely intact—other limbs were dismembered. Skulls sat at grotesque angles, empty eye sockets staring down at them. Clumps of matted hair stuck to some skulls like moss. Teleo wondered how old the bones were and if the mound had once been a pile of decomposing bodies with crows and vultures feasting until they'd had their fill, then worms and rain taking care of the rest of the rotting flesh. What battle had it been? Or was it a massacre? Or did the Stone Guardians pick off trespassers one by one and add their corpses to the pile? Wherever the bones had come from, they served as a stark warning to misguided travelers not to enter the Stone Guardian territory.

They took a short break and ate a few bites of food while the horses foraged for grass and took turns drinking water from the canvas bucket that they filled from their water supply. No one felt safe, so they quickly rubbed sweat off the horses' coats, checked their hooves, and climbed into the saddles again.

Teleo shivered, gripped his shepherd's crook, and guided Benny west onto Demon's Bones Trail. They were leaving the crossroads when a chorus of bleating turned their heads. The four sheep emerged from the wooded trail and bounded joyfully towards them like dogs having found their masters. Teleo was surprised at how happy he was to see the dumb creatures. He dismounted to inspect the tired sheep. Dinsmora hugged each one, and Jessum unstrapped a water bag from Nutmeg's back and poured some into the bucket. The sheep gathered around to drink. Kaspari quartered an apple and fed a piece to each of them.

They rested for a few more minutes to let the sheep catch their breath and graze with the horses until Teleo's patience ended. He gestured to the others and swung into his saddle. "Time to go," he said. "Either the sheep keep up or they don't. We cannot linger here."

The sheep's noses were buried in the grass, but before the line of horses had gone a dozen paces, they scampered down the path and took their places dutifully behind Nutmeg.

The horses and sheep left the clearing at a brisk walk, and Teleo led the small band into the mountains.

◆

Demon's Bones Trail quickly climbed. The trail was faint but there was only one way up. The animals scrambled for footing on the steep rock and dirt path. They rested at the top of a series of switchbacks and Teleo surveyed the landscape below. He was the only one wearing any sort of armor. An arrow could take down the others at any time.

"Do you have a shield up?" he asked Dinsmora.

"No," she said. "They are not here."

"How do you know?" he asked.

She shrugged. "I don't know. I felt them before. Now I don't."

"Don't you think we should have a shield up anyway?" he asked.

Her eyes bored into his. He blew out his breath and broke their gaze. She was so stubborn sometimes.

They continued like that all afternoon. Climb. Rest. Argue. Dinsmora was confident and exhausted. If Teleo knew how to make a magic shield himself, he wouldn't have to depend on an ornery woman. He didn't know why he had wasted his life fighting with a sword when magic was still alive in the world. Although, the Mages had fought with swords, and they were supposedly unbeatable. He needed to dance the sword in a Heliotrope during the Summer Solstice and ignite whatever magic still dwelled in his bones. At least he had been able to help with Dinsmora's shield. But that was small comfort as the day dragged on and the forest pressed in around them.

Demon's Bones Trail angled in a southwesterly direction. The path followed a small stream for a stretch, giving the animals a chance to drink their fill and for Teleo's party to replenish their water supplies. They continued on until the path narrowed and veered away from the stream. The dirt trail led them to the top of a wooded ridge, down the other side, and suddenly they were on Hatchet Pass. Teleo let out a long sigh of relief and inhaled the fresh mountain air. This was officially the border of Stone Guardian territory, according to Mazu the shepherd, and for the first time since they had entered Rock River Gorge, Teleo relaxed.

Hatchet Pass was a single wagon's width wide and stretched east to west, carving a treacherous path of dirt and gravel along the steep mountainsides. There were no wagons or travelers in sight. It was not a well-used pass, although Teleo had crossed this way a few times. The rugged road bypassed the larger border outposts, and the small Hatchet Pass outpost was known for letting through smugglers. Further up, the road ran right through a collection of brigands' camps. Those communities were a two days' climb from here, buried deep in the upper pass where a large mountain lake lay hidden in a forested valley.

They found a flat spot just off the road in a grassy knoll where Teleo dismounted, stiff from days of riding. They unsaddled the horses, groomed them quickly, and then staked them to graze. Teleo unrolled his tarp and lay flat on his back in the weak sunshine, propping his sore legs on his bundle of blankets and shearling coat. Jessum stood watch while the women napped.

Teleo dozed off and awoke with a start. He sat up. Jessum was sitting cross-legged, polishing his sword. Dinsmora and Kaspari were still sleeping. The sheep were lying down, nestled together with their heads resting on each other's flanks, and the horses were asleep standing up—all except BlackJack, whose ear flicked when Teleo looked at him.

The mountain air was cool, with a light breeze wafting up Hatchet Pass. The sun was low in the sky and would descend behind the western peaks soon. He climbed to his feet and examined their surroundings. This was as good a place as any to spend the night, as long as they stayed alert. He ate some food and lay back down, staring up at the fading light.

Teleo had taken the watch from Jessum sometime in the middle of the night. He was sitting on his rolled-up shearling coat with his wool blanket draped over his shoulders, staring out across the hills where first light slowly brightened the sky. His companions were shapeless lumps on the ground, wrapped in their shearling coats against another light frost. The sheep were snuggled together near Dinsmora. The horses were all lying down, except BlackJack, who stood a horse-length apart, keeping watch with Teleo.

The sky grew brighter. Teleo stood up and stretched his arms overhead, trying to work the kinks out of his shoulders. The animals stirred and BlackJack nickered softly. Teleo scanned the forest across the road and froze. A shadow was staring at him. Two shadows. Three.

This time, the Stone Guardians looked like trees. Perfectly camouflaged except for the whites of their eyes, which reflected the golden shafts of sunlight that suddenly streamed over the eastern hills. They stared back at him, unflinching.

Teleo had encountered many groups of men in these mountains. Some were bandits, others were merchants smuggling contraband, and some were simply men trying to eke out a living from the forest. He had developed a strong intuition that guided his sword hand before his head. His hand was calmly resting on the sword hilt at his belt. With his other hand, he reached for his shepherd's crook, which was lying on the ground by his feet, and he held it like a walking stick with its straight end planted on the ground.

The Stone Guardians were not drawing bows or hurling lightning bolts. They looked young, not much older than Jessum. They seemed merely curious, wondering how a band of real-life Mages had arisen from the dust of ancient legends, crossed their hidden territory in a protective net of blue light, and were now calmly sleeping by the side of the road. Not mysterious Mages, not gnarled old men with long white beards, but a family with a boy and a girl their age.

Teleo stared at them, trying to make out details, and they stared back. Their clothing looked like bark and moss. Their hair was tied back, with deerskin caps perched atop their heads. Deerskin boots reached to their knees and blended in with the ground covering of pine needles and autumn leaves. Teleo's gaze shifted from one to the next, and just as the young men had appeared from the shadows, so they disappeared. In the brief instant when his eyes had left one to find another, they were gone. No whisper of boots on leaves. No flicker of movement. Simply gone.

The hair on the nape of Teleo's neck stood on end and he searched the woods for signs of them. Nothing. He blinked hard. Had they been apparitions? His imagination? Was he so sleep-deprived that he'd started to hallucinate?

BlackJack stomped his foot. The big black was staring into the forest, his nostrils flaring wide. "You saw them too?" Teleo asked.

BlackJack tossed his head and snorted, then walked casually over to the sack of carrots and poked his nose at it. Teleo laughed aloud, making his companions stir.

He roused everyone and told them what he'd seen.

Dinsmora scolded him. "They could have put a glamour on you. We're lucky we're not all dead."

Dinsmora paced back and forth along the road's edge, and Teleo could see strands of blue light leaving her fingertips and weaving a hazy barrier. He did not want to suffer her wrath by suggesting she save her energy—or to tell her he told her so.

After a quick breakfast, they left Hatchet Pass and set out on the southern stretch of Demon's Bones Trail, an indistinguishable path that was no more than a deer trail. Teleo would have missed it had the shepherd not told him it was there; he had in fact missed it all the times he had traversed Hatchet Pass. The trail led them into the woods, and they left the Stone Guardians' domain behind.

10

CASTLE TRILLIFORT

The next two days were a steady climb. They fought the wind on long expanses of exposed hills as they picked their way across slopes of scree and washed-out gullies, or trod silently through patches of thick forests as the steep trail led them from one crest to the next. Blue ridges painted misty swaths as far as the eye could see, and snow-capped peaks to the north reminded Teleo that winter was approaching. They had left Verdant Valley just in time. In a few more weeks, this trail would be impassable. They found an occasional stream for the animals to drink from and to top off their waterskins and larger water sacks, and mountain meadows fed the horses and sheep. There were plenty of hares and other small critters, and Dinsmora used her longbow to catch them dinner.

At the end of the second day, they set up camp before dusk. Teleo built a fire in a small open glade while the others went into the nearby forest to collect more firewood. Teleo regarded his companions from a distance as they broke off dead branches and scoured the undergrowth for fallen wood. Jessum's buck-skin shirt and pants and Kaspari's tunic blended in with the forest, but Dinsmora's embroidered tunic camouflaged her so completely that Teleo easily lost sight of her.

Kaspari came back to the campsite with an armful of branches. She set them down and sat on the grass next to Teleo, poking at the fire with a stick and sending a fountain of sparks into the air. She stared into the flames, lost in thought. Her eyes grew vacant and she swiped at her nose and swallowed.

It was a rare moment when the two of them were alone. The days had passed in a blur since the deadly attack on Verdant Castle and had now stretched into weeks. But Teleo knew that the pain of losing loved ones only grew deeper with time.

"How are you doing?" he asked.

Kaspari shrugged and tossed the stick into the fire. "Fine. But I lost my Mage's crook."

"I know. That's too bad," Teleo said. "How are you doing other than that?"

She stared into the blaze. "Fine." This time, her voice was pitched at a higher register.

"Really?" Teleo asked.

"Yes. No," she said, taking another stick and poking at the fire.

He examined the stiff line of her mouth and the deep crease between her eyebrows. "You've been through a lot. A lot of ... loss," he said, prodding gently.

She took in a shaking breath. "I miss my mother. And my father. And my brothers. And Gwen." Her voice was thin, and Teleo could tell she was trying to hold back tears. "Why did they have to get murdered?" she asked, turning to him with red eyes. Her face crumpled and tears trickled down her cheeks. "I can still hear them screaming."

She folded up her knees and buried her face in her hands.

Teleo moved closer and put his arm around her shaking shoulders, knowing there was nothing in this world that could comfort her.

———————◆———————

Late the next morning, Demon's Bones Trail veered southwest, climbed a short rise, and met Southern Mountain Pass. The pass was a major thoroughfare that cut through the landscape in a long ribbon, rising and falling over the folds and ridges of the Blue Mountains. The road was wide and well constructed, the southernmost of three major east-west routes connecting the Verdant Valley with the Sapphire Empire. According to Teleo's map, they were well beyond the Verdant Valley Kingdom's border now, deep into mountain territory—an unincorporated, lawless zone. He doubted that the Verdant Valley border patrols from the Southern Mountain Pass outpost ventured more than a day's ride up the pass into the mountains. Now that the war had ended, the road was mostly used by merchants and travelers. The Sapphire forces manned their own border on the other side of the Blue Mountains. Even so, Teleo was wary of running into units of Sapphire Empire soldiers sent to harass the Verdant Valley's border outposts, or bands of mountain brigands. But compared to the Stone Guardians, those threats seemed manageable. Teleo adjusted the swords on his back and strapped the shepherd's crook to his saddlebags within easy reach.

Three figures on horseback came into view on an eastern rise far in the distance. Teleo watched until he determined they were riding away from them. Teleo's party hung back from the edge of the road until the horsemen disappeared behind a ridge. Another rider appeared over the same rise, moving in their direction, closely followed by a wagon and a second rider. It looked to be a merchant's wagon with two mounted guards—nothing to be concerned about. Teleo and his companions headed west, putting distance between themselves and the wagon.

It was relaxing to ride on a real road after so many days navigating rugged paths. The pass had been paved with granite by the ancient Stone Guardians, if the stories were to be believed. The granite made for a solid roadbed, and over the centuries had accumulated layers of dirt and gravel, packed hard by regular traffic.

The surrounding forest was too steep and treacherous to traverse off-road for any length of time, so Teleo took the risk to stay on the main artery. He kept his swords at the ready, should they encounter bandits, imperial soldiers, or Gerik's henchmen. Teleo doubted that the Staggas' search for the missing prince had extended past the border but, if so, this was one of the routes they would travel.

That afternoon, they came up behind three hooded men riding west on horseback. Teleo examined them from a distance but kept his hands on the reins. They were not mountain brigands or soldiers. Teleo took the lead, Dinsmora and Kaspari rode abreast behind him, and Jessum took up the rear with Nutmeg and the sheep. The travelers moved to the side of the road to let them pass. Teleo led the horses in a fast, thunderous trot, hooves pounding as they bore down on the hooded party. Teleo glared at the men, who turned to face him and kept their hands visible. They were pale and bearded. Verdant Valley folk. A sword hung at one man's side but he was not foolish enough to reach for it. The men glanced at the women, then took in Teleo's soldier garb and the powerful horses.

Benny strutted proudly by, showing off to the travelers' small horses. Teleo watched over his shoulder as Kaspari and Dinsmora followed closely behind, matching in their embroidered tunics.

They could have been mother and daughter. Dinsmora glowered at the men, shepherd's crook in hand. Kaspari, no longer disguised as a boy, rode confidently on the large dapple-gray mare.

BlackJack pranced impatiently, high-stepping as Jessum held him back from a gallop, his muscles rippling and long mane and tail waving. Jessum was long recovered from his injuries, and days of riding had made his posture tall and strong. He was clearly of Hill people stock, and the travelers cocked their heads curiously as he looked down at them. The small flock of sheep scampered along in a tight group, urged along by Nutmeg, who took up the rear and snorted loudly at the travelers. They left the three men in the dust and continued west at a steady pace.

The following day, they encountered three more small groups of travelers, but no soldiers. They mostly walked, maintaining a sustainable pace for the horses and sheep and taking breaks whenever they came upon a grassy shoulder or a mountain stream meandering near the road.

The third morning on the Southern Mountain Pass, a flash of light glinted from the crest of a hill. It was the white obelisk, reflecting the sun like a beacon. Dinsmora gestured at it with a smug look, as if it were an auspicious sign, but foreboding prickled the nape of Teleo's neck. He had always hurried by the landmark in the past. Now he was about to willingly tread down its unknown path. He tightened his hands on the reins and prodded Benny forward.

They reached the marble obelisk and craned their necks to regard its pointed top, towering fifty feet in the air. They inspected the landmark for a few minutes, trying to read the cryptic inscriptions, then turned south onto the branch road. It took them down a gradual slope and eventually placed them at the foot of a white marble cliff, where the trail made a sharp right

turn. These mountains had been quarried for centuries and supposedly had been the source of the marble for Verdant Palace.

Trillifort Trail was a wide wagon road bordered by the cliff
on the left side and a wooded hill on the right that descended
down a gentle slope towards a gurgling stream. As they rode, the
marble transitioned from a sheer cliff to steps of giant building
blocks, each over a head tall, where the quarrymen had cut out
huge cubes. A gyrfalcon perched on a corner four levels up and
watched them pass, its white and gray feathers camouflaged
against the rough-hewn stone.

They passed two travelers, also headed to Castle Trillifort.
One was a farmer driving an oxcart filled with winter squash.
Next, they came upon a tinker's brightly painted wagon-house
jangling with wares hanging from the exterior walls—metal
lanterns and forged tools, leather belts and bridles, glassware
and ceramics, knitting needles and skeins of yarn. They paused
briefly to see if the tinker had anything useful. Dinsmora bought
a few beeswax candles and two small sacks of licorice and birch
beer candies. Teleo bought small whetstones for Kaspari and
Jessum. The draft horse pulling the wagon was large and shaggy
and peered at their horses through its long forelock. It was
shorter than Teleo's and Dinsmora's horses by a hand, and twice
as old. It seemed well-fed and content enough. Teleo slipped it a
carrot stub and removed a burr from under its bridle.

They continued forward at a leisurely pace, stopping to hunt
and then to eat, then to rest. Teleo was not sure what to expect
at the castle and was not overly anxious to find out. Before
nightfall, they made camp down by the stream. At midday the
next day, they arrived at a turnoff flanked by two enormous
white marble pillars, which Mazu had said marked the entrance
to the approach road to Castle Trillifort. They turned onto the
wide, well-maintained wagon path, which cut through a large

meadow and was bordered by tall marble pillars every tenth of a mile and jagged cliffs on either side.

A mile further on, the road ended at another marble cliff. Hemmed in by towering crags on three sides, it was a fine place for an ambush, Teleo reflected gloomily. He scanned the tops of the cliffs for archers and inspected the sunny meadow behind them, half expecting to find a dozen mountain brigands blocking their way out. Birds twittered and a light breeze ruffled the grasses, which the horses and sheep picked at hungrily. They were alone. To their left, a natural arch formed a mouth in the cliff face, flanked by two more pillars carved into the marble. They passed between the pillars and entered a cold shadow, then soon emerged into the sunshine on a rocky bluff.

Up ahead glistened a white marble castle perched atop a towering promontory and standing in brilliant contrast against the azure sky. Three large towers crowned the shining fortress. The central keep was surrounded by a small walled town set atop the cliffs, with rings of blue stone roofs radiating outwards.

Teleo drew his party to a stop and dismounted. He hid his longsword in the rolls of sheepskin rugs, transferred his short sword to his hip, and stuffed the shoulder straps into his saddlebags. He got back in his saddle and they continued on.

As they drew nearer, Trillifort's defensive position came into full view. The sheer cliff the castle was built upon plunged down into a marble quarry that widened into a deep bowl. An entrance road was built atop a narrow ridge, which bisected the quarry and led up to the town.

The raised quarry road appeared to be the only way in and out of the castle town, which was both a benefit and a risk. Such a position would withstand attacks, Teleo determined, but its citizens would be easily trapped. The lower entrance to the quarry was sealed off by a tall defensive wall, which spanned its entire width and met natural cliffs on both sides. The white marble ramparts were topped with battlements that looked like teeth, and there was only one gate. Several guardsmen looked down from between the teeth. Some were behind crossbows or holding longbows with arrows nocked. Others leaned lazily on elbows as they watched them approach. Teleo's band was just a family. No threat.

They made their way down the sloped path. Four armed guards stood under the enormous wooden gate, which was hoisted fifteen feet overhead with ropes as thick as Teleo's forearms.

Teleo drew Benny to a stop several paces from the gate.

"You got an appointment with the queen?" one of the guards asked in a nasally mountain twang.

Dinsmora rode up beside Teleo and they exchanged glances.

"No," Teleo replied.

The guard wore metal body armor and a longsword across his back. The sword's cross guard clanked against his shoulder plate as he stepped forward a pace.

"You here fer the market tomorrow?" he asked, squinting at the sheep. "You got how many? Four? Them ewes?"

"Yes," Teleo replied.

"All right. Market opens at dawn." He waved them through.

Teleo regarded the scraggly sheep with a cocked eyebrow, and Dinsmora flashed him a sly smile. They filed through the open gate and stepped onto the raised road. The marble ridge fell off steeply on either side, and a chest-high marble wall hemmed in the road, which was just wide enough for two wagons to pass each other. The wind sprang up in strong gusts, and Dinsmora stopped to fasten her bedroll more securely on Cinnamon's back. They made it to the top and gathered on a promenade in front of the fortress's open gate. It was the same style of raised wooden gate, and four guards eyed them curiously.

"We're here for the market tomorrow," Teleo said, gesturing to the sheep.

"Them ewes?" one of them asked. "The castellan sent fer you?"

"Yeah, they're ewes. We heard about the market is all."

"The queen will want them ewes. You can spend the night in the town square. Ask fer the castellan. Cutter's his name. Lead yer horses."

They dismounted, passed through the gate, and followed a winding marble-paved road that brought them to a large square surrounded by several blocky buildings. Everything was white marble and of Stone Guardian craftsmanship. They were literally on top of a marble quarry, as though the castle had been carved from the mountaintop itself, and the solid energy of the stone radiated throughout Teleo's body.

A grand staircase at one end of the square led up to another level in the direction of two towers, which soared prominently above an imposing edifice. The third tower stood at the opposite side of the small castle town, poking up above a sea of blue-tiled rooftops. Tall pillars were spaced around the perimeter of the central square, holding up nothing but the cobalt sky. Several merchants were camped out around loaded wagons and bundles of goods. A splashing fountain stood at the center, where two horses drank and several young children held their hands under the spray, giggling loudly.

A tall, barrel-chested, bearded man approached them. He introduced himself as Cutter, the castellan. His abundant facial hair was brown and bushy, and he wore leather armor not unlike Teleo's and just as worn. A bronze plate bore a falcon sigil.

"Nice horses," the castellan said in a lilting mountain accent that stressed the R's, his gaze roving over BlackJack's majestic stature and the powerfully built matched pairs of dapple grays and blood bays.

They were nice horses indeed, Teleo thought smugly, aware
that they stood in sharp contrast to the small mountain horses
of the merchants, who were inspecting the newcomers curiously. He was also keenly aware that people would love to get
their hands on such fine animals. He reached instinctively for
the sword hilt at his hip. At least the gate guards had not made
them surrender their weapons, but everyone else was armed too,
Teleo noted.

Cutter had not missed Teleo's sword hand. "Don't worry," the
bearded man said. "Nobody's goin'a steal yer horses. Thievery
ain't tolerated in Queen Valona's domain. Her dungeons are
empty because she'll just take off yer head. If you should steal
anythin', that is." He smiled, showing a black gap where a front
tooth should have been.

Teleo loosened his grip and dropped his hand to his side.
"That's good," he said.

Cutter turned his attention to the sheep. "Look like four
nice ewes. Nice thick fleece. Ready to be shorn, I'd say. They
make milk?"

"Not at the moment," Dinsmora replied.

"Our whole flock got butchered by wolves o'er the summer,"
Cutter said. "Only an old ram survived. Did Queen Valona
send fer them ewes?"

"No," Dinsmora said. "Lucky coincidence, I guess."

Cutter narrowed his eyes. "Queen Valona is known fer
makin' coincidences happen. Luck has nothin' to do with it."
He met Teleo's eyes meaningfully.

Cutter directed them to a far corner. "Set up there fer the
night, and you can sell yer sheep in the morning. You'll find
shovels and buckets at the side gate to clean up after yer animals,"
he said, gesturing to a gap between two buildings. "Dinner will

be served in the Great Hall after sunset. Come in and tell 'em
Cutter invited you."

They thanked him, and Cutter nodded curtly and left them
to get settled in.

◆

The scent of roasting meat made Teleo's body complain with
hunger, but the big golden sun took its time descending to
the mountaintops. While the kids watered the horses at the
fountain and Dinsmora picked sticks and burrs from the ewes'
fleeces, Teleo found his small leather flask, filled it with hard
cider from the half-empty leather bag, and drank while he
waited for dinner.

He calculated the risk of leaving the animals unattended
versus the risk of his party splitting up so some could guard their
animals and belongings while the others went inside. Missing
dinner was not an option. Finally, they decided to take Cutter at
his word and leave the horses and sheep hitched to metal rings
on the walls. They stacked their bundles between the horses and
carried only their weapons and gold.

The Great Hall was an enormous stone room of unpolished
marble walls and pillars spaced out evenly across the stone floor,
supporting a vaulted ceiling that towered overhead. The ceiling
was made up of thousands of small interlocking stone triangles
of beige and red and black, in an intricate pattern of stars that
glinted and moved in the flickering lantern light. The stonework
had been fashioned by a master, and Teleo stopped to admire it.

Cut into the facing wall were four massive fireplaces—each
big enough for several men to stand inside. Two were blazing
with red and gold flames, crackling loudly and spitting burning
embers onto the stone hearths. The other two were cooking
fires, glowing with orange coals below spits of roasting pigs and

huge steaming cauldrons. At the center of the wall of fireplaces, between the two center hearths, stood a humble marble throne.

An elderly guard and a lad as young as Jessum stopped them and asked who they were.

"We came for the market. Cutter sent us," Teleo said.

"Ahhh, the shepherds with the ewes Queen Valona promised," the old man said, and waved them through.

They walked along the shadowed periphery, observing the various groups of soldiers and families seated at a collection of wooden tables, eating from wooden trenchers, drinking ale, and laughing. At the cooking fires, people approached randomly to be served.

They joined a huddled line and waited their turn. An old woman held a ladle over a cauldron. Her skin was leathery, and she waved her ladle at Teleo and Dinsmora, stew dripping into the huge bubbling pot.

"Who are you?" she asked.

Dinsmora answered, "Came in from the valley with some sheep to sell. Cutter sent us."

The woman's lips were wrinkled, and crow's feet creased her temples. "Sheep, eh? How many?"

"Four."

The woman bunched up her mouth. "Four? Is that all? Are they ewes, at least?"

"Yes."

"That's a blessing. Grab some bowls."

They each took a trencher from a stack, a carved spoon and fork, and a steel knife sharp as a dagger. Tankards of ale were plunked onto the wooden serving table next to them by a big-busted, wide-hipped woman who carried four in each hand. Her forearms were massive. Golden foam slid down the sides of the mugs onto the sticky table. The elderly cook and a wiry old man filled their bowls to the brim with vegetable stew and slices of steaming pork. A young man placed a hot roll and a slab of butter on top of each.

They found a spot on benches at a long table, and Teleo went back for ale, bringing a large stoneware mug of the foamy brew for each of them. They ate and drank without talking. Teleo tried to count the days since they'd had a decent meal. The days and nights since they'd left the shepherds' hut blended together in one long journey of Stone Guardians, treacherous trails, stark mountain terrains, and dark forests. It had been five days. Maybe six. Seven? He went back for another mug of the potent brew.

A group of young teenaged boys and girls came around bearing wooden slabs of more sliced pork, bowls of stewed apples, baskets of steaming rolls, and slices of hard white cheese. Kaspari and Jessum greeted their peers, who were friendly and openly regarded the newcomers. Teleo felt proud, as if they were his own children—they were strong and good-looking, polite and quick to smile. They were good kids. They did not look like sister and brother, but they acted like it, having escaped death together, ridden side by side for endless miles, and lived under the same roof and sky.

The four of them happily filled their bowls again. The woman with the big forearms walked past carrying more ale, and Teleo flagged her down, taking another mug for himself. Next came fruit cobbler and small stone cups of peach brandy, called Ferska, which tasted more like grain alcohol and burnt Teleo's throat in a pleasing sort of way.

The fires were burning down by the time Dinsmora dragged him away from his collection of empty mugs and Ferska cups. He stumbled to their corner of the courtyard and passed out.

It was still dark out when Teleo was awoken by merchants rising all around them and preparing for the market. Lanterns

were perched atop wagon driving benches, casting small pools
of light among the rows of vendors. Teleo rose from his bedding
and shuffled around a corner to the public latrines. He returned
to their huddle of animals and belongings, the sheep bleating at
him as though wondering why he had brought them to this cold
stone square. His head throbbed and he washed away the sour
taste in his mouth with some hard cider and then lifted his nose,
detecting the nutty aroma of Sapphire Hills coffee brewing. He
had not tasted the bitter brew since his quest. He followed the
smell and found the source across the yard at a small wagon
with a coal brazier under a pot of boiling water.

"You have coffee," Teleo said to the hunched-over crone, who
smiled a toothless smile and gestured to several open burlap
sacks of dark roasted beans.

"I have the best," the woman said. "From the shaded hills
north of Sapphire Valley. This here's Bedon's Bane, and this is
Griffin's Growl, and Wolf's Bite."

"Brew me a cup of your strongest," Teleo said.

"Ahhh," she said, her thin eyebrows lifting into sharp points.
"Then you'll want this one." She reached into her wagon and
drew out a smaller sack and opened it, lifting it so that Teleo
could smell the black, oily beans. "This is Mage's Flight. The
finest coffee in the land."

He closed his eyes and inhaled the heady scent. She ground a
handful of beans, then poured water over a cone-shaped funnel,
filling a small stoneware cup with frothy black coffee. She stirred
in a pinch of crushed cardamom seeds and cinnamon stick and
then added a cube of sugar.

Teleo stood to the side and slowly sipped the intoxicating
brew, marveling at how delicious it was.

She charged a fortune, but Teleo paid her a Bronze Bit for
the cup of coffee and a Silver Bit for a small bag of Mage's Flight

beans. For another Bronze Bit, she threw in a cinnamon stick, a few pods of cardamom seeds, and several cubes of sugar. He pocketed his stash and meandered across the square, debating whether he would share any with Dinsmora and the kids or keep it all for himself.

First light had barely touched the sky when the market opened. More vendors straggled in and set up tables or spread out blankets on the ground. Bleary-eyed townspeople walked slowly along the rows where goods of all sorts were displayed. There were baskets of baubles, silver jewelry, and beads of every color. Crates of fruits, tables overflowing with vegetables, and jugs of fresh milk. Dried meats, rounds of cheeses, and crates of squawking chickens. Sacks of grain, fresh baked goods, and candies. Salt, spices, sugar, and honey. Carved wooden utensils, bowls, and plates. Knives, bows, and arrows. Bolts of woven cloth, hats, and ribbons. Candles, lanterns, and oil. Horse tack, farming tools, and wagon wheels. And more goods were being unloaded from wagons and unpacked from baskets and crates. Teleo spied the tinker's wagon and draft horse at the end of a row and nodded to the tinker.

He arrived back at their corner, where Dinsmora and the kids were up and tending to the animals. The scent of peppermint tea wafted through the air, and Dinsmora left to get some. The ringing of a hammer on anvil pierced the air from across the yard where a blacksmith had set up a small mobile forge in the opposite corner. Jessum wandered off to look at the blacksmith's wares.

Kaspari was brushing Daisy's mane and talking to her. Her long mane was streaked charcoal-gray and white, and Kaspari was smoothing the light layer over the dark.

Teleo walked over and rubbed the mare's velvety nose. "She likes you," Teleo said.

"She's a good horse," Kaspari said. "She's very stately and mature. My horse Marigold wanted to play all the time, but Daisy always pays attention to make sure everything is as it should be. Once it's all good, then she likes it when you tell her how strong and beautiful she is."

"That's true," Teleo said. Daisy batted her long black eyelashes at him.

Teleo arranged her forelock and Daisy gazed around the market, standing tall and proud, as though aware that she was now responsible for a princess.

"Benny is her son?" Kaspari asked, turning to Benny, who was nosing her hair. "He must have been a cute colt."

"So Dinsmora tells me," Teleo said. "I was gone his first year."

"At the war?" she asked, her eyes fixed on him.

"No, the war was over by then."

"Searching for your son?" she asked.

He held her gaze. "How did you know?" he asked.

"Gwen told me."

"Ahh," Teleo said, stroking Benny's side. "Yes."

"I'm sorry you didn't find him. But I'm sure he's okay. Like Jessum," Kaspari said, patting Teleo's arm.

Tears sprang to his eyes at her gentleness. "I hope so," he said, drawing in a breath and changing the topic. "Dinsmora told me Benny was very playful, with long spindly legs, and that he liked to chase butterflies."

"Ohhh," Kaspari said, stroking Benny's neck. "Dragonflies too, I bet," she said with a mischievous grin.

"Most assuredly," Teleo said, chuckling. He ran his fingers through Benny's mane, and Kaspari began brushing the gelding's silvery locks.

"I got all the tangles out already," she said, running the brush over his long mane.

"I see that," Teleo said. Benny tossed his head and nuzzled Teleo's shoulder. "He's always been fussy about his mane. He's very vain," Teleo said, pushing playfully at Benny's muzzle. "He believes he is more handsome than BlackJack."

BlackJack stomped at the mention of his name, making them laugh.

"They are both very handsome in their own way," Kaspari said.

"Don't say that around Dinsmora. She believes Cinnamon and Nutmeg are the most handsome horses in all the world."

"They are very beautiful," Kaspari said. "But my Marigold was the most beautiful of all." She glanced up at Teleo with a wistful look, then put on a brave face and asked, "Dinsmora is truly your cousin?"

"Yes. Her father was my father's younger brother. She and I grew up together. Our farms were near each other and we all helped each other build barns and plant crops and bring in the harvests. We spent most of our time together, since we're nearly the same age. We're like brother and sister. We were both only children but had a bunch of other cousins."

"I never got to play with anyone except my brothers," Kaspari said. "And Gwen. And the horses."

They stroked Benny's coat in silence and then wandered over to the aisle and sat next to each other on Dinsmora's rolled-up sheepskin rugs and watched the parade of people stroll by. Of all things, Dinsmora had insisted on carting the bulky rugs over hill and vale and gloated every time Teleo stretched out on one. He still complained about the unnecessary load but was secretly happy for their comfort.

Everyone passing by commented on the sheep and asked if they were ewes. The horses attracted as much attention with their tall statures, bulging muscles, and well-bred lines. Jessum had cross-tied BlackJack in the corner, and Kaspari warned people away from him, though the big horse discouraged anyone from getting too close with his incessant stomping, snorting, and straining impatiently against his bonds. He was a fiery beast, tossing his forelock and tail and flashing his eyes.

Cutter came by. "Those sheep still here? Where's Sonderson?" he demanded, as if Teleo and Kaspari knew who Sonderson was.

Teleo shrugged. "You got me."

Cutter stormed off in a huff.

Dinsmora returned with a large stoneware pot of steaming peppermint tea and a bundle of sweetcakes, which she handed to Kaspari. She had a woman in tow. The middle-aged woman wore a full-skirted, finely tailored gown of burgundy Aldeon silk with gold embroidery adorning the bodice and sleeves. Dinsmora didn't bother introducing her but took the woman directly to their pile of supplies, where she dug into her saddlebags and emerged with skeins of brightly colored embroidery floss. The two women bowed their heads intently over the thread, and Teleo returned to observing the locals.

There were Verdant Valley folk and Hill people, former soldiers, weathered farmers, and skilled craftsmen plying their wares. There were children and elders, families with screaming babies, and dogs nosing through discarded scraps. They all seemed normal enough, despite the reputation of the mountain strongholds harboring outcasts and fugitives.

Three teenaged girls who had been serving food the night before stopped to chat with Kaspari and asked where Jessum was.

"At the blacksmith's, I think," Kaspari replied. The four girls bowed their heads together, whispering and giggling as though they were old friends. The mountain girls spoke with their funny nasal twang, and Kaspari spoke with her proper Verdant City accent. Kaspari turned to Teleo. "May I walk with them?"

Teleo called her over, stepped between Cinnamon and Nutmeg, and said under his breath, "Your name is Kallie. We are your parents. Jeremiah is our adopted son. We saved him from being abused as a Hill orphan. My name is Tesserman. Dinsmora's is … Mora."

She understood and nodded.

"Don't leave the square," he said.

The four girls scampered off in a giggling gaggle, and Teleo shook his head. Teenaged girls were a special breed of human he had never quite figured out and who frankly scared him a bit.

Teleo saw silver change hands between Dinsmora and the woman, who pocketed several skeins of thread. The two women continued talking intently in hushed tones and then walked off together without so much as a glance towards Teleo.

"No problem," he muttered to himself. "I'll watch everything by myself." He ambled over to the supplies and poured himself another flask of cider, ignoring the hot tea that smelled of summertime, then plopped himself back down on the sheepskins. A fiddler on the opposite side of the yard struck up a familiar tune and Teleo hummed along.

The sun was climbing in the sky when a wiry, gray-haired couple strode briskly down the row. It was the cooks who had served them dinner. They stopped briefly at every stand, quickly surveying the goods before moving on to the next vendor. Soon they got to Teleo.

"Sonderson didn't come fer them ewes yet?" the man asked, peering at Teleo.

"No," Teleo said.

The man frowned. "You selling them horses?"

"No," Teleo said.

The man's frowned deepened. "Pity. Nice animals." He trained his eyes on Daisy, examining her powerful haunches and withers. She turned her ear towards him but otherwise seemed uninterested. "Sixteen hands?" he asked.

"Seventeen. The black is eighteen."

BlackJack snorted and pulled at his tethers.

"Looks like a handful," the man said.

"He is," Teleo agreed, chuckling.

"What've you got in them there sacks?" the woman asked, pointing an arthritic finger at the small pile of burlap sacks that had survived Rock River Gorge.

"Not much," Teleo said, rising from his seat. He felt the sacks and listed off their contents.

"Potatoes, carrots, and turnips in this one. Not for sale. Apples in this one, also not for sale. Almonds in this one. I could maybe spare a peck."

"Are they shelled?"

"Yes."

Shelled almonds were worth a lot, and the cook knew it. They agreed upon a fair price, then Teleo measured out the dry quarts into a muslin sack that the male cook produced from his wicker basket, using a measuring scoop borrowed from the dried fruit vendor across the way.

"They make a nice almond tart," Teleo said, scooping the final quart.

"How do you make almond tart?" the woman asked.

"With almond paste."

"What's almond paste? Is that a Verdant Valley specialty?"

Teleo raised an eyebrow. "I guess." He explained how to grind the nuts and mix them with cream, eggs, and sugar. "Do you have the ingredients?" he asked.

"Of course we do," she said with a wrinkled mouth. "I'll make yer almond tarts special fer dessert tonight. You'll need to try them and tell me how I did." Her eyes sparkled.

"That's a promise," Teleo said, silently elated at the implicit invitation to another hot meal in the Great Hall.

The cooks left and Dinsmora returned, clearly distracted. "What happened?" he asked.

Dinsmora frowned, a bit bewildered, and sat down next to him. "The Queen's Lady recognized my embroidery."

"What do you mean?"

Dinsmora stared at him hard. "What do you think I mean?"

"If I knew what you meant, I wouldn't have asked," he retorted, returning her stare.

She sucked her teeth with exasperation, waved her palms across her heavily embroidered tunic, and said in a gruff whisper, "The spell."

"What spell?"

Dinsmora rolled her eyes. "Camouflage. You know."

Teleo's eyes widened. "No. I did not know. You wove a spell into that?" His voice was a low hiss. Dinsmora glowered at him like he was stupid. "Did you weave one into Kaspari's too?" he asked, his skin prickling.

"A few strands," she said sheepishly. She continued in muted tones. "Kaspari laid most of the stitches herself. She does not know how to weave spells, and I did not teach her. She is a princess, after all, and magic is prohibited."

Teleo examined the embroidery on Dinsmora's tunic. It was a simple pattern of leaves and swirls that flowed together in bands of color. He cocked his head. He had always thought it was shades of greens and browns, but now the threads were bone-white, gold, and black, like the surrounding marble bathed by streams of golden sunshine and slashes of dark shadows cast by the towering pillars.

"But the point is," Dinsmora said, "the Queen's Lady *recognized* it."

Teleo's attention followed the black pattern of the embroidery, noticing ever smaller stitches the longer he looked.

"Teleo," she said sharply. "Don't stare at it like that. Look at me."

He pulled his eyes away from the flowing pattern, his vision blurring for a moment. Her face came into focus. "Don't stare at it," she repeated sternly. "Anyway. She wants me to make a cloak for the queen. She said the queen will want to learn how to stitch such a garment herself, and that I should teach her."

Teleo raised one eyebrow. "Do you think that's a good idea?"

"Probably not." Dinsmora's bemused expression turned thoughtful. A tendril of copper-colored hair fell across her forehead and she brushed it away. "But then again," she said, "it could be interesting."

"Interesting," Teleo huffed. "Dangerous, more like."

A sly smile deepened the creases at the corners of her eyes. "Oh, Teleo. Always so cautious."

He broke out in a loud laugh. "Me? Cautious? Look what I've gotten us into." He gestured across the market to where he suspected the teenagers were. "We are calling our 'daughter' by the name Kallie, by the way, and Jeremiah is our adopted son. My name is Tesserman. And you're Mora."

She nodded. "Good idea. You'd better go look for them," Dinsmora said, her tone expressing the same concern Teleo felt for the children. She got up and went to her saddlebags and started pulling out more embroidery floss.

Teleo rose slowly from the rolled sheepskin, his knees popping and crackling, and strolled down the row of stalls. He perused the wares, and the vendors smiled at him with unspoken questions glinting in their eyes. *Who was this stranger who had unexpectedly appeared in their town with a mixed family of Verdant Valley and Hill folk, four healthy sheep, and five magnificent horses?*

And wearing King Elke's armor and a battle sword? Teleo smiled back. The people seemed like a reserved but friendly lot, with a fierce independence in their eyes. They were survivors, living in the Blue Mountains—the wild and forbidding no-man's land between Verdant Valley and the Sapphire Empire.

Teleo found the kids at the blacksmith's forge. Jessum was tending to a bar of iron at the fire while the blacksmith hammered another on the anvil. Jessum buried the iron in a bed of red coals, then pumped air into the forge with a large set of bellows. Kaspari and the three mountain girls stood to the side, watching Jessum and whispering. Two other men were looking on and glanced at Teleo as he took a spot next to them.

"That boy knows what he's doing," one of the men said to Teleo as Jessum took a pair of tongs and pushed the iron further into the coals.

"That's my boy," Teleo replied proudly. "He trained as a blacksmith's apprentice."

The man's gaze wandered over Teleo's graying brown hair and slate-gray eyes, observing silently that he was not of Hill stock, then returned his attention to the blacksmith, who had hammered the iron into a simple hook. The blacksmith hammered a hole into the flat end and then set it aside. Jessum stepped back and continued working the bellows as the blacksmith took over at the fire and waited for the iron to get hot. When it was ready, he removed the metal with his tongs. It glowed a bright yellow and he brought it over to the anvil. Teleo watched him make another hook while Jessum buried another bar in the coals and worked the bellows. The girls wandered off to the ribbon vendor and started trying on hair ribbons. The kids seemed safe—it was a small market with little children running about.

Teleo left them and found a man selling beer out of a keg. He stood around a tall oak-barrel table with three other men and sipped at a mug of frothy brew that tasted of raspberries and hops. He exchanged pleasantries with the men, commenting on the blue skies and the balmy breeze from the south. The men assured him it would soon shift to a howling wind from the north that would not stop until spring.

There was a reason not many people wanted to live in the mountains—it took a special type of person to endure the brutal winters. Teleo silently thanked the shepherds for insisting on making them shearling coats. They would need them. Snows up here could reach higher than a man's head. The sense of urgency Teleo had been suppressing surfaced. They needed shelter for the winter.

"Where do people stay around here?" Teleo asked the men. "Know anybody who will take work for trade? I'm pretty handy. Anybody have a spare hut that you know of?"

The men clammed up and drank their beer. "Nope. Don't know'a nobody," one of them said between swigs.

Teleo read their body language and did not press the issue. He was an outsider. This was the mountains. Trust was earned, not given.

Teleo hid a frown with his mug, taking in a mouthful. Trillifort was a small castle town—there would not be many options here. Maybe randomly choosing this castle had been a mistake, despite it supposedly harboring two Heliotropes. He inspected the marble slabs underfoot. They were pure white marble laid in a grid of perfect squares whose seams were nearly undetectable. The Mage's circles must be hidden away in walled courtyards, Teleo guessed, like at Verdant Castle. Regardless, Heliotropes would do him no good if they had nowhere to stay. But Dinsmora had landed a small job with the Queen's Lady already. That was a start.

He tried not to surrender to negativity and took another gulp. He finished his beer and nodded to the men, then made his way to a farmer who had a wagonload of hay. The long golden shafts were gathered in sheaves that a man could carry. The wagon was half empty already.

"Nice-looking hay," he told the farmer.

The farmer nodded. "Good sun this year."

They chatted about the harvest and eventually came around to negotiating a price. The farmer threw out a number. It was high. He was probably giving Teleo the outsider's rate. Then again, any decent farmland was several days' ride from here. Teleo did not understand how a town ensconced in a marble valley survived. He wanted the whole wagonload but he had no wagon. He worked the price down a little and finally bought a dozen sheaves for a Silver Owl.

He hoped the sheep would sell today—he didn't want to feed them anymore. Everyone seemed happy to see the creatures, but no one was buying. The hay would only feed the horses for a few days. They would need to take them into the forest to forage in the undergrowth, which would soon be buried in snow. They needed to find themselves a dwelling with access to a barn and a supply of hay and oats to last the winter.

Worry niggled at him. Maybe wintering in the mountains was not such a good idea after all. He pondered heading back down into Verdant Valley, but Gerik would surely hunt them down there eventually. They could hide out at Dinsmora's, but she had sold or given away much of her winter stores. They could always get food from their cousins, and he could take back some of the bounty from his own farm, but his cousins would need the food themselves—especially Tams Junior's widow. He took in a deep breath. His guilt wouldn't help her now. The time to help was past.

But there was no reason Dinsmora had to abandon her life and risk starving or freezing to death in the Blue Mountains.

He knew she missed her home, but she had dismissed a recent discussion they'd had of turning back. "The river is flowing," she had said, her freckled nose turning up to sense the air. "It is flowing in the mountains, not in the valleys."

Teleo sighed. Maybe they should press on over the mountains. But Sapphire Valley was too far, and it was a foreign land. They were from Verdant Valley, after all, and age-old rivalries died hard. When he had last been there looking for his son, he had needed to bribe or fight his way out of some close calls. Things had been changing quickly there after the war, with internal strife and politics roiling among the Imperial Ministers and among the seven Hill Tribes who paid tribute. Teleo had not always been kindly received—a Verdant Valley soldier mingling among them so soon after the end of hostilities. He had done his best to lay low while he searched for Oren in the Hill fortresses and backwoods villages, then the valley farms and towns, and finally Sapphire City itself. He had left in defeat, his heart broken.

He snapped out of his reminiscence as the farmer lashed two sheaves of hay to Teleo's back and set one on each of Teleo's broad shoulders. The farmer's two adult sons were likewise loaded up, and they crossed the market square to Teleo's corner. Teleo cut loose one sheaf knot, and Dinsmora portioned out the hay for the animals. They leaned the rest of the sheaves against the wall while the young men admired the horses.

"Want to buy four healthy ewes?" Teleo asked, patting one of the sheep on the back.

"Nay," the tall one said. "The queen'll want 'em. Her flock got butchered by wolves not too long ago."

"Yeah, so I heard," Teleo said.

The men left, and Teleo and Dinsmora sat on their rolled sheepskins and waited. After a time, Kaspari returned for some food. Teleo took her to a stand, which was selling hot pies stuffed with meat, carrots, and potatoes. They bought four. They ate theirs with Dinsmora, then he and Kaspari went together to give Jessum his. The boy stuffed it down in four bites and went back to tending the fire. The blacksmith gave Teleo a toothy smile before hammering out another hook. Teleo and Kaspari wandered by the ribbon stand.

"Do you want a ribbon?" he asked.

Kaspari blushed and ran her fingers through the long silky streams of color hanging from the vendor's display rack. She had fled her life of privilege with nothing but the clothes on her back—simple starched linens that noble boys wore. He wondered if she had ever been allowed to dress as a girl.

"Pick out a couple," he said. She chose a pink one and a green one that matched the embroidery of her tunic, and he paid the vendor. "Where are your girlfriends?" he asked.

"They had to go back to the kitchen to help prepare the evening meal. They said we should come."

Teleo nodded. "We will." He regarded her embroidered tunic, trying to determine which stitches were Dinsmora's. There were trailing vines of leaves intertwined with colorful flowers. The leaves were dark like shadows, and Teleo tried to follow a vine's path as it meandered through the neatly stitched petals, but he lost track of which vine he was following and had to start over at another flower. Kaspari noticed him looking at her tunic. "Dinsmora stitched the vines?" he asked.

"Yes. They're beautiful, aren't they?"

"You could say that," he said, pulling his gaze away from the entrancing needlework.

"Here," he said, as they arrived at their corner. "If you ever get separated from us, you might need some coin. Don't spend any if you don't have to. Especially the Lion." He dug into his stash of coins and handed her one Gold Lion, two Silver Owls, and a few Silver, Bronze, and Copper Bits.

Tears glistened in her eyes as she accepted the coins and stashed them in a pocket inside her tunic. "I never thanked you for saving me," she said, her voice wavering.

"It was my duty and my honor," he said, lowering himself onto one knee. He took one of her delicate hands.

Her hand trembled as she gazed down at him.

"You must stay alive," he insisted quietly, holding her gaze. He squeezed her hand, then dropped it gently and opened the saddlebags at his side, pretending that was why he was on his knee, for the benefit of any nosy neighbors.

The princess stepped away and hid behind Daisy, wrapping her arms around the mare's neck and burying her face in the thick mane.

Teleo held back his emotions and organized his bags, even though they did not need organizing.

◆

It was not until early afternoon that a bustle of activity turned all eyes to the grand staircase. A tall woman who was obviously the queen descended the marble steps, surrounded by the woman who had bought the embroidery floss, and four white-haired armed guards. The guards—two males and two females—strode in an easy, confident manner, swords hanging at their sides and forest-green cloaks billowing behind them.

Queen Valona was not what Teleo had expected. She wore dark brown leathers, not unlike Dinsmora's, and knee-high leather boots of white calf hide. Around her flowed a long, white satin cloak thickly embroidered with starbursts of gold and silver thread and glittering with small crystals. Hanging from her waist belt was a collection of knives. A long thick braid of pure white hair hung down over her chest, though she did not look over fifty.

She was not prim and proper like Kaspari's mother, who wore huge silk skirts, tight-fitting bodices, and mounds of elaborately coiffed hair coiled atop her head. Were it not for the ornate mantle, Teleo might have guessed Queen Valona had just returned from a hunt, and perhaps she had.

The townspeople parted to let her pass, lowering their heads respectfully and then raising their eyes to gaze after her adoringly. Small children hopped and clapped and skipped after her, reaching for her shimmering robe, while parents grabbed them and pulled them back. The queen did not seem to mind, or even notice, and the attendants nimbly avoided tripping over the children. The fiddler launched into a lively tune, the melodic strains weaving through the air, accompanied by the splashing fountain. Bright bands of amber sunlight glanced off the marble pillars and bathed the yard in shades of rose and apricot.

Cutter hurried across the courtyard to speak with the queen. They looked in Teleo's direction, then headed their way. Teleo, Dinsmora, and Kaspari rose from their shearling seats and bowed their heads as Queen Valona and her entourage approached.

"Where are you from?" the queen demanded, dispensing with any pleasantries. Her singsong mountain twang was short and sharp.

Teleo lifted his eyes and said, "From Verdant Valley."

"How did you get past the border outpost? I hear they are conscripting all young males," she said, glancing around. "Where is your boy?"

Teleo considered lying but he was not very good at it. "He's helping the blacksmith," he said, tilting his head towards the sound of the hammering. "We came in the back way."

"Which back way?"

"Demon's Bones."

The queen silently inspected him, then briefly regarded Dinsmora's and Kaspari's tunics. She traded glances with her lady attendant before returning her steely gaze to Teleo.

"You brought yer sheep through the gorge?" she asked.

He blinked. She knew of Rock River Gorge? Her white cloak sparkled in the sunshine. Teleo forced his attention back to her piercing brown eyes. "Yes."

"How many sheep did you lose?" she asked.

Teleo hesitated. "None."

The queen's eyes flitted back to her attendant. "I see."

Silence hung in the air.

"Fine mounts," she said. The horses were lined up, munching on the fresh hay.

"Thank you," Teleo said, ignoring the unspoken questions: *Who are you? Where did you come from? Why are you here?*

"So, yer shepherds, then," she stated, directing her words at Dinsmora this time. A smile softened the queen's masculine, chiseled face.

Dinsmora's shepherd's crook lay at her feet. She bent for it and held it like a walking stick, the blunt end set firmly on the marble paving stones. "You could say that," Dinsmora said, meeting the queen's gaze.

"Good. Because we need someone to care fer these ewes and help build our flock. My shepherd cares more fer his mushroom wine than fer my sheep. You don't have that problem, do you?" She glanced at Teleo with an arched eyebrow.

Dinsmora answered, "No. No, we don't." Teleo kept his mouth shut, hoping he did not reek of beer and hard cider. "We could breed the ewes with your ram," Dinsmora said, "and see to it that the lambs are born healthy. After that, we will be moving on."

"After the spring thaw," the queen said.

"Yes," Dinsmora agreed. "In the meantime, we will need shelter, food, water, and heat—for the three of us and our son, and the horses."

The queen consulted quietly with Cutter, then turned back to them.

"Yer family and horses may shelter with the sheep in their cellar. We will provide you with what you need to survive the winter."

"How much are you offering to pay us for the sheep?" Teleo asked.

The queen's brown and gold-flecked eyes drilled into his. "Food and shelter to survive a mountain winter." Her tone was withering.

He stood up straighter. "I suppose that is a fair trade," he admitted while secretly gloating over their good fortune.

The queen gave him a flat look and returned her attention to Dinsmora, as though she were the adult of the family. "I assume you know how to use yer swords and that bow?" she asked, gesturing to the longbow and quiver sitting atop their pile of belongings. "Wolves are appearing out of nowhere. It is a problem." She looked from Dinsmora to Teleo and back again.

Teleo and Dinsmora shared a silent exchange, and Teleo's hand went to his sword hilt.

"Between the two of us, I think we can protect the sheep," Dinsmora said.

Queen Valona nodded, then her eyes narrowed. "Gracie said you stitched yer own cloak."

Teleo's gaze was drawn to Dinsmora's tunic. Embroidered leaves of autumn red and gold, curling vines with heavy clusters of deep purple berries, and dry sticks covered with lichen made Teleo wonder for a moment if they were not back in the forest.

A sharp clapping pulled him from his reverie. It was the queen, her long fingers heavy with gold rings. Sunlight glanced off her cloak. "Very well, then," she said to Dinsmora. "You will join our daily embroidery circle. We start mid-mornings after our dawn hunts. I will send word fer you in a few days' time after you've had a chance to settle in. Yer husband can tend the sheep while yer away. Agreed?"

Dinsmora bowed her head and Teleo nodded mutely. The jewels adorning the queen's cloak glimmered and reflected shards of light onto her smooth cheeks. Though not a classic beauty, he couldn't help but wonder what her skin would feel like under his hands and if his rough calluses would bother her.

Dinsmora slid her hand into the crook of his elbow and pinched him hard in the tender spot at the elbow crease. He flinched and pulled his gaze away from the queen. Dinsmora's face was placid but her glance held a veiled warning.

"I'll show you the cellar," Cutter said, and stayed with them as the queen left with her attendants to tour the market. A swirl of light reflected off Queen Valona's billowing cloak, and several children scampered in her wake. Teleo stared after her, mesmerized by the gems on her cloak, which glistened like droplets of dew, catching the sunlight and reflecting every color. Dinsmora elbowed him in the ribs, and he reluctantly pulled his gaze away.

"Let's pack up," Dinsmora said, and firmly pulled him towards their mound of supplies.

11

FALCON'S NEST

Teleo wove through the market stalls to the blacksmith's forge to get Jessum. The blacksmith gave the boy a hook and nail for his help. They went back to their corner and loaded the horses with their belongings and sheaves of hay, cleaned up after the animals, and led the horses and sheep from the courtyard, following Cutter out a side gate. The castellan rode a small mountain horse.

They followed a maze of unpolished marble alleyways between tightly packed houses two or three stories tall. All were constructed from the ubiquitous white marble, some with ornate carvings decorating the window and door lintels, while others were simpler structures of unadorned square blocks. They all had steeply pitched, blue stone tiled roofs with over-hanging eaves.

Cutter led them through a small manned gate into an even narrower alleyway, hemmed in by solid stone walls. The alley turned and sloped downward to yet another gate, whose tall timber door was closed. Cutter dismounted and rapped loudly with a metal knocker. A small door hatch slid open, two eyes peeked out, and the heavy door swung open.

The guards greeted Cutter by name and regarded Teleo's small band curiously as they filed through the opening. Another narrow passageway led them into a spacious circular courtyard. The clomping of metal horseshoes on stone echoed back at them as the horses entered the enclosed space.

It was a dead end. Perfect place for an ambush, but Teleo did not sense any threat. He quickly scanned the stonework at their feet, thinking that the round yard would be an ideal place for the Mages of old to have hidden a Heliotrope, but the paving stones were plain marble. The perimeter was lined with stone lean-tos, wooden sheds, a well, and a large fireplace.

The sheep bleated softly and huddled in a group. The yard was big enough for perhaps a hundred people to camp, if tightly packed, and Teleo guessed it was a place for the townspeople to hide out if the castle were under attack. Was this where Cutter intended they live with the sheep? The queen had said they would be wintering in a cellar.

Cutter stopped and faced them. He cleared his throat and when he had their attention, he spoke solemnly as if delivering a prepared speech. "Trill'fort has withstood sieges fer hundreds'a years," he began. "Queen Valona has ruled unchallenged since her father died from the fever twenty years past." He looked sternly at each of them. "Secrets of the castle are shared only with mountain folk who call Trill'fort their home and who're loyal to Queen Valona. Anyone who betrays her trust dies." Cutter clamped his jaws shut. He fixed his gaze on Teleo. "Are you prepared to protect Trill'fort with yer silence?"

Teleo checked himself from grabbing his sword hilt. Teleo had heard the mountain folk were a strange bunch, and he had met a few who were downright crazy. They formed tightly knit clans and some displayed cult-like devotion to their leaders. But Cutter had seemed sane enough so far. This was not the time nor the place to question Cutter's or the queen's motives.

Teleo nodded. "We won't tell anyone about this yard. You can count on that. Looks like a good place to hunker down during an attack. Doesn't look like a cellar, though."

Cutter ignored his observations and asked, "So do I have yer promise and that'a yer family? Upon yer lives?"

Teleo regarded Dinsmora, Jessum, and Kaspari, who met his gaze nervously. What choice did they have? They were trapped. He gave his companions a confident nod until they nodded back.

Teleo turned his attention back to Cutter. "Yes, on our lives," Teleo said.

The castellan held Teleo's eyes for a long moment, then finally said, "All right, then. On yer lives." Cutter turned and pressed his two large palms against the marble wall, and a large slab slowly swung open.

Teleo stared at the hidden doorway. He would never have guessed it was there. What Stone Guardian mastery had carved those invisible seams? And what ingenious mechanism allowed the heavy slab to swing open so easily and silently? Kaspari and Jessum appeared similarly intrigued, and Dinsmora sniffed at the air wafting out from the dark passageway.

They dismounted and filed into a stone tunnel, leading the horses. The sheep followed, uncharacteristically quiet.

Cutter closed the door behind them, plunging the passage into gloomy shadows. A faint glint of yellow flickered from a lantern mounted on the wall up ahead. The tunnel was deadly silent, and thoughts of dungeons whispered in Teleo's head. He took his shepherd's crook from where it was strapped to his saddlebags. Dinsmora already had hers in hand. Teleo felt the familiar weight of his short sword at his belt and considered that if the Trillifort folks had wanted to attack them, they would have done so in the circular yard.

His eyes slowly adjusted to the dim light. They mounted their horses, and Cutter took the lead. The tunnel descended and the air grew cooler. The passageway curved gently, revealing another lantern further on. At the end of the curve, a small underground lake appeared in a cavern to their right. The water was a bright turquoise-green and perfectly clear, reflecting light off the white marble lakebed.

The tunnel continued straight for a mile, lit with lanterns every hundred strides. Occasional piles of fresh manure marked this as a regularly traveled path. Finally, a hint of daylight appeared up ahead.

They left the tunnel through an open archway, its heavy wooden gate raised overhead, and entered a tall argillite cavern lit by two high windows carved into the blue rock and glimmering with leaded glass. Two guards stood up from a wooden bench as the horses crowded into the chamber.

"Afternoon, Cutter," one of them said. "Who've we got here?" The guard squinted up at them. "Ah, must be the shepherd family."

Teleo nodded at the guards. He was happy to be known as the "shepherd family." That description was not something Gerik would readily connect to Teleo.

A second gate stood closed at the far end of the chamber. One of the guards slid open a small metal plate and spoke to someone on the other side. Slowly, the large wooden gate lifted, creaking on thick ropes while counterweights lowered on the other side. A stone path led from the cavern into a yard surrounded by argillite walls thrice a man's height and open to the sky. Four rough-looking men stood guard, swords strapped to their backs and various lethal weapons hanging from their belts. Several male and female archers looked down at them from atop the walls, arrows nocked. Another gate to their left stood open and led out onto a rocky hilltop, and Cutter ushered them through it.

They stood on an overlook paved with blue argillite. Spread out below them, a valley extended southward in a series of gently rolling hills that faded into a bluish-gray mist in the distance. Open rangeland and cultivated fields were interspersed with stretches of mixed forest. Teleo gazed in wonder at the hidden valley, flanked by towering blue stone cliffs. Gentle slopes met the base of the cliffs on either side, gradually descending across the fields and forests to a small river, which cut through the center of the valley.

Teleo estimated the valley to be four or five miles wide, and he could not see where it ended to the south. Dwellings dotted the land in clusters. Some fields were grayish-green, the grass dying off from the recent frost. Others were stubbly and brown from recent harvests, with sheaves of grain standing in stooks. Still others were terraced and lined with orderly orchards or vineyards. Far-off hills were dark green with stands of pines and sprinkled with patches of red and gold. The last warm breath of autumn wafted through the valley, carrying with it the scent of fresh hay and musky leaves. The orange sun was already heading for the horizon.

"Welcome to Falcon's Nest," Cutter said, waving his arm across the idyllic hideaway.

"It's beautiful," Kaspari said. Her cheeks were red from days of riding, and her eyes were bright. Her light brown hair had new streaks of blond from being out in the sun, and it was growing longer—almost as long as Jessum's—brushing her shoulders in unkempt waves which, were she home, her mother would have twisted into tight buns or chopped off to maintain the pretense of a prince.

Jessum craned his neck to watch a white-and-black-speckled falcon lazily riding an updraft above them. It was a gyrfalcon, acclimated to the icy peaks and larger than the brown eagles in Verdant Valley. The wingspan was as wide as a grown child was tall, and the talons were probably as long as Teleo's fingers.

"Nice work," Dinsmora said under her breath, making Teleo squint curiously at the shimmering blue haze that shrouded the valley.

Cutter smiled proudly and urged his little mountain horse forward. He led them onto a road of rough paving stones, and the horses made their way down the gradual grade to the valley floor. Teleo gazed over his shoulder at the small gated fortress they had just left. It was built of blocks of blue stone and was hidden from Castle Trillifort by a jagged ridge of blue and white, where argillite met marble in a fractured line.

They headed south. The paving stones gave way to a wide dirt and gravel road that followed the river. Soon they came upon the first cluster of buildings. Many were half-buried in the turf, with steep A-framed roofs of thatch or wood shakes. The structures were built for heavy snow, and stacks of firewood stood against exterior walls under overhanging roofs. It was a small village, with a carved wooden sign announcing that they had arrived at Mud Flats.

The village consisted of a humble inn with a pub, and a barn with its double doors wide open, revealing a farmer's market with three rows of tables displaying what remained of the day's produce, eggs, and other goods. The rest of the buildings were dwellings, surrounded by small plots of land with vegetable gardens and fruit trees. Dogs barked at them and a donkey brayed while children, chickens, goats, and pigs watched the strangers ride slowly through their village. Adults stood in the doorways and tipped their caps at Cutter or sucked on pipes, puffing clouds of blue smoke into the air. A cow lowed at them from a small pasture at the edge of the village, and a large bull-calf came up next to her and started nursing.

They continued their journey through fields and orchards and came upon a larger village, Bitter's Ford. Blue cobblestones paved its one street, which ran through the center of town. They passed a larger inn with a noisy pub, another food market, a feed store, saddlery, candle shop, yarn and fabric shop, a smithy and farrier, and an herbal pharmacy with a mortar and pestle painted on the wooden sign hanging over the doorway.

They dismounted while Cutter spoke with a couple of men and the three of them inspected the ewes. Dinsmora peered through the window of the pharmacy and then knelt to pet a cat who was sitting on the front stoop. Kaspari lingered in front of the yarn and fabric shop, where several frilly dresses were displayed. Jessum poked his head into the open top half of the wooden door to the blacksmith's workshop, but it was dark inside and the forge had no fire. Teleo guessed it was the same blacksmith who had set up the forge at the castle market. A farm wagon stood outside a second, smaller pub, the *Scythe and Sickle,* where a mule, free from its harness, was nosing around the empty wagon bed for stray bits of hay, and several small mountain horses waited patiently near a watering trough. An accordion crooned sadly from inside. Laughter and lively conversation marked it as a popular place. Teleo peeked inside and wished he could stop for a quick draught with the locals.

They climbed back onto their horses and continued past the village, and as the sun was descending towards the top of the blue cliffs, Cutter led them eastward up a dirt road that cut through a field of mixed grasses. Soon, fieldstone walls flanked either side of the road. The enclosed fields extended eastward to the base of the cliff, as well as stretching north and south into the distance. It was a large piece of land and Teleo guessed it had once held the queen's flock of sheep. His suspicion was confirmed when they came upon an old ram who watched them approach from a slope beyond the fieldstone wall on their left. The ram trumpeted one loud bleep at the four ewes. They scampered away from him, trying to hide behind the horses, and bleated softly among themselves. The ram angled towards a small hillock up ahead.

The sun set behind them, and in the fading twilight they came upon a steep grassy bank with a stone façade and wooden door built right into the earth. They dismounted, and Cutter hitched his horse and then opened the door.

"This is it. Bring yer animals," Cutter said, and led them down a stone ramp.

The horses and sheep clomped down the ramp with them into a dark cellar. Dim light filtered in from two vents on the upper walls. Cutter lit a candle and placed it in a wall bracket.

It was an underground stable with vaulted stone ceilings worthy of a castle. Half of the spacious room held eight stalls and a large pen. Sheaves of straw were stacked in a corner. A large well was built into the stone floor against the wall near the pen fencing. A second wooden door was next to the well.

The other half of the room served as the shepherds' quarters. A large grotto in one corner held a man-sized, open fireplace. An old sheepskin rug and a wooden rocking chair sat in front of the hearth. Along the perpendicular wall to the right of the fireplace, stood a long table and benches. Two large wooden bunk beds were built into a nook between the table and the second door, one above the other, with heavy woolen curtains lending privacy to the bunks. The curtains were pulled back. The lower bed had a stained mattress, a pillow, and disheveled blankets. The upper bed had a mattress cluttered with an assortment of books, clothing, and other items.

Shelving on the other side of the fireplace and its perpendicular wall held baskets, all manner of stoneware dishes and crocks, and metal cooking pots and utensils. A large wooden countertop held a knife rack, an assortment of metal tins, and a water basin. A moldy hunk of hard cheese sat abandoned on the counter next to a sticky honey crock.

Cutter lit another candle, stuck it in a glass lantern, and opened the second door. Teleo followed him up another stone ramp. At the top, they found the ram in a small barn, munching on hay. The walls were stone, and the A-framed roof was of heavy timber. The barn had only one open pen and two large stalls. A loft covering half the area was stacked high with straw, hay, and burlap sacks. Teleo took the lantern and stepped through the open doorway to the outdoors. The barn was mostly buried in the earth, with a short peak of the steep roof poking up and covered with thatch. A half-moon floated ghostlike against the pale sky. The road was not visible from this vantage point. Teleo went back inside, and Cutter pulled the heavy barn doors closed and slid a long wooden bar into metal brackets.

"Damn Sonderson," Cutter muttered. "He cain't even bother to shut in the ram. The queen'll have his head." Cutter shook his head in exasperation. "He likes it up here in the upper stable," Cutter said of the ram. "Till it gets too cold." Cutter climbed a ladder to the loft, brought down a sack, and dumped a small amount of barley into a wooden feeding trough. "You can meet yer ewes another day," he said to the white and brown ram, who ignored him and chewed on the grain. His long horns curled around his ears in an outward spiral.

Cutter showed Teleo an outhouse accessible through a human-sized door next to the large barn doors. When Teleo returned, Cutter slung the sack over his shoulder. "Yer horses like barley?" he asked.

"If we can cook it," Teleo said.

"You've got a fireplace. Cooking pots. Plenty'a water. It's yer new home, you can do what you like."

"Is there any wood?" Teleo asked.

"Uh ... good question."

They went outside and found an open lean-to nearby filled with split, seasoned wood several layers deep and stacked to the ceiling, along with bins of kindling. "At least Sonderson made sure he'd be warm all winter," Cutter muttered.

Next to the woodshed stood an ancient stone building, which appeared to be a workshop, and behind that was a third wooden outbuilding. This place would do just fine, Teleo reflected happily. Cutter loaded their arms with firewood and kindling, and they went back into the cellar through the upper stable.

"Can you ask yer boy to bring water up to the ram?" he asked Teleo.

Jessum was grooming BlackJack but put the brush aside, pulled a bucket up from the well, and disappeared up the ramp, holding the lantern in his free hand. Teleo told the women about the outhouse, and they disappeared up the ramp behind Jessum.

Dinsmora, Kaspari, and Jessum returned and went back to grooming the horses and settling the animals into stalls. The horses each had their own, and the sheep shared one. They put hay in the feeding racks and filled the watering troughs. Cutter gave the ewes a few handfuls of barley, then sat at the table and watched Teleo build a fire and hang a pot of water from a hook over the flames.

"Dinner at the Great Hall should be ready soon," Cutter said. Teleo's stomach growled. "Should we go back?" he asked.

"Ay-yah," Cutter said. "Cook's roasting pheasant tonight."

Teleo's stomach growled again. "The old woman's making a dessert with my almonds."

"If we go at a steady trot, we can make it back to Trill'fort in under an hour," Cutter said.

"Sounds good to me," Teleo said. Dinsmora was over by the wall, looking through her saddlebags. He glanced at her. "Right?"

She looked at him sideways. She probably did not want to eat turnips and dried mutton any more than he did. "I'll stay and watch the sheep," she said.

"Wolves can't get through stone walls or timber doors," Teleo said.

"Bring me back some food," she said, frowning. "The kids can go with you."

Cutter said, "That's prob'ly wise. The queen would agree with Mora."

Teleo shrugged. His cousin always did what she wanted, and if she chose to stay in a musty cellar by herself and guard sheep, she was free to do that. He watched the water impatiently while Jessum stoked the fire and Kaspari arranged the horse tack on hooks and racks in the back corner. Finally, the water boiled and Teleo threw a few handfuls of barley into it.

He unpacked his belongings while the grain cooked. They decided the kids would each get a bunk. Kaspari claimed the top one. They took the mattresses outside under the moonlight and beat them with brooms, sending up clouds of dust that drifted off in a light breeze. Kaspari sneered at the multitude of stains on her mattress cover.

"Hope there are no bugs in those," Dinsmora said quietly to Teleo, then spoke more loudly so Kaspari could hear. "I'll ask the Queen's Lady for some clean sheets when I see her, but we'll need to make do with our blankets for now." Kaspari's face was pinched, but Jessum did not seem at all concerned. "Or you can sleep on the floor on my sheepskin rug with me," Dinsmora continued, noting Kaspari's sour expression.

"I'll put my shearling coat over the mattress," Kaspari finally said.

Dinsmora and Teleo climbed into the bunks and swabbed out the wooden cubbyholes, removing tattered books, soiled clothing, empty bottles, and candle stubs stuck to the wood with globs of melted wax.

When they judged the bunks to be clean enough, they put the mattresses back, and the kids began arranging their private cubbies. Teleo and Dinsmora each took a sheepskin rug and set up their sleeping areas against the opposite wall between the base of the entry ramp and the pen area. When the grain was ready, Teleo set it aside to soak overnight and then prepared to leave.

They saddled the horses again, who were none too happy at being disturbed so soon.

"I know," Teleo said to Benny apologetically as he adjusted his bridle. "You got the day off, at least," he reminded him. "Mostly." Benny snorted and plodded heavily up the front ramp behind Teleo and Cutter, followed by the kids and their mounts.

The ride back to the castle was invigorating. The night air was cool and fresh, and after the horses shook off their moodiness, they settled into an easy trot.

They passed through the guarded gates and dim tunnel. Cutter showed them the release mechanism of the secret door, and Teleo stopped to examine the large steel hinges. They stepped out under the night sky into the circular yard, which was lit by a single lantern, and then passed through the interior gates. The horses trotted briskly over the marble streets to the Great Hall, puffing steam into the chill night air.

They found a spot for the horses in a crowded horse pen at the side of the building, which was covered with a steeply pitched thatch roof and had watering troughs, feeding mangers, and racks and hooks for tack. They unsaddled the horses, gave them a quick rubdown, and then entered the cheerful hall, ablaze with lanterns and hot fires. The evening meal was well underway. They went straight to the cooking fires, loaded up wooden trenchers with pheasant meat, potatoes, wilted greens, and orange squash, and found an empty table. A serving boy brought them a steaming loaf of bread and a large slab of butter, and smiled at Jessum and Kaspari, who smiled back.

"Gibby. Meet Jeremiah and Kallie," Cutter said through a mouthful of pheasant. "Gibby's my sister's boy. Bring us some ale, will you?"

"No, no. None for me," Teleo said. He knew himself—if he got too accustomed to ale every night, it could become a problem. The mountain brew was strong. The kids shook their heads as well. Gibby brought his uncle a tankard and a large pot of steaming tea for everyone else.

Cutter was a hearty eater and drank his ale in loud gulps. They ate quickly and spoke little. Teleo cleared his plate and went back for more. When he was pleasantly full, he relaxed on the bench, nibbling on hard yellow cheese and purple grapes. Soon, the servers came back with slices of warm tarts topped with almond paste and glazed pears. The cook had done well, and the addition of the glazed pears made the almond paste even more delicious. He ate two slices before waving away thirds, then lugged himself off the bench to compliment the cook.

"Did I do a'right?" she asked, grinning. The woman stood with her back against the warm fire.

"Better than all right," Teleo assured her. "Almost better than my aunt's recipe, but don't tell her that."

"Oh, I would'na dare," she said, winking.

"Do you mind if I take some home to my wife? She stayed behind to watch the sheep."

The cook promised to pack a dinner for her and send him home with a whole almond pear tart.

Teleo returned to the table and poured himself more tea. The kids had wandered off to talk with their new friends by another fire where the youngsters had all gathered. Some of the youths sat on benches while others stood in small groups or warmed their hands over the flames. The boys and girls kept separate, mostly. Flirting and joking brought the groups together for a time, then they separated again and watched each other with furtive glances.

"Oh, to be young again," Cutter said.

"Young and awkward," Teleo said, chuckling.

"How long have you and yer lady been married?" Cutter asked, picking at his teeth.

Teleo nearly choked on his tea. "We grew up together," he said.

"Ah, childhood sweethearts," Cutter said, grinning and showing his missing tooth. "Me and my wife were too. She died several years ago from the fever. Got two boys, but they're off seeking their fortunes in Sapphire City."

"Ah. Sapphire City," Teleo said, eager to change the subject.

A tall red-bearded man with long moustaches curled at the tips approached and sat on the bench next to Cutter with a grunt, clunking a heavy mug onto the table. "That woman will be the death of me," he said.

"Meet my brother, Johnswold," Cutter said.

"Tesserman," Teleo introduced himself. He shook the man's large hand, seeing the resemblance. They were both large and broad-shouldered and had put on a few pounds around the middle that hid a core of solid muscle. Teleo could feel in the man's strong, calloused grip, and see from his thick forearms and the way he held himself that he was a former soldier. Judging from the number of men and women guarding the walls, most likely every adult in this mountain fortress knew how to fight.

"What'd she do now?" Cutter asked his brother, then added for Teleo, "The queen."

"Argh," Johnswold muttered. "I'll tell you later. Are you the shepherd?" he asked, turning tired brown eyes to Teleo. "Heard all about you." Unlike Cutter, the man had all of his front teeth, but the perfect circles at the tips of his copper-colored moustaches, shiny with wax, made him look almost comical.

"What did you hear?" Teleo asked.

"Just that you brought the ewes the queen's been waiting fer, and you got some nice horses. Them big ones hitched in the pen are yers, I'd wager?"

Teleo nodded.

"You fought in King Elke's army?" Johnswold asked, eyeing Teleo's chest armor bearing Elke's sigil.

Teleo nodded. "Yes. Years ago. Been retired for a long time now. After the border treaty was signed."

"Ay-yah, me too," Johnswold said. "I fought on the Sapphire Valley side fer Emperor Arnbjorg till he got killed. He paid in gold. Then I came back home to the mountains. The new Emperor Cornwal's a bastard. I got tired'a all that political bullshite."

"I know what you mean," Teleo said. "It gets old. Men are men. I like the honorable ones and try to avoid the others."

"Hear, hear," Johnswold said, and raised his mug of brew. Teleo lifted his mug of tea and clinked it against Johnswold's and Cutter's ale mugs, and they drank.

12

SONDERSON

Teleo's bed was warm and comfortable. Dawn peeked through the air vents overhead. He crawled out of bed, pulled on his roughspun shirt and trousers, slid into his boots, and lit a lantern. He climbed the ramp to the upper stable, where the ram looked at him with big yellow eyes. Teleo stepped out into the cold morning air, the valley spreading out below him in a blanket of thick, gray mist that hung low to the ground, waiting for the sun to rise over the peaks and burn it off. He breathed in the fresh air, visited the outhouse, and then went back down to the cellar, where he threw a couple of small logs on the hot coals in the fireplace and stoked them until they awakened tongues of orange flames. The animals were stirring but he crawled back into bed, closed his eyes, and rolled over. There was no rush to start the day. They were home.

A stick in the back awoke Teleo, and in one swift motion the stick was in his hand and he was on his feet, holding the shepherd's crook over the cowering man like a spear.

"Who are you?" the tall, thin man asked, raising his hands defensively. His long white beard and hair were matted and stuck with straw.

"Who are *you?*" Teleo demanded in return, lowering the shepherd's crook, which was not his own, but of a dark polished wood. He handed the crook back to the man. "You must be Sonderson."

"I am," he said haughtily. The shepherd straightened his spine and made a small effort to smooth his linen cloak, which was gray with grime and wrinkled as though he'd slept in it. "And who are you, making home in my stable?"

"Name's Tesserman. Cutter brought us here. Queen Valona purchased our sheep, and we will be tending them for the winter."

The man's rheumy blue eyes shifted to the stalls where the five horses were watching, waiting for their barley mash, and the ewes' noses poked through slats of their gate.

"Hmph," the man grunted dismissively. He turned his back to Teleo, hobbled to the fire, and proceeded to stoke the coals. Teleo dressed in his leathers and watched as Sonderson shuffled about like he lived there: feeding the fire, moving aside the pot of barley, fetching a bucket of water from the well, and hanging a new pot of water over the coals. He ignored the teenagers, who peeked out from behind their curtains. Sonderson hummed a tune as he opened a crock from a shelf and added a scoop of crushed green leaves to the water.

"Mmmm, is that mint?" Dinsmora asked, coming up behind Sonderson. "And fennel? And cinnamon? Nice mix," she said as she leaned her head over the pot and sniffed.

"Blue spearmint," Sonderson said, lowering himself slowly into the rocking chair.

"What else is in there?" she asked, stirring the pot. "Black tea? And some kind of bark? White willow?"

"Yep."

Dinsmora nodded approvingly, then went to the table and unwrapped the almond pear tart, smelling it with closed eyes. She set it aside and peeled the shells from the last of their hardboiled eggs and sprinkled the eggs with salt.

Sonderson was on his feet again, poking his nose over the tart. "What is this?" he asked, and sat on the bench at the table. He produced a knife from the folds of his robe and sliced the tart into six neat triangles. Teleo raised an eyebrow at Dinsmora, whose dimples were showing. Teleo marveled at how patient she could be—when she wasn't being stubborn.

Teleo stood at the counter and ground a few beans of coffee with a mortar and pestle, along with some cinnamon and cardamom. Sonderson appeared at his side, sniffing the rich aroma as Teleo folded a small square of linen into a cone, arranged it inside a funnel, and put the coffee and spices into it.

"Mmmm, coffee," Sonderson said.

"Yes, coffee for me, tea for you," Teleo said, shouldering him aside and pouring hot water over the ground beans and spices.

"I'll just take the sludge," Sonderson said, and took the funnel after Teleo was done with it, pouring more water over the used grounds. Teleo shook his head and stirred in his sugar cube, tossing one Sonderson's way.

"Thank you kindly," the shepherd said, leaning over his cup of weak coffee and inhaling.

The kids left their bunks, and Jessum fetched fresh water from the well for the animals while Kaspari brought the barley mash to the horses. She went from stall to stall, asking each one if they had a good sleep and if they liked their new home. She fed oats to the ewes while she asked them the same questions.

"They seem to like it here," Kaspari said across the room to no one in particular.

"That's good, Kallie," Teleo said, catching her eye and gesturing stealthily to Sonderson.

"Did you let the ram out?" Dinsmora asked the shepherd, who had already eaten a slice of tart, an egg, and finished his coffee, and was back in his rocking chair with a fresh mug of steaming tea in his hands.

"Yep," he answered.

"Did you sleep in the hayloft?" Teleo asked, surprised Cutter had not found him.

"Nope."

After breakfast, Teleo quickly shaved off his stubble and then went outside with the kids to inspect the grounds in the daylight. The grass was wet with dew, and a low-hanging mist still blanketed the rolling fields. The ram was nosing at the grass nearby.

The workshop was unlocked. Inside were two workbenches and a wall of shelves filled with a collection of rusted tools, cracked leather strips, scraps of milled wood, and mouse droppings. The third building was a small barn with more sheaves of hay propped up in a corner and a mountain of loose straw taking up the rest of the space. A soiled and stinking blanket was tangled in the straw at the edge of the mound, and three stoneware jugs lay uncorked near the blanket. Teleo sniffed one. Mushroom wine. All three jugs were empty.

Teleo avoided the stuff himself. Getting drunk on ale or cider, or even brandy, was one thing. Hallucinating and losing days at a time was another. He had tried mushroom wine a few times as a young soldier until his commander had left him and his three drinking buddies behind during one of their binges. It took them a week to find their unit. The commander let them back in with a warning that the next time they would be out.

Teleo hadn't tried it since. He didn't like the feeling of losing control like that anyway, and the hallucinations scared him.

Teleo told the kids what it was and gave them a stern lecture to keep away from it. They stared at him and nodded.

There wasn't much more to the property except some junk piled behind the workshop, and fields in every direction. Teleo breathed in the moist air, which smelled of decaying leaves and sheep dung.

They went back into the cellar and led the animals to the upper stable while they mucked the stalls down below. Sonderson showed them a wooden hatch that stood at shoulder height on the cellar wall on one side of the pen. Teleo pushed it open, and he and Kaspari used pitchforks to toss the soiled straw up to Jessum, who threw the straw onto a pile a few paces away. When they were done, Kaspari and Dinsmora went upstairs to clean the ram's pen. Teleo could hear the animals through the open door to the upper stable. They were restless.

"Is it okay to let the horses outside?" Teleo asked Sonderson.

"Why wouldn't it be?" the shepherd retorted, sipping on his tea and staring at the low-burning fire.

"Wolves."

"It's daylight."

"I know. I'm just asking. I'm new around here. Are the fields completely enclosed?"

"More or less."

Teleo held his tongue. Mushroom wine hangover was an ugly beast. He served himself a mug of the fragrant tea, sat on the bench, and faced Sonderson, who was rocking slowly. The man was tall and wiry, and his thin form was hunched over the steaming mug. His face was leathery and wrinkled, and his long bony nose curved like an eagle's beak. He wore sturdy boots, but everything else about him was tattered and filthy.

After several minutes, Sonderson spoke in a scratchy voice. "There's a breach in the southern wall. We tried to patch it up. I'll show you later. It'll keep the horses in, but bring them in before nightfall. Or just keep them in the northern field."

Teleo nodded. "What about the ewes? When should we put them in with the ram?"

Sonderson turned a sour eye on Teleo.

Teleo raised his hands apologetically. "I don't know your ram's temperament."

Sonderson sighed, returned his gaze to the smoldering fire, and resumed his rocking. "They'll be fine. Let them rest, though. Fatten them up a bit. Feed them a little grain, and the ram, too. A couple of weeks should be enough. I'll trim the ram's hooves tomorrow." Sonderson could feel Teleo looking at him and turned his irritated gaze on him again. "Now what?"

"Should we let them out to graze?" Teleo asked.

Sonderson's bloodshot eyes bulged. "Are you a fucking child? You look like a man, but looks can deceive."

Teleo laughed. "I just mean, how do we keep them separated? How are your fields laid out? I didn't see any pens."

Sonderson answered in a condescending, overly patient tone. "The southern field is separated from the northern field by the walls behind the barns. There are things called gates back there. Put the ewes in the northern field. Put the ram in the southern field. He won't wander far. His name is Marblehead. He responds to his name."

Teleo went outside and found the fieldstone walls behind the junk piles at the rear of the workshop. The ground fog had mostly burned off, exposing the walls facing each other across a wagon path. The walls formed two straight, parallel lines and met the cliff in the distance, enclosing a large field to the north and a larger field to the south. Marblehead was grazing where they had found him when they'd first arrived, in the northern field.

"Marblehead," Teleo called out, opening the gate.

The ram lifted his head and walked leisurely his way. When he got close, he stopped and looked at Teleo.

"Here," Teleo said, holding up half a carrot. Marblehead moved towards him. Teleo broke the carrot in half again, and Marblehead delicately took the chunk Teleo offered him with big, yellowed teeth, and crunched loudly while holding Teleo's gaze the whole time.

Teleo walked across the wagon lane to the opposite gate, holding out the remaining carrot stub. Marblehead followed close behind. Teleo led Marblehead into the southern field, then fed him the carrot.

"That's all," Teleo said, holding up empty hands.

Marblehead gave him a disdainful look and sauntered off.

"You're welcome," Teleo said, and closed the gate behind him.

Teleo opened the barn doors wide and let the horses and ewes out into the northern field. The animals ran outside like they'd been cooped up for days and immediately started grazing. Teleo, Jessum, and Kaspari hiked through the southern field to explore, and discovered a brook fed by a small waterfall running down the cliff face. The brook meandered through the field and into a small pond, then continued flowing through a culvert under the wagon path and down towards the river. Marblehead followed a short distance behind, trumpeting at them every few minutes.

"Yes, Marblehead," Teleo said. "You can make some lambs in two weeks." Marblehead glowered at him with yellow eyes and trumpeted again, showing Teleo his lower teeth.

After finishing their short tour, they left Marblehead in the field and went back inside. Dinsmora was kneading dough at the table, and Sonderson was looking through the ceramic crocks.

"I have dried currants here somewhere," he said to Dinsmora as he removed the cork lid from a crock.

They left Dinsmora to her bread making, and Teleo and the kids saddled their horses and rode to Bitter's Ford.

At the village's indoor farm market, Teleo purchased a round of hard yellow cheese, a smoked pork loin, two jugs of fresh cow's milk, four stoneware flagons of hard cider, three dozen eggs, a crock of butter, a crock of lard, a sack of wheat flour, a tin of dry baker's yeast, dried peas and lentils, a large bundle of mustard greens, a few onions, a dozen large red peppers, several yellow squash, a small wooden crate filled with bunches of dark purple grapes, a small sack of salt, a larger sack of sugar, and a crock of wildflower honey.

The kids stayed outside, talking to three youngsters whom Teleo recognized from dinner the night before—two teenaged girls and a boy. When he was done shopping, they loaded the supplies into saddlebags and lashed the larger items behind Benny's saddle. They rode back to their new home, which the villagers called Sheep's Haven, and cooked a simple meal of eggs and bacon.

Sonderson was still there, and they shared their meal with him. He had cleaned himself up somewhat. His white hair was combed and pulled back into a long stringy ponytail, and he wore a relatively clean robe. He was not very talkative, but after they finished eating he offered to show Teleo the breach in the stone wall.

Dinsmora stayed behind but the kids wanted to come along. They saddled the horses again, and Dinsmora gave Sonderson permission to ride Nutmeg. Sonderson led them along the wagon path to the southern border of Sheep's Haven, two miles away. Some of the land was divided into smaller fields by stone walls, but most of it was open rangeland. One enclosed section was a recently harvested hayfield, which Teleo guessed was the source of the hay in the barn. Everything else had been left to nature. If it was Teleo's land, he would plant a variety of grasses, partition more of the fields, and move the sheep around in an orderly fashion.

The shepherd told them that the queen had had a large flock at one time. Some died from disease. Others got picked off by wolves one by one until a bloody slaughter took the last ewes and lambs earlier that summer. Marblehead had been in the barn recovering from a gash on his back. Sonderson claimed he had been tending to the ram when the slaughter happened, but Teleo suspected he had been nursing a jug of mushroom wine.

Teleo examined the section of the fieldstone wall where a tumble of rocks created a gap big enough for wolves to climb through. The hole had been filled with a crisscross of logs wedged in between the rocks to keep the sheep in.

"Nice patch job," Teleo commented wryly.

"It does the job," Sonderson said, dismounting from Nutmeg.

"How'd the wall fall down?" Jessum asked, joining Sonderson on the ground.

"Lightning."

A few of the fieldstones were split down the middle, and others had weeds sprouting through cracks. "Wolves can still get over this," Teleo said, climbing up onto the pile of rocks and peering over the top log, noting that the crisscrossed logs formed a sort of ladder. The queen was right to replace Sonderson. "We need to repair this properly," Teleo said, trying to keep the annoyance from his voice.

Sonderson shrugged. "I don't know much about building rock walls."

"Well, I do," Teleo said. "We will start tomorrow morning." Teleo wondered what Sonderson was good for, or cared about, other than getting drunk.

"*You* can," Sonderson said. "I'm not fit fer lugging stones."

Teleo glared down at the shepherd from his rocky perch. He had had about enough of this sniveling excuse for a man. "You will help," Teleo said curtly, "or you will vacate the property. You are no longer responsible for the sheep."

"You won't be ordering me around on my own land, stranger," Sonderson said, narrowing his piercing blue eyes at Teleo. "I don't know where you came from or what yer doing here, or what the queen sees in you. But I've been here all my life, and Sheep's Haven is mine."

"We'll see about that," Teleo said, his patience gone. "Come on, Jeremiah."

Teleo swung into the saddle and Jessum got on BlackJack. Kaspari was still in her saddle and looked back and forth between the fuming men. Teleo met her concerned gaze. "It'll be fine," he assured her. "Let's go."

Kaspari guided Daisy onto the path and took off at a trot. Jessum and Teleo followed. "Nutmeg, come!" Teleo commanded. Nutmeg trotted obediently behind Benny, happy to be rid of the stinking shepherd.

"Hey!" Sonderson protested, chasing after them and waving his shepherd's crook.

Teleo ignored him. "Hi-ya!" he called out, slapping his knee, and the horses took off at a gallop, leaving Sonderson behind.

13

WOOL

The next day, Teleo hitched Benny up to a hay wagon and loaded it with a long straight log and a milled wooden beam he found behind the woodshed, along with several items from the workshop: coils of thick rope, iron crowbars, shovels, pickaxes, sledgehammers, saws, and buckets. Teleo took Jessum and Kaspari with him down to the southern wall, and Marblehead followed them. They carried their swords and shepherd's crooks in the unlikely chance they encountered wolves or needed to rescue the queen's ram.

At the wall breach, Teleo carved one end of the log into a point and mounted the beam perpendicularly on the other end, carving a rough joint and lashing it securely. He dug a hole next to the wall, and the three of them raised the log to vertical and buried the base into the ground. They tested the lever system by tying a large boulder in a rope sling to one end of the beam and hanging buckets filled with rocks from the other end as a counterweight, easily lifting the large rock to the top of the wall.

By the time the makeshift boom crane was done, the day was almost gone.

They headed back to the cellar, with Marblehead leading the way. When they arrived, Dinsmora had already brought in Cinnamon, Nutmeg, and the ewes. Sonderson hadn't shown his face again, and Teleo hoped they had seen the last of him. Teleo swapped Benny's harness for a saddle, and he and the kids rode to the Great Hall for dinner.

The following day, Teleo and the kids returned to the wall. They started by removing the logs that crisscrossed the gap and set aside the loose stones that lay where they had fallen from the lightning strike. Next, Teleo sank stakes into the ground and ran a level line at the height of the first row of stones they needed to lay. They used the crane to lift the stones. Teleo climbed up onto the wall and guided each one into place while Jessum and Kaspari added their weight to the crane's wooden boom to raise and lower it.

Teleo wiped his sweaty brow with his sleeve and regarded the original wall. It had been well built, three layers deep, with through-stones and hearting and without the need for any mortar. He hopped down to the ground and split stones and squared them with his hammer and chisel. Then he climbed back up onto the wall and set them flat across as best he could and made sure they fit snugly.

He was up top when a loud trumpeting bellowed across the field. The horses lifted their heads for a moment and then returned to grazing. Marblehead was ambling towards them through the grass. Sonderson strode behind him on the wagon path, using his crook as a walking stick. Teleo groaned and met the glances of Jessum and Kaspari.

Teleo hopped down and loaded another stone into the rope sling, ignoring Sonderson as he approached. Teleo climbed back up onto the wall and settled the stone into place.

"You need bigger rocks in the middle there," Sonderson said in his annoying nasal twang. He pointed his staff at the wall.

"Actually, smaller stones go in the center," Teleo said. "But this is what we have to work with," Teleo said, gesturing to the displaced stones on the ground. They had carried the stones they could lift by hand from the rockfall on the other side, but it was beyond the range of the makeshift crane, so they had left the larger ones there. He had decided not to bother mounting the crane on both sides but instead to collect smaller stones from the field to fill in the top portion.

"Bigger is better," Sonderson said, planting his staff on the ground.

Teleo inhaled and hopped down to help with the next stone. He and the teenagers worked in silence. They had their technique down—now it was just a matter of raising one stone after another.

Sonderson tapped loudly with his staff on a rock, which was half buried in the grass several paces away. "Here's one," he called out.

Teleo glanced up. "That's downhill from us. Easier to roll one downhill than up."

Sonderson sneered at him but walked stiffly up the slope.

A couple of minutes later, Sonderson found another one and announced it proudly. He was poking at the grass around the buried rock with his crook. Teleo shook his head and muttered to Jessum, "Go help him dig it out. We'll need another row of through-stones, and we need some capstones."

Kaspari and Teleo continued loading stones into the sling while Jessum trudged up the hill carrying two crowbars, a shovel, and a pickaxe. After several minutes of digging, Jessum and Sonderson used the crowbars as levers to roll the large rock down the hill to the wall. Sonderson watched smugly while they loaded it into the sling and raised it up.

Teleo found a spot for it and shifted it into place. He looked sideways at Sonderson. "Well?" Teleo asked. "If you're going to help, then go find more. Try to find long ones. And they need to be flat, not round."

They worked through the day, making good progress. The shepherd did help a little bit, despite getting on Teleo's nerves. The next morning, Sonderson showed up at the cellar again, uninvited. Dinsmora was gracious, as always, sharing their breakfast with him and suggesting that he ride Nutmeg out to the wall. Teleo rolled his eyes behind their backs, making Jessum smirk and Kaspari giggle.

Teleo, Sonderson, and the kids finished the wall two days later. It was late afternoon, and by the time they had disassembled the crane, gathered all their tools, and loaded up the wagon, the sun had set. The sky was slate gray with fading wisps of lavender clouds, and a gyrfalcon circled overhead, hunting mice. The horses and Marblehead waited on the wagon path. It was past their bedtime.

Teleo adjusted Benny's traces between the wagon's shafts, checked his harness, and slipped the dapple gray a piece of apple. The others mounted their horses, and Teleo sat on the wagon's driving bench holding Benny's reins. Sonderson led the way on Nutmeg, followed by Marblehead, the two kids on their horses, and the wagon taking up the rear. It grew darker, and a pale moon shed enough light for them to make out the path ahead of them.

They settled into a comfortable pace when a boom shook the ground, followed by a loud crack and rumble. Teleo whipped his head around to see forks of white lightning fading from the sky. Another bolt lit the sky with a deafening blast.

BlackJack reared and Jessum struggled to keep his seat. Daisy sidestepped off the path, and Benny snorted and stomped, coming to a halt and rattling his heavy harness against the wagon's wooden shafts. Sonderson jumped off Nutmeg and called Marblehead to his side. The shepherd produced a torch from his robes and knelt to light it with a flint. On the third strike, the oil-soaked rag ignited and flames climbed into the air, casting a golden orb around him and the ram. Sonderson's dingy white robe glowed ghostlike in the flickering light.

"There are no storm clouds," Teleo said ominously, standing on the wagon's footboard and holding Benny's reins tightly.

"Stone Guardians," Sonderson said, sending shivers up Teleo's spine.

"Stone Guardians? You knew it was Stone Guardians who destroyed the wall?" Teleo asked Sonderson accusingly. "Why didn't you tell us?"

"Shhhh!!" Sonderson hissed and raised his torch high in one hand and his shepherd's crook in the other, sniffing the air.

The night was silent except for the rustling of grass from a sudden breeze. Teleo grabbed his shepherd's crook from the bench behind him and Jessum pulled his crook from BlackJack's saddle strap. Kaspari glanced nervously at Teleo.

"Stay close," he told her.

BlackJack pawed at the ground and whinnied shrilly.

The attack came from the dark grasses. The pack of wolves formed a circle of shadows around them, snarling and growling. One lunged forward, leaping at Marblehead. Sonderson was a swirl of cloak and fire as he lashed out with his shepherd's crook, striking the wolf with a burst of blue light. The crook drove the animal away for a moment, but two others took its place and lunged forward.

Teleo jumped to the ground and Jessum leaned down from his saddle, and they joined Sonderson, swinging their shepherd's crooks at the leaping wolves. The crooks flashed blue and stunned the wolves for a moment, but they recovered quickly. Teleo drew his short sword, delivering a deadly blow to a wolf who leapt at him. Two snarling wolves turned on Sonderson and BlackJack. The shepherd jabbed the torch at one, and the black warhorse reared and slashed at the other with his hooves, then trampled the screaming beast underfoot.

Jessum frantically wielded his crook against another pair of wolves that were trying to break through and get at Marblehead, who was squalling like a baby and turning in circles. Daisy reared and kicked wildly at another wolf. Kaspari hung on with one hand, brandishing her sword with the other. Nutmeg was at Sonderson's back, protecting Marblehead from the rear, while Jessum hooked a lunging wolf around the neck with his crook and plunged his sword into its chest. Jessum pushed the wolf free of his blade with his boot and swung his crook at another that was snarling at Marblehead just as two more wolves attacked Teleo, one from each side.

Teleo tossed away his crook in favor of his short sword and heavy hammer, and swung at them in a circle, striking one in the head with the hammer and cutting the foreleg off the second, sending it whimpering to the ground, where Teleo hacked at its neck in a fountain of blood, then killed the stunned one with a slash to the throat.

He turned to see a gray wolf lunge at Benny's neck the same time as a wolf leapt at Teleo's arm and another tore at his pant leg. He reached over his shoulder for his longsword but met empty air, having left the longsword in the cellar, thinking it needless weight for him to carry. He was unable to get to Benny, who tried to rear and kick but was hitched to the heavy wagon. Teleo killed the wolf attacking his arm and kicked at the other one while the gray wolf took hold and hung from Benny's throat. The horse shrieked, straining against the shafts, and suddenly Daisy was at Benny's head, battering the wolf with her front hooves and trampling it underfoot.

Kaspari leapt from Daisy's back onto the driver's bench and cut Benny loose from his traces. Teleo's sword met the throat of another wolf who lunged at Teleo's chest while Benny lurched forward with the wagon a pace, then sagged in his harness. Teleo's wolf fell sideways in slow motion while Kaspari turned to meet a black wolf who leapt onto the wagon. She swung her sword with both hands, the force of the blow sinking the length of the blade into the wolf's thick neck and shoulder and wrenching the sword from her hands as the wolf fell over the side of the wagon, taking the sword with it.

Benny was still strapped to the wagon shafts, blood streaming down his neck, and his legs collapsing under him as a wolf lunged at Teleo's thigh and another leapt through the air and landed on the wagon facing Kaspari. Teleo responded by reflex to the one attacking his leg and hacked through the wolf's spine. By the time he had pulled his sword free, Kaspari was on her back in the wagon bed, holding a crowbar crosswise in the jaws of a wolf straining over her.

Snarling wolves and shrieking horses and the smell of singed fur filled the air as Teleo jumped onto the wagon and speared the wolf's ribcage with his short sword, pulling the beast off Kaspari and striking another wolf with his hammer while the first wolf was still skewered on his sword, its writhing weight pulling Teleo off balance. The second wolf had his jaws around Teleo's hammer arm, tearing through his buckskin sleeve. Teleo let go of his sword and the impaled wolf in favor of another hammer and struck at the second wolf's head until it released his arm and fell off the wagon. Teleo finished off the impaled wolf as Kaspari lurched to her feet and swung a pickaxe with both hands, catching an airborne wolf in the belly as it sank its teeth into her face. Teleo swung the pointed end of his hammer at the wolf's skull, then struck again. The wolf went limp and Teleo pulled it off Kaspari, blood covering her face.

Teleo whirled to meet the next wolf, but there were no more. The field was suddenly still and the air was filled with the sounds of panting men and snorting horses. Bloody wolf carcasses littered the ground, and flames licked up from a patch of grass where Sonderson had dropped his torch, bathing the scene in an orange glow and casting grotesque shadows. Benny was hanging in his harness, his head drooping.

Teleo knelt next to Kaspari and dabbed at her face with his sleeve. Jessum jumped up next to him and pulled off his linen shirt, wiping away blood from the trembling girl. She had deep gashes under her cheekbone and above her eyebrow where the teeth had sunk in and torn the flesh. The wolf had missed her eye, and aside from a lot of blood, Teleo did not judge the wounds to be fatal. He showed Jessum how to apply pressure, then jumped off the wagon to go to Benny's side. Dark red blood spurted from gashes in the horse's neck. Teleo quickly cut him loose from the shafts and pushed the wagon back. Benny fell onto his front knees and rolled heavily onto the ground.

Daisy was nosing her offspring's face. Sonderson knelt next to Benny and pressed his palms on the wounds, trying to staunch the bleeding. Benny's throat was ripped open in several places, the arteries severed. Teleo knelt and placed his hand on his beloved horse's wide jawbone. Benny's big brown eye looked up at him. Teleo stroked his cheek and held his gaze while the dapple gray slowly bled out.

◆

They stomped out the grass fire and examined each other's wounds, quickly applying bandages to the worst of them, using strips of linen from Sonderson's shirt. They left the wagon and the corpses of Benny and the wolves where they had fallen. They would bury them in daylight the following morning.

Teleo lifted Kaspari onto Daisy's saddle and climbed on behind her, holding her with one arm and grabbing the reins with his free hand. She leaned back against his chest, her hands pressing Jessum's shirt to her face as they headed across the dark fields in the wan moonlight.

Sonderson and Nutmeg led the way at a brisk trot, followed by Marblehead, Jessum on BlackJack, and then Daisy. Teleo kept his senses alert for more wolves or Stone Guardians, but the shadows were only shadows. Dinsmora, riding Cinnamon, met them when they were halfway home, bearing a bright torch, having heard the thunderclap and seen the lightning. They quickly explained what had happened, and she fell in next to Teleo.

They arrived at the cellar and laid Kaspari on the table. The three adults gathered around and cleaned her bite wounds. Sonderson applied an herb compress to numb Kaspari's cheek and brow, then Dinsmora stitched her up with several neatly place sutures. Kaspari held still and did not complain. The princess would have scars, but Teleo did not think she would be permanently disfigured. She was young yet, and strong. Sonderson prepared another herbal compress, and he and Dinsmora bandaged her up while Teleo examined Jessum and the horses.

Jessum had an ugly gash on his forearm, and Teleo sent him over to Dinsmora and Sonderson to get sewn up. Daisy, Nutmeg, and BlackJack bore an assortment of lacerations, which they treated one by one. BlackJack stood relatively still while Jessum held his bridle and Dinsmora cleaned a particularly deep cut on his hindquarter, which required stitches, adding another battle mark to his already scarred hide. The big horse tolerated the needle without making a fuss. Teleo had several gashes and puncture wounds on his legs and arms. Dinsmora fixed him up last, using the numbing compress to dull the pain.

His and Jessum's wounds would have been worse had it not been for their buckskin clothing, which would need to be cleaned and mended. Only Marblehead and Sonderson escaped unscathed, although the shepherd's robe was stained a deep scarlet from the blood of everyone else. The shepherd disappeared up the ramp and returned in a fresh linen shirt and a clean, if rumpled, robe.

They decided not to make the trek to the Great Hall for dinner but instead sat around the table while Dinsmora dished up leftover stew and served them a heavy brown bread she had made, with slabs of butter and cheese and slices of apple. They ate in silence. Kaspari chewed slowly, every bite seeming to be an effort. Her face was swollen under her bandages, and her right eye was half closed and purplish. She would have a nice shiner come morning.

Dinsmora produced an herbal powder, mixed it with water, and poured a small cupful for Kaspari, Teleo, and Jessum. "For the pain," she said.

Teleo drank the bitter liquid.

"What about BlackJack?" Jessum asked.

"I applied an ointment that will numb his pain somewhat," Dinsmora said. The big black was quiet in his stall.

Sonderson produced a flask of Ferska and poured a small amount into each of their empty cups, and brought over cups for himself and Dinsmora. Teleo sipped on the strong peach brandy, feeling it burn down his throat. Kaspari and Jessum downed theirs, making faces. Kaspari coughed and winced in pain, and Jessum wiped his mouth with the back of his hand. The room fell silent again.

Teleo glanced across the cellar. Daisy's head was hanging over the wooden divider into Benny's empty stall, and Teleo choked back a sudden sob.

"Benny was a good horse," Dinsmora said gently.

"The best," Teleo said, dabbing at his eyes. He took another sip of Ferska, then pushed himself up from the bench and went to Daisy. He hugged her neck and she nuzzled his shoulder. They stood like that for a long while.

When he finally returned to the table, Sonderson poured another round of Ferska.

Teleo narrowed his eyes at Sonderson. "Wait a second," Teleo said. "So the lightning came from Stone Guardians? What about the wolves? Were they sent by Stone Guardians too?"

Sonderson tilted his head noncommittally. "Could be," he said, and poured Teleo more brandy. "That's what the queen thinks."

"You should have warned us," Teleo said grimly, and Sonderson averted his eyes.

"So there are Stone Guardians in this valley?" Dinsmora asked.

Sonderson shrugged. "There's one, sometimes."

"And you're not hunting him?" Teleo asked, rising to his feet.

Sonderson peered up at him through bushy eyebrows. "She hides."

"She?" Dinsmora asked.

"Ay-yah," Sonderson said. "Valona believes that the Stone Guardian witch sends wolves to do her dirty work. She does not come herself. Not very often, anyway, that we are aware of ..."

Teleo paced in front of the fireplace, wondering at the incompetence of the shepherd in front of him, letting a lone Stone Guardian woman roam freely in his territory.

"She sends wolves to kill sheep?" Jessum asked.

"Ay-yah," Sonderson said, turning his eyes to the boy.

"She wants to kill Marblehead?" Kaspari asked.

The shepherd nodded with an ominous glower.

"Why does the Stone Guardian want to kill the ram so badly?" Dinsmora asked.

The shepherd brushed crumbs from his beard with long, knobby fingers, his fingernails still black with dried blood. "He's the last of the ancient Mage's stock."

Dinsmora's eyebrows rose and the kids wore puzzled frowns.

"The queen hopes your ewes will continue the line," he said. "The ewes were raised by Mages, after all. Were they not?" The shepherd directed his question at Teleo, and for the first time, Teleo saw a sharp, astute man behind the unkempt exterior.

Teleo exchanged glances with Dinsmora. He could not deny that statement—the crooks the shepherds had given them were Mages' staffs, there was no doubt about that. But Teleo understood the question behind the question. Sonderson thought he and Dinsmora had raised the sheep and that they were Mages. Teleo shrugged. "Could be."

"Could be?" Sonderson scoffed. "I saw the blue light coming from yer crooks."

It was true. The staffs had flashed blue when he or Jessum had struck a wolf, albeit faintly, but he did not know if it had been the power in the staffs or perhaps the Stone Guardian's wolves that had made them light up. It wasn't him—he was sure of that. Nor Jessum. Maybe it was Sonderson. The shepherd was no Dinsmora—his crook's light was a brief spark compared to her tightly woven net. But still ...

"And you passed safely through Stone Guardian territory," Sonderson added. "Valona told me."

"So what's so special about Mages' sheep?" Dinsmora asked, holding out her cup for more brandy.

Sonderson poured her more of the amber liquid. "They grow magic wool." Sonderson smiled, and goosebumps rose on Teleo's arms.

"What does magic wool do?" Kaspari asked.

"It holds spells," Sonderson said in a dramatically hushed

tone, making his eyes big, and then laughed a big, hearty laugh at the bewildered looks on their faces.

"What kind of spells?" Jessum asked.

Sonderson made his eyes big again. "You'll have to ask the queen. But don't ask the queen." He burst out laughing again. Teleo could not tell if the shepherd was playing with them or if there was some truth to his words.

"But seriously," Sonderson said, returning his attention to Dinsmora, his wrinkled face growing somber. "Queen Valona sent fer you, and you came."

Teleo withheld the urge to dispute his claim. "How so?" he asked instead. "We never got sent for."

"Oh-ho," Sonderson said. "It doesn't work like that. She is not so direct as that. She manipulates the threads of time and space. She doesn't like to do it much. She says it starts things in motion and brings results, but what happens in between she can't predict or control. Unintended consequences fer a greater good, she says."

Teleo chewed on that thought for a moment, then discarded it. What had been set in motion and ended with them arriving at Trillifort was way bigger than anything a crazy mountain queen could have conjured. All their suffering just to bring sheep for Queen Valona?

"No," Teleo said. "Sorry, but no. It was coincidence."

"Oh, yes," Sonderson countered, enjoying Teleo's resistance. "You'll see. Coincidences aren't mere coincidences. Not around Queen Valona."

"She feels the river flowing," Dinsmora said, with a distant look in her eyes. "Then she drops metaphorical stones in it to alter its course."

"See?" Sonderson said to Teleo. "Mora understands." The skinny shepherd smirked and rose to set a kettle of water over the flames. Teleo shook the brandy flask. It was empty. He ground a handful of coffee beans and waited for the water to boil. Sonderson stood by his side, lowering his long nose over the coffee beans and inhaling.

"I suppose you want some," Teleo said.

"Ferska fer coffee. Fair trade," Sonderson said, fetching his mug and clomping it down next to Teleo's.

Before Teleo had a chance to drink his coffee, a pounding at the door was followed by Cutter and his brother Johnswold clomping down the steps. The two big men brought with them the scent of pipe smoke and ale.

"What happened?" Cutter asked. "Guards saw the lightning. Where's Marblehead?" Cutter scanned the shadows until his gaze landed on Marblehead where he stood in the last stall, his nose pressed against a gap in the boards separating him from the ewes. "Ah, there he is. What happened?" Cutter repeated, his attention turning to Kaspari. "You all right, young lady?"

"Yes, sir," she replied. Cutter and Johnswold glanced at the bandages on Teleo's and Jessum's arms.

"Wolves," Sonderson said.

"They broke through the wall again?" Johnswold asked, and Sonderson nodded.

"Where's yer other horse?" Cutter asked Teleo, noticing the empty stall. "Your dapple-gray gelding."

Teleo made a cutting motion with his hand across his throat. He could not get himself to speak.

"Oh, I'm sorry," Cutter said, laying his hand on Teleo's back. "That's rough."

Teleo nodded, a lump rising in his throat.

"Damn wolves," Cutter said, squeezing his shoulder.

"Why doesn't the Stone Guardian come herself?" Dinsmora asked. "Why send wolves? How did the Stone Guardian get into the valley, anyway? Those cliffs are forbidding."

"Ah, so you've heard the tales," Cutter said, glancing pointedly at Sonderson. "That witch has been after our sheep fer a generation. She revealed herself after the first wolf attack, years ago. Sonderson saw her. He's been smitten ever since."

Sonderson's face screwed up into a petulant scowl. "Have not."

Cutter and Johnswold laughed. "What did she look like?" Johnswold asked. "Tell us the story again."

"He always tells it when he's drunk," Cutter said.

Sonderson stirred sugar into his coffee, his brow furrowing, and said, "She glowed."

Cutter and Johnswold laughed uproariously, slapping their knees, their jollity making Teleo and the others laugh with them.

"Like an angel," Johnswold said when he caught his breath. "Come down from heaven." He imitated Sonderson's nasal voice. "The birds sang fer her and the air smelled o' honeysuckle." Johnswold clasped his hands to his heart. "Oh Heart of Stone, Warrior of Love, would that you were not the enemy, I would make you my own."

Sonderson stood up from the bench and went to the fire, turning his back to the laughter and stoking the coals with an iron poker.

"So if we patch the wall, she'll just break through again?" Jessum asked.

The men grew silent. Cutter and Johnswold sniffed at the coffee beans, and Teleo brewed them each a cup.

"We're exposed out here," Teleo said, dropping a sugar cube into each cup before handing them to the brothers. The three men sat at the table, and Teleo continued, "There are miles of walls. We can't possibly defend them all."

"We can stake the sheep close to the barn," Dinsmora suggested. "Or build a small outdoor pen. Or keep them inside the barn."

"Or move them inside the castle walls. Like we did at my ... our ... city ... village," Kaspari said. "There are only five sheep." She was blushing by the time she was done.

"Yeah," Jessum said quickly. "Some of the townspeople used to keep their livestock inside the city walls during the winter."

Cutter and Johnswold exchanged glances.

"There's no room inside the castle walls," Cutter said. "Everyone's already packed in tight fer the winter. Claimed every good spot, they have."

"What about the central square?" Teleo asked.

Cutter raised an eyebrow. "Do you know how much snow we get?"

"No," Teleo said.

"A lot," Cutter said. "We do our best to keep the square clear, but you'd be miserable out there, and in the way."

"There's that round yard by the hidden door," Kaspari said.

"The soldiers take over that yard at first snowfall," Cutter said. "There are only enough shelters for the soldiers to get out of the weather between shifts."

"What about the tunnels?" Jessum suggested.

"It's just a trail. Too narrow. There are no big caverns except at the lake, and the banks there are too steep," Cutter said. "We always talk about building an underground city, but we never have. Haven't needed to. We have Falcon's Nest."

"There's the tower," Johnswold said.

"Nay," Sonderson said flatly.

"What tower?" Dinsmora asked.

"The third castle tower," Cutter said.

"It's abandoned," Johnswold said.

"Why?" Dinsmora asked.

"Nobody wants to go in there," Cutter said. "They're scared."

Johnswold said, "I went in there once as a kid. It's just a tower."

"It is not just a tower," Sonderson said.

Johnswold glared at the shepherd.

"It's haunted," Sonderson said.

Johnswold rolled his eyes. "Old mountain tales. It's a perfectly fine tower."

Sonderson set his jaw stubbornly. "You don't know what yer talking about."

"Neither do you, otherwise you would still be one of the Queen's Guards," Johnswold retorted, and the two men stared daggers at one another.

"She sent me out here to protect the sheep," Sonderson said stiffly.

"Fine job you've done," Johnswold said.

"Boys, boys," Cutter said. "Please."

"I think the tower sounds like a good option," Dinsmora said.

Sonderson exhaled loudly. "Valona will forbid it."

"Have you asked her?" Cutter challenged.

Sonderson turned back to the fire, muttering under his breath, and threw a log onto the flames.

"I'm supposed to be helping Queen Valona ... uh, sew," Dinsmora said. "I promised her lady I would start soon. It would be much more convenient to reside on the castle grounds."

Cutter let out a long sigh and said, "I'll ask the queen tomorrow." He drained his coffee cup, then smacked his lips. "Ahhh, black gold. You got the good stuff," he said, nodding appreciatively at Teleo.

"The best," Teleo said. "Mage's Flight."

Sonderson peered over his shoulder at Teleo and Dinsmora and squinted, as though trying to detect something.

14

THE THIRD TOWER

The kids and Dinsmora went to bed while Teleo and the brothers sat around the table and Sonderson rocked in his chair by the fire. Johnswold produced a flask of blue elderberry wine and they passed it around, trading stories of their soldiering days and of Stone Guardians.

Cutter and Johnswold spent the night in the upper barn with their horses, and Sonderson slept in the hay mow, where he had set up a makeshift living area. At dawn, Johnswold stayed behind to watch the sheep while the rest of them headed out to view the carnage.

Teleo rode Daisy. Kaspari sat behind Dinsmora on Cinnamon, and Jessum rode Nutmeg. They left BlackJack in his stall to heal. Cutter was on his small but sturdy mountain horse, and Sonderson borrowed Johnswold's mount. Johnswold accused Sonderson of selling his own horse for mushroom wine, a claim Sonderson denied.

They rode somberly down the wagon path. Dew was burning off the grass in a rising mist while the towering blue cliffs loomed to their left. Daisy was not herself, but plodded forward at Teleo's urging.

Vultures and crows hopped away as the horses and humans approached the gory scene. A large vulture dragged away a piece of flesh, attracting the others in an undulating sea of gray feathers and orange heads pecking at the bloody morsel. Jessum and Cutter threw rocks to drive them further away.

Teleo stood stoically over Benny's corpse, having shed all his tears the night before when he'd found time alone under the stars. The dapple gray's legs were stiff, and half his neck was gone, exposing raw, mangled flesh. Daisy lowered her nose and touched Benny's muzzle, then wandered off to graze.

As for the Stone Guardian's wolves, Teleo had expected some sort of monsters, but they were just wolves. They lay in scattered clumps of fur caked with blood. Sunken, glassy eyes stared at nothing, and mouths hung open with swollen tongues draped over long fangs. The carrion birds and rodents had not wasted any time. Eyeballs and chunks of flesh were missing, and entrails were spread across the grass like dead snakes.

The wagon stood where they'd left it, sticky with blood. They took up shovels and pickaxes and dug shallow graves in the rocky soil. Teleo removed Benny's harness and bridle and did his best to comb out his forelock with his fingers, avoiding the mutilated neck and blood-matted mane.

They dropped Benny into the first hole, in one great heave and roll. The wolves went into the other, dragged by legs or tails. They shoveled dirt on top of the corpses and piled mounds of stones on each grave. Teleo placed one last round rock on top of Benny's cairn. He had buried too many horses and comrades in his day. The weight of them all pressed down on him like the mound of fieldstones, making it hard to breathe.

His dead wife and daughter and his missing son ached like phantom limbs. He wished he had seen their corpses—the bodies of Bella-Mae and Abigail, whom his cousins had kindly told him had not suffered—that way Teleo could be sure of their fates. Each new death tore open the scars of all the others and let the pain flood back in. Clamping his jaws shut, he stared at the grave. Dinsmora stepped across the blood-stained ground and gave him a hug.

"I'm okay," he said, and patted her back.

They turned away from the cairns and mounted up, then rode south to the fieldstone wall. A hole was blown in it like before, destroying their new patch job and leaving fresh scorch marks on the shattered stones. Teleo shook his head at the power of the Stone Guardian. He slid his shepherd's crook from its strap and dismounted, gripping it tightly and glancing at Dinsmora. She held her crook aloft and gazed about, sniffing at the air. He climbed the pile of rubble and stepped through the gap to the other side, and the others followed. They scouted the terrain for the Stone Guardian's access point. The land was overgrown with bushes, brambles, and clumps of damp, rotting grass.

Dinsmora and Sonderson crept into the brush together while Cutter and the kids fanned out near Teleo, searching for boot prints or some sign of a human—hair, threads, refuse, anything.

"Tesserman," Dinsmora called to Teleo. "Come here."

He joined Sonderson and watched as Dinsmora crouched over a scraggly bush and ran her fingertips through the air next to it. The air shimmered silver and parted, as though a gossamer veil had been cut. A dark slit opened to reveal a brown patch of dirt behind it, then closed again. Dinsmora pulled at it again with both hands. Sonderson stuck his hands through the illusion, and together they pulled it back like a curtain until it rippled and dissolved. A dirt path appeared where before there had been none.

The kids and Cutter came up behind them, gawking at the newly exposed ground. They used their shepherd's crooks as walking sticks and scrambled along the dirt path, which climbed up the steep hill and wove back and forth between spiky bushes. When it met the cliff face, the path continued crosswise up the wall on a narrow ledge.

"Do you think the wolves came down this way?" Jessum asked.

"Could be," Teleo said. "Where are you going?" he asked Dinsmora, who slid her long shepherd's crook through her belt and with two hands pulled herself up onto the ledge. She began edging her way across the cliff face, chest facing the wall and hanging onto the rough rock with her fingertips. Teleo climbed up after her. "Stay here with the kids," he said to Sonderson, who scowled but stayed put.

"It widens out up here," Dinsmora called back to Teleo, and disappeared behind a small outcropping.

Behind the outcropping, the trail became easier to navigate, widening in a hidden crevasse of jagged rocks, dirt, and moss that ran up along the cliff face. He was able to face forward and climbed after Dinsmora, pulling himself up the steep step-like trail with his hands. They were hemmed in on either side by walls of blue argillite. Just when Teleo began wondering if they shouldn't turn around, they came to a small, dead-end platform where the outer spur of the cliff fell away, leaving them with a sweeping view of Falcon's Nest valley. Teleo peered over the edge. The drop from the stone shelf was long, and a cluster of gray fieldstones jutted up from the grass below to meet them should they fall. Across the platform, narrow steps that Teleo had not noticed before led up into another crevasse and disappeared in the shadows.

Standing on an upper step and looking down at them was a very old woman.

Teleo froze and held his breath. The Stone Guardian was small and compact, dressed in a boxy brown skirt and a long tunic of gray animal hide that blended into the rocks. Small metal beads sewn onto her tunic glinted softly. They could have been droplets of water, or light reflecting off the blue stone walls. She held a staff taller than she was, the twisted wooden shaft topped with a clear, tear-shaped crystal that glinted gray and yellow. Her steely eyes bored into his. A shiver ran up his spine, but he could not take his eyes off her.

Dinsmora grabbed his arm and pushed him firmly behind her, lifting her shepherd's crook. Teleo crouched at Dinsmora's back, feeling like a child. He stayed in her shadow, clutching his crook, and waited for a bolt of lightning to hit them. Embroidery was stitched neatly into Dinsmora's buckskin tunic. He had never noticed this design before—a series of gray, blue, and black chevrons that grew smaller and smaller as they followed their winding path. A sharp jab to his chest shifted his attention to Dinsmora's elbow, jarring him from his trance. He peeked over her shoulder through waves of auburn hair. The elderly Stone Guardian woman nimbly climbed the steps, her back to them. She lifted one gnarled hand as though in farewell, then disappeared into the rock in a transparent silhouette that faded like water soaking into sand, leaving behind a dark splotch and then nothing but rough, rock stairs.

Teleo stepped out from behind his cousin. He dared not speak but read her body language. She wanted to follow the woman and explore the trail, as did he, but his feet were heavy and would not move. A scraping and shuffling behind them startled Teleo, but it was only Cutter, squeezing up through the narrow chasm. The large, bearded man stepped onto the platform and gazed out over the valley from the strategic vantage point.

"Wow," he said. "I never knew this was here." He looked around at the ledge, which was barely big enough for the three of them. "This is it?" he asked. "It leads to nowhere?"

"We found a Stone Guardian," Teleo said excitedly, trying to lift his heavy legs. "An old woman. She disappeared up the path." Teleo gestured with his chin to the natural stone stairway.

"What path?" Cutter asked.

Teleo met his questioning gaze and then looked back at the ascending steps. They were gone. A solid rock face covered where the stairs had been, turning the platform into a dead end again. Teleo's legs broke free and he leaned dizzily against the rock face, then sat down heavily. Dinsmora went to the illusion of a wall and pressed her palm against it, then knelt down, feeling for an opening. She passed her crook to Teleo, pressed both hands to the wall, and closed her eyes. The rock shimmered for a moment, ripples of blue and silver radiating from her hand. She breathed heavily, exhaling loudly from her mouth with each outbreath. The rock solidified again, and she bowed her head in defeat. Her face was glistening with sweat.

"It's too strong for me. I need Sonderson's help."

"Let me try," Teleo said, having regained his equilibrium. He knelt next to her and ran a hand over the rock. It felt so real— cool and textured. He knocked on it. It was solid rock. He set the crooks down, pulled a hammer and chisel from his belt, and chipped off a flake.

"This is real," Teleo stated. "I know rock when I see it."

"It's an illusion. You saw the stairs yourself," Dinsmora said, pressing her hands to the rock again and closing her eyes.

Cutter cleared his throat. "Do you really think you should be messing with Stone Guardian magic right now?" Teleo glanced over his shoulder at Cutter, who was glancing nervously around the small platform. "We might get stuck up here," Cutter said. The big man turned, pushed his bulk through the narrow gap, and headed down the steps.

Teleo and Dinsmora locked eyes and then got to their feet and grabbed their shepherd's crooks. Teleo followed after Cutter, trying to control his racing pulse, and Dinsmora was close behind.

———————◆———————

Teleo, Dinsmora, Sonderson, and the kids kept watch at the base of the cleft while Cutter left to alert the queen.

"You didn't know that path was there?" Dinsmora asked Sonderson.

"We suspected something," the shepherd said. "Old maps showed a path, but we could never find it. The old folks used to tell stories of Stone Guardian raids coming off the rock wall, but we thought they were just trying to scare us. Then when the wolves started attacking the sheep, we started wondering again. A pack of wolves doesn't just show up out of nowhere. But we thought they had snuck in from the south or were living in a den in the woods."

"Are there other ways into the valley?" Teleo asked. "There could be hidden paths like this all over the place."

Sonderson poked at the dirt with the blunt end of his crook. "I hope not. There's only one other way into the valley, that we know of. It's down at the southern end. The cliff is tall but jagged there. Mountain goats can scale it, and men, but very slowly, and yer totally exposed on the rock face. We keep a contingent of archers at the southern fortress to guard it, and scouts patrol the top. Accessing the ridge from the other side is almost as treacherous. Haven't had much trouble there since I've been alive, aside from two bands of brigands who didn't survive the archers." His face twisted into a grimace. "I had to help cart away the bodies the last time."

Sonderson cast his gaze over Jessum and Kaspari. "You young'uns will have to serve down there, if you end up staying here, once yer ready to leave home, that is. Everybody has to serve at least two years as a guard, and everyone gets a rotation down there at the Southern Gap." Jessum and Kaspari exchanged glances and then looked at Teleo, who didn't respond one way or the other. Sonderson continued, "You'll be a fine archer by the time yer southern tour is up. There ain't nothing else to do down there besides practice yer archery and hang out with the other teenagers." He gave Jessum and Kaspari a half-smile, showing a glimpse of crooked teeth.

Sonderson wasn't such a bad sort, Teleo reckoned, once the mushroom wine wore off. The kids looked intrigued, but Teleo gave them a quick shake of his head. They were headed to the Sapphire Valley once spring broke, he had decided. Jessum deserved a shot at finding his people—and what if, like Teleo, Jessum's father was desperately searching for his lost son, hoping against hope that he still lived?

Just as importantly, Kaspari needed to flee further from the reaches of the Staggas, who were not likely to forget about the missing "prince." Once Gerik suspected that Teleo was behind Prince Kaspar's disappearance, he would be furious and redouble his efforts to root them out.

"What did the Stone Guardian look like?" the shepherd asked, interrupting Teleo's musings. One bushy white eyebrow quirked up. "You said it was a woman?"

"Yeah," Teleo said. "Your angel is an ancient crone."

Sonderson looked disappointed. "How ancient? It was years ago when I saw her. Maybe she's my age now?"

Teleo guessed Sonderson's age to be about fifty. "No, she looked about eighty, give or take a decade."

Sonderson looked like he had lost his best friend, and Teleo felt bad for ruining the man's fantasy. "She's powerful," Teleo said. "You don't want to cross her, I can assure you of that. I don't think our shepherd's crooks would do any good against the likes of her. She had her own staff, with a big crystal on top."

"That's probably what she uses to make her lightning," Dinsmora surmised.

"Where is your crook, girl?" Sonderson asked, turning to Kaspari.

"Lost it," Kaspari replied.

"Hmph," Sonderson grunted. "Lost it? How does one lose such a thing?"

She shrugged, frowning. "Dropped it in a river," she said, glancing at Dinsmora.

"She lost it in Rock River Gorge," Dinsmora said. "A bolt of Stone Guardian lightning hit it. Isn't that right, Kallie?"

Kaspari responded with a small nod of her head.

"It probably saved her life," Sonderson said. "But to lose such a tool, that's unfortunate." Kaspari's expression fell even further, and Teleo wished the nosy man would shut up.

Dinsmora asked Sonderson about the plant species in Falcon's Nest valley, and the conversation turned to more mundane things.

The sun was well past its zenith when a sharp neigh from Nutmeg was answered by a distant thundering of hooves, followed by Cutter and the queen surging over the rise. The queen cut a regal figure against the bright blue sky, with her gem-studded cloak casting tiny starbursts of green, blue, red, and gold. Her bronze helm shone like the sun itself, and a large plume of white ostrich feathers cascaded from its crown. Teleo lifted his hand to shield his eyes against a sudden flash as her bronze chestplate caught the light.

Accompanying her were her four white-haired guards and another dozen riders, male and female, wearing leather-and-bronze armor, shiny bronze helms, and holding aloft an assortment of staffs. The dozen guards rode small mountain horses, as did Cutter, but the queen and her four guards were on sleek Sapphire Empire steeds who, although not as large as Verdant Valley horses, were as fast, if not faster—and beautiful—pure white, with long wavy manes and tails that fluttered in the wind. The white-haired guards each wore velvet cloaks of forest green that billowed like banners from their broad, metal-clad shoulders. The queen and her entourage galloped down the slope and drew to a halt in a noisy flurry of snorts and jangles.

Queen Valona, Cutter, and the four Queen's Guards dismounted. "Tell me what you saw," the queen said, cutting to the chase while casting a brief, sympathetic glance at Kaspari's swollen face, followed by an icy glare at Sonderson.

They related the stories of the wolf attack, the ancient Stone Guardian, and her perplexing escape path.

The queen removed her feathered helm and tucked it under her arm. "Did she see you?" the queen asked Dinsmora.

Dinsmora hesitated. "Yes, I think so, at first. And she saw Tesserman, but then I pushed him behind me."

"But she didn't attack you? Then she left?"

"Yes, that is correct," Dinsmora said.

The queen was inspecting Dinsmora's cloak the way a crow looks at a bauble.

"Don't stare at it," Dinsmora said.

The queen continued to gaze at it, mesmerized, as did Cutter and three of her guards. The fourth guard was watching Queen Valona's face with concern. Dinsmora stepped forward and the fourth guard put his hand out to stop her, but she took his hand and moved it firmly aside with a stern glare and then took a final step towards the queen. Dinsmora gently lifted the queen's chin until her caramel-brown eyes broke away from the pattern and met Dinsmora's. "Don't stare at it," Dinsmora repeated gently.

"Oh," the queen said, taking Dinsmora's hand and holding it for moment before letting it drop. "I see." A smile quirked up her lips. "You will join our embroidery circle on the morrow."

Dinsmora nodded.

"Good, then," the queen said. "Take me to see this hidden pathway."

They showed her the entrance to the lower crevasse, which was as they had left it, and she climbed up with Teleo, Dinsmora, and her four guards. The queen was nimble and fit and wore her ornate cloak as though it were a simple shawl. The three of them squeezed onto the platform while the guards waited on the lower staircase. The blue rock wall was still in place where the Stone Guardian's escape path had been. They described how the upper stairway had looked and related every detail of the Stone Guardian woman that they could recall.

They descended the path, then the queen rattled off a short list of instructions. One of her Queen's Guards was to ride down to the Southern Gap and ask for volunteers to field a unit to guard the path day and night. In the meantime, she would consider whether she would ask the quarrymen to destroy the crevasse or if she would try to access the upper path and use it as another route in and out of the valley. Sonderson was to lend his aid to the guard unit and would be in charge of the barn and cellar, which they would turn into a guards' barracks.

Teleo, Dinsmora, and the kids would move into the Third Tower with the sheep and horses. They would move the next morning. The queen left one of her White Guards and a half-dozen of her riders with Sonderson at the base of the wall, then took off at a canter with her remaining guards.

The rest of them went back to the grave site. Dinsmora cleaned Benny's harness, knotted the severed traces, then hitched Cinnamon to the wagon and drove it back to Sheep's Haven while the others trailed behind her. Back at the upper barn, she offered to clean out the bloody wagon. Teleo gladly accepted her offer and went downstairs to cook dinner.

He made lentil stew and potato omelets, which were not half bad, if he did say so himself. After dinner, Cutter and Johnswold took food, blankets, and canvas tarping out to the guards at the wall, then returned to spend the night in the upper stable again.

The next morning, the brothers helped Teleo fashion a wooden crate from scrap wood, leaving gaps between the side boards and lining it with hay. Dinsmora coaxed Marblehead inside, and Teleo nailed the crate closed. Johnswold hitched Sonderson's wagon to his mountain horse, and they loaded the wagon bed with Marblehead, their personal belongings, and as much feed as would fit. Marblehead glared at them through the crate's slats, butting his forehead against the wood.

Teleo and his party saddled the horses, but they decided to leave BlackJack at Sheep's Haven and come the next day to check on him, in order to allow his haunch to heal. Jessum cross-tied the big black and suffered the horse's baleful look. The horse knew they were packing up to go and were leaving him behind.

Kaspari and Dinsmora went into the northern field to find the ewes. The sheep came when they were called and gathered around, expecting treats, and followed them out of the gate. Everyone mounted up and headed down the long dirt road, with Jessum on Cinnamon, Kaspari on Daisy, Teleo on Nutmeg, and Dinsmora sharing the wagon's driving bench with Johnswold, followed by Cutter on his mountain horse.

Pounding and a loud crash came from the barn behind them, followed by sharp neighs and more pounding. Teleo exchanged glances with Jessum. The two of them turned around and went into the barn. The warhorse strained at his ropes and kicked at the wooden hay manger with his front hooves, splintering the wood and littering his watering trough with hay and wood debris. An empty metal trough that had been left within reach of his rear hooves was turned over with a dent on its side.

"BlackJack!" Jessum scolded, standing beyond the reach of the angry horse.

BlackJack leered over his shoulder at him, ears back and showing the whites of his eyes.

"What has gotten into you?" Jessum asked.

The horse pulled against his restraints and pawed at the floor angrily.

"Are you afraid of being left here alone?" Jessum asked gently. "Maybe you're afraid more wolves will come?"

The horse snorted and pawed some more, throwing his head up and down and jerking back against his ropes, trying to break them.

"You are something else," Jessum said. "Hold still." His voice was commanding this time, and BlackJack looked at him from the corners of his eyes but stopped pawing the ground. "We wanted your stitches to heal, but this behavior will not do. Come here," Jessum said, and approached the horse along the wall near his head. "Don't bite me," he said firmly and loosened the knots on the wall bolts. BlackJack pulled away from the wall and pranced in a circle, snorting and blowing dust from his big nostrils. "What a baby," Jessum said, but his voice was kind. "Come."

BlackJack pawed at the ground again, then stepped slowly towards Jessum, his head lowered. Jessum stroked his mane and talked softly to him.

The boy harnessed and saddled the horse, put him on a short lead, and met Teleo outside. Teleo closed up the barn and they headed down the road again, with Jessum leading BlackJack on foot and Dinsmora riding Cinnamon. They kept their pace to a walk, for the sake of BlackJack and his injury, as well as the wagon carrying Marblehead. The big black favored his left hind leg, taking short, deliberate strides, but pressed stubbornly forward.

Teleo brought up the rear on Nutmeg. He missed Benny but chose not to be distracted by sorrow. Nutmeg was a powerful, energetic mount who had been raised with love—he would serve Teleo well.

It was a sunny morning with a sharp chill in the air that felt good as they walked. Villagers waved from their doorsteps. Kaspari and Jessum knew many of the teenagers by name, and some ran over and walked with them for a ways. Word had spread of the wolf attack, and Jessum and Kaspari told the story of their battle. They didn't have cause to embellish—the battle was gory enough and they had fought bravely. Kaspari had a shiny black eye and a swollen face, and Jessum said the wound on his arm was nothing—he had been hurt much worse before. When asked about the Stone Guardians, they glanced at Dinsmora and Teleo, then said there had been lightning and that they had found a hidden trail, but they hadn't seen anything else. Some adults caught up with them as well—the blacksmith and the harness maker, the brewer and the baker. Teleo told them the short version, promising to tell them more details at the Great Hall that evening over dinner.

In due time, they traversed the tunnel and arrived at the castle town, where they wended their way through the narrow streets. The Third Tower stood alone near an outer wall, unlike the other two towers, which were attached to the palace on the opposite side of town. The large tower was tall and cylindrical, constructed with huge white marble blocks shaped to appear as one monolithic chunk of perfectly carved rock. It was a master-piece—Stone Guardian craftsmanship that made Teleo jealous. He strived for such perfection, but the ancient stonemasons were in another league entirely. The pure simplicity of their work was stunning.

They dismounted and walked up to the imposing tower.

"It doesn't look haunted," Kaspari said, craning her neck to take in the full height of the tower.

A few small round windows with colorful leaded glass sparkled amidst the stark stone façade. The top bore the standard tooth-shaped ramparts. Carved under the overhang of each tooth was a large falcon's head with a curved beak and shiny black eyes, which gave Teleo the uncomfortable feeling that he was being watched.

"It *feels* like it's haunted," Teleo muttered.

Cutter pulled a large brass key from his pocket. "Here, let me see if this still works. No one's been inside this tower fer ages." Cutter fiddled with the key in the brass lock. It turned, and he pushed the large, heavy timber door open. It squealed on its hinges, and a breath of stale air escaped. They followed Cutter inside.

It was a spacious, round chamber. It did not look like a stable. Like at Sheep's Haven, a well was built into the bone-white marble floor at one edge, and a large fireplace dominated another section of the curved wall. The ceilings were high and slightly vaulted. On one side of the room was a double door, split horizontally so that the two tops could swing open. Four small round windows were set halfway up the walls, facing the cardinal directions. Their colored panes of glass let in rainbows of light, which lent a cheery feeling to the otherwise dreary, dusty chamber. An imposing wooden chair with ornate carvings of bats and griffins decorating the back and arms stood by the hearth, covered in dust. Other than a stone bench built into a wall near the fireplace, the chair was the only furniture. Metal brackets with ashen stubs of torches were set into the walls. Steel rings were driven into the stone—some at ankle height, others shoulder height, and still others were mounted further up at the perfect height for suspending someone by the hands or feet.

"What was this place?" Teleo asked. "A holding cell?" He imagined the unlucky captives chained to these walls, waiting for the queen's judgment before she lopped off their heads.

"It was an inquisitor's chamber. Back before my grandparents were born. In the days of Ismerelda the Terrible," Cutter said.

"No wonder the place is haunted," Dinsmora said. "It's probably crawling with tormented souls."

Teleo shivered. "Home sweet home."

Cutter chuckled. "Ay-yah. Better you than me."

They took a look around. Cobwebs were strung along the walls, mouse droppings littered the perimeter, and an old wasp nest was set into a window casing.

"I'll get you some brooms," Cutter said. "The animals will fit in here. You guys can sleep on the second floor. You can make up some straw beds," he said, leading them to a stone stairway that hugged the curve of the wall. "Don't go to the third floor, though. That's where the ghosts are."

"Wonderful," Teleo said wryly, following him and Dinsmora up the well-worn steps and running his hand along the rusted wrought iron banister. Cutter unlocked the second floor with the same key and pushed open the heavy wooden door. The second floor was the same as the first, but without the well, built-in bench, or steel rings. Another stairway climbed up the curve of the wall and terminated at a thick wooden door at the top. Two dusty wooden chairs faced each other in the center of the floor, and the large fireplace held a small mound of gray ashes.

There wasn't much else to see, so they went downstairs and out into the side yard, which was walled-in, with one large wooden gate at the end. It was a good-sized, rectangular yard—a perfect place for a Heliotrope, Teleo reflected, but alas, the ground was covered with the usual square, rough-hewn marble paving stones. The yard held an outhouse and a larger outbuilding where they could store the feed and firewood. In the center of the yard stood a circular, dry marble fountain with a large lower pool empty of water, a small upper basin, and topped with a carved rampant griffin clawing the air. The animals would be miserable in this enclosed stone yard after the wide-open fields and abundant grazing land of Sheep's Haven. Ah well, Teleo mused, it would snow soon anyway.

They led the animals into the yard through the gate, unloaded Marblehead but kept him in his crate, and let the horses and ewes explore their new yard. They nosed around for a time, before standing and looking at them.

"This is it," Teleo told them, spreading his arms wide, but the animals continued to gaze at them. "Sorry," he said.

They unloaded the wagon and unsaddled the horses, then Teleo and Cutter stole a sip of Ferska from Cutter's flask. It was like liquid fire and Teleo took a second swig. Cutter knelt and struck a flint down the blunt edge of a knife into a wisp of hay until it produced a flame. He lit a tobacco pipe, then stood up, stomping out the flame with his heel and puffing clouds of fragrant blue smoke into the air.

Johnswold left with the wagon and returned after a time with the wagon piled high with hay, straw, and burlap sacks filled with grain, as well as buckets, wooden hay racks, metal feeding and watering troughs, shovels, pitchforks, brooms, and feather dusters. He was followed by another wagon loaded with lumber.

While Dinsmora and Kaspari cleaned the upstairs and got settled in, Teleo, Jessum, and the brothers unloaded the lumber and woodworking tools into the ground floor chamber. There they built a sturdy stall for Marblehead near the well and another larger stall for the ewes across the room under the staircase. They fenced in a good portion of the remaining space for a shared pen for the horses, leaving the hearth, well, and the passageway between the two doors and the foot of the stairs open for the humans.

Dinsmora came downstairs to greet an attendant who arrived with a parade of teenaged assistants bearing water pitchers, basins, ladles, drinking mugs, linen towels, linen sheets, feather pillows, soft wool blankets of various colors, and large, fluffy featherbeds. She led them upstairs while another crew followed, bearing a crate of fresh torches, several lanterns, crocks of lantern oil, and a box of beeswax candles. Cutter's nephew returned with a wagonload of firewood. Another wagon arrived carrying a pinewood storage cabinet, a cedar chest of drawers with ornate brass pulls, a butcher's block, storage racks, a mahogany washstand with a marble top and mirror, and a bearskin rug for the second-floor hearth. The men lugged the heavy furniture upstairs. It seemed the queen was doing her best to make the haunted tower feel homey.

Yet another wagon arrived with cooking pots, wooden trenchers, and utensils, along with crocks, sacks, and crates of foodstuffs. Cutter told them they were welcome to dine every night at the Great Hall and were free to ask the cooks for anything they might need, and that they could purchase food and other essentials from the villages in Falcon's Nest and charge them to the queen's account. Teleo thanked the castellan and took in a deep breath, knots of tension unwinding in his neck and shoulders.

When the stalls and fencing were completed, they brought the animals inside, released Marblehead into his stall and the ewes into theirs, and led the horses into the open pen where they milled around for a time before lining up at the feeding racks.

Cutter and Johnswold left, and Cutter returned an hour later in clean, tan linen trousers tucked into polished black boots, a wine-red velvet doublet with puffy sleeves, and a ruffled white silk collar spilling over the jacket under a freshly combed beard.

"What in Stone Guardian's name are you wearing?" Teleo asked.

"I know," Cutter said, lifting his arms to show the fullness of his sleeves. "The queen made me. There's to be a ceremony tonight at the Great Hall. You must come to dinner."

"Uh-oh," Teleo said.

"Ay-yah," Cutter said. "Try to look nice."

"This is all I have," Teleo said, gesturing down at his leathers.

"You have linen pants and shirt," Dinsmora said.

Teleo frowned, feeling suddenly ashamed of his tradesman's clothing and tattered soldier's garb. But it was what he had. He hadn't anticipated attending a royal banquet.

They went upstairs and changed into their wrinkled linen clothing. The women wore their embroidered tunics, and Teleo and Jessum polished their boots. Teleo put his body armor aside. The leather cuirass was ratty, and the sigil plate was dented. He stood at the washstand, gazing into the mirror at his reflection. He had aged since the last time he had regarded himself in a mirror. His skin was leathery from being out on the trail, and his graying stubble was scruffy. He washed his face, shaved, and tried to comb his hair. It was still unruly, so he tied it back into a short ponytail. Jessum did the same with his long, dark locks. The boy was showing a shadow of facial hair. One day, Teleo would teach him how to sharpen a straight razor and shave it off.

Cutter came knocking at the downstairs door. He let himself in as Teleo and Jessum descended the stairs. The Queen's Lady was with Cutter. She came bearing silk brocade dresses, the luxurious fabric draped over her arms in a cascade of pale blue, dark purple, ivory, and gold. Teleo directed her upstairs where Dinsmora and Kaspari were fussing over their hair.

Cutter held up two velvet doublets, one in each hand. "Here," he said to Jessum. "This was my son's when he was about yer age."

It was forest-green velvet with gold piping. Jessum took the formal jacket and ran his fingers over the soft fabric.

Cutter handed the other to Teleo. "This one was mine but I outgrew it long ago," he said, patting his ample belly. "It should fit you, though. You need to tell me the secret of staying trim."

"Ride cross-country on a diet of dried mutton and water for a couple of weeks," Teleo said with a grin, accepting the doublet with a gracious nod. It was finely tailored, made of sapphire-blue velvet and black piping. Teleo slid it on over his shirt.

"It's yers if you want it. Sorry, but I don't have any more fancy shirts," Cutter said.

"No worries, ruffles don't suit me," Teleo said. He buttoned the jacket and stretched his arms. It fit well. "It's a fine garment, much obliged."

Cutter nodded deeply. They turned to Jessum, but he was gone and the back doors were cracked open. The green doublet lay on a pile of burlap sacks.

Teleo shook his head. "I'm sorry. Let me get him."

"Don't worry, I was a boy once. Let him be. I hope it fits him. My wife made it special—I would be happy if it came to some good use."

"Thank you for thinking of us. You're very kind," Teleo said, with a small bow.

"It's the least I can do," Cutter said. "I'll see you later."

Cutter left and Teleo took the green velvet jacket out back. Bands of gold and orange lit a cloud-streaked sky as daylight faded. Jessum was across the courtyard throwing pebbles at the wall.

"Here. Try this on," Teleo said, walking over to him. "It was rude to walk out on Cutter."

Jessum threw another pebble, ignoring Teleo.

"Jessum," Teleo said. "What's wrong?"

"I don't want to wear that." He threw another pebble. *Clink.*

"Why not?"

"I just don't." *Clink.*

Teleo sat on the edge of the griffin fountain and watched silently as Jessum gathered another handful of pebbles and continued throwing at his invisible target. It took another two handfuls of stones before Jessum said, "I don't want to look like them. I don't want to *be* like them."

Teleo let Jessum gather more pebbles before asking, "Like who?"

Clink. Clink. "Johan. And Bryce. And the others."

Teleo vaguely recognized the names as the young bullies at Verdant Castle. They liked to wander around in a pack, dressed in their noble finery, throwing rocks at dogs and causing other mischief.

"I don't blame you," Teleo said. "But wearing a piece of fabric doesn't make you who you are."

"Wearing rags gets your ass kicked." *CLINK.*

"Sit here with me," Teleo said gently. "Please."

Jessum stood for a long moment, then shuffled over to Teleo. His hair had fallen loose from its ponytail and covered his eyes. He sat stiffly next to Teleo.

"Cutter's dead wife made it for their son long ago," Teleo said. "From what I know of Cutter, I'd wager his son is a fine man. You could do worse than to wear his hand-me-downs. Looks like it was barely worn, actually. He probably hated it as much as you do." Teleo smiled, but Jessum's face remained stony as he stared at the ground in front of him.

Teleo tried a different tack. "Look," he said, smoothing the plush fabric. "It feels like it's cotton and silk. Made from a plant and worms. It has no power to make you kind or mean. If you had grown up with boys who loved you and who wore this kind of jacket, you would associate it with happiness."

Jessum turned a pebble over and over between his thumb and forefinger. "Who wants to wear worms? That's gross."

Teleo chuckled. "I can't argue with that." He kept his eyes on Jessum, but the boy avoided his gaze.

"I'd feel stupid wearing that," Jessum said under his breath. "I'm a Hill orphan. I can't pretend to be a nobleman."

Teleo ventured, "Maybe your parents were nobles."

"No," Jessum said flatly. "I grew up in a small village. We were peasants."

"You remember?"

"Yes. A little." Jessum pushed his overgrown bangs away from his face and glanced at Teleo.

Teleo did not have the heart to ask if he had watched his parents being killed. He put his arm around Jessum's shoulder. "I know it hurts."

They sat like that, side by side. The sky had deepened to a burnished copper on the horizon and a dusky purple overhead, and the air was already growing cold. A falcon called from the ramparts above, and they watched its silhouette float on an updraft and disappear behind the tower.

"I don't think Cutter is a nobleman," Teleo said, breaking their silence. "I think it's just a nice jacket for a ceremony the queen is throwing. For us, I think. For killing the wolves, or something. The mountain kingdoms are different from the valley kingdoms. People do what they want here."

"Then I don't want to wear it," Jessum muttered.

"I know," Teleo said, "but I'm afraid it would hurt Cutter's feelings. He might think you don't like it or that it doesn't fit. Sometimes it's important to think about other people before yourself."

"I can tell you're going to make me wear it, no matter what I want. I'm your slave boy." Jessum grabbed the jacket from Teleo's lap and stood up, pulling the sleeves roughly over his linen shirt and flinching as the fabric rubbed across his bandaged arm.

Teleo stood up and grasped Jessum's shoulder. "You are not a slave. You do not belong to me. You can do whatever you want. You're free and can leave right now if you want to."

"Where would I go?" Jessum's voice was taut.

"I'm sure someone in Falcon's Nest would take you in. The blacksmith likes you, you could apprentice with him. You're almost a grown man."

Jessum slowly buttoned the jacket, then looked up at Teleo. "Are you telling me to leave?" Jessum asked.

"No," Teleo's heart was full. Full of hurt, full of love. He wanted so badly for this boy to be happy, but he could not save him from his past. "Of course not," Teleo said. "Do you want to leave?"

"No." Tears glistened in Jessum's eyes as he spoke. "Why would I want to do something as stupid as that? You're the only person who's cared for me. You saved my life. You are the best man I have ever known."

Teleo held Jessum's eyes. "And you are a courageous young man. You make me proud." Teleo rested his hands on Jessum's shoulders and smiled gently. "All this over a silly jacket."

Jessum's expression softened. "It fits," he said, stretching his shoulders.

Teleo adjusted Jessum's collar. "It does. You look nice. Come on, let's find the girls."

15

GIFTS

Johnswold appeared at the tower, saying that he had been sent to watch the sheep while they went to the Great Hall. He smiled at the not-so-secret secret. They thanked him and left him sitting in the carved bat-and-griffin chair in front of a crackling fire with a flagon of hard cider.

Teleo walked with Dinsmora, who had been transformed into a noble lady by her new dress. The skirts were not as voluminous as was the fashion in Verdant Castle, but they were of fine Aldeon silk—light blue, bordered with a pattern of ivy leaves embroidered with metallic gold thread on an ivory background—with a tight bodice and big bell sleeves. Dinsmora wore her tunic over the dress for warmth. Teleo was impressed that the tunic's embroidery now perfectly matched the dress—blue and gold trailing vines and flowers. The two garments could have been a set. Subtle stitches of black and gray wove through the tunic's pattern, blending in with the shadows cast by flickering lanterns lining the road.

They approached the back of the Great Hall and headed around the large building. The street was abandoned, the cold night driving everyone indoors. Jessum and Kaspari walked behind them, and Teleo eavesdropped on their conversation.

"You like it?" Kaspari asked, rustling her skirts.

"It makes you look like a princess." His tone was not complimentary, and Teleo tensed up.

"I know," she said sheepishly. "I hate skirts. But this was the queen's when she was a girl. Look, it's actually pants—split skirts—so I can still ride."

"You're not going to ride around in that, are you?"

"No, but I could if I wanted. I prefer to dress as a boy. It's much easier. But this is comfortable, surprisingly. Better than I thought."

Teleo glanced behind him. Jessum was scowling, and Teleo suppressed the urge to take him by the collar and give him a stern shake.

Kaspari was resplendent in her aubergine gown, which was indeed fit for royalty. The pink and green embroidery of her tunic took on tones of spring violets and deep forest moss, beautiful against the purple silk brocade dress. Her hair was twisted on top of her head, and the pink and green ribbons he had bought for her were woven into her gleaming locks, curling down with tendrils of loose hair and artfully placed around her bruised and swollen face. Teleo caught Jessum's eyes and glared at him. Jessum shifted his gaze away and looked at the ground.

"I know," Kaspari continued. "I probably look ridiculous. I never got to dress up as a girl back home."

There was a momentary pause before Jessum replied, "No, you look nice. It's just ... all these fancy clothes, they remind me of home. Not my home, I mean. Your home. Verdant Castle. I didn't like it there very much."

"Oh. I'm sorry," she said.

"It's not your fault," he said gruffly.

"It is," she said. "Sort of. It was my uncle who stole you. Then he went back to the war and got killed. My parents should have taken care of you. I should have told my mother to."

"Your uncle?" Silence echoed off the paving stones. "Queen Eleanor's brother stole me."

"I know. My uncle Osborn. My mother's brother. He stole you but then he didn't take care of you. Well, he died, so he couldn't. My parents should have taken you in."

Teleo clamped his mouth shut, wanting to turn around to see their faces, but he kept walking forward as though he was not listening.

"Y-you're a ...? You're a ...?" Jessum stammered.

More heavy silence.

"Yes. You didn't know?" Kaspari asked.

Teleo felt as confused as the princess. It had never occurred to him that he had not told Jessum who Kaspari really was. Hadn't he? He tried to remember. Dinsmora was staring askance at him. He met his cousin's gaze and shrugged sheepishly as her eyes smoldered with the full import of their situation.

"No, I ... How would I have known?" Jessum asked. "I thought King Elke had three sons. He didn't have any daughters."

"Oh. Yeah, well," Kaspari said. "We didn't tell anybody I was a girl. We didn't want anybody to know. My mother said it was not safe for me. It was better they thought I was a boy. I'm Prince Kaspar."

A fraught silence hung in the air.

"Oh," Jessum said haltingly. "Well ... um ... I didn't know that. I'm sorry, Kaspari. Or, Kaspar? I mean ... um ... Your Highness?"

Kaspari broke out in a fit of giggles. "You don't have to call me that, silly." She laughed harder. "That sounds so funny when you say that. *Your Highness.* I'm Kaspari. Just Kaspari.

Or Kallie, to you. Don't tell anybody. Swear it." Her voice was suddenly grave.

"I swear," Jessum said.

"Swear upon your heart," she demanded.

"Upon my heart, I swear I won't tell anyone."

That seemed to satisfy her, for her voice lightened a touch. "Like I said. I should have told my mother to take care of you. I'm sorry."

"It's not your fault. You were just a kid. Like me. But the queen ... your mother ... gave me to Teleo. I mean ... let me apprentice with him. She saved me."

"Oh ... That's good, I guess," Kaspari said, her voice trailing off.

"Yes, it is," Jessum said. "I'm happy now."

Teleo kept pace with Dinsmora's steady steps, swallowing an upwelling of emotion.

They walked around the front corner of the large building, awkward silence filling the air.

"Now we're both orphans," Kaspari said, her voice resounding off the hard stones.

Their leather soles clicked on the marble walkway and Dinsmora's hand slid into the crook of Teleo's elbow. He drew in a deep breath and patted her hand.

They climbed the front stairs and the huge doors swung open, lantern light spilling out onto the portico.

"I was just coming to get you," Cutter said cheerfully. He spread open his big arms and ushered them inside.

———◆———

The Great Hall hummed with excitement, and almost everyone was dressed in some sort of finery, the various styles from many kingdoms creating a patchwork of colors. Apparently, whatever was going to happen tonight was a big deal and word had spread.

Teleo and his companions walked around the periphery of the crowded hall on their way to the cooking fires. The wooden tables and benches were already filled with families, castle staff, and city guards. Teleo could feel dozens of eyes following them.

They joined a short line at the bubbling cauldrons, where the old female cook hunched over the pot with a ladle. Those in line stepped aside to let them go first.

"No, no," Teleo said, standing to the side with Dinsmora and the teenagers. "No need. We're in no hurry."

Two female guards and a man with his wife and son smiled obsequiously and reformed the line. Teleo exchanged glances with Dinsmora as they grabbed wooden plates and bowls from the sideboard.

The old cook beamed and complimented them on their clothing as she served them chicken stew thick with onions, potatoes, and carrots. Next, they picked up a loaf of warm bread from a nook in the side wall of the stone oven and then took slices of goat meat from a steaming carcass, which had just been taken off the spit and laid out on the butcher's block. Stewed apples and raisins, dandelion roots and mustard greens, and slabs of butter filled their plates.

They found a small square table with straight-backed wooden chairs. They sat down, and Teleo accepted a mug of frothing ale from a serving boy. They were famished and ate without talking. Teleo was the most relaxed he'd been since leaving Dinsmora's. His worries about surviving the winter had melted away under the prospect of an easy job tending five sheep while being housed and fed inside the castle walls. They would be safe and comfortable for the winter, and secure in the heavily guarded Trillifort stronghold.

Tending the sheep had already proven to be a dangerous task, in fact. But fortune was a fickle master. He had learned throughout his life that what would normally be considered trouble could very well turn into a blessing, and vice versa. Having killed a few wolves, encountered a Stone Guardian witch, taken some injuries, and lost his dear Benny, they had more than earned their keep. *Queen Valona must really love her sheep,* Teleo mused, as he took a long draught of ale and recalled the shepherds referring to the queen as "odd."

They were just finishing a dessert of pastry stuffed with cherries when a flurry of activity drew everyone's attention to a side door. Queen Valona strode into the hall with her lady, her four Queen's Guards, and several lesser guards. They filed to the front of the room and everyone stood up, wooden chair legs scraping against the marble flooring. A hush settled over the chamber. The queen lifted her full, gold brocade skirts and climbed three steps onto the marble dais between the two center fireplaces, upon which stood a modest marble throne. She did not sit but gazed out over the crowd, her eyes landing on Teleo, Dinsmora, Kaspari, and Jessum.

The queen wore her sparkly cloak, and Teleo stared, fascinated by her shapely nose and winged eyebrows, which were white as the hair on her head. Her lips, too, were intriguing—red like cherries, as though she had eaten a pastry before coming out to the dais. The cloak cast shimmering reflections across her skin from hundreds of tiny gems decorating the luxurious satin fabric.

Dinsmora jabbed her elbow into his ribs. "Look at the floor," she hissed. She grabbed his chin and turned his head to face her, breaking his gaze away from the queen. She brought her lips close to his ear as though she were a wife with her husband. "We need to keep our wits about us," she whispered. "Do not look at her cloak. Keep your eyes on the floor in front of her."

He grunted his understanding and turned back to the dais, keeping his eyes glued to the marble steps.

Queen Valona's voice rang out. "I stated my intention to the mountains. I sent my falcons to spread the word. I buried the bones of my beloved sheep and cast jasmine petals upon their graves." The crowd was transfixed by the queen as her lilting mountain twang rose and fell in an even cadence. "I envisioned every night the future I wanted to create, and it hath come to pass, and more. Tonight, you stand in this hall with four great Mages, who brought four ewes to answer my call. All hail the Mages!"

A shout went up from the hall and echoed off the high, vaulted ceiling. *"All hail the Mages! All hail the Mages!"*

Everyone was looking at them and cheering. Teleo stole a glance at Dinsmora, trying to conceal his horror. Her face was like marble, with a stiff smile turning up her lips. Jessum and Kaspari were staring innocently at Queen Valona's bejeweled cloak and cheering along with the crowd. Teleo returned his attention to the throne, avoiding the glimmering aura of the flowing satin. The Queen's Lady had her eyes fastened on Teleo and Dinsmora, as though aware that they were not entranced by the queen's mantle. She nodded knowingly—of course Mages could resist the queen's charms, and a small grin spread across her face.

Teleo took a deep breath as the cheering subsided. *Mages.* Claiming his heritage was a death sentence in the valley kingdoms. He was no more a Mage than he was a king. Dinsmora, on the other hand ... she was accustomed to avoiding attention by sharing her peculiar skills only with her extended family and close friends, and dwelling in her secluded forest hideaway. Now he had brought her out into the open. He stood rigidly, feeling like a fox surrounded by baying hounds. The queen gestured at them to approach the dais. Dinsmora stepped out from behind her chair and rested her hand in the crook of Teleo's elbow. He gathered his composure and motioned for the teenagers to follow them to the front of the hall.

What was the likelihood of the queen beheading them for practicing magic? Sonderson had spoken openly of the magic wool of the sheep, but perhaps the queen intended to keep all magic for herself. But no, the queen wanted Dinsmora's help with her strange embroidery, and they were supposed to breed the sheep and take care of them over the winter. Teleo focused on calming himself as they faced Queen Valona and her attendants. He pulled Jessum into the shelter of his arm, and Dinsmora took Kaspari's hand and drew her close.

The queen motioned for the crowd to sit. When the hall had quieted down, she said, "We have been waiting fer you a long time." The queen's face glowed in the firelight. Teleo focused on her eyes, studiously avoiding the sparkling cloak. She smiled broadly at him. "Together, we will rekindle the ancient ways." Queen Valona bowed deeply.

Teleo glanced at Dinsmora, and the four of them awkwardly returned the bow.

"You have already rendered a great service to my humble queendom. In addition to bringing the ewes we need, you have saved the life of our one remaining ram, killed the wolf pack, and found the enemy's entry point. Please allow me to express my gratitude." She flicked her hand towards the side door, and four attendants strode across the floor, their arms filled with bundles wrapped in white linens. The four young men knelt in front of the queen, laid their bundles on the dais, and headed back to the doorway.

"Fer the young man who defended Marblehead," she said, gazing warmly at Jessum.

Teleo glanced at Jessum's startled expression, then looked around for Sonderson, surprised that he would miss the ceremony. Queen Valona's white-haired guards unwrapped the bundles. The first guard held up a long hauberk of fine quality chainmail. Jessum stared at it as the crowd applauded and murmured with approval. "This was my grandfather's," Queen Valona said. "He was a fierce warrior. Like you, he was descended from the Hill Tribes."

Teleo examined the queen's face and could see signs of Hill heritage. A slightly swarthy complexion, a flatter nose than the Verdant Valley people had, and a strong bone structure.

The guard held up the mail shirt for Jessum to try on. Jessum turned to Teleo, his wide eyes asking permission.

"Go ahead," Teleo said, smiling at the boy's excitement.

Jessum took off his green velvet doublet and Teleo held it while the guard helped Jessum slip the mail over his head and linen shirt. It fell to his knees, with a slit in the front and back. It was loose in the chest and fell all the way to his wrists, leaving room for the boy to grow, and would fit over his gambeson.

Jessum shook out his arms. "It's not too heavy," he said, glowing.

The guards opened more bundles and helped Jessum with the other pieces. First, they handed him a blood-red velvet brigandine. Teleo helped him put it on over the hauberk. The long, sleeveless brigandine fell to just below his hips and closed at the chest with black leather straps. Teleo had seen this type of armored doublet before, mostly worn by those with financial means. The velvet outer layer and pigskin lining hid many small steel plates between the two layers, which were riveted together with metal studs forming triangular patterns on the velvet face and pigskin lining.

The next piece was a black leather armor skirt that cinched at the waist under the brigandine and was fashioned with overlapping vertical panels that fell to his knees, backed with the same style of flexible plate armor and pigskin lining. Long, heavy leather gauntlets and steel-plate wrist cuffs etched with scrollwork protected his hands and forearms. Teleo helped strap steel-plate spaulders to his shoulders. It was a fine set of armor. Made for a king—one who intended to fight. Strong but lightweight. A black padded skullcap and chain mail coif covered his neck, and finally, a dome helmet of undecorated, hammered steel fit his head fairly well. Teleo nodded with approval at Jessum, who looked proud and embarrassed.

"I would give you the shield," the queen said, "but it hangs upon my wall. My grandfather never carried it anyway, said it weighed as much as a slab of marble."

The crowd chuckled and Teleo nodded. The old iron and wood shields were strong but impractical for anything but jousting. The last shield Teleo carried had been hacked at one too many times by a battle-axe. He preferred to wield a blade in each hand, anyway, or a two-handed longsword, and so had stopped carrying one altogether.

The final bundle was still on the ground. The queen herself bent to unwrap it. She pulled out a roll of red cloth and unfurled it. "This pennant was passed down to my grandfather from his grandfather before him, who received it from an heir to the ancient empire for his loyalty," she announced. "It bears the sigil of Bedon, the family that first united the Hill Tribes in what is now called the Sapphire Empire. They lost their rulers to sabotage and assassinations during the chaos of the wars between the Mages and the Stone Guardians, but their blood still flows among us. One day, the Bedon will rise again." The crowd cheered and servers threaded through the crowd distributing mugs of ale.

The Bedon emblem was a gold griffin rearing over a dead blue wolf whose black tongue lolled out of its fanged and bloodied mouth. Shivers ran up Teleo's spine and he exchanged glances with Dinsmora.

"The river flows," she whispered, and Teleo nodded.

The banner was long and swallow-tailed, with loops for a staff. Queen Valona handed it to Jessum, who looked overwhelmed. Teleo was not sure if Jessum realized he had just been given a valuable treasure, a relic of an empire long gone.

"It's a sign," the queen said, running her fingers over the embroidered wolf, and the crowd murmured in astonished agreement.

The guards helped Jessum roll up the pennant, then he clutched it to his chest and returned to Teleo's side.

The queen gestured to the door again and an attendant came forth, bearing another large bundle and a shepherd's crook. The queen took the crook and held it high. "Fer the brave young Mage who fought off Stone Guardian wolves and bears the scars to prove it." The crowd went wild, cheering and hooting and pounding mugs on the wooden tables. The queen waited for the cheering to subside and then continued, "The hook is made from the horn of the ram who fathered Marblehead. I understand you lost yer shepherd's crook in the Rock River Gorge, battling Stone Guardians. A true heroine." She handed Kaspari the crook.

Teleo had never seen Kaspari's eyes so bright, and he silently thanked Sonderson and the generous queen. The crowd was clapping, and some were singing the old song, *"Oh heroine of the light, may she shine forever."* But the show was not over yet. The queen pulled from the bundle a floor-length cloak of ivory silk, embroidered with garlands of stars and wheat ears. The embroidery was of gold and silver metallic thread and beaded with lustrous seed pearls that added a soft sheen to the cloak—similar in nature but of a different design than the queen's.

The crowd let out a long sigh of admiration as Queen Valona draped the mantle over Kaspari's shoulders and adjusted the large hood that hung down her back. Kaspari looked like a winter princess. If Gerik had known he was looking for a girl, and if word of the glorious stranger at Castle Trillifort got out, he would have found his quarry. Jessum stared at his foster sister as though seeing her for the first time.

Teleo hoped the queen was done—being the center of attention was the opposite of his purpose for selecting this secluded castle to retreat to—but she was not.

An older gentleman emerged from the side door. A large hooded gyrfalcon perched on his leather gauntlet. The falconer strode across the marble floor, and whispers of excitement rippled through the crowd. He stopped before Dinsmora, and the queen carefully removed the miniature molded leather hood from the bird's head. The gyrfalcon blinked and tilted its head. White chest feathers were speckled with black and gray, and its wing and tail feathers were darker. Its round black eyes were ringed with pale yellow, and the flesh above its gray, hooked beak was bright yellow.

Dinsmora's face lit up like a child's on New Year's morning. Teleo could not have thought of a more perfect gift for his cousin. The Queen's Lady took a bag from the attendant's shoulder and produced a green-and-black tasseled leather gauntlet, and Dinsmora pulled it on. With her gloved hand, Dinsmora reached into another sack the Queen's Lady opened for her and pulled out a small morsel of bloody flesh.

"Fer finding the Stone Guardian's hidden passageway," Queen Valona announced, bringing forth thunderous applause. The falconer moved his hand close to Dinsmora's. Dinsmora gave a short whistle, and the bird hopped onto her gauntleted wrist with a small spread of its wings and shifted its large yellow, taloned feet over onto her outstretched hand. The bird dipped its head and took the fresh meat from Dinsmora's fist and then tilted its head up and swallowed. Dinsmora gazed at the magnificent bird. It did not wear ankle bracelets or bells but perched comfortably and gazed at Dinsmora.

"We call her Hunter," Queen Valona said. "She will be yer loyal companion if you show her kindness and feed her properly."

"Thank you," Dinsmora said, inclining her head graciously to the queen and the falconer and then resting her eyes on the bird once again.

A commotion drew Teleo's attention to the side door. A tall woman with long black hair led a spirited white mare into the crowded, noisy hall. The horse pranced nervously and the crowd hushed. The groom held the mare's harness and quieted her with soft words and then led her to the dais. Teleo's heart pounded in his chest. The horse was pure white except for a charcoal-gray dusting on her muzzle and around her eyes and ears. Her finely sculpted face and high carried tail marked her as Sapphire Empire stock, the same as the queen and her four guards rode.

"I understand you lost yer horse to the wolves," Queen Valona said to Teleo. "I hope Star will help ease your sorrow. She is strong and swift—of the same bloodline as my own Zeta." Teleo gazed at the queen, speechless. She held his gaze, the corners of her eyes crinkling into a smile. "She is yers."

Teleo's heart surged with gratitude. The groom handed him the lead rope, and Teleo gently stroked the high, arched neck of the mare, overcome. Star was a spirited beauty, her eyes alert and intelligent. He had always found mares to be fierce fighters and fast friends. She was calm under his touch and lowered her muzzle to his palm where he stroked the velvety skin.

The queen lifted her arms and called out, "Hail to the Mages!"

"Hail to the Mages!" the crowd echoed, then broke out in song. Teleo found himself singing along to the old ballad, which he hadn't heard since he was a child.

When the Mages arise from the light of the dawn
The Guardians will hide in the stone
We kneel at the tombs of our fathers
We lay down wreaths and garlands
Let them not have died for naught
Let them not have died for naught
Let us shed blood and take heart
When the Mages arise from the light of the dawn
We pray it will be anon, oh, we pray it will be anon

When they left the hall with their royal gifts, the wind was howling in from the north, cold and biting, and clouds were racing across a half moon. Kaspari pulled up her hood and pulled the shimmering cloak around her. Jessum creaked in his armor, and Hunter had her hood on again, perched docilely on Dinsmora's gauntlet. Star walked at Teleo's shoulder, her hot breath forming clouds in the air.

They waved to Sonderson, who was heading the other way, his shepherd's cloak wrapped tightly around his wiry frame.

"Sonderson!" Dinsmora called out, her words taken by the wind.

The shepherd turned his head and walked briskly towards them, his head bowed against a strong gust and hands buried deep in his cloak's pockets.

"Where were you? Did you see the ceremony?" Dinsmora asked.

"I caught the end of it," he said, avoiding her eyes. "I was in the back."

"Are you walking all the way back to Sheep's Haven?" she asked.

"I have to. I've got the midnight shift. I'm goin'a be late already. Congratulations on yer rewards."

"Thank you. No reward for you? You protected Marblehead from the wolves as much as the others did and helped me reveal the hidden path," she said, furrowing her brow.

Sonderson gave her a sour smile. "Valona gave me back my home. That is my reward. Even if it is a barracks now."

"Well, it's too cold to walk all the way there," Dinsmora said.

Sonderson laughed. "I'll be fine. I do it all the time. This weather is nothing—wait until winter."

"I guess I'm just a valley girl," Dinsmora said, shivering and pulling her tunic closer with her free hand. "Why don't you borrow Nutmeg," she offered. "Until you can get a horse of your own. He thinks you're okay. He told me so."

"Oh, he did, did he?" Sonderson asked, a grin spreading across his face. "I think he's okay, too. That is very kind of you."

They went together to the Third Tower, where Dinsmora and Sonderson quickly brushed and saddled the big draft horse. They bid Nutmeg and Sonderson farewell, and Teleo settled Star into Nutmeg's spot against the curved stone wall, fetching her fresh straw, hay, and water. The falconer came knocking at the door, and Teleo went to the outbuilding with him and Dinsmora, holding up a lantern. The falconer covered the piles of straw, hay, and stacks of firewood with burlap sacking. He had brought a shoulder-high T-perch, which Teleo helped mount onto the center of the wooden floor with iron stakes and covered the flooring below with fresh straw. Dinsmora gently nudged the bird onto her perch.

"She should be happy in here," the falconer said. "She'll probably perch on the wood pile too, if you don't tether her. She likes to be outside during the day. She won't stray if you keep her fed."

He left and returned with a shallow ceramic tub, and they filled it with a couple of inches of water. He fussed over the bird and her equipment, showing Dinsmora the anklets and leashes, should she want to use them, and discussed Hunter's diet. Dinsmora told him she had raised a kestrel, a merlin, and an owl, and assured him that the bird would be well cared for. They removed the hood and left the bird to sleep in her new mews.

The falconer left, and Dinsmora and Kaspari went upstairs to change out of their finery. Downstairs, Jessum removed his layers of armor and Teleo helped him pull the chainmail hauberk up over his head.

"So I assume you'll be returning the queen's generous gifts, since you don't like fancy things?" Teleo teased.

Jessum pushed his hair back from his face and gave him a lopsided grin. "No. I'll keep them."

Teleo laughed. "I thought you might." He clapped the boy on the back. "The armor suits you."

"Thank you. The mare suits you. Sorry about Benny."

"Thank you. Everything dies. I'm glad for my years with him. Now I will get to know Star. She is a beauty."

Jessum nodded. "Speaking of beauty, Kaspari's cape is incredible, isn't it?"

"It is, but I wouldn't be surprised if that cape had a spell woven into it. You be careful not to stare at it, or soon you'll be wanting to marry your sister."

Jessum looked horrified. "A spell? Well ... even so, she's not my sister."

Teleo laughed. "Just be careful."

"Yes, sir," he said, and pulled off his boots. "She'd never marry me anyway. She's a princess and I'm a Hill orphan."

Teleo frowned. "That doesn't matter out here. We're in the mountains, where everyone is equal. But regardless," Teleo said, his tone hardening, "don't touch her. You guys are too young. You hear me?"

A deep blush stained Jessum's cheeks. "Yes, sir. I won't."

Jessum glanced up at him and said, "She is my sister, after all. It wouldn't be right."

Teleo rolled his eyes and gave a wry chuckle. "Just don't touch her. Not even a little bit."

"Yes, sir," Jessum repeated. "I won't, sir." Jessum turned his back to Teleo and stripped down to his shorts. The boy was filling out. Despite a disturbing array of scars across his back, including the sword wound Teleo had sewn up himself, the boy's skin was smooth, his shoulders were widening, and his muscles thickening. Soon he would be a full-grown man, just like Teleo's son, Oren, would have been. *Would be ... Is.* The familiar stabbing pain pierced Teleo's gut, and he went to his own corner to change out of his velvet doublet and linen pants.

After the women had changed into their sleeping gowns, Teleo and Jessum went upstairs in their linen shorts and put on their roughspun clothing. Two more wooden chairs had appeared, placed with the other two around a wooden table. An additional matched pair of large cushioned chairs upholstered with a green-and-gold brocade faced the fireplace, flanking the bearskin rug. A new sideboard was set against the wall, stocked with a fresh assortment of breads, fruits, cheeses, and dried meats, alongside a rack filled with blue-and-white porcelain dishes, glass goblets, and silverware.

"Where did all this come from?" Teleo asked.

Dinsmora shrugged.

"The queen," Teleo guessed, feeling terribly spoiled.

He fed the fire, then sat in one of the cushioned chairs. Dinsmora sat in the other, and the kids lay on their bellies next to each other on the bearskin rug, propped up on their elbows and staring into the flames.

"You know there's a good chance your cloak has magic woven into it, don't you?" Teleo asked Kaspari. She sat up and swiveled around to face him. The look on her face made him almost sorry he had told her. But she needed to know. "Yes," he assured her. "It will charm people and make them love you, if my hunch is correct. And that crook may have powers, too. Magic is outlawed in Verdant Valley, and Sapphire Valley, too," Teleo warned. "It is punishable by death."

Kaspari's expression hardened. "I'm not in the valleys." She looked fierce with her bruised face.

"Verdant Valley is your home," Teleo reminded her gently.

"Not anymore, it's not. I'm never going back there."

"Well, if you do, I don't want you to be punished, or killed, for something I've brought upon you."

Kaspari glowered at him, her black eye swollen and half-closed. "*You've* brought upon me? First of all, you didn't send the wolves. I earned that cloak and crook all by myself, fighting off three wolves with a sword, a crowbar, and a pickaxe. You helped me, and I'm forever grateful, but you didn't give me the cloak and crook—Queen Valona did. And if they are magic, then maybe they will protect me."

Teleo held his tongue, reminded by her tone that she had been raised by King Elke and Queen Eleanor—both headstrong in their own right. Kaspari's eyes flashed and Dinsmora stifled a grin as the young woman got to her feet and continued speaking.

"Second of all, you saved my life back at Verdant Castle. If anyone pushed me into the arms of magic, it was Gerik and his weasel of a father. My mother never liked that old man. She said my father was trapped by his charms. I didn't know what she meant then, but now I am beginning to understand." She took a breath.

"Thirdly, if I ever go back home, it will be as Queen of Verdant Valley. I don't see how that would ever come to pass, but if it did, I would make magic legal, like it was in the olden days."

The round tower room echoed with her words. She was not wearing her new cloak but she glowed with the mantle of authority. She was her mother's daughter—there was no doubt about that.

"And another thing," she said, her eyes still blazing. "Your shepherd's crooks are magic too, and you all have been carrying them this whole time. Now I have one for myself again, and I am happy. And that is all," she said, suddenly sounding like a young teenager again. She crossed her arms with a huff, turned back to the fire, and glared into the flames.

"Well. Huh-hum," Dinsmora said, clearing her throat. "With that, I think it's time we turned in. It's been a long day."

Dinsmora, Teleo, and Jessum began preparing for bed while Kaspari sat on the bearskin rug by herself, staring into the dying fire.

16

WINTER

The next morning at dawn, Teleo went to the outhouse and found Dinsmora already outside in the courtyard, bundled in her shearling coat and working with Hunter. She stood several paces from the outbuilding, facing the open doorway where Hunter sat on her T-perch. Dinsmora whistled and the bird swooped down with three quick flaps, glided to Dinsmora, landed on her gauntleted wrist with a flurry of feathers, and daintily plucked the piece of raw meat from her hand. After swallowing, the bird stared at Dinsmora, waiting for more. Dinsmora lifted her arm, launching Hunter into the air. The speckled white gyrfalcon returned to her perch in an effortless glide. Hunter was a large bird, her long, pointed wings spanning nearly four feet and flapping noiselessly. Dinsmora whistled, and Hunter flew to her hand again.

Teleo left them to their feeding ritual and went inside to tend the horses and sheep. Star was high-strung but gentle. She danced on her feet and strained against her tethers as he approached from the side, then she lowered her head for him to scratch her ears.

He mucked the soiled straw and cleaned up the ewes. After Dinsmora came inside, he let Marblehead out into the courtyard. The ram ambled across the stone yard, searching out stray bits of hay. Teleo peeked into the outbuilding-turned-mews. Hunter was on her perch. Teleo stepped slowly around her and gathered an armful of hay. The door was a split door, and Teleo closed the bottom half behind him, leaving the top half open so that Hunter could get out but Marblehead and the other animals could not get in and raid the grain stores. Teleo scattered his armload of hay around the yard. Marblehead nosed about, exploring and eating. Teleo went inside, opened the gate to the ewes' stall, and stood at the double stable doors, swinging the tops wide open to the crisp morning air. He opened a lower door and waited for the curious ewes to make their way outside. The first one squeezed past him and scampered out into the yard, and the others followed.

Marblehead bleated and trotted over to meet them. Teleo watched as Marblehead circled the group, sniffing them. The ewes sniffed him back, then didn't pay him much mind, preferring to eat. It wasn't long before Marblehead sidled up to one of the ewes and held a soft, grunting conversation with her, head-to-head. He pawed gently at the ground in front of her with one of his forelegs. It took less than five minutes for him to get her permission, nuzzle her flank, and mount her several times in quick little thrusts. She was mildly interested. When she'd had enough, she turned away and went back to eating hay. Teleo shook his head. If only it were that simple for men and women. He sighed and went inside to brew himself some coffee.

Dinsmora took Kaspari with her to embroider with the queen and her ladies. Teleo and Jessum spent the day grooming the horses and walking them around the small courtyard on a lead rope, coaxing Hunter onto their gloved fists with bits of raw meat, and taking turns napping. When Teleo went outside to clean up after the animals, Marblehead had herded his ewes into a corner and stood glaring at Teleo.

"Excuse me, Marblehead," Teleo said as he walked past to shovel up some horse droppings. He scooted a ewe out of the way and turned to see Marblehead lowering his head and backing up, getting ready to charge Teleo.

"Hey, whoa now," Teleo said, as the ram ran at him.

Teleo laughed and stepped to the side, grabbing the ram by a horn. They circled around each other. Teleo dropped the shovel and grabbed the other horn, flipped Marblehead onto his back, and straddled him. He held the ram's yellow eyes. "I'm bigger than you, Marblehead," Teleo said. "Don't try that again." Teleo shook the ram by the horns, then stood up. The ram got to his feet and sauntered away.

Teleo went upstairs to rouse Jessum. "I don't want that ornery old ram charging Kaspari," he said as Jessum rubbed sleep from his eyes. They spent the rest of the day getting lumber and carpentry tools from Cutter and building a fence to keep the sheep penned in the rear portion of the yard.

The next morning, they awoke to a dusting of snow. Dinsmora exercised Hunter and fed her every time the bird responded to her whistle and glided to her hand. Teleo quickly shaved, then prepared a breakfast of eggs and applewood-smoked bacon. The kids got up when they smelled the food. Afterwards, they tended the animals and let them outside, herding the sheep into their pen and giving the horses the rest of the snowy yard. The sun topped the jagged horizon and cast slanted, golden rays down on them, slowly turning the snow into slush puddles. Dinsmora left for the queen's embroidery circle with Kaspari, and Teleo and Jessum shoveled the slush into a corner and scattered straw around the wet yard.

When they were done, Teleo stood with his hands on his hips and considered another day of confinement. He examined the fine lines of Star, wanting to ride her. He sent Jessum to find the groom and get Star's tack. At least he could oil the leather and be ready for the next opportunity to steal away for a bit and get to know the white filly.

Jessum returned with a saddle, two saddle blankets, and two bridles. The tack was in pristine condition—there was nothing for Teleo to do.

They ate their midday meal in front of the upstairs fire—stale bread and a thick soup of peas, ham, onions, carrots, and potatoes—then spent some time practicing sword against staff, staff against staff, sword against sword. Then they groomed the horses, cleaned manure from the yard, and split some kindling. Jessum sat on a cross-section of a log by the ground-floor hearth and started a wood carving of a falcon, then went upstairs to take a nap. Teleo visited with Hunter, talked to the sheep, stoked the fire, and stared into the flames.

The next day, it was more of the same. And the next day. And the next. A week passed, and Teleo was starting to reevaluate their luck. Boredom could kill him faster than any blade. The boy was pleasant to spend time with and was a fast learner, but Teleo was already becoming claustrophobic from their confinement to the tower and courtyard. The queen had made it clear that the sheep were to be guarded at all times, and Teleo was starting to develop a distinct resentment towards the dumb creatures. His only respite was in the evenings after Dinsmora and Kaspari returned from their embroidery circle and took a shift watching the sheep while he and Jessum stole away for a few hours to dine at the Great Hall.

One day, Jessum left in search of Cutter with the excuse of asking where they might get more firewood, and he returned two hours later with Johnswold driving a wagonload of split wood. Teleo frowned. Even the joy of splitting wood had been taken from him.

"Johnswold said he'll watch the sheep for a while," Jessum said, "if we want to take a ride out to Falcon's Nest."

Teleo nearly fell to his knees with relief and shook the tall man's hand vigorously. "Bloody hell, I can't tell you how grateful I am. Remember to always be careful what you wish for," Teleo told Johnswold. "I wanted security for the winter, and I got it. This place feels like a prison."

"It was, as you can see. But it's a perfect place fer me to hide out from the queen," Johnswold said. "She won't come looking fer me in the haunted tower." He curled his waxed moustache tips and smiled.

"Great," Teleo said. "Come hide out here as often as you want. Here, let me make the place comfortable for you." Teleo placed a log on the downstairs fire and brought Johnswold a mug of hard cider. "What do you do for the queen?" Teleo asked.

Johnswold sat in the bat-and-griffin chair and rested his feet on the log that stood upright like a small table. He took a draught of cider and smacked his lips. "An endless assortment of random, trivial tasks. Ever since Cutter took the job of castellan, she thinks all his brothers came with the deal." He took a loud gulp of cider. "I'm the only one not married, aside from Cutter. We both lost our wives to the fever. I stupidly thought it would be nicer to live in the castle than on my little farm. Now I'm her errand boy. Very annoying. But every time I start to tell her I'm moving back home, she asks me to do just one more little thing, as though she's reading my mind. I get all soft and completely lose my resolve, and say, 'Okay, Queen Valona, if it pleases you.' She's very charming, that one."

Teleo didn't want to say it was her cloak. If Johnswold hadn't figured that out already, Teleo didn't feel it was his place to tell him about the queen's magic. "Uh-huh," Teleo said. "Maybe you're in love," he teased. She was a compelling woman, cloak or no cloak.

"Not. A. Chance," Johnswold said.

Teleo laughed out loud, tilting his face up towards the vaulted ceiling, which sent his laughter back at him.

They went back outside and helped Jessum unload the firewood and stack it in the shed, disturbing Hunter, who flapped lazily to the top of the griffin fountain and perched on the beast's gaping marble beak.

When the wagon was empty, Johnswold went inside to relax, and Teleo and Jessum fetched grooming brushes and headed into the courtyard to ready the horses. BlackJack's laceration was healing nicely and he was itching to get out of the yard as badly as Teleo was. Jessum saddled the big black, and Teleo saddled Star. It would be his first time riding her, and she seemed as ready as he was. Daisy and Cinnamon eyed them jealously, and Teleo decided to take them along on leads.

There had been a light snowfall overnight, but the skies had cleared. He mounted Star, and they walked through the snowy streets. In the circular, dead-end yard, Teleo greeted four guards who were taking a break in one of the lean-tos. They nodded in recognition and one of them opened the wall for them. Teleo patted Star's neck and talked to her softly. She danced lightly underneath him, ready to run.

"Whoa, there," he said, chuckling and working the reins to try and keep her still.

They removed Daisy's and Cinnamon's leads and walked single file into the tunnel. Teleo held Star to a trot through the silent passageway, hoofbeats echoing off the stone walls. They emerged onto the hilltop and picked their way down the slick paving stones to the slushy dirt road, which was quickly turning to mud in the midday sun. The two riderless horses trailed dutifully behind. When they got to the straightaway on the valley floor, Teleo brushed Star's flanks with the slightest touch of his heels, and she leapt into a full gallop. Teleo nearly lost his seat. He recovered and bent his head into the wind, enjoying the sleek beauty between his knees. BlackJack raced her, nose to nose, and the big draft horses thundered behind them, happy to finally be out in the open.

Star was the opposite of Benny. Benny had been bred from draft horse stock and Teleo had to coax him into a gallop. It had taken Benny a few lengths to feel his stride, but then he would barrel along like a wagon loaded with logs on a downward slope. He could trample over a man and not even notice. When Star ran, it felt as though her hooves barely touched the ground. She deftly dodged and leapt over clumps of dirt and slush puddles, which Benny would have plowed right through. Now Benny was gone. If Teleo weren't enjoying the wind whipping his face so much, he would have been sad. As it was, the mare was exhilarating and paced BlackJack, who rolled his eyes at the lightning-fast newcomer. Teleo glanced over his shoulder. The two draft horses ran side by side, in step as though they were a wagon team, their long manes and tails fanning out like banners.

They ran past fields dotted with patches of snow and arrived at Mud Flats, where they slowed to a trot and waved to the folks who stood in front of the market building enjoying the sunshine. The small village quickly transitioned to tidy homesteads, and they galloped again, then slowed to an easy, rolling canter, then a trot. They slowed to a walk through Bitter's Ford, then turned up the familiar road to Sheep's Haven. Nutmeg neighed from the north field and trotted to the fieldstone wall to greet them. A fine white mare followed after him. Several small mountain horses were clustered together under a leafless black oak and looked up to see if there were treats to be had.

Teleo and Jessum dismounted, removed their saddles and bridles, and put their horses out into the pasture. Nutmeg and Cinnamon trotted to one another and met heads, nuzzling each other, and the two white horses did the same. Daisy joined Nutmeg and Cinnamon. BlackJack trotted in a circle around them all, thinking himself a stallion managing his herd. Then the six horses headed over to join the mountain horses and began pawing at the slush and grazing.

Teleo and Jessum arranged their tack on top of the wall, then Teleo knocked at the thick wooden door, using a rusty piece of iron that hung by the door for that purpose. When there was no response, they let themselves in. Sonderson and four young guards were sitting around the table, eating stew while arguing and laughing loudly between spoonfuls.

"Why, you old goat," Sonderson said, rising from the bench and slapping Teleo on the shoulder. "And the young buck. Where's yer armor?"

Jessum blushed and nodded to the guards, two of whom were young women not much older than he was.

Sonderson dished them up bowls of stew, and they ate with the fire blazing warmly at their backs. The guards had seen no sign of the Stone Guardian crone, and her secret passageway that rose from the upper platform was still a smooth, impenetrable rock face. Sonderson made him describe their encounter for the guards. Teleo related the story of the old woman staring down at them from the steps and how the stone wall had suddenly appeared, blocking the path, and how he had chiseled off a flake. The guards exchanged skeptical glances. Teleo hardly believed it himself. Maybe the old woman had been the illusion and the stone wall was real.

"Look," Teleo said, as much to convince himself as the others. He dug into his pocket and pulled out the small shard of rock he had chipped off and carried around as though it were a good-luck talisman. It was the size of his thumbnail. He felt the sharp edges. It was real. He passed it around and they took turns examining it.

"Looks like a piece of rock to me," one of the male guards said with a snicker.

Teleo shrugged. "I don't know what to tell you," he said helplessly. "Maybe I made it up."

"You and Mora both?" Jessum asked.

Teleo shook his head. "I don't know," he repeated.

"You didn't make it up," Sonderson said. "At least not the part about seeing the Stone Guardian woman." He pulled out a small bit of leather and handed it to Teleo. "I found this snagged in the brambles on the side of the path."

It was a scrap of gray deer hide not much smaller than Teleo's palm. Metallic silver thread and seven hematite beads were sewn onto the soft leather in a spiral pattern. "It's hers," Teleo said, his fingers trembling. The hematite beads felt almost like they were buzzing. He did not like the way it felt—or the way it made him feel. He remembered the old woman's eyes boring into his, and he shivered. "Here," he said, handing the leather scrap back to Sonderson. "She's powerful."

"Ya think?" Sonderson asked sarcastically.

"The part about the magic wall must be real, too, then," Jessum said. "Remember how the Stone Guardians melted into the wall in Rock River Gorge?"

Teleo nodded thoughtfully, and Jessum related their adventure to the rapt guards.

As the afternoon waned, they gathered the horses and returned to the castle. Dinsmora was already at the tower, exercising Hunter and feeding her again, and Johnswold was gone.

"Where's Kaspari?" Teleo asked.

"Upstairs napping," Dinsmora said. "Her face hurts. I gave her some herbs to dull the pain. Maybe you can bring us some dinner from the hall again?"

"Sure," Teleo said, pulling off Star's saddle. "We visited Nutmeg. He was happy to see us."

"I'll bet he was," Dinsmora said. "Is he lonely?"

Teleo chuckled. "No. He's got a pretty white filly who follows him around and a bunch of mountain horses to keep him company. He's just fine."

"Oh, good," she said. "You finally rode Star? How is she?"

"Magnificent," he said.

Dinsmora smiled kindly, knowing that no horse could replace Benny. She gave him a hug. They parted, and she whistled for Hunter again, digging into the feed bag and holding out her hand. The falcon swooped from her perch and landed on her gauntlet, then lifted a small bird's leg from Dinsmora's hand and swallowed it whole.

"Yuck," Jessum said.

"Pheasant," Dinsmora said. "One of Queen Valona's falcons caught it this morning. I'm taking Hunter out with her tomorrow morning. She's going to show me the best hunting spots."

"Great," Teleo said, trying not to sound jealous. "I'll watch the sheep."

She laughed at the face he made.

The next morning before dawn, Teleo rose to find Dinsmora leading Cinnamon out of the courtyard with Hunter on her fist. Teleo wished her luck and closed the courtyard gate behind her.

Kaspari was still in bed, complaining of a headache, and Teleo let Jessum sleep in as well. Teleo fed the sheep and horses, then turned them out under a high, tin-gray cloud cover. The air hung heavy and motionless and smelled like snow. When Dinsmora returned late in the morning, bragging about a big hare Hunter had caught, snow had started falling. It continued all afternoon.

Dinsmora spent a few hours at the queen's sewing room and returned in time to go to the Great Hall with Kaspari. When they returned, Teleo and Jessum went over, ate their fill, and then spent the remainder of the evening talking with friends by the fires.

Teleo drank too many mugs of ale with Cutter, Johnswold, and two of their brothers, who were both skinny and quiet— the opposite of Cutter and Johnswold.

Jessum was at another fireplace, wedged between two young men on a bench at a table packed with boys and girls his age. Ripples of laughter floated over from the group of teenagers. Teleo's heart warmed that the mountain people had accepted his boy so readily. Many were of mixed blood, some with tawny Hill skin and black hair, and others displaying lighter, Verdant Valley coloring. One family was even of the dark, Far Shell Island tribes, and socialized easily with everyone else.

Jessum fit right in and looked happy. Teleo wondered if Jessum had ever had any friends at Verdant Castle, and grimly guessed that he had not. The Verdant City inhabitants always thought they were superior to everyone else and talked about the Hill Tribespeople as though they were stupid, dirty crim-inals. Teleo preferred the down-to-earth folks at Trillifort over the snobby citizens of Verdant City any day.

The snow had reached their shins by the time they trudged through the streets on their way to the Third Tower, bending their heads against icy jabs of tiny, falling flakes. Teleo thought of his shearling hat back at the tower somewhere as the snow blanketed his hair. The area in front of the Great Hall had been cleared, but the streets in the residential quarters had not. Teleo sank his boots into the fresh snow, and Jessum kicked it up in white plumes. They tried making snowballs, but they fell apart in clumps of dry powder when they threw them at one another.

The next morning, Teleo was awakened by scraping at the front door and went downstairs to see what all the noise was. He pulled the door open, and snow cascaded in a small avalanche inside the threshold. Johnswold held a wide shovel and grinned at Teleo. "Good morning, my good man." Snow sat an inch thick atop his hat and shoulders.

Teleo whistled in wonder at the banks of snow on either side of the narrow path, which Johnswold had shoveled to their door. The banks were nearly chest height, and snow was still falling in a thick white curtain, muffling the morning in an enchanted, cottony silence.

"You've been up since dawn?" Teleo asked.

"Nope. We started last night. Gotta keep ahead of it," Johnswold said, scraping the snow away from the doorway and patting down the banks with the flat of his shovel.

"Why didn't you get me?" Teleo asked.

"It was late by the time we stumbled outside. You had already left. I'll get shovels fer you and yer boy now, though, if you don't mind. Maybe we can hook up yer draft horses to one of the carts?" he suggested hopefully.

"Sure. Daisy can help, and I'll ask Mora about Cinnamon."

She agreed, and Teleo and Jessum spent the better part of the day with a team of men shoveling snow into a fleet of wagons. Daisy and Cinnamon each pulled a wagon and seemed to enjoy the work. When the wagons were full, they drove them to the top of the raised entrance road where a promenade spanned the base of the castle wall, and dumped the snow over the side into the deep quarry. The wagons had been built for that purpose, with a hoisting mechanism that tilted the beds to dump the snow over the walls.

At dusk, the entire crew left their wagons and shovels in the central square, and a new shift took over. Teleo and Jessum watered their horses at the fountain, which was now steaming with warm water mixed upstream from a hot spring.

The new crew was nearly all women, so Teleo and Jessum went to find Dinsmora, who had just finished feeding Hunter and was scraping the courtyard with a shovel.

"Cutter came by and helped me clear it all," she said, pushing a strand of red hair away from her ruddy face. "We piled it into a wagon." She gestured to the side gate.

Teleo described the castle's snow removal process. She agreed to take a shift and called for Kaspari to come downstairs. After a few minutes, Kaspari shuffled down the steps, looking like she had been napping again.

"The cold will make your face numb," Dinsmora told her. "It will feel good." The swelling had gone down, and Dinsmora had promised to remove the stitches soon. Kaspari's black eye had turned a mottled purple and green.

Kaspari nodded gloomily and put on her shearling coat, hat, boots, and mittens.

Dinsmora turned to Teleo. "If we still had Benny and Nutmeg, we could trade out the horses as well."

Teleo nodded. More horses were always better, in his opinion. They were useful for all sorts of things, not the least of which was friendship.

"As it is," she continued, "I'll work them for a few more hours and then bring them in."

True to her word, she brought the horses back three hours later, leaving them for Teleo and Jessum to rub down. Dinsmora and Kaspari took a short break, drank some hot tea, and then left again to join the shovel crews. Jessum went with them, and Teleo relaxed in the bat-and-griffin chair in front of the stable's fireplace. The chair had mysteriously acquired a large moss-green velvet pillow, and a proper footstool had appeared, its padded top embroidered with twining ivy and a gray hare peeking out from the foliage. Teleo leaned back, stretched out his legs, and dozed off.

He woke up when Jessum came in with a bowl of steaming hot stew and fresh bread for him from the Great Hall. The venison stew was thick and redolent with onions, potatoes, garlic, and rosemary. The boy left again, and Teleo ate in front of the fire. After midnight, his three haggard companions came back, and Teleo bundled up for another shift.

It snowed steadily for three days and nights. Had they not removed the snow as they had, the entire interior of the castle would have been one solid snow pack. When the snowfall finally ended, Johnswold volunteered to hide out in the tower and watch the sheep while the four of them took the horses for a ride out to Falcon's Nest.

The valley's roads had been cleared and were banked by towering snow walls, and mounds of snow dotted the fields. They rode out to Sheep's Haven to check on Sonderson and Nutmeg. Guards in the cellar directed them to the southern wall. They rode the two miles to the wall along the wagon road, which had been plowed along the entire stretch. Two guards met them at the breach in the fieldstone wall and led them through the gap that had been cleared for wagons to pass through.

Below the cliff, near where they had found the Stone Guardian's hidden trail, they came upon an open area of hard-packed snow bordered by tall mounds of snow. Two newly constructed, wooden lean-tos formed a right-angle to each other, and several young men and women were gathered around a campfire, seated on logs.

A figure rose to greet them. It was Sonderson, standing tall and strong. He strode over to them, exuding a grace and confidence Teleo had not noticed before. The effects of the mushroom wine addiction had worn off, and Sonderson glowed with good health. Teleo understood now how the man had once been a Queen's Guard.

They greeted one another with firm handshakes. Nutmeg whinnied from where he was staked with several shaggy mountain horses in a cleared area, and Cinnamon nickered in response. They led their horses over to the others and tied them to Nutmeg's stake. Nutmeg and Cinnamon touched noses and nuzzled one another's neck and shoulder, and Dinsmora fawned over Nutmeg, rubbing his cheek and talking to him.

Sonderson led them to the fire circle and introduced everyone. The guards—males and females of various ages—shifted over to make room for them on the logs. They all knew about the shepherd family by now, with their fine Verdant Valley horses and magic ewes, and how they had fought off the Stone Guardian's wolves and gained the favor of the queen.

Teleo accepted a mug of hot tea and warmed his feet by the fire as an icy wind whipped along the cliff face with a low moan.

"Are you planning to man this post all winter?" Teleo asked.

"No," Sonderson said. "Only until the witch's cliff trail is made impassable by snow and ice. One more storm like this one should do it."

"How many storms are there going to be?" Jessum asked. Teleo followed his gaze to the towering snowbanks.

"We only got six feet," Sonderson said, as though that were not very much.

Teleo traded glances with Jessum. Down in Verdant Valley, it was a rare year when they got a few inches of snow over the entire winter.

Sonderson laughed, reading their looks. "This is nothing. Just you wait. Last year we got over thirty feet."

"My goodness," Dinsmora said. "No wonder the mountain passes are closed during the winter."

They finished their tea, then mounted up and headed back. They stopped at Bitter's Ford for some supplies, visited the blacksmith, who was also a farrier, and arranged to bring the horses by to get them shod with new horseshoes for the snow and ice. They made one more stop at the pub in Mud Flats for a quick mug of ale before making their way to the Third Tower to let Johnswold go about the rest of his day.

* * *

Life settled into a predictable rhythm. Dinsmora spent early mornings hunting with her gyrfalcon, with Queen Valona and her hunting party, bringing back rabbits and grouse. Dinsmora related the location of the best hunting spots: the edges of fields and forests north of Sheep's Haven, or past Castle Trillifort's front gate in the fields bordering the pillar-lined approach road, or down by the stream beyond Trillifort Trail.

Teleo and the kids went with her one morning while Johnswold babysat the sheep and Queen Valona was busy with some other royal duty. They hiked out to the hunting grounds past Trillifort Trail. The snow in the forest was thick. Hard-packed deer and hunting trails wound between snow-laden trees and cut through open spaces. Dinsmora carried snowshoes, which she strapped on before tramping out to the first kill and taking the pheasant away before Hunter could devour it. The falcon caught another two pheasants that day.

On normal days, Dinsmora started the day hunting with Queen Valona, then afterwards, took Kaspari to the queen's embroidery circle. Teleo stayed with the sheep and trained Jessum out in the courtyard. The boy was getting better with a sword and was deadly with a stave. He used the shepherd's crook as his stave and perfected hooking Teleo's limbs or neck and pulling him in for the kill. The teenager was getting noticeably stronger. Hunter watched them spar from her favorite perch on the gaping beak of the stone griffin atop the dry fountain. Marblehead herded the ewes into the back corner away from the noisy humans or glared at Teleo to let them back inside if it was too cold out. The horses preferred to stay inside munching hay.

The women ate lunch with the queen and her ladies, then returned to the Third Tower. Most afternoons, Dinsmora trained the kids in archery and knife fighting and Teleo drilled Kaspari on sword fighting. Kaspari was already an expert archer, but Jessum had not practiced with a bow and arrow since he was a young child. He was quick with a knife, however. They herded the sheep inside and shot arrows across the length of the yard into bundled-straw targets, and Hunter followed the course of every arrow with her eyes, occasionally swooping down to inspect one embedded in a target, causing them to tether her to the perch inside the mews.

Some afternoons, weather permitting, Dinsmora would stay with the sheep while Teleo and the kids took the horses for a quick ride to Falcon's Nest. They returned at sunset when the air grew bitterly cold. Teleo and Dinsmora took turns taking the kids to dinner at the Great Hall and bringing food back for the one assigned to sheep duty, or they sometimes asked Johnswold to watch the animals so that they could go to the Great Hall as a "family."

One afternoon, pale blue skies turned soot gray and smelled of metal. Snow fell the next morning and did not stop for a week. This time, they got eight feet. Cinnamon and Daisy were called upon again. Finally, the skies cleared to a brilliant periwinkle blue, and the crisp air made Teleo glad to be alive.

Teleo went back to his daily routine of caring for the animals and sparring with the kids. The queen seriously expected that the sheep would never be left unattended, and Teleo started to share the opinion that Queen Valona was a little odd. Sonderson now lived alone in Sheep's Haven, the queen having judged that the deep snows would keep the Stone Guardian away for the winter. Sonderson had acquired a little mountain horse. The other mountain horses were gone, as was the white mare, so Dinsmora continued stabling Nutmeg at Sheep's Haven to keep the mountain horse company and to draw Sonderson's snow plow.

Snowstorms came at regular intervals, bringing out the castle's shoveling brigades. Then the snow would stop and the sun would come out, turning the white castle into a glittering winter fairyland, and life would resume as normal.

Dinsmora and Kaspari returned from embroidery early one afternoon, and Dinsmora sat with Teleo upstairs by the cooking fire while the kids shoveled the courtyard after a light snowfall.

"Have you looked for a Heliotrope in the palace's courtyards and gardens?" Teleo asked. "I know everything's mostly covered with snow these days, but the Heliotropes must be here somewhere."

"I've been in a couple of the queen's private yards," Dinsmora said, sipping on a large mug of tea, the steam rising in front of her hazel eyes. "But everything is paved with white marble. The queen doesn't have gardens, as far as I can tell. She seems to like stone. I did find out why she is so obsessed with the sheep, however."

"Oh, really? Do tell," Teleo said, folding his arms across his chest and leaning back in his chair.

"The wool protects against Stone Guardian magic, or so she thinks," Dinsmora said, a dimple marking her cheek.

"Ah," Teleo said. "So that's what Sonderson was hinting at. What makes her think that?"

"She said Trillifort troops raided Stone Guardian territory several years ago, and all her guards were killed except for the ones wearing cloaks lined with wool from her sheep."

Teleo pondered this for a moment. "Seems like a stretch. Could be coincidence."

"Maybe. She said they've proven it several times. So long as her guards are wearing the wool, they have been protected. She thinks that's why the Stone Guardians have been killing the sheep. The wool repels the Stone Guardian magic and makes it hard for them to defend their territory."

Teleo was skeptical. People loved to believe in magic and attribute normal things to some mystical force. But certain things he could not deny, like Dinsmora's hidden forest, or the blue net she had made with the shepherd's crooks, or the old Stone Guardian woman and her rock wall.

"That's interesting," he admitted. "Is it any wool or just wool from her sheep?"

"Just from her sheep, she says. But she suspects the sheep we brought are magic, too. They were with us when we safely crossed the gorge. Plus, the shearlings we were each carrying were from that same flock."

"I thought it was the crooks that protected us," Teleo said.

"Me too. They did protect us," Dinsmora said, furrowing her brow.

"Isn't most of your clothing a mix of linen and wool?" Teleo asked.

"It is. Some of my embroidery thread is wool too," Dinsmora

said, inspecting an embroidered leaf on her tunic. "From Aunt Bralla's sheep. So maybe ..."

"You think Bralla's sheep are magic?" Teleo asked. "She is descended from Mages, after all," Teleo said. "Hell, maybe all sheep are magic." His mouth curved up in a mocking smile.

"It does sound ridiculous," Dinsmora admitted. "Queen Valona is a little weird. Anyway, she said the cloak she gave Kaspari is lined with it. It was one of her old cloaks from when she was younger. She never wears it anymore, not since she made the one with the diamonds."

"Diamonds? Real diamonds? She made that herself?" Teleo asked.

"Yes," Dinsmora said. "She said there's a diamond mine in Stone Guardian territory. It's hidden, but she figured out how to access it. Half her crew got killed there. The ones wearing wool escaped. Anyway, you guessed it, she thinks they are magic diamonds. She behaved really strangely when she talked about the diamonds, ranting about how only she was allowed to wear the diamonds and that I shouldn't try to get any for myself. It scared Kaspari."

Teleo's hackles rose. He did not like anyone threatening Dinsmora or scaring Kaspari. "You shouldn't go back to her embroidery circle anymore," he said.

"It's fine," she said, waving it off. "We're half done with her cloak. It's very beautiful."

"Are you teaching her how to ... do whatever it is you do?" he asked, eyeing the stitching on her tunic, which was now muted whites and grays that blended in with the stone walls and shadows.

"Not really. It's hard to teach. Besides, I don't trust her completely. There's something off about her, even aside from that diamond rant. I can't pin it down exactly."

"For example?" Teleo asked, prying his gaze away from the tunic.

"I don't know," Dinsmora said, lifting her cup to her lips and blowing on the hot tea. She took a sip and then rested the mug on her knee and said, "Valona's eyes get all shifty when she talks about magic. She's desperate to be more powerful. As if she's not powerful enough already. I mean, she runs the whole place. She's the queen, after all. Everyone defers to her. But she's paranoid. She wants the cloak we're embroidering so that she can lurk around unseen and discover who's betraying her. And everything is about her. Even the gifts she gave us, she always mentions them as though we owe her something, even though they were supposed to be rewards for killing the wolves and finding the Stone Guardian's path. She has to be in charge all the time. Even when we're embroidering, she tries to tell me what to do, even though she doesn't know what she's talking about."

"How do you deal with that?" Teleo asked. "That would drive me nuts."

"Oh, I just smile and say, 'okay.' She just likes to be bossy. I wait until she gets distracted by something else and then I go ahead and do what I was going to do anyway. I can handle her."

"Okay," Teleo said reluctantly. "Just be careful. Maybe Kaspari should hang out here more."

"Yeah. Maybe," Dinsmora agreed. "Valona fawns all over her, and Kaspari follows her around like a puppy dog. I don't like it. Yesterday I caught Kaspari snapping at one of the serving women like Valona does."

Teleo scowled. "Keep her home. I can drill her and Jessum together instead of two separate sessions. That will save me time and energy."

"Deal," Dinsmora said.

Teleo clenched his jaw. If he was to raise Kaspari, he would raise her as he would have raised his own daughter, Abigail. He would do his best to make sure she was safe, strong, humble, kind, and honest. Princess or not, Kaspari would not grow up to be a spoiled brat—not if he could help it. Nor would she be subject to the whims of a crazy mountain queen. He gazed around the circular chamber, wondering what he had brought them all into.

17

THE CELLAR

The next day, Kaspari complained about not going to the embroidery circle, but she was happy to train with Jessum, and Jessum seemed glad to have her around. After they finished their sword and staff drills and a few rounds of sparring, the kids amused themselves feeding Hunter and carrying the large raptor around on their gloved fists while Teleo heated a big pot of water to wash their clothing. The cauldron hung in the lower fireplace on an iron hook that swiveled on a post over the flames. They were due for a trip to the hot springs, and he wanted clean clothes to change into afterwards.

Cutter had shown him the springs one day between snowfalls, situated in the rocky crags of Falcon's Nest near the tunnel gate. There were several stone pools to collect the water, which bubbled up and flowed down the rocky slabs in tiered waterfalls, spilling over the lips of natural stone pools and running down rock faces in glistening sheets, or arcing through the air in steaming spouts as though from massive teakettles.

There were pools for men, others for women, and mixed pools

for those who weren't shy. There were hot pools, as well as cold pools, which people plunged into after getting overheated, enjoying the drunken rush from the shock of the icy water. Some of the pools were covered by pitched roofs and surrounded by stone walls to protect against the weather. Several small stone huts were lined with fragrant wooden boards and served as saunas or dressing rooms. It was a weekly bathing ritual for the Trillifort and Falcon's Nest residents that went on year-round, even in the depths of winter.

Teleo tested the laundry water, swung the pot away from the fire, and submerged the first batch of clothes to soak.

The animals were outside in the courtyard, and the kids had come inside and were cleaning the stable area.

"Teleo," Jessum said. "Look at this." Jessum had swept away the straw and was poking at the stone floor. "Look at this gap. The stones are loose here."

Teleo went over and examined the slabs. Sure enough, unlike the rest of the floor, a small section of squares was not tight-fitting, and one stone had a notch in it. "Wait a minute," Teleo said, and went out to the storage shed. Hunter was on her T-perch and tilted her head at him. Teleo went to the far side of the cold mews, where shovels and rakes and other tools leaned against the wall or hung from hooks. He found a crowbar and returned to the tower.

He levered up the notched stone, and Jessum helped lift it and set it aside. Wooden floorboards were underneath. They took away five more stone squares and uncovered a trap door. Four handle grooves were carved into the wood, and they lifted the heavy cellar door and moved it aside. Cold, dank air wafted up at them. Jessum and Kaspari got on their hands and knees and gazed down into the black hole.

"I don't see a ladder or stairs, or anything," Kaspari said.

Teleo lit a torch, lay down on his chest, and lowered the torch into the void. He hung his head inside and looked around. It was a dirt pit. The floor of the pit was a good fifteen feet below ground level, surrounded by smooth stone walls. The dirt floor pitched gently downwards towards the center, then fell steeply into a cone buried in shadow.

"Ew, creepy," Kaspari said.

"Look," Jessum said, aghast. He pointed to the opposite wall. Teleo and Kaspari crawled around next to him.

The torchlight flickered orange in the stale air. Lying down on the dirt next to a wall were two skeletons. One was curled in a fetal position. The other was lying on its back with its bony fingers resting across its ribcage. Their skulls were still attached to their necks, and tufts of hair lay next to their skulls like clumps of dried feathers. There were no chains or ropes. No blankets or shreds of clothing clung to their bones. A metal cup lay next to one of them, and a wooden bucket sat on a small ledge nearby.

Shivers ran up Teleo's spine, and Jessum backed away from the hole. Teleo and Kaspari gaped at the human remains. It was Teleo's nightmare to be trapped in a dungeon and left to starve. He preferred a quick death. A sword to the heart. A slit throat. Losing his head would be fine—better than losing his mind. Teleo guessed that these poor souls weren't victims of Queen Valona, since she supposedly liked beheading those who crossed her. Maybe it had been her father's or grandfather's doing. It was impossible to determine the age of the skeletons, but since there was no flesh remaining and no fetid stench of rotting meat, their deaths had not been recent.

"What should we do?" Kaspari asked. "Should we bury them?"

"No. They're in their tomb," Teleo said. "Besides, I'm not going down there. We shouldn't touch them. They're not ours to worry about. We will seal them back up and forget about them."

"I will never forget about them," Kaspari said with a look of strangled horror. "That's why this place is haunted."

"Perhaps," Teleo said, pulling up the torch and getting to his feet. "Help me put this door back. Jessum, where did you go?"

The boy came in from the yard, slightly pale. They slid the wooden hatch into place, put the stones back where they had been, and kicked straw over top. Jessum and Kaspari wiped their hands on their fronts and hurried outside to groom the horses. Teleo washed his hands in the warm laundry water, then dunked a pair of his flax-and-wool pants into the cauldron, grabbed the bristle brush and bar of soap, and began scrubbing them—trying his best not to think about what rested down below.

———————◆———————

They tried to forget about the skeletons in the cellar and went on with their lives. Weeks crawled by and the snow built up in the quarry. Dinsmora went hunting with her falcon some mornings when there was no blizzard, and spent more and more time with the queen. Teleo passed his time with the kids and the animals and did his best to maintain a clean and cozy home in the haunted tower. Kaspari's face healed, and he hoped that in time the angry red scars would fade to fine white lines. She was not bothered by them but wore her scars proudly. She had fought off Stone Guardian wolves and bore their teeth marks like a badge of honor.

Kaspari found a pickaxe in the outbuilding, and Johnswold told her she could keep it, along with an iron crowbar that lay rusting in a corner. She polished them and wrapped the pickaxe handle in pigskin. Dinsmora helped her sew a leather sheath on each side of the rear of her saddle, and Kaspari began riding around with the pickaxe and crowbar at her hips and her sword and knife hanging from her waist belt. She kept her shepherd's crook in hand, with its butt-end set into a leather flag boot she had added to her stirrup. She also took to wearing the white mantle over her shearling coat. She was an imposing sight with her weapons on full display and her cloak flowing behind her as they galloped down Falcon's Nest Road.

One sunny afternoon, Dinsmora sent word that she would be spending the remainder of the day with the queen, and dining there. The next evening, she dined with the queen again, and the following evening as well. After a week of taking care of the animals and kids all by himself, Teleo asked Johnswold to babysit the sheep for the day, luring him with fresh currant cake, hard cider, and the prospect of a peaceful nap in front of the fire. Teleo left him with a dollop of fresh whipped cream and clove sugar for his cake, then he and the kids saddled the horses and left for Falcon's Nest.

Cinnamon ran free by Star's side, as had become the big bay's habit, knowing he was headed to visit Nutmeg. The roads were well-sanded and the horses were sure-footed. Enormous snow-banks had built up in the fields, and several children slid on wooden sleds down the mounds outside of Mud Flats, laughing and yelling, their voices chiming across the snow. Jessum and Kaspari eyed the sledders curiously, but Teleo hurried them along.

They got to Bitter's Ford and dismounted to visit with the villagers, many of whom were outside enjoying the sun. The blacksmith, Goff, asked if Jessum wanted to help him make an axe. Jessum turned to Teleo, who nodded his permission. Jessum grinned and went to the forge with the broad-shouldered man. Kaspari asked if she could spend the afternoon with two sisters who were around her age. Teleo chatted with the sisters' parents, the Spinners. They had all gotten to know each other at the Great Hall and at the hot springs, so Teleo let her go.

Teleo was suddenly free to spend a moment without another soul to worry about, so he went for a mug of ale at the *Scythe and Sickle.* He chatted with the bartender and three other men, then left with Star and Cinnamon to pay Sonderson a visit.

Teleo found Sonderson sitting in front of the open cellar door in the sunshine. He was leaning back in a wooden chair, smoking a pipe, and stood to greet Teleo. Blue smoke billowed around his head, smelling of fragrant mountain pine. Nutmeg's whinny came from the back, and Cinnamon replied. Teleo took the horses to join the big bay and Sonderson's mountain horse, who were outside on a plowed patch in front of the barn doors, standing in the sun. Cinnamon and Nutmeg whinnied and touched cheeks. Teleo went back out front, sat on an upside-down bucket, and gazed out over the snowy landscape.

"Where's Mora?" Sonderson asked. "With Valona again?"

"Always," Teleo said. "I hardly see her anymore. She's even started eating dinner with the queen in her chambers. She comes home late at night and leaves first thing in the morning. We can't even eat at the Great Hall unless I bribe Johnswold to watch the sheep."

Sonderson puffed on his pipe, rings of smoke drifting through the air. "Valona's got her hooks into her."

"Yeah, I guess," Teleo muttered.

"I wouldn't play that game," Sonderson said. "That's how I ended up out here. Valona has some sort of soft spot fer me, otherwise I would be gone, like the others." He made a slashing motion across his throat. "Yer wife needs to be careful."

"Why? What 'others?'" Teleo asked.

"Her last batch of White Guards," Sonderson said. "I'm the only one left. She was convinced the others were plotting to sneak off to the diamond mine behind her back, so, *thwack,* off with their heads. She keeps her father's axe and chopping block in her audience chamber just fer that purpose. So if you ever get invited there, be warned." Sonderson peered at him through the smoky haze. "I was her lover when that all went down, so she spared me. I guess. I don't know. That bitch is crazy." He puffed on his pipe and blew a smoke ring.

"What's really messed up," he continued, "is that they knelt and put their heads on the block of their own free will. 'Show your loyalty!' she told them, and they knelt. One by one. With her little minion guards all puffed up around her, swords in hand. They'd lick her boots if she asked. I was there watching the whole thing, cowering like a frightened child. I hate myself fer it."

Sonderson stared into the distance and Teleo held his tongue while the shepherd went on. "She hacked their heads off herself. Sometimes it took several blows. It was the most gruesome thing I've ever seen. The whole floor was a pool of blood by the end. She's got some fearsome magic, that one, and a heart of stone. Soon as I could, I contrived a lover's spat and convinced her that the sheep needed watching day and night. A good dose of mushroom wine cleared my head of her foul influence. Now, I stay as far away from her as I can."

Teleo couldn't find any words, so he gazed out over the fields to the stone fortress up on the hill in the distance, guarding the tunnel to Trillifort. It all began to make sense. The prickles on the nape of his neck whenever Dinsmora mentioned the queen. The glazed look when Dinsmora described the hunts or distractedly deposited Hunter on her T-perch before rushing off to attend to the queen again. The burning intensity when she had whispered to Teleo about Queen Valona's continued obsession with diamonds and how she had shown Dinsmora a diamond tiara in secret, but only for a moment before she hid it away again.

"What's so special about the diamonds?" Teleo asked Sonderson.

"Ah. What, indeed?" the shepherd replied, puffing on his pipe. "They inspire total love and devotion, far as I can tell.

Whoever gazes upon them long enough becomes hopelessly entranced. Valona hoards diamonds and wears her cloak all the time—it's covered in them. It's some sort of Stone Guardian magic. She mines them out of a cavern past Demon's Bones. I actually helped her find it. Her grandfather had told her about the cavern, and had a map, but he had never been able to find it himself. She and I searched fer it together fer years. We finally discovered the entrance hidden behind a magic shield, sort of like the path Mora found. The cave walls are covered with rough diamonds—feels like yer inside a geode. It's a bitch to chisel out. Harder than steel. Comes off in tiny chunks, usually. After we went into the diamond cave," Sonderson continued, "our hair turned white the very next morning. We go every year—or I used to, but not anymore. Her new guards must have gone with her the last trip, because their hair is already white. She'll trust them until she gets paranoid again, and then ..." Sonderson made a cutting motion across his neck.

The shepherd gazed at Teleo through the smoke, his bushy white eyebrows perched above somber blue eyes. Sonderson went on, his voice raspy. "A few years ago, the Stone Guardians ambushed us as we were making our way to the mine, and that's when we discovered that Trillifort sheep's wool defends against their magic. Everyone was killed except Valona, me, and her three other Queen's Guards. We were immune to their attacks somehow. She observed that all of us who survived were wearing cloaks lined with wool from her sheep."

Sonderson leaned back, balancing on the two rear legs of his chair. "You guys were all wearing wool from yer magic sheep when you escaped the Stone Guardians, too, I'd wager," Sonderson said, cocking an eyebrow at Teleo.

Teleo shrugged. "Yeah, I suppose the wool might have had something to do with it," he said, not bothering to mention that the shearlings from the shepherds' flock were rolled up on top of their saddlebags, and he stayed silent about Dinsmora's web of blue light. *Unless Aunt Bralla's sheep ...,* Teleo considered silently, recalling that they had all been wearing Dinsmora's gambesons of flax-and-wool weave.

"From bits of gossip I've been able to piece together," Sonderson said, gazing thoughtfully through the veil of smoke, "I suspect Valona hopes that with the embroidered cloak Mora is making fer her, the Stone Guardians will no longer be able to see her. Then she'll be able to go to the diamond mine alone and not reveal its location to anyone else. She can have it all to herself, like she wants." Sonderson's voice trailed off and he stared after the swirling smoke.

"But first she will kill anybody who knows where the cave is," Teleo finished, goosebumps rising on his arms. He met Sonderson's eyes.

Sonderson returned his sullen gaze. "I know. I need to leave here before it's too late. But it's my home." He gestured sadly across the fields. "I already lost all my sheep. And my lover. All I have left is this ramshackle farm."

"What about the seed pearls?" Teleo asked. "Are they magic too? Kaspari has some on the cloak the queen gave her."

Sonderson took a puff that produced no smoke and turned the pipe over, tapping out the dead ashes. "I think so," he said. "But not the same kind of magic. The pearls come from the Far Shell Islands. Frightfully expensive. I haven't figured out what they do, but they are not as strong as the diamonds. Valona got much crazier after she got hold of the diamonds and made herself that cloak. When she only wore seed pearl cloaks, she was charming and kind of untouchable—eccentric maybe, and demanding—but people didn't *die* fer her."

"So some people can resist the diamonds?" Teleo asked.

"Fer a time," Sonderson said. "The more yer exposed to them, the harder it is to resist. Mora is most assuredly enchanted by now. Although, people with their own magic are somewhat immune. Valona always gathers those people closest to her, and eventually turns them to her will. She's devious that way."

Teleo pondered Dinsmora's increasingly fervent devotion to the queen. The long hours she was spending at the palace. Her anxiousness to return to the queen's side and irritation whenever Teleo tried to get her to spend time with him and the kids. It was not like her. At first, Dinsmora had been the one warning Teleo about the queen—turning his eyes away from her cloak and sending Kaspari away from the embroidery circle. Now it was Teleo trying to get Dinsmora to use caution, only to be pushed aside with an edge of hostility.

He and Dinsmora may have fought some in their younger years, and Dinsmora was more stubborn than a goat, but she had never been hostile towards Teleo. His blood chilled as the full import of Sonderson's words sank in. Dinsmora may have been immune to Valona's powers at first, but no longer. Teleo had been witnessing Dinsmora's ensnarement with his own eyes but had not wanted to admit the full truth. His cousin was caught in the queen's web and was being wrapped tighter and tighter like a hapless fly. He swallowed, worried that his realization had come too late. What if he could not save Dinsmora and had to choose between her and protecting Kaspari? His jaws tightened as he considered the impossible choice. Dinsmora was an adult, and a smart one at that. Kaspari was young yet, and the only hope for the Verdant Valley Kingdom. He gazed glumly at Sonderson, feeling as though a fieldstone weighed heavily on his chest.

"I'm surprised Valona hasn't pulled you into her circle yet," Sonderson said, raising a bushy eyebrow.

"She wouldn't be interested in me. I'm not that powerful," Teleo said with a wry chuckle. "I don't know any magic."

Sonderson looked at him sideways. "Yeah, right."

"It's true," Teleo replied. He sometimes wished he understood the nature of things like Dinsmora did, but the only things he had mastered were sword and stone.

"You wield that shepherd's crook well enough," Sonderson said, his eyes glinting.

"That's the crook's magic, not mine."

Sonderson laughed out loud. "Okay, whatever you say, Mage Tesserman."

Teleo smiled, but his bones were cold with dread. "How does one get out of the queen's snare?" Teleo asked.

Sonderson laughed again and smoothed his moustaches. "Mushroom wine."

Teleo cracked a true smile. "No, seriously."

"I am serious. At least I suspect it's so. I was able to distance myself by leaving the castle and losing myself in the sheep fields and jugs of mushroom wine. When I snapped out of it, I was no longer under her spell. But I don't know fer sure. Maybe she just got sick of me and let me go. Most people only escape through death." He made the cutting motion across his throat again, and Teleo's smile vanished.

18

ℰNCHANTED

It was a cold, windy evening, and Teleo was upstairs with Kaspari, sitting at the table. Dinsmora was still with the queen, and Jessum had left to play cards with Cutter's and Johnswold's nephews. Teleo was oiling the horses' bridles, and Kaspari was drawing on smooth linen paper that Dinsmora had procured from the queen's scribe, along with a fountain pen carved from Trillifort marble and a small pot of Aldeon indigo ink.

"That's very good," Teleo said, leaning over to look at three horses and riders she was sketching. "Horses are hard to draw," he said.

"Master Wendell taught me how to draw," she said. Teleo watched as she carefully drew a bow in the hand of one of the riders.

"Who's that?" Teleo asked, pointing to the archer.

"That's me," she said, biting her lip as she drew the bowstring in a wide V shape and then sketched a straight arrow nocked at the gripping hand.

She detailed the arrow tip and fletching, then exhaled and looked up. "It's hard to draw in ink," she said. "I can't make any mistakes."

"That looks like a boy," Teleo commented.

"Yeah," she said. "That's me, at home. This is my brother Tristan, and this is my brother Severin." She pointed at two figures, then wiped at her nose with the back of her hand and met his eyes.

"I'll bet you miss them," Teleo said carefully, knowing that sometimes avoiding tender topics was more hurtful than facing them.

She nodded and lowered her eyes to the paper. "And this is my horse, Marigold. She's a golden palomino. Severin's horse was a blue roan, named Blade. And Tristan's was a black horse, like BlackJack, only smaller. His name was Spirit."

"Now I'm going to draw the pear tree," she announced, and turned to a fresh sheet of paper. She glanced up at him with a mischievous glint in her eyes. He grinned, and she leaned over her paper.

Teleo oiled the tack and watched as her sketch progressed. The tree slowly took form, filling the top of the page with individual leaves, large pears, and the trunk surrounded by bushes. He leaned in as she drew eyes peeking out from among the branches, and Teleo laughed out loud.

"I see you," he teased.

"How did you know I was there?" she asked, peering up at him.

"I could smell your mother's jasmine soap."

"Ugh!" she said, and they both laughed. "My mother always made me take baths."

He smiled as she drew a dragonfly hovering above the branches.

"Did you make those dragonfly and finch tiles?" Teleo asked. "Or was it your mother?"

"It was me," she exclaimed, feigning offense. "Well, she helped a little bit. She got the mortar from one of your bags on the terrace."

Teleo threw back his head and laughed. "She did? That little sneak. She was smart, your mother was."

"Yeah, she was," Kaspari said, her cheeks flushing, and Teleo hoped he hadn't made her sad.

"And strong," Teleo said gently. "And kind. And beautiful. Like her daughter."

Kaspari's face crumpled and a tear fell on the dragonfly, splotching the ink of a gossamer wing.

"Oh, no," she said, wiping at her cheeks. "Now look what I've done."

"I'm sorry," Teleo said, rushing to get her a towel to soak it up.

She patted at the ink spot. "The wing's still blurry, but not too bad," she said, tilting her head as she inspected her work.

"Why don't you draw some finches?" Teleo encouraged her.

She dipped her pen into the ink well and started on a small bird pecking at the border of the bushes. After she drew several birds, he watched in fascination as she began sketching the Heliotrope in a fair representation of the complex pattern. She worked her way from the edges inward and then drew the black rays and round center stone. She drew a slightly lopsided urn and glanced up. "I messed it up," she said, pursing her lips. She bent over the paper again and began filling in the urn with crosshatches, trying to correct its shape.

"Do you know what that circle is?" Teleo asked. "The pattern of the stones?"

Kaspari shrugged. "I don't know. It's just garden stones. It's pretty, though, isn't it?"

"Lovely," Teleo agreed.

"My mother used to say it was a dancing circle," Kaspari said, dipping her pen nib into the well.

Shivers ran up Teleo's spine. "She did?"

"Yes," Kaspari said. She finished the urn, then started filling in the pattern between the rays. "We used to dance around it sometimes, with Gwen and mother's other ladies. Gwen would move the urn away and someone would twirl on the center stone, then we would all try to push her off and steal the middle." Her eyes glistened with a fond smile. "It was fun," she said. "They let me win sometimes. The boys didn't join us because they said dancing was for girls, but sometimes they would play-fight with swords around the circle."

"I see," Teleo said, his skin prickling.

"Why?" Kaspari asked, narrowing her eyes at him. "I saw you swinging your sword and a broom that time. Were you play-fighting with swords, too?" she asked. "Or dancing?"

"Both," he said.

She gave him a quizzical look, and he held her gaze.

"It's an old game," he said.

She nodded slowly, then returned to her sketch.

◆

Teleo got up at first light, and Dinsmora was already out in the yard feeding Hunter.

"Aren't you going to take her hunting?" Teleo asked. "It's been over a week."

"I know. I've been so busy."

"Busy doing what?"

"We've been training Valona's juvenile falcons," Dinsmora said, whistling to Hunter.

Teleo examined his cousin's profile as the large bird landed on her gauntlet, snatched a morsel of bloody flesh from her grip, and flew back to its perch.

"We've hardly seen you lately, Dinsmora. You barely even say hello to Cinnamon anymore. Can't you take a day off and spend some time with me and the kids? We can go hunting in the morning, or go to Falcon's Nest and visit Sonderson and Nutmeg."

"Oh, I wish I could," she said, leaving Hunter untethered on her perch with the mews door propped open. Teleo followed Dinsmora into the stable. She pulled on her shearling coat. He blocked her way and glared at her. "Maybe tomorrow," she said, her gaze glancing across his eyes for a moment.

"Good," he said with finality. "We will go hunting with you tomorrow morning. You promised the kids you'd take them out with Hunter weeks ago."

"Okay," she said distractedly, walking around him, then left the tower, closing the door behind her. Teleo stared at the closed door. She hadn't even said goodbye.

◆

The next morning, Johnswold arrived before dawn, bleary-eyed.

"I owe you one," Teleo said, handing him a cup of hot tea.

Johnswold sat heavily in the bat-and-griffin chair in front of the fire. "You owe me more than one," he muttered. "No coffee?" he asked.

"All gone," Teleo said, wishing spring would arrive, and with it the market of itinerant traders.

Teleo had roused the kids, and they had already groomed and saddled the horses when the upstairs door creaked open and Dinsmora came downstairs.

"What are you all doing up so early?" she asked. "What are you doing here at the crack of dawn, Johnswold?"

"We're going hunting with you and Hunter," Teleo reminded her, glancing at Cinnamon, who stood patiently, already saddled and bridled.

He saw the flash of annoyance before she quickly masked it and smiled apologetically. "Oh, no. I'm so sorry, the queen needs me this morning. We are training her juveniles."

"You can train them later," Teleo said. "Queen Valona somehow managed without you all these years. Get your bird. Dawn only comes once."

"Tomorrow," she said, heading towards her shearling coat where it hung from a hook by the door. "I need to feed Hunter real quick and then get over to the falconry yard."

Teleo stood in her way. "You said today, and I am holding you to your word. The queen is not more important than your family." He glanced at Johnswold and then back at Dinsmora, raising one eyebrow, daring her to blow their cover.

Her lips thinned to a straight line and she stared daggers at him, his cheeks stinging as though struck with tiny barbs of ice.

"Get Hunter and get on your horse," he said in the iron tone he reserved for when he needed to send young soldiers into battle, knowing they might meet their deaths.

She gaped at him. It was not a tone he had ever used on her before. She blinked twice, then held out her hand for her coat. He took it from the hook and handed it to her, keeping his body between her and the front door. He folded his arms and watched as she left through the side door. He had locked the courtyard gate and held the only key in his pocket. The kids watched the power struggle with interest, and Johnswold fed the fire, pretending he wasn't listening.

Dinsmora returned with Hunter on her gauntlet and the

truculent expression of a five-year-old. "Let's go, then," she said, her eyes ablaze. "I need to stop by the palace and tell the queen I will be late."

Teleo bowed his head and opened his arms wide in mock submission.

She set Hunter on Cinnamon's saddle, clipped her snowshoes to the saddlebags, and then led the big bay out to the courtyard without another word.

Teleo rolled his eyes at Johnswold, who suppressed a smirk. "Women," Teleo said to him under his breath, then followed the kids and horses out the side door.

Dinsmora mounted Cinnamon, her head held high. Hunter hopped onto the shepherd's crook's handle, which Dinsmora had wound with rope for that purpose, setting the crook firmly in the leather flag boot she had strapped to her stirrup.

Teleo unlocked the gate, then he and the kids climbed onto their mounts in the frigid morning air, the horses puffing clouds from flared nostrils. They filed behind Dinsmora over the snowy streets to a gate Teleo had never been through. Dinsmora pulled a rope that set a cowbell clanging. A minute later, one of the female White Guards pulled the gate open. She ran her eyes over their hunting party and gestured for the four of them to enter.

It was a large stone yard situated behind the palace. Three T-perches were lined up at one end, and a young, pure white gyrfalcon sat on one of them, tethered with anklets and a long training line. The walled yard was another perfect location for a Heliotrope, Teleo considered, frowning at the white marble paving stones peeking out between stripes of shoveled snow and clumps of scattered sand. He was sure Dinsmora's map had shown two small Heliotrope symbols at Trillifort, unless the small floret icons were not indicators of Mage's circles, after all. Maybe Trillifort's Heliotropes had been covered with paving stones for some reason. He scanned the walls for a Focal Point but found no round window opening to the sky. Perhaps the high wall and window had been shorn off and the Heliotrope hidden when magic was outlawed.

The queen stood several paces away, wearing a leather gauntlet, and turned to greet them.

"I forgot I promised my husband and children," Dinsmora said, looking pointedly at Teleo, "that we would go hunting this morning. We shouldn't be long."

Queen Valona smiled graciously, splendid in her white cloak. Dozens of tiny diamonds caught the amber hues of sunrise like snow crystals. She beamed at Teleo, and he couldn't help but smile back at her.

"That's wonderful," the queen said. "No one is as gifted with animals as yer wife," she said. "I swear she can read their minds sometimes. It's uncanny."

"True," Teleo said, nodding.

"How is my Hunter? And my Star?" she asked, holding out her gauntleted hand for Hunter to hop onto, and then walked over to Star to scratch her ears. "Is my brave filly serving you well?" she asked Teleo.

"She's magnificent," he said, bowing his head. "Thank you."

"She is the full-blooded sister of my own Zeta."

"And a beauty at that," Teleo said. Star was indeed a royal steed. He dismounted so as not to be looking down at the queen, and felt a rush of warmth for the generous woman. Joy radiated off her like the pink and yellow morning light. Dinsmora was grinning at her as well, and Teleo understood why his cousin liked to spend time in her presence.

The queen turned her attention to the teenagers.

Kaspari was wearing her ivory cloak, and the queen praised her. "You look like a snow princess in that mantle."

Kaspari's face glowed and her eyes sparkled with gratitude.

"And you, my handsome young man. Where is yer armor? You should be wearing it to grow accustomed to its weight."

"Yes, ma'am," Jessum said, looking abashed. "I will next time."

"Before long, you and yer sister will be old enough to train to be Trill'fort Guards," she said, lifting her gauntleted hand to Dinsmora's crook. Hunter hopped from her hand onto the makeshift perch.

Jessum and Kaspari gazed at Teleo hopefully. He traded glances with Dinsmora and then found himself smiling at Queen Valona.

She smiled back. "It's settled, then. As soon as you turn fifteen, at the following Summer Solstice Festival you will be inducted into the Youth Guard. Tesserman, you must join us fer dinner tonight in my chambers. I will send Johnswold to guard my sheep so the children can dine at the Great Hall. Surely they are old enough to dine by themselves?"

Teleo nodded, realizing he was accepting her dinner invitation.

"I trust the ewes are pregnant?" she asked.

Teleo nodded again. "I imagine you will have four fine lambs come spring. Or perhaps there will be twins."

"Such great fortune you have brought to Trill'fort," she said, bathing them with her radiant smile.

Teleo bowed to the queen, then swung up into the saddle. They bid their farewells and left Trillifort through the front gate, then made their way over the raised road and out to the stream down the hill from Trillifort Trail. Coveys of grouse lived in the thick undergrowth bordering the stream, which was fed in part by the hot springs, keeping the water running clear of ice all winter. It did not take long for Hunter to dive at an unfortunate grouse who had ventured out into a clearing. Dinsmora tramped through the snow on her snowshoes, took the struggling bird from Hunter's talons, and broke its neck. She returned to the horses and tied the dead bird by its feet to the back of her saddle.

They caught three more grouse before returning to the castle. Dinsmora gave the birds to the queen's private cook for their dinner that evening. They all returned to the Third Tower together. Dinsmora fed Hunter strips of fresh meat from the leg of a grouse she had saved for that purpose, then left the gyrfalcon sitting on her griffin perch and rushed off to serve the queen.

The kids groomed the horses while Teleo invited Johnswold upstairs. They built up the fire and sat in the cushioned chairs, drinking hot tea and eating yesterday's stale bread, which they dipped into the fragrant fermented black tea flavored with cinnamon, cardamom, and honey.

"I can't help but love Queen Valona when I'm in her presence," Teleo confided.

"I know. That's why I try not to be in her presence," Johnswold said. "It's not natural."

"Mora spends every day with her," Teleo said, worry creeping into his voice.

"I noticed," Johnswold said, smoothing back his thick moustaches with a thumb and forefinger.

"She invited me to dine with her and Mora in her private chambers tonight," Teleo said.

Johnswold cocked an eyebrow. "Did you accept?"

"How could I refuse?" Teleo asked.

"I do it all the time," Johnswold said.

"She invites you, too?" Teleo asked.

"Yes. Every week, at least once. She's trying to recruit me and Cutter to be her next White Guards."

"What do you mean, 'her next?'"

Johnswold laughed. "We always joke that hanging out with Valona speeds up yer life. You age fast, get white hair, and die." He gave Teleo a broad smile that was anything but cheerful.

Teleo winced, dunked a heel of bread into his tea, and recalled the adoring look on Dinsmora's face when she gazed upon the queen.

◆

That evening, Teleo left the sheep and horses in Johnswold's care, dropped off Jessum and Kaspari at a table with a bunch of their friends at the Great Hall, and went to the palace. He waited outside in the cold at the front entrance. The pair of doors were twice the height of a man and were covered with sheets of bronze embossed with rampant griffins. Although he was dreading spending time with Queen Valona and afraid of succumbing to her charms, he was excited to finally gain access to the interior of the palace.

One of the tall doors swung open and Teleo stepped inside, welcomed by the Queen's Lady, Gracie. The foyer was white marble with high ceilings, cold and austere. A king's face stared down at him from an imposing oil painting on the wall, and a portrait of a white stallion adorned the facing wall. Hallways extended right and left, and before them stood a wide staircase. Gracie led him up the stairs, down a short hallway, and through heavy wooden doors into a dining room with a fire blazing on a large hearth.

Dinsmora rose from the table to greet him. The table was long and rectangular, with six carved wooden chairs on each side and one at each end. Dinsmora was the only one at the table. Gracie left through the door they had entered, and Teleo sat across from his cousin with his back to the door, and the fireplace to his left. Plates of pickled cucumbers and eggs sat in the middle of the table, untouched. Teleo took a small pickle and ate it, examining the large room. The floor was made of square, unpolished white marble tiles with nearly invisible seams. The table was heavy oak. Two large brass candelabras stood on the table, each flickering with a half-dozen tall tallow candles, and several oil lamps shone weakly in wall sconces, casting more shadow than light across the marble walls. A tapestry hung on the wall facing Teleo, depicting a hunt with several mounted archers chasing a buck through a forest. A smaller door stood closed at his right, near the foot of the table. There were no windows.

"Is this where you always eat?" he asked Dinsmora.

"For dinner. Other meals we eat in her private reception room or the sewing chamber."

"It's rather gloomy in here," Teleo muttered. Despite the bright candles and crackling fire, the room felt heavy and stuffy, as though the burdens of generations of rulers had soaked into the stone walls.

"You think so?" Dinsmora asked, lifting a delicate glass goblet of water to her lips.

The small door swung open and Queen Valona entered the room with a bustle of fabric and a nimbus of light shimmering from her diamond cloak. The long white cloak was tossed back over her shoulders, voluminous indigo-blue skirts reached to the floor, and a ruffled black silk blouse was fastened at her neck with a blue sapphire brooch. Her long white hair was twisted up into a large bun and studded with pearl pins. Her face lit up at the sight of Teleo, sending a surge of warmth through him. He and Dinsmora rose to their feet. He realized he was grinning at her like a fool, but he couldn't help himself.

"Ah, Tesserman, so good to see you. It was rude of me not to invite you sooner." She extended her hand to him.

He took it and kissed the back of it. Her hand was strong and her skin was smooth and cold as marble against his lips. She wore a large gold ring on her middle finger—a fox with red ruby eyes.

They waited for the queen to sit at the head of the table before sitting down again. The fire blazed behind her, sending shards of light from her bejeweled cloak as she settled into the large cushioned chair and beamed at them.

They spent the evening around the table, just the three of them. Servers quietly came and went, bringing roasted grouse and several dishes of heavily spiced vegetables that warmed his blood, and soft fresh bread still warm enough to melt chilled butter. They drank a sweet elderberry wine, which went to his head and made him laugh and tell stories of his youth. Dessert was thick egg custard topped with stewed plums in a sweet syrup. Before he knew it, the candles had burned down, and they were rising to leave. He bowed graciously to the queen, and Gracie escorted them out.

The wind hit them as they left through the bronze doors. The air was biting cold and a cloud cover obscured the stars. The fresh air cleared his head, and he realized he had no sense of how much time they had spent with the queen and had only a foggy recollection of what they had discussed.

He and Dinsmora trudged silently through the empty streets, many of the lanterns having guttered out, leaving long stretches of dark shadows. Remnants of snow had melted in the midday sun and were now sheets of black ice. He grabbed Dinsmora's elbow as she slipped, and they walked arm in arm back to their tower.

He went to the palace again for dinner the next evening. The evening after that, Dinsmora came to get him and stood by the tower door. "Are you ready?" she asked.

"No," he said. "I'm not going."

Johnswold was already there, squaring off with Jessum in the open area in front of the stable fireplace, with the bat-and-griffin chair and embroidered stool moved out of the way. Jessum held his shepherd's crook, and Johnswold held a normal staff. Kaspari was in the sheep pen, petting one of the ewes.

"What do you mean?" Dinsmora asked.

"I mean, I am not going with you. I'm going to eat at the Great Hall with the kids."

"What do you mean?" she repeated.

"I mean, I am not eating with the queen."

"Why not?" she asked.

"It's creepy, that's why," Teleo said, placing his hands on his hips and tilting his head, mimicking her pose. "I lose all sense of myself when I'm with her, and I don't like it."

Dinsmora's cheeks flushed. "That's nonsense." She dropped her hands from her hips and folded her arms across her chest.

"You, my dear woman, are thoroughly enchanted," Teleo said, folding his arms to mirror her.

"I am not." Dinsmora's face hardened, turning her normally cheerful dimples into angry gashes.

Teleo uncrossed his arms, then took his shepherd's crook from its hook and lunged at Johnswold, going at him two-on-one with Jessum.

"What will I tell the queen?" Dinsmora asked over the clacking of staves.

"You'll figure it out," he said, striking Johnswold's thigh. Teleo ducked and dodged as Johnswold's stave whizzed by at shoulder level. A gust of cold air was followed by a loud slam, and Dinsmora was gone.

The next morning, Dinsmora took them out again with Hunter. Kaspari wore her pearl cloak over her shearling, Jessum wore his chainmail hauberk under his shearling, and Dinsmora gave Teleo the silent treatment. They didn't catch anything. The sky was heavy with low black clouds, and the air smelled of snow.

Back at the tower while they were grooming the horses, Dinsmora said to Teleo, "The queen wants to see you today. She has a job for you."

Teleo scowled at her over Star's withers. "What kind of job?"

"She wants you to make her a mosaic."

"Who told her I make mosaics?" he snapped.

"You did. The other night."

Teleo clamped his jaws shut, and Johnswold said from across the room, "Don't worry, Tesserman, I can stay and watch the sheep." Johnswold cast him a jovial glance from where he sat in the bat-and-griffin chair, and Teleo returned a sneer, making the moustachioed man snicker.

Teleo walked with Dinsmora to the palace, and Gracie met them at the bronze doors. Dinsmora went off to the sewing chamber while Gracie led Teleo to a set of large double doors and left him with one of the male White Guards.

"The queen is waiting fer you," the thin-faced man said. He did not smile but held a door open for Teleo.

Teleo found himself in a cavernous hall with a high, wood-beamed ceiling. A fire blazed in a large hearth, but the hall was still frightfully cold and fog left his mouth with every breath. The queen was standing by a window with her back to Teleo, light framing her silhouette against the clear leaded glass and refracting into rainbows around her. She wore her diamond cloak, as usual. Teleo avoided looking directly at it and quickly scanned the room. He noted immediately that the stone floor was not a Heliotrope. Blue argillite alternated with white marble in a repetitive pattern of large diamond-shaped tiles. On the wall next to the fireplace hung a long-handled axe with a wide blade shaped like a meat cleaver. Nearby on the floor was a square knee-high wooden block. Several white marble floor tiles near the block were stained brown. He resisted putting his hand to his sword hilt and began plotting his escape should the queen grab the headsman's axe. There was only one guard outside the door. Easy.

Queen Valona turned to him with a broad smile. "Ah, Tesserman. I was sorry to hear you were feeling unwell last night. I trust yer feeling better?"

He forced a smile. "Yes, thank you for asking."

"The dead of winter always brings on a brief fever, does it not?" she asked. Light sparkled around her, and Teleo kept his eyes on the floor at her feet.

"It does," he said, wondering what other stories Dinsmora had told her. He cleared his throat and fumbled to fill the awkward silence. "I look forward to the long, warm days of summer."

"As do I," she said, her voice pleasant. Teleo lifted his eyes, meeting her piercing gaze, and then lowered his head again. The queen wore a heavy woolen sweater and simple riding leathers and boots under her sparkling cloak. He liked a woman who knew how to ride a horse.

"There's something I've been wanting fer a long time," Queen Valona said, striding across the room. "Finally, the mysterious weaving of life has brought me what I need. An artist. Not just a stoneworker—goodness knows we have more than enough quarrymen in this town—but someone who can give life to stone. That's what I'm seeking. I was afraid gifted stoneworkers had all been born Stone Guardians, but Mora assures me that you are such a one. A rare breed. A Mage Stone Master. I had heard some existed, far in the distant past."

Teleo felt a surge of pride. Did Dinsmora truly think so highly of his work? She had never seen the pear tree, which he considered the pinnacle of his artistic achievements. She had seen several smaller pieces, though—tiles he had sold at the market—plus a mosaic he had made for a wall inside their village community hall of a wheat field during harvest, which was second only to the pear tree, in his opinion.

"She says you specialize in mosaics of nature and animals. I have always wanted a gyrfalcon throne." She walked to a blue stone dais that dominated the room, and he followed her, their footsteps echoing in the cavernous chamber. An imposing white marble throne topped the blue dais. Teleo climbed onto the dais with the queen. The high-backed throne had been carved from a single block of marble and was elegant in its simplicity. He almost did not want to disrupt its stark lines.

"I want it here," she said, running her fingers over the broad, flat stone where her back would lean against were the throne small enough to lean back upon, which it wasn't. Any monarch, no matter how large, would need to sit upright on the oversized chair—either that or slouch horribly backwards or rest against mounds of cushions—or fold their legs up onto the seat like a child, which a monarch would never do.

"What color gyrfalcon do you envision?" he asked. "Is there a bird of yours you would model it after?"

"I want a black, gray, and white falcon, like my father's, similar in coloring to Mora's Hunter."

"I can do that," he said, hearing his mouth agree to the task before his mind had decided.

"Wonderful," she said, clasping her hands together.

"Do you imagine the falcon amongst the trees, or perched on a rocky mountaintop, or perhaps a snowy cliff?" he asked.

"Snow. Definitely snow," she said, her eyes bright with anticipation.

That was easy. White marble was in no short supply in this town, and much of the ubiquitous argillite was steel gray in color and would work nicely for the accent feathers and winter sky. "I will need a bit of black stone," he said. "Though pure black stone is often hard to come by."

"You may take yer pick from the stone collection at the masonry and use any of the tools in the mason's workshop."

Teleo smiled and nodded. He had poked his head inside the masonry a few times but had not had reason to purchase anything. From what he had seen, it stocked only the local marble and argillite. A dark blue argillite would work just as well as black, he mused as he measured the back of the throne with a length of cord he kept in his pocket. The queen hovered at the periphery of his vision, the diamonds on her cloak trying to draw his eye. He quelled the urge to gaze upon them, focusing instead on the throne.

He rushed out of there as soon as he was done measuring and headed directly to the masonry—a collection of large buildings close to the castle's front gate. He greeted the two brothers who ran the masonry and told them his business there. One of them led him past the slabs of local marble and blue argillite and into a back warehouse filled with a large assortment of granite and other igneous rock of various colors. The slabs were stored vertically in wooden racks, arranged by type and color. Teleo was mesmerized by the collection of rare and exotic specimens and looked through the slabs one by one. He noted several that would be good for the small tesserae that made up the outer circles of a Heliotrope. This collection rivaled that of the stone yards in the Guild Zone outside Verdant City.

"You have an impressive assortment here," Teleo said.

The man beamed at him proudly. "Thank you. My father and his father before him knew their rocks. While other families quarried marble, my grandfather got into trading. My father used to sit at the side of Southern Mountain Pass and flag down every wagon carting stone between Sapphire Empire and Verdant Valley. Collected stones from far and wide. Even the Far Shell Islands." The man's eyes crinkled at the edges as he smiled, and his hand rested lovingly on a slab of dark burgundy stone glittering with cinnamon-gold flecks. "This one here is Ruby Red Sparkle, from the Aldeon Coast."

They walked down the next row. Teleo stopped, frozen in front of a dusty rack. He rubbed at the grimy slab with his sleeve, then tilted the heavy slab back against the rear rack support and cleaned a bigger section. The black rock grew darker as he polished it.

"What did you find there?" the brother asked, peering at the stone. "Ah. Down in the Deep. That'll make the perfect black feathers fer yer gyrfalcon mosaic."

Teleo nodded, nearly dancing in his boots. It was the stone of the black central rays of a Heliotrope—the very stone he needed for the training yard in Verdant Castle, even though he would never get the opportunity to complete it.

"Where is this from?" Teleo asked. "The Far Shells?"

"No. This here's from a cave over yonder," the man said, gesturing southward. "It's under water. That's why it's so expensive. It's a bitch to quarry."

"I imagine so," Teleo said, rubbing another section clean and noting that it absorbed all light, reflecting a dark void back at him. "What is it?"

"It's argillite," the man said, shrugging. "Just an unusual variety that holds exceptionally strong when you carve it and gets blacker the more you polish it. Very unique."

Teleo nodded thoughtfully. He selected a slab, and they loaded it onto a cart. His heart tripped over itself when, at the end of the same row, he found a slab of white translucent stone. It shone up at him, the same material used for a Heliotrope's round center stone. "What is this? Where did this come from?" he asked, his blood singing.

"Right here at Trill'fort. It's marble from a vein right down where we dump the snow. It's gorgeous, isn't it? We call it Angel Wings. Can you use it fer the feathers?"

"Absolutely," Teleo said, polishing a section with his sleeve and gazing into it. He helped pull out the slab and transfer it to the cart. From the main room, Teleo selected several shades of blue and gray argillite and a few small slabs of opaque marble of pure white, ivory, and cream, and charged it all to the queen's account.

19

Dancing with Shadows

The mason's workshop was next to the warehouse in a large, well-lit building with multiple carving stations and an enviable collection of hammers, chisels, and saws. Teleo made several drawings of a falcon perched on an icy cliff. When he was satisfied with the design, he ran it by the queen. She asked him to adjust the angle of the bird's head from profile view to three-quarters, and she wanted partially open wings, so he started over. After three versions, she approved his design. He then began the meticulous work of measuring and cutting each stone feather and the contrasting flecks that gave gyrfalcons their distinctive mottled look.

He and Dinsmora and the kids adopted a new routine. Every other day, they started the morning with a pre-dawn hunt, weather permitting. Dinsmora left soon after to spend the day embroidering with the queen and her ladies. Alternate mornings, she trained the juvenile falcons or hunted with the queen while Teleo and the kids slept in until the animals complained down below. Teleo spent the remainder of the morning drilling the kids with their weaponry, tending to the chores, and preparing their midday meal. Dinsmora had long since stopped returning to the tower in the afternoons, sending a page at first to tell him she was dining with the queen and then eventually not even bothering to send word at all.

Johnswold showed up early afternoons to play shepherd, thereby avoiding queenly errands, and Teleo took the kids and horses to Bitter's Ford. There, Jessum helped Goff at the forge, and Kaspari and the horses, including Cinnamon, stayed with the Spinners. Teleo stocked up on food supplies at the local market, dropped off the foodstuffs and left Star at the tower, and then walked over to the mason's workshop.

Teleo arranged for Sonderson to accompany the kids back to the Great Hall and meet him there for dinner, which the shepherd agreed to do, grateful for the use of Nutmeg, but he refused to stay and eat. Kaspari reported that Sonderson usually showed up at Bitter's Ford mid-afternoon, left Nutmeg at the Spinners' to visit with Cinnamon, and waited at the *Scythe and Sickle* until Kaspari and Jessum were ready to head back to the castle.

Sundays, the castle market was still closed for the winter, and so people gathered at the hot springs to soak off a week's worth of sweat and grime, stave off the bone-chilling cold, and socialize. Teleo took the day off each week to partake in this ritual and spend time with the kids. Even Dinsmora stole a few hours away from the queen to join them.

After one particularly monstrous snowstorm, they never resumed their family hunts. They didn't need to hunt for their survival, and Teleo's desire to rise before dawn and brave the frozen forests had long since waned. The kids didn't ask about it and Dinsmora did not remind them, and so Teleo feigned sleep and let her creep off at first light to join the queen. Most days, she left Hunter and Cinnamon behind, and had somehow convinced Jessum and Kaspari to take turns feeding the gyrfalcon at dawn, so she didn't even need to do that anymore. Teleo assumed the queen had also tired of the frigid hunts, and he pictured the ladies gathered around a fire drinking tea and gossiping. He took it upon himself to feed the gyrfalcon at dusk, and Dinsmora didn't need to ask them to tend to Cinnamon, which of course they did. Dinsmora stayed away from daybreak until well past dinnertime, and often shuffled in after the rest of them had already gone to bed.

In late winter, their routine was disrupted five times in one week—once when a blizzard dumped several feet of snow in two days, and the other times when the lambs were born, including a pair of twins. There were four ewe lambs and one ram lamb. The queen herself came by to see the lambs, sweeping into the humble tower stable with a burst of light and personality, and then leaving ten minutes later, pale and complaining about ghosts.

◆

Teleo's attention was consumed by the mosaic. He was a perfectionist when it came to his work, but he stretched out the job because he liked being in the mason's shop and working with stone again, but even more than that, he was reluctant to step foot inside the palace and run into Queen Valona in her diamond cloak. He acted like a teenager with a crush whenever he was around her, and it made him feel stupid. But of greater concern, he did not want to get caught in her net and die an early death. Dinsmora was hopelessly trapped, and he dreamt up various schemes to free her, discarding one idea after another. The only solution was to leave Trillifort, and he was not looking forward to the battle with Dinsmora to drag her away from the queen. He was not at all sure who would win.

As he worked with the stone, he thought about the elusive Heliotropes. He considered asking the queen for a tour of the palace, with the excuse of looking at the stonework, but then he would have to spend time with her. Although the two Heliotropes at Verdant Castle were outdoors, he supposed that in a cold climate like this, they could just as well be indoors. He hinted vaguely to the masons about stone floors with patterns of stars and petals, but they didn't know of anything like that on the castle grounds.

One day, after cutting, chiseling, and grinding the tesserae for the falcon's feet from yellow alabaster, he left the shop when the sun was still well above the mountaintops. He relieved Johnswold from shepherd duty, and the big man left with a promise to return in a few hours so that Teleo could dine at the Great Hall. Teleo stood out in the back courtyard, rubbing the small of his back. He'd forgotten how sore he got from bending over a workbench.

Teleo puttered around, happy to have the place to himself for a short while. He swept the yard and carried wood inside for both fireplaces, then broke up the ice in Hunter's water tray and filled it with warm water from the cauldron. He visited with Star, combed out her mane and tale, cleaned her hooves, and gave her some grain. He then filled the sheep's feeding racks with hay, stepping aside as Marblehead and the ewes pushed past him to eat.

He watched the lambs frolic together in the open pen area, then yawned and stepped out into the yard where the air was crisp. The sun had just set, and he gazed up at the sky as it transitioned from golden apricot to a dusky lilac. The stone yard faded to muted grays, and Hunter was a silhouette on her griffin perch. It was time for her feeding.

A flit of shadow caught Teleo's eye, and a moment later, Hunter followed it towards the tower and disappeared from view. Teleo craned his neck, trying to get a view of the topmost section of the tower, backing towards the far courtyard wall for a better angle. The falcon was sitting in a round window set into the thick tower wall, high up on the third floor, looking inside. Teleo had never noticed before that the glass was missing from that window. Hunter flapped her wings and disappeared into the tower.

Teleo regarded the window and gathered his courage. How silly that he was too afraid to go to the top floor. He was a grown man and had faced worse than ghosts. Besides, they'd already found the skeletons in the cellar, which were most likely the basis for the ghost stories. He went inside and climbed to their sleeping chambers, lit a candle from the fire and set it in a brass candleholder, and then mounted the stone stairs leading up to the third floor. The heavy wooden door at the top of the staircase was locked. He fetched the tower key and tried the lock. After a bit of jiggling, the key turned with a raspy clunk, and he slowly pushed the door open. It creaked on its hinges and a gust of cold air escaped. He held his breath and stepped into the circular chamber.

The space was dimly lit by the disappearing daylight from four round windows, one of which was bare of glass and let in the outside air. The circular room was laid out like the second-floor chamber, with a large fireplace and not much else. The walls were rough-cut marble and the stone ceiling was slightly arched, like the two stories below. There was no furniture, save for an ash bucket and a wooden chest next to the fireplace, secured with a large padlock. Teleo set the candle on the mantelpiece, pulling away thick cobwebs, and looked around. Another stairway hugged the curved wall up to a hatch, which Teleo assumed opened to the roof. Several small brown bats hung from the ceiling and stared down at Teleo with beady eyes of obsidian black, reflecting glints of candlelight. Two of them dropped from the ceiling and swerved out the open window. Hunter was on the floor in the shadows, pulling the guts from another, unfortunate bat. Teleo watched with fascination as the falcon ate the remains whole, a webbed wing disappearing down her gaping yellow beak.

The floor.

Layered with years of dust and mounds of bat guano, it could not hide its secret from Teleo. He hurried to the center and brushed away the grime with his boot. His heart beat in his throat. A milky white marble shone up at him—a circular slab of Angel Wings. He brushed away the dust around the edges of the center stone. Long triangular rays of Down in the Deep extended outwards in a ten-pointed star. The round eastern-facing window was the windowless one—twilight-gray against the marble walls and larger than the other three. The Focal Point. He noted with appreciation how the window frame flared out to allow a circular ray of light to shine at various angles through the thick wall.

He ran downstairs for another candle and ran back upstairs to set it in a wall sconce, then hurried to the ground floor for a broom, shovel, mop, and water bucket. He swept the Heliotrope clean, then mopped it until the concentric rings of alternating star and petal tesserae came alive, released from years of disuse. It was perfect. Not one tessera was missing or even chipped. Blues and purples, tans and reds, stones from near and far came together in a perfect harmony of shape and color, rippling in expanding circles that swirled in a slowly spinning vortex.

Teleo tore himself away long enough to return the cleaning supplies and fetch his two swords, and then he danced.

Teleo oiled the third-floor door hinges and locking mechanism, then stuffed burlap sacking into the three recessed window frames to block any candlelight from revealing his secret. He left the Focal Point window as it was—it was higher up on the wall than the others and Teleo did not feel the need to fetch a ladder to reach it. The Third Tower and its private courtyard was perched on the promontory at the edge of the walled town, and the Focal Point faced east over the uninhabited hinterlands. Besides, the bats lived there and needed access to the open window to hunt, and he saw no reason to evict them.

A gust of air wafted upstairs through the open doors, and Marblehead's bellow was followed by Johnswold clomping into the ground floor of the tower. Teleo extinguished the candles, locked the door behind him, and crept downstairs to greet his friend, smiling innocently. They chatted briefly before Teleo bid him goodbye and hurried to the Great Hall, where he found Jessum and Kaspari at a table by themselves, already eating. He grabbed a plateful of food and a mug of ale from the servers and joined the kids at their table.

"Sorry I'm late," Teleo said breathlessly, taking a seat across from them. He could barely contain the excitement of his discovery but decided to keep it to himself for now. The two teenagers had each stepped foot on a Heliotrope themselves, many times, without realizing they were treading upon an ancient Mage's circle. Dinsmora would be as excited as Teleo to have found a Heliotrope, but she was under Queen Valona's spell. He did not trust his cousin enough to keep her mouth shut while under the queen's malign influence.

"How's the blacksmithing going?" he asked Jessum, who was shoveling stew into his mouth.

"Good," Jessum mumbled through his food. "I made myself a battle-axe."

"An axe?" Teleo said. "Wow."

"Yeah," Jessum said, swallowing. "Goff's teaching me how to fight with it."

"He is?" Teleo asked, happy that Jessum was happy. The Hill orphan was growing up. The lines of his face were hardening, and actual whiskers were growing back more stiffly where he had shaved his chin and upper lip.

Jessum nodded. "Goff set up wooden posts for me to hack at. But mostly he sends me out back to split firewood," he said sheepishly. "He says it will build battle muscles."

"He is right about that," Teleo said, appraising Jessum's shoulders, chest muscles, and upper arms, which were straining against his buckskin shirt. His hands were calloused, and his forearms and the backs of his hands were webbed with blood vessels from swinging a sword and staff in the mornings and a blacksmith's hammer and axe every afternoon.

"And what do you do all day with the Spinner girls?" Teleo asked Kaspari, who was spreading soft butter onto a thick slice of bread.

She turned her golden eyes to Teleo and smiled. "We practice archery and ride horses. Sometimes we ride and shoot at the same time. Yesterday I got a rabbit." She raised her chin proudly. "Their dad says I'm a natural."

Teleo returned her smile. He was thankful for the kind people in Bitter's Ford taking the time to raise the teenagers while Teleo and Dinsmora were busy with their projects for the queen. It was a good community in which to raise children, except for the constant specter of Stone Guardian attacks and the stories of Queen Valona's deadly temper. His plan had always been to spend the winter there and then move on to the Sapphire Valley, far from the politics and intrigue of Verdant Valley. Already, buds were forming at the tips of branches, and water carved channels through the muddy roads of Falcon's Nest as the mounds of snow melted.

Even if Teleo were not convinced Gerik would find his way to Trillifort sooner or later in search of the missing Verdant Valley heir, he did not want to grow too comfortable under the rule of Queen Valona and her unpredictable ways. He was anxious to distance himself and his charges from her. Teleo sipped at his ale and recalled the other morning when he had confronted Dinsmora again.

He had blocked her way at the Third Tower's door as she went to leave, crossing his arms and leaning back against the heavy timber.

She faced him, her hands on her hips. "What now?" she asked.

"I think you are under the queen's spell," he said.

Her moss-green eyes rolled towards the ceiling.

"You're so hypnotized, you don't even see it," he said.

She huffed out an impatient breath. "You're the one who's delusional, Teleo Stonemason."

"No, Dinsmora," he said, reaching out to touch her shoulder, but she drew away. "I'm worried about you," he said.

"You're jealous," she replied, her lips pinching together as she pulled her canvas sack onto her shoulder.

He chuckled sardonically. "Jealous?"

"Yes. Jealous. Now if you don't mind, I'm already late."

"I don't think you should spend time with her anymore," he said, standing his ground. "Finish her cloak if you must, but tell her you can't spend time at the palace any longer. Finish the cloak here at the tower. Tell her your husband demands you stay at home."

Dinsmora's face flushed and she pointed a finger at him. A sharp jab seared through his cheek, though she had not touched him. He did not flinch, refusing to give her the satisfaction of her petty magic tricks. "Now you look here, cousin," she said. "I am not your wife, and I answer to no one. Now step aside."

He held her angry glare. Her hand darted out and twisted his ear, dragging him away from the door as though he were a child. She always had been adept at finding points on the body that caused pain. He could have easily immobilized her, but he did not want to humiliate or hurt her.

"Don't say I didn't warn you," he called after her as a rush of cold air hit him in the face. She marched down the stone path without looking back.

"More ale, Mister Tesserman?"

A serving woman was standing over him with two frothing mugs.

He took a mug with a grateful nod and regarded the kids sitting across the table from him. Jessum shoveled a last heaping spoonful of stew into his mouth and started wiping his trencher with a hunk of bread, and Kaspari was pushing cooked carrots to the side of her otherwise empty bowl. Teleo blew at the cap of foam and took a draught of the bittersweet brew.

"You know we have to leave here soon," Teleo said, wiping at his mouth.

Their faces fell and Jessum stopped chewing. Teleo suddenly wished he had chosen a different time to raise the topic.

"Nooo," Jessum said plaintively.

"Nooo," Kaspari echoed. "I don't want to leave."

"Me neither," Jessum said. "Why do we have to go?"

Teleo sighed. "It's time to move on. Spring is almost here. The snows are melting."

"Where are we going?" Jessum asked unhappily.

"I was thinking we would go to Sapphire City and see if we can find your family," Teleo said, holding Jessum's eyes.

The boy's gaze darkened. "My family is dead. You are my family. You and Kaspari and Dinsmora."

Teleo's heart softened. "Don't you want to find out where you came from? Maybe one of your relatives is looking for you—waiting for you to come home."

Jessum held his eyes. "I don't think anyone is looking for me," Jessum said quietly. "But if you want to search for your son, I can help you look."

Teleo set his mug down. The young man had seen into Teleo's soul. They exchanged a long poignant look and Teleo wondered how Jessum had survived his years of abuse and still turned out to be such a good person.

Teleo turned his attention to Kaspari, whose eyebrows were knit together.

"I like being a girl," she said. "I like having girlfriends. I like being free."

"I know you do," Teleo said, wishing Kaspari were not heir to Verdant Valley throne, hunted by the Staggas. Wishing Queen Valona were not spinning Dinsmora in her web. Wishing he himself did not have a constant restlessness flowing underneath the surface, bubbling up like a mountain spring, too cold to ignore.

"You can be a girl and be free on the road," Teleo said.

"Will we ever come back here?" she asked, dropping her gaze to her bowl and pushing at the carrots with her spoon.

"We might," he said gently.

"When are we leaving?" Jessum asked.

"I don't know. Soon. Please don't tell anyone. Don't even discuss it with Dinsmora. She doesn't want to go either, and it will make her upset. We may need to leave without her."

The teenagers' eyes widened. "Nooo," they said in unison.

"I know," Teleo said, agreeing with their sentiment. "But she's not been well lately. She might not be fit for travel."

Short of kidnapping her, he did not know how he could convince his cousin to leave the queen's side. The choice he had made after fleeing Verdant Valley Castle came rushing back. Choosing to defend Kaspari over his own farm and family. The death of Tams Junior. His damned sense of duty. He set his mug down, his hand shaking. He lifted his eyes and examined Kaspari's face. Her scars were fading to pink, puckered worms. She was the last of the line of Elkes who had ruled Verdant Valley justly for generations. The kingdom Teleo had sworn his life to and served on the battlefield for, killing scores of men. Would he risk her life now to stay with his cousin? Duty to kin and kingdom warred in his head. His gaze fell to Kaspari's shoulder, where her pearl-laden cloak was pushed back, revealing the wool lining. Valona's old cloak. A hand-me-down mantle from a mad queen.

"Then I will stay with Dinsmora," Kaspari said, her mouth set in a stubborn line.

Jessum was silent, looking between Teleo and his foster sister.

"It is not safe here," Teleo said quietly, owing them some sort of explanation. "Do you trust me? Have I protected you before?"

They both nodded mutely, eyes like saucers.

"Do not say a word," he warned in a hushed tone. "Cutter!" he said to the big man who strode over to their table with a cheerful smile. Teleo's gaze brushed over the teenagers' eyes. "Go visit with your friends," he said. "We'll head back to the tower when Cutter is finished talking my ear off."

"That could be all night," Cutter said jokingly.

The kids got up from the bench and went across the room to join their friends at the far hearth, and Teleo braved a smile for Cutter.

After a long afternoon at the mason's workshop, Teleo returned to the Third Tower to find Johnswold out in the yard standing in the griffin fountain and shoving a long copper wire into the griffin's gaping beak.

"If I can ... just ... clear this—" Johnswold was interrupted by a spurt of brown water shooting out of the griffin's mouth and nearly hitting him in the face.

"Aha!" Johnswold chortled, continuing to clean out the fountain's spout with the wire before climbing out.

"It works," Teleo said, stating the obvious. He climbed into the dry pool, reaching up and holding his hand under the stream of clear water, which made an arc in the air and splashed into the top basin. The small basin soon filled up and began spilling over the edges into the larger, lower pool. "It's warm. Is it spring water?" Teleo asked, hopping out onto the paving stones next to Johnswold, who was curling his moustache tips and admiring the results of his work. Hunter was perched on the wall, regarding the fountain with interest.

"Ay-yah," Johnswold said. "Comes from the same underground aqueducts as the ones feeding the fountain in the main square. Mechanism works the same too, I just needed to fiddle with the inflow." He nodded towards the gate. "It's out there. I'd better check the outflow, so we don't flood the yard. He leaned over the lower pool and poked around with the wire, finding exit holes.

Star came up next to them and started drinking, and Teleo let the sheep out of their outdoor pen and released Marblehead from a separate enclosure they had built for the aggressive ram. The sheep ambled over and started drinking. Even the lambs were big enough to get their heads over the rim and slurp up the water.

"You mean to tell me we could have had water out here all winter?" Teleo asked.

Johnswold shrugged abashedly. "Yeah, sorry. Should have thought of it sooner. I got tired of raising buckets from the well to fill their watering troughs out here," he said.

"You and me both," Teleo said, and followed him out the gate and around the exterior of the courtyard wall. The courtyard stood at the very edge of the castle town, and its wall was bordered by only a narrow ledge that overlooked a jumble of boulders crowning a sheer cliff that plunged to the forest below. Johnswold and Teleo edged one by one around the corner. "Oh, good," Johnswold said as a dribble and then a spurt of water exited a gap in the wall and flowed down the jagged escarpment.

"When it gets warmer out, I'll turn off the hot water valve completely."

Teleo nodded and edged back around the wall to the gate. He followed Johnswold to a small wooden door he had never noticed, tucked into a stone nook not far up the alley from the tower's main entrance. Johnswold showed him the lever mechanisms that controlled the hot and cold water streams.

"We should install a proper commode and water pump in there," Teleo said, gesturing at the tower. "Like civilized people."

"Maybe someday. The queen has a proper water closet," Johnswold said. "I prefer outhouses myself. Painted porcelain and shit don't really go together."

They laughed and then Teleo thanked him and offered to take the dinner shift with the sheep. Johnswold readily agreed and promised to invite the kids to eat with him and his nephews at the Great Hall and accompany them back to the tower afterwards. Teleo closed and locked the courtyard gate behind his friend and then went over to the fountain. It was full now and made a pleasant splashing sound. The kids would be delighted.

The sheep were still gathered around, as happy as Teleo was to have a source of clean, flowing water. Hunter swooped over and landed on the beak of the rampant griffin and immediately ducked her head into the stream of water flowing from its open mouth. The gyrfalcon shook her head, spraying water into the air, and then hopped down to the lip of the upper basin and proceeded to step into it and take a bath.

Teleo smiled and left the animals to their fountain.

He went inside and locked the front door, slipping the only key into his pocket. He ate a quick meal of brown bread and hard-boiled eggs, washed it down with well water, and then got fresh straw and scattered it around the pen. The ram lamb, whom Kaspari had named Bo-bo, came inside and tugged at Teleo's pant leg and then butted its little head against Teleo's shin.

"Yes, you're very cute, Bo-bo," Teleo said. "Now go away. I'm not your friend." Bo-bo bounced a few times, butted Teleo's leg again, and gazed up at him. Teleo bent down and scratched the lamb under his chin. "If you were mine, you'd make a delicious lamb stew. But since you belong to the mad queen, you will grow up to be old and fat like your sire." Teleo glanced over at Marblehead, who was glowering at them from the open doorway. Teleo fetched hay from the outbuilding, and Star and the sheep followed him inside. Teleo held out an apple and lured Marblehead into his stall.

With the animals taken care of, Teleo grabbed a broom, a dustpan, and a cleaning rag from the back corner, then grabbed his swords and climbed the steps to the third floor.

He pushed the door open. Cold air enveloped him as he closed the door behind him. The large round room was murky in the fading twilight that leaked in through the Focal Point window. Bats squeaked and dropped from the vaulted ceiling one after another, flying out the open window in a fluttering line as Teleo's eyes adjusted to the faint light.

Teleo lit the candles from his ember box and a twist of straw, swept fresh mounds of bat guano into the ash bucket by the fireplace, and then dusted the mantelpiece. After sweeping the Heliotrope to a polished gleam, he took his short sword and longsword from their scabbards and set the leather sheaths on the mantel.

The Heliotrope lay before him—a slowly undulating circle of stones glinting in shades of saddle-leather brown and ruby red, ochre yellow and jade green. Teleo walked slowly across the perfectly laid stones in the direction it spun, counter to the sun's passage across the sky. He examined the mosaic as he walked, trying to understand how the intricate pattern of triangles, diamonds, and petals created the optical illusion of movement, even up close. The tesserae were expertly laid out around the white center stone and black rays in a large spiral of interlocking shapes, the glinting minerals shifting naturally through the color spectrum. He thought back on his years of sword practice in the Verdant Castle training yard, having never noticed the subtle colors underfoot. The yard's neglected mosaic had been covered with grit and grime, coated gray and brown from years of boots tramping across them, hiding their magical secret.

The sword hilts in his hands were growing warm. He swung the blades through the air and crouched into a sword form. He took a step. Then another. Right foot over left. Turning, turning. The Heliotrope circled with him as he sped up, his polished blades flashing. Steps became leaps, the rotating circle making him light on his feet. Soon his boots skimmed the surface, his leather soles barely brushing the marble and lapis lazuli, granite and feldspar, jade and olivine, wind and air. He leapt and spun, as though his swords were the steel feathers of wings he never knew he had.

When the first candle guttered out, he came to a stop on the center disk of Angel Wings marble. The room still felt like it was turning around him. He set his swords on the floor, resting his hands on his thighs to catch his breath. His hands were vibrating and his heart thudded in his ears. He hung his head down and sweat dripped from his forehead onto the marble, leaving dark splotches on the pearly white moon that gleamed up at him.

He stood up straight and took in great lungfuls of air. A single bat was hanging from the stone frame of the Focal Point window, its velvet wings folded over its chest like a cape and its coal-black eyes glinting down at him in the yellow light of the remaining candle.

Teleo snuck up to the Heliotrope every afternoon that week, aided by the fact that Johnswold had come down with a cold and was holed up at his cottage in Falcon's Nest. Sonderson came every day to share their midday meal and then take the kids and horses, including Cinnamon and Star, out to Bitter's Ford. The shepherd brought them back to the Great Hall at dinnertime, and Cutter delivered the kids and horses home to the tower afterwards.

While dancing the sword on the Heliotrope, Teleo kept the door cracked open and listened for Marblehead's bellow, which announced their approach and gave Teleo enough time to extinguish the candles, lock the third-floor door, hurry downstairs, and unlock the courtyard gate for them.

Teleo was not concerned about his cousin discovering him— she ate all her meals with Queen Valona and did not return home until late in the evenings. He wished he could share his discovery with her—the old Dinsmora—before she had come firmly under the sway of Queen Valona. Teleo did not want the mad queen to find out about the Heliotrope and amass any more power, although the map showed a second Heliotrope at Trillifort—so for all he knew, the queen was already using it.

He wondered what powers were truly bestowed upon those who danced in a Heliotrope during the Summer Solstice. There were stories of the solstice sun streaming in and filling the Mage with a magical fire. In the stories, it was always only one Mage in the Heliotrope during the solstice—the most powerful among them. Mages battled one another to earn the honor of dancing in the blessed fire of the solstice sun. There were tales of plots and betrayals, even assassinations, to get rid of the oldest Mages, making room for the next in line to take his or her turn at the center stone of the Heliotrope. Now here he was—Teleo, dancing in a Heliotrope.

But it would be months before the Summer Solstice sun would shine its rays through the Focal Point. They could not stay at Trillifort that long. Dinsmora's insightful personality had already dulled to a blunt edge. The only time she was somewhat herself was the rare Sunday she showed up at the hot springs. The mineral water and fresh mountain air seemed to clear her head, but as soon as they returned to the castle, she hurried off to Queen Valona's side. He had considered various strategies of dragging his cousin away from Trillifort, but none of the scenarios he came up with ended peacefully.

When he danced the sword, all of his worries fell away, and so he danced. His two-handed sword forms were improving daily. A strange energy filled him when he danced around the circle, making him feel like he was flying. He practiced cartwheels off his gloved fists, hilts in hand, and advanced to front and back flips, something he had been adept at as a younger man. It felt easier now, and he attributed it to the Heliotrope lifting him as if on a cushion of air.

During daylight hours, Hunter liked to sit in the Focal Point window and watch as the bats slept overhead. At night, the bats flew in and out, sometimes watching upside-down from their ceiling perches, and sometimes darting about his head as he danced.

It was late afternoon and Teleo was making the most of his free time—Johnswold was returning to tend the sheep the following day so that Teleo could finish the falcon mosaic for the queen. Teleo made one more circuit of his flying leaps and slashes, then took a break. He set down his swords, crossed the room, and sat on the wooden chest next to the fireplace. The chest was locked with a hefty iron padlock. He examined the lock's fine metalwork. It had been fashioned by a master. He considered getting his tools and breaking it off, but he did not want to destroy the queen's property.

"The key's on the door lintel."

Teleo jumped to his feet, nearly stumbling backwards into the empty fireplace.

A figure stood in the center of the Heliotrope on the Angel Wings marble. Teleo edged towards the door. The figure was transparent, a shimmering mirage, but it had clearly spoken. But wait. Now it was solid. It was a she, and the phantom looked directly at him from under thick black eyebrows. She appeared to be no more than forty years old, an amused smile on her red lips.

"Over the door," she said. "The key. To the box."

Teleo stood frozen. She looked real, with a prominent brow over a wide flat nose, and thick black hair wound up into two large buns, one on each side of her head.

"Who are you?" he demanded, clutching the cold stone frame of the fireplace. His swords were on the floor where he had left them, not far from where she stood.

"I am Sigrid."

"You are the ghost?" he asked with a tremor in his voice.

She held a folded-steel sword, the blade shimmering like water, with a steel pommel studded with pink rubies. Her red velvet gown reached to the floor, a plain design with trailing sleeves and simple gold and black embroidery decorating the bodice, wrist cuffs, and hem. Her feet were bare.

"No, I am not dead," she said, chuckling.

"Are you one of the skeletons?" he asked, his pulse throbbing at his neck.

Her mouth opened in a silent circle. "What skeletons?" she asked after a long pause.

"D ... downstairs," he said. "In the cellar."

"How many skeletons?" Sigrid asked, her voice tight.

"Two," he said.

She held his eyes. Hers were dark brown, almond-shaped, and slightly slanted. She was of the Hill people. Teleo swallowed, his palms sweaty. "You dance the sword," she said simply.

He blinked. "Yes."

"You are a Mage, then," she said.

He swallowed again. "I suppose so. Some say that I am."

"Ah, so. How curious," she said, her brow wrinkling in thought. "Don't you want to know what's in the chest?"

He had forgotten all about the chest. Stepping over to the door, he reached up and ran his fingers along the dusty lintel, keeping his eyes on Sigrid until he found a cold metal key. He tossed the iron key and it landed with a clatter on the floor in front of the wooden chest. "You open it," he said.

She hesitated for a moment, then left the center circle. With a swish of velvet, she stepped across the floor to the chest, set her sword down, and fiddled with the key in the lock until it opened. She removed the padlock, lifted the top of the chest, and stepped back.

Teleo peered at the chest but could not see the inside from where he stood. Sigrid went back to the Angel Wings circle and held the sword at her side, her face flushed.

He caught a whiff of her perfume. Amber. "Are you really real?" he asked, still befuddled.

"Yes," she said.

"Why do you stand on the center stone? Where did you come from?" he asked.

"Why do I stand in the Sun Circle? I must. I came from another Sun Circle. I'm afraid I must leave now." She bowed her head, closed her eyes, and was gone.

He stared at the spot where she had been a moment before. He blinked hard and shook his head, trying to clear it. Maybe there had been something in the ale Sonderson had brought him for their midday meal. But the air still held a hint of amber, and the chest sat open. He met the black eyes of Hunter, who was perched in the window.

"Did you see that?" he asked the gyrfalcon.

Hunter tilted her head, then turned with a hop and flapped out of view.

Teleo crossed the room and looked inside the chest. A half dozen yellowed skulls stared up at him, neatly arranged in the bottom of the black-velvet-lined box. He dropped the lid and fastened the lock, his hands shaking. He returned the key to the lintel, his fingers brushing against another key. He took down the second key and inspected it. It was brass, and he tried it in the door's lock. It turned easily.

"Hmph," Teleo grunted to himself, and returned the spare key to the door lintel. The lingering scent of the red-robed woman still haunted him. He grabbed his swords, locked the door behind him, and ran down the two flights to the stable.

He splashed cold water on his face, then went into the pen and picked up Bo-bo. He buried his face in the ram lamb's soft wool, wanting to feel something real. Bo-bo squirmed in his arms and nuzzled Teleo's ear.

Teleo wished Star were there—he would ride out to the *Scythe and Sickle* in Bitter's Ford. Or the pub in Mud Flats— that was closer. He had finished the ale Sonderson had brought and was fresh out of hard cider. He needed some Ferska. He put down the lamb and paced in a circle, pondering the beautiful phantom up above and the tortured skeletons down below.

Cutter brought the kids home later that evening, along with a jug of ale that the two of them finished in front of the fire, but Teleo could not shake the sight or scent of Sigrid. The next day, after making little progress on the mosaic, he returned to the tower instead of dining at the Great Hall, relieving Johnswold of duty early. He immediately went upstairs and knelt on the Heliotrope by the center stone. The "Sun Circle," she had called it. He peered into the translucent marble.

"Sigrid," he whispered, feeling foolish. "Sigrid," he hissed more loudly, then with his full voice called out, "Sigrid!"

The marble reflected a dim image of his own face. Unsuccessful in summoning the mirage, or ghost, or whatever she was, he took his swords and began to dance. She was a Mage, he concluded as he spun and crouched, swinging the blades overhead. That was the only logical explanation. A Mage who had unlocked the mystery of the Heliotropes. He wished she would come back and teach him what she knew.

The third day after he had met Sigrid, he was dancing the sword when she appeared again. She was in the same red dress, sword in hand.

"Don't stop dancing," she said. "It gives me energy."

He resumed his forms, circling in an outer ring of the Heliotrope. She joined his dance, on the opposite side of the floor, spinning with lightness and grace, her blade cutting through the air with deadly strokes. He imitated her movements, reminiscent of a form his father had taught him long ago. Soon they were moving in harmony, and he became lost in the rhythm, his boots barely touching the floor before leaving again. The floor was glowing beneath them as they danced over it, the circular pattern spinning slowly. Teleo flipped forward, then backward, flying effortlessly through the air. Sigrid flew and spun across from him, a ribbon of light trailing from her sword.

They landed on the stone floor and stopped, breathless, and gazed at one another.

"You're good at that," she said, panting and wiping sweat from her brow with her embroidered sleeve.

"Where did you come from?" he asked. "Teach me what you know."

She returned to the Sun Circle and sat cross-legged on the Angel Wings marble. Her long red dress was draped over her knees and ankles, with bare toes peeking out. He sat on the wooden chest across the room from her.

"I know that if you dance in the Heliotrope during Summer Solstice," he said, "you become unbeatable in battle."

"Really?" she asked. She seemed surprised.

"Have you danced during the solstice?" he asked.

"Yes, many times," she said. "But that is not required to access the power of the Heliotrope, only to master it."

"Oh? Where do you come from?" he repeated.

"From a Hill fortress overlooking the Sapphire Valley. Where are you from? You are not of the Hill Tribes nor do you have a mountain accent."

"I am from Verdant Valley," he said.

"Ah, I see. Why are you all the way up here in the mountains?"

"I am wintering here," he said.

"Strange place to spend the winter," she said with an arched eyebrow. "Most people flee the mountains before the snows come."

He nodded. "Yes, most sensible people do," he said with a wry grin.

"You are the one who danced in the courtyard with the overhanging trees," she said, her eyes shimmering.

"It was you," he exclaimed. "You warned me." He recalled the image from that fateful day in the Royal Garden. It was the same face, although calm now.

She inclined her head in affirmation.

"How did you know I was in danger?" he asked.

"There were soldiers sneaking through the palace, with swords drawn," she said. "That could only mean one thing. That was Verdant Castle, was it not? I heard they suffered a coup last summer and have a new king."

"Yes, it was," he said. "That was the moment when they overtook the palace. How did you see them?"

"I can see through the Sun Circle. My vision expands. It's hard to explain."

"Can you teach me?" he asked.

"Maybe one day. It's an acquired skill," she said.

"Ah, okay," he said. "Could you see into the training yard, too, at Verdant Castle?"

"I used to be able to. A little bit. Through broken fragments, but you replaced them, did you not? You are the stonemason."

"Oh," he said, aghast. "I ruined it?"

"Well," she said. "It is very grainy now. I can only see faint shapes. I don't think it will work like the original stone. I would not recommend traveling to it."

"It's only a temporary replacement," he rushed to explain. "I needed to find the source for the proper stone. But I have found it now," he said, excited to share his discovery with someone. "It comes from the marble quarry right here." He stomped his foot and pointed downwards.

"Ah, that makes sense," she said, running her fingers over the polished stone at her side. "Of course."

"I feel horrible," he said glumly. "I knew I shouldn't have taken the old stones away."

"It's okay," she said. "The broken circle was useless for anything besides viewing, anyway. If you ever do repair it, you'll be able to travel using it."

She smiled and he relaxed, enjoying her presence.

"Travel?" he asked.

"Yes. You could learn to travel between the Heliotropes, as I'm doing," she said, tucking a stray lock of black hair behind her ear. "If you had an amulet, that is. You are fortunate to have found this Heliotrope. In fact, there are two small Heliotropes at Trillifort, as I understand it, although the second one is always darkened in shadow. But there are apparently no battle circles, which is unusual."

"Shadow," Teleo said, scratching at his chin. "Do you think it's been paved over?"

She narrowed her eyes in thought. "I think not," she said. "I see vague shapes moving from time to time."

He considered this information, concluding that the second Heliotrope must be indoors as well. "What is a battle circle?" Teleo asked. "The larger ones? Marked by the sunray symbols on the map?"

"You have a map?" she asked. A dark eyebrow quirked up, but not waiting for his reply, she continued, "Yes, battle circles are the large Heliotropes. They were traditionally used for swordplay and competitions among Mages, sometimes to the death. In any case, it is best to train for traveling in a castle with two Heliotropes. They built a second, smaller Heliotrope in some locations for that purpose. That way, if you do not have the energy to return home, you can simply walk." She grinned. "Now most all the Heliotropes are unused, as far as I can tell. In fact, I know of only one other living Mage using the Heliotropes. She is locked inside the Sapphire Palace. She could escape if she wants, but she holds out hope."

"Hope for what?"

"Hope that the Sapphire Empire will return to its former glory. She thinks she can do that best from the inside. I think it will kill her." Sigrid shook her head sadly.

There was so much Teleo did not know and so much that she could teach him, but she stood to leave.

"I will try to come back tomorrow at this same time," she said.

"I will be here," Teleo said, and watched as she closed her eyes and was gone.

20

ᴛʜᴇ Sᴜɴ Cɪʀᴄʟᴇ

Sigrid appeared after the sun had left the sky and the bats swooped out the window. The twilight air shimmered, and suddenly she was standing there, her flushed cheeks the color of her dress, and the air scented with amber. Teleo had a primal urge to take her in his arms, feel the velvet dress under his fingertips, and taste her raspberry lips. But he just stared at her, then raised his swords and began to dance.

She joined him. The floor glowed brighter and brighter, spinning in a slow vortex of color as they danced and twirled and leapt through the air.

Teleo's feet grew lighter and he jumped higher, his head swirling with energy as her lithe form danced opposite him, matching his pace as they circled the room, turning and flipping and cartwheeling through the air like autumn leaves caught in the wind.

They stopped and smiled at one another. They were both breathing heavily and she wiped sweat from her brow with the back of her wrist. She walked to the Sun Circle and stood there, one hand on her hip, blowing at a strand of hair that had fallen over her cheek. The luminescent glow of the Heliotrope faded. Teleo sat on the wooden skull chest and leaned back against the wall, bathing in the beauty of the woman standing across from him.

"I will need to go soon," she said. "I have had a busy day, but I can talk for a minute. How was your day?"

"Busy waiting for you," he said, holding her gaze. She did not shy away from his flirtation, but he felt silly all of the sudden and asked, "How do you make the floor glow like that? It doesn't happen when you're not here."

A half-smile turned up her lips. "That started happening after I danced in the Summer Solstice one year. That was the same year I discovered traveling locally within the same Heliotrope— hopping from place to place across the floor. But that takes pure concentration. You have to be completely in the moment, if you know what I mean."

He thought he did. Like in the midst of battle.

"I will show you the local traveling sometime," she said. "It is not something I can always do at will; I've only managed to do it a few times. I'm not sure what it's good for. Maybe it's just a practice technique."

"What about traveling to other places? Can you do that at will?" he asked.

"Yes, but it only works if you have already been to a Heliotrope in person and touched the Sun Circle."

"So you've been here before," he said. "In person."

"Yes," she said, her expression turning somber.

"When?" he asked.

She tucked another stray strand behind her ear, and her mouth turned down. "I was captured. Many years ago. My brothers and I were on our way to Verdant Castle for peace talks and were ambushed on the Southern Mountain Pass. Our guards were killed, and my brothers and I were brought to this tower. I was dragged up here, alone, but before my captors could assault me, I fled. I stood in this circle and went home. I never saw my brothers again."

Teleo watched the struggle of emotions play across her face. "I'm sorry," he said.

She smiled sadly. "Trillifort did not want peace," she said. "They were afraid Verdant Valley and the Sapphire Empire would combine forces and conquer the mountain kingdoms. Anyway, I came back a few times, traveling using the Sun Circles, hoping to learn something about my brothers' fates. Now I just come to practice traveling. Plus, I kind of like this place. It's peaceful. Just me and the bats. At least until now." She gave him a teasing grin.

"I'm sorry," he repeated, returning her smile.

"I am glad to have found another Mage," she said. "I could teach you how to travel if you had an amulet, but I do not know where they come from. I inherited mine. Once you have an amulet, the rest is fairly easy."

"What kind of amulet?" he asked.

"One passed down from the Mages," she said, pulling a gold chain and large gold disk pendant out from under her bodice.

Teleo tried to recall if he had ever seen a gold amulet among his father's or Aunt Bralla's trinkets. He leaned forward and rested his elbows on his knees.

She tucked the amulet back under her bodice and continued, "First you need to dance the sword in a Heliotrope. The more practice, the better. You are already strong in it. How long have you been here? Not long, from what I have observed."

He shook his head. "I just discovered this Heliotrope, but I have danced in others. Once briefly in the garden where you saw me. The other was the one I was repairing and which I ruined," he said, grimacing sheepishly. "I trained there for many years in my youth. You said that it was a battle circle, made for Mage battles?"

"Yes. Battles of magic. Tourneys, of a sort, which helped establish the Mages' hierarchy." She examined him curiously, her gaze running over his scarred face, down his muscled arms and legs straining against his buckskin pants and half-open shirt, and resting on his scuffed riding boots, then flitting back to meet his eyes. "It is good you have danced the sword for many years. That explains your skill. With what knowledge were you repairing the battle circle?"

He shrugged his shoulders. "I was just replacing broken and missing stones. I was following the pattern from the intact one in the Royal Garden."

Her eyes narrowed. "Are you a Mage Stone Master?"

"I don't know," Teleo said, his pulse quickening. "I suppose I may be. I come from a long line of Mages—and stonemasons."

"Take a look at this," she said, revealing her amulet again and letting it dangle from her fingers.

He stood up and walked over to her, her amber scent filling his head. The nearness of her made his skin tingle as he took the amulet from her fingers and cupped it in his palm. He took in a sharp breath. It was a miniature replica of a Heliotrope, mounted in a simple gold setting. A round white center stone was surrounded by ten black rays. Tiny triangular, diamond, and petal-shaped bits of every color formed the outer rings. Teleo inspected the familiar pattern and looked down at the mosaic at his feet. They were exactly the same.

"I can make one of these," he said, a shiver of excitement brushing across his skin. He handed the amulet back to her. "What else do I need to know to travel?" he asked, stepping back a pace.

She locked eyes with his, her brown irises and black pupils melding together in a deep, dark pool. He could see her trying to decide if she could trust him with the ancient, secret knowledge.

She took in a small breath and raised her chin. "You must wear the amulet. Then, you must think of the Sun Circle that you want to travel to. You must have touched the other Sun Circle and know how it feels. Stand or sit in your Sun Circle with concentration and a quiet mind. Then bring yourself back to the target circle. You must feel it under your skin as if you were there, and you will find yourself there. Just like that. Returning is the same process."

He nodded. That was simple enough, he supposed.

"A few other things you must know," she continued. "Staying within the white Sun Circle disk is the easiest and safest way to travel. Leaving the Sun Circle takes energy. Leaving the Heliotrope completely takes even more energy. Sword dancing in the Heliotrope is a way to maintain your strength. Other Mages dancing with you gives you more energy." She waved her hand across the complex pattern of radiating stars and petals. "When you are first learning, you must remain in a calm state of mind. Holding onto the amulet helps. When you first travel, you may feel sick when your body solidifies in the new location, especially when you set foot off the Heliotrope. I don't recommend that. I have only left this Heliotrope a couple of times, when I went downstairs looking for my brothers. Once, I almost didn't have the energy to travel back home. That is why you must first train in a castle with two Heliotropes, to grow strong in the magical art, unless you are okay with being stuck in another place. You're lucky to be at a castle that has two."

"I don't know where the other one is, though," he said.

"Hmmm," she said, wrinkling her brow. "You must try and find it."

"I have been trying," he said.

"Try harder," she said, grinning kindly.

"I touched the Sun Circle in the Royal Garden where you saw me, I think," he said, wracking his brain to recall his inspection of the Heliotrope in the Verdant Palace courtyard. Had he touched the center stone? Yes, he could feel the cool, smooth Trillifort marble under his hands. He could hear the finches chirping, and the fragrant garden made him miss the fertile valley. He shook his head to clear the vivid sensations.

"I could travel to Verdant Castle to practice," he said, "but I don't want to get stuck there."

"It is always a risk," she said.

"You came back here after you escaped your abductors," he said. "You could have been captured again."

"I've been traveling in Sun Circles since I was ten years old. You've never done it before."

She was right. He couldn't risk it. He couldn't abandon Dinsmora, Jessum, and Kaspari here with crazy Queen Valona. Nor did he want to find himself alone in the center of the Staggas' heavily armed palace.

"Make your amulet," she said.

"I will," he promised.

"I must go." She held out her hand to him, and he held it, her fingers slender and strong and as real as his own flesh. She dropped his hand, closed her eyes, and disappeared in a shimmer of red shadows.

She appeared the next evening at the same time. He smiled at her, trying to conceal how delighted he was to see her. He felt like a teenager. "Sigrid," he said in greeting. "I was hoping you'd come tonight."

She smiled, but her expression was strained. "I have a favor to ask you," she said, then quickly added, "but you can say no if you want."

"What is it?" he asked. "I'll help if I can."

She hesitated, then said, "The skeletons. I want to see them."

He held her dark gaze. "Are you sure?" he asked.

She nodded.

He led her down the two flights of stairs to the stable and swept aside the layer of straw. The ewes bleated and surrounded them, wanting food. Sigrid petted the lambs, and he herded the sheep into their stall.

They levered away the stone flooring and wooden hatch, and Teleo lit a torch. He and Sigrid knelt down, and he lowered the torch into the black pit. They peered down into the flickering dungeon.

The skeletons gleamed white against the dark earth.

"It's them," she whispered.

"How do you know?" he asked gently.

"Devan always slept like that, curled up. And Gagan always slept on his back with his hands folded across his chest." She swallowed loudly. "At least they died in their sleep." Breathy sobs shook her chest. Teleo held the torch, letting her look upon her brothers.

When she was ready, he doused the torch and replaced the flooring. Sigrid was leaning against the stall gate, petting a ewe through the slats.

"She likes you," Teleo said.

"She's soft," Sigrid said, keeping her face turned away from him.

He visited with Marblehead over in his own pen, and the ram glared up at him, as though angry with Teleo that he was locked up.

"I know," Teleo said quietly. "Life is not fair."

After a time, Teleo followed Sigrid up the stairs. She held his elbow as they walked across the Heliotrope and stopped at the Sun Circle. She released his arm and gazed up at him, her eyes glistening. "I feel better, in a strange way," she said. "I finally know their fate."

Teleo nodded somberly. "I understand. Not knowing is the hardest."

She lowered her head, and he took a step back. "Thank you for finding them," she said, lifting her eyes. They smiled sadly at one another. "Dance for me," she said.

He took up his swords and moved into his forms, slashing and turning. The next time he glanced at the Sun Circle, she was gone.

———————◆———————

Sigrid came again the next evening, and the next. They danced silently, exchanging only a few words. When she stood on the Sun Circle to leave on the third evening, she asked, "Have you started your amulet yet?"

"I drew the stencil and found the proper stones. Trillifort's masonry is well stocked," he said. "I will start tomorrow."

"Good," she replied.

"I am unable to meet at this time for the next several days," he said with regret. "I have some responsibilities to tend to." He did not want to abandon the kids as Dinsmora had done.

Sigrid nodded. "When you wish to meet again, place a sword outside the Sun Circle on a black ray, and if I am free, I will dance the sword with you."

He inclined his head, and she disappeared in a shimmer of crimson.

Teleo spent the next many days filing tiny slivers of stone. It was meticulous work and took longer than cutting the feathers for the falcon. The other stoneworkers left him alone—Queen Valona's business was none of theirs.

When all the pieces of the puzzle were complete, he set the miniature Heliotrope into a round, gold setting he'd made by melting two Gold Lions and hammering out a backplate and bezel. He had carved each micro-tessera to such perfection that there were no gaps to seal. He set the stones in the epoxy and let it set overnight.

The next day, he admired his work. The finished amulet fit into his palm. It was mesmerizing the way the pattern shifted before his eyes—one moment it formed an intricate star, the next moment a multi-petaled flower. The entire pattern seemed to swirl towards the center. He was astounded that he had made this masterpiece and attributed its wonder to the Mages of old who had conceived of such a design.

He did not have a gold chain, so he strung it with a simple leather cord around his neck, hid it under his shirt, and left the workshop, excited to show Sigrid. That afternoon, he placed his sword on a Down in the Deep ray, and she appeared that evening.

"You are indeed a Mage Stone Master," she said breathlessly as she examined his amulet. "It's incredible." She lifted her eyes and met his.

His skin grew warm from the praise and her touch as she handed back the miniature Heliotrope, her hand lingering in his as she passed it to him.

"You must find the other Heliotrope and practice traveling," she said.

"I know," he said. "I'll try."

One afternoon in early spring, Teleo and one of the other stonemasons carried a square board with a large piece of parchment onto which Teleo had reverse-mounted the falcon mosaic tiles in place.

Gracie let them into the queen's audience chamber. Teleo mixed up some mortar and adhesive, spread it onto the marble surface with a trowel, and with his companion's help transferred the design in one piece to the back of the throne. The stonemason left and Teleo fussed over his handiwork, making sure every tessera was in its proper place. The stone gyrfalcon gazed at him, and he smiled back. It was a stunning likeness. Queen Valona should be pleased.

Teleo added a border of marble tiles to create a smooth transition between the mosaic and the edges of the throne's back. The mortar needed to cure for a couple of days. He draped the throne with burlap sacking and hurried from the palace.

Two days later, he grouted the mosaic. He replaced the burlap and left to tell Gracie he would return in a few days for a final polish, then it would be ready to present to the queen.

Outside, a steady breeze blew in from the south. It was early afternoon and he stopped by the Third Tower, where he found Johnswold napping in the chair in front of the cold fireplace. He awoke, and Teleo told him to go back to sleep. Johnswold grunted and closed his eyes. Teleo quickly brushed and saddled Star. The kids had taken Cinnamon with them but left Star behind so that Teleo could ride out to Bitter's Ford and meet them. Jessum wanted to show him the weapons he had made, and Kaspari and her friends were having an archery competition.

Teleo made his way through the tunnel to Falcon's Nest and galloped along the flat, loamy shoulder of the wagon road. The mountains of snow in the fields had diminished to small clumps, and rivulets crossed the road in places as the snow melted and drained to the river. He approached Mud Flats, where the small homesteads divided the open fields into tidy parcels. Two dairy cows were nosing around in the soggy forage of a fenced pasture, and several pigs had already turned another small field into mud.

He arrived in Bitter's Ford and stopped first at the smithy. Jessum and Goff greeted him as he stepped into the shop. Teleo peeled off his gambeson and pushed up his buckskin sleeves in the heat cast from the glowing forge in the center of the room.

"Yer boy's made a lot of progress," Goff said, slapping Jessum on the back.

Jessum smiled and led Teleo to the wall where several axes were on display.

"This is the first one I made good enough to sell," Jessum said, pulling a small throwing axe from its display hook. "Goff's going to give me half the money."

Jessum handed Teleo the axe. It was well-balanced. The wedge-shaped steel head was straight and sharp. "Well done," Teleo said, examining the cutting edge.

Jessum puffed up with pride. "I had to melt ... how many?" he asked, turning to Goff. "A dozen? Before I made one good enough to keep?"

Goff nodded. "Something like that. Yer a fast learner. Took me two dozen." Goff laughed heartily and smoothed his moustaches. "Of course, yer boy had a head start. Whoever taught him the basics knew what he was doing."

Jessum rolled his eyes, and Goff arched an eyebrow at him.

"The blacksmith back home had a drinking problem," Teleo hurried to explain. "But that just meant my boy had more time at the forge. Isn't that right, Jeremiah?" Teleo asked, giving Jessum a firm frown.

Jessum scowled but held his tongue.

"Show him the battle-axe you made," Goff said.

"Oh yeah," Jessum said, brightening up, and pulled a long, straight-handled pole axe from a cabinet. "Goff's letting me keep this one for myself."

Teleo replaced the throwing axe on its hook and hefted the battle-axe. The polished steel head was a wide crescent shape. Simple and deadly. "Nice," Teleo said, stepping away and swinging it overhead. "You'll be dangerous with this."

Teleo grinned at Jessum, who nodded and said, "Yeah. Nobody better mess with me."

"That's no joke," Goff agreed. "He's got a mean swing."

Teleo followed Jessum out back where Jessum demonstrated his prowess against a thick post, notched from many previous attacks.

Teleo took a turn hacking at the post. The blade sank deeply into the wood. It was a respectable weapon.

"He made a knife, too," Goff said. "He's getting the hang of folding steel."

Jessum led them back inside and removed a knife from a case. "This is the first folded-steel blade that didn't go back into the fire," Jessum said. "After I make a few good knife blades, Goff said I'll be ready to start learning swords."

Teleo inspected the knife. It was a rough blade—the transitions from soot gray to shining silver of the many layers were random and inconsistent. Still, the blade was straight and the edge was sharp. "Not bad," Teleo said.

Jessum shrugged. "Goff said it's good enough to fillet a fish."

They laughed. "I'm sure it can handle a fish," Teleo agreed. "Folded steel takes a lot of practice to master, as I understand it," Teleo said.

"It does," Goff agreed. "Years. But he's made a lot of progress in a short period of time. Give him a few more seasons and he'll be making fine sword blades, mark my word."

After some time chatting and inspecting Goff's wares, Teleo prepared to leave. "How much for the throwing axe?" Teleo asked, taking Jessum's creation down from the wall. "I need a new axe. I left most of my tools back at the farm."

They agreed on two Silvers, and Goff tossed one of the Silver Bits to Jessum, who pocketed it with a satisfied nod.

"Are you coming to watch your sister's archery competition?" Teleo asked.

"Yeah. Let me clean up real quick," Jessum said, and disappeared into the back.

When Jessum returned, they headed over to the field behind the Spinners' house—a broad, flat stretch of land with sodden gray grass newly exposed from the melted snows, and bright green shoots already showing themselves. They hitched their horses with others along the fence bordering the Spinners' apple orchard. Teleo visited briefly with Nutmeg, who stood between Daisy and Cinnamon, brought down for the day by Sonderson, as was his habit. The horse seemed in good health.

Teleo and Jessum walked over to the field where eight targets were set atop eight mounds of wet straw. Eight young women were spaced out across the field, facing the targets at fifty yards and checking their arrows and bowstrings. Kaspari was third from the right. Jessum left Teleo's side to join a group of young men sitting on the fence rail.

Teleo waved as Kaspari caught sight of him. She stood alone. All the other young women had their father or mother, or both, at their sides, preparing for this apparently important event. Teleo ducked, stepped between the fence rails, and crossed the mushy ground.

"You ready, princess?" he asked, arriving at Kaspari's side.

"Don't call me that," she said, blushing.

"Here, let me check your arrows," he said, taking the first one and looking down its length. "This one's straight," he said, taking the next one.

"They're all good," she said. "I checked them twice. I don't have any others, anyway. I broke two of Dinsmora's and lost one. I borrowed these others from Maddie."

Teleo frowned, noting the mix of cedar and poplar shafts. "I should have been paying more attention," he said. "I thought you were just doing this for fun. I could have helped you get more arrows. How is Dinsmora's bow working out for you?"

"It's a little heavy for me," Kaspari said. "But it's a nice bow."

Teleo nodded and sighed, disappointed with himself for being so distracted with stonework and magic circles and a certain red-robed woman that he was neglecting his foster daughter. He took the next arrow, running his thumb lightly over the fletching. "These feathers are a little soft," he said. "We've got some grouse wings back at the tower. We can make you stiffer ones tonight."

"Okay," she said.

"Have you warmed up?" he asked. "Want to take a few practice shots? It's windy out."

"I know," she said, nocking an arrow and drawing it back.

Other parents were fetching arrows from the targets.

When the way was clear, Kaspari shot six arrows, landing them all within the three center rings of the target, with one bull's-eye. They retrieved the arrows together.

"I was better back home," she said, kicking at the grass as they walked back to the wooden slat that marked her shooting position. "I used to always beat my brothers, but these girls are better than me."

"You got a bull's-eye," he said. "It's not easy to do with a headwind."

"Should have had more," she said grimly.

"It seems archery is all the youngsters talk about here," he said, trying to think of something to cheer her up. "Back home, you had to divide your time between your studies and riding. Right?"

She nodded glumly. "I guess so." She pressed at the scar on her cheek. "I had to change where I press my hand against my cheek when I draw, because this hurts."

"Ah, yes," Teleo said. "That would change things. You'll get used to it." He patted her shoulder and tucked a loose strand of hair behind her ear. "You'll do fine," he said. "Just have fun."

Jeb Spinner hailed Teleo. He left Kaspari's side to help Jeb replace the practice targets with new ones from a stack behind the straw mounds.

"You take your archery seriously around here, don't you?" Teleo asked jovially as they set a target in place and clamped it down.

"It's how we defend our valley," Jeb said. "We start the kids shooting at three years old. Some of these gals are getting ready to graduate to guard training. Two turned fifteen this year."

Teleo glanced at the young archers huddled in the center of the field. They ranged from around twelve to fifteen years old, as far as he could tell. Kaspari was right in the middle of the pack, having turned fourteen the prior August. The transition from childhood to womanhood was evident in the group of girls, in a confounding mix of awkwardness and graceful beauty.

When the new targets were set up, Teleo wished Kaspari luck and went back to the fence to watch. *They started their kids with archery at three years old.* That's when he and Bella-Mae had started their own children. Teleo had made the child-sized, lightweight bows himself, and crafted arrows from reeds. He could still see his baby girl, Abigail, at four years old, biting her lip as she drew back the bow and loosed an arrow, hitting the target with a squeal of delight.

Teleo swiped at his eyes as the whistle blew for the first shot and Kaspari loosed an arrow. It hit the target in the second ring from the center. Her shoulders sank with disappointment. She glanced over her shoulder at him. He nodded and raised his thumb in encouragement. The judges ran forward, removed the arrows, and marked the shots. Kaspari nocked another arrow and swiveled towards the target, waiting for the next whistle.

Sonderson showed up and leaned his elbows on the fence rail. "She's pretty good with a bow," Sonderson said. "She'll be a good addition to the guard."

Teleo nodded and they both yelled out with approval as her next arrow hit a bull's-eye.

She ended up coming in third place, behind the two oldest girls. Teleo gathered with the others, congratulating the winners. He gave Kaspari a hug. "Good job, Kallie," he said. They parted, and she smiled up at him.

"Not too bad, I guess," she said.

Sonderson congratulated her and headed towards the *Scythe and Sickle,* released for the day from accompanying the kids back to the castle.

The top three archers each received a new bow, and Kaspari accepted hers, beaming with delight. It was a fine bow of blond wood, with a leather-wrapped grip.

"Test it out," Jeb encouraged her.

Kaspari walked to her marker, drew back the bow, and hit a bull's-eye on the first try.

Jeb folded his arms across his chest with a smug grin. "I made that bow. Made it from a plum branch."

"Nice job," Teleo said.

"But you made the girl," Jeb said. "She's a strong one—and pretty. Brave, too. You should be proud."

Teleo nodded. "I am," he said, imagining what Abigail might have looked like at fourteen. She would have had a strong back and shoulders, like Kaspari's. And her chubby cheeks would have sculpted to her cheekbones by now, like Bella-Mae's.

Kaspari took a few more shots, then ran to retrieve her arrows, crossing the field with long, lithe strides. King Elke and

Queen Eleanor would have been proud of their daughter—and had likely been terrified of her fate as they fell under the Staggas' traitorous swords. Teleo stood up straighter. The princess was his responsibility now, and by the Light of the Mages he would do his best to keep her safe.

"Before you know it, Kallie will be old enough join the Youth Guard," Jeb said. "I'd wager yer boy can join now. Is he fifteen yet? Is he as good with a bow and arrow as his sister?"

"He turned fifteen not long ago," Teleo said—Jessum had said he was born in the winter—and glanced behind him at the lad, who was standing with the other teenaged boys at the fence. "He's not so great with a bow and arrow, but he's deadly with a stave, and he's learning the sword."

"And axe, I hear," Jeb said, chuckling.

"True," Teleo said, and smiled as Kaspari returned and thanked Jeb Spinner for her new bow.

"Fit fer a queen," Jeb said, putting his arm around her shoulder.

Teleo and Kaspari exchanged glances while Jeb prattled on about how he used to make bows for Queen Valona back when she was still just a princess.

◆

"Where's Sonderson?" Teleo grumbled later that week, pacing in front of the tower's ground floor fireplace. "He's late."

The shepherd had agreed to pick up the kids again that day and Teleo wondered if Sonderson had forgotten, or perhaps he had lost himself inside a jug of mushroom wine. Teleo needed to polish the falcon throne that afternoon and be done with his commitment to the queen once and for all.

"We can ride to Bitter's Ford by ourselves," Jessum said.

"Yeah," Kaspari agreed, her chin held high. "We're not kids anymore."

Johnswold had sent one of his nephews in his place to watch the sheep, and the young man stood with the teenagers, facing Teleo.

Teleo examined Jessum. Teleo had been only sixteen when he'd gone to war for the first time. His gaze turned to Kaspari, the lone surviving heir to the Verdant Valley throne and bearing the scars from the Stone Guardian wolf attack.

"I know you're not kids," Teleo said. "I'm sure you'd be fine. But I need to take a ride out there anyway and shop for a new file at the blacksmith's," he lied.

"Goff has lots of files," Jessum said.

They waited a few more minutes, then when Sonderson had still not arrived, Teleo saddled Star, Kaspari put Cinnamon on a lead, and they headed out on their horses, lowering their heads against a stiff wind.

At Bitter's Ford, Teleo dismounted and stepped inside the *Scythe and Sickle.* "You seen Sonderson?" Teleo asked the brewmaster.

"He was here this morning," the man said, leaning his large hands against the wooden bar.

"This morning?" Teleo asked. "He was supposed to pick up my kids, but he never showed up."

"Hmm," the burly man said. "He seemed a little out of sorts. But then again, it was Sonderson, who's as moody as spring weather, so I didn't pay him much mind. One of the queen's White Guards came in looking fer him and they left together."

"Really? Okay. He must have been summoned by the queen. Visiting with her could take all day, if he's not careful," Teleo said.

The brewmaster laughed. "True. Perhaps they decided to patch things up." The brewmaster wagged his eyebrows and Teleo shook his head in amusement.

Teleo left the pub and told the kids that Sonderson had been called to help the queen with something. They continued up the road to the Spinners. Jeb Spinner came out to greet them, and Kaspari and Jessum dismounted and led their horses and Cinnamon into the barn to remove their tack and stable them out of the wind.

"Looks like spring's blowin' in," Jeb said, clamping a brimmed hat down over his ears before a gust could lift it off his head.

Teleo eyed the trees in the orchard swaying back and forth. "Hope it doesn't bring down any of your apple trees," he said.

"Nay," Jeb said. "Falcon's Nest is usually sheltered from the worst of it. But up top on the castle side it might get a little blustery."

"Not many trees in the castle town," Teleo said. "I need to head back there. I'll stop by later for the kids. I've got some work to finish up for the queen this afternoon."

"We can take them back to Trill'fort later, if you want," Jeb said. "We're due fer a dinner at the Great Hall."

"That's kind of you. I'll meet you there," Teleo said. "Thank you."

Kaspari ran off with the Spinner girls to get their bows, and Teleo led Star and walked with Jessum to the smithy.

Jessum put on his apron, and Goff showed Teleo his collection of files. Teleo bought a set of small files, like the ones he had used at the stonemason's workshop, to shape the tiny tesserae for his amulet.

Teleo left Jessum at the forge, rode Star back to Trillifort, and stopped by the mason's workshop for some polishing cloths.

"Here you are! I've been looking all over fer you."

Teleo looked up from the workbench to find Cutter standing there. The castellan was wearing his frilly white shirt and wine-red velvet doublet.

"Uh-oh," Teleo said. "Why are you all dressed up?"

"The queen has summoned us to her audience chamber," Cutter said. "Johnswold and Dinsmora are already there."

Teleo hid his displeasure and gathered the polishing cloths and a small flask of rock oil. He thought he had told Gracie the falcon mosaic needed a final polishing before presenting it to the queen.

He and Cutter stopped by the Third Tower, where Teleo handed off Star to Cutter's nephew for grooming, then quickly cleaned himself up, changing into his linen trousers and shirt and the sapphire-blue velvet doublet Cutter had given him. He gave his boots a quick polish and joined Cutter on the ground floor.

"You can come back fer that stuff later," Cutter said as Teleo grabbed a canvas sack to carry the polishing cloths and oil.

Teleo frowned. "Fine," he said, setting down his supplies and following Cutter out the door.

They wended their way through the back streets to the palace and let themselves in through the bronze doors. They found Dinsmora, Gracie, and Johnswold waiting outside the audience chamber, flanked by three guards on either side of the heavy wooden doors. The guards were young and stared straight ahead.

Gracie's fingers fluttered nervously together. "Oh, good. You found him. Are we all here, then?" she asked with an uneasy smile, avoiding Teleo's eyes.

"Looks like it," Cutter said.

Teleo's hair stood up on the back of his neck and he wished he had brought his swords.

Gracie pushed one of the doors open. They filed through, and Gracie closed the door behind them.

Queen Valona was seated on her falcon throne in her glittering white robe, flanked by six guards on each side. A foul stench filled the air. It took a moment for Teleo's mind to register what was displayed before them.

Lined up in front of the dais, impaled on bloody iron stakes set on heavy metal stands, were five heads. Sonderson's blue eyes stared at Teleo from the center stake, his white beard and hair caked with dried black blood. To each side of him were the heads of the queen's four White Guards. Teleo glanced around the room. The bodies had been removed and an attempt had been made to mop up the blood around the headsman's block, but several marble floor tiles were freshly stained.

He turned a stony gaze onto the queen, his heart hammering. She wore a cocky smile and met his eyes. Under her sparkling cloak, an ivory silk brocade dress was splattered with blood. Atop her head perched a diamond tiara, which winked at him. He swallowed, trying not to let the glamorous cloak and crown distract him from the horror she had just committed.

Cutter and Johnswold stood stiffly at Teleo's side, and Dinsmora fell to her knees, clasping her hands to her chest. "Oh, my queen, what has happened?" she cried, openly weeping.

"Mora, my faithful servant," Valona said, her arms outstretched. "Come kneel before me and I will tell you. Come, all of you." She smiled graciously at the four of them, as though inviting them to tea.

Teleo's battle blood was up and he surreptitiously glanced at Johnswold and Cutter, but their eyes were on the queen. Teleo followed behind the brothers. Johnswold's big shoulders blocked Teleo's view of the queen for a moment, and he stole a look at the six guardsmen to his left. Their eyes were also on Queen Valona, the glimmer of her diamonds reflecting in their eyes and sword hilts resting under their hands at their belts. As Teleo and the others approached the dais, two of the guards unsheathed their blades with sharp ringing sounds, amplified in the cavernous space. Teleo kept his eyes lowered, concentrating on the alternating white and blue floor tiles.

Teleo stepped past Sonderson's head, trying not to notice the white hairs growing out of his ears and the yellow snot crusted on his moustache.

Dinsmora climbed up onto the dais and fell to her knees in front of the throne, her arms in the queen's lap in supplication, clasping her hands with the queen's. Tears stained Dinsmora's cheeks as she gazed with concern up at Queen Valona's flushed face. Johnswold and Cutter stepped up onto the dais and knelt heavily in front of Teleo. Teleo joined them on the platform, edging himself in awkwardly alongside Johnswold, and lowered himself to his knees, keeping his eyes glued to the dais floor.

Queen Valona's paranoid voice scraped his eardrums as he tried to tune her out. Her words faded in and out of his awareness as he focused instead on the rasping of his breath entering and leaving his nostrils.

"... royal diamonds ... plotting against me ... would follow me to the source ... stab me in the back ..."

Burning oil from the wall lanterns mingled with the stench of death. Teleo lowered his head, sizing up the room from the corners of his eyes, and tried to work out Queen Valona's next move. She needed allies. She would not attack the four of them. Not right now, in any case. He hoped. Teleo did not have much choice but to continue kneeling on the cold stone and hope the queen's manic rant would exhaust itself.

Teleo did not think he could fight their way out, even if he had wanted to—particularly since Dinsmora was hopelessly enthralled by the queen and the two brothers looked like they were on their way to being spellbound themselves. The dozen guards were all young, but fit. It would be nearly impossible for Teleo to defeat them all by himself, even if he did get hold of a sword or two, which should not be an issue—the young man nearest him held an unsheathed blade that looked so new Teleo doubted it had ever severed a bone. Better yet, the queen's headsman's axe hung in its place on the wall. Teleo curled his hands into fists and waited.

"... and Tesserman, you will stand watch outside my chambers until nightfall ..."

Teleo jerked his head up and laid his eyes upon the queen's face. Her granite-brown eyes were hard and her pupils were tiny pinpricks. The halo of diamonds above her brow teased him, trying to capture his attention.

"Yes, Queen Valona," he said. "As you like."

She bored her eyes into his. "I understand you were a renowned soldier," she said, flattery sugaring her raspy voice.

Teleo tried to lower his eyes but he could not, locked as they were onto the queen's relentless gaze. "I survived a few battles," he said.

"And you have the scars to prove it," she said.

He always forgot about the scars on his face. "Yes, Your Grace," he said.

His words softened her visage. She liked him calling her that. He would use it more often. Her eyes smoldered at him. "The falcon mosaic is a masterpiece," she said, the corners of her lips turning up.

"It needs a final polishing," he said, his eyes flitting to the stonework over her shoulder. Her cape's glittering diamonds reflected off the translucent marble tesserae he had pieced together to look like an icy peak against a blue argillite sky. The bird itself was obscured behind her back and head. He examined the diamonds on the queen's shoulder. They were so perfectly cut. Each tiny facet caught the silvery daylight filtering in through the leaded-glass windows. Yellows, greens, reds, and blues flashed off the precious gems as she moved.

"I need trustworthy companions," she said, her gaze shifting to Johnswold and Cutter. "Those equal to me in loyalty and strength—and humility." Her eyes shot to Teleo again.

Yes, that made sense, he reasoned. Of course a ruler needed trustworthy companions. Those equal in loyalty and strength and humility. She knew him so well already, and they had only just started to get to know one another.

Her voice rang out in the grand hall. "Imagine our strength together, the five of us, riding across the kingdom on our white steeds."

Teleo envisioned his Star and Valona's Zeta, such glorious mounts. Dinsmora, Cutter, and Johnswold would each get their own royal white. They would make an awe-inspiring entourage. Teleo's blood warmed at the thought. He had always wanted recognition for his loyalty. Always wanted to be rewarded with a place by the ruler's side. All his life, he had been blocked by his heritage. But not here. Not with Queen Valona. She judged people by their merit, not their bloodline. She smiled at him, and he smiled back.

"Yes," he murmured.

"Yes," chorused Johnswold and Cutter.

"Oh, my queen," Dinsmora said, kissing the back of her hands.

Queen Valona talked more about their duties. They would guard her day and night on a rotating schedule. Stand with her during public appearances. Assist her on hunts. Advise her on trade deals. Resolve minor disputes among Trillifort's citizens on her behalf. She would have royal-green capes made for them and new leather-and-bronze chest armor emblazoned with her falcon sigil. And bronze, feathered helms.

Teleo found himself nodding as she spoke. Yes. He would finally have some authority. The townspeople would come to him to settle their squabbles. They would gaze upon him as he stood next to the queen on her falcon throne. All that he had secretly longed for while serving King Elke would finally come to pass, here in this marble palace with its gracious queen. He smiled.

Queen Valona shifted on her seat, and the eyes of the falcon mosaic peered at Teleo over her shoulder. The two black stones he had fashioned from Down in the Deep shone with the all-seeing eyes of the predator. Teleo froze. The falcon stared back. Goosebumps prickled his skin. The queen kept talking but Teleo did not hear her. With stark clarity, he observed the scene as though from above. She had nearly trapped him with her enchantment, slowly pulling him down into the warm pool of her spell. It had felt so natural. So right. The horror of it chilled him. He held his breath, then exhaled slowly, afraid of taking his eyes off the falcon.

At long last, the queen finished speaking. With a rustle of crinkling silk, she arose from the throne, Dinsmora helping her to her feet. Teleo closed his eyes until the queen was standing, then lowered his head as though in deference.

"Tesserman," Queen Valona said sharply.

He lifted his head, focusing on the stone falcon, its majestic feathers fluffed and ready to launch for the attack, its wings partially unfurled. "The falcon," he said, keeping his gaze fastened on the mosaic. "Do you like it?"

"Oh, yes," she said, glancing over her shoulder at the falcon. "Of course I do. I love it. You are so talented."

"That is good," he said, braving a glance at her eyes. Diamonds surrounded her face like the open jaws of a bear trap. Teleo quickly lowered his gaze to the floor, feigning humility. He could not look at the sparkling gems. He closed his eyes for a moment, resting in the darkness, then opened them again, staring at Johnswold's shiny boots as they followed the queen past the mounted heads.

They left her audience chamber and strode down the long hallway, their footsteps echoing off the cold stone. The windowless passageway was dimly lit with wall sconces, and Teleo exhaled silently. He did not know how long he could withstand her spell. He had to do something about her. Tonight.

21

WALLS

"These are my chambers," Queen Valona said as she turned the key and opened the heavy wooden door, set into a recess in the stone hallway of the private wing of the palace. Teleo peered into the chamber from the hallway. Against the facing wall of the spacious room stood a large canopy bed with carved wooden bedposts and sheer white drapery pulled back to reveal a high mattress covered in white down-filled bedding. The queen did not invite him to enter but remained with him in the recess and went to pull the door closed.

Teleo put his hand out and held the door open. "I should take a look around inside," he said. "If I am forced to defend you in the dark, I will need to know the layout of the room."

She looked him in the face and he returned her gaze, staring at the deep vertical crease between her eyes. If he kept his gaze right there in the center, almost cross-eyed, he could withstand the allure of the diamonds.

She lowered her head in a brief nod of assent, the tiara's diamonds glinting. He pushed the door open and stepped inside the chamber. The queen, Dinsmora, and Johnswold entered behind him while the six young guards stayed at their posts—three guards at either end of the long hallway. The queen closed the door and slid a thick metal bar across it, letting the bar fall with a clunk into a heavy metal bracket. A second door set into the eastern wall was similarly barred shut.

The room was filled with heavy wooden furniture. The high ceiling was vaulted and of plain blue stone, its dark hues calming the bright white of the marble walls. The bed dominated the southern wall, flanked by two rectangular windows, which murmured as the wind battered against them. Teleo walked over and peered through the clear leaded glass. Three stories below lay the falcon training yard, its T-perches empty and the door to the mews shut tight against the spring gale. It was a long drop, each castle story twice the height of a normal dwelling.

Across from the bed, set into the corner next to the main door, was a fireplace whose hearth glimmered with orange and gray coals, dulling the sharp edge of the stone-cold room. Above the fireplace hung a kite-shaped shield lacquered bright red, with a rampant griffin in the center in what looked like gold leaf.

On the other side of the bed, along the western wall, a third, smaller doorway was cracked open to what smelled like a commode. Between the bed and the toilet stood a bare dress form. The lifelike posture of the upholstered torso gave Teleo pause. A wooden knob poked up from the top of the torso like a tiny head on a long skinny neck. The beige, fabric-covered bust and abdomen were embroidered with a falcon standing on a dead pheasant with a shred of bloody flesh in the falcon's yellow beak. The embroidered falcon was not nearly as realistic as the mosaic he had made for the queen—the eyes did not study him knowingly, nor follow him as he moved across the room—they merely stared blankly into space.

Teleo peeked into the water closet. It was small, with one round stained-glass window. A small vent high in the ceiling let in a breath of fresh air. A fancy ceramic commode, painted with red roses, stood closed on a wooden pedestal. A matching ceramic water basin sat on a polished wooden counter with a water pump arching its metal head over it.

He felt the queen standing behind him. He turned, keeping his gaze cast down to the floor, and left the little room, brushing against her cloak as he passed. Shivers ran across his skin, and the diamonds glimmered as the folds of the cloak settled around her. He closed his eyes against a wave of lightheadedness and clenched his teeth, breathing slowly. He quickly understood that not only should he avoid gazing at the diamonds, but he should not touch them either. Sweat broke out on his brow and he wiped it away with his sleeve. He opened his eyes and focused on his inspection as the queen hovered closely behind him.

Several large Far Shell Island rugs covered the bedchamber's white marble floor. Tall chests of drawers, a mirrored dressing table, an ornate inlaid-wood desk with a matching chair, three large wardrobes, and two straight-backed chairs with small side tables completed the furnishings.

"May I?" he asked, his hand upon the knob of one of the wardrobe doors.

She nodded and he opened it, releasing a puff of musty air. The wardrobe was stuffed full with silk dresses, each one probably worth more than the entire collection of clothes of any of the women in Falcon's Nest. The second wardrobe held an assortment of velvet cloaks, shearling coats, hunting leathers, a fox-fur shawl, and an ermine cape. The third wardrobe contained shelves of boots, belts, and some personal items. Though the wardrobes were big enough to hide a person inside, they would need to be emptied of their contents first. He knelt and checked under the bed—it was bare except for several dust bunnies.

He climbed to his feet. "What's in there?" He gestured to the second barred door.

"My sewing chamber." The queen pulled the heavy metal bar back.

It was almost impossible not to gaze at the diamonds as she stood in front of him, the glittering cloak draping down from her outstretched arm. The diamonds seemed to be everywhere he looked. Teleo stared up at the ceiling. Queen Valona pulled open the door and they entered the room.

The sewing chamber was round, filling an entire floor of a tower. Another dress form stood in his path like a woman greeting him. It was of plain, polished wood. Next to it, a long, embroidered cape was draped on another form, its hood pulled up over the small knob head. A second cape was spread out on a large rectangular wooden table, which dominated the center of the room. The table was surrounded by several chairs and was littered with small baskets of embroidery floss. Yet another form stood against the wall beside a second barred door, exiting, Teleo assumed, into the hallway. The form held a full suit of chain-mail armor with the queen's feathered bronze helm perched atop the wooden knob. Weapons were displayed on the wall by the door—swords, daggers, a halberd, a crossbow, and two longbows with quivers of arrows.

A stone hearth glimmered with a mound of dying coals, and two wardrobes stood open, displaying stacks of folded fabric and skeins of yarn of every color. A large floor loom stood against one wall, with a half-finished tapestry of a blue-and-white floral design, and a smaller loom sat on a side table. Nearby, a spinning wheel was flanked by a basket of fleece on one side and a basket of coiled, undyed yarn on the other.

Far Shell Island rugs covered the floor, but Teleo immediately recognized the pattern peeking out from between them. His breath caught in his throat, and he looked for the Sun Circle. It was under the table—the subtle gleam of the translucent white Angel Wings marble hidden in the shadows, surrounded by exposed portions of Down in the Deep rays underneath the chairs. He looked up high on the eastern wall and the Heliotrope's Focal Point gazed down at him, filled with one pane of clear, round glass.

"As you can see," the queen said, waving her hand across the circular room, "not much goes on here besides spinning, weaving, and stitching, to while away the long winter months." She walked to the hallway door and pulled the security bar back, indicating that the tour was over.

Teleo's pulse raced. "Wait," he said, scrambling for an excuse to stay in the room. "Is this where my wife has been hiding from me all these months?" He tried to turn his mouth up into a charming grin and turned his attention to Dinsmora in an effort to avoid looking at the queen's cloak. Dinsmora tightened her mouth at him.

"Yes," the queen said, stepping away from the door. "She does beautiful work. Look." She walked to the embroidered cloak hanging from the form. She lifted it off the wooden torso and swung it around her shoulders, the fabric draping down and concealing the diamond cloak. It was as though gray, soothing clouds suddenly covered a blazing sun. He could hear the outbreath of the others as they sighed in audible relief. Teleo could not tell if the queen realized she was shielding her magic. Perhaps she was not conscious of it, he considered, although her obsession with diamonds hinted otherwise. Teleo wished she would keep the embroidered cloak on forever. The diamond tiara still glistened from her forehead, but it was easier to avoid than the voluminous cloak. The queen was describing the embroidery and how long it had taken to stitch.

Teleo's eyes wandered over the embroidered design. Dinsmora had outdone herself. Red foxes chased gray hares around mossy stones, under pine boughs, and over snowbanks, leading Teleo down a path through the forest that blended so perfectly with the white marble walls and embroidered seat cushions and multi-colored Far Shell Island rugs that he forgot where he was.

"Tesserman," Dinsmora said, tugging at his sleeve. She caught his gaze with her forest-green eyes, bringing him back to the present. "Here's a new one we're working on," Dinsmora said, diverting his gaze to the table.

"Dinsmora needs a proper cloak made of linen and wool," the queen said. "Not that sleeveless leather tunic she wears all the time, although that is lovely, too."

Teleo turned his back to Queen Valona and regarded the cloak spread out on the table.

"I only have the basic pattern down, so far," Dinsmora said.

The design reminded Teleo of a gyrfalcon—gray, black, and white scallops in alternating rows, like a falcon's wing and tail feathers. He leaned his hand on the table to get a better look, nudging aside a small wicker basket filled with skeins of embroidery floss. The basket fell to the floor, scattering the small bundles of thread.

"Oh, how clumsy of me," he said, and knelt down under the table, collecting the many twists of gray and black thread with one hand, while resting his other hand on the Heliotrope's Sun Circle. He filled the basket and rested both palms on the round stone, pretending he was searching for lost thread, and absorbed the sensation of the cool, smooth marble. He closed his eyes for a moment, then gazed down at his dim reflection. Finally, he pulled himself out from under the table and returned the basket to its place. The women ignored him, already standing around the table and examining the embroidery. Johnswold was gazing out the southern window overlooking the back courtyard.

"Ready when you are," Teleo said. He averted his eyes as the queen removed the embroidered cloak from around her shoulders and exposed the radiance of the diamonds.

"Mora and I will stay here until dinner," Queen Valona said, arranging the fox-and-hare cloak on its stand and then sitting at the table next to Dinsmora. She shooed Teleo away with a wave of her hand. "Please stand guard outside the door, Tesserman. Make sure no crazy relatives of the traitors come looking for vengeance. Johnswold will relieve you at sunset."

"Yes, Your Grace," Teleo said with a small bow. "First, I will need to run home to get my weapons."

"You can borrow a few of mine," she said, gesturing idly at the wall.

Teleo chose a sword and dagger, found their sheaths hanging on a hook, and strapped them to his belt. Johnswold held the door open for him and they stepped out into the hallway. Johnswold closed the heavy door behind them, and Teleo leaned his back against it.

"Whew," Teleo said, wiping at his brow. He still had his wits about him, as far as he could tell, but his hands and knees were shaking.

"She's something, isn't she?" Johnswold asked, his eyes gleaming with admiration.

"Ay-yah," Teleo drawled. "She's something else, that is for sure."

A scraping at his back made Teleo stand upright. The metal bar clunked into place, securing the door from the inside.

"See you later," Johnswold said, and headed down the dimly lit hall.

"Later," Teleo called after him, and brought his hand to his chest. He pulled the Heliotrope amulet out from under his shirt collar and clasped his fingers around it, in an effort to ground himself.

———◆———

Johnswold came to relieve him at dusk. At the same time, Gracie arrived to bring the women dinner. There was a scrape as the door was unbolted from the inside. It swung open and Dinsmora held it for Gracie and Teleo. The queen was bent over the cape, laying stitches, and spared him only a brief glance before returning to her embroidery. Dinsmora helped Gracie with the covered platters, and Teleo turned away from the queen's glittering diamonds as he returned the weapons to their spots on the wall. He closed the door silently behind him, bid farewell to Johnswold, and strode down the corridor.

The three guards standing at the head of the stairs bowed their heads deferentially as he passed. He descended to the ground floor, then walked down the long hallway and out the front door, passing more small groups of guards as he went. They all seemed to know who he was and let him pass without question.

A gust of wind caught him sideways, threatening to lift him off the marble paving stones. He bowed his head, turned into the gale, and hurried along the side wall of the palace where he came upon Sonderson's mountain mare hitched by herself on a covered walkway, standing forlornly near a watering trough with her head lowered against the wind.

"Oh, you poor thing," Teleo said, and untied the mare. "Come on." Sonderson must have only expected to be at the palace for a short time, Teleo determined, otherwise, the mare should have been put into the palace's guest stables. Teleo shook his head and led the seal-brown mare through the alleyways to the Third

Tower and opened the door. The wind swung the heavy door open and slammed it against the inside wall. He stepped aside for the mare to enter, then shouldered the door shut, thankful for the warm shelter of the stone tower. The sheep bleated and Star nickered at them. A new young man was sitting in front of the fire and stood up to introduce himself.

"Hi, I'm Gabe. My uncle Johnswold says I'm supposed to watch the sheep while you go to the Great Hall."

Teleo nodded graciously. "Much obliged, Gabe," he said.

"You must feel honored to be serving the queen as a White Guard," the young man said with a note of awe in his voice. "I hope one day to be so honored."

Teleo swallowed. "Ay-yah. What an honor," he managed to say.

Teleo herded the ewes and lambs into their pen, checked on Marblehead in his pen, and then removed the mountain mare's saddle and bridle and rubbed her down. She and Star seemed to know one another, so Teleo let her roam freely in the open area. He fed the animals, freshened their water, and then went to use the outhouse. The door to the mews was banging in the wind. The falcon was not on the griffin fountain nor on her T-perch. He spotted her grayish-white shape huddled in a corner of the shed on top of the woodpile. He fed her and then latched the door closed against the wind. He finally ran upstairs, where he quickly changed into his leathers, strapped on his swords, knives, and stonemason's belt, heavy with hammers, and left for the Great Hall.

He spotted Kaspari and Jessum sitting with the Spinner family on the other side of the large hall. Teleo went to the cooking fires for a plate of food, then threaded his way between the crowded tables and benches to join them. Shifting eyes and whispers followed him. Word must have gotten around about the beheadings and that Teleo had been chosen as one of the new Queen's Guards. It was a small, tight-knit community, and the four dead White Guards and Sonderson must have been related to many of them—but people also loved the queen. Were they ashamed that the guards had betrayed the queen, or did they know she was crazy? Were any of them secretly plotting against her? Either way, Teleo was an outsider and had taken the place of one of the dead.

Teleo sat down with his foster children and friends.

"Did you hear?" Teleo asked.

Jeb Spinner nodded silently. His wife and daughters looked down and picked at their food. Kaspari and Jessum gazed at Teleo, wide-eyed.

Teleo cut into his roasted pork and chewed slowly.

Jeb cleared his throat and talked about the strong winds and how the river was swollen from the spring thaw.

Kaspari pushed her plate away. "Sonderson is dead?" she asked.

"Yes," Teleo said grimly, holding her stricken gaze.

"What did he do?" she asked.

Jessum listened curiously and the Spinners shifted in their seats.

Teleo cleared his throat. "I don't know exactly. But I'm sure the queen had her reasons."

Kaspari held his eyes. He returned her gaze with a firm frown. They could talk more about it later, but not here. He took another bite of meat.

"Where's Nutmeg?" she asked.

Teleo stopped chewing. He had forgotten all about Nutmeg. A wave of dismay washed over him. He had convinced himself that he had escaped the queen's foul influence, but clearly her claws were embedded into him, addling his mind—despite his best efforts. Worse, Dinsmora had said nothing about her beloved horse. The Dinsmora Teleo used to know would have headed to Sheep's Haven straightaway to fetch Nutmeg. He suddenly lost his appetite and pushed his plate aside.

"Let's go check on him," Teleo said.

Teleo, Kaspari, and Jessum thanked the Spinners and bid them farewell, then left the warmth of the Great Hall and headed around the corner to the Great Hall's horse pen where BlackJack, Daisy, and Cinnamon were waiting. They led the horses through the keening wind to their tower, where they greeted Johnswold's nephew and asked him to stay a bit longer. Kaspari checked on Sonderson's mountain mare while Teleo saddled Star. They pulled on their shearling coats and hats to protect against the wind and then trotted through the walled town. After cantering through the soothing stillness of the tunnel, they emerged out onto the promontory overlooking Falcon's Nest. The wind was biting, and the moon was waxing towards full, bathing the valley in an eerie glow. Wisps of high clouds raced across the moon's yellow face, chasing shadows across the rolling hills.

They headed down into the valley. Jessum and BlackJack led them single file along the edge of the road where it was dryer and flatter. They alternated between trotting and cantering and soon passed through Mud Flats and Bitter's Ford. The road to Sheep's Haven was lit by moonlight and the wind howled in from the north.

The upper barn, half-buried in the hillock, stood like a hunched troll against the pale fields. The barn doors were wide open to predators and the cold night, and the relentless wind sent straw spiraling into the air. The barn was dark, but Nutmeg's whinny led them to the back corner where the big draft horse stepped forward to meet them.

"Hey, boy," Teleo said, hugging the horse's neck. Daisy stepped forward and touched noses with the gelding. Teleo turned to the kids. "Give him a quick brushing and saddle him up."

Teleo closed the barn doors and lit a lantern, and Kaspari and Jessum took brushes to Nutmeg's dusty coat. Teleo went down to the lower barn and lit another lantern. The underground space was sheltered from the wind, aside from a high-pitched whistling from the hatch and small gusts from the air vents. He raised the lantern and looked around. Sonderson's belongings were as he had left them, as one would when leaving home on a normal day and fully expecting to return. Teleo had heard talk of sending guards back to the encampment near the Stone Guardian's secret path after the snows melted, but there were no signs of guards inhabiting the cellar.

A ceramic jug sat on the floor by the bunk. Teleo uncorked it. Mushroom wine. It was half full. He found a leather satchel and placed the jug inside it. He searched the food shelves and found Sonderson's metal flask. It was filled with Ferska, and Teleo added it to his stash. Folded neatly on the upper bunk was a relatively new set of clothes made of homespun wool: shirt, pants, and a hooded cloak. He rolled them up and stuffed them into the satchel. He looked around for anything else that might be useful. A small bag of silver and gold coins he found hidden under a mattress would come in handy, but Teleo figured Sonderson might have family somewhere who needed it, so he left the bag on the fireplace mantel.

Various tools were scattered on a bench. A small scrap of buckskin caught his attention. Hematite beads glinted up at him, and a shiver ran up his spine. He picked up the Stone Guardian's shred of clothing. The tiny stones were cold and an inaudible vibration flowed through his fingers. He pocketed the beaded scrap, then searched for Sonderson's shepherd's crook. It was not there.

Teleo slung the satchel across his shoulder, extinguished the lantern, and went upstairs. Nutmeg was saddled, and Kaspari was adjusting his bridle. Teleo stroked Nutmeg's cheek, then tied the reins to his saddle to keep them from dangling. Jessum blew out the other lantern, Teleo clicked his tongue for Nutmeg to follow, and they left the shelter of the barn.

Teleo latched the barn door shut, ducked his head against the steady wind sweeping across the open fields, hoisted himself into Star's saddle, and led them at a brisk walk down the moonlit road.

⸻ ◆ ⸻

Dinsmora finally came home, well after midnight.

Teleo was waiting for her and stood up from the bat-and-griffin chair as she shut the door against the moaning wind.

"You forgot about Nutmeg," he scolded as she hung her quilted gambeson on the hook.

Dinsmora's brow furrowed as she turned to the horses. Nutmeg and the mountain mare were standing quietly with the other horses. "Is he okay?" She crossed the stable and spoke into Nutmeg's ear. The big bay's black tail flicked back and forth.

Teleo watched her through narrowed eyelids. She seemed concerned but not horrified with herself like she normally would have been. She left the horse pen and took Teleo's seat, stretching her hands out towards the fire to warm them.

Teleo stood by the fireplace and glared at her. "Are you sorry at all that Sonderson is dead?" he demanded.

"Of course," she said defensively. "But he shouldn't have betrayed the queen."

"What did he do, exactly?" Teleo asked.

Dinsmora shrugged. "I don't know."

"You spent all day and evening with her," he pressed.

"She didn't say, and I didn't ask," she said curtly.

Teleo snorted. "Here," he said in a conciliatory tone. "Want some of this?" He poured a mug half full from Sonderson's ceramic jug and offered it to Dinsmora. She had always boasted about how she had never been stupid enough to try mushroom wine. "It's made with a rare mountain berry," he said. "One of the guards gave it to me."

She sipped it and crinkled her nose. "It's sweet."

"It is," he said as she took another sip.

He sat with her until she drained the mug and asked for more. Mushroom wine had that effect on people. He gave her another half cup and watched guiltily as she drank it all. Her face glowed and a lopsided smile cut across her face, her dimples deep like when she was a teenager. They talked and laughed about when they were younger until the fire died low and the wind wailed outside and Teleo felt a glimmer of hope.

Sonderson had said mushroom wine cleared his head from the queen's bewitchment. Teleo hoped it was true but dared not take a sip himself for fear he would drain the entire jug and lose track of the next three days. Dinsmora suddenly arose from her chair and ran into the stable area. He could hear her vomiting into a bucket. It was working. Next, she would fall into a deep sleep with vivid dreams and then awaken with a pounding head-ache. The only thing that would dull the headache was more mushroom wine, and if she indulged in it a second time, the fantastical visions would take over her waking life as well as her dreams and she could get lost in the mushroom haze for days.

She retched a few more times and came stumbling back.

"Gosh, I don't know what came over me," she said, wiping her mouth. "I'd better go to bed."

"You'd better," Teleo agreed.

He sat by the upstairs fire and waited until she and the kids were asleep, then gathered his courage and stood up. He knew what he had to do—he just wasn't sure he could do it.

He slipped his short sword into its belt sheath, strapped on his knife and hammer belts, and crept up the steps to the third floor. The door swung open silently, letting through a cold draft. He closed it softly behind him and let his eyes adjust to the room, which was lit by a stream of moonlight shining through the open Focal Point window. Several bats fluttered overhead, startling him. He watched their dance as they swooped after tiny bugs that swarmed like dust motes in the moonlight. He stood in the shaft of light, took the amulet out from under his jerkin, and compared its likeness to the Heliotrope. It was perfect.

Teleo kept his heavy belts on and danced the sword until he broke a sweat. The dance invigorated his body and calmed his mind. The night was at its deepest, and he needed to get this done. He knelt by the Sun Circle and pressed his palms onto the cool Angel Wings marble, leaning on his hands and closing his eyes to let the feeling of the stone soak in. Nothing happened, so he lowered his head and pressed his forehead to the circle, then lay prone, resting his cheek on its smooth surface. He wished he could sleep but pulled himself upright and sat cross-legged in the center of the disk and closed his eyes.

Teleo brought his mind back to that afternoon in the sewing chamber. He could feel its polished Sun Circle under his palms. It was warmer than this one, and the room smelled of wood smoke. Cedar. The odor of women's sweat. And wool. He breathed evenly. He could feel the brush of his fingers over the translucent marble as he picked up skeins of embroidery floss. The windows rattled in the wind.

His eyes flew open. Embers in the fireplace gave off a faint orange glow as he stared through chair legs. The dark wooden table spanned just above his head. He held his breath, checking that he was really in the sewing chamber, then exhaled in a moment of surprised satisfaction. Getting onto his hands and knees, he crawled silently out from under the table and stood up, the room tilting from a sudden onslaught of vertigo. He closed his eyes and held onto the edge of the table until the lightheadedness passed. When he opened his eyes, pale moonlight from the large leaded-glass windows and the Focal Point filled the room.

Teleo turned around, moving his hand to his sword hilt by reflex. For a moment, he thought Johnswold and the other guards had caught him stealing into the queen's private chambers, but it was just the dress forms. The one with the chainmail was the most realistic, but even the bare wooden form and the one draped with the queen's fox-and-hare cloak gave him pause. He imagined Johnswold standing in the hallway on the other side of the thick wooden door, bored or irritated, or perhaps dozing off. Both of the sewing chamber's doors were closed— the hallway door was bolted shut, but the interior door was not.

Teleo stepped over to the queen's fox-and-hare cloak and silently undid the clasp. He swung the cloak around his shoulders, pulling on the hood until it nearly covered his eyes. Clasping the cloak at his neck, he padded silently to the door leading to the queen's bedchamber. He hesitated at the edge of the Mage's circle where the mosaic met the plain marble border. Sigrid had warned him against leaving the Heliotrope—that it made it harder to travel back. But what choice did he have? The windows were too high off the ground to jump from—he should have brought rope, just in case. Too late now. He should have planned better. Part of him had doubted that he could actually travel using the Heliotropes. But here he was. A flush of accomplishment warmed his skin. Sigrid would be proud of him.

If he could not travel back, he could always fight his way out. But that would mean injuring or killing Johnswold, which he did not want to do. If he made a scene, leaving a trail of bodies like he had at Verdant Castle, then he would need to flee Trillifort—either abandoning Dinsmora and the kids or risking their lives along with his. No. Best to stick to his plan, as crazy as it felt.

He held his breath and stepped off the Heliotrope. His eyes went black as another wave of vertigo washed over him. He leaned his forehead against the door until he regained his balance. Slowly, he turned the handle and pushed. The door did not budge. He stepped aside in frustration, biting at his lip. Of course she would have locked herself inside her bed-chamber—even though the sewing chamber's hallway door was already barred shut. She was completely paranoid. Maybe with good reason, he admitted.

Now what to do? His options were limited. He could stay here, ambush her in the morning, and slit her throat. But that was messy. He could probably break her neck, but she was not small, nor was she weak. Strangling her would be easier. Or he could just go home to the Third Tower and forget this whole foolish scheme. But then the queen would get him under her thrall—it was only a matter of time. He and Dinsmora would turn up dead at some point, and the kids would be left on their own. He would never find Oren, and Oren would never know Teleo had been searching for him.

The best option was to return to the Third Tower, take the family hunting in the morning, and never come back. That's what he should do. If he could just travel one more time through the Heliotropes. He was so exhausted. He turned and leaned his back against the stone wall. The cold seeped into his bones, and the grain of the rock enveloped him in its pattern. Blackness engulfed him as he felt himself falling. He stepped backwards to catch himself and lifted his head, pressing his palms against the stone wall for balance. Nausea welled up in his throat and he leaned his forehead against the cold wall, taking deep silent breaths, then opened his eyes. He was standing next to the barred door to his left. To his right was a polished, inlaid wood desk, its intricate pattern faintly illuminated by ghostly moonlight. He slowly turned around.

He was in the queen's bedchamber. He stared at the canopy bed, confused. Somehow, he had passed through the wall. Sigrid had not told him about this, and he did not know how he had done it, nor how he could do it again. His body felt like it had passed through a meat grinder—his once-solid form chopped up and stuffed back into a sausage skin.

Queen Valona was breathing softly under a mound of covers. The wind battered at the windows, and moonlight reflected off the white marble window casings, bathing the room in a silvery sheen. The gold griffin gleamed faintly from its shield above the fireplace, the hearth glowing with a hint of red beneath a pile of ashes. Beyond the bed, the queen's diamond cloak glinted, draped over the dress form. Teleo grimly pondered the cursed diamonds that had everyone falling over their feet to serve Queen Valona and forgetting who they were in the process, then ending up with their heads chopped off. Evil gems from a Stone Guardian diamond mine. No wonder the Stone Guardians were such powerful foes.

He averted his gaze and briefly considered killing the queen, but his options for escape would remain the same as before. Besides, he did not relish the thought of killing a woman in her bed. It felt wrong.

He tried to discern the effect of the embroidered cloak draped over his shoulders. Did it work the same way as Dinsmora's tunic and serve as camouflage? He gazed down at the foxes chasing the hares across his chest. Gray and white, reflecting the muted tones of the moonlit room. But more intriguing, he cast no shadow.

Regardless of how he had gotten into the room or the power of the embroidered cloak, he was here now. He was committed. He steeled himself against a wave of dizziness and took a step forward. Then another. He trod slowly and silently across the carpeted floor and around the foot of the bed to the other side. The hood of the queen's white-satin, gem-encrusted cloak draped over the wooden knob of the dress form, and the faceless head stared out at him, diamonds glimmering in starburst patterns around it. The cloak took on the queen's shape, but no ... the shoulders of the dress form could be anyone's shoulders. They could be Teleo's. He could be the object of desire, the one who attracted admirers like moths to a flame.

Teleo did not pause to consider his vagrant thoughts but reached for the glittering cloak, unclasped the silver leaf catch at the neck, and slid it off the form. The fabric whispered as Teleo turned it inside out and rolled it up, hiding the diamonds and exposing the white wool lining. He tucked it under his arm like one of the lambs.

The queen stirred and rolled over. Teleo froze. When her breathing evened out, he backed silently into the shadows of the commode chamber to wait until he was sure she was in a deep slumber. A floor tile tilted slightly under his foot with a soft scrape. He stepped back a pace and listened to see if the sound had awoken the queen. Her breathing continued as before, and Teleo exhaled silently. Moonlight filtered in through the small stained-glass window above the commode, and Teleo glanced down at the floor. He squatted to get a closer look. The loose tile had no grout around it, which he found to be odd, given that it was in the middle of the floor and all the other tiles were set in grout. Teleo carefully unsheathed a knife, levered up the tile, and set it silently aside. There was a void underneath where the tile had been. Teleo reached his hand down inside and felt around, finding plaster and a supporting beam, and then his fingers sank into plush velvet. He pulled out the soft fabric.

It was a small sack. He unknotted the silk rope. Inside glimmered a handful of uncut diamonds. He lifted out a few of the rough, glistening chunks. Such wealth and power, sitting in his hands. Just one of the larger diamonds, if cut properly, would be worth more than a soldier's salary over an entire lifetime. He closed his eyes and let the gems fall noiselessly back into the sack. He quickly tied it closed and stuffed it inside the rolled cloak before he lost his self-control and slipped a few diamonds into his pocket.

His hands trembled as he felt around the rest of the dark hole. Finding nothing, he carefully replaced the tile and stood up. Could she have more diamonds stashed away in her chambers? She had not seemed overly concerned when he had searched her chests and cabinets, and had paid him little mind when he had explored the sewing chamber—a room where many women frequented. He hoped he had found all of her precious jewels, but if not, there was nothing he could do about it. He could not very well ransack the queen's private quarters while she was asleep in her bed.

Teleo steadied his pulse and then slunk out of the commode chamber. Taking care with each step, he crossed the room the way he had come, moving slowly to let the camouflage cloak conform to his surroundings. He reached the wall and pressed his back against it like before, hoping he could repeat the mysterious magic. He surrendered his thoughts and his body to the cold stone. It enveloped him like an icy pool of water. He stumbled backwards and landed in the sewing room on his rear end, knocking the breath out of him. The wall was solid in front of him.

Relieved, he turned and crawled across the floor on his knees and one hand, clutching the cloak with the other. Climbing to his feet, he staggered to the dress form and returned the fox-and-hare cloak to its stand. After draping it carefully and clasping it closed, he crawled between chair legs and under the table, sat cross-legged on the Sun Circle with the white cloak in his lap, closed his eyes, and thought of the Sun Circle in the Third Tower.

He sat there. And sat there. And sat there.

The wind wailed a mournful cry. His body ached as though he had been beaten up, and he wanted to sleep. He clutched the amulet hanging from his neck. It was cold.

He had to dance.

He placed the diamond cloak on the Angel Wings marble and climbed out from under the table and chairs, struggled to his feet, unsheathed his sword, and began to turn and crouch in his sword forms. He awkwardly edged around the large rectangular table and chairs, between dress forms and looms and cabinets bursting with fabric and yarn. His leg muscles shook from exhaustion, and the back of his head felt like it had been hit with a hammer. Still, he danced. He danced for his life. For Dinsmora's. For Jessum's and Kaspari's. For Oren's. For Johnswold's and the half-dozen young guards outside in the hallway who wanted to live out their lives, not die for a mad queen by the sword of an interloper.

He danced until he could dance no more. The sword was heavy in his hand, and his arms were like jelly. He sheathed his blade and crawled back to the translucent circle. Sitting with the cloak warm in his lap, he closed his eyes, remembering the feel of the Sun Circle in the Third Tower. He felt his hands pressing against the smooth, cold stone. The bats were hunting overhead, diving and dodging, their chirps filling the air. His cheek rested on the hard marble, his body prone and heavy, all of his energy gone.

He was freezing. Shivering. A puff of air brought a cloud of white billowing up and settling over him, warm and soft. Gentle hands smoothed it over his back and tucked it around his shoulders. He cracked open his eyes. Petite toes peeked out from under a red velvet hem.

"Sigrid?" he croaked from a dry throat.

"Yes, I'm here," she said, kneeling by his side. "I was getting worried. I saw you leave through the stone. I've been dancing for you for hours. The bats and I. Trying to give you energy and bring you back."

"Thank you," he mumbled. He curled onto his side, drew the covering up under his chin, and peered across the pattern of the Heliotrope to the rough-hewn walls of the Third Tower. He could hear the high-pitched chirping of the bats, and their shadows flitted across the slowly swirling Heliotrope. He closed his eyes.

"You must be cold," he said.

"I'm sweating, actually," she said. "But I will get cold soon. I must go before I grow any more tired."

"You'd better," he agreed, reaching out from underneath the warm wool. She took his hand and squeezed it.

"That's a beautiful cloak," she said, releasing his hand and fingering the diamond-laden satin. "Where did you get it?"

"Oh ...," he moaned. "Don't look at it. You should go."

She rose to her feet. "As you wish. Goodbye, then," she said.

"Thank you," he said again, and pulled himself up onto his knees, drawing the cloak around his shoulders. Pale moonlight filtered in through the Focal Point window, and wind gusted through the opening. The velvet sack sat on the Sun Circle. He grabbed it and clutched it to his chest.

Teleo shuffled backwards on his knees off the center circle and watched Sigrid step onto the Angel Wings marble, shimmer, and then disappear. Gathering his last bits of strength, he climbed to his feet. He removed the cloak and rolled it up quickly around the velvet sack, exposing the wool lining and hiding the sparkling gems from view—not allowing himself to bask in their beauty one last time.

He crept downstairs. On the second level, Dinsmora, Jessum, and Kaspari were silent lumps in their beds. On the ground level, the horses shifted and made sleeping sounds. The ewes and lambs were huddled in a fluffy pile in their pen, and the ram was sleeping in his. Teleo fetched a crowbar and then nudged Cinnamon aside with his shoulder.

"Move over, buddy. Sorry." The big gelding stepped away and found a spot between Nutmeg and Daisy. Teleo dropped the cloak onto the straw bedding, levered the floor tiles off the hatch, and slid the heavy wooden slab to the side. The pit was dark and musty. He tried not to think about what was lying in the dirt down below. He fetched a burlap sack, stuffed the diamond cloak and velvet bag inside, and tied it shut. He lit a torch and lowered the flame into the dungeon. The dirt floor fell away at the center into a deeper, darker hole where no light reached. The skeletons watched him toss the burlap sack into the hole. A moment later, he heard it land with a soft thud—the hole was deep but not bottomless. He grabbed a shovel and threw heaps of sheep dung and horse manure down after it. He checked his work with the torch. The dark pit would not reveal its treasure.

After sliding the wooden hatch back into place, he set the stones where they belonged and pushed soiled straw over them. His back ached and his muscles shook, but he stood tall and breathed a deep sigh of relief, then crept upstairs and over to his pile of belongings. He tried not to wake the others as he removed his weapon and hammer belts and emptied his pockets of a collection of nails, a hoof pick, a handful of Silver and Copper Bits, and a small scrap of gray buckskin. He stared at the scrap he had taken from Sonderson's cellar. The hematite beads were icy cold under his fingertips and arranged in a spiral pattern.

"Stone Guardian magic," he mumbled. "I'll be damned." Stone walls had melted like butter for him. He gazed at the polished hematite beads—shining bits of magical iron ore. He raised his other hand and pressed his palm against the stone wall near the fireplace. After a moment, his hand sank into the rock up to his wrist. He pulled it out and stared at it, then regarded the scrap of hematite-beaded leather. He crossed the room, set the buckskin scrap on a step, and then returned to the fireplace and pressed his hand to the wall again. It was solid stone. Creamy marble, rough to the touch. Left unpolished intentionally to provide muted light and a natural texture. Hard and unyielding. He ran to fetch the buckskin, then returned to the wall and tried again. His hand sank into the stone as though it were a mud pit after spring thaw. He pulled his hand out again, his arm trembling.

Such a little piece of deer hide. So few hematite beads. He could not fathom the power that the Stone Guardian crone must wield wearing an entire tunic covered in these stones. He shook his head and wondered how her body had survived a lifetime of walking through rock. His head felt like an anvil being struck by a hammer every three seconds. He searched his saddlebags. At the bottom, he found his small leather medicine bag and stuffed the scrap of Stone Guardian magic into it, then hung the medicine bag around his neck next to the miniature Heliotrope. He held the stone mosaic for a moment, rubbing his thumb over the intricate pattern. The amulet was smooth and warm and calmed his throbbing pulse.

Teleo went back downstairs to the stable, put a log on the dying fire, and poked at it until flames crept up around it. He gulped down two mugs of well water, ate a sandwich of stale bread and cheese, and then pulled his shearling coat off its hook, tossed it down in front of the stone hearth, crawled onto it, and passed out.

———◆———

The animals woke him at first light. Teleo struggled to his feet, his head still pounding. He splashed cold water on his face and drank from his cupped palms. Traveling between Heliotropes and stepping through rock had thrashed his body worse than a battle or a mushroom wine binge. The mushroom wine jug sat on the stump by the hearth. There was still some left. Next to it was Sonderson's flask of Ferska. Teleo took a swig of the peach brandy, then went upstairs to the living area where he poured half of it into a mug and set it quietly on the table. He then drained the rest of the mushroom wine into the flask with the remaining Ferska, tossed in a few crushed cloves and black peppercorns, added a dollop of honey, and shook the whole thing. He took a small sip and scrunched up his face. It was awful. It would do perfectly.

Dinsmora was still sleeping—probably due to the mushroom wine. If she looked for the wine jug when she awoke, it would be empty. She might find the mug of Ferska, which would help a little bit, and then she would go straight back to bed. He chuckled to himself.

Jessum rolled over and went back to sleep, and Kaspari was motionless in her bed. Teleo crept downstairs and out into the courtyard, where he let Hunter out of her mews, slipped on a leather glove, and fetched the falcon's bag of meat from a wooden cabinet. Soon it would be too warm to store fresh meat like this, and Dinsmora would need to go back to hunting every day. He whistled for the bird. Hunter flew at him, landed on his cuff, and delicately took a piece of meat from Teleo's hand.

Teleo fed the bird until she was satisfied, then left her on the griffin fountain perch, where she sat on its stone beak, watching the water spew from its open mouth. The wind was not as strong as it had been the night before, but it still whipped in from all directions, fluffing the bird's feathers and slamming the mews door shut. He propped it open, then went back into the tower. He fed the horses and sheep, fetched Sonderson's flask, and then left for the palace as the sky brightened to a pearly gray.

Inside the palace, he passed three groggy guards at the top of the stairs and found Cutter leaning against the wall outside the queen's chambers.

"What are you doing here?" Teleo asked the scowling man. "Where's your brother?"

"We split the night shift," Cutter said, standing up straight and grabbing the flask from Teleo's hand. "This woman is going to be the death of me." He took a swig and made a face. "What in demon's name is this?" He took another mouthful.

"It's called wildfire," Teleo said, smiling deviously. "A Verdant Valley specialty."

"Tastes like horse piss," Cutter said, tilting the flask to his mouth again.

"It'll kick your ass," Teleo warned. "Be careful."

"Will it put me to sleep?" Cutter asked. "I haven't slept in two days."

"It will."

Cutter took another gulp and coughed, then wiped his mouth and smoothed his bushy beard. "I'm off to bed. Have a *great* time." He took one more gulp and capped the flask, handing it back to Teleo.

He took the flask, resisting the temptation to sip from it himself, his temples already pounding and his vision too sharp.

A shriek came through the thick wooden door. Teleo and Cutter started, and Cutter shook the door handle. "Valona?!"

She screamed again.

"Goddamned woman insists on bolting the damn door." Cutter pounded on the wood. "Valona, open the door!"

The metal bar rattled, and the door swung inwards. Queen Valona was turning wildly in a circle, then rushed to a wardrobe and began dragging out silk dresses and tossing them to the floor.

"My cloak! My cloak!" She went to the next wardrobe and pulled out velvet cloaks and furs. She turned to Teleo and Cutter with frenzied eyes, her white hair mussed and sticking to her moist face, and her rumpled white nightgown showing hints of large drooping breasts underneath. *"Look fer my diamond cloak, you idiots! It's gone!"*

"Where?" Cutter asked.

"If I knew where it was ...," the queen screamed, then went to the third wardrobe, boots thudding to the floor as she swept her arms across the shelves.

Teleo rushed past the empty dress form. The form's embroidered falcon, with bloody flesh hanging from its mouth, stared into nothingness—it would not reveal Teleo's secrets. Teleo pretended to search the commode chamber. The cold room was small and empty and could not hide him for long.

When Teleo emerged from the smelly chamber, Cutter was on his knees, looking under the bed. Teleo checked under the bed from the other side.

"Are you sure you didn't leave it on the bed?" Cutter asked, climbing to his feet and pulling an embroidered coverlet off the bed, then pushing aside a fluffy white featherbed comforter. Teleo inspected the sheer drapery tied at each bedpost.

"I did not leave it on the bed! I always put it on its stand. You idiot. You know that!" she yelled, throwing pillows to the floor.

Cutter exchanged glances with Teleo. "It's okay, Yer Highness," Cutter said soothingly. "We'll find it. It's got to be here somewhere." He started opening chest drawers.

She pushed him aside and opened them herself, throwing metal bracelets across the room.

Cutter ducked, and Teleo unbolted the connecting door and escaped into the sewing chamber. The fox-and-hare cloak gazed calmly at him, and the chainmail armor and feathered helm watched with interest.

Teleo conducted a cursory inspection. The black-and-white cloak lay spread across the table, and the Sun Circle was a waxy white underneath. He leaned against the doorjamb leading into the bedroom and watched Queen Valona peel off her night-gown and pull on her linen underclothes and riding leathers right in front of them, her bare skin pale and her muscles toned.

"Well, are you just going to stand there?" she demanded, hands on her hips and glaring at Teleo.

He stood straight. "I'm sorry, Your Grace. I'm trying to figure out how anyone got in here with all the doors bolted shut." He strode to one of the windows flanking her bed, pulled down the latch handle, and pushed the window open. It creaked on its hinges. He looked down into the empty falconry yard. The fresh air felt good, and he gazed out over the misty blue peaks.

Queen Valona elbowed him aside and stared down to the ground, sixty feet below. The Stone Guardian-fashioned exterior walls of the palace were rough-hewn, not polished, but there were no gaps or bumps big enough for fingers or toes to grab hold of.

"It's unlikely anyone could have climbed up here," he said. He leaned out the window and peered up at the ramparts. A line of griffin gargoyles stared down mockingly at him. "What's up there? Can I inspect the roof?"

They spent the whole day tearing apart the palace. Queen Valona became more agitated as the day progressed and the cloak did not turn up. She sent for Dinsmora and Johnswold. Dinsmora arrived with dark circles under her eyes. Her hair was dull and uncombed, and her normally lively gait dragged. She shuffled along quietly at the queen's heels, and Johnswold and Cutter stole sips of wildfire.

They ended up back in the bedchamber, looking at one another.

Queen Valona slumped despondently in a chair. "Stone Guardians," she said. "That vile sorceress." She took a glass vase sitting on a side table and flung it into the cold fireplace, where it shattered with a loud crash. A curved chunk of glass rocked on the stone hearth until it became still and the room returned to an uncomfortable silence.

The queen hopped to her feet and pointed, straight-armed, at Johnswold. "Search every household. Anyone who looks the least bit suspicious you will bring to me and I will chop off their head." She then pointed at Cutter. "You will get the quarrymen, and they will start shearing off that witch's cliff. Today!"

"Yes, Queen Valona," Cutter said, with a small bow.

"Yes, Queen Valona," Johnswold echoed.

Cutter turned on his heels, and Johnswold and Teleo followed him, taking the opportunity to escape her wrath. They pulled the hallway door closed, leaving poor Dinsmora with the queen. The iron bar clunked into place on the other side, and they let out a combined sigh.

"That woman is completely losing it," Johnswold said, with the dazed clarity of the mushroom wine burning in his eyes.

Cutter nodded. He was not smiling. "Something must be done about her."

The two brothers exchanged glances, and their eyes landed on Teleo.

"I completely agree," Teleo said quickly. "She's nuts, and frankly, she's dangerous and she's taking my Mora down with her."

The brothers nodded somberly. Cutter put his hand to his sword hilt and led the way down the dim hallway.

"Yer relieved fer the day," Cutter barked at the three guards at the head of the stairs. "You, too!" Cutter called to the three at the other end of the hallway. "Go get some food and some sleep."

"Should we get replacements?" a guard asked.

"No. I'll take care of it," Cutter said sharply, and the guards scurried by and hastened down the stairs.

"She has been running this place like a tyrant fer too long," Cutter grumbled.

Johnswold nodded vigorously and followed his brother down the steps.

Teleo took up the rear and rubbed his aching head.

———◆———

Johnswold and the Captain of the Guards organized the search of every household for Queen Valona's missing cloak. Teleo could tell they did not believe they would find it and thought the queen had lost her mind. The search took three days, and no one was hauled in to put their neck on Queen Valona's chopping block. They didn't even ask to inspect the Third Tower, and Teleo did not remind them.

During the same time period, Cutter called on the quarrymen to strip away the Stone Guardian's access path. The burly men took to the task with relish, bringing chisels, wedges, hammers, iron mallets, levers, saws, scaffolds, water barrels, and wagons to Sheep's Haven, and setting up shop at the base of the cliff near the guards' camp. There was a small contingent of archers stationed there already, but they had seen no signs of wolves or mysterious old crones creeping down the cliff path.

Teleo accompanied a couple of quarrymen up the narrow crevasse to the Stone Guardian's platform, where they discussed their stone cutting. Teleo reminded them about the staircase hidden behind the stone wall at the head of the platform, and the men regarded him with furrowed brows.

"We'll cut away the stone and see what's behind there," one of them said. Teleo couldn't tell if the man believed him or thought he was delusional.

Teleo left them there, squeezing back down through the crevasse, and then wandered over to a makeshift table. An architect was drawing up plans for a stone watchtower to be built below the witch's lookout. In addition, a small fortress was to be constructed in the fields where the wolves had attacked them.

"After we remove the stone facing from the cliff, we will use the Stone Guardian's blue stone fer our fortress," the architect said with excitement. "It will be impenetrable. Now if we only had a Mage Stone Master," he added slyly, eyeing Teleo.

"I don't know any of those," Teleo said, feigning ignorance. He was not going to commit to a multi-year project at Trillifort. He intended to go west to the Sapphire Valley—sooner rather than later. Spring was arriving with a vengeance, and as soon as the winds died down and they got a clear patch of weather between rainstorms, he and the kids would be on their way.

He needed to figure out how to present their departure to Queen Valona—and to Dinsmora. His cousin was still loyal to the deranged queen. The mushroom wine had worn off, and the diamond cloak was gone, but Dinsmora still spent her days holed up in the queen's sewing chamber. Whenever Teleo suggested she stop going there, Dinsmora snapped at him and shot her little energy barbs at his face. That's the thanks he got for trying to save her life.

That Sunday, Teleo went with the kids to the hot springs. He did not bother finding a babysitter for the sheep. The queen had suddenly become a recluse and nothing was going to befall the sheep.

He lowered himself into a small unoccupied pool, stealing some time for himself. He scratched at a week's worth of stubble on his chin, thinking maybe he would grow a beard. He sank all the way into the hot water, letting it flow over his head and dull the surrounding sounds to distant murmurings. He surfaced, water dripping from his hair, and leaned his head back against the pool's edge.

Dinsmora showed up, surprisingly, and settled into the water next to him, disturbing his moment of peace and quiet. She slid down into the hot water until it covered her head, then rose up again, water streaming from her dark red hair, her freckled cheeks glistening. They were alone. Most people preferred the larger pools and catching up with friends and family. Jessum and Kaspari were with their peers at an upper pool, the youths screaming and laughing as they challenged each other to wade across the hottest spring at the top.

"What are you doing here, Dinsmora?" he asked.

"Glad to see you, too," she said dryly. "I need to speak with you."

"Why?" He hoped the queen was not calling him and the brothers back to the castle for guard duty. Last he'd heard, she had dismissed all her guards and locked herself inside her chambers with Dinsmora, only opening the door for Gracie to bring food.

"I will be gone for a few days," she said. "I did not want you to worry."

He blinked. "Kind of you. Where are you going?"

"The queen and I are going to get her some more diamonds. From a mine near Demon's Bones—she would not tell me exactly where. We leave tonight. She told me not to tell you."

"Dinsmora ..."

"Shush," she said, cutting him off.

"The queen is crazy, Dinsmora," he said.

"She's fine," Dinsmora said dismissively. "She's just upset someone stole her cloak. Her bag of loose diamonds was also stolen. She's sure it was the old Stone Guardian woman. That's the only explanation. Valona needs to get more diamonds to defend Trillifort from the Stone Guardian magic."

"You know those diamonds give her power, don't you?" he asked.

"Yes. I just told you that. They defend against Stone Guardian magic."

"No. Not that kind of power," Teleo said.

Dinsmora looked slightly confused. "What, then?"

"A spell that makes everyone love her," he replied.

Dinsmora's mouth drew into a thin line. "I love her with or without diamonds. She's a fantastic human being."

Teleo snorted. "She killed Sonderson and the others."

"They betrayed her," Dinsmora said.

"Says who?" Teleo asked. "They are not around to defend themselves."

Dinsmora's eyes flashed. "She would not have killed them for no reason."

"Oh, she had a reason," Teleo said. "They knew where the diamond mine was, and she was paranoid they would take the diamonds for themselves. Now you will be next in line. Once she gets what she wants, it will be your head on a pike."

Dinsmora looked flustered. Teleo could see the war waging in her head between Teleo, her cousin and longtime friend who always spoke reason and looked out for her, and Queen Valona, her new best friend who was volatile and irrational and had just murdered five people.

Her eyes narrowed. "You're the one who sounds paranoid, Teleo Stonemason. If I didn't know you better, I would wonder if you weren't plotting against her yourself."

She challenged him with a hard glare, but he was speechless. She stood up, water dripping from her glistening skin. Stepping over to the bench, she drew a linen towel around herself and stalked off to the women's changing huts.

Teleo stared after her. His heart broke a little bit in that moment. He had lost his dear friend to a monster. Anger simmered in his blood, drowning his sadness and filling him with resolve.

22

♦

ᗰIAMONDS

The Spinners were at the large hot spring pool, wrapped
in towels and sitting on the edge with their feet dangling
in the water. Teleo sat down next to them. "I have a big
favor to ask you," he said. "Is there any way Jeremiah and Kallie
could stay with you for a few days? Maybe a week? Just until the
drama at the castle calms down a bit. It's very tense over there
right now."

They nodded sympathetically. "The queen is acting very
strangely, I hear," Jeb Spinner said.

"Very strangely," Teleo agreed.

Teleo called the kids down from the top to tell them, and
they were happy to stay in Bitter's Ford. They went with him
to the tower to gather some belongings, then Teleo rode with
them to Falcon's Nest, taking Nutmeg to stay with them at the
Spinners' farm.

After dropping them off, there were only a few hours of daylight left. Not much time to act. He went to the new quarry
site at the Stone Guardian's wall, where he found Cutter and

Johnswold. He stood with them and watched a huge chunk of blue argillite being pushed down a ramp of logs and levered onto a waiting wagon. "You guys work fast," Teleo said.

"There's a job to be done," Cutter said. "So we do it."

"I like your attitude," Teleo said. "I'm going to stay close to home for a week or so. You guys don't need me here."

"Are you guarding the queen again?" Johnswold asked, curling the tip of one moustache between grimy fingers.

"Hell no," Teleo said, chuckling. "I just need a break from everything. Mora's being weird. We need to work some stuff out. I left the kids with the Spinners."

"Need to patch things up with the wife, eh?" Cutter asked, giving him a big wink. "A little one-on-one time?"

"Something like that," Teleo said.

"Well, we'll be out here," Cutter said. "If you need anything, just give us a holler."

"Will do."

Teleo rode Star back to the Third Tower to prepare his things. Cinnamon was already gone, as were Dinsmora's shepherd's crook, her bow and quiver of arrows, and her sword. Dinsmora had left Hunter loose in the yard, with the top half of the mews door propped open. The falcon could hunt for herself for a few days, or maybe the majestic bird would never come back.

Teleo went to the third floor, knelt at the Sun Circle, gazed into it, and waited a few minutes to see if Sigrid would show up. It was too early for her, but he could not wait any longer. He went back downstairs and found the bundle of clothes he had taken from Sonderson's bunk. They were on the floor by his bedding, just where he had left them, still rolled up. He quickly changed into them. Sonderson had been taller and thinner than Teleo, and he had to hitch the pants all the way up to his waist and turn up the sleeves, but they would do. The homespun cloak was long and hooded. He looked down at himself. It was just the sort of clothing many of the mountain people wore. Perfectly nondescript.

He mucked the animal pens and laid down a thick layer of fresh straw, then brought in armfuls of hay, filling all the feeding racks and mangers to overflowing, hoping it would be enough to last Star and the sheep until he got back. He brought in more hay and piled it in a corner just to be safe. He then filled the watering troughs and hung extra buckets of feed along the walls. He fastened the sheep pen gates open to the larger horse pen, and chained the courtyard doors open to give the animals access to the outdoors and the fountain.

He finally saddled the mountain mare, whom Kaspari had named Petunia. Star paced restlessly. "You need to stay here, my beauty," he said. "I'll be back soon. And Marblehead," he said, eyeing the old ram, "don't hurt Bo-bo, or your name will be Mutton Stew." The ram ignored him and munched on hay.

Teleo filled his saddlebags with food and water, packed a leather jerkin, gloves, a coil of rope, fabric strips, a burlap sack, and tied a bedroll behind the saddle. He rubbed his face with dust, strapped on his short sword at his waist, along with his weapon and stonemason belts, and covered himself with Sonderson's homespun cloak and hood. He hid his longsword and shepherd's crook in a sheaf of hay lashed on top of the bedroll. With a parting word to the animals, he locked the front door from the inside, went out into the yard and bid farewell to Hunter, who was perched on the griffin's beak, and led Petunia out the courtyard gate, locking it behind them.

If Dinsmora and the queen had already left, he would need to ride hard to catch up with them. He led Petunia to the palace and walked around its perimeter, keeping his hood on and his head down. The covered walkway where visitors' horses were normally hitched was abandoned. He stopped outside the gate leading to the queen's stables and stood in the shadow of the wall. The gate was locked and he did not want to find a groom and draw attention to himself. He whistled softly and listened. Cinnamon's whinny answered him. Petunia whinnied back and Teleo nodded to himself, hoping that Dinsmora had not also recognized his whistle.

Teleo headed back the way he had come and turned towards the main castle gate. The sun was already making its descent, but he was not the only one leaving the castle walls. It was springtime—days were growing longer and people were on the move. Streams were thick with trout, and game was abundant. He rode closely behind a group of men with bows and arrows slung across their backs and lined up with them at the gate. Guards were patting everyone down, probably searching for the queen's missing cloak and sack of diamonds.

When it was Teleo's turn, he dismounted, kept his head down, and spread his arms to be frisked. No one seemed to recognize him. They were used to seeing him on Star in his Elke chest armor and short sword displayed prominently on his back, with a clean-shaven face and his hair tied back in a neat ponytail. Or on a snow wagon drawn by fine draft horses, bundled in his shearling coat and hat. Now he was just a downtrodden peasant on a mountain horse. They patted him down quickly and peeked inside his bedroll.

"What's this?" one of the guards asked, tapping the blunt end of the shepherd's crook that stuck out from the hay sheaf.

"Walking stick," Teleo said, putting on a nasal twang.

The guard grunted and waved him through.

When he got to the bottom of the raised road, he exited through the lower gate and natural stone arch and emerged onto the approach road. He rode Petunia at a walk between the pairs of white pillars until the road intersected Trillifort Trail. He urged Petunia into a trot and headed for the Southern Mountain Pass and Demon's Bones.

He rode all night, stopping only long enough to drink and grab a few mouthfuls of food. The night was lit by a waning gibbous moon, casting enough light for easy riding. Before dawn, he came upon the obelisk and turned east onto Southern Mountain Pass. He left the road and found a sheltered area near a spring where he staked Petunia to graze and dozed off for a few minutes, forcing himself awake before he fell into a deep sleep. He climbed to a lookout point with a clear view of the road and settled in to wait.

It was mid-morning before Zeta and Cinnamon came trotting down the road. Queen Valona and Dinsmora were wearing their embroidered cloaks, which made it difficult for Teleo to keep his eyes on them. It was a strange sensation—the horses sometimes appeared riderless or blended into the shadows themselves. At other moments, the women's forms were visible and captured Teleo's attention in a fascinating study of light and shadow. He closed his eyes and shook his head. He could hear them coming—that was good enough. Petunia nickered behind him and Teleo tossed an apple at the mare's feet. She grabbed it with long teeth and munched loudly. The vantage point was a good distance away from the road, but Cinnamon turned his head towards them. Teleo climbed down behind the rocky outcropping and waited until the pounding of hooves passed them by.

He mounted Petunia and trailed them at a distance, keeping the women's flickering forms in view as dots on the horizon. The women each carried a shepherd's crook, and the curved handles jutted above their heads, serving as markers for Teleo to track.

They were riding hard. Petunia was a solid little creature and was in moderately good shape. Still, the pace was grueling.

They encountered few travelers. One large covered wagon was pulled by a team of horses and flanked by guards, heading west. Teleo hid behind a jumble of boulders until they passed by, then hurried to catch sight of the women again.

The pair turned off the road at sunset. Teleo left the road as well and after a time, smelled hints of wood smoke. He found a flat bit of ground behind a boulder in a thicket, fed Petunia some hay, and stretched out on his bedroll.

He slept for a few short hours, then when the moon was high in the sky, he crept closer to the women's camp. They rose before dawn and he was on their trail. The next night, Dinsmora and the queen camped off the side of the road again, rose at dawn, and by noon, left Southern Mountain Pass. He recognized the turnoff—a faint trail that went downhill in a scramble of dirt and gravel. Demon's Bones. He pulled the shepherd's crook from his bundle and held it aloft, scanning the trees and shadows for Stone Guardians, though he was not yet at Hatchet Pass. Seeing none, he followed the women carefully at a distance, catching occasional glimpses of them traversing the rugged hills, which were blanketed with tender spring grasses, wildflowers, and stunted, stubborn trees clinging to life in the harsh terrain. Other trees had fallen in the recent windstorm, their roots upturned, wrenched free of the sodden earth.

It wasn't until he came upon a distinctive fallen tree with its roots fanned out like a giant spider's web that he realized he had traveled in a circle. He cursed, dismounted, and pissed into the tangle of roots. The last time he had gotten lost and traveled in a circle was in Dinsmora's hidden forest. That damn woman was up to her old tricks. He wondered if she knew he was following her, or if she was hiding her and the queen's trail for their safety—or more likely, to soothe the queen's paranoia that someone would discover the location of her precious diamond mine.

Teleo looked around. The sun was sinking towards the western peaks. If he did not find the women before nightfall, he might never find them. He let Petunia forage for a few minutes, then gathered his strength and proceeded on foot, leading the mountain mare slowly along the path. He came to a fork, and he stopped and closed his eyes. Last time, he had taken the left fork, so he should probably take the right one this time. He quieted his thoughts and let his senses guide him left again.

Teleo and Petunia walked slowly along the dirt and stone path, and soon, Teleo drew to a halt. The downward slope to his right was a rockfall of fist-sized stones and lingering patches of snow. The faint deer path he had followed the first time lay before him, but the cascade of rubble exerted a stronger pull. He left the trail, and he and Petunia picked their way across the scree and onto a patch of dirt. Teleo knelt down. Hooves had left half-moons in the chalky soil. Teleo followed the hoofprints until bare rock hid their trail again.

He crept forward, relying on his inner senses to guide him. His intuition was confirmed by the occasional hoofprint, a pile of fresh manure, a breadcrumb, a milled oat, or the scent of human female urine. The women were getting careless, thinking Dinsmora's glamour spell protected them.

Dusk had darkened to a murky shroud when the moon peeked over the horizon and showed its face, illuminating the landscape. Teleo stood still and listened, then turned his nose to a gust of air, which carried the faint smell of smoke. He tied Petunia to a stake under a copse of scrubby trees, removed her bridle, and loosened her girth. She nosed at the sparse forage. He strapped his homespun cloak, shepherd's crook, and short sword to Petunia's saddle, and then prepared for what he had to do.

Teleo crept across the shadowy fields, following the scent of smoke until firelight danced off gnarled tree trunks. The women had made camp in a grove near a stream, which flowed noisily in a gully. He lay in the underbrush and watched Dinsmora and the queen move around their campsite. Dinsmora left the firelight and disappeared down into the gully with a leather water sack over her shoulder.

Teleo made his move. He crept silently to the gully and moved upstream on the muddy bank, wincing at the squishing sound his boots made. The water thundered over the rocks, rushing with the spring thaw. Up ahead, Dinsmora bent over the stream, filling the sack, her new black-and-white embroidered cloak blending in with the rivulets of water in an ever-changing pattern. Her shepherd's crook hung from her elbow.

He came up behind her and in the same moment that she sensed him, locked his arm around her neck in a stranglehold. With his free hand, he shoved a wad of fabric into her mouth, muffling her startled yell. He levered his forearm tight, cutting off her blood flow.

She struggled and they fell to the ground, her feet kicking in the water and the leather sack sinking and bobbing in the stream. He wrapped his legs around her and tightened his arm around her neck until she went limp. Releasing his hold, he quickly tied a strip around her eyes in a tight blindfold, then tied another strip around her face to secure the gag. He pressed his fingers to her neck. Her pulse throbbed. It would be a matter of seconds before she came to. He bound her wrists tightly behind her back as she regained consciousness, kicking and choking. He pounded lightly on her back, helping her to breathe through the gag. When he was sure his gag wouldn't suffocate her, he dragged her away from the water and tied her bound wrists to the roots of a tree on the muddy bank, then managed to tie her ankles together without getting kicked in the face. She was strong and fighting for her life. But he was stronger and was also fighting for her life.

She stopped struggling when she realized she could not fight her way free and lay on her side, panting through her nose in the dark mud. Teleo took the knives from her waist belt and the one from inside her boot and tucked them into his belt. He then removed her muddy cloak and draped it over himself and pulled the hood up over his head.

He took her shepherd's crook, grabbed the half-filled water sack from where it was snagged on a rock, and walked confidently up the bank and into the campsite. Queen Valona was adding sticks to the crackling fire. Teleo came up behind her. Cinnamon nickered at him, and Zeta looked up from her oats.

"I found some dry wood," Queen Valona said, the embroidered hood of her fox-and-hare cloak hiding him from her peripheral vision. "It doesn't need to be a big fire. I only want to scare away the shadows."

Teleo laid the water sack and crook on a rock, then stepped behind her and in one swift motion, had her in a headlock. She was as strong as Dinsmora and thrashed back and forth, bringing them to the ground near the fire. Zeta neighed angrily and stomped, pulling at her rope. The queen tried to roll Teleo into the flames, but he pressed his weight onto her back and shifted his chokehold. He squeezed his arm around her neck and when she went limp, he did not stop. He held the position for several minutes to be sure she was dead, then turned her over onto her back. Her eyes had rolled up into her head, exposing the whites of her eyes, and her hood had fallen back, exposing the glittering tiara on her forehead. The diamonds blinked and Teleo blinked back.

"Damn it," he said. How had he forgotten about her crown? He had lost his edge completely. Her magic was so strong, his mind so dulled, that even as he had broken into her chamber and stolen her gem-laden cloak and sack of diamonds, he had never thought to look for the diamond tiara, nor had he thought of it since. He fought back a flood of shame and guilt. Gritting his teeth, he gently closed her eyelids. Her face was so beautiful and peaceful, and the diamonds were dazzling.

"You're a fool, Teleo," he muttered angrily, and removed the crown from her head, pulling it free from her white hair. Seven little diamonds. That was all. Seven. They looked like a thousand stars in the sky, the way they glittered with their enchantment. He could have just taken the crown and spared her life—but then she would have just gone to the mine and brought back more of the magical gems. It would have never ended. He tossed the tiara onto the dirt and dragged the queen's body away from the fire.

He checked her neck for a pulse, afraid the diamond-magic had kept her alive. There was no pulse, but he took a dagger from her belt and pressed the point up into the artery at her throat, piercing it, then pulled the blade out and stepped back. Blood drained in a thick flow from her neck and stained the ground black, and a rasp of air escaped her lungs. Teleo rested the hilt of the bloody knife in her open palm.

He left in search of more dry wood. When he had gathered a good stack, he piled it onto the fire and watched it catch. It would take over an hour for it to burn down into a bed of hot coals. In the meantime, he dragged Dinsmora up to the camp-site and tied her behind a tree. She had pissed herself, and he felt terrible. He removed her gag, and she assaulted him with a stream of curses.

"*You no-good, demon-cursed spawn of a Stone Guardian ...,*" she said, and spat in his direction. "*Valona? Valona!!*" she called out. "Did you kill Valona? I heard you struggling. Why did you do it? Why?!"

He did not respond.

She moaned and sobbed and rocked back and forth. "I know it's you, Teleo," she said, little sobs escaping her throat. "Cinnamon knows you," she said, snot running down her lips. "And I know how you smell."

He refused to acknowledge her guess and could only hope she would keep her suspicions to herself. If not, then he was truly dead to her.

"Valona," Dinsmora said, weeping. "Oh, Valona."

Teleo sat on a rock and let her cry herself out.

When the coals were hot enough, he untied his cousin from the tree, saddled Cinnamon, and hoisted Dinsmora belly-down over the saddle, her head and legs hanging down on either side. He tied her securely so that she couldn't slide off, fastening her wrists to her ankles underneath Cinnamon's belly. She was yelling angrily, but he ignored her protests. Cinnamon stood quietly through it all. Teleo lashed her sword belt, shepherd's crook, and water sack to her saddlebags and then saddled Zeta, who was nervous but did not fight him.

He left Queen Valona lying in the dirt. After a moment of hesitation, he hooked the diamond tiara with a stick and shoved it into the red-hot coals, then hurried the horses away from the fire. They were halfway across the field when the diamonds started exploding—loud cracks booming across the hills. One. Two. Three. He counted all seven and then exhaled with relief.

Teleo reached Petunia and got her ready to ride, then swung into the saddle and led Zeta and Cinnamon, with Dinsmora slung over Cinnamon's back, all the way back over the moonlit hills. His cousin alternated between cursing at him, crying, and hanging silently.

It was morning by the time he trudged wearily onto the wide thoroughfare of the Southern Mountain Pass. Teleo ground-tied Cinnamon and Zeta, then pulled Dinsmora off Cinnamon's back and sat her on the ground, tying her bound wrists to her bound ankles in front of her. She didn't bother fighting, but gulped in air and spat his way. "You no-good dirty pig," she said.

He ignored her insults and put the nozzle of his waterskin to her lips. He let her drain half the sack, keeping the blindfold on.

"Are you going to let me go to the bathroom, or are you going to make me piss myself again? Talk to me, Teleo Stonemason, you piece of horse dung. You bastard fiend of a Stone Guardian."

He considered whether or not she had the strength to cause him much trouble. Finally, he cut the rope that he had just fastened between her wrists and ankles, but kept her limbs tied together, then tethered her to a tree and let her struggle to relieve herself with bound wrists and ankles. When she was done, he pulled her to the ground as gently as he could, cut her wrist bonds, pushed her onto her belly, and pulled her arms behind her back.

"Ow," she said. "What are you doing, you shit-stained demon spawn?"

He gritted his teeth as she struggled against him. He was intent on keeping his silence and maintaining the pretense of anonymity. He was forced to straddle her, pressing his full weight on her hips, and tied her wrists tightly behind her back, deafening himself to her protests. He checked the bonds around her ankles as she tried to kick him away. He sat on her legs and tightened the rope a bit more, then pulled her up to sitting.

He removed her black-and-white cloak from around his shoulders, rolled it up, and tied it to the back of Cinnamon's saddle, then brushed the dried mud from his clothes as best he could. He tethered Cinnamon and Zeta to a rock, tied

Dinsmora to a different rock, and left her there on the side of the road with the two horses, her wrists and ankles still bound and curses streaming from her lips.

Teleo took off eastward down Southern Mountain Pass towards Verdant Valley, kicking Petunia into a gallop. Beyond a rise, he circled back and led Petunia through the steep, tangled forest and hid behind a bluff until two riders found Dinsmora later that day. They were simple travelers and helped her to her feet, cutting her loose. He could not hear what they were saying, but once he was sure they were not going to harm her or steal the horses, he followed a deer trail westward until he had put enough distance between them. He then took to the road and headed towards Trillifort at a full gallop to ensure Dinsmora would not catch up with him.

When he was confident she was far enough behind, he alternated between a trot and a brisk walk, intent on staying ahead of her. He traveled through the night, only resting for a short while before dawn, for Petunia's sake. They rode without seeing another soul all the next day, stopping when night fell.

The following morning, he arrived at the obelisk turnoff and headed south on Trillifort Trail. He traversed the trail quickly and by afternoon, reached the pillars at the entrance to the castle's approach road.

Teleo didn't have a good plan for getting back inside the fortified castle. What if someone recognized him this time and connected him to the murder of the queen? He could try passing through stone walls again, but what about Petunia? Besides, the only place to enter through the ramparts was at the guard station at the base of the raised road, otherwise he would plunge to his death in the deep quarry. He took in a deep breath. He had no choice but to enter through the gates and hope his disguise worked again. However, the guards did not let any random stranger enter the castle town without good reason.

On his way up Southern Mountain Pass, he had passed two wagons loaded with spring crops from Verdant Valley. He counted the days. Tomorrow was Sunday already. He recalled Cutter mentioning the market would be opening for the season. Teleo didn't have any produce or sheep this time. He needed to hunt. He stood at the first pair of pillars leading up to the castle and decided to head the other way, towards the stream where he had spotted several hares and pheasants last time they had been hunting.

He led Petunia down into the forested land that bordered the stream, hitched her to a tree, and took a coil of rope and a burlap sack with him. He clambered over rocks to the other side of the water, where the forest thinned out and sunny glades were lush with spring grasses, and crept along the edges of the clearings on foot, looking for game. He didn't have a bow and was contemplating building a simple snare when a gyrfalcon circled overhead. Joy leapt in his heart. He whistled and held out his hand, wrapping it with rope and burlap. Hunter landed on his fist with a flurry of wing feathers.

"Hunter, my girl," he crooned.

He crept along the border of a meadow where the grass met brush and brambles, the raptor perching contentedly on his wrist. He beat the undergrowth with a stick, flushing a hare, and Hunter took off after it. Teleo ran to the kill and tied it to his belt. They caught two more hares and two pheasants by the time twilight began to darken the sky.

"One more," Teleo said, but he didn't have to flush anything this time. Hunter took off in low flight over the field. Teleo watched the falcon pounce on its prey. A struggle ensued and Teleo ran across the grass. It was a small red fox, still alive and staring up at Teleo as Hunter pinned it to the ground with her large talons. Teleo found a thick stick and jammed it between the fox's jaws, then struck the fox's skull with a hammer, killing it in one stroke.

The falcon had hopped away, and Teleo tied the dead fox by the hind legs, then headed towards the stream crossing. By the time he reached Petunia, Hunter had flown off. He tied the furry creature to his saddlebags with the pheasants and hares and then rubbed dirt onto his forehead and cheeks. He mounted Petunia and trotted towards Trillifort's gates.

The white pillars hovered like ghosts in the deepening dusk, and when he turned the corner and passed through the rock arch, the castle town sparkled atop its stony perch, lanterns glistening from the myriad windows. The guard at the lower gate held up a lantern and inspected him as he approached. The hood hid Teleo's eyes in shadow, and his jaws were covered with whiskers.

"Here fer the market tomorrow," Teleo said, sharpening his R's in a mountain twang.

"We have our own hunters," the guard said gruffly.

"Yessir," Teleo said, head bowed. "But I got three big hares and two pheasants. An' a fox. I hear yer queen loves fox fur."

The guard traded glances with his partner and frowned, then examined the fox carcass, sinking his fingers into the thick fur.

"Okay," the guard said, gesturing for Teleo to enter.

The guards moved aside and Teleo walked Petunia over the raised road to the upper gate. He had the same conversation there, and the guards let him pass. "You can sleep in the central square," the guard said. "Look fer Cutter in the morning."

"Yessir," Teleo mumbled, and rode into the castle grounds.

He dismounted and led Petunia towards the center of the dark city. He made his way to the large square, where several merchants were camped out near their wagons. Sounds of revelry floated through the air from the Great Hall at the far end of the square, where the townspeople would be finishing up dinner and drinking ale at the fireplaces. Teleo's stomach rumbled, but he focused on his task.

The merchants were gathered in small groups, eating and drinking. Teleo took stock of the merchants and approached a husband and wife who looked to have come up from Verdant Valley. Their sturdy farm wagon held crates filled with crocks of jellies and honey, beeswax candles, crates of bundled greens and beets, and bushels of eggs.

"Excuse me," he said, clearing his throat. "I was wondering if you'd want to buy these and sell 'em for me tomorrow." He motioned to the hares and pheasants hanging from his saddle, then held up the fox. "I'll sell 'em to you cheap. Came real easy to my traps. Springtime, you know. I need to head out before dawn to check my other traps. Lots of thievery going on in the backwoods this year. Can't believe people have the nerve to steal my game, but I guess that's what the world's come to these days."

The man eyed him curiously, and the woman inspected his catch and ran her hand over the fox's coppery fur.

"The queen here loves fox fur," Teleo said. "I'll sell the whole lot for a Silver Owl."

"A hundred bits?" the man scoffed. "What do you think I am? I'll give you two Bronzes. No more."

"Ten bits?" Teleo laughed in his face.

They settled on twenty-five bits. After all, the fox was special. Teleo pocketed his five Bronze Bits, handed over the carcasses, and left the yard the way he had come, leading Petunia.

When he was out of sight of the yard, he scanned the empty street and then stepped around a corner and removed his peasant's cloak, lifted his chin, and strode confidently through the maze of back streets to the Third Tower. He unlocked the side gate and led Petunia into the courtyard. Hunter was sleeping on the T-stand inside her mews. "Good girl," Teleo said, and fastened the door closed.

Teleo and Petunia went into the cold stable. Star whinnied and ambled over to them, and Marblehead stood up from a mound of straw and trumpeted at Teleo. The ewes greeted him with a bleating chorus, and the lambs frolicked around him. He felt guilty for leaving them unattended for so long, but they appeared to be in good health. Teleo petted the animals and quickly rubbed down Petunia. He then changed out the filthy watering troughs and filled the hay racks and feed buckets, the animals pushing him out of the way as though they were starving. He forced himself to muck the huge mess in the stable and yard, piling it outside the gate for a wagon pick-up, then spread out fresh straw in the stable.

Teleo dragged himself upstairs, carrying a bucket of warm water from the fountain. He filled the basin and washed his hands and forearms, lathered his scruffy facial hair, and passed a sharp edge down his face and neck, cutting back the itchy overgrowth to a manageable stubble. He scarfed down a few chunks of smoked sausage and hard cheese and drank a tankard of cold well water. Finally, he peeled off his dirty clothes and collapsed into bed.

◆

Teleo hid out in the tower with the animals all the next day. Dinsmora hadn't returned by nightfall, and he finally fell into a fitful sleep. The following morning when she still had not appeared, he began to wonder if leaving her with two strangers had been such a good idea. Then again, knowing Dinsmora, she probably convinced the men to go with her to retrieve Queen

Valona's body. He assumed that was the case and decided to enjoy having the tower to himself.

Teleo was upstairs dancing around the Heliotrope when a pounding set Marblehead to bellowing down below. The insistent rapping continued. Someone was knocking at the front door. He hurried downstairs, unlocked the door, and pulled it open. Dinsmora was standing there, her face hard with anger. Cutter and Johnswold stood behind her, with Cinnamon nosing Cutter's shoulder.

"Queen's dead," Cutter said breathlessly. "Stone Guardians butchered her. Stole her diamond crown. Nearly killed Mora. The Miller brothers found yer wife on the side of the road at Southern Pass, tied up and left to die."

Teleo met Dinsmora's glare. If eyes were a sky, hers were a thundercloud rolling over a jagged cliff. He said nothing, only took her in his arms and buried his face in her tangled hair. Her arms slowly circled his back and she hugged him.

◆

The week was chaotic with Queen Valona's funeral, the crowning of Cutter as King, and packing to leave. Teleo had convinced Dinsmora it was time and broke the news to the kids, then told Cutter and Johnswold. After a day of objecting, they all finally accepted his decision. A flurry of activity followed as they wrapped up loose ends. Jessum helped Goff shoe the horses. Kaspari competed in another archery competition, this time from horseback, and came in second. Dinsmora helped Gracie clean out Queen Valona's chambers, taking nothing from all of the queen's riches for herself aside from a few skeins of yarn. And Teleo said goodbye to Sigrid.

He danced the sword while the others were at the Great Hall, having claimed a headache. Sigrid appeared on the Sun Circle and began dancing around the Heliotrope across from him. She stopped, then he stopped.

"You have something to tell me?" she asked.

He stepped forward and they met at the Sun Circle. "I'm leaving," he said. "I'm coming to the Hill country. I need to look for the family of my foster son. He was stolen during the war from the Sapphire Empire and taken to Verdant Valley, where I found him." Teleo did not mention his own son, afraid to voice the hope buried deep in his chest.

"How old is he?" she asked.

"He thinks he turned fifteen over the winter."

"What does he look like?"

Teleo described Jessum as best he could. His tall stature, the growing thickness of his arms and neck. His sense of humor. His good heart.

"I know of several families who lost their sons or grandsons," she said. "I will ask around."

Teleo grasped her hand without thinking, and she gazed up at him, her hand warm in his. "Thank you," he said, and loosened his grip, but she kept her hand in his. Her amber fragrance seeped into his head, making him feel giddy.

"You must come find me," she said. "I can help you. I'm in Red Flag Fortress at the southeastern edge of Sapphire Valley, up on the cliffs. You can't miss it."

"Ah, okay," he said, her soft skin velvety under his calloused fingers. "I stopped by there once, briefly, after the war. I do not believe I had the pleasure of meeting you." he said, holding her gaze.

"I'm sure I would have remembered," she said, blushing.

He cleared his throat and said, "I will see you there, then." He smiled and she smiled back, their eyes lingering on one another's. He wanted to kiss her but did not dare. "How will I find you?" he asked.

"I'm not hard to find," she said. "Just ask for me by name and someone will come find me. The castle town is not very big, as you know. So I'll expect you in a couple of weeks?" she asked.

"In a couple of weeks," he said. "As long as the passes stay clear of snow."

"Safe travels," she said, and pulled her fingers from his.

He backed away and pivoted into his flying sword form, leaping and spinning through the air. When he had completed two circuits, she was gone. He walked around the Heliotrope, bowed to the Sun Circle and to a lingering bat who hung overhead, then blew out the candles and locked the door behind him. He went down to the ground floor, sat in the bat-and-griffin chair, and recalled the feeling of Sigrid's hand in his.

◆

On the morning they were to leave, Teleo found King Cutter in his audience chamber, looking out the window. The throne's falcon mosaic followed Teleo with its eyes as he walked across the room to join the new king. Teleo had never given the mosaic a final polish, but only he would ever notice. He glanced around the room. The headsman's axe and block were gone, leaving a clean square surrounded by blood-stained tiles. Teleo raised an eyebrow at Cutter.

"I will only rule if the people want me to," Cutter said. "If they don't want me to, I'll be glad to return to my normal life. This king garbage is overrated."

Teleo laughed and slapped his friend on the back.

"Where's Mora?" Cutter asked.

"Saying goodbye to Gracie."

"I have something you guys might want," Cutter said. He pulled a woolen bundle from a burlap sack and unrolled it. It was the queen's fox-and-hare cloak. "She was wearing this when she was killed. I was going to burn it, but Johnswold thought Mora might want it, seeing as how she embroidered most of it. Or that's what Gracie said, anyway. There was some blood on it, but Gracie cleaned it. You can't even notice. I understand if you don't want it—coming from a dead body and all."

"No, no," Teleo said, reaching for the cloak and tucking it under his arm. "I'll let Mora decide. It might make her sad, or it might make her happy. We'll see."

"We definitely want Mora happy, right?" Cutter joked, nudging him with his elbow. "Glad you guys made up. I never want to see you in that sorry state again."

"Me neither," Teleo agreed. Teleo had lied to Cutter and Johnswold the night after Mora had returned, over a flask of Ferska in front of the stable's fireplace after the others had gone to bed. He told them Dinsmora had stormed off after a fight and gone with the queen to find diamonds for a new cloak while he had lost himself in a jug of mushroom wine he'd found at Sheep's Haven, and had shown them Sonderson's empty jug. The brothers knew about Sonderson's habit and the diamond mine, bemoaning the fact that no one else knew where the mine was. Anyone who had ever been there was dead, and Queen Valona had been killed before revealing its location to Dinsmora.

Cutter walked with him to the audience chamber doors and gave him a hearty hug goodbye. "I need to meet with a bunch of Falcon's Nest farmers who're complaining about the sawmill dumping sludge into the river. Otherwise, I'd see you guys off. Johnswold's out at the Stone Guardian witch's wall overseeing the quarrymen. The two quarry families keep fighting."

"I'll pay him a visit before we leave," Teleo said.

"Say goodbye to Mora and yer son and daughter fer me. They're good kids."

"They are," Teleo agreed.

"Tell me something," Cutter said, meeting his gaze. "How did you get that Hill boy? Did you steal him during the war?"

"No. I rescued him from an abusive situation."

A wide smile split Cutter's face. "I figured as much. He's way too happy to have been yer slave."

Teleo nodded. "I'm going to try and track down his family."

Cutter patted him on the shoulder. "Good luck to you. Come back when you can. Yer always welcome at Castle Trill'fort and Falcon's Nest."

"Thank you, my king," Teleo said, and laughed at Cutter's smirk.

"Remember yer vow not to reveal Falcon's Nest's existence," Cutter said, poking Teleo's chest armor with his index finger.

"We will all remember. Your secret is safe with us. Thank you for everything," Teleo said sincerely, and bowed. Cutter returned the bow and Teleo left the new king to his duties.

Teleo rode Star through the tunnel to Falcon's Nest and then headed directly to Sheep's Haven and out to the wall. At the cliff quarry site, he found Johnswold leaning back in a wooden chair, curling his moustache tips between his fingers and watching the quarrymen do their work. Teleo wished he could stay and learn everything the quarrymen knew about stone, but a deep restlessness was driving him to move on. Johnswold rose to greet him.

"The sheep are with the Spinners," Teleo told him. "What should I do with Sonderson's mountain mare? Marblehead likes her, so I was thinking she could stay with the Spinners too, unless you know Sonderson's family. They might need her."

"Sonderson has no family," Johnswold said. "You can have

his horse if you want. But do you really need more horses?" Johnswold lifted a bushy eyebrow.

Teleo shrugged. More horses were always better, from his experience, as long as you could feed them. Petunia had proven her mettle on his clandestine mission. "It's springtime," he said. "There will be plenty of forage and water on our way to Hill country."

"True. I suppose you could sell her once you get there."

"We could," Teleo agreed. "Thank you. She's a good horse."

Johnswold nodded. "You guys about ready to go?"

"Ay-yah. We cleaned out the tower. Good as new. What are you guys going to do with it? You moving in? Haha."

"No way," Johnswold said, shaking his head. "That place is haunted."

"I thought you didn't believe in ghosts," Teleo said.

"I didn't. Not until I started spending time there. An actual ghost lives there. You haven't seen her?"

Teleo felt himself pale. "Does she wear a red dress?" Teleo asked.

"Ay-yah, that's her." Johnswold's eyes were round.

"I saw her when I was drunk on mushroom wine," Teleo lied. "I thought I was seeing things."

"Nay." Johnswold shook his head emphatically. "She's real. Or as real as a ghost can be. I saw her creeping down the stairs last time I was sheepsitting. She saw me and ran back upstairs. Kinda pretty fer a dead person, but it gave me the creeps. I meant to tell you, but then the queen went crazy. Nobody wants to set foot inside that place, except you. Especially after you guys move out. You made it feel almost homey. We'll lock it up and wait fer you to return. You can move back in anytime you want." Johnswold smiled, his moustache curls rising.

"That's very kind of you," Teleo said. "It is a nice tower, despite roaming red-dressed phantoms."

Johnswold laughed and slapped Teleo's back. "It is. You've got a good day fer traveling."

"Weather's perfect," Teleo said. "I want to get over the pass before more rains come, or a late snowstorm."

Johnswold sniffed the air and looked at the sky. "You should be good. A wind's coming up, but it's from the south."

They hugged and said goodbye. Teleo swung into Star's saddle and went to get the kids from Bitter's Ford. He found them at the Spinners with Goff the blacksmith and other friends who had gathered to wish them well. Marblehead was in a paddock with an old shaggy pony, and the ewes and lambs grazed contentedly in the large field alongside Petunia, BlackJack, and Daisy.

Kaspari went out into the field, and Bo-bo ran over to her. She bent down and hugged the ram lamb, then took turns petting all the ewes and ewe lambs. Jessum and the Spinner girls joined her, and Teleo watched, tearing up a little as he regarded the sweet sheep who had shared this odd journey with them. Marblehead bleated loudly, glaring at Teleo.

"Bye, you old goat," Teleo said, walking over and letting himself into the ram's enclosure. The ram walked up to him, and Teleo rubbed the thick fleece around Marblehead's neck. The ram pressed his forehead against Teleo's leg. "You behave for the Spinners, you hear?" Teleo said, stroking the ram's head. "Jeb will put Bo-bo in here with you when he gets a little bigger. You be nice to him." Marblehead bleated plaintively. "I know," Teleo said. "You miss Sonderson and now we're leaving too. But the Spinners will treat you well." Teleo gave him a slice of apple and then gave one to the pony. After giving Marblehead a parting pat, Teleo went to join the others.

He whistled for the horses and they trotted over, followed by the sheep. He doled out slices of apple and tied a rope halter around Petunia's head.

"She's coming with us?" Kaspari asked brightly.

"Ay-yah. Johnswold said we could take her."

"Oh, good," Kaspari said, and hugged the little mare.

Teleo said goodbye to each ewe and ewe lamb individually, then knelt and gave Bo-bo a parting hug. The ram lamb kissed his face, and Teleo wondered if the cute little bundle of fleece would grow up to be as proud and ornery as his sire.

Finally, they saddled the horses, and the kids stood awkwardly as they waited to leave their friends. Jessum had his battle-axe and showed Teleo a rampant griffin he had etched into the axe head.

"Nice work," Teleo said.

The blacksmith smiled proudly at his apprentice. "He's a good boy. I mean, man," the blacksmith said, putting his arm around Jessum's shoulder.

Teleo thanked Goff and the Spinners for taking such good care of the teenagers.

"Ready?" Teleo asked Jessum and Kaspari.

The kids nodded reluctantly and said a final farewell to their friends.

Teleo took Petunia's lead rope, then they mounted their horses and rode out of Bitter's Ford, with a steady breeze at their backs.

"Look, Teleo," Jessum said, trotting up to ride at Teleo's side. Jessum held up a shiny Silver Owl coin. "Goff gave this to me for helping him all winter. And this too." Jessum grinned and unsheathed a folded-steel knife.

"Wow," Teleo said. "Your fish knife and an Owl. Lucky you." He had been planning to give the boy some coin in case they got separated, but it was even better that the boy had earned it himself. This hidden valley had been good for them, all things considered.

They rode through the tunnel to the castle town and made their way to the Third Tower. Dinsmora was loading up Nutmeg with food, water, bundles of clothing, lanterns, candles, a cooking pot and ladle, a wooden cutting board, bags of yarn, and other sundries. Teleo noted scraps of color peeking out from the bundles of clothing—the silk dresses Gracie had given her and Kaspari, and the velvet doublets from Cutter. She was wearing her riding leathers and her old embroidered tunic.

"We need to travel light," Teleo said. "Nutmeg should be carrying feed for the horses."

She scowled at him and secured another bundle. "What's that?" she asked, as Teleo unlashed Queen Valona's fox-and-hare cloak from Star's saddle and unrolled it. Dinsmora's frown deepened and she glared at Teleo accusingly, his cheeks stinging. He ignored her dagger eyes. She had accepted what he had done but was still sore at him. They hadn't spoken of it, but he hoped she realized he had saved her life.

"Cutter thought you might want it," Teleo said. "Gracie told him you did most of the stitching."

"I don't want that," she said sharply. "That was Valona's. She *died* in it."

He held her stony eyes. At least she hadn't used the word "murder."

"I'll take it, then," he said, secretly pleased she didn't want it, and draped it around his shoulders, ignoring her disapproving scowl. "Where's your other cloak?" he asked. "The one you worked on all winter. Is it still at the palace?"

"No, Gracie brought it over. But I'm leaving it behind," she said. "It brings bad memories."

"You're taking everything under the sun, but not that?" he asked. He found it bunched up next to the fireplace in the burn pile and shook it out. The black, gray, and white feather design reminded him of Hunter. The scalloped pattern played with the shadows, flickering in and out of focus. Seed pearls added a subtle gleam, mimicking the light that glanced off the marble walls. The lining was a fine black wool weave.

He walked over to Jessum, who was working out a tangle in BlackJack's mane. Teleo fastened the long cloak around the boy's shoulders. Jessum was wearing his blood-red velvet brigandine over his chainmail armor and red gambeson, and the black-and-white cloak made a nice contrast. "Here," Teleo said. "Your very own magic cloak."

"It's not magic," Dinsmora said icily.

"Your very own camouflage confusion cloak that is not magic," Teleo said dryly.

Jessum looked from Teleo to Dinsmora and back again. "Okay. Thanks." A hesitant smile lifted the corners of his mouth.

"You look like a falcon," Kaspari said. "A red falcon."

Jessum's chipped teeth shone in a real smile, and Teleo agreed. "I like it," Teleo said. "Jessum the Red Falcon."

Dinsmora glared at them darkly but did not object.

"Are you taking Hunter?" Teleo asked her.

"Of course I'm taking Hunter," Dinsmora snapped.

He bit back a smart retort, then took a breath and said, "You don't have a cloak now. It's windy out."

"Yes, I do. I found this in your bundle of trash," she said, pulling the plain peasant's cloak from a saddlebag. "I needed some good homespun."

"That was Sonderson's," he said.

"I figured," she replied, and swung the cloak around her shoulders.

They burned the last of the trash, doused the fire, checked the shelves and outbuildings one more time for anything they might have forgotten, and gave the floors a final sweep. Teleo and Dinsmora loaded up Nutmeg and Petunia with as much feed as the horses could carry, then lashed a fifty-pound sack of oats atop the saddlebags of the other four mounts.

Teleo placed the key on the downstairs mantelpiece and left the doors unlocked. They stood with the horses out in the yard. No one was there to bid them farewell. They had said all their goodbyes, and their friends had moved on with their daily tasks. They led the horses to the fountain for a drink and Teleo gazed up at the empty Focal Point window, then to the rampant griffin, who he realized for the first time was gazing up at the Focal Point as well.

"Goodbye, friend," Teleo murmured to the griffin.

Teleo opened the yard's gate. "Shall we?" he asked, taking Star's bridle. The horses and riders filed out, and he closed the gate behind them. They rode single file to the upper castle gate and down the raised quarry road to the lower gate, where Teleo waved to the guards in parting.

He looked back at the gleaming castle on the hill—a white beacon set starkly against a cerulean sky. They passed through the arch and took off at a brisk walk down the pillar-lined road towards Trillifort Trail and Southern Mountain Pass, the wind catching their cloaks and speeding them on their way.

PART THREE

SAPPHIRE EMPIRE

23

$\mathscr{S}$APPHIRE $\mathcal{V}$ALLEY

In the first few days of their journey, they made the arduous climb to the upper reaches of the Southern Mountain Pass. The air grew cold again, snow clung to rocky peaks, and trees were replaced with standing monoliths of sentinel stones. At the overlook on the highest point of the pass, peaks and valleys spread out in every direction in a stunning panorama. The wind whipped at them, catching their cloaks and lifting Hunter off Dinsmora's shepherd's crook to soar joyfully overhead.

The weather grew warmer as they descended towards Sapphire Valley. The road twisted back and forth along the edges of mountainsides and led them across stone bridges spanning thundering waterfalls. By the second day of their descent, Jessum had shed his chainmail and helm, rolling up the hauberk with the griffin pennant Queen Valona had given him. Kaspari rolled her heavy satin, wool-lined cloak into her bedroll and strapped it behind her saddle, and the others removed their cloaks as well.

They looked almost like a peasant family again, except for their well-bred mounts, Jessum's velvet brigandine, and their weaponry. In fact, they looked a little too well-off for Teleo's comfort but strong enough to discourage opportunistic attacks. Over the next two days, they passed two mounted units wearing the blue and gray uniforms of the Imperial Army of the current Sapphire Emperor, Cornwal. The small units of four and six soldiers ignored them and trotted by while Teleo herded his band to the side of the road to let them pass.

The next day, the skies darkened. Over the next four days, they suffered sudden, drenching downpours. They rode through the storms, covering themselves against the cold rain with their waxed canvas tarps and making rough shelters at night. Despite their best efforts, they were soaked to the bone and the horses were miserable. On the fifth day, the sun came out. They spent the day drying their clothing and bedding on rocks next to a rushing stream and let the horses graze in lush foliage bordering the streambed. Hunter and Dinsmora caught a pheasant, Jessum caught a large yellow trout, and Teleo and Kaspari foraged for fresh greens for their dinner.

The next day, Dinsmora came down with a cough and hunched over her saddle, hacking and sucking on herbs as they descended into the foothills.

The following afternoon, BlackJack alerted them to the approach of another traveling party. The jangling of tack, the creaking of wagon wheels, and the hollow coughing of a child reached Teleo's ears before the travelers came into view over a rise ahead of them. It was not a family as Teleo had assumed, and he examined the party darkly as they passed.

A dozen Sapphire soldiers guarded a wagon filled with as many children—boys and girls ranging in age from about five to ten, all of them skinny and dirty and scared. The children were roped together and followed Teleo's party with pleading eyes, and the soldiers glowered at them to mind their own business.

Teleo urged Star and the other horses up the hill, and the wagon trundled downhill behind them, heading away from Sapphire Valley. When the hill separated them from the wagon, Dinsmora wheeled Cinnamon around.

"What was that?" she demanded.

"Slaves?" Jessum asked.

"Boys *and* girls?" Kaspari asked.

They glared at Teleo as though it were his fault.

"Looked like it," Teleo said, angry with himself for choosing their own safety over confronting the slavers. "I didn't know they were trading in slaves," he said. "That's new."

"Staggas," Kaspari said, spittle flying from her mouth as she said the name with contempt.

"Staggas," Jessum echoed.

"Staggas," Teleo agreed.

"Emperor Cornwall tried to establish a slave trade with my father," Kaspari said. "My father said he was a cruel man and refused."

"Now Cornwal has an evil partner on the Verdant Valley throne," Dinsmora said.

The four of them looked at one another with equal parts anguish and rage, then turned wordlessly and walked the horses down the granite-paved road.

The next day, the road took a turn along the edge of a steep hillside, and the expansive Sapphire Valley came into view. They stopped to admire the vista. The large round valley had a bluish tinge to the grasses in the pasturelands and was ringed by tall blue cliffs and sloping escarpments. It appeared to be a giant crater with a mountainous rim.

Sapphire City glistened in the center of the flat valley like a gem, encircled by three concentric defensive walls. Seeing the shining blue city brought back a rush of memories of the war and his quest to find his son. During the Valley Wars, Teleo had attacked the outer wall with his unit, ultimately unable to breach the massive barrier. The Verdant Valley Army had retreated after they had suffered too many casualties to carry out with them, leaving the dead for their enemies to deal with.

After the war, he had returned to the enemy's territory and walked through the City Gate, losing himself in the labyrinth of mansion-lined boulevards and market squares, inns and alleyways, pubs and brothels. He had bribed his way into the Castle Ring and perused the expensive shops and castle workshops, looking for a Verdant Valley slave boy. He had even lied his way into the inner Palace Ring and reached the Imperial Palace courtyard, posing as a dignitary from Verdant Valley. He had been unable to enter the palace building itself, lacking an invitation bearing the seal of a minister.

He gazed down upon the magnificent city, which made Verdant City look like a humble trading post. The outermost City Wall was a tall fortification of blue argillite, surrounded by an expansive grassy defensive zone separating the city from the cultivated fields and small villages of the flatlands. The middle ring of defensive walls, known as the Castle Wall, was also of the ubiquitous blue stone. At the very center, the Imperial Palace towered above the Palace Wall, both of which were built of lapis lazuli, the rich indigo stone polished to a watery shine, with streaks of gold sparkling as though the sun reflected off a tranquil sea.

Teleo squinted and could not make out details at such a distance, but he recalled the emperor's purple banners flapping in the wind from the high castle, a prominent terrace on the upper level of the main palace where Emperor Cornwal liked to stand and look out over his domain and loyal subjects.

Teleo examined the landscape below and picked out the seven smaller castles glinting from the ring of cliffs and steep trails surrounding the cultivated valley. He found one perched on a southeastern bluff and looked for red flags, but the fortress was too far away.

Two days later on a sunny morning, they reached the empire's Southern Mountain Pass border town. Cutter had told Teleo that the gates to the Sapphire Valley were still open to civilian traffic, with a toll, as they had been since the war ended.

The border town had changed from the sleepy, drunken soldier's outpost Teleo remembered to a bustling little trading hub. Merchant stalls lined the main road, and soldiers, travelers, and mountain men inspected the wares.

They dismounted and led their horses through the street market, looking over the goods for anything of interest. Teleo bought himself a hunting hat like many of the mountain men wore—deer hide decorated with quail feathers. He bought birchbark and cinnamon hard candies for the kids, and a grooming brush made with wild boar bristles for the horses. Dinsmora bought silk embroidery thread of various colors, steel needles, and a small sack of Far Shell Island seed pearls. There was no horse feed for sale, and a merchant told him he might be able to buy some in the valley. "Not many horses around these days," the man said, with a furrowed brow. Teleo noted several horses hitched outside a pub with matching cavalry saddles and saddlebags, but he did not press the issue.

The sun was high in the sky by the time they went to the gate and got in line behind a few peasants and peddlers.

"Twenty bits per head," the guard said, when it was their turn. "Including the horses." He turned his gaze on Hunter, who was perched on Dinsmora's crook.

Teleo glowered at the man. That was highway robbery. "It used to be five per person, and animals were free," Teleo said.

"It used to be Verdant Valley folk weren't allowed inside the empire," the soldier retorted, eyeing the Elke sigil on Teleo's chest armor plate.

Teleo shook his head and dug into his coin purse. "They didn't tell us how expensive peace would be," he joked. The soldier did not laugh. Teleo handed him two Silver Owls.

"No hunting in the emperor's valley," the soldier said sternly, waving them through. "Keep your falcon tethered."

Teleo exchanged glances with Dinsmora as they passed through the gate—he was unsure if they had even brought Hunter's anklets and leashes. They rode between shoddily constructed wooden buildings, which had sprung up around the border wall, and emerged onto the straight Emperor's Toll Road leading to Sapphire City, twenty-five miles ahead. As the valley opened up before them, Teleo regarded the vast patchwork of green pastures and tilled fields. The land had been transformed in the five years since he had last crossed the valley, after giving up on the search for his son. Back then, the valley had been dotted with small landholdings with barns and cottages and tidy garden plots—amidst tracts of open, public grazing land, and horse farms that bred the famed Sapphire Empire white steeds. Now, chest-high fieldstone walls flanked the road on either side, enclosing large tracts of tilled land and fenced pastures, as far as the eye could see. The narrow shoulders between the blue argillite road and the gray fieldstone walls had been grazed down to brown stubble and trampled dirt.

They had gone through most of the horse feed on their journey down the mountain, not wanting to spend time grazing the animals. He noted the remaining feed Petunia carried: two forty-pound sheaves of hay and two fifty-pound sacks of oats. Enough for a day or two at best for the big draft horses. He inspected the southeastern hills and located Red Flag. He tried to remember where the switchback trail snaking down from the castle cut across the fields and intersected the Emperor's Toll Road. He would ask at the next town.

The first stream they came upon flowed under the road through a culvert. They dismounted and led the horses down a dirt path to drink but were met by a small contingent of guards who sat lazily in front of a guard shack. One stood and rested a pike on the ground. "Emperor's water," he said, chewing on a long piece of grass.

"What do you mean?" Dinsmora asked.

"I mean you can't water your horses here. Take them to the town pump at East Haverly."

Dinsmora traded glances with Teleo. "What's the fee to water here?" Teleo asked. It was a warm day and the horses were tired and thirsty.

The guard scowled at him, and three more got to their feet. "There is no fee. Go to East Haverly."

"How far is East Haverly?" Teleo asked.

"Twelve miles," the guard said, and waved his hand for them to move along.

Teleo signaled at Dinsmora not to argue, and their party climbed up to the road. "What the hell," Teleo muttered. They poured some water from their leather sacks into the canvas bucket and let the horses drink, then fed them some hay before continuing down the road.

East Haverly was a muddy little town with moss-covered roofs. Stooped men, old women, and children in dingy clothes formed a long line at the water pump in the town square. They carried all manner of containers: buckets, jugs, and leather water bags. There were no troughs for the horses—and no one else led horses. Save for a few stray dogs lurking at the edges of the square, theirs were the only animals and drew open stares. Dinsmora and Kaspari took the horses and hitched them in the shade, then came back and rejoined Teleo and Jessum to the hostile glares of those behind them. Teleo glared back at them, and they averted their gazes.

It was finally their turn.

"Five bits per gallon," the water tender barked.

"Two," Teleo snapped back.

"Five." The man glowered at him over drooping lower eyelids.

Teleo held his gaze, sizing him up. He probably had to hand the money over to the mayor, who then gave a percentage to the emperor.

Teleo exhaled loudly. They had twenty gallons of empty water sacks between them, which they would need for themselves, plus each of the parched horses would need several gallons. "Where are your troughs?" Teleo asked.

"No troughs," the man said.

"How do you water your horses?" Teleo asked.

"Don't have no horses. Now hurry along." The man gestured impatiently at Kaspari, who held the canvas water bucket open on the ground while Jessum pumped.

"You don't have any troughs?" Teleo pressed. "Got a pond? We've got six tired and thirsty horses."

The man's face could have been a statue for the amount of emotion he displayed. "No public watering holes."

Teleo stared the man down, wondering if his hands would fit around the man's pudgy neck.

"They sell buckets at the coopers," the man said, tilting his head towards a line of shops across the square.

Teleo scowled and took a turn at the pump while Dinsmora placed a leather water sack under the spigot. The kids had carried the canvas bucket to the edge of the yard where the horses were hitched, and BlackJack was already hogging it and splashing water on the ground. When they were done filling all the water sacks, Kaspari and Jessum came back with the empty bucket.

"Go to the back of the line," the water tender said, waving the kids to the end of the long queue.

Teleo held his tongue and gestured to the kids to do as the man said. It would take all day to water the horses at this rate. Teleo left Dinsmora with the kids and stomped across the dirty cobblestones to the cooper's shop. The shop smelled of fresh-cut wood. Staves were soaking in a large vat, and others were being shaped for barrels. The cooper looked up.

"Good day. I need a bucket to water my horses," Teleo said.

"What size?" The cooper was friendly and relaxed, a welcome relief from the grumpy water tender.

"Ten-gallon, I guess. Won't be able to lug much more than that away from the pump."

The man pulled out a stack of buckets from behind the soaking vat, and Teleo chose one with rope handles.

"How much?" Teleo asked.

"One Silver Bit," the man said.

"A Silver Bit?" Teleo asked. "For a bucket?"

The cooper shrugged, looking embarrassed. "Can't harvest wood in the emperor's valley no more, and they charge a hefty tax to bring it into the valley from the hills."

Teleo grumbled and dug into his coin purse.

"Nobody has horses around here?" Teleo asked.

"Only soldiers. And draft horses who work the emperor's fields. Or oxen. Some royalty still have horses. You royalty?" The man eyed Teleo's beat-up Elke armor and raised his bushy eyebrows.

Teleo laughed. "No, we're farmers. On our way to visit a friend up in one of the Hill fortresses. We left our wagons behind."

"Ah," the man said, peering out his open doorway. "Fine horses."

"Yes, indeed," Teleo said, not bothering to hide the pride and affection he felt for the animals. Daisy, who had served Kaspari well—a lesser horsewoman would not have been able to handle the massive dapple gray; Dinsmora's two matched bays, big and husky; the fiery black and the high-strung white, who, if they had been left whole, would have bred fine offspring together; and the little mountain horse who had more stamina than any of the larger horses and ran just as fast as Nutmeg and Cinnamon.

"Can't get to the fortresses from here," the man said as Teleo counted his coins. "Roads are closed."

Teleo glanced up. "Closed? Hmph," he grunted unhappily. "Then I guess we'll have to head out from Sapphire City." Roads radiated out from the center like spokes on a wheel. It was the long way around but Teleo bit back his annoyance. It was not the cooper's fault.

"Them roads are closed, too," the cooper said.

"What? Why? What is going on here?"

The man dropped his eyes. "Cornwal owns all the roads. Only official empire business is allowed. The only open highway is the Emperor's Toll Road, from the eastern gate off the Southern Mountain Pass to the city, the road I assume you came in on. All others are restricted." He stood up straight and faced Teleo, more words dwelling behind a frown of disapproval, words the cooper would not dare utter to a stranger.

"We can't pay a toll to use the other roads?" Teleo asked.

The man shrugged his shoulders. "I don't know. I don't think so. The emperor doesn't take kindly to bribes, either. Says it's the same thing as stealing from him."

"Ah. I see. Where can I buy feed for the horses?" Teleo asked.

The cooper shook his head grimly.

"No feed stores?" Teleo asked, concern for the horses edging out his annoyance.

The man shook his head again and said, "Cornwal owns all the grain and all the horses."

Teleo's pulse quickened. "How can he own all the horses?"

The cooper hesitated before speaking, casting a dour look at Teleo. "Taxes are so high, people couldn't feed their horses, so they either sold them to the emperor for his cavalry and fields or the horses died. Some people ate theirs. The last couple of winters were hard. Wiped everybody out."

Teleo's stomach grew heavy.

"If I were you," the cooper said, "I would turn around in the morning and head out the way you came. Best way to the Hill castles is to take the Fortress Trail. Would hate to see you waste another day going to Sapphire City only to find out the roads are closed, like I said."

Traveling to Red Flag Fortress would take a day or two from Sapphire City but three or more days to turn back and travel over the rugged Fortress Trail. They were running short on feed for the horses, and all the pastures were enclosed behind stone walls. Plus, he had told Sigrid he would see her in two weeks. That was now.

"That your falcon?" the cooper asked, peering out into the sun-filled square.

"It's my wife's." Hunter was perched on Dinsmora's gauntlet, eating out of her hand. Two barefooted children watched with fascination.

"Falconry's outlawed on the emperor's land. No hunting in the valley."

Teleo pursed his lips and raised his brow in exasperation, and the cooper mirrored his expression.

Teleo thanked the cooper and took the bucket out to the pump. They had to wait in line three times to satisfy the horses.

By the time the horses were done drinking, the sun was descending towards the rooftops.

"I suppose there's no place to stay around here, either," Teleo said to the water tender.

The man would not meet his eyes but had softened up a touch after three rounds of buckets. "You can camp outside the miller's at the end of town," he said.

"Good, we'll be back in the morning," Teleo said.

The man did not reply, turning his attention to the next person in line.

Teleo, Dinsmora, and the kids walked their horses to the edge of the densely built town. They were directed to a muddy lot bordered by fieldstone walls on three sides and the mill on the fourth side.

They paid the miller ten bits for the night, horses included. They spread out their wax tarps on the muddy ground and tried to make the best of it, sharing a meal of dried pheasant and hardbread. At least it was not raining.

The gristmill was powered by a water wheel in a river beyond the southern wall, and Teleo could hear the gears turning and the hiss of grain being processed inside the mill. Rage simmered in Teleo's blood. Two tall granaries stood next to the mill and water flowed freely beyond the walls, but both were controlled by the emperor.

At nightfall, a steady stream of men and women trod along the road on the other side of the northern wall, coming home from a long day out in the fields. They eyed the strangers and healthy horses in the miller's lot as they shuffled past.

Teleo and Dinsmora weighed their options. The horses could go hungry for a day, but not more—not with all the miles they were pushing them. They needed a reliable water source, and Hunter's meat was almost gone. If they continued on to

Sapphire City and the spoke road to Red Flag was closed, it would be a two-day journey back to the border town. Or, they could turn around now and be back in the mountains in one day, where forage and water were still free.

Besides, what kind of reception would they get in the city? Teleo did not like the way people regarded the horses and their relatively fine clothing, with all their goods and weapons on full display. People were poor here. Poorer than he remembered—and they had been poor then. Would the emperor's men demand they register their horses and pay some exorbitant fee or else they would confiscate them? Sapphire Valley had not felt this hostile before, even soon after the war had ended, when he had been searching for his son. At that time, he had been a retired soldier among retired soldiers, all farmers at heart and exhausted from war. Now, people were under the thumb of a tyrant, and he could see the oppression in their eyes.

They watered the horses at the pump first thing in the morning, getting something close to a smile from the water tender, then strapped the empty bucket on Petunia's back and headed back the way they'd come. At midday, they passed through the eastern gate to Southern Mountain Pass, paying the same high toll to get out of the valley as they had paid the day before to get in. Teleo dug into his coin purse, grumbling. Dinsmora appeared at his side and offered to pay, and he let her.

Teleo's mood grew worse when he peered over a wall and saw stooks of hay in a barn next to a cavalry horse stable, Cornwal's purple banner hanging limply from a flagpole nearby. Teleo was glad they were skipping Sapphire City, where he would have had to endure the sight of the emperor's officials walking the streets in their fine velvets and silk ruffles and wearing the fancy white wigs that the bureaucrats and their ladies liked to wear. So

much powder and pomposity while common folk were suffering would have been more than he could stomach.

Leaving the town, they climbed into the foothills and turned
right onto the well-marked Fortress Trail. They found a campsite at dusk in a clearing bordering a brook and let the horses
graze. They ate a dinner of pinecone buds, fiddlehead ferns,
miner's lettuce, and half a skinny hare Hunter caught, which
they roasted on sticks over a small fire, saving a portion of the
uncooked carcass for the falcon. Dinsmora and the kids settled
in early while Teleo stood watch under the shelter of an old oak
near the flowing brook, breathing in the fragrant forest air and
silently thanking the cooper for his advice.

24

RED FLAG

The Fortress Trail hugged the hillsides and afforded magnificent views of Sapphire Valley before heading into the dense forest. The trail went all the way around the valley's perimeter, winding across rugged crests and through mountain vales and eventually leading to each of the seven Hill Tribe castles—all of them built as defensive fortresses centuries ago when the seven tribes were independent and fighting for dominance. Red Flag was the first fortress they would encounter.

Teleo had traversed the Fortress Trail once himself, asking after his son at each of the fortified castles and any forest hamlet he found. He had ended his search down in the Sapphire Valley, where he had crisscrossed the cultivated fields, stopping at farmhouses and villages and asking at the local pubs. He had ended up in Sapphire City, where he had finally abandoned his search and turned to alcohol and enterprising young women. He shook his head to clear away the dark memories.

On the second day of their trek along the Fortress Trail, Teleo sensed he was being watched. He was in the rear and whistled to Dinsmora, who was in the lead. She stopped and he turned Star around, scanning the forest behind them. He was wearing his fox-and-hare cloak, Jessum was in his falcon cloak, and Dinsmora and Kaspari wore their embroidered tunics, but they were not invisible—not with the horses, and not to a skilled scout. When he glanced back over his shoulder, Dinsmora and Kaspari had arrows nocked and Jessum held his axe. All of them stayed still, listening and watching.

Hunter gave the location away. Teleo followed the falcon's line of sight to a copse of trees they had just passed through. Teleo remained motionless until the form of a man training an arrow on him resolved from among a screen of leaves and branches. The man was leaning against the trunk of a pine, partially obscured behind bushy undergrowth, but his hunter's hat, like Teleo's, stuck out, the quail feathers glinting in the dappled sunlight. Behind him, peering around another tree, was another, younger man. Teleo met the younger man's eyes, and the man drew his bow.

"Don't shoot," Teleo called out, as much to Dinsmora and Kaspari as to the men. None of his party was wearing armor, except for him with his tattered leather cuirass.

"What do you want?" Teleo called to the men. He scanned the forest for more men but found only trees.

"Put your bows down," he said over his shoulder to Dinsmora and Kaspari, who slowly lowered their weapons.

"What do you want?" Teleo repeated.

Birds twittered merrily in the tree branches. The older man lowered his bow. "What business do you have here?" The man's voice was deep and resonant.

"We're going to Red Flag Fortress," Teleo called out.

"For what purpose?"

"To visit a friend," Teleo said.

"What friend?" the man asked.

Teleo had told them enough. "What do you want?" he asked again.

The older man was about the same age as Teleo, and the younger man looked to be his twenty-something son. They were thin, their faces gaunt, and their clothing worn. Teleo noted the men's silence. They did not look to be brigands.

"Are you hungry?" Teleo asked.

"We're fine," the older man said haughtily. He did not look fine. It was difficult living in the forest without adequate shelter and food reserves, and it had been a tough winter.

"We have two pheasants," Teleo said, gesturing to Dinsmora's saddlebags, where the two fowl hung. They had flushed them on the grassy banks of a stream earlier that day, and Hunter caught them with ease. Kaspari had found a clutch of ten eggs. "We'd be happy to share."

The man and his son traded glances.

"Come on," Teleo said to Dinsmora. "Let's cook these up." It was late afternoon, and all they had eaten that day was hardbread and cheese from Trillifort. They had been keeping a steady pace since dawn, and everyone was tired.

They dismounted and began setting up camp in a gully behind a thicket of holly bushes. The two men had moved down the hill parallel to them, and Teleo could feel them watching as he plucked the birds' feathers. The kids started a fire, and Dinsmora gathered dandelion leaves near where the horses were grazing. Hunter perched on Cinnamon's saddle and watched Teleo dress the birds. He whistled for her, and she swooped down and landed on his wrist, plucking choice morsels from his hand. Once the fire was going, they roasted the pheasants on green willow spits and boiled the eggs in the cooking pot. They sat around the fire and removed the smaller bird from the willow rod and cut it up on Dinsmora's cutting board.

"Come on over," Teleo called into the woods. "We don't bite." The smell from the roasted meat would lure the men in, Teleo predicted. A few moments later, the undergrowth rustled at the edge of the clearing, and the two men stood hesitantly under the hanging boughs of a willow.

Dinsmora placed the quartered bird on a wide piece of bark, juice and fat dripping, added four hard-boiled eggs and some greens, and placed it on a log a few paces away. She motioned to the men and returned to the fire.

The men approached slowly and then knelt by the log and tore into the meat, watching Teleo and the others curiously while stuffing hot meat into their mouths.

Teleo, Dinsmora, and the kids let them eat in peace, and shared the remainder of the food amongst themselves.

After the two men finished eating, they sat back on their heels and did not leave the clearing.

"How long you been living in the hills?" Teleo asked. "You're welcome to join us over here if you'd like. I'm Tesserman."

The father and son exchanged a few quiet words and then slowly approached, sitting on rocks within easy speaking distance. "I'm Will," the older man said, "and this is my son, Waite. We've been out here since the emperor kicked us off our land."

"Oh? When was that?" Teleo asked.

"Last summer, right before harvest," Will said bitterly.

Teleo shook his head. "That's rough."

"It's criminal," Will said, and Waite nodded.

"Can't argue with that," Teleo said. "Seems like this Cornwal character is making up whatever laws he pleases."

"He's a despot," Will said.

"We couldn't buy feed for our horses," Teleo told them. "I heard the emperor owns all the horses."

"True fact," Will said. "That is, he owns all the grain and grasslands and won't sell whole grain to common folk for their livestock. So ..."

"So ...," Teleo echoed.

Teleo and Will shook their heads.

"You're going to Red Flag?" the man asked. "Been there before?"

Teleo nodded as he gnawed on the end of a leg bone. "Once," he said. "A few years ago. Seems like another lifetime."

"We can show you the way. There are a few tricky turnoffs. If you miss them, you could get lost for days."

Teleo nodded. He had wandered aimlessly in these hills, hiding out from brigands and then following them to find his way from one settlement to another. He caught Dinsmora's eye and she gave a small nod.

"Okay. Much obliged," Teleo said.

Will and Waite set up camp on the other side of the gully. Teleo ended up sharing a midnight watch with Waite, who told him about their family farm and all that had befallen them. His brothers had died in the war and his mother had died when he was a child. All Waite and his father had in the world was each other.

———◆———

The next morning, Will and Waite led them on foot and stopped at a branch in the trail. "Red Flag is this way," Will said. The turnoff was marked with a simple wooden post topped by an arrow-shaped board that looked to have been painted red at one time but had since faded.

Teleo nodded and his party followed the two guides, leaving Fortress Trail. Will and Waite helped them navigate a series of turnoffs. Later that day, the high stone walls of Red Flag Fortress appeared on a stone bluff overlooking Sapphire Valley. Red flags embroidered with gold rampant griffins flapped from staffs placed at the corners of the fortified castle walls and over the main gate.

A dozen guards peered over the battlements, some with longbows at the ready, others aiming crossbows. A small iron plate on the closed wooden gate slid open and two eyes looked out at them.

"What's your business here?" a gruff voice asked.

"We're here to see Sigrid," Teleo said, swinging down from his saddle and lifting his new hat in greeting.

"What business do you have with the princess?" the guard asked.

"Princess ...? Um ... I'm her ... friend. She is expecting me." Teleo tried to gather his wits. She knew him by his real name. He stepped closer. "Tesserman is my name. She calls me Teleo."

The iron hatch slid shut.

Princess?

Several minutes later, the gate creaked open. The guards let Dinsmora and the kids pass, along with the horses and their weapons. Teleo followed, but the guard stopped Will and Waite. "Who're they?" the guard asked Teleo.

"Friends," Teleo said.

"They wait out here," the guard said.

"No problem," Will said. "We'll be on our way."

"Okay," Teleo said. "Sorry to send you back out into the wild so soon. I was hoping you could at least get a proper meal and a real bed for the night." Teleo glanced at the guard, who met his eyes with an unrelenting stare. Teleo sighed and counted out a few Silver Bits and held them out for Will.

"No need to pay us," Will said, refusing the money.

"Take it," Teleo insisted. "Times are hard."

Will glanced at his son, then reluctantly accepted the coins. "Many thanks. Good luck to you."

"And to you."

They shook hands, and Teleo passed through the gate into a walled yard that had weeds sprouting between worn flagstones. He and his companions followed another guard through a long stone archway, their steps echoing off the damp walls. They emerged into a small square hemmed in by tall edifices. The buildings were constructed of plain blocks of blue argillite, with small recessed windows and tooth-shaped ramparts lining the rooftops.

A group of workers shuffled by. They were lean and wore threadbare clothing. Though they were gaunt in the face, their eyes were sharp and curious. The workers left the yard through an alleyway leading to a cobblestone lane of row houses, and Teleo noted a placard depicting a tankard of ale hanging from a signpost over one building. He vaguely recalled the small castle town from his brief visit there. He had stopped at the few pubs and inquired about Verdant Valley war orphans. He had drunk too much and rented a bed in a humble inn for the night, sleeping on a horsehair mattress on the floor with three other snoring men squeezed into the small chamber. At least the room had been free of rodents and lice.

The guard motioned for them to hitch their horses to iron rings mounted on ancient stone posts. There were no signs of other horses. Dinsmora stayed outside with Kaspari and Jessum. Teleo left his swords and knives with Dinsmora and followed the guard into one of the large stone buildings.

They stepped into a small foyer, and the guard closed the door behind them. It was dim, silent, and cold, the only light filtering in through narrow slits set high into the stone wall. Teleo's palms were sweating. He hoped Sigrid's invitation had been sincere and not just a polite gesture. Maybe she hadn't really expected him to take her up on her offer. She hadn't told him she was a *princess*.

Did she mistakenly think he was nobility? Teleo took a breath and followed the guard down a long stone hallway lit by more wall slits. No one was about. Their boot soles clicked against the stone-tiled floor. Stern portraits of men and women stared after them. The guard rapped on a large wooden door and then pushed it open, leading Teleo into a library.

Sigrid's amber scent greeted him before he saw her. She was sitting in a simple wooden chair by a low fire. She stood and crossed the floor, hands outstretched. Her face shone and he clasped her hands in his, his heart warmed by her smile.

"Sigrid," he said, overcome with the rush he got whenever he was in her presence.

"Teleo." She motioned for the guard to leave them. The door closed softly, and they were alone in the library. They gazed at one another for a long moment, then she lowered her eyes and stepped back a pace, releasing his hands.

He glanced around the room. Scrolls and books littered a large wooden table. Shelves lined the walls, floor to ceiling, and were filled with books, boxes, and carved animal figurines. A ladder provided access to the upper shelves.

She went to the fireplace and pulled up a second chair for him. They sat across from each other, smiling. Her black hair was twisted into buns at the sides of her head, as usual, and she wore the same red dress.

"I'm so glad you arrived safely. Was the journey difficult?" she asked. "I expected you days ago. I thought maybe you'd changed your mind." Her cherry-red lips relaxed from their smile and turned down a bit.

A knock came at the door and an old woman entered with a tray carrying hot tea and wedges of apple raisin tart. Sigrid pulled a small, linen-covered table between them for the tray to rest upon. The old woman inspected Teleo openly, her little bird eyes taking in his unkempt hair, scarred face, and scruffy beard, then dropping to regard his tattered Elke chest armor, stained and patched buckskin pants, and unpolished boots. Teleo hadn't seen a mirror since leaving Trillifort, and judging by the frown on the woman's face, he was not pleasing to the eye.

"That'll be all, Tildie. I'll be fine," Sigrid said. She waited until the door closed behind the serving woman, then turned her gaze on Teleo. "My aunt. She disapproves of most men."

They laughed together, and he relaxed. "The journey was a bit rough," Teleo said. "Lots of rain over the pass. Then the valley was surprisingly ... inhospitable."

"How do you mean?" she asked.

He described the grain and water situation and the exorbitant border fees. "I was told the roads from the valley to the Hill fortresses were closed, and so we turned back and came the long way around, on Fortress Trail. I'm sorry I'm late."

"Oh, I should have warned you," she said. "I'd heard they closed the valley roads a few weeks ago but I haven't been down there myself."

"Emperor Cornwal is tightening up everything, it seems," Teleo said.

"He is," she said. "It's bad. But let's enjoy our tea."

Teleo sipped the hot, spiced tea, his big thumb and forefinger clumsily holding the fine porcelain cup handle. He tried not to eat the fruit tart in two bites. It took him four. The room was well lived in, with a worn rug in front of the fireplace and a ten-point deer head mounted above the mantelpiece. A single log glowed in the fireplace. Though the air outdoors was pleasant, castles were always cold—one reason he preferred his small farmhouse.

He turned to her. "It's good to see you in person," he said. "I mean ...," he faltered.

"I know what you mean. It's good to see you, too." She wiped her red lips with a white handkerchief. "I did not know you were married." A smile strained her lips.

"Oh," he said, taken aback. "You mean my ... traveling party? Outside?"

"Yes." She sipped her tea, watching him over the rim of her cup.

"I'm sorry," he said. "I should have told you. But that is not my wife." He held her gaze.

"Who is she?" Sigrid asked, holding her teacup in the air, with her pinky outstretched. "My guard informed me that you are with your wife and two teenaged children. Is that not your family?"

Teleo let out an awkward chuckle. "Can I be honest with you?" he asked.

"Please," she said, setting her teacup on its saucer.

He set his on his saucer as well, the delicate cup clattering a bit too loudly.

"I trust you with my life, Sigrid," Teleo said. "I don't know why, but I do. Mora is my cousin. The boy, Jeremiah, is a war orphan and, as I told you, I intend to search for his family. The girl is also an orphan. We adopted her, so to speak, but we tell people she is our daughter to protect her. That is something I beg you not to speak of to anyone. However, if you'd like, you may say Mora is my cousin and Kallie is her daughter. I trust you to help protect Kallie as well." Teleo was no longer smiling and neither was Sigrid.

Sigrid studied his face, as though trying to determine if he was telling her the truth.

"You can ask Mora, if you want," he said. "I guess I assumed you saw their things when we went downstairs in the tower, but it's my fault for not explaining our situation. And please call me Tesserman. We do not want to be found."

Sigrid blinked at him. "We should invite them in," she said, brushing crumbs from the tablecloth.

"As you like," he said. "We will need someone to guard the horses and our belongings. And Mora has a falcon."

Sigrid blinked again. "No one will steal your horses or your belongings. This is my father's castle. Your cousin may bring the bird inside."

They went together down the long hallway. It felt good walking by her side, even though they did not say a word. She was the perfect height for him, and her dress hugged her breasts and hips.

His companions were waiting outside where he had left them. Guards were watching curiously from the ramparts, and three women pretended to sweep the courtyard. There was no fountain, only a vacant square of blue argillite paving stones. The cling-clang of several hammers rang out in the distance and the acrid odor of a smelter reached his nose.

"Mora," he said. "I'd like you to meet Princess Sigrid. Sigrid, meet Mora. This is Kallie." Kaspari gave a slight curtsy, managing to make her riding leathers and embroidered tunic look stately. "And this is Jeremiah." Jessum inclined his head shyly.

Dinsmora carried Hunter on her gauntleted fist, and they went inside. The three adults walked abreast down the hallway, with the teenagers trailing behind. In the library, Sigrid stacked books and scrolls out of the way and invited them to sit at the large table. She pulled on a bell rope and then sat down, gesturing for Teleo to sit next to her. Aunt Tildie appeared at the door, and Sigrid asked for more tea and tart while Dinsmora settled Hunter on the back of a wooden chair by a window and then sat across from Sigrid.

When they were all settled around the table, Sigrid turned to Dinsmora and asked, "So, how long have you and Teleo been married?"

Teleo felt a pinprick of disappointment that she still did not trust him and felt the need to test him.

Aunt Tildie chose that moment to come in and set a pot

of tea and a whole tart on the table. She distributed cups and poured the steaming tea as they silently watched.

When she left, Dinsmora glanced at him. He waved his hand and said, "You don't have to lie. Go ahead. Tell her how we're related. Sigrid is my friend."

Dinsmora turned to Sigrid, whose face had softened.

"He's my cousin," Dinsmora said. "We grew up together. Our fathers were brothers." Dinsmora glanced at Teleo again.

"And we adopted the two orphans for their safety," Teleo finished.

The kids and Dinsmora looked at one another and then at Sigrid and Teleo, wondering who this Hill Tribe woman was and how she had earned Teleo's trust.

Teleo turned to Sigrid and raised his eyebrows. Sigrid's lips quirked up as she sliced the round fruit tart into six triangular pieces and handed Dinsmora the plate. Dinsmora took a slice and passed the plate around the table.

"Please call me Tesserman in public," he reminded Sigrid. "As I said, you can tell people that Mora and I are cousins and that Kallie is Mora's daughter—and that I will kill anyone who touches her. Or the boy. Or Mora, for that matter, although she can defend herself. As can the kids at this point. Right?" he asked, nodding to each of them in turn.

Kaspari and Jessum nodded mutely, and Dinsmora wore an amused expression. "He's a hard man," Dinsmora said, turning to Sigrid, "and stubborn. He likes to have his way."

"Don't most men?" Sigrid asked Dinsmora, tilting the teacup to her lips as though it were only the two of them sharing a bit of tea and gossip.

"He more than most," Dinsmora said.

"Really?" Sigrid asked. "He does seem a bit strong-minded." She turned to him, her eyes crinkling at the corners in a warm smile.

Teleo melted under her gaze. "What's the feed situation here for the horses?" he asked, steering the conversation away from himself. "Do you have a granary? Can we purchase some?"

Sigrid's cheeks flushed. "We're short on grain. We don't have livestock anymore, except goats, and they eat mostly kitchen scraps or fend for themselves in the yard. We often take them into the hills to forage."

"No horses?" Teleo asked, scarcely able to imagine a kingdom without horses.

Sigrid shook her head, looking embarrassed. "We lost the last of them over the winter."

Lost or ate? Teleo did not want to ask.

Sigrid rushed to explain. "Cornwal took control of our fields in the valley last summer, right before harvest. Our farmers couldn't defend themselves against Cornwal's troops, and we couldn't spare any men to help fight them off. We were being harassed by brigands at the time. We think the emperor paid the bandits to harry the castles while he stole our land. Our men in the valley had to let them take the land or else he would have killed them and their families. Same thing happened to the other Hill Tribes. Cornwal controls the entire valley now. We think he wants to starve us out and take over the hills as well."

Teleo grimly examined her pained eyes and the slouch of her shoulders. That explained the same red dress and the gaunt faces of the castle inhabitants. There was nothing of value in this room aside from books. No weapons hung on the walls, as was the custom in most castles. The only wall decorations were the stuffed buck's head over the fireplace and a boar's head mounted above the doorway, its long tusks curving up from bared lips. Only one gold band adorned Sigrid's fingers, set with a small pink star-ruby. Her neck was bare but for a gold chain, which he knew held the Heliotrope amulet under her bodice.

"How do you survive?" he asked.

"We have iron and an armory. We sell weapons and armor to the emperor." Sigrid winced as she said this, and Teleo grimaced with her at the bitter irony. "My father has been negotiating with him for food," she continued. "However, Cornwal refuses to sell whole grain. He sells only milled flour, and he controls the mills, of course. You can't feed horses milled flour."

"No," Teleo agreed. "You lost the horses but not the goats?" he asked.

"We had to make a choice," she said painfully. "Goats are smaller and give milk, and they eat anything."

"If I had to make a choice, I would have eaten the goats and saved the horses," he said, wishing he hadn't as her face flinched. "I'm sorry," he said quickly, touching her arm.

"I know," she said glumly. "It's horrible." She took a deep breath and straightened her spine. "What's done is done."

"What's next?" he asked.

She pushed aside her plate and said, "We think Cornwal's next move will be to attack the Hill fortresses, once he's weakened us enough. That won't take long, the way things are going. You'll meet my father at dinner," she said, brightening. "You will stay, won't you? We can put you up for a few nights."

"We would appreciate that," Teleo said, nodding at Dinsmora, who smiled at Sigrid. He and Dinsmora and the kids would hunt in the morning and try to feed themselves.

Sigrid showed them to two bedchambers with a large bed in each. Teleo and Jessum took one room, and Dinsmora and Kaspari took the other. The rooms were furnished in old but high-quality furniture. The castle had been grand at one time. They changed into less grimy clothes, then one of the guards showed them to a vacant horse stable with twenty-four empty stalls. They fed the horses what grain they had left. They would take them out to the forest during the day to forage. The spring undergrowth was thick. At least Red Flag had plenty of water from a river that tumbled down a rocky hillside nearby.

They dined in a small hall with Sigrid's father, King Jarnsmidt, and Aunt Tildie. They were served wild boar with stewed apples, fresh greens, soft goat cheese, warm bread, and cold ale. Teleo ate his fill and grew rather drunk with Sigrid's father, who had an acerbic sense of humor that had Teleo laughing until his sides hurt. Dinsmora and Sigrid sat by the fire, talking quietly, while Kaspari flipped through books and read passages to Jessum, and Aunt Tildie knitted in a rocker near the hearth.

King Jarnsmidt was in his seventies, and although he showed his age with loose spotted skin and sparse white hair, he walked with a spring in his step. He shook Teleo's hand with the iron grip of a blacksmith, or that of a soldier—apparently he had been both, having earned his crown through hard work and victories on the battlefield. But now, with no sons and few resources, Teleo could not see how Jarnsmidt could withstand the relentless pressure from Emperor Cornwal.

Jarnsmidt said that many young men had left the small Hill castles to go work in Sapphire City or the fields. Some even became soldiers for Cornwal, who paid in gold. The Hill Tribes had kept their independence and landholdings under the previous emperor, Arnbjorg, while trading freely and contributing men and resources to the war with Verdant Valley. After the peace treaty, life had been returning to normal under Arnbjorg. But within a few short months, a coup put Cornwal on the throne, and things had been getting worse ever since.

"What are you going to do?" Teleo asked him.

"The problem is Cornwal. He's greedy for power and wealth," Jarnsmidt said, taking a long draught of his ale.

"How does he maintain power if nobody likes him?" Teleo asked.

Jarnsmidt belched loudly and continued in hushed tones to Teleo. "He told everybody we should be rich, not second-rate. He said Verdant Valley and the Far Shell Islands were all rich, and that they laughed at us for being simple Hill folk. He convinced everyone that only he knew how to make us rich. If we did things his way, blah blah blah. Far as I can tell, he's the only one getting rich. He and his cronies. Everybody else makes just enough to get by. Now he wants my iron and my armory. He told me he'd lease it back to me and it'd be better for me." Jarnsmidt belched again.

"Do you believe him?"

"Hell no," the king said, wiping ale from his white beard. "He's a lying sack of shit. I was onto him from the very beginning, but nobody listened. All anyone could think about was gold. Now everyone is focused on how to get their next meal. He's got us over a barrel. When he stole our fields, he claimed they legally belonged to the emperor, saying that the four-hundred-year-old Bedon edict that divided the fertile land among the seven Hill Tribes was supposed to expire after one hundred years. He said he could produce grain more efficiently on large tracts of land, store it in the large granaries, and mill it in the large mills—that it would be cheaper for everyone that way. But he didn't tell us that he would not sell whole grain or that we would need gold to buy his flour—and gold is hard to come by. So he tills our fields using our own people, takes all the harvest for himself, and guards the fields and granaries with our own soldiers while we starve." Lines of anger and frustration scored his brow.

"Don't people hate him for killing Arnbjorg? How did he manage the coup?" Teleo asked. There had been rumors burning through the empire when Teleo had last been there, not long after the assassination had taken Arnbjorg's life—stories of intrigue and lies, alliances and betrayals. Rumors were that Cornwal had murdered Arnbjorg with his bare hands. Or with poison. Or magic. Or that the ministers had cornered him and backed him into a fire. Or shackled him to a stone wall and executed him with a barrage of arrows. Or the military commander had slain him with a sword. Or knives. Or a garrote. In short, no one knew.

Jarnsmidt shrugged. "One day, Cornwal appeared at the high castle holding up Arnbjorg's head on a pike. No one knows who actually killed him. Probably Raedwald, Cornwal's thug general. But anyway, before the coup, Cornwal had been the trade minister. He was responsible for all goods passing in and out of the empire. He made it seem like he was the reason we could suddenly buy things that were not available during the war. Then he started rumors that Arnbjorg was using magic. He made people afraid that the Mages would come back and start the chaos all over again and Stone Guardians would start raiding, and then we would be back in the bloody Magic Wars that brought us down in the first place."

Jarnsmidt scratched at his bearded chin, and Teleo kept silent. Teleo took a swig of his ale, which was piss-warm by now, and wondered if Jarnsmidt knew about the Heliotropes in his castle and what his daughter had been up to. Teleo's own Heliotrope amulet hung heavily around his neck, barely hidden under his leather jerkin, which was partially unlaced. Jarnsmidt's large brown eyes pierced his.

Teleo took another draught of ale. When he lowered his mug, Jarnsmidt's eyes were still fixed on him, expecting a response. "Yeah," he managed to say. "Stone Guardians are trouble."

"Cornwal is more trouble," Jarnsmidt grumbled, seeming almost angry that Teleo agreed with something Cornwal had said. "I would rather be free and fighting Stone Guardians than starving under that scumbag's rule."

Teleo did not know what to say and stole a glance at Sigrid.

"More ale!" Jarnsmidt bellowed, and lurched to his feet, fetching a full pitcher from the sideboard and sloshing ale into Teleo's mug. "You'll help me beat that bastard Cornwal, right Tesserman? You're a soldier, I can see it in your bones." Jarnsmidt sat heavily in his chair and lifted his bushy eyebrows. Teleo took a large gulp of ale.

Sigrid rose from her chair and placed her hand on her father's shoulder. "Papa, let Tesserman relax. They've been on the road for days."

"Poff," he scoffed. "Soldiers are on the road their whole lives. It never ends. Right, Tesserman?"

Jarnsmidt raised his mug to Teleo and they clinked their mugs together.

"I'm retired," Teleo said.

"So are you, Papa," Sigrid said.

"Retired, poff. We'll have time enough to rest when we're dead. In the meantime, I'll squish that bloodsucker Cornwal between my fingers."

"Ewww, Papa." She pulled up her chair next to Teleo's and sat down.

Dinsmora joined them, and Kaspari came over with a large open book and placed it on the table in front of Teleo.

"Look," Kaspari said, pointing to an illustration of a white griffin on a red background, clutching a golden spear and silver sword in its black claws. "The Bedon sigil. Same as on the castle flags here."

"So it is," Teleo said, glad for the diversion.

"Kind of like Jeremiah's banner but without the wolf," Kaspari said.

"Griffin is the Bedon sigil," Jarnsmidt said. "We've got Bedon blood. All the Hill fortress kings do. But not Cornwal. He's a mongrel. Some say he's descended from Stone Guardians. He's been stealing from all of us and hoarding the fruits of the most fertile valley in the world." Jarnsmidt slammed the mug down, splashing yellow ale onto the table. "The only solution is to band together and defeat that mangy wolf. Bury him in the dirt and let the worms eat his flesh."

"Papa!" Sigrid scolded.

"Don't *Papa* me," he said, leaning past Teleo to peer at his daughter. "Cornwal wants me to marry you off to one of his poofy ministers. Is that what you want? Do you want to live in a cloud of powder and perfume the rest of your life? Wear white wigs and bodices so tight you can't breathe? Locked in some stone tower making lace with the *ladies?*"

Sigrid gave her father a long-suffering look, as though this were an old conversation. She glanced at Teleo. "No. Of course not," she said.

"Well, then. Let the men talk. Jeremiah, sit down here, young man. You're about fighting age. Do you know how to wield a sword?"

Jessum sat across the table from Jarnsmidt. "Yes, sir."

"He's even better with a stave," Teleo said proudly. "And he's learning the axe."

"Are you of Bedon blood?" Jarnsmidt demanded.

Jessum shrugged. "I don't know."

"You look like you are. What is this banner your sister speaks of?"

"A gift. From the queen, uh ... former queen of Trillifort."

"Let me see it," Jarnsmidt said.

"Yes, sir," Jessum said, rising to his feet. He left the room with Kaspari on his heels.

"Don't put ideas into the poor boy's head," Sigrid said. "He's a war orphan."

Jarnsmidt turned a bloodshot eye on Sigrid. "So? You think that changes his blood? He's a Bedon as sure as my teeth are gold," he said, grinning widely and revealing several gold molars.

Sigrid pursed her lips and sat back in her chair.

The kids returned with the red banner and spread it out on the table. The two points of the long swallowtail pennant hung off the end of the table. The gold embroidered griffin stared up at Teleo, with one foreleg raised, its wings unfurled, and its beak gaping with a long silver tongue curling out. The dead wolf stared up at the griffin, blood dripping from its mouth.

"Hmm," Jarnsmidt said, standing up to regard the pennant. "I haven't seen a sigil like this since I was a child. The ancient Bedon griffin always vanquished a wolf, like this one." The king leaned in to get a better look.

Aunt Tildie came over and inspected the design. The detailed griffin bore scales and feathers and had a lion's tail with a pointed arrowhead at its tip. "Where did you get this, you say? Trillifort?" she asked, squinting curiously at the embroidery.

"Yes, ma'am," Jessum said.

"It's quite a fine piece of work," Jarnsmidt said. "It's a war banner. It's meant to take into battle, not hang from ramparts. Do you have a stave for it?"

Jessum shook his head.

"We'll make you one," Jarnsmidt said.

Jessum nodded and ran his fingers over the gold thread of the griffin. Hunter ruffled her wings from her perch and Dinsmora stood up. "We should turn in for the night," she said. "It's getting late. We'll take our falcon hunting at dawn. Where is a good place to hunt?"

Sigrid and Jarnsmidt stood up and insisted on accompanying them in the morning.

They retired, and at dawn they convened in the cold dining room, quickly consumed hot tea and honey cakes, and left for the stable. Jarnsmidt rode Nutmeg, and Sigrid rode Petunia. Game was scarce, and after three hours, they had only bagged three small quail. They returned to the castle, and as they approached the gate, two men were trudging towards them with a full-grown buck suspended by its legs from a long pole propped on their shoulders. Teleo recognized the men as Will and Waite, and they smiled broadly at him.

"Wow. Good catch," Teleo said. "But why are you bringing it here?"

"Thought the castle might need some meat. The forest is overhunted around here. We were lucky with this one. Can't eat this whole thing by ourselves, anyway. We'd just attract wolves before getting a chance to smoke it."

Jarnsmidt came up behind them and agreed with Will's assessment. He offered Will three Silver Owls for the buck and invited them inside the castle grounds, showing them the way to the butcher.

25

LARISSA

L ater that evening, they shared a venison dinner in the dining room with Will and Waite, who had been given space in the stable for the night. A fire blazed on the hearth, warming the large room, which featured a long, heavy oak dining table. Situated around the room were a half-dozen full suits of plate armor—hollow steel sentries standing tall and holding polearms with gauntleted fists. Tapestries softened the severe stone walls, depicting hunts through tangled forests, and one featuring a white unicorn standing in the center of a lush, manicured garden.

After a long evening around the table, Sigrid invited Teleo to walk with her. He had been waiting for time alone together. She took a lantern and led him through the cold hallways of the castle and into her bedchamber. She did not lead him to her bed but climbed the stairs set against the curving wall of the round tower room. She unlocked the door at the top and they entered another round chamber. The Heliotrope gleamed up at him. It was similar in size to the one in the Third Tower but polished to a bright sheen. The room was warm from a mound of coals glimmering orange on the hearth.

"Is this where you visited me from?" he asked, crossing the slowly swirling floor. He knelt down and pressed his palms to the translucent Sun Circle.

"Yes," she said, kneeling next to him and gazing at the round slab of Angel Wings marble.

Teleo sat back on his heels and gazed around the room. Four large, rectangular, leaded-glass windows faced each cardinal direction. Between the northern and western windows stood the fireplace, and above the mantel hung a collection of swords. A small round wooden table with two straight-backed chairs and a built-in stone bench sat under the western window, and another chair and a cushioned bench sat in front of the fireplace, both embroidered with a repeating pattern of red and gold griffins. Above the eastern window, set high into the stone wall, the round Focal Point stared down at Teleo, its clear glass glistening at him.

Sigrid stood up and hung the lantern from the wall, then lit another, setting it on the mantelpiece.

"Here," she said. He joined her at the fireplace, and she handed him a sword from the wall rack, took one for herself, and they began dancing in the lantern light.

After a few circuits, Teleo stopped and faced her. She met him at the Sun Circle, and he wondered if she liked him the same way he liked her. He thought she had flirted with him a few times, but he could not be sure. Women were confusing. Especially Hill women, who were strong and confident and would stick a knife in you as soon as kiss you, as he had found out one drunken night in Sapphire City when he had narrowly avoided being stabbed by a woman he had mistakenly thought was interested in him.

Sigrid took a step closer and looked up at him.

He gazed down upon her smooth, tawny cheeks and tiger-eye irises.

"Do you find me pretty?" she asked, tilting her head slightly to one side.

"I do," he said, his voice catching in his throat.

She gave him a tight smile. "I heard Verdant Valley men don't like the darker skin of the Hill Tribe women."

"You heard wrong," he said.

She took another step towards him, lowering the sword to her side. She reached out and took his sword hand, wrapping her fingers over his, clutching the hilt. He slid his free arm around her waist and drew her close. She raised her mouth to his, and he kissed her.

She was soft and strong, sweet and spicy. He resisted taking her to the stone floor, and ended up standing with her head cradled on his shoulder. He rocked her gently back and forth, swords dangling from their hands.

"I want you to meet someone," she said, drawing away and stepping across the floor to the northern window. He joined her and gazed out at the star-filled sky. "She should be here soon," Sigrid said.

She held her hand out for his sword and set their blades on the rack over the fireplace. He stood behind her and wrapped his arms around her belly. They stood together, gazing into the flickering embers. "So you've danced the sword during the Summer Solstice sunrise?" he asked.

"Yes," she said, tilting her head back and kissing his bearded chin.

"What does it do?" he asked, meeting her lips in a brief kiss.

"You told me it makes one unbeatable in battle," she replied. "But I have never been in battle, so I don't know."

"Do you know how to fight?" he asked.

She nodded, leaning back against his chest and entwining her arms with his. "I can kill prey with a bow and arrow. I've hunted many times but have never killed a man. My father trained me to fight with a sword, but I suppose, like anything, I would need real-life experience to become good at it. I would probably get killed."

"That's no attitude," he said, scolding her playfully. "You would probably be victorious." The amber scent was strong in her hair, mixed with a heady lemon-verbena perfume, and he breathed it in, brushing his lips against the crown of her head and stroking his fingers over the plush velvet of her dress.

Teleo felt the visitor's presence before he heard her.

Sigrid pulled away from his embrace, and they turned together to face the Sun Circle. Teleo stepped back with surprise. A woman had appeared, standing tall on the center disk. She appeared to be about the same age as Sigrid but had a more severe countenance. Her nose was thin and straight, her eyes jet-black and somber.

"Larissa," Sigrid said, moving to the Sun Circle and grasping the woman's hands. "This is Teleo. He's come." Sigrid motioned for Teleo to approach.

"Ah," Larissa said. "I told you he would." She took Teleo's hand, falling to one knee and pressing her forehead to the back of it.

Teleo was surprised at the greeting and pulled her gently to her feet. She gazed into his eyes with fierce desperation. "We have been hoping for another Mage to help our cause."

"I don't claim to be a Mage. But what is your cause?" he asked.

"We must overthrow Cornwal," she said with a steely voice.

Teleo withdrew his hand from Larissa's, not liking where this conversation was going.

"She tells you this at the risk of death," Sigrid said, squeezing his arm with a clawlike grip.

He took Sigrid's hand and tucked it into the crook of his elbow. "Hold on, now, tell me what is going on," he said.

"She is the empress," Sigrid said in a loud whisper.

Teleo turned to Larissa. She wore a floor-length, sky-blue silk dress trimmed with spotted lynx, and a gold-and-white brocade cloak. Long tumbles of wavy black hair fell past her waist, held back from her forehead with a red velvet ribbon that brought out her rosy cheeks and lips.

"You want to overthrow your husband?" he asked.

"I am his prisoner," she said, her eyes cold.

"You are here, in Hill country," Teleo said. "Don't go back. Run to the Blue Mountains."

"No," she said, shaking her head vehemently. "I can fight him best from within."

"Why do you want to fight him?" he asked. "You can easily escape from here."

"I can escape," she agreed. "But what about everyone else?"

Teleo nodded slowly. "Do you have a plan?"

Larissa and Sigrid exchanged glances. "If we could get an assassin inside the palace, then we can start a rebellion from within," Larissa said.

The two women fixed their eyes on him.

"Oh-ho, no," Teleo said, chuckling warily. "I am not an assassin. No," he repeated. "I'm sorry. Even if I could kill the emperor, then what? He has hundreds of troops in the valley. Thousands. The imperial advisors would replace him with another one of their own. There's too much wealth under his control. His cronies won't let go of it so easily."

Larissa responded with a bitter laugh. "His ministers are a litter of suckling pigs. They would grovel in the mud at the sight of you." Larissa ran her eyes up and down Teleo's body.

Teleo glanced down at himself. He was still wearing his riding leathers. "Me?" he asked, spreading his arms. "I'm just an old, washed-up soldier."

Larissa and Sigrid exchanged glances again. "He doesn't see himself, does he?" Larissa asked.

Sigrid cocked an eyebrow. "I think not."

"See what?" Teleo asked.

"Look," Larissa said, pointing down at the translucent Angel Wings marble. "Look at yourself."

Teleo stood over the Sun Circle and looked down. He didn't see anything but the smooth white marble glowing in the lantern light.

"Look closer," Larissa said, pointing down at the floor.

He raised an eyebrow, but she was the empress, after all, and so he lowered himself onto his hands and knees and gazed at his faint reflection in the stone. His image became clearer the longer he stared at himself, but only his aging, scarred face gazed back at him. The weight of the amulet pulled the miniature Heliotrope out from under his jerkin, and it swung down, arcing across his reflection. A flash of white encircled his head and left a lingering glow. He drew back, startled.

"What was that?" he asked, looking up at the two women, who wore smug smiles.

"You are a Mage," Larissa said, her eyes glittering. "You wear the Mage's Halo."

Teleo stood up, his breath coming faster. "What does that mean? Can people see it? They would kill me." He pushed the amulet under his jerkin.

"No, they cannot see it," Larissa said. "Only other Mages can see it, and there are precious few of us."

"They see something," Sigrid clarified. "But they don't know what. They just respect you and maybe fear or admire you—depending on if they are honest people or if they are trying to deceive others. The good people will admire and be drawn to you. Others will feel threatened and try to kill you. Or they will try to get you to serve them so they can use your power."

"Fabulous," he drawled sarcastically. "Can I undo it?"

Both women laughed.

"No. The best thing to do is grow stronger," Sigrid said.

"How can I do that?"

"Dance the sword," Sigrid said. "As you have been doing. Dance at the solstice."

"That's nearly two months away," he said.

"It will be here before you know it," Larissa said.

It was tempting to stay with Sigrid for the next several weeks and dance in the rays of the Summer Solstice in her Heliotrope. Ignite the legends he had always thought were myths. See for himself what a Mage really was. But Red Flag was already struggling.

"I don't think I can stay here that long, much as I would like to," he said. "You have little food and no grain for the horses." He instantly regretted his words as Sigrid's smile faltered. Larissa caught his eye. The empress knew exactly what her husband was up to, and Teleo could see that she suffered from guilt.

"Besides," he said quickly. "I have to search for Jeremiah's family."

Sigrid nodded and said, "I know of some families whose young boys were kidnapped by Verdant Valley marauders during the war. There's one back in the mountains south of here. Their veins flow with ancient Bedon blood. You should start there. Jeremiah has their stature and the same slant to his eyes as they have. Maybe you will find his family there."

Teleo swallowed. The two women were watching him. His mouth opened and closed, but no words came out.

"What is it, Teleo?" Sigrid asked, taking his trembling hand.

"My son," he choked.

"Your son," she repeated, trying to understand.

"My son. My own son. Oren. He was stolen too." He could feel tears running down his face. "I can't find him."

"Oh," Sigrid said, pulling him into her arms, and he sobbed, the dam of years of grief breaking and a river of anguish rushing out.

"I wish I knew," he said through his tears. "I wish I knew if he was dead or not." Sigrid hugged him, kissing his cheek, and let him cry. After several wracking sobs, he sniffed back his tears and stood up straight, holding Sigrid's concerned gaze.

"I'm so sorry," Larissa said. "That is such a barbaric practice. We can help you look." The empress patted his back. "There are two Verdant Valley orphans in the palace. I will introduce you."

He drew away from Sigrid, wiping his cheeks with his sleeve. "Okay," he said to Larissa. "Thank you."

"As if war raids and kidnappings were not bad enough," the empress said, "my husband has started a slave trade in peacetime. The most despicable of his many despicable acts."

Teleo nodded. "Yes. We saw slavers on the way over the pass. We must put an end to that."

Larissa grabbed his hand. "Then you will help us?"

He took in a deep, shaking breath. "If I can."

"Good," Larissa said, taking Sigrid's hand and forming a circle with the three of them in a silent pact.

26

THE ARMORY

The next day, Jarnsmidt took them to see the armory. A smelter took up an entire building, where they watched orange molten steel flow from large crucibles into molds. Another building housed four large forges where a half-dozen men worked at each, hammering steel into blades of various types. The enormous room was noisy with the roar of bellows and the clanging of hammers.

Jessum walked around in wonder, and Teleo stared at the floor. It was a large Heliotrope, as big as the battle circle in the training yard at Verdant Castle, but fully intact. The Sun Circle was grayish-white, obscured by layers of sooty boot prints. It appeared as though the Heliotrope had once been in an outside yard and the building had been constructed around it. Whoever designed the building knew what it was, because a large Focal Point window stood high in the eastern wall in a section of ancient stone wall surrounded by newer walls.

Teleo proposed they take a tour of the forges, for Jessum's sake, and maneuvered himself so that he was standing in the

Sun Circle while he admired the vast space. The stone at his feet was solid and quiet, imbuing him with the sense of grounding he had felt at Trillifort. He knelt down, pretending to fiddle with the sole of his boot, and pressed both palms to the Angel Wings marble for a long moment before rising to his feet.

Jessum was mesmerized by the swordsmithing, and Teleo had to drag him away by the elbow. Jarnsmidt promised Jessum he could come back whenever he wanted and help tend the fires, and Teleo offered to accompany him, secretly wanting to immerse himself in the masterpiece of interlocking tesserae.

A third building was dedicated to powered hammers that flattened sheets of steel, run by a waterwheel. Fleets of female polishers filled another building, grinding and rubbing plate armor to a brilliant shine, while others were busy engraving or embossing sheets of metal. The next building was for leather-workers and sewers who fashioned straps, stitched brigandines, and bound armor plates together into their final form.

The last building housed rows of shining steel cuirasses displayed on wooden posts, standing in ranks like an army. The walls were lined with shelves filled with helmets and spaulders, hip faulds and armored skirts, and leg and arm guards. There were racks of chainmail and bins of gauntlets. Red Flag's armory was the biggest Teleo had ever seen and put the distributed armory craft houses of Verdant Valley to shame.

Jarnsmidt poked Teleo in the chest. "You need better protection."

"This has served me well," Teleo said, rubbing his worn leather chest guard.

Jarnsmidt pulled at Teleo's shoulder panel that was flapping loose and stuck a finger through a hole in the leather back piece. "It's seen better days, Tesserman."

"Plate armor is too heavy," Teleo said.

"Ours is light. Lighter than chainmail," Jarnsmidt said,

calling Jessum over, who had worn his full armor at Jarnsmidt's request. "This brigandine is fine work, I must admit," the king said, feeling the blood-red velvet and inspecting the pigskin lining and hidden metal plates. He inspected the chainmail, shoulder armor, and gauntlets. "Looks like Trillifort work. They had some good craftsmen back in the day. The old mad king knew metal." He tapped his knuckles on Jessum's helmet and suggested he join Kaspari, who was trying on gauntlets on the other side of the warehouse.

"Let me see that thing," Jarnsmidt said.

Teleo handed him the steel helmet he had taken from one of Gerik's thugs months ago—it had never fit quite right.

"I'll melt this down," Jarnsmidt said, tossing the helm into a wooden crate. "Let's fit you with a new cuirass."

Teleo loosened the straps of his armor, pulled the whole thing up over his head, and set it on a post. "I like my Elke sigil," Teleo said, tapping the metal plate.

"You like that? Doesn't mean anything anymore," Jarnsmidt said. "I heard King Elke and his family were slain. Seems like coups are in fashion these days."

Teleo frowned. "Can you transfer it to a chestplate for Kallie? She always liked this. She misses Verdant Valley."

Jarnsmidt glanced at Kaspari. "Sure. We'll outfit your ladies. They can fight, you say?"

"Kallie fought off three Stone Guardian wolves. One with a sword, one with a crowbar, and one with a pickaxe." Teleo grinned proudly and Jarnsmidt raised bushy eyebrows. "I had to finish off the last one for her," Teleo said. "The one who had his fangs buried in her face."

Jarnsmidt whistled. "Well, well. Stone Guardian wolves. That is something. I was wondering how she got her scars. They match yours. Very cute."

Teleo snickered. "Mine came from a broken bottle," he said, touching the one above his eyebrow. His fingers dropped to the scar under his eye. "And a horse's hoof. Not nearly as heroic as Kallie's."

Jarnsmidt chuckled and said, "Stone Guardian wolves are a much better story."

"A true story," Teleo insisted.

"Oh, I believe you." He threw Teleo a knowing glance and lifted a new cuirass off a post. "Try this one on."

At the other end of the building, Sigrid was helping Dinsmora find a helm. Teleo caught Sigrid's eyes for a brief moment, and his skin tingled.

"My daughter likes you," Jarnsmidt said, following his gaze. He dropped the metal armor over Teleo's head and tugged on the straps at his side.

"She is a fine woman," Teleo said. "Ow. That's a bit tight."

"Her husband died in the war," Jarnsmidt said. "They lost their only two children as infants. I think she is wary of love." Jarnsmidt tugged harder.

"Ouch. She and I, both," Teleo said, buckling the other side himself. "My wife and daughter were killed in the war during a raid, and my young son disappeared."

"Sorry to hear that," Jarnsmidt said.

Their eyes met. They could have faced each other across enemy lines. But the war was over and now they were just men.

The armor dug into Teleo's muscles. He removed the cuirass and Jarnsmidt chose another.

"My wife died of pneumonia one winter when the kids were teenagers," Jarnsmidt said. "My two boys disappeared during the war. They were young men at the time. I sent them on a diplomatic mission and they never returned. It was my fault."

His voice was heavy. "My daughter was the only one who came home."

Teleo met the man's gaze again, wondering if Sigrid had told her father about the skeletons in the dungeon.

"How's this one?" Jarnsmidt asked, lowering it over Teleo's head and fastening the straps.

"Feels good," Teleo said, shrugging his shoulders and twisting his torso back and forth. "Nice craftsmanship," he said, rapping his knuckles on the shining steel.

"The finest," Jarnsmidt said proudly. "Cornwal will take this armory over my dead body."

"He won't take it," Teleo said, squaring his jaw.

"Not if I can help it. Let's find you a helmet."

"How can I pay you?" Teleo asked Jarnsmidt, afraid the old man mistook him for a wealthy man and thought he was about to make a lucrative sale.

"Well," Jarnsmidt said, "I would try to trade for one of your horses, but I'm afraid I wouldn't be able to feed it next winter. How about you lend us your two spare mounts for the summer? You won't need pack horses to carry water or feed in the forests here, there are plenty of streams and forage. You can store your winter gear here. I noticed your shearlings and snowshoes. You won't need those in Sapphire Valley. Come for the horses and your winter gear before the snows come, if you intend to head back over the pass, that is."

Teleo rubbed his chin. "The draft horse is Mora's. The mountain horse is mine. Let me ask her. But first, tell me, where are all the Sapphire Empire white horses? There used to be horse farms all over the valley."

Jarnsmidt's placid expression turned suddenly stormy. "Where do you think?" he growled. "Cornwal took them all. Raises them in the bluegrass pastures in the northern valley.

Purple Flag still has some—the grass in their tribal lands is the best. Supposedly, Cornwal's grandparents bred racehorses up there. Anyway, the horses are Purple Flag's primary source of revenue, and so far, they've resisted Cornwal's arm-twisting, as I have with my armory. But I don't know how long any of us can hold out before giving everything over to that mangy wolf."

Teleo nodded in commiseration. The terribly expensive white steeds were not generally used as war horses, and definitely not as plow horses. They typically competed in jumping events and racing, and occasionally were used in royal hunting parties. Mostly, they were used for show—favored by noblemen and women for public events and processions, and for generally riding around in their velvets and silks, flaunting their wealth.

Teleo left to consult with his cousin about Nutmeg, and she agreed to Jarnsmidt's proposal, her eyes roving over the walls of exquisite armor.

Teleo ended up with a few carefully selected pieces, favoring lightness and flexibility over full coverage. He chose steel-plate hip faulds with a short chainmail skirt attachment, steel-plate spaulders with overlapping panels, chainmail chausses, long steel gauntlets that strapped on over heavy leather gloves, and a smooth, domed helm with an optional chainmail aventail, and a padded skullcap to line the helmet.

Dinsmora had chosen a simple chainmail hauberk similar to Jessum's, a plated brigandine of black-dyed buckskin suede, metal gauntlets with heavy black buckskin suede gloves, and a simple steel helmet and chainmail aventail of the same style as Teleo's.

Sigrid fitted Kaspari. She chose a steel-plate cuirass similar to Teleo's, a helmet and aventail, black leather shoulder guards with overlapping panels, a black leather warrior's skirt similar to Jessum's, and black gloves with steel gauntlets.

Teleo and Dinsmora got together and each chipped in five Silver Owls to make the trade fairer. After that, they all went to the stable to turn out the horses.

"We've got a small shop that makes steel-plate barding, for custom orders," Jarnsmidt said, "if you want to armor your mounts."

"No thanks," Teleo said with a wry grin. "The horses would hate that. We're not planning on pitched battle, or any tourneys that I know of."

"We could stitch Jeremiah a caparison with the Bedon sigil to match his standard," Sigrid said with a glint in her eye.

"When he becomes king," Teleo joked, "then we'll get him one for his inauguration parade. BlackJack would look majestic with his own flowing cape, don't you think?"

Jessum did his best to ignore their teasing, patting BlackJack's shoulder while the big gelding snorted and stomped.

They turned their attention to the horses. Jarnsmidt had already ridden Nutmeg, and Sigrid had ridden Petunia on their hunt. They were both good horsemen, and the animals were comfortable with them. Everyone groomed their own mounts, mucked their stalls, then saddled up and rode out to a meadow not far from the castle gates, where they let them loose to graze while the humans bathed in the river—the women upstream, and the men down around a bend. They spent the warmest part of the day picnicking in the meadow and listening to Jarnsmidt recount the history of the Bedons as he knew it. Jessum and Kaspari listened intently.

"Those are your people," Jarnsmidt said to the boy. "Brave and strong. Ancient. Of noble blood."

Jessum nodded, transfixed. Teleo noticed a new light in the boy's eyes, even though Jessum had said he did not want to find his family. They spent the rest of the afternoon flying Hunter and practicing archery. The women were by far the best with bow and arrow. Although Teleo could bring down a deer if he had to, the women were hitting pinecones from across the field. Jessum faced off with Jarnsmidt with staves and gave the old man a workout. The king was clearly a skilled warrior, but Jessum had the advantage of youth. Before they left, Jarnsmidt went into the woods with Jessum, and they returned with a linden branch to carve into a staff for his Bedon pennant.

Back at the castle, they enjoyed a dinner of venison stew, after which Jessum carved the branch in front of the dining room hearth under Jarnsmidt's watchful eye. Will and Waite had joined them for dinner and excused themselves early. They had agreed to guide them to the forest community Sigrid had told them about to look for Jessum's family. Sigrid left her father and Jessum in front of the fire and took Teleo, Dinsmora, and Kaspari into the library.

Sigrid stoked the fire to ward off the chill, and Dinsmora went around the room, lighting candles. They spent the evening sitting around the table, poring over books and scrolls on Mages and Stone Guardians. Teleo sat next to Sigrid and showed her the Heliotrope map, and she studied it with interest. He pointed out the two Heliotrope symbols over Red Flag, and she nodded. "I know," she said under her breath. "The armory is built over a Heliotrope, but don't speak of it."

After some time discussing the various Heliotrope symbols scattered across the lands, they set aside the map and Sigrid took down a big book from a shelf.

"Look at this," Sigrid said, opening to a bookmarked, illustrated page. "We can have this etched onto your chestplate."

"What is it?" he asked, leaning his shoulder against hers.

A sigil of a forked lightning bolt striking a crossed hammer and chisel was sketched in fine detail with indigo ink. She draped her arm across his shoulders, playing with his hair and making his skin tingle. He wanted to pull her onto his lap and run his hands over her body, but he pretended to be interested in the book.

"It's the ancient mark for the craftsmen's guild—Mage Stone Masters."

"Ah," he said with genuine delight.

She held his gaze and he leaned over and kissed her lips. She kissed him back, and their hands started roaming.

"Hey. Knock it off over there," Dinsmora said. "There's a child in the room."

"I am not a child," Kaspari complained.

Teleo eventually released Sigrid's lips but their arms remained entwined. She pulled his Heliotrope amulet out from under his jerkin and rubbed the miniature mosaic with her thumb. "It's amazing," she said breathlessly. "I can't believe you made this."

"Thank you," he said. "I can't believe it works. If I had never met you, I would have never learned about it." They compared their amulets, foreheads leaning close together. His was a little larger than hers but otherwise they were nearly identical. He shook his head in wonder and she kissed his cheek.

"What is this?" she asked, pulling the medicine bag out from under his shirt.

"My good luck charm," he said, taking the small pouch gently from her fingers and tucking it under his jerkin with the amulet. She hid her amulet under her embroidered bodice, and he tugged playfully at the bodice's laces. She blushed and turned back to the guild mark. He rested his chin on her shoulder and nuzzled her ear. She giggled and gently pushed his face away.

He inspected the Mage Stone Master sigil more closely. Sketched subtly in the background behind the hammer and chisel and lightning bolt was a labyrinth. He sat up straight. "I can't display what I am for all the world to see," he said.

"No one will know what it is. This book is six hundred years old," she said.

"What if they do?" he asked.

"Then they deserve to know you."

"What if they want to kill me?" he countered.

"Then they deserve to die," she said.

The practical tone of her voice surprised him and he realized she was indeed the daughter of a king. "You shouldn't need to hide who you are," she went on, raising her chin. "None of us should. We should own it."

"Does that mean we should display our amulets?" he asked for her ears alone. Dinsmora and Kaspari were talking softly on the other side of the room, lost in a book.

"No," she said with a wry turn of her mouth. "Those are too powerful to show off. But the sigil is just a mark, not a power object."

The idea of displaying the guild mark of the Mage Stone Masters sent a shiver up his spine. A good shiver. "Okay," he said. "Let's do it."

It took him a full hour to meticulously copy the mark onto a piece of parchment. By that time, the fire had burned low and Dinsmora and Kaspari had retired to their bedchamber.

Teleo spent the night with Sigrid in her bed, lost in the bliss of skin against skin. He had forgotten what pleasure felt like and never wanted to go without it again. They got little sleep, but the next morning, Teleo had more energy than he could remember, and they both wore permanent smiles.

Aunt Tildie looked like she had swallowed a bird, and Jarnsmidt scowled at him over breakfast and clapped him on the back as they walked to the armory together. "You hurt my daughter, I'll kill you," he said jovially.

"Yes, sir," Teleo said. "I won't, sir. She is a wonderful human being."

"She's an adult and can take care of herself. Still, I will kill you." Jarnsmidt smiled menacingly, showing his gold teeth.

"I understand," Teleo said somberly. He could not hold his serious expression for long, however, and soon the smile crept back across his face.

Jarnsmidt shook his head. "Ah, to be young again," he said, sighing wistfully, and opened the door to the polisher's shop.

Sigrid was already there with Dinsmora and Kaspari. A craftswoman was engraving the Mage Stone Master sigil onto Teleo's new chestplate, and he left her to her work.

"Look," Kaspari said, excitement lighting up her face. She pulled Teleo by the sleeve to a workbench. His old steel sigil had been soldered to Kaspari's new cuirass. Dents had been hammered out and the metal had been polished to a bright shine—the molded Elke sigil looked like new. The soldering was clean, and the Elke plate appeared as one piece with the underlying armor. He put his arm around her shoulder and gave her a half-hug.

"Thank you," she said, tears pooling in her eyes.

"It's your sigil," he said. "Wear it proudly. Though I am no longer wearing it, I will always defend you."

"I know," she said, wiping away a tear.

His engraving would take a while longer and the horses were hungry, so they took the horses to the meadow to graze. Sigrid sat with him by the stream's edge, interlacing her fingers with his. "Can I come with you?" she asked.

His heart skipped. "Yes," he said, surprised at the elation he felt. "Isn't it dangerous in the forest, though?" he asked, not wanting to face Jarnsmidt's wrath.

"Yes, a little," she admitted. "The farther back into the hills you go, the wilder it becomes. Many people have fled the valley and are trying to survive out here."

He nodded. What was one more woman to defend, he reasoned. Besides, she knew the terrain and the Hill culture. She was also an expert archer. "Will your father take good care of Nutmeg?" he asked, fondly regarding the big bay who was grazing next to his brother.

She laughed. "Are you kidding? That horse will be so spoiled. Papa misses his own horses terribly. This past winter broke his heart. Nutmeg is a beautiful horse."

"He is," Teleo agreed.

They returned to the castle for the midday meal, then turned the horses out again in a fenced meadow within sight of the battlements. The next day, the armor was ready. The engraving added an unexpected dimension to the plate armor, drawing Teleo's eye to the labyrinth where he found himself wanting to puzzle out its path.

They spent the next two weeks lazing around at the castle. Early mornings, Dinsmora, Sigrid, and Hunter went in search of game while Teleo went with Jessum and Kaspari to fish and search for crawdads under rocks in the river upstream of the armory. During the day, Teleo took the horses into the forest to forage and passed the time gathering edible greens for the kitchen. Sometimes, Sigrid joined him, spreading out a blanket in the privacy of the leafy glens. She always carried her bow in the forest and sometimes got a hare or wild turkey.

Teleo spent two days trailing a group of wild boars with Will and Waite, bringing back a fat male to share with the castle and giving the tusks to Jessum to use for knife handles.

Jessum spent his days assisting at the forges, and Jarnsmidt began teaching him how to make sword blades. Kaspari befriended three young women her age, and they entertained themselves with archery practice and sewing velvet bodices from an old rose-colored curtain Aunt Tildie had given them. Dinsmora spent most of her time at the leather shop and made them all fresh sets of buckskin pants and jerkins. Nights, Teleo danced the sword with Sigrid and then shared her bed.

But as the days wore on, even though they contributed to the food supplies, Teleo could tell that their added numbers were a strain on the castle's resources. And so, they prepared to leave.

On the morning they were to depart, Sigrid met them at the stable and saddled Petunia. They led the horses outside when the sun was climbing above the horizon. Sigrid wore a simple set of armor, consisting of a tight-fitting gray gambeson that fell, slitted, to her knees, covered by a simple steel cuirass and a black padded vest over that. A black leather archery bracer was laced over her left forearm. A hunter's cap similar to Teleo's, with short reddish quail feathers, perched on her head, her long black hair tumbling loose down her back. A sword and dagger hung at her side, and a bow and quiver were slung across her back. High black leather boots folded over her knees, and dark-green leather riding pants hugged her thighs.

"That's it?" Teleo asked. "That's your armor?"

Sigrid shrugged. "I'm an archer."

"Your father dressed me up like I'm competing in a tourney," Teleo said.

Sigrid laughed. "You let him. He loves his metal." She rapped her knuckles on his steel chestplate, and he smirked at her.

He secretly admitted to himself that he had always envied the fine plate armor the nobles wore but had never been able to afford it himself. He shrugged his shoulders. "It feels good," he said, "and it's lighter than I expected."

"My father is a master," she said. "Not even a crossbow bolt can pierce that."

Jarnsmidt came to bid them farewell, admiring their party all suited up in their new armor. Aunt Tildie took Nutmeg from Dinsmora. The elderly woman smoothed the bay's mane and gazed into his big brown eyes, cooing nonsense words to him and slipping him a sugar cube.

Will and Waite met the traveling party at the front gate and led them on foot up a steep, twisting path into the forest.

27

ḤILL ℂOUNTRY

Their destination was called Pine Top and was a three days' journey with their foot guides Will and Waite, forcing them to travel at a walk. It was just as well—the rugged terrain was treacherous for horses. They dismounted and led their mounts half the time, letting them pick their way over rocks and washouts without the burden of a rider. They also had to let the horses forage whenever there was anything worth eating, having no grain to supplement their diet.

Their armor transformed them from a peasant family into nobles. Teleo weighed the risks of looking rich versus deflecting arrows, and chose to look rich—the horses and swords screamed that fact anyway.

The second day in, Will held up his hand for them to stop and be silent. Will was good—he had detected the threat before Teleo or Dinsmora had, and even before BlackJack or Hunter. Teleo's party were in their saddles and grabbed their weapons, holding them at the ready. After a full minute of sitting frozen in place, Teleo spotted several men slowly emerging from the forest. He counted half a dozen and could feel others lurking in the shadows. Dinsmora, Sigrid, Kaspari, Will, and Waite all had arrows trained on the interlopers. Teleo chided himself for not carrying a bow, or at least a spear and shield, and for not insisting Jessum practice archery instead of blacksmithing. He hefted his Aldeon longsword and gripped Star with his knees.

"Lower your bows," Will called out to the band of men.

"Says who?" a gruff voice answered from the trees.

"Says Will Millerson."

The rustling of underbrush was the only reply, creeping closer.

"Son of Willy Millerson?" another voice asked from the woods.

"The same. Who goes there?" Will asked.

"Gray Wheelwright," the man said, stepping into view. He was large and muscle-bound, with a long brown beard. "What are you doing out here?" Gray asked, shielding his eyes against the sun.

"Cornwal kicked us off our land before the harvest last summer," Will said.

"He stole my shop last summer too," Gray said, stepping further into the clearing. "He claimed he owned all the wood in the valley and had his own wheelwrights, and therefore did not require my services. I hate that man."

"Me too."

"What have we got here?" the first, gruff voice interrupted. The man who stepped out into the open was even larger than Gray, with a barrel chest, and arms and thighs like logs. He waddled over the grass carrying a woodsman's axe and wearing a hunting hat that formed a tall conical point, crested with long quail feathers.

"I'll handle this, Kegger," Gray said.

"What've you got to share with some poor refugees?" Kegger asked with a sinister edge to his voice, ignoring Gray. He stroked his axe handle.

"They're valley folk," Gray said.

"I see Verdant Valley blood," Kegger said, squinting at Dinsmora. "And a pretty young thing, too." Kegger licked his lips, leering at Kaspari.

"You touch my daughter and I'll chop your nuts off with your own axe," Teleo promised.

Kegger turned his gaze on Teleo. "Oh, yeah?"

"Kegger, knock it off," Gray said.

"They've got some nice armor," Kegger said. "Horses, too. We could use some horses. And a falcon." Kegger shifted his greedy eyes back to Dinsmora. Hunter was perched at her shoulder on the shepherd's crook and extended one wing, grooming herself. "Give us half your stuff and we'll call it even," Kegger said, as though doing them a favor. "I'll take the black and white warhorses and the two plow horses. You can keep your little mountain horse and the sweet lady on it. We'll take your daughter—keep her safe, we will." He smiled at Teleo.

Kaspari drew her bowstring tauter, her eyes trained on the fat man's chest.

Kegger let out a hearty laugh. "She's feisty. This will be fun."

Teleo unsheathed a dagger with his free hand, prepared to throw it should the man try to make good on his threats. Jessum sneered at Kegger, holding his battle-axe with two hands and his new linden staff ready across his lap.

"Kegger!" Gray turned on his companion. "Shut up!"

"Make me," Kegger snapped, his round cheeks reddening.

Gray ignored him and turned back to Will. "Where are you going? This is our territory."

"Really?" Will asked. "We've been hunting here all season. First time I've seen you."

Gray shrugged. "Must have missed each other. Where you coming from? Out Red Flag way?"

Will nodded.

"Red Flag," Kegger chortled. "Home of Old King Syphilis with the forged-steel prick?"

"Kegger …" Gray rolled his eyes.

"I hear he's giving Cornwal blowjobs to keep his armory," Kegger said.

"Say one more thing about my father and you'll regret it," Sigrid said.

"Oh, such big threats from such a little lady," Kegger said, grabbing his groin and ogling her.

Sigrid let loose her arrow with a thrum, and Kegger's hat flew off his head, wispy brown hair fluttering from his balding head. All eyes turned to Sigrid, who nocked another arrow. Petunia stood solid beneath her, tail flicking.

"Don't mess with Princess Sigrid," a new voice said from the trees. "She'll take your eye out." A tall, lean man strode into the clearing, picked up the arrow-impaled hat from where it had landed in the brush a few paces behind Kegger, then handed the hat to Kegger and returned the arrow to Sigrid.

"Pytor," she said, greeting the tall man and accepting the arrow. "I wondered where you'd disappeared to."

"Game is scarce out Red Flag way," Pytor said, smiling up at Sigrid. "Y'all didn't need another mouth to feed. With the horses gone, there was nothing for me to do." He stroked Petunia's neck. "Where'd you get the mare?" he asked.

"She belongs to my friend," she said, glancing at Teleo.

Teleo sheathed his blades and Jessum holstered his axe. Teleo's companions lowered their bows. Other men stepped out from the trees, lowering longbows. Kegger brushed off his hat and returned it to his head, the quail feathers askew.

"Why didn't you tell us you were accompanying the princess?"

Gray asked, bowing his head to Sigrid. "Where are you off to?" he asked, addressing her.

"We're on our way to Pine Top," she said. "We're searching for this boy's family. He's a war orphan."

Jessum reddened and reined in a restless BlackJack.

"We're their guides," Waite said.

"I'm from Pine Top," another man said, stepping out from the shadows. "What's your name, boy?" he asked, peering up at Jessum.

"Jeremiah, sir," he said, glancing at Teleo. Teleo nodded, and Jessum said, "Or they might know me as Jessy."

The man came closer, inspecting Jessum's face. "You don't look like Laney's boy, but I was gone fighting most of the time when you were little. I can take you there and we'll see."

"We're their guides," Waite repeated.

"It's my village," the man said.

"We already agreed to guide them," Will said stubbornly.

Teleo broke in. "I can't pay all of you."

"You don't need to pay me," the Pine Top man said. "If he's Laney's boy, that'll be pay enough."

They agreed to all go together to Pine Top, then headed south on the trail through the trees.

"We have nothing better to do," Gray said as he and Teleo walked side by side in front of Star, who tugged at her lead to snatch a tuft of grass. "There's something about you guys," Gray said. "I smell adventure."

"I hope not too much," Teleo said. "I've had enough adventures to last a lifetime."

The man laughed with him as they kept pace along the wooded trail.

Teleo had a talk with Kegger around the fire that evening and determined the man was all bark and no bite, so he refrained from breaking his pudgy, purple nose. Even so, Kaspari slept between Teleo and Jessum. Sigrid slept in Teleo's arms, and Dinsmora slept next to Will or Waite, whoever was not on watch.

The next day, they arrived at Pine Top. The villagers gathered around them. Laney, a middle-aged woman, rushed out of a stone hut, looked at Jessum for two seconds, and shook her head. Disappointment was plain on her face, and Jessum's as well. She hugged him anyway. "You'll find your people," she said, and directed them to another hamlet called Hog Hollow, deeper in the hills.

At Hog Hollow, two days later, aptly named for the dozens of hogs that wallowed in a muddy field, the locals examined Jessum like he were a horse, inspecting his teeth, his hands, his legs, his ears. "Nope, not our boy," they determined, and sent them to yet another hamlet deeper into the forest, sending along two guides to show them the way.

The hamlet was called Cedar Creek. When they reached it three days later, the scent of cedar and the musical babbling of a brook greeted them in a broad sunny meadow ringed by small round huts and larger cottages with cedar shake roofs. The brook fed a small pond at one end of the meadow, and another, wider creek rushed with a steady hiss on the other side of the settlement. Lush grazing lands sloped up behind the cottages. Across a plank bridge, on the other side of the creek, tilled fields stretched out in straight green lines. An orchard bordered the cultivated fields to the south, hay fields lay to the east, and the forest took over beyond that.

They filed into the clearing with their horses and band of twenty. A boy and girl looked up from a vegetable garden, two oxen lowed from where they were grazing in a fenced pasture, and a scruffy brown pony ambled over. The pony tossed his head and then turned and led the horses to the pond. The humans followed, and Teleo knelt next to Jessum as they washed their hands in the cold water. Lily pads floated on the glassy surface, green buds showing edges of pink and yellow.

"It won't be them, either," Jessum said glumly, shaking off his hands. His black hair was long and thick and hung down over his eyes.

"Pull your hair back, so they can see your face," Teleo said, handing him a short length of leather cord.

"I don't want to meet anyone else," Jessum said, reluctantly tying his hair into a ponytail. His brown eyes flashed up to meet Teleo's. "I feel like a horse at an auction."

"I know," Teleo said, straightening Jessum's brigandine.

"I feel stupid in this thing," he said, tugging at the blood-red velvet. "Everyone here is poor. I just want to wear my jerkin."

"What do you wear every day?" Teleo asked him.

"This," he said, looking down at himself. He was wearing the chainmail under the brigandine. Over his buckskin pants hung the black leather armor skirt, which was getting broken in from the road.

"Then wear that. Be yourself. There's nothing to be ashamed of. You came by that armor honestly. A gift from Queen Valona for fighting Stone Guardian wolves. Be proud."

Jessum lifted his chin a little, which was sprouting random black whiskers. A feathering of black fluff grew over his lip. His chin and jaw were strong and square, and his body was filling out by the day.

"You look fine. You're a good-looking lad," Teleo said, patting his arm. "Come on." Teleo rested a hand on his back and they walked together up the grassy slope.

Dinsmora and Sigrid went off to speak with a woman who was peering at the strangers from her front stoop. Teleo and

Kaspari waited with Jessum, who kept tugging at his brigandine and crushing clods of dried mud under his heel.

A few minutes later, several men tramped down the sloping grasslands, eyeing the band of brigands warily as they approached the road. A small herd of bleating goats and two barking dogs followed the men. Dinsmora and Sigrid walked down the road with the woman and children and were joined by an older gray-haired woman. The older woman hurried her steps when she caught sight of Jessum and was nearly running by the time she reached him.

"Are you my Jessy?" she asked, holding out her hands to him. She gazed into his eyes. He was taller than her by a head. She reached up and cupped his face in her hands.

"Grandma?" he asked, covering her hands with his.

"Jessy," she said, and started weeping. "Jessy." She wrapped him in a bear hug and he returned the hug, tears streaming down his face.

"What happened to you? Let me look at you." Jessum's grandmother gazed up into his face. "Come, tell me everything." He was still crying and couldn't talk. She took his hand and led him towards the pond.

Teleo watched his foster son walk away. His heart tightened and a wave of unexpected sadness rolled through him. Kaspari stood at Teleo's side, staring after Jessum with tears glistening in her eyes.

Teleo went with Sigrid and Dinsmora to meet the Cedar Creek men. He told them why they had come and how Jessum had ended up in Teleo's care. An older man broke away and ran to join Jessum and his grandmother. Teleo could hear them talking, crying, and laughing.

Teleo excused himself and went to stake the horses, who were wandering into the brush bordering the field. He wiped at his eyes and wrapped his arms around Daisy's neck, pressing his wet cheek against her warm coat.

They were standing around a corral where they had penned the horses at the small farm of Jessum's grandmother, Flora, and great-uncle, Bron. Several neighbors were with them, leaning against the fence and watching the sun descend towards the treetops.

"How do you know it's him?" a neighbor demanded.

"I know my own grandson," Flora retorted, her brown eyes flashing.

"He was only a child when he was taken," the man said.

"He was six," Flora replied curtly.

"Looks just like his father," Bron said, puffing on a pipe.

Murmurs of agreement came from the villagers.

"All Hill people look the same," the man said.

Flora turned her mouth down at her neighbor. "Thank the stars we don't, Mitchman. Hate to have your ears and nose."

"Now that was unnecessary," Mitchman said, feigning hurt feelings. Large ears stuck out from the sides of his head, and his nose was long and hooked. "I'm just saying, we need to be sure it's him."

Jessum leaned against the fence rail, listening and watching, his expression unreadable.

"Why do *you* need to be sure, Mitchman?" Bron asked. "The only people who matter are our boy Jessy, Flora, and myself. We're the last of his family and we know our own blood. It's none of your business, to be honest."

"It's everybody's business. You know why," Mitchman said.

"Now don't start that," Bron said. "He's just a boy and he's just returned home. Leave him in peace."

"Who's got time for peace around here? I don't. That Cornwal scum sent scouts out here just last week, searching for springs and claiming the emperor owns the headwaters and will be taxing everyone downstream." Mitchman raised his brow in a challenge.

"I know very well what they said," Bron said, annoyance rising in his voice. "I was the one who talked to them and told you what they said."

"So, then you know better than I. Why do I have to convince you?"

Bron looked sideways at Mitchman and then turned to Flora. "Let's get the boy some dinner." He peered over at Teleo and the women, then glanced at the band of brigands who were camped out in the field behind them, making a cookfire.

"We've got food for ourselves," Teleo lied. They did have some hard cheese and harder bread, but that was it. They would take Hunter out before dusk fell and hopefully catch something. He met Dinsmora's eyes. She was thinking the same thing.

"There's only one way to find out," Mitchman said.

"No," Flora said flatly. "Come on inside, Jessy. I'll show you where you can sleep."

Jessum glanced awkwardly at Teleo.

"It's okay, Jessum," Teleo said. "Go with your grandmother. We'll see you in the morning."

"We need a Bedon, and we need one now," Mitchman said stubbornly.

"We are all Bedons," Bron retorted.

"Not from the ancient bloodline, we're not. Only his father was, and now Jessy. He's back. Just in time, too. If it's really him, that is. We need to find out."

"What are they talking about, Grandma?" Jessum asked.

"Oh," she said, her shoulders drooping. "Your father and grandfather. They were descended from the ancient Bedons."

"The kings. The ones who united the tribes," Mitchman said.

"That was a long, long time ago," Flora said. "Many generations

past. Blood mixes, times change. What mattered once is meaning-
less now."

"No, it means more than ever now," Mitchman insisted.
"Let's at least check, then I'll shut up."

"Do you promise?" Flora asked.

Mitchman nodded.

"Swear on your next harvest," Flora said.

"I swear," Mitchman said. "I will not say another word." He
smiled, revealing crooked teeth.

Flora sighed in resignation. "Get the shears," she said to Bron.

Bron went into their cottage and returned with sheep-wool
shears and a straight-edged razor.

"What are you doing?" Jessum asked as his great-uncle came
towards him with the blades.

"Let me do it," Flora said. "Jessy, honey, can I please shave
the side of your head?"

"Cut my hair?" he asked, putting his hands to the side of his
head with a look of horror. "Why?"

"You have the mark of Bedon on your scalp, and we just
want to prove who you are."

"What is the mark of Bedon?" Jessum asked.

"We'll show you. Bron, get the platter."

Bron disappeared inside and returned with a polished steel
serving platter, which reflected the sky and treetops.

Jessum reluctantly sat on a stool while his grandmother
trimmed the hair above his ear.

"Take off the whole side," Bron said. "So it's even. He doesn't
want a hole in his hair."

"Unless you want me to cut it all off?" Flora asked.

"No," Jessum said, holding his head protectively.

Flora trimmed the entire left side of his head, locks of long
black hair falling to the dirt, and then lathered his scalp and

began shaving it. "Where did you get all these scars, honey?" she asked.

"Long story," Jessum replied. "Do I have the mark?"

"Let me see." She shaved another section. "Yep, here it is. Told you, Mitchman. I know my own grandson."

Everyone gathered to look. She shaved off the last of the stubble and wiped away the soap so they all could see.

It was a finely detailed, colored tattoo. An orange-gold griffin stood victorious over an indigo wolf lying upside down with its legs in the air and red tongue hanging out of its fanged and bloody mouth. One of the griffin's forelegs clawed the air with long, black talons.

Teleo's breath caught in his throat.

"Let me see," Jessum said.

Bron held up the platter, and Jessum examined the side of his head in the reflection. "Nice tattoo," he said with a puzzled grin. "I never knew that was there. But anybody can tattoo their child. That doesn't prove anything."

"People can, but people don't," Mitchman said. "Nobody but those crazy ancient Bedons. Your father had the mark, and your grandfather, and his father before him. My grandpa told me he saw your great-grandfather's tattoo with his own eyes."

"But they weren't kings, were they?" Jessum asked.

"No," Flora said. "Not since they fled after the Magic Wars and went into hiding. They were Mages."

Jessum gaped at his grandmother. "Mages?" he asked, his voice nearly a squeak.

"My grandpa said your great-grandfather was descended directly from the last Bedon king. That means you are too," Mitchman said matter-of-factly.

"Mitchman ...," Flora warned.

"Magic is still illegal," Jessum said to his grandmother,

ignoring Mitchman. "Cornwal won't like somebody from an ancient Mage bloodline walking around. Right, Tesserman?" He cast Teleo a sidelong glance.

"Cornwal can go to hell," Mitchman said. "We're taking our kingdom back."

"Mitchman," Flora scolded. "You promised."

"Oh, yeah. See you tomorrow." He grinned mischievously. "Welcome home, Jessy," Mitchman said, bowing his head, and turned to leave.

"It's like my banner," Jessum said, still examining the tattoo in the mirror.

"What banner?" Mitchman asked, turning around.

Flora gave them both a stern look.

"I'll show you tomorrow," Jessum said, fascinated with the tattoo.

They left Jessum with his family. Teleo and Dinsmora took Hunter out as the sun fell behind the trees, casting shafts of golden light through cedar branches. The falcon caught a grouse. It was small, but better than nothing. Sigrid and Kaspari gathered wild rhubarb and cattail shoots, which made for a decent meal.

Bron offered them space in the barn, but it was a nice night, so they decided to camp out in the meadow under the stars. Will and Waite were camping with the other men by the pond. Teleo, Dinsmora, and Sigrid divided the night into three watches.

"I miss Jessum," Kaspari said when Teleo lay down between her and Sigrid in the middle of the night, passing the watch to Dinsmora.

"Me too," he said. "We'll see him tomorrow."

"Then we won't see him anymore?" she asked.

"I don't know."

"Is he really a king?" she asked.

"If times were different, he might have been," Teleo said. "As it is now, he's just a normal person."

"Like me," she said quietly.

He turned his head and caught the whites of her eyes gazing at him.

"Like all of us," he said. "Just people."

Kaspari closed her eyes and did not ask any more questions.

The night was quiet. Sigrid nestled her head on his shoulder, and Teleo stared up at the stars.

———◆———

"How old are you, Jessy?" Mitchman asked.

Flora had invited them for breakfast, and Mitchman had appeared at the door and invited himself in. They sat around the table, drinking tea, their empty plates pushed away after a hearty meal of fresh eggs, smoked trout, millet cakes, and apricot jam.

"Fifteen, I think," Jessum said.

"Fifteen, this past January seventh," Flora said, nodding decisively as she cleared the dishes. She smiled warmly at Jessum, whose face transformed momentarily into that of a five-year-old, open and bright and loved. She kissed the top of his head and carried the dishes to the water basin.

Jessum looked like a different person—older and younger at the same time. Long locks of heavy black hair hung across his forehead and down the back and one side of his head, while the shaved side displayed the triumphant griffin poised over the dead wolf, and his scarred scalp told of the hard life he'd led.

"Where's that flag of yours?" Mitchman asked.

"Over here," Jessum said. He went to the corner of the room where his belongings were piled next to a mattress and patchwork quilt.

He unrolled the long pennant and he and Kaspari each held up an end. A large version of the tattoo design was embroidered with a bright gold griffin and sapphire-blue wolf.

"It's a sign," Mitchman said, gazing at Jessum in wonder.

"It's a coincidence," Flora said.

"I don't believe in coincidence," Mitchman said, drawing looks from Dinsmora and Kaspari. "Everything happens for a reason. He is the young Bedon, returned from the dead, come to lead us in battle."

Jessum met Teleo's eyes with a pained expression. "Our last name is Drake, not Bedon," Jessum said.

"Descended from King Drake Bedon," Mitchman said matter-of-factly. "Your family dropped the Bedon surname when you went into hiding. But you are a true Bedon, of the pure, ancient bloodline, sure as the sun rises in the east."

Jessum rolled up the banner and returned it to the corner. "I need to check on BlackJack."

"I'm coming with you," Kaspari said.

The two youths escaped out the front door, and the adults sat around the table, looking at one another.

"He's the last Bedon," Mitchman said.

Flora and Bron nodded silently.

"He was stolen away to Verdant Castle, you say?" Mitchman asked Teleo, who nodded. The gaunt-faced man continued in a somber voice. "They must have known his heritage. They liked to keep the valuable ones at the castles. For ransom, or leverage, or whatever."

Flora's brow creased with worry. "Cornwal must not find out," she said, twisting a linen napkin in her hands.

Teleo took a deep breath and the conversation drew to a halt.

Dinsmora and Sigrid helped Flora clean up, and Bron and Mitchman headed out to the fields. Teleo sat on a log by the pond where the horses were drinking while Jessum and Kaspari crouched on the muddy bank beyond the cattails, tending a fishing line. Hunter perched on a fencepost near their small camp. The field was almost cleared of men. Will and Waite ambled over.

"Where'd Gray and Kegger and everybody else go?" Teleo asked.

"I don't know," Will said. "They took off. Said they'd be back. Is it true the boy is a Drake?"

Teleo shrugged. "So they say."

"Does he really have the mark of Bedon on his scalp?" Waite asked.

"He does. Who told you?" Teleo asked.

"The skinny guy with the big ears," Waite said.

"Mitchman," Teleo said.

"That's right, Mitchman. Jeremiah's the last Bedon, then?" Waite raised a curious eyebrow.

"Mitchman's got a big mouth," Teleo said, standing up and glancing over at Jessum who was baiting a hook.

"Then we've got a chance," Will said, his eyes brimming with hope.

"A chance for what?" Teleo asked.

"To defeat Cornwal and take Sapphire Valley back. Take our kingdoms back. The way it used to be, when everyone tilled their own land or worked an honest trade and lived as free people. We can't hide out in the hills forever, and nobody wants to become a serf to that bastard. Bad enough our young men think it's an honor to serve in his army."

"Do they?" Teleo asked.

"You know young men. They love to fight," Will said, glancing at his son.

"I don't," Waite said. "They don't want to fight for him, but they need work. Cornwal pays gold. Better than slaving in his fields for a couple of Copper Bits."

"Would they turn against him if it meant they would be free to return to their family farms and trades?" Teleo asked.

"In a heartbeat," Waite said. "At least, the guys I grew up with would. They want families. Cornwal makes them live in barracks. And nobody likes the new slave trade Cornwal started, it's making everybody uncomfortable. They say they're only selling orphans, but what happens when there are no more orphans? Are they going to start kidnapping people's kids?"

Teleo glanced painfully over at Jessum and Kaspari.

Waite went on, "Rumors are Cornwal plans to cut soldiers' pay once he's got the Hill fortresses under his control, then he's going to start raiding the mountain kingdoms."

"That'd be a bloody, miserable war," Will said. "Nobody wants that."

Teleo smoothed his beard, which was filling in nicely and had finally stopped itching, and watched Jessum tug at the fishing line. He pulled in a small sunfish and whistled for Hunter, who launched off her perch and flew to Jessum's hand, taking the flopping fish to the mud and plucking at it.

Teleo said, "I don't see how these small hamlets and wandering bands of displaced men could defeat Cornwal, even if they did band together under one leader, and even if the fortresses combined forces. Red Flag barely had a company's worth of men."

Will sighed and took the bow from his shoulder. "We're going to try to catch some dinner. How long do you plan on staying here? What's your next move?"

"I'll head back to Red Flag with the women in a few days," Teleo said. "As soon as Jeremiah gets settled in."

Teleo silently considered his own journey. Now that Jessum had found his family, it was time for Teleo to resume his search for his own son. He would meet with Larissa again and try to figure out how to get into Sapphire Castle and find the Verdant Valley orphans there, to see if one was Oren. He tried not to get his hopes up. He had been disappointed so many times in the past, suffering the bitter pang of despair every time a Verdant Valley orphan was not his boy.

"We'll go to Red Flag with you," Will said.

"Sounds good," Teleo said. "I'll see you later. Good luck hunting."

Teleo walked around the pond's edge to talk with Jessum.

"We'll be leaving in a few days," Teleo said, laying his hand on the boy's shoulder. "Looks like you'll be happy and safe here." Bron and Mitchman were former soldiers, from the looks of them. No harm would come to Jessum under their care.

Jessum rose and moved into the circle of Teleo's arm. Teleo squeezed his shoulder. They parted, and Teleo looked proudly at the young man he had become.

"Thank you for everything," Jessum said, wiping at his nose. "You saved my life. You've been my best friend, and like a father to me."

"And you've been like a son."

They embraced again and then pulled apart, struggling to smile.

"But I don't want to stay here forever," Jessum said, making a face. "I don't want to be a farmer. I want to spend some time with Grandma, then I want to go back to Red Flag. King Jarnsmidt said I could apprentice as a bladesmith in the armory."

"Really?" Teleo said, his heart growing lighter. "When?"

"I told Uncle Bron I'd stay through the fall harvest and then start my apprenticeship in the winter."

"Great idea," Teleo said.

"What about me?" Kaspari asked.

They turned to her. She was listening from the muddy bank. "What's going to happen to me?" Tears were pooling in her eyes.

"You and Dinsmora will come back to Red Flag with me and Sigrid," Teleo said.

"Are you going to marry Sigrid?" Kaspari asked.

"I don't know. We haven't known each other that long."

"You knew her before, though, right?" Kaspari asked.

He hesitated. "Yes. It's a bit complicated."

"When are you and Dinsmora going to stop fighting?" she asked.

Teleo stared at her and swallowed. "We're not fighting."

"You hardly talk, or laugh, or look at each other anymore," Kaspari said, dabbing at her eyes.

Teleo did not know what to say. She was right, and he had barely noticed, having been distracted ever since Sigrid had come into his life. It was as though Kaspari and Jessum were really their children, and he and Dinsmora were their parents who were splitting up.

"You can stay here with me if you want," Jessum said to Kaspari. "I'll ask my grandma."

"I can?" Kaspari's face brightened, and Jessum looked slightly relieved.

"I don't know ...," Teleo said. "Let's ask Dinsmora." He led the way back to the cottage.

After a long discussion, they decided Dinsmora and Kaspari would stay at Cedar Creek through the summer. Flora said the hamlet needed an herbalist and leatherworker, and there was an abandoned fishing shack upstream that they could fix up. Kaspari would live with Dinsmora and learn about herbs and healing and how to tan hides. Come autumn, they would decide if they would winter at Cedar Creek or go with Jessum to Red Flag and see about working with the leatherworkers at the armory, or perhaps return to Trillifort. Teleo would go to Red Flag with Sigrid and use that as a home base while he searched for his son.

The main thing Teleo was worried about was Kaspari the Princess and the distant chance that Gerik would track her down. Cedar Creek was about the most out-of-the-way place he could imagine while still being a safe community. It was the perfect hiding place. Bron had told him that the Drake family had settled there precisely because of its remote location. But Cornwal's scouts had found it while searching for headwaters, which did not give Teleo comfort. Regardless, Kaspari was growing up and couldn't stay with him forever, and Dinsmora was a master at keeping a low profile.

Teleo pulled Jessum aside that evening after grooming the horses and putting them in the pen behind the barn.

"I want you to keep your eye on Kaspari," Teleo told Jessum.

The boy nodded and brushed the long bangs away from his eyes.

"Keep a lookout for anyone from Verdant Valley who might appear, or from the Coastal Kingdom. I'm afraid Gerik is still after her."

Jessum's face hardened. He hated Gerik as much as Teleo did, if not more. "I'll watch out for them," Jessum promised.

"And other men," Teleo said. "She's growing up. Men might try to take advantage of her. Make sure they know you are protecting her and that they are not to touch her."

"Yes, sir," he said.

Teleo held Jessum's gaze and lowered his brow. "You, too," Teleo said gently. "Don't touch Kaspari." Jessum's eyes dropped to the ground. "Do you know what I'm talking about?" Teleo asked. "Look at me."

Jessum raised his gaze and met Teleo's. "I know what you're talking about," he said. His eyes were stormy and petulant. "Why? Because she's a princess and I'm a peasant?"

"No," Teleo said. "You both have royal blood now, I guess.

But neither of you have thrones. No, it's because you're a handsome young man and she's a beautiful young woman, and nature is a powerful force. But you are both too young to raise a child."

Jessum's cheeks darkened.

Teleo sighed and put his arm around Jessum's shoulder. "Let's walk," he said.

They strode slowly up the road away from the small settlement. Moonlight reflected off a sea of rippling grass.

"When a woman is pregnant, she's very vulnerable," Teleo said. "What if wolves attacked again, but she was nine months pregnant? She wouldn't be able to fight them off. Or what if you had a child to care for, but food was scarce? Would you want to put that burden on your grandmother? What if Kaspari died in childbirth?" The more Teleo went on painting dire pictures, the more Jessum's steps dragged and his head hung low.

"What if Gerik came," Teleo said, "and stole her for his bride, then found out that she already had a child? He would kill it."

At that, Jessum raised his head.

"I would kill him," Jessum said through clenched teeth.

Teleo laughed. "That's the spirit. But you get my point, right?"

Jessum rolled his eyes. "Yes, Teleo, I get your point. I won't touch her. Besides, she's still a kid," Jessum said. "Plus, she's my sister."

"That's right," Teleo said, chuckling. "Take care of her."

They spent the next two weeks fixing up the fishing shack. It was built on pilings at the creek's edge, upstream from the central cluster of homes, with a small deck overhanging the water. Hunter perched on the peaked roof, looking out over her new domain.

Spring rains came in from the south, dumping a deluge on the small settlement and flooding the field by the pond. Will and Waite and the horses took shelter in the barn, squeezing in with Bron's goats, his two oxen, an old mare, and several barn cats. Teleo and Sigrid slept on the floor of Dinsmora and Kaspari's shack, the rain hammering on the new cedar shake roof. The creek, which was already high from spring thaw, rose and rushed around the pilings under the floor where they slept.

After three days, the skies cleared. Two days after that, the water receded and the trails turned from soupy mud to normal mud.

Teleo and Sigrid packed up to leave and stood outside the fishing shack to say their goodbyes. Dinsmora hugged him and wished him well. He gazed fondly at his cousin, grateful that she had accompanied them on their journey.

Hunter swooped down and landed on Teleo's bare wrist. "Ow," he said, laughing and moving her taloned feet over onto the buckskin sleeve of his forearm. The gyrfalcon held Teleo's eyes with her sharp black ones. He stroked her smooth feathers. "Take care of the girls for me," he said.

Teleo transferred Hunter onto Dinsmora's shepherd's crook, then took a private moment with Kaspari out on the back deck overlooking the creek. She was looking more and more like her mother. He faced her and gently grasped her shoulders.

"You do as Dinsmora tells you, now. You hear?"

"I will," she said.

"Don't wander off, and do not talk with any strangers."

"I won't," she said.

"If you should see any strange men, run and hide. Always carry your bow and arrows. And your sword … and your knife."

She nodded and he furrowed his brow, wondering if he shouldn't take her with him back to Red Flag.

She tilted her head, examining his face, and stood taller. "I'll be fine," she said. She looked directly into his eyes, reminding him of that sunny afternoon when the dragonfly had perched on her fingertip in the Royal Garden a whole lifetime ago.

He sniffed loudly and squeezed her shoulders. "Okay. You did fight off Stone Guardian wolves, after all."

She smiled and nodded again.

"And remember," he said. "Boys are not to be trusted. Not even Jessum. You do not want to have a baby at your age."

She blushed and glared at him. "I know that!"

He laughed and drew her into a hug. "Okay. Good. We'll visit soon, okay?"

"Okay," she said, returning his hug.

They rejoined Dinsmora and Sigrid out front, and the four of them walked to Flora's cottage, where she and Bron and Jessum were waiting for them.

Flora thanked him for all he'd done for her grandson. They walked to the barn and saddled Star and Petunia. The other horses were outside in the muddy corral. He called them over and fed them carrot stubs. It was almost harder to leave Daisy than the humans. He nuzzled her cheek and she batted her eyelashes at him as he arranged her forelock. Cinnamon snorted and stomped his hoof, and Teleo patted his neck. Even BlackJack let him scratch his ears goodbye.

Gray had returned with Kegger and their companions, and they were skinning a deer carcass at the edge of the woods. Mitchman was helping them. Teleo would have kicked the vagabonds out by now, but Bron had given them permission to camp there.

Teleo gave Dinsmora and Kaspari one last hug, and Jessum and Bron walked with Teleo and Sigrid, leading their horses across the field to the head of the meadow where the forest trail began. Dinsmora, Kaspari, and Flora waved goodbye from the front porch of Flora's cottage.

Will and his son were waiting for them in the shade and stood up from their seat on a log. Jessum and Bron would be heading out with them on foot, on their way to check Bron's traps.

The six of them entered the dappled sunlight of the forest and started the slow descent to the main trail that would take them back through Hog Hollow and Pine Top. It was an hour later when they reached the wide wagon trail. Bron and Jessum stopped to say goodbye at their turnoff onto a faint deer trail when Will stopped and cupped his hand to his ear, listening.

"Men," Will said softly. "Many men."

They stood still and Teleo listened to the gentle wind wafting in from the south. Then he heard it. Distant talking. The scraping of a blade on a whetstone. The whinny of a horse.

They ducked into the woods and approached the sounds through the screen of trees. They ground-tied the horses and lay on their bellies on a small slate bluff, overlooking a forest of deciduous trees. Teleo counted fifty men in small groups of twos and threes and caught glimpses of more men beyond them. They had staked out camping areas and seemed to be setting up for an extended stay, clearing brush and making shelters with branches and tarps. There were a few mountain horses, several goats, and even a pen of chickens.

"What is this?" Teleo whispered to Bron.

"Kegger said they brought a few more men, but this is more than a few."

It did not look like a war camp, though some men were sharpening weapons. If they were brigands, they were of the unusually well-behaved sort. By Teleo's estimation, it was simply a gathering of woodsmen setting up camp together.

"Do they always camp out here?" Teleo asked.

"No," Bron said. "Come on. Let's see what they want."

Teleo, Sigrid, and Jessum exchanged glances. Teleo did not

believe Jessum's great-uncle would lead them into a trap, and Bron did not appear afraid or even cautious.

They got the horses, returned to the main trail, and continued towards the encampment on foot. Will and Waite held their bows at their sides, arrows nocked.

When they came upon the camp, which flanked both sides of the path, men looked up and several walked towards them.

"Ho, young Drake," one of them called out, raising a sword.

"Drake ... Drake ... Drake." The name passed through the camp like the whisper of wind through a wheat field.

Jessum's eyes darted from his great-uncle to Teleo, then out at the people who were gathering along the trail, craning their necks to get a look at Jessum. The boy was in his new buckskin pants and jerkin, sword and axe strapped crosswise on his back, and his partially shaved head showing off the tattoo.

"Are they talking about me?" he whispered loudly to his great-uncle.

"Yes," Bron said, waving at the men, and kept walking. More small camps dotted the wooded hillsides. Tall men, skinny men, and portly men. Teenaged boys Jessum's age, gray-haired men Bron's age, and wiry women dressed in traveling leathers. They could have been folks from any village— tavern-keepers, lumbermen, and shepherds. They gazed at Jessum as their small party strode by. Star was prancing and tossing her mane while Petunia snatched at every tuft of grass they passed.

Teleo was dumbfounded at the number of folks who had gathered. He counted over two hundred, and more people came into view beyond the next rise.

"Princess Sigrid," one of the men called out, waving at Sigrid.

She smiled and lifted her hand in return, sending another ripple of murmurs through the camp.

"Bedon! Bedon! Bedon!" someone chanted. Others took up the chant. Up ahead, a red banner flew, displaying a white satin griffin clawing at the air. The flag flapped in the breeze, and the chanting grew louder. *"Bedon! Bedon! Bedon!"*

Jessum stopped walking and faced Teleo. His eyes were like Hunter's, intense and alert, and his mouth hung open. "What do they want?" He turned his attention to his great-uncle. "Uncle Bron?" he asked.

Bron shrugged helplessly. "Looks to me like they want a leader and they think they've found one."

"I'm not a leader," Jessum hissed.

"You *are* a leader—you just don't know it yet. You've got Bedon blood." His great-uncle held Jessum's confused gaze.

"Everybody out here has Bedon blood," Jessum said.

"None of them are directly descended from Drake. You're the only one." Bron smiled and patted his grand-nephew's shoulder.

"Why is everyone gathering here?" Teleo asked Bron. "What are you going to do?"

Bron's weathered skin was brown and wrinkled, but his slanted, fiery eyes were those of a young man. He said, "There's only one thing we can do, and not much time to do it. Cornwal's talons are sinking deeper and deeper. Soon he'll bleed us to death. We have to fight."

"Tesserman's the best fighter in Verdant Valley," Jessum said.

"Oh, come on," Teleo said humbly, glancing at Sigrid, who inspected him curiously.

"I'm serious," Jessum said. "Everyone knows it. Gerik hated you for it. I heard him say so."

"You did?" Teleo asked, raising his brow.

"Yeah. He said, *'Teleo ...'* I mean, Tesserman *'thinks he should be in charge just because he's the best warrior in the kingdom. But he doesn't have the right blood, so he can suck my ...'* you know what."

Teleo burst out laughing and then cleared his throat. "Maybe at one time I was okay. But I'm old now."

Jessum wrinkled his brow. "Kallie told me what you did to Gerik's soldiers when you rescued us."

Teleo grimaced.

"We could use your help," Bron said. "If they start taxing water, then what next? Are they going to say they own all the game in the forest? That we're not allowed to raise our own livestock? Grow our own apples? Eat our own chicken eggs? Breathe the open air? If that Cornwal sticks his grubby mitt any deeper in my pocket, I'm going to have to chop off his hand." Bron shook his fist and continued, "I'm sorry, but he's crossing a line. He's crossed many lines already. Will he come for our daughters next?" His eyes bulged at Teleo.

Teleo shifted uncomfortably. Sigrid was listening pensively and he searched her eyes.

She shrugged. "He's right, Tesserman. Cornwal will not be satisfied until he's taken everything. He won't stop unless someone stops him."

"Come back to Cedar Creek and let's discuss it," Bron said. "At least help us map out a plan."

Sigrid's lips thinned to a hard line, and Jessum's big brown eyes pleaded with him. Teleo couldn't very well abandon Jessum at a time like this. He motioned for Will and Waite to follow, then turned around and headed back to Cedar Creek.

"An assassin is what we need," Bron said, sitting around Flora's table with her, Teleo, Jessum, Sigrid, Dinsmora, and Kaspari. "Put Cornwal's smug head on a pike."

"I know an assassin," Dinsmora said, staring pointedly at Teleo.

Teleo frowned. "I might be able to figure something out," he muttered.

Sneaking into Sapphire City's Imperial Palace was even crazier than breaking into Queen Valona's chambers. He could die for his efforts this time. His luck was bound to run out eventually—but some things were worth dying for. He cast his gaze upon Jessum and Kaspari, who gazed back with total trust and confidence. Sigrid reached out and held his hand.

Sigrid was the one who knew the most about the internal workings of the Sapphire Empire. She had been inside the Imperial Palace several times and had been friends with Empress Larissa for years.

Teleo considered sending the kids outside, but if they were both the rightful heirs to their kingdoms, then they deserved to hear the conversation. He wondered to himself how Empress Larissa would feel about a Drake Bedon descendant showing up, but put that concern aside. First, they must deal with Cornwal.

"I can get you a map when we return to Red Flag," Sigrid said. "Cornwal stays inside the palace walls, except to show his face briefly from the high castle during celebrations. He has seven ministers who make most of the decisions. The ministers spend most of their time in the palace chambers and live on the palace grounds. There's a castellan named Pfaff, and the Supreme Commander is General Raedwald. Raedwald will give you the most trouble. He led the Sapphire troops throughout the war. He is merciless."

Teleo knew of Raedwald. He was a legend. But he was getting old—older than Teleo. If Sapphire Palace was anything like Verdant City's Royal Palace, then it was heavily guarded, but it would also have service entrances and a network of service staircases and passageways. The palace would be surrounded by service buildings, administrative buildings, gardens, baileys, alleys, barracks, stables, and yards for soldiers and horses.

If Teleo could get inside the palace and find Larissa, then she could guide him. Larissa wanted Cornwal gone probably more than anybody, and she knew the palace intimately, having grown up there.

"I can try and get inside," Teleo said, rubbing his chin. "My goal will be to weaken the defenses inside the palace and distract their commanders long enough for the Hill people to stage an attack. When I've secured the palace, I'll ring the tower bell."

"We will come down off the hills," Bron said. "But it will take time for our troops to cross the valley. It's a full day's march from the foot of the hills below Red Flag. Longer from other fortresses."

"How many fortresses do you think will join us?" Teleo asked. "How many men do you think are hiding out in the hills?"

"Thousands," Bron said. "And many of Cornwal's troops will turn, if they sense victory."

"My father and I know the rulers of the other six Hill Tribes," Sigrid said. "I believe they will join us. Cornwal intends to put us all out of business. It will take a couple of weeks to get the word out to everyone, seeing as how we can't cut through the valley."

"What if Cornwal discovers the plan beforehand?" Flora asked.

"It won't matter," Bron said. "If we attack from all sides, they won't be able to withstand us."

"Or it could be a bloodbath," Dinsmora said.

"It could go either way," Teleo said. "If Cornwal has more men, or if they're better equipped, which they will be, or if his troops do not flip sides, it could be a long and bloody battle."

He had been in one such battle on the floor of the Sapphire Valley. The Battle of Fallow Field. An attack by the Verdant

Valley forces on a moonless night. The battle had lasted three days and three nights until Verdant Valley admitted defeat and retreated. Gerik had been watching from the hills the entire three days, safely watching the carnage. Teleo had lost track of the number of men he killed, and suffered a blow to his head that almost killed him. His horse, Thunder, died underneath him. His uncle Brady had hauled him to safety on Silver Moon. But that had been an attack by an enemy on foreign soil. This would be a rebellion by people who had been kicked off their own land.

"We can die under the sword or we can die of starvation—or our spirits can die from cowardice," Bron said, leveling his gaze at Teleo. "How do you choose to die?"

Teleo turned to Sigrid, and her expression reflected his own.

"The sword," they said in unison.

28

THIRTEEN

They spent a week at Cedar Creek, working out details of a coordinated assault and dispatching messengers to the other Hill fortresses. They envisioned seven armies flooding the valley, Hill sigils flying, trampling the emperor's defenses and storming Sapphire Castle.

It was finally time to leave. They said their goodbyes again, then Teleo, Sigrid, Will, and Waite traveled the wagon trails to Red Flag, slogging for nearly a week through rain and mud.

Teleo spent a third week plotting with Larissa in Sigrid's Heliotrope chamber, examining maps of the Imperial Palace and its surrounding structures. One afternoon, they were sitting around the small round table, the pattern of the Heliotrope floor moving in a slow circle as they talked. Sigrid was barefooted, her feet resting on the shifting pattern. They moved the table fully onto the outer rings of the Heliotrope, where Teleo removed his boots and Larissa removed her delicate ivory velvet slippers. The mosaic was warm under Teleo's feet and its heat spread throughout his body.

"Aren't you concerned," Teleo asked the empress, finally broaching the subject he had been fearful of, "that my foster son, Jeremiah, has the blood of Drake Bedon?"

"Concerned?" she asked, her eyes searching his. "Concerned about what? That he would take my place on the imperial throne?"

He shrugged. "Yeah. Well, you know ..."

She gave a mirthless laugh. "What I know is that the tribes are rallying around a young man who is inspiring them to fight against Cornwal. Honestly, I am thrilled. Should this young Drake Bedon of yours desire to ascend to the throne, well then, he will not need to kill me to take it—assuming he is a good man and a capable leader. My concern is for the freedom of our people. Whatever government returns our land to honor, peace, and prosperity, I am in full support of. In the meantime, shall we discuss getting rid of my despicable husband?" She raised her eyebrows, and Teleo inclined his head.

"As you wish, Your Highness."

The conversation turned back to their plans, and Teleo asked Larissa about her Heliotrope.

"The Heliotrope is in my tower," she said. "It adjoins my chambers. That had always been the guest wing until Cornwal decided I couldn't be trusted and locked me up. I convinced him to put me in that wing, away from everything. That suited him fine—he wanted me out of the way. I keep the floor covered with rugs unless I'm using it. He doesn't know the Heliotrope is there or what it's for. No one does. He never goes in there. When he wants me, he calls for me, and I go to his ... bedchamber."

The woman's pained expression fueled Teleo's growing hatred for the emperor.

"Do you have children?" Teleo asked.

Larissa looked as though he had stabbed her in the gut, and he was immediately sorry he had asked.

She took a breath and met his eyes. "Arnbjorg and I had two sons. They were eight and ten. Cornwal killed them. He took them hunting. He said it was an accident, which, of course, is ridiculous. He didn't even bother to make up a believable lie."

They locked eyes and Teleo swore to himself that he would kill Cornwal, if it was the last thing he did.

"He wants his own sons," she continued, exchanging glances with Sigrid. "But I am having difficulty ... getting pregnant."

Teleo nodded slowly. Women knew herbs that men did not, and he steered the conversation away from her personal business.

"When I was here last, there were rumors he was studying magic," Teleo said. "But then he blamed Arnbjorg for using magic. I always wondered if that was deflection."

"Yes," Larissa said. "I believe he is trying to amass power any way he can, including with magic. He's fascinated with history and legends. But many of the important mystical manuscripts were in my personal library, and I gave them to Sigrid to hide here at Red Flag. They are not very helpful, to be honest. A few do discuss Heliotropes, but they don't mention traveling—Sigrid told me about that after my husband was murdered."

"Do you travel to Larissa's chambers?" he asked Sigrid.

"No, I cannot. I have never visited that Heliotrope in person," she said.

"I always welcomed guests in my reception chambers," Larissa explained. "Before Cornwal. By then, it was too late to get Sigrid into the tower. He does not allow me to receive guests anymore. Sigrid recognized my necklace and told me its purpose at Arnbjorg's funeral. That was the last time we saw each other the normal way." She pulled her Heliotrope amulet out from under her bodice. "I had always thought it was just a trinket my mother left me." She rubbed her thumb over the miniature Heliotrope pattern.

"I've been to the large one, though," Sigrid said. "The battle circle at Sapphire Castle. I retrieved flowers from the center stone one time when my brother had taken first place in a Sword and Shield tournament. I've never traveled there, but I still remember the feeling of the cold stone under my fingertips. It's too dangerous for me to go there now. Raedwald and his guards train there."

Teleo nodded and asked Larissa how she was able to travel to this tower.

"I was here many times as a young girl," she said. "My mother was friends with Sigrid's mother. They would drink tea and make lace by the fire, and Sigrid and I would play on the bare floor, skipping and doing cartwheels around the shifting pattern, then napping on the center stone. Now in retrospect, it's clear that our mothers knew exactly what they were doing, having us play here for hours."

Larissa pulled out a map and showed him where her Heliotrope tower was located, then continued explaining how the extensive and sprawling Imperial Palace was laid out. Reception halls, meeting rooms, and administrative chambers filled entire wings, connected in a labyrinth of corridors and stairways. The imperial residence was its own wing, a small castle in itself. Lacking maps of the lower levels, Sigrid provided her with a blank parchment and fountain pen, and Larissa sketched the kitchen wing and adjoining service entrances and subterranean passageways, tracing for Teleo possible paths to Cornwal's chambers.

After a time, the women took a break and left Teleo alone in the Heliotrope chamber. He watched the slow swirl of the floor, marveling at its powers and wondering what other secrets it held.

———————◆———————

Teleo spent the final two days at Red Flag in bed with Sigrid. Finally, the morning came when he reluctantly pulled himself from the clutches of pleasure and prepared to depart on his mission. He intended to head out with Will and Waite on horseback to the border town, cross the valley alone on foot, and then walk right up to the palace. It was an audacious plan, but Teleo had found in life that taking big risks was the only way to do anything worth doing.

Teleo was checking Star's hooves, and Will and Waite were saddling Nutmeg and Petunia when a guard ran into the stable. "Sir, Tesserman, sir. King Jarnsmidt needs you in his office, right away," she said.

Teleo followed the guard to the armory. She led him up several steps into Jarnsmidt's office, which looked down upon the Heliotrope and blacksmith forges through leaded glass.

"Tesserman," Jarnsmidt greeted him curtly, then shut the door, leaving the guard outside. "Take a good look at that man," Jarnsmidt said, peering through the glass to the floor below.

Teleo examined the only person who was not in a black-smith's apron. His skin was noticeably fair, and his fine, light hair marked him as Verdant Valley stock. "Who is he?" Teleo asked.

"He came in here posing as a buyer from some mountain fortress I'd never heard of. Looking to buy several dozen swords, he said. It's the only way he got in here. I don't sell one-offs. Usually," he said, with a quirk of his brow. "So I go down to talk with him and he shows me a handful of Gold Lions. I listen to what he has to say. It's all good, he wants to order four dozen short swords. Then he starts saying how he heard about the armory from a friend. This friend, he says, was a retired soldier, a big guy with scars on his face, and did I know him. So I play dumb because I know you didn't know we had an armory before you got here. That's how I knew you liked my daughter for herself and not for her money. Not that we have much gold these days, with that dirtbag Cornwal in power. But I knew he couldn't have run into you while you were off to the Bedon villages, otherwise I would have heard about it. It's not every day you see Verdant Valley folk in these parts. Anyway, I know this guy is lying, so I act like I didn't know what he was talking about. So then he tries to remind me of who you were. 'You know,' he says, 'he was with a Hill boy and a pretty young teenaged girl, and a peasant woman.' So I say, 'No, I don't know.' I left him with the foreman so you could take a look at him. Foreman won't tell him anything, don't you worry."

Jarnsmidt cocked an eyebrow at Teleo. "What'd you do? Who's after you, and why?" Jarnsmidt spoke to him like a man interrogating the potential husband of his daughter.

Teleo's heart dropped into his stomach. He met Jarnsmidt's birdlike eyes. "He's not after me," Teleo said despondently. "He's after Kallie."

Jarnsmidt's eyebrows knit together. "Kallie?" he asked with surprise.

Teleo did not answer but turned his attention to the stranger down below. A glimmer of hope allowed Teleo to breathe normally for a moment. Maybe the man was a rebel friendly to the Elke rulers. Maybe he was part of a plot to overthrow Henrik Stagga and return the Verdant Valley throne to the only Elke heir. Teleo's burst of excitement fizzled out quickly. No one except the Staggas would venture all the way across the Blue Mountains searching for Kaspari. Teleo himself wasn't important enough to track all the way out here—all he'd done was kill a few soldiers, and for good reason. No one would try to track down an escaped Hill orphan. Lastly, few men had a handful of Gold Lions.

Had the scout tracked them to Trillifort first and then to Red Flag Fortress? Maybe the man had come straight to the Sapphire Valley, and Cornwal's border guards had told him about the strange family who had passed through. Teleo tried to remember who he had told that their destination was Red Flag. The village cooper and the border town merchant. Teleo was truly an idiot. He had been an idiot all his life but had somehow managed to survive. But this was Kaspari's life he was talking about now. The Staggas had obviously figured out the prince was a princess. That probably hadn't been too hard after ransacking the Royal Palace's private chambers, which would have held personal effects and maybe even family records.

Teleo tried to discern the heritage of the man below. Did he have the upturned nose of the Aldeon Coast folk, like Gerik and his people? It was difficult to tell. "Did he have an Aldeon Sea accent?" Teleo asked Jarnsmidt.

"I couldn't say," Jarnsmidt said, shrugging.

Teleo tried to imitate the accent, but Jarnsmidt shook his head. "It all sounds strange to me. You eastern folk all talk like you have straw in your mouth."

Teleo scowled, thinking.

"Why Kallie?" Jarnsmidt asked.

"Do you mind if I don't tell you everything right now?" He met the man's curious gaze. "She's the daughter of someone ... important to me ... and I'm trying to keep her alive."

Jarnsmidt nodded slowly. "Good enough," he said. "What can I do to help?"

"We have to track this guy and see if he's alone," Teleo said. "If he's got a band of soldiers with him, which I suspect he has, I might need some help putting them out of commission."

"I have some good men who can help," Jarnsmidt said.

───────────◆───────────

Jarnsmidt put a guard, Dunbarden, on the man's tail.

Less than an hour later, Dunbarden sent a runner to tell them he was at the *Sword and Shield,* one of the two remaining pubs in the small Red Flag castle town. Jarnsmidt called in another guard, Soren, and briefed him. Teleo told Soren to strike up a conversation and gave him some questions to ask the scout.

"Ask him if the artichokes are ready," Teleo told Soren. "Tell him you know someone who can help him sell them at the capital. And ask him what kind of blades he looked at in the armory. Make him say dagger. Ask him if he looked at any. Tell him your friend is a bladesmith and makes daggers. Then ask him if he looked at the dirks. Watch his reaction."

Soren understood. He came back a few hours later, staggering somewhat as he walked, and Jarnsmidt sent a third guard, Finister, to join Dunbarden and tail the scout through the night.

"I got him to talk," Soren said, dropping heavily into a chair in Jarnsmidt's office.

"What'd he say?" Teleo asked, standing and leaning back against Jarnsmidt's desk and folding his arms.

"He said he doesn't know any artichoke farmers," Soren said.

"How did he say artichoke?" Teleo asked. "Arrrtichoke, or Ahhhtichoke?"

Soren thought for a second. "Ahhhtichoke."

"What'd he say about the dirks and daggers?" Teleo asked.

"He said he looked at the daggers. 'Dahgahs,' is how he pronounced it," Soren said, catching onto Teleo's line of questioning.

"Did he know what a dirk was?" Teleo asked.

Soren nodded. "He did. He didn't look at them."

Teleo paced the room, hands clasped behind his back, pondering. The scout was an Aldeon Sea man. A Stagga crony. They were definitely after Kaspari. "We have to follow him," Teleo told Jarnsmidt.

"We already are," Jarnsmidt said.

"Let me send Will out with one of your guys," Teleo said. Will was one of the best trackers Teleo had ever encountered, and that was saying a lot.

They sent Will to find Dunbarden. The two trackers would tail the Aldeon scout by foot. Waite and Finister were to follow behind Will and Dunbarden with Petunia and Nutmeg, to hand off the horses at the right time. The Staggas' scout had not crossed the mountain pass on foot. He had a horse somewhere.

The Staggas' scout left Red Flag at dawn. A few hours later, Waite and Finister burst into the office, out of breath.

"There are thirteen of them," Finister panted. "They all have horses. Big Verdant Valley horses, except one Hill man with a mountain horse. Probably a guide. They headed west."

"Towards Pine Top and Hog Hollow," Waite said, locking eyes with Teleo.

Someone at Red Flag had talked. Teleo gripped the handle of the knife at his belt. Thirteen? Henrik was serious. Then again, the usurper knew Kaspari was with Teleo. Or at least she had been. Now Teleo had abandoned her at Cedar Creek. "How much of a lead do they have? Do Will and Dunbarden have the horses?" Teleo asked, thinking quickly.

"Yes, my father took the horses," Waite said.

Finister continued, "The thirteen men left a couple of hours ago, but they'll have to take the long way around, the same path you guys took. It's the only way to get there on horseback. But there's a shortcut if we go by foot. We'll have to climb a rock face and cross the river on a rope bridge. We can get in front of them before they get to Pine Top."

Jarnsmidt nodded in agreement. "We can cut them off at Fern Cliff Pass. Ambush them." Jarnsmidt turned to Teleo and asked, "Do we have to kill them?"

Teleo thought about it. He recalled Fern Cliff Pass, a narrow stretch of trail two hundred yards long, flanked on both sides by thirty-foot slate cliffs with hanging ferns and water dripping down the mossy rocks. Thirteen was a lot of men and they would be the Staggas' best fighters. Teleo wondered if Gerik was among them.

Teleo said, "If we only mildly injured them—even if we took their weapons, horses, and coin—they could still recover and find their quarry on foot."

"We could capture them and throw them in our dungeon," Jarnsmidt said. "But that would take a lot more men, and perhaps horses, which I don't have. I can't afford to feed prisoners. Do you need to interrogate them?"

Teleo shook his head. "No. I know what they want and who sent them. We should finish them off."

"You say there's a big band of men guarding Jeremiah's home village?" Jarnsmidt asked.

"I'm not sure if they're necessarily guarding it," Teleo said, recalling the simple folk who had set up camp outside Cedar Creek. "I'm not sure they would stop a single scout if one came through. He would be able to alert the others and find another route into the village."

Jarnsmidt grew pensive and looked through the window, scanning the armory floor down below. It was late morning and the four forges were glowing orange, the blacksmiths busy at work. "Okay," he said to Teleo. "You take your horse and catch up to Will and Dunbarden. You guys will seal the pass from the rear. I'll send my people to ambush them at the gap. Meet me at the guard house in thirty minutes so you can brief my troops, then you can take off."

Teleo gathered his things and readied Star while Waite sketched out a rough map for him. Teleo had passed that way twice now and thought he knew the trail.

"You'll catch up to my father by dusk," Waite assured him. "Then it will take you most of the next day to reach Fern Cliff Pass. We will be waiting there."

Teleo was in his new armor and strapped his short sword and Aldeon longsword across his back. At his waist, he belted on his knives and hammers. He drew the fox-and-hare cloak over his shoulders and clasped it at the neck.

Teleo stopped by the tower to tell Sigrid what was going on. She was not there, so he left her a note on the table by the Heliotrope and ran downstairs. At the guard house, Jarnsmidt had assembled a group of two dozen. Some were in red guard uniforms. Others had clearly just left the forges, their arms bulging and clothes soot-stained from work. Two of the guards were women, and Sigrid was there in her archer leathers. He joined Jarnsmidt and Sigrid.

"I'm sending my best archers and strongest swordsmen," Jarnsmidt said. "Sigrid will command the archers." Jarnsmidt gestured at his daughter.

Teleo frowned at her. He did not want her to face Gerik and his henchmen. She met his frown with a hard, level gaze before he could object. How was it that he had attracted someone as stubborn as Dinsmora, he wondered wryly, but held his tongue.

Jarnsmidt continued, "Sorry to say, but I will stay here and hold down the fort. I could use a good fight, but I'm not as young as I used to be."

Teleo regarded the fighters, who were waiting for instructions. They all looked seasoned. Jarnsmidt had chosen well.

"Are the Verdant Valley scouts in plate armor?" Jarnsmidt asked Finister.

"Yes, sir," Finister said.

"You'll need polearms," Jarnsmidt told Teleo. "Take a couple for Will and Dunbarden, too."

They explained the mission to the ambush party, then dispersed to get ready. Teleo went to the armory with Jarnsmidt and chose halberds for Will and Dunbarden and a pole axe for himself.

On his way out of the armory, Sigrid met him, carrying her longbow and two quivers across her back and a sword and three daggers on her belt. Teleo stood facing her.

"Take a polearm," he said.

"I'm on my way to get one," she said.

They looked at one another, wasting precious seconds. "I don't want to see you hurt," he said finally, a poor summation of his jumbled emotions.

"And I don't want to see *you* hurt," she replied, her eyes locked onto his.

He sighed. "Okay, then," he said. "See you at the cliffs." He leaned down and kissed her briefly on the lips, and they went their separate ways.

◆

Will found Teleo before Teleo found him. As light was fading from the sky, the hoot of an owl made Teleo rein in Star. He listened until Will appeared on the trail in front of him, an index finger crossing his lips. Will led him into the woods to where Nutmeg and Petunia were staked, and they found a place to rest. Dunbarden was watching the Aldeon soldiers' camp a mile up the road.

The next morning at first light, the thirteen Stagga soldiers were on their way, and Teleo and his companions were on their trail, riding forward until they detected the horsemen, and then hanging back to put some distance between them.

Tree shadows were already lengthening to long black lines as the sun made its descent when Will determined by the landscape that Fern Cliff Pass was up ahead. They stopped the horses, listening for signs of battle, then hearing nothing, continued on. Twigs crunched under the horses' hooves, and Star snorted as they paced slowly forward, three abreast.

Distant yells floated down the trail. Teleo and his two companions broke into a gallop. Teleo had his pole axe in hand, and Will and Dunbarden were hanging onto their seats with their knees, bows in hand and drawing arrows from their quivers. The fern-covered cliffs came into view. Trapped between the slate walls, Gerik's men were on horseback, fighting off Jarnsmidt's foot soldiers with swords and axes. Jarnsmidt's men had sealed off the two ends of the narrow gorge and swung long polearms at the ambushed horsemen. Arrows flew from the ledges on both sides, bouncing off armor amidst screams and spurts of blood. One after another, Gerik's horsemen were pulled from their mounts by halberds topped with glinting axe heads and steel spikes, and those who were still standing faced off, swords clashing. Teleo and his two companions charged their horses into the fray. Arrows flew, finding purchase in armor gaps and exposed faces. One of Gerik's men fell in front of Teleo, and Star leapt over him. Teleo swung his pole axe at a mounted Aldeon man, piercing his armor and throwing him off balance long enough for two of Jarnsmidt's men to pull him from the saddle.

Another horseman pivoted and charged Teleo. He abandoned his pole axe, which had gone to the ground with the Aldeon, and drew his longsword. Star reared and the two horses slashed at each other with iron-shod hooves. Teleo and the soldier pulled their horses back and circled one another.

"Rickhart," Teleo said, sneering at Gerik's lackey, who resembled a huge bullfrog sitting atop his warhorse.

"Teleo," Rickhart replied, hefting a long-handled axe with a beefy, gauntleted hand. Rickhart wore dented plate armor and an open-faced helmet similar to Teleo's but made of bronze. "Prince Gerik's onto you," Rickhart sneered. "And your little adopted *daughter*. He sent me to fetch him his bride." Rickhart's smile was wide and devious, showing a mouthful of missing teeth.

"Too bad you won't make it back home," Teleo said. "It'll take Gerik months to retrace your steps. By that time, his prize will be beyond his reach."

"So you think," Rickhart taunted, and swung at Teleo with his axe.

Teleo deflected the first, heavy blow but not the second that came in reverse, an unexpectedly agile move by the fat frog, striking Teleo's chest armor with the blunt end of the axe-head as Teleo's sword hit Rickhart's steel-plate pauldron and glanced off. The axe shook Teleo's bones and set him back in his saddle. He recovered and dodged another swing of the axe and then lashed out with his longsword and ducked, but Rickhart caught him on the side of his helmet with the butt end of the axe. Teleo's head rang from the blow. Before he could regain his balance, Rickhart's horse lunged past him and barreled down the trail, back the way they had come. Teleo wheeled Star around and took off in pursuit, his brains jiggling like jelly and his vision blurring.

Rickhart's horse was fast, but Star was faster. Teleo was nearly on his flank when an arrow whizzed by, hitting Rickhart's horse in its right hock. The horse shrieked and Rickhart launched off the horse's back as it stumbled and fell.

Teleo reined in Star. If Star had been Benny or Daisy, Rickhart would be in shreds already, but the elegant white filly pranced uncertainly. Rickhart crouched and approached Teleo, swinging his axe at Star's forelegs. She danced out of the way, neighing shrilly. Teleo jumped to the ground and the two men faced off, circling one another. Rickhart lifted his axe and lunged at Teleo.

Teleo dodged and held his longsword with two hands, half-swording it into Rickhart's overhanging belly, where pale skin drooped below the fat man's chest armor and above the steel skirt belted below his gut. The blade sank into Rickhart's abdomen, and before Rickhart could bludgeon him with the axe again, Teleo withdrew the blade and leapt aside, his head still muzzy. Rickhart bellowed and charged Teleo.

An arrow struck Rickhart in his open mouth, the shaft quivering from his gaping maw. Rickhart staggered, blood gurgling from his mouth and his eyes bulging. The big man fell in a twitching heap at Teleo's feet. Teleo stared, panting, as dark red blood pooled in Rickhart's mouth and spilled down his cheek. Teleo turned and Sigrid ran up behind him, an arrow nocked in her longbow.

"Good shot, my love," Teleo said, resting his hand on her shoulder for balance.

Teleo glanced behind him. The rest of the battle appeared to be under control, with a lone man surrounded by six of Jarnsmidt's fighters. Teleo turned his attention to Rickhart's horse, who was lying on its side, trying to get up on its forelegs.

"We normally try not to hurt the horses," Teleo said to Sigrid. He circled around the rear of the fallen horse. Its hind leg was twisted unnaturally, the tendon severed.

"These are not normal times," Sigrid said. She backed away a pace and aimed her arrow. She let it loose, and it pierced the horse's throat with a thwack. The horse screamed, and she shot another. Blood oozed around the sunken shaft, the horse's head flailing and eyes wild, its front hooves scraping at the ground. Teleo turned away, leaving Sigrid to finish off the horse, and ran to help with the last man standing.

It was a Hill man, pleading for his life.

"I didn't know who they were," the man said, his hands raised. "I was just their guide. I know these woods. They paid gold. Here," he said, fumbling for a leather pouch and holding it out. "Take it. Take all my gold."

Sigrid came up behind Teleo, and the Red Flag soldiers turned to her as the other archers rappelled down off the cliffs.

"We can take him back with us," Sigrid said. "We'll throw him into the dungeon until this whole mess is over with."

She walked over to a Red Flag man, who was lying on the ground with others crouched around him. He was fatally wounded. Sigrid and the others knelt by his side, comforting him as he died.

Teleo and the rest of the party checked each other for wounds and bandaged the worst of them. Teleo gingerly removed his dented helmet and aventail, then peeled off his quilted skullcap. His head was tender and a lump was already forming. The Red Flag armory's steel helmet and cuirass had likely saved his life.

Sigrid came to check on him. "That doesn't look good," she said, feeling the lump on his head and examining the dent on his helmet. She soaked a rag in water from her waterskin and pressed it to his head.

"I'll be fine," he said. He held the cool rag against the lump for a minute, then went with her to help gather the horses and weapons and deal final blows to any of the Aldeon soldiers who were not quite dead. They then tended to the injured horses, none of which were badly hurt, other than some bloody gashes—and Rickhart's dead horse, which they field dressed to bring the meat back to Red Flag. Finally, they dragged Rickhart's body and the Aldeon corpses to a gully away from the path, pilfered anything of value, and then covered the dead bodies with stones. The land was too rocky for an in-ground burial, and so they kept stacking stones until a proper cairn took shape.

"I killed my first man," Sigrid said to Teleo as they lugged stones.

"You did," Teleo said. "How does it feel?"

She placed a stone on the cairn. "Not very good," she said.

Teleo nodded. "It's a difficult thing."

They walked silently back to the foot of the cliff, searching for more fallen rocks. "If it makes you feel any better," Teleo said, "I knew him, and he was not a good man."

She did not respond but found a suitable stone and bent to lift it.

It was dark by the time they finished with the cairn. They built a fire and shared a meager meal around the crackling flames. One by one, people wandered off to the edges of the firelight, where they curled up to steal a few hours of sleep.

Teleo remained seated by the fire. His ear was still ringing from the blow to his skull. His head pounded, and surges of nausea made it impossible to eat. He kept himself awake and did not let on to Sigrid that he suspected he had a concussion. He sat up all night drinking water and stroking her hair as she slept at his side.

At the first hint of daylight, they prepared to depart. They cut the horsemeat into manageable pieces and wrapped them in canvas from the Aldeons' bedrolls. Others wrapped the dead Red Flag soldier in a blanket and lashed him onto one of the mounts, then threw the complaining guide across the back of his mountain horse, bound hand and foot. Sigrid and others rode the remaining warhorses, divvying up the horsemeat between them to carry behind their saddles. The horsemen took the wagon trail while the others cut through the forest on foot.

"What will you do now?" Sigrid asked as they rode side by side.

"I'll continue the mission as we had planned," Teleo said. "I'll stop by Red Flag briefly to restock and then head down into the valley."

Now, more than ever, he had to succeed in gaining access to Sapphire Palace and help these people reclaim their lives. The Red Flag community had sacrificed one of their own for a stranger. Teleo wondered how Jarnsmidt and Sigrid would feel if they knew their soldier had died to protect the heir to the kingdom they had fought against for much of their lives. Teleo took in a shaking breath, his vision wavering. He shielded his eyes from the rising sun with his hand and rode on.

29

◆

SAPPHIRE PALACE

Back at Red Flag, Teleo finally succumbed to his headache and spent three days in bed, tended to by Sigrid and Aunt Tildie. After he finally could hold down food and stand up without the world tilting around him, he spent three more days gathering his strength. If he'd had his way, he would have spent another month healing, but the plan was already in motion and seven Hill Tribes were waiting for him.

The days were long and it was only a few days until the Summer Solstice. More than anything, he wanted to dance the sword in its sacred light. He, Sigrid, and Larissa discussed it in the Heliotrope chamber.

"See? I told you two months would go by before you knew it," Larissa said with a smug smile.

"Yeah, but I can't wait another week," Teleo said. "I'm already several days behind schedule. The tribes will get restless. Things could go wrong. Cornwal could get tipped off."

If things were unfolding as they had planned, militias were already waiting around the perimeter of the valley for the

Sapphire Castle's bell to toll, something that only happened for royal life events: coronations, marriages, births, or deaths. When the bell tolled, the militias would flood into the valley and converge on the castle. The plan hinged on Teleo gaining entry to the Imperial Palace and killing the emperor. No big deal, he thought sardonically—it was merely an emperor protected in a fortified palace, and only thousands of people's lives were riding on the success of his mission.

Larissa's smile had vanished and Sigrid was frowning at her.

"What's the matter?" Teleo asked.

Larissa's face was pinched. "I think Cornwal already suspects something."

"Why? What makes you think that?" Teleo asked, chiding himself for letting Rickhart land a blow with his axe. Two blows. He had warned the women he was getting too old for this.

Larissa twisted a gold ring on her finger. "He said that the people were coming down off the hills and that he would need to teach them a 'lesson' if they thought they were going to challenge him."

"What kind of lesson?"

"I don't know, but his generals have assembled the cavalry outside the City Wall and they've been doing drills day and night."

Teleo sank his forehead into his hands.

Sigrid laid her hand on his arm. "Are you okay? Is it your head?" she asked.

"No," he said, lifting his head, which was still swimming a bit, but he did not want to worry her. "I'm just upset I wasted a week."

"It wasn't your fault."

"I know," he said, holding Sigrid's hand. Although it was his fault. He had not hidden their trail well enough. He had let that toad Rickhart beat on him. His younger self never would have been so careless. He should have spent the winter training with Cutter and Johnswold instead of lazing around with a bunch of dumb sheep and drinking too much ale at Trillifort's Great Hall.

"When do you think they'll expect an attack?" Sigrid asked Larissa.

"The morning of the solstice," Teleo answered. "It is the most propitious day for battle. Every soldier knows that."

Summer Solstice and Winter Solstice. Mead Moon and Harvest Moon. The best days to wage war. The only problem was, both sides thought the same thing. Bron had mentioned it and Will had mentioned it, and Mitchman, and Kegger—that if Teleo could somehow time it so that the bell tolled at dawn on the solstice, then the fight would go in their favor. Teleo had suffered many a bloody battle on the "best" days for war and had advised them that they should not wait. The sooner the better, he'd said, and they had reluctantly agreed. Mostly, he just wanted to get it over with.

"A smarter strategy," Teleo said to the two women, "would be to launch our offensive before the solstice. They won't be expecting that. How many days until the solstice, exactly?" he asked, walking to the western window.

The sun had just set and he could see where the brightest glow still lingered on the mountaintops. Sigrid came to his side and pointed to the ridgeline.

"See that peak?" she asked. "The one that looks like a witch's nose?"

Teleo leaned in and tried to follow where her arm was pointing. "No," he said.

"Well, that's where the sun will set on the night before the longest day. Four nights from now."

Teleo calculated the journey. They could make the ride in three days to the border town. Then one long day to cross the valley to Sapphire City. And then he would need to somehow get through the three concentric rings of defensive walls, gain access to the palace, kill Cornwal, and call forth the Hill Tribes with the tower bell—and that did not even take into account the possibility that he might need to confront General Raedwald. He did not have enough time.

Teleo rubbed his chin, thick with a beard that needed trimming. He had no choice but to move faster and take advantage of the nights. Without pack animals, he should be able make it to the miller's in three days, then he could arrive at the castle before midday on the fourth day and hopefully accomplish his task before nightfall on Solstice Eve. The Solstice Festival and heavy drinking would have already begun inside the city, distracting the city guards. The tolling bell would catch Cornwal's troops by surprise and the Hill Tribes would have a chance.

He stood. "I must leave before dawn."

The women stood with him and did not object.

"Let us dance," Sigrid said.

The three of them took up swords, spaced themselves out across the Heliotrope, and danced.

Teleo, Will, and Waite left when the moist night air was still thick and black. Two great horned owls hooted to one another along the river, and the rustle of four-legged creatures scurried away through the underbrush as the horses snorted and tramped across the dark trail. At least it was not raining.

They pushed the horses, setting a grueling pace and taking advantage of the long days. They arrived at the Southern Mountain Pass border town on the second day after the shops had closed and the few small pubs were filling up. Off-duty soldiers, merchants, and travelers spilled out of the pubs and gathered around tall, upturned barrels, enjoying the fine evening over mugs of frothy ale. The sun was descending down its long western arc. The next day, its path would be even longer. Then the following day would herald the solstice, when on the fifth day the sun would take its longest journey before heading in the other direction and shortening the days with every turn.

They spent the night sharing a large bed in an overcrowded and overpriced inn. Teleo paid even more to keep the horses in the inn's stable. The innkeeper grudgingly agreed to provide water for the horses but was not allowed to sell them feed.

The next morning, Teleo put Star in the care of Will and Waite, who were to return her to Red Flag. The father and son wished him luck and accompanied Teleo to the border gate, where he doled out the toll fee. His money purse was worryingly light. It didn't matter, he reasoned. In two days' time, he would either be dead or at the center of a new administration indebted to him. He inspected the guardsmen's faces, trying to discern if any of them had betrayed him to the band of Rickhart's riders. None of them registered recognition, but they inspected the Mage Stone Master insignia on his chestplate.

"Mountain tribe," Teleo explained.

"What do you need armor and all those weapons for?" one of them asked, eyeing the sword hilts poking up over his shoulders. Teleo tried not to scowl. They had not given him trouble the first time through.

"Needed them to cross the mountains," Teleo said. "Brigands are crawling all over the place, and I'll need them on the way back. Plus, I hear people are hungry in the valley. Can't be too careful." He adjusted the new helmet Sigrid had given him to replace his dented one—this one was a fancy decorated bronze thing with pompous red and black pheasant feathers, and she had giggled when she had slid it onto his sore head.

"What's your business here?" the guard asked gruffly.

"Setting up a deal with the trade ministers," he said, flashing a Silver Bit. "They are expecting me."

The guard eyed Teleo's shiny armor and the two mounted guards and purebred Sapphire Empire mare he was leaving behind as Will and Waite watched from the side of the road. He looked the part of a successful merchant braving the Southern Mountain Pass for a lucrative trading deal, but not rich enough to have a wagon train or pack horses with feed that would sustain them in the emperor's valley. The guard pocketed the coin and waved him through.

Teleo pulled out the fox-and-hare cloak from his travel bag, slung the leather sack over his shoulders, and clipped his gauntlets to his belt. He draped the long cape over his armor and swords, raising the hood over his helmet and tucking in the feathers. The less attention he attracted, the better.

He took off on foot down the Emperor's Toll Road. Clouds rolled in, and by the time he arrived at the miller's, they were low and dark.

The miller led him out into the dirt lot. "Rain's coming," the man said, sniffing the air.

Teleo paid the miller and climbed into the shelter of a covered wagon he'd paid an extra Bronze Bit for, and waited for night to fall. A pounding rain on the canvas covering woke him before dawn. Teleo ate a quick breakfast of hardbread and smoked fish, then headed down the road at a brisk walk, bowing his head against the driving rain and trying to ignore his lingering headache.

After long miles of trudging past other miserable, sodden travelers, he arrived at the City Gate and joined a long queue waiting to enter through the massive City Wall, the first of three fortifications he would need to get past. People were arriving already for the city's Solstice Festival, and even the rain wouldn't dampen the night's drunken celebration. The sun was somewhere behind the thick clouds, and Teleo judged it to be late morning. The guards were as wet as the travelers and waved them through the entry arch, not even checking for weapons.

Teleo emerged into the walled city and got his bearings. This sector of Sapphire City was a warren of narrow streets and alleyways, its drainage gullies gushing with dirty water and clogged with refuse. He stepped over a sputtering ditch and stood under the eaves of a saddlery. He found a dry wall to sit on and forced down some hardbread and cheese and the remainder of the smoked fish. His head was throbbing as though Rickhart's axe had gone through his skull instead of just denting his helmet, but at least the dizziness had subsided. The rain was letting up. Teleo shook out the fox-and-hare cloak, most of the water having been repelled by the wool and silk embroidery, then draped it over his armor again. He drank some water and then entered the cobblestone maze, passing crowded tenements, small eateries and pubs, bustling markets, and workshops of every kind.

He headed towards the Castle Wall, its ramparts jutting above the roofline and encircling the old castle town. He finally stepped into the large open square in front of the Castle Gate, the main entrance to the Castle Ring where grand homes and various administrative and service buildings surrounded the walled Imperial Palace.

Sodden garlands were festooned above the Castle Gate and strung between pillars bordering the square, the green ivy and braided wheat ears drooping from the earlier downpour. Tents and tarps were being erected in the square for the solstice celebration, and workers rushed around in the light but steady rain. Casks of mead were being rolled across the cobblestones and coal braziers carted in for the food and mead stands. Musicians were setting up under canvas tarps. The festivities would not start until sundown, but people were already dressed in their finery. This was the rich part of town, and gentlemen and their ladies ducked into shops surrounding the square or hurried towards the Castle Gate, scarves covering their tall white wigs and rain staining their velvet clothing with dark splotches. Government officials strode importantly, hooded cloaks protecting their wigs, velvet doublets, and puffy pants.

Teleo told his trade minister story to the guards at the Castle Gate, dispensing more Silver Bits into their greedy palms. He entered the Castle Ring, leaving the hubbub of the City Ring behind. Everything in this elite enclave was quiet and orderly. Imperial business was conducted here, and master craftsmen and exclusive shops served only the most discerning patrons. High-ranking ministers resided in stately homes hidden behind tall stone walls.

Teleo followed a group of administrators up a wide boulevard towards the lapis lazuli Palace Wall—a towering fortification hewn from the indigo-blue stone slashed with veins of gold, its polished surface slick with rain. The magnificent wall, topped with ornately carved battlements, surrounded the palace. An architectural masterpiece, the Imperial Palace crowned the city, its lapis lazuli walls glistening in the muted light and its towers and spires piercing the overcast sky.

Teleo made his way to the Palace Gate, where he would need to beg for an appointment and wait several hours to be admitted for an audience with a trade minister—if they let him in at all. He would probably run into the same requirement for an invitation with an official seal as he had the last time he had tried to sneak in, years ago. He considered turning around and searching for a back-alley shop where he might procure forged documents.

He slowed his pace and considered his options. A half-dozen

soldiers flanked either side of the open gate. They were staring straight ahead, motionless, and holding long spears that rested butt-end on the paving stones. More guards stopped people as they entered the gate, and another dozen guards were marching in formation inside the palace bailey, no doubt preparing for a shift change. Teleo inspected what he could see of the palace from his vantage point. The building was surrounded by more walls, stone ramps, and staircases. The main entrance was a wide staircase flanked by another half-dozen guards. He eyed the thickness of the wall at the open gate. It was at least two arm spans thick.

Teleo passed the gate by and continued alongside the thirty-foot high wall. Guards manned the ramparts above and peered out through arrow slits. Teleo pulled his hood down over his brow and walked slowly, gauging people's reactions as he passed. Most people did not notice him in his embroidered cloak. Or if they did, their eyes flickered as though they had seen a shadow before returning to their thoughts or conversation, lowering their heads against the drizzle. Teleo turned a corner, hugging the shadowed base of the wall. This side of the palace was less busy. He turned another corner, continuing forward until two workers passed him unnoticed, then stood with his back against the wall and waited. He reviewed Larissa's map in his head and tried to place his exact location.

No guards sounded an alert at the presence of a man lurking below, and no one else passed by. When he was convinced he had not attracted attention, he turned slowly and leaned his face and chest against the polished wall and felt it give way to the pressure. The hematite-beaded Stone Guardian talisman in its leather medicine bag burned cold against Teleo's sternum. The stone wall was cold. *He* was cold. He pressed his whole body into the lapis lazuli until he was surrounded on all sides. He sank into the stone matrix, abandoning himself to its icy clutches. He pushed his legs forward as though through quicksand, and finally his foot broke loose, stepping out onto solid ground.

He emerged from the wall's tomblike embrace on wobbly legs. His head could have been a piece of steel, hammered and folded a thousand times. He sucked in a mouthful of air and tried to focus his eyes. He was in a walled, paved courtyard. No one was about except the guards on the ramparts, and their backs were to him. A curtain of rain fell across his cloak's shifting pattern of indigo hares and silver foxes, shimmering insubstantially against the wet stones.

Exhaustion washed over him, and his knees shook. He closed his eyes and breathed, trying to steady himself and resist a fresh wave of nausea. He leaned back against the wall for support. He could feel his back starting to merge with the stone, and he jerked upright. The paving stones felt soft under his feet, and panic pricked at him. He fended it off and gathered his strength, breathing deeply. The leather bag holding the hematite beads was still cold against his skin. Next to it, the Heliotrope amulet was hot. He pressed his chest armor against the amulet, and its warmth seeped into his bones, steadying him.

He stood camouflaged against the bailey wall, waiting until his lightheadedness passed and his muscles stopped shaking. His head still pounded, but there was nothing to be done about that. He adjusted his hood and walked slowly along the wall until he found a set of narrow stairs that led up to a side service entrance. Teleo ducked and crouched behind the walls of the staircase and climbed stealthily through the shadows until he reached the top. He then darted across a ramp and up another service staircase to a wooden door that led into the palace.

He tried the handle. It was locked. He stepped to the side and pressed himself against the palace's stone wall and pushed through in slow motion, feeling as though he were naked and plunging through jagged ice into a frigid lake.

He emerged into the dry air on the other side and inhaled deeply. He was in a dimly lit foyer that led to a service stairway built of blue argillite. He pressed his armor against the warm Heliotrope amulet again and leaned back against the wooden door until his head stopped spinning. He recalled Larissa's map and thought he knew roughly where he was. He shook the rain off his cloak and wrapped it around himself again, then staggered to the stairs, gripping the wooden banister for support, and climbed.

The stairway was abandoned, and Teleo climbed gingerly from one platform to the next as the staircase turned. The stone steps felt odd beneath his leather boot soles. He cracked open the door at the top, peering side to side down a long, dim service hallway lit with flickering wall sconces. The corridor was empty. He stepped through the doorway, checked his memory of Larissa's palace map, and turned left. He stashed his travel bag in a dark alcove, then navigated a series of service corridors and stairways, pausing in the shadows to orient himself and slipping into a broom closet when a serving girl rushed by. He crept out into the empty hallway and continued on.

When he determined that he had reached the main administrative wing, he slowly opened the door at the end of a corridor, slipped out, and quickly climbed another, wider staircase. At the top, the thick wooden door was propped open to a grand, well-lit hallway, resplendent with polished lapis lazuli floors and walls, and lined with stained-glass windows and small tables displaying blown glass vases overflowing with spring flowers. If he had navigated correctly, he was standing in the corridor leading to the offices of the Imperial Ministers and Emperor Cornwal himself.

A velvet-clad administrator swept by, followed by two attendants. So wrapped up were they in their own importance, they did not notice the change of pattern in the grain of the polished blue stone wall where Teleo stood like a statue. Teleo exhaled silently and stalked after them. The administrator and attendants disappeared down a side corridor and Teleo continued straight along the main hallway, walking confidently as though he belonged there.

Further down, two administrators walked slowly towards him, heads leaning close to one another, absorbed in conversation. Based on their extravagant fur-trimmed cloaks, Teleo judged them to be two of the seven senior Imperial Ministers who made up the Cabinet directly under the emperor—the men who actually ran the empire, according to Larissa, while Cornwal was holed up in his study. The two ministers did not see—or ignored—Teleo and stopped in front of a large wooden door. A guard opened the door for them and they went inside, the guard closing the door behind them. If Teleo was correct, they had entered the Imperial Ministers' chamber.

The tall guard stepped back, blocking the door and clasping his hands in front of him. The man gazed straight ahead at a large stained-glass window that depicted a peacock at a pond. Teleo hesitated next to a cascade of flowers.

His destination was the emperor's study, the last door at the end of the hall. It was several paces away, where another man stood guard across from a second stained-glass window, its colors bathing his face. Past the emperor's study door, the hallway terminated at a stone wall, which displayed Cornwal's purple banner. The banner featured a gold-embroidered balance scale—Cornwal's sigil. People referred to it as the scale of justice, but to Teleo it looked more like a money changer's scale. To the left of the banner, an alcove leading to another service stairwell darkened the far corner.

Teleo needed to cross in front of both guards to reach the emperor's study. He did not know if the fox-and-hare cloak could adjust to the many colors of the stained-glass windows were he to walk in front of them. He contemplated turning back but hesitated, having come this far already.

Across the wide hallway, facing Teleo, was a large curved alcove. At the center of the alcove wall, double doors stood open to the damp air and a spacious terrace overlooking the mist-covered city and valley. Cornwal's purple banners hung limply from their flagpoles—no one had bothered to take them down during the rainstorm. The nape of his neck prickled as Teleo realized he was gazing upon the high castle terrace, the platform from which the emperors addressed their subjects, and which had been the crown jewel—the ultimate prize—of the invading Verdant Valley forces years ago when Teleo had fought outside the City Wall. They had never captured the city, fleeing in defeat like a pack of hungry, beaten dogs. Now here he was, looking out from within.

He froze while another minister strode by, the man's satin cape billowing in a gust of rain-swept wind. The guard turned to let the man into the Imperial Ministers' chamber, and Teleo made his move, darting across the hallway and treading silently over the polished floor in front of the peacock window to the safety of the stone wall beyond. He stepped back against the lapis lazuli wall between two tables of flowers and stood still as stone, watching the fox-and-hare cloak with fascination as it conformed to his surroundings. The guards stared straight ahead, and Teleo plotted his next move.

Larissa had assured Teleo that her husband spent most of his time alone in his study, poring over ancient texts. He was not a sociable man, convinced everyone was scheming against him, and only emerged when the ministers could not agree on terms of a trade deal or some new law they wanted to impose.

The guards at each door looked to be more doormen than soldiers, wearing blue velvet brigandines and black silk pants and caps instead of the standard blue-and-gray uniforms, steel cuirasses, and steel helmets of the guards manning the walls. They carried only one ceremonial sword and a dagger at their sides, more for show than for defense. Cornwal must think his palace walls impenetrable, with the single gate, towering ramparts, and guard units marching in formation out front—the cocky stupidity of a man with total power.

But although Teleo had permeated the defenses and was so close to his quarry, he stood on the wrong side of the corridor, trapped between stained-glass windows and tables of floral bouquets across from the chambers' doors. He held still, poised against the blue-and-gold shimmering walls and hoping the fox-and-hare cloak's magic was strong enough to conceal movement.

He got his chance with a shift change. Two new velvet-brigandine-clad soldiers marched down the hallway and stood in front of each of their posts. They didn't think anyone else was in the corridor and so the men relaxed and joked briefly before exchanging positions. Teleo stole across the hallway as the men traded spots, just another shadow in the shifting light.

He stood camouflaged against the wall between the two new guards as the original guards left, one walking past him while adjusting the sword at his side. Teleo exhaled silently and estimated the distance between the doors of the ministers' chamber and the emperor's study. Where did the interior wall that separated the adjacent rooms fall? He edged sideways along the corridor wall and slunk around another decorative table, and then another, sidling closer to the emperor's study.

When he got as close to the guarded door as he dared, he

turned and pressed face-first into the wall. This wall was thinner than the bailey wall, and its icy grip held him for only a brief moment before releasing him. Teleo emerged into a spacious wood-paneled chamber, knocking his knee against a heavy wooden chair and nearly falling over it as he entered the room. The chair scraped against the polished lapis lazuli floor, and the emperor looked up from his seat behind a large mahogany desk.

Teleo froze, his vision blurring and a stabbing pain slicing through his head. Cornwal stared across the room at the chair. The emperor slowly arose from his seat and crept around the desk towards Teleo. Cornwal was a short, stocky man, with thinning black hair, puffy gray silk breeches, black knee-high boots, and a purple silk brocade doublet that was tight against his ample belly. The doublet's slashed sleeve panels were edged with gaudy gold piping, and white ruffles fell from his wrists and neck. His powdered wig sat on a small table behind the desk. Around his waist, he wore a thin black belt with a single dagger. His eyes were intelligent and alert. Emperor Cornwal squinted in Teleo's direction and trod warily across the floor, his footsteps falling silently on a Far Shell Island rug depicting great blue herons fishing at a pond thick with lily pads and pink lotus flowers.

Teleo did not think Cornwal saw him, otherwise he would have yelled for the guard—although the thick timber doors would have been built for privacy, silencing everything. Or maybe the emperor was lost in the pattern of Teleo's cloak, busily chasing hares and foxes through a tangled forest. Teleo held his breath and tried to still his quivering limbs.

Teleo slowly edged sideways and pressed himself against a large wooden wardrobe as the emperor approached. Cornwal tilted his head, listening and sniffing the air. He stood like that for a long moment and then suddenly released his pose and bent to straighten the chair.

Teleo lunged from his hiding spot. The emperor jerked his head around, and their eyes met. The chair stood between them. Teleo edged around it, preferring to inflict a bloodless death. The emperor lashed out with his dagger. Teleo dodged the slash but the sharp blade caught the clasp of his fox-and-hare cloak, tearing it open at the neck. He had not been expecting the small pudgy man to be so quick, but he supposed the man was Emperor, after all, and must have some redeeming qualities.

Teleo drew his short sword and stepped around the chair, his cloak sliding to the floor.

The emperor backed away, glowering at Teleo's steel chestplate and pointing accusingly with his dagger. "You bear the mark of ...," Cornwal said, his brow wrinkling. "... a ... a Mage Stone Master?" Cornwal gazed at Teleo in a moment of puzzled curiosity that quickly turned to terror.

The emperor pulled a gold chain from under his doublet and pushed a round pendant at Teleo, as if trying to fend off dark magic. A circle of diamonds glittered at Teleo.

"Diamonds?" Teleo scoffed. "They don't defend against magic, they *are* magic. But not strong enough for me, I'm afraid."

Teleo knocked the dagger from the emperor's hand and clamped him in a headlock, his arm closing off the blood flow to Cornwal's head. They wrestled and struggled, staggering across the room. The emperor scratched at Teleo's arm, then scrabbled for the weapons at Teleo's hip. Teleo was ready for that and held Cornwal's wrist with his left hand and maintained pressure on the neck with his right arm while Cornwal's other hand flapped uselessly at his side.

"Why are you so greedy?" Teleo growled as they lurched together across the rug in a macabre dance. "When is enough gold enough? Or perhaps it's more diamonds you crave?"

Cornwal spasmed and his knees buckled. Teleo held the

emperor upright as he grew limp. He released Cornwal's wrist and used his free hand to lever his arm tighter around Cornwal's throat. The emperor died in his arms, just as Valona had. Both rulers had been so arrogant they were easy prey. Paranoid and overconfident at the same time. In both cases, their greed and lust for power had gotten the better of them.

Teleo wiped sweat from his brow and laid the emperor behind the desk. Cornwal's dead eyes stared up at him, as though daring him to slit his throat. Teleo worried about the magic of the diamonds, and just as he had done with Valona, pierced Cornwal's carotid artery and watched as blood oozed out, no heartbeat left to pump it. Cornwal had been dead already, and now Teleo had made a bloody mess. The emperor's glassy eyes fixed on him, taunting. Teleo lowered Cornwal's eyelids so that the dead man could not look at him any longer.

Teleo strode across the room, locked the door to the hallway by sliding the metal bolt into its bracket, and then collapsed into the wooden chair, shaking.

He breathed deeply, trying to calm his pounding heart while battling vertigo and flashes of white light, which randomly sparked across his field of vision. He pulled the warm Heliotrope amulet out from under his armor and held it, eyes closed, then finally rose and poured himself a glass of cold water from a copper pitcher wet with condensation. He drank another glassful and helped himself to sweetcakes from a covered tray, and little pork sausages. The meat made him feel better and he ate more. Things were going well—better than Teleo had anticipated.

He hardened his will to finish the job, reminding himself that hordes of rebels were waiting on the hillsides. He could go straight to find Larissa or he could go into the ministers' chamber. According to Larissa, the seven Imperial Ministers would resist crowning her Ruling Empress and would vote instead for one of them to take the throne and then probably force her into marriage. Teleo leaned against the side table with both hands as a wave of dizziness washed over him. He was not in any condition to fight seven men, even seven soft men in powdered wigs and puffy sleeves.

He stumbled across the floor to an overstuffed chair of purple velvet. He would rest a bit more and then decide. He swayed as he reached the chair, grabbing for its arm. The room turned sideways as he missed the chair and fell against the wall, tumbling into the cold, dark stone.

Teleo's helmeted head struck the floor, hitting the sore spot on the side of his skull. He winced and pulled his feet from the icy clutches of the stone wall and then drew his knees up to his chest, the stone floor spongy beneath him. All strength had left him, and his muscles were flaccid as a wet rag. He wondered idly if he would fall through the stone floor to the level below.

"What was that?" a deep voice asked, followed by the scraping of chair legs against the floor. Teleo's eyes flew open. His view was at floor-level, the polished lapis lazuli floor tiles stretching out before him. Legs of wooden chairs stood around carved wooden pedestals holding up a long table. Black polished boots and stockinged calves moved.

Teleo grasped the Heliotrope amulet and struggled to his knees, propping himself up on one hand. He climbed to his feet, trying to keep his balance while the stone floor grew mushy underfoot. The room tilted, and he reached out, steadying himself against a wooden bookcase.

"Stone Guardian!"

The screeching voice hurt Teleo's head. He squinted, trying to bring his double vision together into a single image.

"Did you see him come through the wall?" the screeching voice asked.

"He came through the wall?" another voice asked. "Black magic! Get him!"

"You get him, you're closer," the high-pitched voice screamed. "Hurry up, you fool."

An ink well flew across the room, barely missing Teleo's head and splattering black ink across the wall. Teleo gripped the amulet and took in his surroundings.

Seven men were gawking at him—some were standing while others were still seated around the large rectangular wooden table, their mouths agape. A collection of weapons decorated one stone wall, and the other walls were lined with benches, bookcases, and serving tables. Leaded-glass windows reached all the way to the ceiling and were festooned with green-and-gold brocade curtains.

Teleo staggered across the room and threw the bolt to lock the only door, then stood in front of it, arms folded. He leaned gratefully against the solid wood and took stock of the Imperial Ministers, foggily considering his course of action. The other ministers scraped up from their chairs. Four of them scurried behind the table, keeping their eyes on him as though he were a rabid dog. The other three edged slowly around the table towards Teleo. One ran for the wall and grabbed a headsman's axe from its display hooks and waved it threateningly at Teleo.

"Get back!" the minister cried. "Or I'll yell."

A laugh escaped Teleo's lips. No one was going to hear him yell. Even if the guard did hear him, the door was bolted shut.

The minister's hands were large but soft. He had pushed more parchments than he had ever swung a sword. Teleo lurched at him, ducking a wild swing of the axe, and tackled the heavy man with his armored shoulder, taking him to the ground. A quick dagger to the throat left the man glaring up at him as blood gurgled from his mouth.

The other ministers stared in horror. Teleo went for the next closest minister, dagger in hand. The lapis lazuli floor was boggy beneath his boots. The minister grabbed a heavy wooden chair and tried to throw it at him. It fell short, landing on its solid legs in front of Teleo, who hopped onto it and kicked the minister in the face, knocking him to the ground. The man scrambled away with the third minister, joining the others in the back of the room. Teleo hopped onto the table, the wood solid underfoot. "Who wants to be a prisoner, and who wants to die?" Teleo asked.

The ministers babbled incoherently. Teleo pondered the situation as the ministers huddled together, whispering frantically. He could use the silk ropes holding back the curtains to hog-tie a few of them, then make strips of their silk robes to bind the others. They suddenly burst across the room, three running for the door and three turning to the windows, tugging at the latches. Teleo would have run for the wall and grabbed weapons. There were swords, shields, daggers, spears, and axes. But they were bureaucrats, not soldiers, a useless class that only existed in Sapphire City.

Teleo jumped down and met the one closest to the door with a swipe of his longsword at the shins, tripping him and then half-swording him in the back. The puncture made a sucking sound as air escaped the minister's lungs. Teleo took down the other two in short order, then stalked to the back of the room where the three remaining ministers had abandoned trying to unlatch the windows, which were probably nailed shut at the orders of the paranoid emperor. Two were trying to lift a chair to break the glass. Teleo pulled the chair away and killed one man, then the next. The last one quivered against a window, begging for his life.

"I'm sorry," Teleo said. "I don't trust you now."

Teleo slit his throat and backed away as blood spurted over the minister's frilly white collar and the man slid to the ground.

Teleo rolled the writhing body over so he wouldn't have to see his face as life bled out of him.

Teleo's boots sank slowly into the stone floor. He sat in a solid wooden chair and took the weight off his feet, then wiped his sword and dagger with a linen napkin and cleaned splatters of blood from his armor. His muscles were shaking again and he was sweating. Not the hot sweat of battle but the cold sweat of sickness. He clutched at the Heliotrope amulet and breathed deeply. If the ministers had known how to wield more than a writing quill, he would be dead by now.

Teleo lifted silver food tray covers from platters arrayed across the table and examined their contents, pulling them over and arranging them before him. There was sliced pork loin with plum sauce, a dish of fresh greens, roasted onions and mushrooms, a plate of cheeses and sliced fruit, and bread and butter. Teleo ate with bare hands, suddenly ravenous. Walking through walls sapped his strength like nothing he had ever experienced. Meat seemed to help, as did water. He ate his fill, drank from a pitcher of water, and wiped his mouth, perusing a ledger that lay open on the table.

Two slave girls, sisters, ages 8 and 9 – 3 Gold Lions each
One slave boy, age 7 – 3 Gold Lions
One slave girl, age 14, virgin – 4 Gold Lions

Teleo closed the book with disgust and wearily got to his feet. His legs were heavy and the floor was growing squishy beneath his feet again, which concerned him, but he had forgotten a couple of things.

Teleo clutched the Heliotrope amulet at his neck, which solidified the floor to something less like mud and more like sand. He crossed the room and passed through the wall into the emperor's study, emerging from the cold embrace on trembling legs. His feet sank into the stone floor. He pulled up a foot but the other foot sank deeper, the lapis lazuli swallowing his boot up to his ankle. He panicked and fought against it, trying to climb out, but the more he struggled the deeper he sank. The stone engulfed him up to his knees and he reached forward, grabbing at the only thing within reach, the edge of the blue heron rug. He pulled himself forward and his legs plowed through the stone floor behind him, cold and numb. He dragged himself onto the wool rug and lay prone, panting, his cheek resting on a pink lotus blossom, the carpeted floor solid beneath him.

Wool.

Valona's crazy obsession with wool ... those blessed, bleating, smelly sheep. The queen had not been completely nuts, after all. There was some truth to her superstition—that wool granted protection against Stone Guardian magic. He stroked the soft rug, an island of safety amidst a sea of quicksand. He wondered despondently if the shepherd's crook would have helped as well—the crook he had left behind with Sigrid, thinking he would not be encountering any Stone Guardians in Sapphire Valley. He held onto the Heliotrope amulet. It gave him strength, but it was not enough.

Teleo marshaled his courage and climbed up onto his hands and knees on the rug, unsure of what to do other than the next task in front of him.

He crawled across the carpet and retrieved his fox-and-hare cloak, throwing it over his shoulders, then stood up and hopped onto another carpet of blue waves and sea creatures. He crept around the emperor's desk, keeping his feet on the rug and stepping over Cornwal's sprawled legs, and opened the center drawer. He shuffled through parchments and in the back, he found what he was looking for. A long brass key. Teleo pocketed the key and peered down at the corpse.

Cornwal lay mostly on the stone floor, in a puddle of blood. The emperor's diamond pendant winked up at Teleo, as though it still lived despite Cornwal being dead. Teleo frowned and placed one foot on the stone floor, with the rear foot still anchored on the rug. The front foot started sinking immediately. Teleo quickly pulled Cornwal closer. He hesitated for a moment, the diamonds drawing his eye, perfect in their symmetry. He did not need diamonds—they were poisonous to the soul. But he would not keep them for himself. He would give the pendant to Larissa to prove to her that her husband was dead.

Teleo quickly unclasped the gold chain from around Cornwal's sticky neck. As soon as Teleo held the diamond pendant, the stone floor congealed around his foot. Teleo pulled his foot out with a sucking sound and cautiously placed it on the floor again, which was suddenly solid underfoot. He stood, confused for a moment, unsure of what had just happened. But the floor was definitely solid. He tested it, putting his weight on both feet on the lapis lazuli tiles and bouncing up and down. It held firm. He clutched the diamond pendant in his fist and then gazed down at it in wonder, his hand opening to reveal its glittering glory.

"Stone Guardian magic," he said aloud, the bloody diamonds staring up at him. He had been mistaken when he'd told Cornwal that diamonds did not defend against magic. It was something even greater than that—it was the other half of the Stone Guardian magic. The balancing aspect. The solidifying force.

Teleo laughed out loud, his body flooded with warmth, as though the summer sun had just broken through heavy clouds. He hurried across the rug to the pitcher and poured water over the necklace, washing away the emperor's blood. The diamonds sparkled, reflecting every color of the rainbow from their tiny facets. A shiver ran up Teleo's spine as he gazed down at them. He closed his fingers around the pendant. If the diamonds had made the stone floor solid again, could he still walk through walls?

He went to the wall separating the study from the ministers' chamber, then held his breath and pressed a finger against the polished lapis lazuli. His finger pushed through easily. He exhaled with relief, inhaled again, and then stepped into the wall. This time, instead of entering a numbing sheet of ice, it felt as though he were pushing through layers of velvet curtains. He stood still, encased by stone on all sides, and turned in a full circle, retaining his full awareness. The stone flowed and parted around him like water. He exhaled and inhaled. He could breathe. The air was the thick, stagnant air of a deep cave, but breathable. And he could see, in a fashion. Flecks of gold glimmered in a sea of midnight blue, the mineral's crystals parting as he slowly waved his hand and then reforming their matrix after his hand had passed through.

Diamonds and hematite, the magical pairing of light and ore.

Teleo stepped easily into the ministers' chamber, delighting at how the floor was sturdy under his feet and his head was clear, although his skull still throbbed from where he had been struck by Rickhart's axe. He examined the diamond pendant more closely. Six gold creatures formed the outer circle of the pendant—three lions alternating with three eagles, each holding a small diamond. In the center was a rampant griffin—part eagle, part lion—clasping the seventh diamond in its raised talons. It was not a solid disk—light shone through the meticulously sculpted gold between unfurled wings and flowing manes as the creatures danced around the center griffin. Teleo pulled out the scrap of Stone Guardian buckskin, which was no longer cold.

Metallic embroidery thread and seven hematite beads formed a spiral pattern, a perfect balance for the seven diamonds.

He tucked the hematite talisman and diamond pendant together into the little leather medicine bag and pushed it under his cuirass along with the Heliotrope amulet, grinning to himself like a thief who had just pulled off an impossible heist. He crossed the room and searched the ministers' clothing, pilfering silk money purses and a fine dagger with a whale tooth handle and finally finding a brooch on one man's collar. The brooch was a simple gold bar inset with two large pearls on either side and a center stone of pale blue moonstone. Teleo pinned his fox-and-hare cloak closed with the brooch, carefully cutting away the original clasp from the torn cloak and pocketing it.

He then lifted a crimson cloak trimmed with gold brocade from the back of a chair and draped the heavy silk over his fox-and-hare cloak. Next, he found a minister whose white powdered wig was unbloodied and peeled it off his head. Teleo gingerly removed his helmet and skullcap, then fitted the wig over his tender head, tucking in loose strands of his own hair and arranging the ridiculously long white curls over his shoulders. He peered at his own reflection in the windowpanes. He would pass.

Teleo took a deep breath, then walked to the door, stepping off the Far Shells rug onto the solid floor. He unbolted the lock, pressed on the handle, and cracked open the door.

"Guard," Teleo said, poking his wigged head out the doorway. "We require your assistance."

The guard gave him a respectful bow and entered the room. Teleo closed the door with his foot as the guard gaped at the corpses littering the ground. Teleo grabbed the guard from behind and neatly sliced his throat. He waited patiently while the man bled out, disliking this assassin's role more and more.

He sighed and steeled himself for the next guard.

Teleo called the guard who stood outside Cornwal's study. The man hesitated for a moment, then trotted down the hall.

"We have a small situation," Teleo said. "It won't take but a moment of your time."

The guard nodded and entered the room. The guard saw the bloody scene as Teleo pushed the door closed and threw back his cloaks from his shoulder, drawing his short sword. He knocked the man against the wall, pressing the tip of his steel blade into the hollow above the guard's sternum. The guard grabbed the sword blade, and Teleo stabbed him in the gut with his dagger and then again in the neck, twice. He died quickly, like the others, and Teleo wondered how the Sapphire Empire had kept the Verdant Valley soldiers at bay for so many years.

Teleo sighed and got a napkin from the table, dampened it with cold water, and cleaned blood off his hands and armor. Splatters of blood were soaking into his crimson robe, and he absorbed it as best he could, dabbing it with cold water, and then took a moment to make sure he had thought of everything.

He stepped back through the stone wall into the emperor's study. Taking out the key from his pocket, he went to the door to test it, sliding the key into the keyhole. He turned the key, and the lock mechanism responded silently. Teleo slid back the bolt, pulled open the door, and peeked out. The hallway was empty, the stained-glassed windows bathing the polished stone corridor with kaleidoscopes of color. The window across from him depicted a mounted warrior with a falcon on his gauntlet. Teleo pushed the door closed again, locked it with the key, and went back through the wall into the ministers' chamber, where he searched for the key to that room. After looking through every drawer in three ornate, inlaid-wood desks set against the walls, he found it hanging in plain sight next to the door at the edge of the weapons display.

A small bell tinkled over the door and Teleo jumped back. He held his breath, and the bell rang again.

Teleo unsheathed his dagger, then slowly opened the door and peered out.

A boy was standing there holding a covered serving tray. He couldn't have been more than twelve. He was chubby with round cheeks, red hair and freckles, and wearing bright blue velvet pants and tunic.

"Who are you?" Teleo asked.

"Serving boy, uh ... sir?" His big blue eyes gazed up at him. "I've brought dessert." He held up the tray. "Peach cream puffs."

"Are you a Verdant Valley orphan?" Teleo asked. His own Oren was older, light-haired and gray-eyed, and slim, with pronounced cheekbones and a straight nose—not the freckled, plump boy who stood before him.

"Yes, sir."

"What's your name?"

"Stephan, sir."

"Wait here, Stephan," Teleo said. "Here, give me that." Teleo took the tray from the boy and left him standing out in the hallway, closing the door between them. He gathered his thoughts. Everything was done. He set the tray on the table and stole a cream puff, ate it in one bite, ate another, and then tucked his helmet under his arm and left the room, joining Stephan in the corridor and locking the door behind him.

"Do you know where the empress's chambers are?" Teleo asked.

Stephan nodded. "Yes. Who are you?" the boy asked. "Where are Shane and Johnny?"

Teleo hesitated for a moment. "You mean the guards?" The boy nodded again. "They're inside," Teleo said. "I'm a doctor.

Something terrible has happened. Now take me straight to the empress." He nudged the boy across the abandoned corridor. The minister's crimson-and-gold robe flowed around Teleo and brushed the floor, the Aldeon silk probably more costly than a suit of armor. "Take me the shortest way, but past the fewest people. Can you do that?"

Stephan nodded and stepped into the alcove that led to the servant stairway.

◆

Stephan led Teleo down the stairs and along a dim hallway, then down another, winding staircase to a subfloor, where they followed a low stone hallway lit with wall sconces. They passed two servants, who glanced curiously at Stephan and Teleo. More musty hallways and a short tunnel led to another steep, narrow service staircase, which wound up in a tight corkscrew of smooth stone steps. They climbed it and emerged onto a wide hallway that ended at a stone wall. A red satin banner embroidered with a gold rampant griffin hung on the wall above a small table and a vase of dead flowers. A large wooden door was guarded by two men. These were soldiers, not doormen, and they watched curiously as the child servant and Teleo-the-Minister-Physician strode towards them.

The soldiers stood with a wide stance, hands at their sword hilts.

"I am here to speak with the empress," Teleo said in his best Sapphire Valley accent.

"She does not take visitors," the older of the soldiers said flatly.

"I am a doctor and have been summoned to check on her health," Teleo said.

"We have not heard of any ill health with the empress. If she were unwell, we would have been informed."

"Stephan, wait on the stairs," Teleo said softly, and the boy scurried to the stairwell from which they had come and disappeared into the dark recess.

"I don't recognize you," the soldier said with an edge of wariness.

"That's true," Teleo said. "I'm new." He smiled at the soldier and dipped his head in a polite bow. "May I pass?"

"No. I'm sorry."

"The emperor sent me," Teleo said.

"That is unlikely," the soldier said, his eyes narrowing. "Prove it."

Teleo pulled out the diamond pendant from the leather bag at his neck and held it up until it caught the light. "Do you recognize this?"

The man scowled at the glinting diamonds, and his face softened. "No, I don't."

Stupid Cornwal had not known its power and had kept it hidden. Unfortunately, the diamonds' influence accumulated over time and did not turn the soldier to pudding immediately.

"I'm sorry, you still cannot pass," the soldier said, with sincere reluctance. "Ask the emperor to tell Raedwald, and he will let me know."

"Good idea," Teleo said. "Is the general in the lower bailey?"

The soldier shrugged his shoulders. "I believe they are training in the yard now, yes."

Teleo took a tired breath. "You can let me in and live," he said, "or put up a fight and try your luck."

The older soldier chuckled derisively, his eyes sliding up and down Teleo's luxurious cloak and powered wig. His gaze stopped at the helmet under Teleo's arm and flitted to the scars on his face and his Verdant Valley features.

Teleo tucked the pendant away and considered his next move, then set the helmet on the floor, stepped forward, and punched the man in the face. He took the soldier by surprise, but the man recovered quickly and the second soldier jumped into the fray. After a bit of a struggle, Teleo prevailed, killing the first one with a knife to the throat, and the second with a headlock that turned into a grappling session on the floor and ended with a broken neck.

Teleo picked up his helmet and pounded on Larissa's door with his gauntleted fist.

"Stephan," Teleo called out.

The boy emerged from the stairwell and gaped at the dead guards.

"Don't look," Teleo said, pulling the boy to him. Teleo tugged on a silk cord that hung near the door. After a minute, Larissa cracked open the door. It took her a moment to recognize Teleo in his disguise, but she appraised the situation quickly and held the door open. Teleo pushed the boy inside. She bustled Stephan into a sitting room while Teleo dragged the soldiers' bodies into a vacant maid's chamber and cleaned the floor tiles of blood. Teleo pulled off his gauntlets, his wig, and his two cloaks, tossing them onto the narrow bed. He took the opportunity to relieve himself in the maid's water closet and washed up using the marble basin, which was outfitted with its own water pump, orange blossom soap, and starched linen towels.

Feeling almost human again, Teleo joined them in the sitting room.

Empress Larissa was formally dressed in an emerald-green gown and was seated on an overstuffed blue velvet couch, her satin skirts draped to the floor. She gestured to a large leather chair, and Teleo gratefully took a seat.

The boy regarded him quizzically. "You're a doctor?"

"Of sorts," Teleo said, to the amusement of the empress.

"Is it done?" she asked, her eyes betraying hope and fear.

"Yes," Teleo said, casting a wary glance at the boy.

Her gaze turned to the orphan and then to Teleo. "Tell me, do you … recognize each other?"

"No," Teleo answered. "He's too young. My boy would be fifteen by now."

"Oh, yes," she said, frowning, then turned to Stephan. "Come upstairs to my roof garden. Have you ever been up there?" She led the boy into the foyer and up a set of circular metal stairs, chatting as they went. "I have hummingbird feeders up there, and a goldfish pond. Do you like hummingbirds? They like a gentle rain. It's not too cold for you, is it? Come underneath the awning." Her voice drifted away and a gust of fresh air flowed down into the sitting room.

A few minutes later, the empress returned alone. "Poor child," she said. "Come, Tesserman, you must tell me everything."

Larissa led Teleo through a series of rooms: a library, a bedchamber, a dressing room, and finally into the Heliotrope chamber. Like Sigrid's Heliotrope and those at Trillifort, it was in a round room of a tower. The diamond and petal mosaic was unobstructed, with several small rugs rolled up and stacked against the wall, and sparse furnishings lining the perimeter. The stone pattern gave him strength just gazing upon it. He stepped onto the Heliotrope, and warmth flowed up through his legs, filling his body.

"So. Cornwal?" she asked, her eyebrows pinching together.

"Dead," he said, handing her the diamond pendant.

She examined it for a brief moment and then pushed it back at him with a scowl. "I don't want this. Take it as part of your payment."

He inclined his head and returned the pendant to the leather bag at his neck, secretly pleased.

"Was it … painful for Cornwal?" she asked.

Teleo couldn't tell if she was asking out of some sort of sadistic vengeance or if she harbored some affection for the tyrant.

"Not very," he said.

She swallowed. "What about the ministers?"

He made a cutting motion across his throat.

"All seven?" she asked.

"Yes. Everyone was right where you told me they would be."

She threw her arms around his shoulders in a hug, surprising him. He patted her back awkwardly. She let go and held him at arm's length. "You are truly my hero. I was afraid my hopes were unreasonable and you would have sacrificed yourself for naught."

Teleo shrugged. "None were fighting men."

"No," she said, shaking her head. "They were only good at counting money. How did you get through the Palace Gate and inside their chambers?" she asked.

"I snuck in," he said.

She narrowed her eyes at him. "Impressive," she said. "Only one more problem to take care of before we ring the tower bell and call forth the Hill Tribes."

"Yeah, I know," he said reluctantly. "Raedwald." Teleo sat carefully in a delicate wooden chair at a small round table. "What about the castellan—Pfaff, is that his name?"

Larissa sat across from him and said, "Pfaff is mine. He has kept me sane these past few hellish years. But Raedwald would kill his own mother to get what he wants. It is thought that Raedwald orchestrated the coup and was the one who murdered Arnie. All because Cornwal promised Raedwald riches. Pfaff says it was Raedwald's idea that Cornwal should marry me, because of my Bedon blood." Her voice was bitter. "I am his connection to the old ruling lineage. Without me, he is nothing. I suppose it is better than the alternative," she said wryly. "Cornwal had wanted me killed. Or so he liked to tell me whenever I angered him."

"You were in a tough situation," Teleo said. He leaned his elbow on the table and rested his head in his hand.

"What's wrong?" she asked, pouring him a glass of water.

He drank it and sat back, wiping sweat from his brow. "It's been a long day. Do you travel to Red Flag from this room?" he asked.

"Yes," she said.

"Would you allow me to dance the sword? It may give me energy."

"Yes, of course."

Teleo drew his swords and went into his forms, circling the room a few times until his blood was flowing and his muscles loosened up. He did not leap as he liked to do, wanting to spare his throbbing head, but he felt invigorated nonetheless. He wished Sigrid were there to dance with him, to make the floor light up and the tiles flow in a swirling vortex and infuse him with energy. He came to a stop, wiped his brow, and drank more water.

The empress watched from her seat, which was situated under the Heliotrope's Focal Point. Her hands were clutched together, her knuckles white. "We cannot delay," she said. "Where did you leave the ministers' bodies, and Cornwal's?"

"In their chambers," Teleo said.

"Someone will find them and raise an alarm," she said.

"They will notice something odd eventually," Teleo said. "But I locked the doors. The guards are ... um, gone. And they recently had a shift change." He set the brass keys on the table and pushed them towards her. "What is our next move?" he asked. "Your guard thought Raedwald would be in the training yard."

"Yes," she agreed. "Probably in the lower bailey or the adjoining office, meeting with his officers or drilling his personal guard." She stood up and unlocked a wooden chest, then returned to the table and unrolled a map. "His training yard is the site of the other Heliotrope," she said, pointing her quill at a rectangular yard with a diagram of a ten-pointed star at its center.

"Has he danced the sword during the Summer Solstice?" Teleo asked.

"I do not know," she said, leveling her gaze at him.

"Have you?" he asked.

She shook her head. "No, I have not. Sigrid only told me about that recently. We are all discovering different pieces of the lost art of magic."

"We are," he agreed. "How many soldiers will be with Raedwald?"

"I don't know," she said. "A dozen? Two dozen? And they will know how to fight."

Teleo shook his head tiredly and leaned his elbow on the table again as a wave of dizziness passed over him. Maybe he should just step on the Sun Circle, go to Red Flag, curl up with Sigrid, and sleep for a few days. But duty called, and so he stood up, waited for his lightheadedness to pass, and walked to the center of the room.

He knelt at the Sun Circle and rested his palms on the smooth Angel Wings marble, absorbing the texture and committing the sensations to memory in case he needed to travel to this room in an emergency. Shadows flitted inside the stone, and he imagined Sigrid on the other side, watching him. He pressed his hand against a shadow that could be her hand. She came into focus, gazing up at him through the circle, and suddenly he was in Sigrid's tower, kneeling on the floor next to her, both their palms pressed on the Sun Circle.

"Oh," he said, laughing. "I didn't mean to do that."

She gently pushed him onto his back on the stone floor and straddled him. He pulled her down and they kissed and rolled around until he was on top. He moved onto his side to keep the weight of his armor off her and stroked her cheek.

"Would that I had the time and energy to quench that fire in your eyes," he said, kissing her on the lips. "You are not going into the valley with the archers?" he asked.

"Someone had to stay and guard Red Flag," she said, pulling his head down for another kiss. She released his lips and looked up at him. "We are waiting for the tower bell to chime. Is the emperor dead?" she asked.

"Yes," he said.

"That's good," she said, raising herself up onto one elbow. "Are you okay?"

"I'm fine," he said. "The emperor was not expecting to be attacked in his own study."

She pursed her lips thoughtfully. "No, I suppose not." She peered at him. "You are indeed an assassin. Mora was not exaggerating."

Teleo lifted a shoulder in a half-shrug. "I do what needs to be done." He sighed and lay on his back, gazing up at the vaulted ceiling and stroking her hand, a wave of exhaustion overtaking him.

"But why has the bell not rung?" she asked.

"I still need to confront General Raedwald," Teleo said. "Victory is not assured until he is out of the way." Wearily, he rose to his feet and stood on the Sun Circle.

"How's your head?" she asked, standing with him and holding his hands.

"It's okay, but I'm exhausted. I don't know if I can finish the job," he said. In addition to his head feeling like an anvil under a hammer, his muscles were weak and trembly. He was unused to wielding the Stone Guardian magic, even with the aid of the diamonds. Although killing Cornwal, the seven ministers, and the guards had not been particularly challenging, every life he took sapped a little of his own will to live. But Raedwald stood between the Hill Tribes and their freedom, and Teleo needed to face him—the most celebrated of the Sapphire Empire warriors. Teleo was not sure he would survive this one. "Will you dance with me?" he asked Sigrid. "Can you make the floor light up like you do?"

She squeezed his hands. "I'll try."

They danced the sword. Sigrid leapt and spun through the air, steel blade swinging overhead while Teleo moved deliberately through his two-handed sword forms, crouching and turning.

Slowly, the Heliotrope accelerated its rotation, the mosaic's tiles folding over themselves, blurring into a spinning disk of white light. Teleo was lifted off his feet, as if caught in an updraft and spiraling in lazy circles—a gyrfalcon on the wing. His blades flashed and sparkled, lightning and fire. Time slowed down, or perhaps it sped up—because soon he was dropped onto his feet. He fell to his knees, panting and overcome with a silent buzzing that vibrated his bones.

He rolled down onto his side and cradled his head on his bent elbow and closed his eyes, sliding helplessly into a velvety blackness.

He awoke with Sigrid sitting by his side and holding his hand. She assured him he had passed out for only a minute.

"Are you ill?" she asked.

"No," he said, rising to his feet and stretching with a big yawn. "I don't think so. I feel good, actually." He pulled her to him and kissed her lips. "You smell amazing. You put lemon verbena in your hair again," he said, nuzzling her ear.

"Stop that," she said, giggling.

"I love lemon verbena," he said, squeezing her and making her giggle more.

"Teleo!" she scolded. "Be serious. We don't have time."

"Oh, okay," he said, letting her go. "You're no fun."

"The tribes are waiting," she said, straightening her collar. "Wait," she said. "Let's take a look at Raedwald's battle yard. It was empty earlier."

"Good idea," he said. He was not very skilled at seeing things through the Sun Circle, but Sigrid was. They knelt side by side and peered down into the murky stone.

"What's that?" he asked as two shadows flitted by.

"Soldiers," she said, gazing fixedly at the white circle. "It looks like they are slowly gathering. For practice, I think. They are too casual to be gathering for war."

"How many of them?" he asked.

"I see four. No, six. I'm not sure. It's fading in and out." She looked up at him, worry creasing her brow.

"I must go," he said, standing and sheathing his swords. "Goodbye, my love," he said.

"I'll see you soon," she said, fear burning in her eyes.

"Of course you will," he said, steeling his heart against any other outcome. After one last kiss, he stepped onto the Sun Circle. He closed his eyes and when he opened them again, he was standing in Larissa's chamber.

———◆———

"Where did you go?" Larissa asked, hovering tensely near the Sun Circle.

"Sigrid is fine," Teleo replied. "Thanks for asking."

A smile almost cracked the empress's lips, but the strain of the day was too much. "You need to find Raedwald," she said. Her severe look and stiff posture made her appear as though she had already assumed the mantle of empress. She was dressed the part in the emerald-green dress with large puffy sleeves trimmed with red and gold, and a thin circlet of gold holding back her long black hair.

"I will need help," Teleo said. "I don't really feel like dying today."

"Yes. I mean, no, of course not," she said. "I will get you some help. Come with me to the kitchens. If you can take care of Raedwald, I will take care of the rest."

They discussed their plan. Teleo would try to kill Raedwald and subdue his officers or, at least, trap them in the bailey. Larissa would organize a takeover of the palace by the servants. They would draw as many guards as possible outside the building with some sort of disturbance or festival distraction and then barricade the palace and wait for the Hill Tribes to come to the rescue.

"It could work," Teleo said. "Get Stephan. I need his help."

Larissa went up to the roof and returned to the sitting room with the orphan. Teleo met them there and sat in a chair facing the child.

"I need you to do something for me," Teleo said.

Stephan's eyes grew round.

"Don't worry," Teleo said. "It's not hard. I need you to climb the bell tower. Have you ever been up there?" Stephan nodded, relief plain on his face. "Good. Larissa, can the lower bailey be seen from the bell tower?" Teleo asked.

"I think so, yes," she said.

"Good," Teleo said. "Stephan, I need you to climb up there and watch the lower bailey. If all goes well, I will be fighting down there. You will see me either win or lose."

Teleo hesitated. In all their planning, they had never discussed what they would do if he were killed. The plan was that Teleo would clear the way by killing the emperor and Raedwald—the ministers had been Larissa's idea. Then the Hill Tribes would flood the valley and surround Sapphire City. Once the imperial soldiers learned that Cornwal and Raedwald were dead, they would change sides and support the Hill Tribe rebellion. It was a gamble but not an unreasonable one. They had not considered what they would do if Cornwal were slain but Raedwald were victorious. Would the soldiers change sides then? Perhaps Raedwald would seize power and the Hill folk would be slaughtered by soldiers still loyal to the general or afraid to defy him.

"If I win," Teleo continued, holding the nervous gaze of the twelve-year-old, "I need you to ring the bell. Can you do that?"

Stephan blinked. "What if you lose?" His voice was a squeak.

Teleo exchanged glances with Larissa.

"You will still ring the bell," she said, getting to her feet and lifting her chin. "Either way, when the fight is over, you will ring the bell."

Stephan slid off the chair onto his feet. "Yes, Your Highness," he said with a deep bow.

The empress patted the boy's shoulder. "Very good. Once you start ringing the bell, don't stop until you hear the Hill fortresses ring their bells in reply. Do you understand?"

Stephan nodded.

Teleo wanted to object, but Larissa was standing right in front of him. If Teleo lost and Raedwald became Emperor, there was a good chance that Raedwald would take Larissa for his wife, or perhaps execute her. Teleo swallowed. When the Hill fighters answered the tower bell and streamed into the valley, a civil war would break out. Father against son. Brother against brother. The Hill rebels would be sorely outmatched. Groups of woodsmen and farmers—hungry and on foot, bearing old swords and hunting bows, hoes and scythes—would be up against well-fed soldiers and cavalrymen, who rode mounts stolen from the citizens and were outfitted with the finest armor and swords from Red Flag's own forges.

Teleo held his tongue. He had to win. That was the only acceptable result.

He left the wig and silk robe on a chair, clasped his fox-and-hare cloak around his shoulders, donned his feathered helm, and followed Larissa and Stephan from the empress's chambers. They navigated the servants' hallways and stairways, brushing past an elderly cleaning woman who stared after them, and then hurried across the sprawling complex to the bell tower. They sent Stephan up the narrow circular stairway towards the giant bell, and Teleo and Larissa headed to the palace kitchens.

30

RAEDWALD

The kitchens were abuzz with festival preparations for the feast the following day. Mounds of dough were rising, vegetables were being chopped, and pies were in the ovens.

Larissa gathered the cooks and quickly told them that the emperor and ministers were dead and she was taking the throne. Joy, relief, and worry played across their faces. Some dispersed to gather more servants; some stared at all the food, no doubt wondering what would come of the solstice feast; and others lined up knives and meat cleavers on the butcher's block, taking stock of their weapons.

The castle staff were clearly Larissa's people. Castellan Pfaff showed up—a tall, thin, elderly man who displayed genuine affection for the empress. He and a group of household staff huddled to plot a distraction for the palace guards. Teleo stepped out into a quiet hallway with Larissa.

"There are weapons on the walls of the ministers' chamber," Teleo reminded her.

"I know," she said. "I will make my way over there in due time."

"Okay. I am going to find Raedwald now," he told her. "By myself. Send men to be ready outside the lower bailey. I will try and kill Raedwald and then escape through the Heliotrope. Your men should secure the bailey from the outside, locking the other soldiers inside."

She understood. Teleo turned and strode down the hallway, pulling his fox-and-hare hood over his helmet and closing the cloak across his chest, concealing him from head to toe in its shifting shadows.

Teleo exited the western wing through a rear service entrance. The lower bailey was down the hill, beyond the kitchens and herb gardens. The fragrant gardens were quiet except for birds flitting about. He descended blue stone steps two at a time and then peeked around a curved lapis lazuli wall. The interior of the lower bailey was partially visible from this vantage point, sitting down below and surrounded by twelve-foot walls. Several soldiers were conducting a training exercise in the large yard, swords clashing, steel against steel.

Teleo drew his cloak more tightly around his armor and crept down a stairway, which meandered through budding lavender and rosemary bushes and past a stone gazebo. He stealthily approached a rear gate to the bailey. The rain had stopped and a gentle breeze wafted in from the north. Hints of mint and honeysuckle mingled with the heavy scent of moist earth. A fine day to die, he considered, as he often did when about to enter battle. One thing he had determined long ago: if he had to die, let it be outdoors under the sky and the sun, the rain or the snow, the moon or the stars. It did not matter which. Just not in a stinking, rotting dungeon.

He stood against the wall outside the closed gate, listening. It was quiet at this end of the yard. The clanging of swords had stopped and several men's voices drifted over the wall. There were the gravelly voices of war veterans, resonant voices of men in their prime, and the fiery voices of young men feeling their strength.

A commanding voice barked orders, and the clang of swords resumed, sweeping gradually across the yard as the men sparred. Teleo stepped into the wall, letting the rock matrix engulf him. He halted in the middle of the blue lapis lazuli, gold flecks floating alongside him. Sound was muffled, as though he were underwater. He stepped forward, poking his face out of the wall but leaving his body inside.

The Heliotrope spread out before him, dominating the long, rectangular yard with its concentric rings of stone and the large Sun Circle at its center, surrounded by ten black Down in the Deep rays. Grime dulled the colors of the surrounding stones, but the pattern was clearly evident to Teleo's eye. There were two dozen men training on the circular mosaic and two men moving along with them, instructing. Others watched from the sides of the yard, seated on benches. A few men looked down from ramparts on the outer wall, leaning their elbows between the teeth of the battlements, longbows poking up behind their shoulders.

It was not difficult to pick out Raedwald. He was standing at the head of the yard, his arms folded as he observed his men with a thoughtful expression.

"Put your weight behind it, Blackman," he shouted. "Keep your elbow in, Jimbo," he told another.

Raedwald was a large man, with black hair hanging in several braids below his helmet, long black moustaches, and a trailing goatee. He had a strong brow, calm eyes, and a voice that conveyed care and concern, not criticism. Teleo was immediately drawn to the man and wondered how the Verdant Valley forces would have fared under his leadership, versus the constantly changing commanders he'd served under, the ilk of Gerik Stagga and worse.

The Sapphire Valley general wore lightweight metal armor of many small, square, overlapping plates hanging from his shoulders and hips, painted blue and decorated with leather tassels and feathers. Unlike the steel helmets of the soldiers, Raedwald's helmet was polished bronze, with two boar tusks protruding from the sides and a blue chainmail coif covering his neck. A long black leather vest hung open over the chest armor and draped to his knees. Four sword handles held the vest open, two at each hip, sparkling with gem-covered pommels. Rows of small black throwing knives were sheathed in two bandoliers crossing his broad chest.

Four other men stood outside an open door to a room Teleo assumed was the office. The stone room appeared to be a recent addition and took up a corner of the yard. The four men's heads were bent together in quiet conversation. They also wore bronze helms, with tufts of stiff boar's hair sticking up from the conical peaks. Teleo determined that they must be Raedwald's senior officers.

Soldiers crossed swords up and down the yard, oblivious that under their feet lay a magical circle of stone—a Mages' battle yard as large as the one at Verdant Castle. The Angel Wings marble at the center peeked out in gleaming patches between muddy footprints, and the Focal Point window stood high on the eastern wall, in an arch built up to support the proper position of the open circle. Beyond the arch, poking up from inside the palace compound, stood the bell tower. Teleo hoped Stephan was watching from the belfry.

Teleo waited patiently for the right moment to confront the general. The moment came when they took a break and

Raedwald headed for the office door not far from where Teleo was encased in stone. Teleo stepped silently from the rock and moved slowly along the edge of the yard, letting the filtered daylight play off the fox-and-hare cloak against the lapis lazuli wall. When Raedwald was four paces away, Teleo pushed back the hood and threw the cape over his shoulders, exposing the sword handles poking up from behind his back.

Raedwald stopped and regarded him, unperturbed. "Who are you?" he asked.

"I am Empress Larissa's champion," Teleo replied. "She has rid the palace of the emperor and his ministers. The throne is hers now. I give you the opportunity to stand behind her."

Raedwald's face puckered as if he were eating a sour plum, then he threw back his head and laughed. His laughter trailed off and he wiped at his moustaches, his officers glancing over curiously. "Oh?" he asked, raising thick black eyebrows. "She fought them off with her embroidery needles, did she?" He threw back his head and guffawed again. "Oh ... wait, let me guess. *You* killed them. By yourself." The man waggled his eyebrows at Teleo, as though they were old friends trading jokes.

Teleo's initial warmth for the man cooled. "Are you refusing my offer?" Teleo asked.

Raedwald's smile dropped, replaced by a dark scowl. "You don't deny that you killed the emperor?"

"He fancied himself a knife fighter," Teleo replied. "He should have been training with you instead of trying to learn magic."

Raedwald drew two swords, the steel blades ringing. Light glinted off them as Raedwald lunged forward, the long blades cutting crosswise through the air where Teleo's neck had been. Teleo had seen the man's hands move before the blades followed, and ducked, springing off his hands and landing in a crouch several paces away, drawing both swords. Teleo stepped onto the dust-covered Heliotrope and danced the sword to the center stone, leaping and flying through the air as the soldiers backed away to give their general room to deal with this stranger.

Raedwald entered the outer fighting circle, his eyes narrow slits as he inspected Teleo. The soldiers crowded around the perimeter, and the gaps on the battlements filled with guards, arrows nocked. Raedwald jumped forward and they crossed swords, testing each other's strength and mettle. They were well-matched, and perhaps Raedwald was even stronger. Teleo backed away, conserving his energy and looking for an opening. They crossed swords again, then backed off.

"Where are you from?" Raedwald asked, not even breathing heavily. "Verdant Valley?"

"Aye," Teleo said.

"I believe I've seen you fight before. You killed my best general."

Teleo shrugged and adjusted his grip on the short sword. "It was war."

"It was. Why are you disrupting our long-sought peace?" Raedwald asked.

"Because Cornwal was a tyrant," Teleo answered.

"No worse than any other," Raedwald said.

Teleo cocked his brow, and replied, "He was basically enslaving his own people."

"For their own good," Raedwald said, and Teleo leapt forward, his respect for the general falling another notch.

Teleo went in with one of his best moves, flipping sideways through the air with simultaneous slashes to the backs of Raedwald's arm and thigh. Raedwald responded with his own spinning leap, avoiding the blades by a finger's width and leaving a shorn feather floating in his wake. Raedwald had been dancing the sword as well, Teleo feared. At least the Heliotrope was not lighting up. It looked neglected. Perhaps Raedwald had not known to dance during the solstice. Teleo could only hope. His last move had ceded the center to the general, and Raedwald stood on the Sun Circle, grinning smugly.

"Too bad we did not have the chance to become better acquainted," Raedwald said. "You should have approached me earlier and we could have worked out our problems together."

"Could have," Teleo said, not liking the look in Raedwald's eyes.

The general sheathed his swords in one practiced motion and started spinning. Faster and faster he spun, the square panels of his blue armored skirt fanning out around him, black braids flying, tassels and feathers swirling in a blur.

Teleo watched, mesmerized, as the Heliotrope began spinning as well. A wind kicked up, flapping Teleo's cloak and sending puffs of dust into the air. Teleo crouched, his swords at the ready, and crept around the circle, preparing to attack.

Black knives flew from the spinning vortex. Teleo dodged them with a sideways flip, and soldiers grunted behind him. Teleo landed on his feet, panting, as the circle of soldiers fell back and ran for cover. Two soldiers lay fallen, black knives protruding from their faces.

More knives flew from the swirling general, and Teleo dodged again with a flying cartwheel. He realized he should have reversed direction as a knife bounced off the back of his steel cuirass and the punch of two knives struck him in the calf and back of the thigh, pain lancing up to his groin. He did not stop dancing but spun and leapt, circling closer to the center, knives stuck in his leg. A blade struck his upper arm below his shoulder guard, making him drop his short sword. He spun away and hopped into the air as more knives flew at ankle level. A blade caught him in his foot, impaling him through the top of his boot. He landed on his feet, the searing pain of the steel bringing him to his knees. Another knife bounced off his shoulder armor and another pierced the chainmail curtain at his neck, dangling from the side. Teleo bowed his head, panting, his vision going black, then a blow to his jaw sent him sideways. The blade lodged in the meat of his jaw and another struck him in the armpit. Teleo opened his eyes and the yard blurred and wavered.

Raedwald came out of his spin and landed on his feet. The wind died down and the Heliotrope grew still. Teleo watched dizzily as the thick legs of Raedwald approached. Both Teleo's swords were gone. He pulled a hammer from his belt and flung it at the boar tusk helmet and reached for his knives. Raedwald dodged the hammer, raised his steel gauntlet, and easily deflected the knives and another hammer Teleo flung with the last of his strength. Teleo struggled up onto his good foot, and Raedwald kicked him in the gut, sending him sprawling onto the stones, the blade in Teleo's arm hitting the ground. He screamed and pulled the blade out, blood soaking his elbow as he forced himself onto his foot and one knee.

"Tie him up," Raedwald ordered. "I want to question this bastard at the tip of my knife."

The deafening clang of the tower bell made Raedwald stop and turn to the sound.

DONG. DONG. DONG.

Thwack. Thwack. Thwack.

Raedwald pivoted. Three arrows protruded from his back, harmlessly lodged in his armor.

Sigrid stood on the Sun Circle, longbow drawn.

Thwack.

An arrow lodged in Raedwald's neck coif. His hand went to his knife bandolier but came up empty.

DONG. DONG. DONG.

Arrows rained down from the battlements and landed harmlessly on the Sun Circle.

Thwack. Thwack. Thwack.

Sigrid was across the Heliotrope, on the far edge.

Thwack.

Suddenly, she appeared on the opposite edge.

The Heliotrope glowed as she flitted from spot to spot, archers
targeting her from the ramparts but their arrows meeting empty
stone as she disappeared and reappeared in different places,
loosing arrows as she went.

Thwack. Thwack. Thwack.

DONG. DONG. DONG.

The tower bell stopped ringing, the sonorous gonging fading
away as Teleo dragged himself towards the Sun Circle, coughing
up blood as he went. Bells tolled in the distance—the frantic,
ominous pealing coming from the north, south, east, and west. An
arrow whizzed past his ear. Another bounced off his armor. Two
lodged in his legs. Teleo grunted and glanced over his shoulder.

Raedwald was clutching an arrow shaft protruding from his
eye as he fell to his knees, blood trickling down his face. The
general fell forward as Teleo reached the Sun Circle and pressed
his palms onto its surface.

Teleo closed his eyes and felt the smooth stone of Red Flag
tower's Sun Circle, and when he opened his eyes, he was in
Sigrid's Heliotrope chamber. The Red Flag bell tolled nearby.
He crawled away from the Sun Circle and moments later, Sigrid
was kneeling at his side.

She stood up, crossed the floor, and threw open a window.
"Tildie, get the doctor," Sigrid yelled over the gonging. "Hurry!"

Teleo's cheek rested on the cold stone floor and he watched
as blood seeped from his mouth, forming a small puddle on a
Down in the Deep ray.

31

SUMMER SOLSTICE

Teleo woke up in Sigrid's bedchamber with a doctor leaning over him. The doctor explained that he had sutured Teleo's knife and arrow wounds, put a tube into his punctured lung under his arm, bandaged his broken foot, removed two broken teeth in the back of his mouth, and wrapped a bandage around the crown of his head and under his chin to keep his broken jaw clamped shut. Teleo spent the next few hours throwing up the medicine the doctor had given him and painfully coughing up blood, which he spewed through his nose and clenched teeth into a basin.

Finally, he collapsed into bed with his bandaged legs propped up on pillows.

He awoke again to find Aunt Tildie sitting in a chair at his bedside, mending a tear in his fox-and-hare cloak. The windows were dark and a small fire flickered over a bed of coals in the fireplace. Aunt Tildie looked up. "Ah, you are awake. Good," she said, tying off a thread and clipping it with a small knife. "Your cloak should be good as new. Quite an interesting weave," she commented, standing and draping the cloak over the back of a chair. She shuffled to his side and tried to stick a waterskin spout between his lips.

"Wait," he mumbled, unable to open his mouth. "I've got it," he said through his teeth, and took the flask, wincing as the rib under his armpit felt like a hot poker was stabbing it. He drank, then sank back into the pillows, exhausted from the effort. He hurt everywhere. "Where's Sigrid?"

"Watching the battle."

"What battle?" he asked, trying to remember how he had gotten there.

"The battle to take Sapphire Valley. The Hill forces have entered the valley from every direction. They are drowning Cornwal's troops slowly but surely." A light blazed in her eyes, which reminded Teleo that she was indeed Sigrid's aunt and must have been a force to be reckoned with in her younger days.

"I want to watch," he said, trying to sit up.

She pressed firmly on his chest, pushing him back into the bed. "You're not going anywhere, young man."

"Hmph," he grunted, the fight with Raedwald coming back to him in bits and pieces. Sigrid had killed the general with an arrow through the eye socket, he recalled, reminding himself never to get on her bad side.

"You're lucky you're husky as an ox," she said. "Doctor Jackson said two blades just missed major blood vessels. But you still lost a lot of blood, your lung is pierced, and you broke a rib, bones in your foot, and your jaw."

"Right," he said, straining to breathe.

"He's also worried about infection," she added.

"Uh-huh," Teleo said. "Sounds like I'll live." He pushed himself up with one arm and gingerly swung his legs off the bed, to the loud protests of Aunt Tildie.

He brushed her hand gently aside and asked her to find something he could use as a crutch. She *tsk'd* with disapproval but left the room. He awkwardly pulled on a clean pair of linen pants and shirt he found folded on the bedside table, pulled the fox-and-hare cloak over his shoulders, and hobbled over to the window.

The dark valley was alight with fires and thousands of dots of torchlight scattered across the flatlands, mirroring the star-speckled sky. Teleo wondered if the soldiers knew that Cornwal and Raedwald were dead. He opened the window and a dull roar rose from the valley, as though he were overlooking the sea—but instead of waves crashing, the low rolling thunder was that of hordes of men killing each other.

Down below, he spotted Sigrid, Jarnsmidt, and several house folk standing on the bluff overlooking the valley, watching the battle.

Aunt Tildie returned with a proper crutch and helped him slide his uninjured foot into his boot. "I want to go down there," he said, hunching over in a coughing fit.

Aunt Tildie frowned with disapproval but did not argue. Teleo pushed blood and saliva through his teeth into a basin, then headed for the door. With the aid of the crutch and Aunt Tildie, he managed to hop down the stairs. He rested at the bottom, wheezing and bathed in sweat. She continued to scold him but helped him out to the overlook. Sigrid saw them and hurried over.

They joined Jarnsmidt and the rest of the castle staff at the wall at the edge of the cliff. Teleo was overcome with anger and helplessness as the din of battle and the stench of scorched flesh wafted up from down below. What had he unleashed? Where were Dinsmora and Jessum and Kaspari? Where were Will and Waite and the horses? He had done everything wrong. Abandoned those he loved. Handed the responsibility of the children over to his cousin. Sparked a civil war.

Teleo leaned against the stone parapet, wincing in pain. He was hot and shivering at the same time.

"We should go inside," Sigrid said, putting her arm around him. "You need to lie down."

He wanted to be down in the valley, fighting, but he could barely walk, or even breathe. He nodded reluctantly.

With Sigrid's help, he hobbled back upstairs and insisted on going up one more flight to the Heliotrope chamber, where they would have a better view of the valley. She left him there and returned with a feather bed and blankets and laid them out on the Heliotrope. She made him drink a foul herbal brew and changed his bloody bandages, bathing his sweaty skin as she went. When she was done, he sank into the puffy embrace of the bedding.

"Does your father know the power of the Heliotropes?" he asked groggily.

"I don't know. We never discussed it. I'm afraid to speak with him about it. I'm afraid he would prohibit me from practicing magic if he knew. I used to travel to the armory's Heliotrope in the middle of the night to practice, after he'd gone to bed. Sometimes, he makes criminals kneel in its Sun Circle when they state their case. He says they always tell the truth when they kneel upon that stone. It is widely known that my father is the most just king of all the seven kingdoms. He is always fair and kind, when possible."

"Fair and kind, when possible," Teleo mumbled. "That's a good way to be." He turned onto his side, trying to find a comfortable position. "Dance for me," he said.

He closed his eyes and listened as she removed her boots, took down her sword from the wall, and padded barefooted onto the Heliotrope. He felt more than heard her dancing. The breath of wind as she leapt by. The warmth of the floor as it began to glow. He cracked his eyes open and watched as she flew and spun, her skirts floating around her legs, her ruby-hilted sword flashing in the lantern light. He closed his eyes again, letting the heat of the Heliotrope sink into his bones, and drifted off to sleep.

He dreamt of little workmen trudging through his body—pushing wheelbarrows, carting away debris, and bringing fresh stones to build new walls. They shaped and shimmied the stones so they fit just right, then stepped back to admire their work. Then the workmen knelt and polished. More men came with baskets of gems—amber, diamonds, pearls, and sapphires. They strung them from threads in three-dimensional spiral patterns and hung their creations from the ceilings where they twirled slowly, catching the light and casting rainbows in all directions. Women came with baskets of embroidery floss and sat in a circle with lengths of linen and wool and silk, laying neat stitches in repeating patterns of stars and diamonds and flower petals. Red, tan, and brown. Black, white, and gray. Blue, pink, and purple.

Teleo awoke from his dream and opened his eyes. Sigrid was dancing in a trance-like state, weaving and turning slowly across the floor, which seemed to dip and swirl with her in waves of undulating light. He was hot and threw back the covers, then crawled half-naked onto the glowing Sun Circle. He lay on his back, spread-eagled, limbs outstretched. The stone was hot against his skin and soothed his aching bones and muscles. He closed his eyes and drifted off.

When he awoke, Sigrid was on the floor next to him, sleeping soundly on her side, her head cradled on her folded arm. The Heliotrope glowed and shimmered, and it seemed to Teleo that the pattern extended up into the air, or that they were down inside the stone matrix. He reached for the small leather medicine bag around his neck. It was still there. He felt inside for the diamond pendant and the scrap of hematite-beaded buckskin. Satisfied that they were safe, he closed the bag and let himself sink deeper into the Heliotrope, surrounded by grains of crystal sand. He was floating in a warm slurry, as though in the hot mineral baths at Trillifort. He let his mouth and nose stay above the surface and slept again.

He awoke with a start, afraid for a moment that he had become part of the stone mosaic and would never come out. He rolled onto his hands and knees, and Sigrid looked up at him, her eyes flashing with concern. She raised herself on one elbow and wrinkled her brow at him.

"What happened to your bandages?" she asked, sitting up.

Bloody bandages were coiled on the floor to either side of him. He felt his face with his hands and opened his mouth, working his jaw gently back and forth. With his tongue, he felt the gap where his molars had been. The teeth were still gone, but his gum was no longer sore. He locked eyes with Sigrid. She reached out and touched his arm. Teleo looked down. The sword wound on his bicep was a thin white line. Sinewy sutures hung off his skin, dried up. He picked them off and they crumbled at his touch. He inspected the wounds on his legs and under his arm. They were all healed. The flexible chest tube hung from a bandage still stuck to his skin. He drew in a deep breath and his lungs filled and deflated like normal. His head no longer ached, and his vision was crystal clear. He bent his leg and held his foot. There was a red spot on the top and a matching one on the sole where the blade had gone through. He wiggled his toes and felt along the metatarsal bones. Aside from a tingly feeling, he would never know his foot had been impaled by Raedwald's blade.

Sigrid ran her fingers over his smooth skin in wonder.

"It healed me," he said, his voice rasping with emotion. "The Heliotrope healed me. *You* healed me." Tears ran down his face, and Sigrid inspected his wounds in disbelief.

"I have seen the Heliotrope described in manuscripts as a healing circle," she said. "But I did not believe it was meant in the literal sense. They say its healing power is most potent in the light of the Summer Solstice sun."

"The solstice dawns this morning, right?"

"Indeed," she said, glancing at the dark window.

"Will you dance in its light with me?" he asked.

"I would love to," she said, sitting up. "But only one person can dance in a Heliotrope on the solstice. You should. It also imparts strength, and you'll need all the strength you can get if you're going back out onto the battlefield."

He smiled and ran his hand lightly over her smooth cheek. "But you said you wanted to learn to do that trick at will," he said. "The one where you hop across the Heliotrope in the blink of an eye."

"Ah, yes," she said. "That would be helpful."

"You did it with Raedwald," he said.

"I did," she said, smiling. "I don't know how. It just happened."

"I'll dance in the armory," he suggested. "You can dance here."

"Okay. Good idea," she said, her eyes brightening as she leaned in for a kiss.

◆

Teleo gazed out the tower window when the first hint of light appeared in the sky. Fires had burned down in the valley below, and the night was blessedly silent—but only for a while. At dawn, the fighting would resume, if he knew anything about men. They would all think the solstice was on their side and fight harder than ever—and more would die.

He had changed into his leathers, with the two swords Sigrid had lent him sheathed at his hips. Teleo pulled the fox-and-hare cloak around his shoulders, drawing the hood up over his head, then knelt on the Sun Circle. He pressed his palms to the Angel Wings marble and closed his eyes. He recalled the Heliotrope of the armory, feeling the sooty stone of its Sun Circle under his fingertips, smelling the acrid stench of coal smoke and hot steel.

He opened his eyes and found himself kneeling in its shadowy interior with his palms pressed against its Angel Wings marble disk, the pre-dawn gloom faintly illuminating the cavernous space through large windows. The four forges stood like black tombs against the walls. Teleo glanced around the empty armory. During a normal solstice, the blacksmiths would be taking the day off for the holiday. But today, most of the men were down in the valley, wielding swords instead of hammers.

Teleo pushed back his hood and stood up, inspecting the grimy pattern of the Heliotrope and the ash-coated Sun Circle, wondering if he should sweep the tiles. As he went looking for a broom, the door creaked open, and Teleo faded into the shadows.

Jarnsmidt locked the door behind him. He was carrying a lantern and a long cloth bundle. The elderly king crossed the floor and carefully unwrapped a sword and placed it on the Sun Circle, then went to the well and returned with a bucket of water. The king left and returned again with a footstool and a block of wood, which he placed in the center of the Sun Circle. He covered the block with the cloth, put the sword on the block, and sat on the footstool, folding his legs under him and examining the glinting steel blade.

Teleo glanced nervously at the Focal Point window. The sky was growing brighter. He held his breath, considering what to do.

Jarnsmidt cocked his head and turned Teleo's way. "Ho!" the old man called out. "Who's there?"

Teleo hesitated and then stepped forward into the lantern light.

Jarnsmidt squinted at him. "Tesserman? How'd you get in here? How come you're walking? Where are your bandages?" A look of fright crossed his face. "Are you a ghost? Have you died?" Jarnsmidt stood up, wavering on unsteady legs.

Teleo chuckled. "No. I just got better, that's all. Your daughter is a master healer. She gave me the key to get in."

Jarnsmidt frowned. "What? Why?" Understanding slowly softened his features. "Ah," Jarnsmidt said, narrowing his eyes at Teleo. "You are here to dance the sword."

Teleo approached the center of the Heliotrope. "You know about that?" he asked.

Jarnsmidt laughed. "Of course I know. Who do you think set Sigrid up in that tower? She is my daughter, after all, and I know what goes on in my own castle." Jarnsmidt winked, with a sly grin curving his lips.

"Well, then, what ...," Teleo said, looking down at the bucket, the block of wood, and the footstool. "Why are you not dancing the sword yourself? What is all this?"

"I am polishing a sword," Jarnsmidt said and then sat down again, pulled out a small square stone, and balanced it on his fingertips. "The final polishing. Done in the light of the Summer Solstice." He grinned up at Teleo.

"Ah," Teleo said, excitement rushing through his veins. "You are a Mage Swordsmith."

Jarnsmidt chuckled and shrugged. "Perhaps I am. These swords sell for more gold than a dozen normal swords—I know that much." He laughed again. "Each one takes two years to make. During the first solstice, I roll my wagon forge out here and fold the light into the metal. I spend all year hammering it to perfection. The second solstice, I begin to sharpen it, then spend the next twelve months sharpening and polishing. Today's dawn, during the third solstice, I will give it its final polish. Just like my ancestors have done throughout the ages." Jarnsmidt held up the blade, and its edge shone like a mirror.

"It already looks perfect to me," Teleo said, admiring the wave-like pattern of the steel.

"It will be perfect after today," Jarnsmidt said. He looked up at Teleo, concern etching his brow. "But you came here to dance the sword," he said to Teleo. He carefully set down the blade and rose slowly to his feet. "You must dance," Jarnsmidt said, stepping away from his footstool. "Then you must go down to the valley and help our men win," he said gravely.

"But what about your blade? Would that I had such a Mage's sword," Teleo said, admiring the crystalline blade, its honed edge pure white. "I didn't know any still existed."

"Oh, they exist. I've made at least a dozen Mage's Blades. Sigrid has one."

"The one with the ruby hilt?" he asked.

"One and the same," Jarnsmidt said. *Raven's Blood*. Too bad you can't dance the sword while I polish the blade. Then I would give you the finished sword to take into battle. But only one person can be in a Heliotrope during the Summer Solstice light. Duels were waged between Mages for the right to claim the sacred circle." Jarnsmidt bent down and began wrapping his sword.

"No, don't go," Teleo said. "I have an idea. I will travel to another Heliotrope and dance there. You must finish your blade."

"Brilliant idea," Jarnsmidt said, a broad smile lifting his moustaches. "Back to the Sapphire Palace?" he asked, with a knowing wink.

"No, I was thinking of another place," Teleo said. "If I could just access the Sun Circle for a moment, I will be on my way.

We don't have much time." The round Focal Point window was a pearlescent white and growing brighter.

"Morning comes," Jarnsmidt agreed.

Teleo carried the bucket and footstool to the perimeter of the Heliotrope. Jarnsmidt took the block and sword and stood to the side while Teleo approached the Sun Circle.

He knelt and placed his palms on the stone, looking down at it like he had so many times in the Third Tower when he had been searching for Sigrid. The Angel Wings marble was smooth, and he could smell the bat guano and hear their chirping. When he looked up, he was in the abandoned tower at Trillifort, a gust of cool mountain air wafting in through the open Focal Point window. Bats circled overhead, darting and weaving, as though glad to see him.

He stood up and stretched his arms, filled with contentment as though he had returned home after a long journey. He pivoted slowly, surveying the room. The chest of skulls sat closed by the cold fireplace, and the door was shut. Everything was just as he had left it.

He took the broom and quickly brushed away accumulated bat guano and dust. The many-colored stones of the Heliotrope took on a lustrous sheen, and the subtly undulating pattern came to life. When he finished sweeping, Teleo removed his boots and walked barefooted across the polished stones to the center circle, unsheathed his swords, and gazed up at the Focal Point.

The light in the round window slowly burnished from silver to copper to gold. Teleo pushed his cloak over his shoulders, the embroidered fabric draping down his back, and stood on the Sun Circle in anticipation, swords in hand, eyes fastened on the round opening.

He drew in his breath as a pink shaft of Summer Solstice morning light caught the edges of the window frame. His pulse quickened and he crouched into a defensive pose. Slowly, he began dancing—twirling and pivoting on the translucent marble center circle—on the stone quarried from the mountain-top Trillifort stood upon. He felt the weighty, grounding power of the local stone under his feet and wondered if the Trillifort Heliotropes were more powerful than the others because of it. An entire castle town built of Angel Wings marble.

Bats darted and swooped overhead as they fled the sun and settled into the upper recesses of the vaulted ceiling. Teleo stayed within the Sun Circle and danced, cutting the air with his blades, trying to catch the first ray of light as it crept down the western wall in a pure, golden shaft. He turned to face the stream of light and it blinded him for several beats of his heart. His face soaked in the blessed sunrays and shivers ran through his body. He pivoted in the beam of light, letting it touch him on every side.

Teleo's steel blades flashed as he carved the ray of light in a pattern of figure eights, as though unfurling the radiating petals of a flower. The flying blades reflected flashes of rainbow colors and sliced the vibrating beam into droplets of golden sunlight that landed like rain on the Heliotrope, merging with the carved bits of colored stone and setting them aglow. His consciousness melded with the rays and stars of the spiraling mosaic as it flowed around him. He was in it and on it at the same time. He was every stone tessera, whose shapes he knew by heart. He was the small pattern feeding into the larger pattern and shifting back to a single stone again. He was molten lava flowing through the earth and transforming into granite. He was the shells of sea creatures turned to sand in pounding waves and settling to the ocean floor. He was their essence merging and solidifying under the weight of the ages. He rose with mountains pushing up from the sea to tower over the land. He was the block of

marble cut by quarrymen. He was the Sun Circle carved by a
Mage Stone Master. He was the cosmic pattern that beat with
the pulse of the stars.

The sunray landed on the Sun Circle in perfect alignment.
The center stone ignited with a burst of golden light, radiating
through Teleo until he was glowing himself—a dazzling torch
lit from within. The entire room exploded in a brilliant flash,
lifting Teleo in a pulsating orb, as though he were inside the
sun itself. He could no longer feel the Sun Circle under his
feet as he slashed and swirled, his cloak fanning out around
him. Time lost all meaning as every fiber of his being vibrated
with light—became light—dispersing throughout the room
like so many tesserae of pink and gold and white, petals and
diamonds, blooming and dying, melting and crystallizing, over
and over again.

He gradually became himself again, a man wielding two
swords and dancing in the sunlight. He vaguely wondered
if he was floating, when the soles of his feet landed softly on
the marble. The circle of light tiptoed away from him across
the floor, and he edged forward with it, longing to stay in its
magical brilliance forever.

The sun slipped past the window, the yellow sunbeam
casting one final flicker, and suddenly the room was gray again.
Teleo sheathed his swords at the border of the Heliotrope and
slumped against the wall. He slowly slid down, sitting on the
cold stone floor and closing his eyes. His entire body vibrated.

He breathed deeply, letting the life-giving air permeate his
body and quiet his buzzing mind. The chirping of the bats
drew his attention to the vaulted ceiling. Their black, beady
eyes stared down at him from where they hung upside down
in furry clumps. His senses were acutely alert and he cocked
his head, listening for the sounds of the waking castle. A horse

neighed. A chicken loudly announced an egg she had laid. A gyrfalcon keened.

Rising to his feet on shaky legs, he stood at the edge of the shimmering Heliotrope, his body still buzzing. He pulled on his boots and then closed his eyes, focusing his thoughts on the pattern on the opposite side of the Third Tower's Heliotrope, and found himself standing on the spot he had intended. He focused his mind again and popped around the circle, practicing his newfound local traveling ability and wondering if his skill would fade with the waning solstice light. He finally landed on a black ray next to the Sun Circle, where he knelt and peered into the Angel Wings marble.

Sigrid gazed up at him from the translucent stone and smiled. "Oh, good," she said. "I found you." He heard her faintly but clearly and returned her smile.

———————◆———————

Teleo traveled to Sigrid's Heliotrope and wrapped her in his arms.

"How do you feel?" she asked.

"Better than ever," he said, gazing down at her. Her eyes shone like polished bronze.

She took his face in her hands. "Your old scars are gone now," she said, running her fingertips above and below his eye.

"They are?" he asked, touching his face. He felt almost sad—those scars had been a part of him for so long. He peeled off his jerkin, examining his bicep and the ribs under his armpit, and then kicked off his boots and rolled up his pant legs. All signs of his recent scars were completely gone, replaced by smooth, pink skin.

"Your whiskers are brown. No more gray," she said. "Your hair, too."

He rubbed his hands over his beard. "That, I'll take," he said. He gazed into her eyes. "And you are younger than ever." He took both her hands in his.

They examined one another, wondering at the secrets of the Heliotropes and the powers of the Mages.

"I must go find your father," he said.

Her brow wrinkled. "I saw him through the Heliotrope at the armory. I think he was polishing a sword."

"Yes," Teleo said. "He's a Mage Swordsmith, and he knows all about you dancing the sword."

Her mouth fell open. "He is? He does?"

"Yes," Teleo said. "Your ruby sword is a Mage's Blade."

Her mouth widened further.

Teleo shook his head and laughed. "Come on, let's walk over there."

They found Jarnsmidt still sitting on the Sun Circle, burnishing the blade. He looked up from his work.

"Almost finished," he told them, and turned back to the sword.

Teleo stepped outside into the sunshine with Sigrid. A short time later, Jarnsmidt joined them at the overlook, and together they watched the churning masses of humanity push and pull at one another, the roar of the battle already at full force.

Jarnsmidt turned and presented the sword to Teleo, holding it flat atop both his palms. The steel blade shimmered, and the sun flashed on its watery surface. "For you," Jarnsmidt said.

Teleo was tongue-tied. "I ... I can't accept it," he finally said. "It was rude of me to ask for it. I cannot pay you the gold it's worth."

"You didn't ask for it," Jarnsmidt said, extending the blade towards Teleo. "I offered it, and not because you are my daughter's suitor but because you killed Cornwal." Jarnsmidt lifted a bushy eyebrow. "That is worth more than its weight in gold, don't you think? Now, please accept the sword. I have named it *Heart Fire*."

Teleo bowed his head and took Heart Fire by its hilt. The blade had a single cutting edge, deep and razor-sharp and sparkling like a diamond. A fuller ran along the flat edge, stained red as though filled with blood. The grip was also red—crimson-dyed pigskin, spiral-wrapped in silver wire, with a large reddish-black garnet inset on each side of the thick, disk-shaped steel pommel.

Teleo hefted the long blade. The balance was perfect, making the heavy sword feel weightless. He swung the blade through the air, and it sang.

He bowed to Jarnsmidt again. The Mage Swordsmith handed him a sheath—polished black leather embossed with a red twining knot design.

"I am humbled," Teleo said.

"Don't be too humbled," Jarnsmidt said. "We have a war to win. Let's go."

"What do you mean, '*Let's go?*'" Sigrid asked, frowning at her father.

"Go get your armor and meet me back here," Jarnsmidt said to them both, and hurried towards the armory.

In Sigrid's chamber, Teleo pulled on his gambeson and steel-plate armor and then donned his plumed helm. He strapped the two swords he'd borrowed from Sigrid across his back and sheathed Heart Fire at his hip, along with his remaining hammer and chisels. He had lost all his other weapons in Raedwald's yard, so Sigrid gave him two daggers from her collection. He draped his fox-and-hare cloak down his back between the sword hilts and turned to Sigrid.

Sigrid wore her archer's leathers and was armed with Raven's Blood, several knives, her longbow, and two quivers of arrows. They traveled back to the armory one at a time through the Sun Circles. Teleo went to a forge and selected two hammers and hung them from his belt.

Jarnsmidt appeared, wearing a full suit of armor and a single sword hanging at his side.

"Don't you need more weapons than that?" Teleo asked.

"One good sword is all a man needs. *Dragon's Tooth,*" he said, patting the hilt. "Are you ready?"

They stood around the Sun Circle. "Should we go to the Sapphire Palace's battle yard?" Teleo asked. "Have you ever touched the Sun Circle there?" he asked Jarnsmidt.

"I have traveled to every Sun Circle in the Sapphire Empire, and then some," Jarnsmidt said. "You youngsters act like you invented Heliotropes." He cocked his eyebrow at Sigrid, who gaped at him.

"You could have helped me all these years, Papa, and given me some training. And you could have traveled to the other fortresses to alert them to the uprising."

"The Heliotropes do the training," he replied. "And how do you know I didn't travel to them?" He grinned mischievously. "Come. We are wasting precious time. Lives are being lost while we stand here yammering."

"Raedwald's warriors could be locked in the yard," Teleo warned them. "Although they may have escaped or been killed by now." He froze and stared at Sigrid.

"What's wrong?" she asked.

"Raedwald," he said, his throat tight.

"Raedwald?" she asked. "What about him?"

"If I was healed in the Heliotrope, he may have been as well. Arrows to the eye are not always fatal."

Sigrid stared back at him.

"I sold that pompous ass a Mage's Blade many years ago," Jarnsmidt said, frowning. "One of my best. *Black Lightning*. But he is not a Mage."

"Oh, he's a Mage," Teleo assured him.

"He's definitely a Mage," Sigrid agreed.

Worry wrinkled Jarnsmidt's brow. "Well. Nothing to do but face that bastard. We can't have him running around leading his troops against us, now, can we?"

Teleo and Sigrid shook their heads.

"Okay, that's settled," Jarnsmidt said. "One at a time. Who's first?"

"Wait," Sigrid said, kneeling and peering into the Angel Wings disk. She shook her head and stood up. "No one is there."

"Good. I'll go first," Teleo said, pulling on his gauntlets and unsheathing Heart Fire.

"Then me," Sigrid said, stepping aside and brandishing Raven's Blood.

"See you there," Jarnsmidt said, moving away from the Sun Circle.

Teleo stepped onto the round slab of marble, crouched into his guard position, and felt the soles of his boots resting flat on the smooth stone. He recalled Raedwald's battle yard and the snarling grimace when Sigrid's arrow pierced the general's eye.

Teleo blinked and the lapis lazuli walls reflected back at him. He was standing in the center of the Sapphire Palace's lower bailey with the intricate pattern of the battle-sized Heliotrope catching the morning sun. The yard was empty. Birdsong from the kitchen gardens drifted over the walls, and the rumble of war bled in from further afield. The bell tower loomed silently overhead, casting a long shadow like a sword blade splitting the yard in two. Teleo straightened and took a breath, then stepped aside. A moment later, Sigrid appeared, followed by her father.

They looked at one another, then the office door creaked open.

Raedwald shambled through the doorway, his blue scaled armor hanging from his tall frame, tassels and feathers dangling limply. One good eye inspected them while the other stared straight ahead, glassy and unseeing.

"I see the solstice magic didn't completely heal your eye," Teleo said to the man who hitched slowly across the Heliotrope. Black Lightning hung from his hand—Jarnsmidt's handiwork evident in the crystalline blade and diamond-studded pommel. "That's a shame," Teleo taunted, while Sigrid and Jarnsmidt warily watched Raedwald approach. "Too bad your men did not have the knowledge to lay your body on the Sun Circle during the solstice light," Teleo said. "You would have been good as new."

Raedwald fumbled for a knife in the bandoliers crisscrossed over his chest and flung it at him. Teleo ducked and the small blade whizzed overhead, clattering against the stone wall behind him.

"Let me pass," Raedwald croaked, heading towards the Sun Circle. "I must go home to see my daughter."

"Where is home?" Teleo asked, struck with a momentary pang of empathy for the distraught father.

Raedwald did not reply but continued shuffling across the yard, breathing heavily and using his Mage's Blade as a walking stick.

"The western Hill fortress," Jarnsmidt answered for him. "Gray Flag. Home of the silver mines."

"Ah, Jarnsmidt," Raedwald said in a raspy voice. "You still live, you old goat. My father always said you'd outlast us all.

Is this your daughter? She's good with a bow and arrow. You taught her well."

Raedwald approached the Sun Circle. Sigrid and Jarnsmidt stepped aside to let him pass.

"I honor you as a warrior," Teleo said, taking the center circle and blocking his way. "But I cannot let you live."

"No one *lets* me live," Raedwald said, brandishing his blade.

Black Lightning and Heart Fire clashed, sending sparks flying across the yard. Teleo parried, keeping Raedwald off the Sun Circle. The blades shimmered and glowed. Black Lightning slashed at Teleo's head and Heart Fire repelled the diamond blade. Teleo spun, infused with white light from the Trillifort marble, and swung his sword. The steel caught Raedwald in the neck and as the general stumbled, Jarnsmidt sank Dragon's Tooth into his back and Sigrid slashed him behind the knee with Raven's Blood.

The general's armor was no match for a Mage's Blade, much less three, and blood welled up and spilled over. Jarnsmidt yanked his sword free and Teleo wiped his own blade while Raedwald convulsed at their feet.

"He defied death once," Teleo said. "That is one time too many." He raised Heart Fire and let it fall across Raedwald's neck, severing his head in a single stroke. The head rolled to the side and blood spurted over the Angel Wings marble. Teleo kicked the head away from the spouting neck, long black braids trailing like dead snakes. He retrieved Black Lightning and handed it to Jarnsmidt.

"No, you keep it," Jarnsmidt said, stepping back a pace and staring down at the twitching, headless body. Sigrid turned away and Teleo heard her panting against the wall. Teleo went into Raedwald's office, where he found the sheath to Black Lightning, and slid it onto his belt opposite Heart Fire. He found his short sword and Aldeon longsword, cleaned and arranged neatly on a bench alongside Raedwald's other swords, none of them Mage's Blades. He unsheathed Sigrid's two swords from his back straps and laid them on the bench, leaving them there with his old weapons.

"Come on," he said to Sigrid, who was still huddled against the wall outside the office. "Let's go find Larissa." He supported her arm and crossed the yard to Jarnsmidt, who was cleaning his blade, his back turned to the sprawled corpse. "Wait a second," Teleo said, and disappeared back into the office. He found a polearm propped in a corner, grabbed Raedwald's boar tusk helmet, and returned to the yard.

"Wait outside," he said to Sigrid, motioning to the gate.

It was unlocked, and she and her father slipped out. Teleo dragged the headless corpse into the office, leaving a trail of smeared blood. He hoisted the body onto the table draped with white linen where the general must have been laid out. He folded Raedwald's arms over his chest and bandoliers, then frowned as blood from the neck stub stained the linen. A bundle of white linen was on the floor at his feet. Teleo poked at it and recognized it as a burial shroud. He used the shroud to wipe Raedwald's blood off his own armor, then went outside and cleaned the blood off the Heliotrope as best he could. He knelt and gazed into the Angel Wings marble, looking for Larissa's Heliotrope. To his delight, an image came into focus and expanded to show him Larissa's circular Heliotrope chamber. The room was empty.

Not having the time to dwell on his newly enhanced vision, he stood up and gingerly approached Raedwald's severed head, where it lay in a tangle of blood-soaked hair. Teleo held his breath and rolled the head upside down onto its crown. He held the skull steady between his boots and shoved the point of the polearm down into the pulpy mess of what was once a neck. When the polearm's blade was firmly lodged, he raised the head, strapped the boar tusk helmet under the bloody, bearded chin, and arranged the long mass of braids. Raedwald's good eye stared angrily at Teleo and the glassy eye stared off into space. Teleo left them open. He wiped up the rest of the blood, tossed the stained linen into the office, and left the yard with his prize on a pike.

Sigrid and Jarnsmidt were waiting in the shadows and gaped at Raedwald's head.

"Let's find Larissa," Teleo said, swiveling the general's grotesque face away from their horrified eyes. "She's not in her Heliotrope chamber. Where do you think she'd be?" he asked. "Where is the central keep?"

"The old keep is where the high castle is," Jarnsmidt said, swallowing and shifting his gaze onto Teleo. "That's where I'd go."

"Good enough. I know exactly where that is. Come on," Teleo said, and led them through the gardens.

———◆———

They passed through the abandoned kitchens and into the servants' corridor—a long dimly-lit hallway with low stone ceilings and dank air.

"Hold this," Teleo said, shoving the pike bearing Raedwald's head into Jarnsmidt's hand.

Jarnsmidt grimaced and pushed Raedwald's long bloody braids away from his arm.

Teleo clipped his gauntlets to his belt and drew his fox-and-hare cloak closed across his body armor, pulling the hood up over his plumed helm. The folds of the cape draped around him.

"Your cloak," Sigrid said. Her expression grew puzzled as her eyes meandered over the embroidery.

"Don't stare at it," he said, pulling the hood off. He locked eyes with her. "It helps conceal me."

"It's strange," she said, "I never noticed ..."

Jarnsmidt's eyes widened. "You have a Mage's Shroud?"

"A Mage's Shroud," Teleo mused, trying not to look at Raedwald, whose head stood at the same height as Jarnsmidt's. "Is that what it's called?"

"Hey. You didn't tell me that cloak is magic," Sigrid said accusingly.

Teleo quirked a smile at her. "There's a lot I haven't told you."

"Like what? More secrets? When are you going to tell me?" she asked, raising both eyebrows.

"Not *now,*" he said, raising his eyebrows back at her.

She faced him stubbornly, her hands on her hips.

He rolled his eyes. "I walk through stone walls," he said simply.

"You *what?*" she asked.

"I walk through stone walls," he repeated, shrugging.

"Like a Stone Guardian?" Jarnsmidt asked. Disbelief and horror flickered across Jarnsmidt's and Sigrid's faces.

"Yeah. I guess. But I'm *not* a Stone Guardian. I just learned some of their powers."

Sigrid's jaw dropped open.

"Come on, let's go," Teleo said, turning her gently by the elbow. "We can talk about it later." He raised his hood again, tucking the overly large plumes into its folds, tempted to slice them off with his dagger—and he would have, were the ornate helmet not a gift from Sigrid who stood there glaring at him. "Don't stare at the embroidery," he repeated as she scowled at him. "You either," he said to Jarnsmidt, who nodded and dropped his gaze. Raedwald's one good eye peered at him, and Teleo turned away, a shiver running up his spine.

Teleo guided them through the maze of tunnels and up a narrow set of servant stairs. They emerged into a wide, formal corridor, brightly lit with leaded-glass windows. No one was about.

A dull pounding thudded in the distance. They followed the sound down the corridor, stepping around streaks of dried blood. A glass vase was in pieces on the tiles, and a dead body lay twisted against the wall. It was a servant with his arm outflung and a carving knife still in his hand. They hurried past him, the thudding growing more intense.

The sound drew them to the main stairs leading to the upper level, which housed Cornwal's study, the ministers' chamber, and the high castle. They climbed, following the sound and stepping over two more servants where they had fallen dead on the stone steps.

At a turn in the stairwell, Teleo could hear men up around the next bend. He, Sigrid, and Jarnsmidt crept back down a level. The pounding echoed off the stone walls.

"Harder," a gruff voice said from above.

The distinctive thud of an axe sinking into solid wood struck once, twice, three times—each stroke accompanied by a loud huff. "Fucking ironwood," the voice said, and the pounding continued.

Teleo took Sigrid's hand and guided Jarnsmidt back downstairs and along another hallway in the direction of the servants' back stairwell. The hall turned and led to a long, windowed corridor. Vases of flowers decorated small tables, potted trees leaned towards bright windows, and wall hangings adorned the walls, depicting hunts with horses and hounds and fleeing bucks. Doorways stood open, revealing ornate reception rooms.

They were all empty. Teleo stopped and tugged on Sigrid's hand. The three of them backed into a small alcove. More pounding came from up ahead. They hesitated, then crept down the hallway towards the noise and peeked around another turn. A small group of soldiers waited while a large man hacked away at the door to the servant stairwell, where Stephan had guided Teleo from the ministers' chamber an entire lifetime ago. There were six soldiers, plus a seventh swinging the axe, all dressed in the blue and gray uniforms of the Sapphire Army.

Teleo and his companions retreated, hiding behind a potted fern tree. Teleo unclasped his fox-and-hare cloak and draped it across Sigrid's shoulders. He pulled the hood up over her head and clasped the pearl and moonstone closure at her neck. The embroidery around her face was exquisite. Dinsmora had outdone herself. Braided patterns intersected swirls, and pine boughs with tiny pinecones studded the edges.

"Don't stare at it," Sigrid breathed in barely a whisper. She reached up and turned his chin away.

He blinked and tried to focus on the task at hand. *Mage's Shroud,* he thought, intrigued. The crack of the axe brought him back to attention. The door's thick wood had split. They did not have much time.

He gestured to Sigrid and Jarnsmidt, and the three of them darted across the corridor and pressed their backs against the stone wall.

"Wait here," he whispered into Sigrid's ear, closing his eyes against the glamour of the cloak. He slipped on his gauntlets, gestured to Jarnsmidt to stay with Sigrid, and then stepped backwards into the stone.

The lapis lazuli flowed around him until he was totally submerged in it. He walked parallel to the hallway through the thick stone blocks, as though pushing through water, and emerged next to the door frame. The axe bit into the wood, and Teleo ducked up under the axeman's armpit and stabbed him in the neck. Blood spurted out, splashing onto Teleo's gauntlet. Teleo pushed the man down and wrested the axe from his grip, finishing him off with a well-placed blow of the sharp, heavy blade to the throat. Teleo stepped over the body and glared at the six soldiers, who watched in stunned horror, trying to understand what they had just seen.

"Raedwald's dead," Teleo said, wishing for a moment that he still carried the general's head, but his death did not appear to be news to them. "As is the emperor," Teleo continued. "The Imperial Ministers too."

Doubt twisted their faces as they gripped their swords. "We haven't seen Cornwal's head on a pike," one of them said. "How do we know he's dead?"

"Yeah," the others agreed. "Or the ministers. Where are their heads?"

"Maybe they're just hiding up there," another said. "The empress ran up there. Why would she still be alive if the emperor were dead?"

Teleo hefted the axe. "I will be happy to get the heads of Cornwal and his ministers for you. In the meantime, you can join me in supporting Empress Larissa, who rightfully rules the land now. Or you can die. Your choice."

The soldiers exchanged glances. Teleo shrugged and said lazily, "It's as good a day as any to die. For you, that is. But I'm tired of killing."

They traded glances again and two soldiers rushed him, swords raised. Sigrid's arrows hit the soldiers from behind while Teleo took one down with the axe and another with a hammer. The others turned to flee but were met with Sigrid's arrows from the front and Heart Fire from the rear. Soon they were all dead or twitching on the floor. Teleo wiped his blades and looked down at the bodies. One stared up at him, still alive, with blood seeping out of his mouth. The man gurgled as he gasped for life. Teleo knelt and slit his throat, like he would a goat. Teleo rose wearily to his feet as the man stopped struggling and grew limp. He slowly wiped his blades clean, sheathed them, and stuck the long axe handle through his belt. Sigrid and Jarnsmidt crept out of the shadows. Raedwald's head on the pike in Jarnsmidt's grip bobbed along as though the general were still embodied. Teleo waved them forward.

"All this armor is damned hot," Teleo complained to Jarnsmidt as he pulled off his helmet, sweat streaming down his face and neck.

"Better a hot warrior than a cold corpse, I always say," Jarnsmidt said.

"I'll die of heatstroke," Teleo muttered.

"That's why you should always carry water," Jarnsmidt said, handing him a plump waterskin.

"Thanks," Teleo said, and gratefully took a few mouthfuls, then passed the waterskin to Sigrid. "I lost mine somewhere along the way." He wiped his hand across his mouth, still thirsty.

Raedwald's gargoyle face leered at him. "Turn that thing around," Teleo said. "It's creepy."

Jarnsmidt swiveled the pike until Raedwald faced the wall.

"Much better," Teleo said.

The sound of an axe striking the other door filtered faintly through the hallways.

"Let's take care of the other crew," Teleo said, donning his helmet. "Wait here for a moment."

He stepped through the stone wall bordering the door, unlocked the ironwood door from the inside, and opened it for Sigrid and her father. They stared at him as though he were

a ghost. He ushered them through the doorway, then bolted
the door behind them. They followed him up the servant staircase and out into the wide corridor, past the closed doors of
Cornwal's study and the ministers' chamber, past the stained-
glass windows and the high castle alcove, whose doors were
drawn shut, and stopped at a set of closed double doors. The
doors sealed off the top of the main staircase where an axe was
relentlessly striking the heavy timber from the other side.

Teleo passed through the stone wall, dispatched the startled
axeman, and fought with two decent swordsmen in the stairwell while Sigrid and Jarnsmidt opened the door and attacked
the other four soldiers with their Mage's Blades. It ended with
Sigrid chasing the last soldier down the stairs and felling him
with arrows to the legs as he fled along the corridor past the
empty reception halls. Teleo and Jarnsmidt followed after him
and ensured he was dead.

They dragged the dead soldiers' bodies down the long
hallway, seven from each end, retrieving arrows and stray swords
as they went. They stashed the bodies and weapons in a reception room. When the bodies were all lined up, Teleo regarded
the corpses. They were men like him, just doing their jobs. This
morning they had awoken, taken a piss, eaten some breakfast
if they were lucky, and daydreamed about women they loved.
Then they had met their fate.

When he looked up, Jarnsmidt was tightening the strap of
Raedwald's boar tusk helmet around the general's blood-caked,
bearded chin, and Sigrid was waiting at the door, the shadows
of the fox-and-hare cloak playing against the grain of polished
lapis lazuli behind her. Jarnsmidt propped Raedwald's pike in
a corner and hefted an axe he had retrieved from a dead man.
"This is a Red Flag axe," Jarnsmidt said, pointing to a small
griffin etched in the steel by the haft. "That one, too," Jarnsmidt

said, pointing to the one hanging from Teleo's belt. Teleo checked it for the griffin mark.

"Yes, Papa," Sigrid said. "Half their swords are ours. We should be more careful who we sell to next time."

"Easy to say, my darling daughter. Not so easy to do when winter is approaching and the larders are empty."

"Let's go," Teleo said, interrupting their familial banter.

Sigrid lifted her chin at her father. Jarnsmidt slipped the axe handle through his belt and retrieved Raedwald's pike. They strode down the corridor, stepping around puddles and streaks of blood.

"Can you please take that hood off so I can look at you?" Teleo asked Sigrid.

She shook the hood off her head. "I like this cloak," she said, strands of hair sticking to her sweaty forehead.

"It is beautiful," he agreed. "Mora has many talents."

They climbed the stairs to the upper corridor, bolted the door closed behind them, and rapped on the ministers' chamber door. Teleo pounded his fist repeatedly and then pulled at the silk bell tassel, with no response. "Wait here," he said, and walked through the wall.

In the back by the windows, Larissa, Stephan, and three men were huddled together, the adults clutching swords and Stephan holding a steak knife. Larissa was the first to see him. She knit her brows together. "How did you get in here?" she asked.

"Never mind," he said, and unbolted the door for Sigrid and Jarnsmidt to enter.

"What happened to the soldiers?" Larissa asked, tilting her head, listening to the silence.

"They're dead," Teleo said.

"How?" she asked, looking between Teleo, Sigrid, and Jarnsmidt. Her eyes landed on Raedwald's head.

Teleo shrugged. "We took care of them."

The eyes of the three strangers and Stephan were fastened on Raedwald's head.

The corpses of the ministers were laid out along a wall, covered by a large brocade curtain, which left one of the windows lopsided with a single floor-to-ceiling curtain pulled back from the leaded panes. Teleo strode across the room and peered through the glass, but the view was of an interior courtyard, devoid of people.

"The soldiers didn't know Cornwal and the ministers were dead," Teleo said to Larissa. "They want to see heads on pikes."

"We have all the heads," Larissa said. "Cornwal's too." She gestured to the curtain covering the bodies. Teleo noticed a collection of pikes next to them on the floor, and what was once a white linen tablecloth bunched in a corner and stained completely red. "Jiggs is a butcher—he took care of it," she continued, nodding at one of the three men. Jiggs looked slightly ill. "We're getting ready to mount and display them," she said. "You can help."

"I want to see the battle," Teleo said.

"We're taking the heads out to the high castle terrace," Larissa said. "We can watch the battle from there."

Teleo sighed. "Sigrid, why don't you and Stephan look out the window?"

She gladly took the boy to the window as Larissa and Jiggs pulled back the drape covering the corpses.

Twisted, frozen faces grimaced up at Teleo, heads severed from their bodies and positioned above their bloody necks. He went to Cornwal's decapitated body and lifted the emperor's head by his wispy hair. He turned the head upside down and shoved the tip of a pike into a food or windpipe, he couldn't tell which. Larissa plopped a white wig on top of her husband's head and pressed down on it none too gently.

Soon, the seven ministers' heads were secured on their pikes. In one hand, Teleo carried Cornwal's mounted head. In his other hand, he carried the head of the minister whose wig he had taken, which had been returned to its rightful owner, the long white curls bloody and bobbing below the severed neck.

"Wait," Larissa said, leaving the room and returning with a gold crown laden with blue sapphires and green emeralds, which she placed atop Cornwal's head. She then led them from the ministers' chamber out to the large alcove off the corridor. She pulled the doors open and they stepped out onto the stone terrace of the high castle.

Teleo went to the balustrade and gazed out over the broad valley. The clatter and din of fighting rose from all directions, throngs of men pushing at one another, blades slashing and thrusting, shouts drowned out by screams. Directly below, the large entry yard to the palace, the bailey where the guards had been marching in formation when Teleo had first arrived, stood empty. The ramparts surrounding the Imperial Palace were also empty. The guards appeared to have abandoned the palace and concentrated their forces atop the Castle Wall and outermost City Wall, the latter a thick, blue stone fortification built by Stone Guardians to withstand anything. Lines of archers manned the ramparts, watching the battle rage in the surrounding fields. Teleo squinted and peered at the front lines of Sapphire troops where they encircled the city at a good distance from the walls, defending the muddy buffer zone against the surging Hill Tribes, and seemed to be holding steady.

Teleo searched the southeastern quadrant for BlackJack and Jessum, Daisy and Kaspari, Cinnamon and Dinsmora, Will, Waite, Nutmeg, Petunia, or Star—anyone he knew. But all he saw were clusters of the empire's blue-and-gray-uniformed soldiers—some on horseback, others on foot, clashing in the mud with crowds of the tribesmen's brown-and-red-clad foot soldiers—peasants and Hill people in their leathers and home-spuns, waving home-made flags dyed crimson and painted with rampant griffins.

Jiggs and Jarnsmidt tore down Cornwal's purple banners from where they had been flapping noisily in sporadic gusts of wind. They then took Teleo's pikes bearing the heads of Cornwal and the minister and mounted them in the upright flagpole brackets mounted to the balustrade. Soon, all the heads were leering out over the battlefield. Cornwal's and Raedwald's stood next to each other—the gold crown and the boar tusk helm flashing in the sunlight. Archers on the castle ramparts began to take notice, and word spread quickly. The soldiers turned their way, staring at the heads and shifting nervously.

Larissa raised her arms and cried out. "I have freed you from the tyrant Cornwal. Stand by my side and live in freedom!" Her voice rang out over the yard, drifting in the wind to the Castle Walls. The soldiers on the ramparts whispered among them-selves. Some nocked arrows. Others looked around in confusion.

"I can't see the battle properly from here," Teleo complained. "I'm going to the bell tower." He wanted to view the fighting in all directions and then go down to the battlefield, where he felt comfortable. Let Larissa deal with this political quagmire.

Sigrid came to his side, longbow in hand. "We'll stay with Larissa and the others," she said, glancing at Jarnsmidt and Larissa, who stood side by side gazing out over the valley.

Stephan appeared beside Sigrid and gazed up at Teleo.

"You did well ringing the bell," Teleo said.

The boy reddened and attempted a smile. "Did you find Owen?" Stephan asked.

"Who's Owen?" Teleo asked.

"The other Verdant Valley orphan. The empress said you were looking for him."

Owen. Oren. Could be. "Where?" Teleo asked, his heart in his throat.

"He's a guard."

Teleo's brain could not process the words. "A what?"

"A guard."

"Where?" Teleo asked. Oren was only fourteen. Fifteen now. Maybe sixteen already. He tried to count the years in his head but couldn't.

"I'm not sure," Stephan answered. "Last I knew he was guarding the Castle Wall. Maybe he moved up to the Palace Guard, I don't know."

Blood drained from Teleo's face. "What does he look like?"

"Tall," Stephan said. "Like you. Kinda mean, but nice. Like you."

Teleo swallowed and scanned the ramparts beyond, but the helmed archers were too far away for him to make out any features. His flesh was suddenly cold and his tongue was wooden, but he managed to force out a response. "No. I didn't find him. I'll look for him. I've got to go." He turned on his heel and strode from the terrace, then turned back. "I need my cloak," he said to Sigrid.

She removed the fox-and-hare cloak, and he swung it around his shoulders.

"Are you okay?" she asked.

"No," he said, and left the terrace.

32

SURRENDER

Out in the corridor, Teleo clasped the cloak closed, pulled his hood up over his feathered helm, and trotted down to the reception room where the fourteen soldiers who had been trying to breach the doors were laid out on the floor. One by one, he pulled off helmets and chainmail coifs, terrified of finding Oren's light hair and eyes. One dead face after another looked up at him. Long black hair. Short black hair. Brown, slanted eyes. By the time he got to the last body, his hands and legs were shaking uncontrollably. It was another Hill Tribesman, and Teleo fell to his knees. It was a young man, no more than twenty-five. Someone else's son. Someone's brother. Someone's husband. Someone's father. Teleo closed the soldier's eyes and crossed the man's thick arms over his chest and tried not to weep.

He struggled to remember if the two soldiers who had fallen to Raedwald's flying blades had died. He had not noticed, he realized guiltily. There had been no other corpses in the battle yard when he'd returned—he knew that much. What if one of the fallen soldiers had been Oren? He repelled the horrific thought. But other thoughts snuck in. His son might be on the Castle or City Walls—or he could be out in the battlefield, dead already.

Teleo pulled himself together and closed his eyes. He needed a plan. He thought for a few long moments, then left the reception room and swept down the hallway. He navigated the palace complex to the bell tower and climbed to the top, where the great bronze bell hung silent. He went around to the arched openings—north, east, south, and west—analyzing all sides of the battle.

He was able to distinguish the armies of each of the seven Hill Tribes by their flags. Red. Green. Gray. Gold. Blue. Purple. Black. The tribes were all there and bled into one another to form one coagulated, pulsing offensive.

The Sapphire forces were holding an unbroken blue line around Sapphire City. They were well disciplined, well-armed, and fielded a significant cavalry. Raedwald had done an admirable job. It was almost a shame he was gone.

Teleo searched the southeast again for Dinsmora, Jessum, and Kaspari. Cedar Creek was located between Red Flag and Green Flag Fortresses, so he looked for where red flags met green—but red flags were mixed in across the entire perimeter, all the Hill fortress militias having taken up the ancient Bedon clan's banner. He raised his hand against the sun and scanned the crushing forces. A cluster of red-flag-bearing horsemen had formed a point and were slowly penetrating the blue defenses. A big black horse reared, hooves slashing, its rider's steel helm glinting in the sun, sword raised. A red pennant flew from a bearer behind him. A flash of white caught his attention above the fray. A gyrfalcon slowly circled on an updraft. *Hunter.*

Teleo ran down the steps and through the long stone hallways. He came upon two Sapphire soldiers hurrying down the corridor away from him. He called out to them. "Hey. You. What're you doing in here?"

The soldiers turned, surprised.

"The palace has been taken," Teleo said in his best commander's voice. "The Sapphire forces are surrendering. Wait in Raedwald's battle yard in the lower bailey. If you are not there when I get there, you will die in a dungeon."

He pushed the hood off his head and glared at them. "Did you hear me?"

Fright froze their faces. One nodded, and he elbowed his partner.

"To the battle yard!" Teleo commanded, pointing towards the kitchens.

He pulled his hood back on and trotted past the men.

Teleo made his way to Larissa's residential wing and tore down the Bedon griffin banner from the wall outside her door. He bundled the red and gold satin in his arms, stepped through the stone wall, and crossed her sitting room and bedchamber to the Heliotrope chamber. He knelt and peered into the Sun Circle, conjuring up the image of the battle yard. The yard came immediately into focus. He leaned in closer and was able to look all around the yard as though he were looking through a window. The yard was empty. He got to his feet, wanting to practice traveling from a standing position. He closed his eyes and felt the stone under the soles of his boots. He caught a whiff of lavender and honeysuckle. Birds twittered in the kitchen gardens, enjoying the longest day of the year. Teleo opened his eyes and found himself standing on the Sun Circle of the battle yard. The sun blazed overhead. He set the banner on the ground as the two soldiers rushed through the gate, stumbling to a halt at the sight of him, mouths agape.

"Good," Teleo said, removing his hood and approaching them. "You know how to follow orders. What are your names? Take off your helmets. Let me see your faces."

They removed their helms, staring at him as though he were a phantom.

Black hair. Brown eyes. Swarthy skin.

"Bing," one said.

"Philip," said the other.

"Good. Bing, Philip. Do you know Owen, the Verdant Valley orphan?"

They looked at one another and then nodded at Teleo.

"You do? Where is he?" Teleo demanded, his heart hammering.

"I don't know," Bing said, stepping back as Teleo glowered at him. "He's out there somewhere, I guess," he said, gesturing towards the dull roar of the battle. "I haven't seen him since I moved up to Palace Guard."

"Me neither," Philip said.

"Okay," Teleo said, trying to steady his raging pulse. "Go into the kitchens and find white tablecloths. As many as you can. Slice them crosswise into big triangles. Then get onto the Castle Wall and hang them from the outer ramparts, one facing in every direction, so the guards on the City Wall can see them. You got that?"

They froze, speechless.

"Take the rest of the white flags to the City Wall ramparts and hang them there, facing the battlefield."

They looked horrified. "How can we do that?" Philip asked.

"Easy. Just do it. Take the flags and say the new commander said we should surrender or we will die."

They did not respond but only stared at him, bug-eyed. Teleo exhaled. He did not have time for this.

"Do you recognize this?" Teleo asked, unsheathing Black Lightning and waving it through the air, the diamonds on the pommel sparkling in the midday sun.

Bing's mouth flapped open and shut without uttering a word. Philip managed to croak, "General Raedwald's sword?"

"Correct," Teleo said, sheathing it again. "Do you believe that he is dead?"

Philip cleared his throat and answered, "We heard rumors he was killed by a Mage witch. They said she appeared out of nowhere and killed the general with magic arrows blazing with blue fire."

The mix of wonder and terror on their faces reminded Teleo of children telling ghost stories around a winter hearth.

"Come with me," Teleo said, and herded them towards Raedwald's office.

Inside, the general's headless body lay where Teleo had left it. Bing and Philip stared down at it and began backing away, hands on their sword hilts.

"Raedwald is dead," Teleo said. "Cornwal and his ministers, too. They're all dead. Larissa is Ruling Empress now. You can choose the winning side or the losing side. But you need to decide now, because I don't have any more time to convince you."

"Who are you?" Bing asked.

"Are you a Mage?" Philip asked.

"I'm just a soldier from Verdant Valley," Teleo said. "Our kingdom was recently taken over by a man as cruel, or crueler, than Cornwal. I don't like cruel men and I don't want to be one. So let me let you live." He removed his gauntlet and held out his right hand. He could see Bing's fingers twitching, deciding between his sword and his life.

"Why should we trust you?" Bing asked.

"Because I rescued a Hill war orphan and brought him home, here, to the Hills," Teleo said, gesturing south. "He is the direct descendant of Drake Bedon. He is on his way here. He is Empress Larissa's champion. You will want to welcome him home."

Teleo held Bing's eyes, curiosity and hope transforming the young man's face. Slowly, Bing extended his hand and gripped Teleo's. Philip followed suit.

Teleo forced a smile. Convincing people to live was so much harder than killing them. "Who else knows Raedwald is dead?" Teleo asked.

Bing shrugged. Philip was looking at the fox-and-hare cloak.

"Who is the commander now?" Teleo asked.

Bing's eyes dropped to the diamond pommel of Black Lightning at Teleo's belt. "They were fighting over who's in charge," Bing said.

"Who was fighting?" Teleo asked.

"The other generals," Bing said. "The ones under Raedwald."

"How many of them are there? What are their names?" Teleo asked.

"Generals Ezios, Lander, Petros, and Vasilios."

"Four? Is that it?" Teleo asked.

Bing nodded.

"Thank you," Teleo said, then turned to Bing's companion. "Philip, look at me." Teleo reached out and shook the young man's shoulder.

Philip disentangled his gaze from the fox-and-hare cloak and met Teleo's eyes, looking a little drunk.

"Go get those surrender flags and then tell everyone that Raedwald is dead and to let Drake pass."

"Yes, sir," Philip said.

"Thank you, sir," Bing said.

The young soldiers turned and left the yard.

Teleo wished there were Heliotropes all over the palace so that he could hop from place to place. But there weren't, so he grabbed the griffin banner and trotted all the way across the palace and up the servant staircases. He found Sigrid, Larissa, and the others still outside on the high castle terrace.

Sigrid rushed over to him, and he gave her a quick kiss.

"Has anything changed?" he asked, walking to the balustrade. Larissa and Jarnsmidt shook their heads from where they stood next to the severed heads, gazing out over the ramparts at the battle beyond. Soldiers were still posted atop the Castle and City Walls. The ones closest to the high castle glanced nervously over their shoulders at the empress and the row of heads, then returned their attention to the battle, where the front lines of blue and red soldiers pushed against one another.

Teleo stepped between Cornwal's and Raedwald's heads. Their dead eyes were beginning to sink into their skulls, and Raedwald's long braids hung limply below the boar tusk helmet.

Teleo unfurled Larissa's griffin pennant and hung it over the wall, securing the loops on hooks sticking out of the stone.

"Is that my banner?" Larissa asked.

"Yes," Teleo said.

The red and gold satin stood out starkly against the midnight-blue lapis lazuli wall. Details of the golden griffin were embroidered with metallic thread and glittered in the sun. Black front talons clawed the air, a red tongue hung down below sharp, white fangs, and coal-black eyes gazed out over the battle. Soldiers on the walls turned and looked at it, unsure of what to make of it all.

Teleo told Larissa about the surrender flags and then gestured to the battle. "I am going out there to kill Raedwald's generals. Then the Sapphire Empire will be yours."

Larissa gazed at him with gratitude, then lowered her eyes to Black Lightning's pommel.

"You are wearing Raedwald's sword," she said, her eyes glazing over with that look people got when they gazed upon diamonds for too long, and Teleo's heart dropped.

"Yes," Teleo said, covering the diamond-encrusted pommel with his hand. "Jarnsmidt forged it and thought I should have it. Unless you want it."

"No, no," she said, shaking her head vehemently. "I don't want anything of his. Besides, it suits you."

Teleo swallowed and gazed out over the killing fields, looking for Jessum and the others.

Jarnsmidt nudged his shoulder and handed him a magnifying scope.

Teleo extended the brass tube and lifted the looking glass to his eye. Beyond the teeming front lines, clusters of men dotted the trampled fields. Some were huddled in makeshift camps or field hospitals. Others were forming ranks and marching forward in small units. Mounted rebels were heading towards the front lines in groups of twos and threes. Teleo guessed that some of the farmhands had stolen back their own horses and that other Hill people had come down from small villages, where they had managed to hang onto their horses and feed them through the winter. Teleo searched for BlackJack, Cinnamon, and Daisy near where he had seen BlackJack last, but he could not find them. The myriad of red flags all looked the same. He searched the sky for a gyrfalcon, but all he saw were vultures circling over mounds of corpses.

"I thought I saw BlackJack and young Drake from the tower," he told them. "But I don't see them now." He pointed in the general direction and handed the scope back to Jarnsmidt, who scanned the fields.

"I'm off," Teleo said. He bowed to Larissa and Jarnsmidt and then turned to Sigrid. He clasped her to him and kissed her long and hard.

When he released her, she frowned up at him. "Don't kiss me like that," she said.

"Sorry. Did I hurt you?"

"No. You kissed me like you don't expect to see me ever again," she said, tears glistening in her eyes.

He was struck silent. She was right. He always went into battle expecting to die. But not since he had kissed his wife Bella-Mae goodbye for the last time had he had a lover whom he would leave behind.

"I'll be back," he lied.

Sigrid frowned at him again, and he kissed her gently on the mouth, not letting go until she pulled away and pursed her lips at him in a tearful pout. He smiled at her, holding her eyes. She reluctantly smiled back. He kissed both of her wet cheeks, then turned and left her.

◆

Out in the grand hallway, Teleo stood in the multi-colored light of the peacock window to think. His chest was burning. He pulled the medicine bag out from under his steel cuirass, the little bag hot to the touch. A strange longing pulled at him. Slowly, he dug his fingers into the leather bag and felt for the diamond circlet. He drew it out and inspected the detailed gold carving of lions and eagles, each animal holding a small faceted diamond in its claws. The central griffin's yellow-topaz eyes drew Teleo's gaze. The tiny gold beast clutched a large diamond in its talons, as though offering it to Teleo.

The precious metal was hot in Teleo's hand, and he polished the seven diamonds one by one with the flat of his calloused thumb. What had he gotten himself into, he wondered, by leading a coup in the Sapphire Empire? Suddenly, it felt completely insane. He was an old, washed-up Verdant Valley soldier. What kind of madness had taken hold of him? He rubbed the center diamond. It had so many facets. He tried to count them but got lost at twenty. What had felt like bravery was more like sheer stupidity. But now it was too late. He had personally killed the emperor and beheaded the Supreme Commander, spearing their heads onto pikes. He, himself. Teleo Stonemason. Mage Stone Master. The most celebrated warrior in Verdant Valley, now wielding two Mage's Blades. A walker through walls. A traveler of Heliotropes. A royal assassin. He should just take over. If Larissa were a strong leader, she would have gotten rid of Cornwal a long time ago. But no, Teleo had to do the dirty work for her and then stay in the shadows while she got all the glory. It was the story of his life. He deserved better. It was *his* time. He stared angrily at the stained-glass window. The peacock stared back at him with its two purple amethyst eyes set alight from the sun shining through them. He was reminded of his gyrfalcon mosaic on Queen Valona's throne and then he recalled the dead queen and her diamond tiara.

"Diamonds ... Damn it," Teleo said, closing his fingers around the sparkling pendant. "Devilish magic. This thing is too powerful for me. It's messing with my head." He considered tossing it down a refuse chute. "What if I don't look at it?" he asked the peacock. The stained-glass creature gazed blankly back at him. He sighed and drew the gold chain from the bag, clasped it around his neck, and let the amulet fall atop his cloak. He couldn't see it resting there unless he tucked his chin and really tried. "I'll just expose the diamond pendant for now, for others to see. To make them more pliable and agreeable. Just until this mess is over with and I've found Oren. What do you think?"

The peacock's amethyst eyes reflected back at him, offering no help.

Teleo's chest was cold. He reached into the medicine bag and drew out the Stone Guardian's buckskin scrap, rubbing his thumb over the icy hematite beads. He hated being in the spotlight. He detested court politics, bureaucracy, pomp and circumstance. Besides, the Hill people would never accept a Verdant Valley leader. When all this was finished, he could go back to his farm and plow his fields. He wondered if Sigrid would enjoy being a humble farmer in the Verdant Valley.

He tucked the buckskin scrap back into its bag. His hand dropped as though of its own accord and landed on the diamond sword pommel at his hip. It was hot to the touch. The fiery magic seeped into his hand. "Ah, so ...," Teleo muttered. "No wonder Raedwald was so strong." He considered tossing the blade to the floor and leaving it there, but it was a Mage's Blade, forged in the Summer Solstice sun by a Mage Swordsmith. Deadly in battle.

"Just don't look at it," Teleo said to the peacock and clasped his hand tightly around Black Lightning's burning pommel.

Teleo turned abruptly, his fox-and-hare cloak billowing around him, and hastened to the stairs. He made his way through the palace corridors, stopping to straighten dead servants' bodies as best he could, but many were too stiff already. He donned his hood and trotted to the kitchens.

Bing and Philip were sorting through a mound of white tablecloths on the large butcher's block. They looked up, startled, as Teleo pushed back his hood and threw the cloak back over his shoulders.

"Are you guys still here?" Teleo asked, huffing out his breath in exasperation. "Here. Each of you grab two corners."

They spread out a tablecloth and Teleo sliced it in half, crosswise, making two large, triangular flags. They did the same for all the tablecloths. He gave them each ten flags. "Now go," he told them, handing them coils of sturdy cord the cooks used to lash the legs of goats and pigs onto roasting spits. "Hang eight from the Castle Wall, two on each side. Then give two to the gate guards and tell them to wave one at either side when Drake rides through. Then do the same at the City Walls."

They started to complain but Teleo interrupted. "You can do it," he said encouragingly. Their eyes flashed to his diamond pendant. Teleo continued, "You weren't promoted to the Palace Guard for nothing. If I see you holding the flags at the Castle Gate, I will put in a good word for you with Drake."

They shifted their eyes between Teleo's diamond pendant and the diamond pommel of Black Lightning. With a few more words of encouragement from Teleo, they grabbed their flags and left.

Teleo stole a few minutes to fill a tankard from the water pump and drink his fill, then raided the larder and ate standing up. Solstice Festival food had been stored away in various stages of preparation, some no doubt spoiled by the sudden coup. But there was plenty for Teleo to choose from: fruit pies and sweetcakes; sharp white goat cheese and green olives on flatbread; hard, cured sausages and boiled eggs.

When he had eaten his fill, he went to an outhouse, removing his layers and cursing at the armor, then finally returned to the kitchen. He rolled together the rest of the white flags and tied the bulky bundle to his back. He strode briskly through the gardens past the battle yard, crossed a cobblestone bailey, and stopped at the rear Palace Wall. Two guards peered at him from where they were huddled in the shadows, looking slightly lost.

"Larissa is Ruling Empress now," he said, unsheathing Black Lightning and flashing the diamond pommel at them. "Protect her with your life!"

They gaped at him but did not try to stop him.

"Go to the City Gate and prepare to welcome the young Drake Bedon."

They looked even more confused.

Teleo shook the crystalline blade at them, and they scurried off.

He sheathed his sword and walked along the base of the fortification until he found a sheltered area with no guards lurking, then walked through the lapis lazuli wall.

Teleo emerged into the Castle Ring in an alleyway behind a row of storage sheds. Hurrying along abandoned streets, he veered south, away from the main gate. Doors and shutters of castle workshops were closed up tight, and a stray dog wandered the street, nosing around behind trash bins. Teleo could smell the stables, but all the horses would be out carrying soldiers into battle. He pulled the hood low over his eyes and padded silently across the paving stones, letting the folds of the cape mingle with the light and shadows of his surroundings.

He reached the Castle Wall and walked through the thick stone blocks as easily as if he were walking through water, then emerged into the sprawling City Ring.

Everything was closed up here as well, silent as a graveyard, with distant shrieks of dying men floating through the air. Shops and market stalls were empty. Festival decorations were strewn across the streets, garlands and dead flowers clogging the gutters. Mead stands stood abandoned, with half-finished mugs of golden mead still sitting on upturned barrels.

If there were any mothers and children or elderly folk about, they were locked up tight in their homes and shivering with fear. The same as he imagined the white-wigged bureaucrats were doing—hiding out in their velvet-and-silk-furnished sitting rooms with shutters drawn, frantically counting their coin.

Teleo navigated the maze of streets to the towering City Wall, found a sheltered spot, and passed through the thick argillite. He stepped out onto the muddy buffer zone between the City Wall and the battlefield. The familiar smell of earth and sweat and dead bodies greeted him, and he breathed in deeply, filling his lungs. He threw back the cloak, rested his hand on the diamond pommel, and took stock of his surroundings.

The front lines were clashing a few hundred yards away. Injured and dying Sapphire soldiers were lined up along the base of the towering City Wall near white medic tents. Clusters of soldiers milled about on the wide stretches of trampled mud. Some soldiers were queued up at water stations, filling water-skins from large oak tanks hauled in on wagons, or waiting at one of several water pumps to wash up and drink their fill. At another group of wagons, women were distributing rations of hardbread and cheese. Officers yelled for their soldiers to get back to the fight. Some obeyed but others seemed lost, wandering aimlessly. Many stood with their backs to the battle, gazing up at the City Walls.

Teleo walked slowly along the rows of the injured, looking for a boy with light brown hair. How would he ever find his son among so many? Scores of men were groaning and bleeding. Medics were helping some while others had been left to die. Teleo went up to one soldier who might have had Oren's build and removed his helmet. The black-haired man was dead, sitting up against the wall as though taking a rest. Teleo replaced his helmet and moved on to the next one.

Two soldiers carrying an injured man set him down near Teleo. The man's thigh had a deep gash, seeping blood. Teleo helped them lay him on his back, then propped his leg up on a dead body. Teleo took a white flag from his bundle and tore it into bandages.

"You'll be okay," Teleo told the man as he wrapped his leg tightly. "The blade didn't reach the bone." The soldier was sweating and panicking, gasping for breath. "Calm down," Teleo said firmly, holding the man's hand and feeling the racing pulse at his wrist. "Look at me," Teleo said, holding his gaze until the man breathed more normally and his pulse evened out. "You'll be fine. You're not going to lose your leg. Relax." Teleo propped up the man's head and gave him some water. The soldier's eyes were fixed on the diamond pendant hanging from Teleo's neck.

"Wait here," Teleo said, resting the man's head on the ground. "I'll find a medic to stitch you up."

Teleo approached a medic who was leaning over a man several bodies away. The man's abdomen was a pulpy, bloody mess and he was clutching the medic's wrists, screaming at him to help him. Teleo transferred the man's clawlike grip to his own arms and looked down into the man's wild eyes. "There's a man needs his leg stitched up," Teleo said to the medic, cocking his head behind him. The medic hurried away and Teleo looked down at the man clutching his gauntleted forearms. The soldier's belly was torn open, exposing a mass of lacerated intestines.

"What happened?" Teleo asked.

"Pitchfork," the man said, panting. His face was pale, and his grip loosened on Teleo's arms.

"That's unfortunate," Teleo said. "You're going to die, but it's okay."

"It's not okay. My wife just had a baby, I can't die," the man said, taking short gasps.

"We all die," Teleo said. "Now is your time." He twisted his arms free, made the man drink from his own waterskin, then poured a little water on a bandage and washed away blood and grime from the man's face. "What's your name? I'll tell your wife you died bravely."

The man's words tumbled from his mouth: his name, his wife's name, his baby's name, the name of his village and how to get there. Teleo nodded and covered his belly with a white flag. The man was half-sobbing and half-groaning in pain. Teleo could not bring himself to do the merciful thing and end the man's life. Let him think of his wife and child for as long as he could. Soon, the blood loss would render him unconscious and his torment would end. Teleo stood up and walked away as the man wept behind him.

Teleo gritted his teeth. He would never find Oren at this rate. He was wasting precious time. He needed to stick to his original plan and stop the fighting. That was the best chance he could give his son.

Teleo strode out beyond the shadow of the wall and walked eastward until he could see the high castle perched up on the polished lapis lazuli façade of the Imperial Palace. Cornwal's head was easy to spot in his gold, bejeweled crown. Raedwald's polished bronze helmet shone yellow in the sun, and the ministers' heads stood in a row, all proper with their white powdered wigs, as though watching a tourney. Larissa's red-and-gold Bedon banner flapped in a light wind.

A splash of emerald marked the central, robed figure standing behind the parapet as Larissa, flanked by a tall male figure looking through a spyglass and a feminine form with a longbow drawn. His gaze rested on Sigrid for several heartbeats before turning to the Castle Wall. The archers manning the ramparts glanced over their shoulders at the high castle occasionally, but no one was shooting at the empress. Neither was anyone cheering. The soldiers were in a state of limbo, awaiting orders.

Movement atop the far end of the Castle Wall drew Teleo's attention. Two heads poked up over the battlements, and a white flag unfurled, hanging point down over the stone wall. Teleo nodded with approval, then turned away and headed towards the fighting.

With his cloak thrown back over his shoulders and his fancy bronze helm with its gaudy pheasant feathers, Teleo looked like he could be a Sapphire Empire officer. He was outfitted with fine Red Flag armor and weapons, unlike the foot soldiers, many of whom wore only gambesons or chainmail and carried a standard-issue sword. Cornwal had not invested in enough armor for all his men, Teleo reasoned, although properly outfitting thousands of men was nearly impossible. Teleo had survived in only a gambeson for years, as a young man.

No one looked at him twice as he trod over churned-up earth towards the front lines. He tried not to see his son in every helmeted soldier and focused on the task in front of him. He came upon a group of three soldiers.

"Where are the generals?" Teleo asked. "Lander? Petros? Ezios? Vasilios?"

"Petros is holding the Emperor's Toll Road," one of them said, pointing to a company of Sapphire soldiers blocking the wide stone road that led from the city's front gate to the border crossing. "I don't know where the others are."

The main road and surrounding land, like everywhere else, were held by lines of foot soldiers in blue gambesons, gray pants, and steel helmets, swords flashing and clanging. Small units of cavalry were pushing back mounted rebels who managed to pierce the lines, and a cluster of foot soldiers bearing pikes and a unit of mounted soldiers were beating back a team of oxen drawing a wagon filled with rebels who were trying to break through.

Teleo headed towards the noise and mayhem.

He needed a horse. He veered towards one that was plodding through the mud, its rider slouched over. Blood was seeping through a gash in the gambeson covering the man's chest, and he was coughing up blood.

"This way," Teleo said, taking the horse's bridle, and led them back to the field hospital. He helped the rider dismount and called to a medic whose forearms were bloody to his elbows. Teleo found a free patch of ground between two motionless bodies, quickly spread a white flag over the blood-soaked mud, and helped the man lie down as blood trickled from his mouth and nose. He had been wounded by a halberd in the chest and again in the belly. It did not look good for him. Teleo tore bandages from another of his surrender flags and did the best he could to staunch the bleeding. The medic finally came over with an assistant. Teleo stepped back to give them room.

"My horse," the soldier gasped between choking coughs, his eyes meeting Teleo's, pleading. "She's a good horse."

"I'll take care of her," Teleo promised. The man fell into another coughing fit, spitting up blood, and the medics leaned over him. Teleo took the mare's reins and led her away, weaving through rows of injured men.

The filly was a pretty chocolate palomino with a dark brown coat, flaxen mane and tail, and a white blaze down her nose. She was young and spirited but followed obediently. Teleo scoured the ground as he walked, picking up abandoned spears and polearms while scanning each soldier for familiar features—a strong nose, gray eyes, fair skin. They had none of those—they were all of Hill stock, but Teleo couldn't stop himself from checking. After he'd gathered thirteen weapons, he knelt in the shade of a medic tent and tied a white flag to each, then lashed them all together.

He balanced his bundle of flagstaffs across the withers of the palomino and swung into the saddle. He trotted over the muddy ground towards the Emperor's Toll Road and approached the shifting mass of soldiers, regarding the battle scene from his elevated vantage point astride the mare. A couple of Sapphire battalions manned the eastern front, primarily made up of infantry—swordsmen, spearmen, pikemen, archers—and with small units of cavalry interspersed. The heaviest fighting was at the road, and the lines thinned out from there.

Teleo was pleasantly surprised at the number of Hill Tribesmen who had joined the fight. Thousands of men, and some women, had come down off the hills, and it looked as though many of their brethren who worked the fields in the emperor's valley had joined the rebel side. Battles were being waged all around the perimeter, concentrated at certain points.

While the peasants and Hill rebels outnumbered the Sapphire soldiers, the Sapphire soldiers were better organized. They were cycling to the front in ranks, waging short, coordinated assaults, and then falling back to let the next row take a turn, pulling injured comrades out with them. The rebels, on the other hand, were trying to push through with brute force. The Hill men at the front were trapped in their positions until they were cut down, forming a barricade of screaming, dying bodies. Teleo was tempted to break through and organize the rebels but kept to his plan, searching the throng for a Sapphire commander.

It was easy to pick out the shiny bronze helmet of a senior officer among the lines of steel-helmed men. *General Petros.* The general was a short, stocky man, and his bronze helm appeared and disappeared behind his cavalrymen as he rode a large chestnut stallion back and forth, calling out commands that got lost in the hubbub. A stiff tassel of black boar bristles stuck up from the pointed peak of the general's helmet. Teleo reached the defensive lines of infantrymen, eight ranks deep at the road.

Teleo guided his palomino through the ranks, which parted to let him pass. He reached the third rank, where Petros was ranging back and forth. Teleo drew up his horse and pulled out a surrender flag from his bundle of staffs, raising it overhead, where it caught the wind and fanned out. Nearby soldiers glanced up at it and turned surprised eyes on Teleo. Petros followed their startled gazes and wheeled his horse around to face Teleo, scattering his ranks. Petros's momentary confusion quickly turned to anger, and he rode towards Teleo, forcing the palomino to dance backwards as Petros pulled the red stallion up short, its ears laid back.

"What's the meaning of this?" Petros bellowed, narrowing his eyes with disbelief. "You!" he said. "I thought you were dead."

"You thought wrong," Teleo said, balancing the bundle of staves at his knees as he tried to calm the mare. "Your side is surrendering."

"We are not. We are winning. Lower that flag!" Petros demanded.

Teleo backed the palomino out of the crowded ranks to a clear area. Petros followed, his face flushed. "How did you disappear from the battle yard? You're a Mage," he said, pointing his sword accusingly at Teleo. "Lower that flag, I say."

Teleo could feel confusion among the Sapphire troops and curiosity in the rebels. The fighting faltered, everyone's eyes on the general and the strange officer bearing a flag of surrender.

"Look," Teleo said, waving his flag towards the castle. White flags hung over the Castle Wall. Beyond that, the Imperial Palace towered over the castle and city. Displayed prominently from the high castle, the row of dismembered heads stood like grotesque puppets next to Larissa.

"She will not rule," Petros said scornfully. "She will marry the next emperor, and I will be Supreme Commander." A leer spread across Petros's square face.

"No, you won't," Teleo said.

Petros sneered. "Ezios, Lander, Vasilios. None of them have what it takes."

"Drake Bedon does."

Petros's sneer bent into a frown, and his gaze dropped to the diamond pendant resting on Teleo's chest armor. "Drake's line is dead," he sputtered.

"No, it isn't," Teleo said. "He's out there. He is coming." Teleo smirked and then lunged at Petros with the long steel tip of the flagstaff's halberd, aiming at Petros's throat, which was arrogantly unarmored. Petros dodged the jab and grabbed the flag, pulling the halberd from Teleo's grip. Teleo grabbed another flag from his bundle and pushed the other staves off his horse, swinging the flagstaff butt-end at Petros. It met the general's sword blade, which sliced off the end of the wooden staff and sent it flying. Teleo dug his knees into the palomino's flanks. The mare jumped forward, and Teleo flung the flag across Petros's face and leapt from the mare's back onto the stallion, taking Petros to the ground. They landed with a jarring thud. Teleo was on top and punched Petros's face with his steel gauntlets, knocking a knife from the general's grip with a strike across the wrist. He levered Petros's arm into an elbow lock, wrenched him face down in the mud, and slit his throat with his own blade.

Teleo climbed to his feet to let the general bleed out. Men like that weren't used to being challenged. Petros should have followed in Raedwald's footsteps and danced the sword instead of plotting about how to take his place.

Teleo retrieved his flags, and Petros's soldiers shifted uncomfortably. The nearby fighting had diminished to grunts and groans, and yells of, "*Wait, wait, a surrender.*"

Teleo distributed six white flags to the closest horsemen. "Ride around the perimeter," he said sternly, pointing clockwise towards where he'd last seen Jessum. "Drake Bedon is waiting to be welcomed home. The battle is over."

The men took the flags, holding the poles awkwardly and steering their horses around the sprawled body of the general.

"Hurry up," Teleo ordered.

They hesitated until one spurred his horse and raised his flag. The others followed.

Teleo went to Petros's limp body and wriggled the bronze and boar-hair helmet loose. He tied it by the bloody chin strap to the top of a flagstaff, where it dangled, staining the top corner of the white flag red.

He chose the most frightened of the foot soldiers looking on and gestured to him. The man hurried over, visibly trembling. "What are you afraid of?" Teleo asked.

The man's mouth opened and closed. His gaze shifted from Petros's helmet to Teleo's diamond amulet.

"Can you ride a horse?" Teleo asked, adjusting his cloak and flipping the embroidered fabric out of the way to drape down his back.

The man nodded mutely, as though he'd swallowed a salamander.

"What's your name?" Teleo asked.

The man's mouth worked again, and finally he choked out, "Alvin."

"Hold these, Alvin," Teleo said, shoving the six remaining flagstaffs into his arms, then walked over to where Petros's stallion was prancing in a circle. He grabbed the reins and turned with the horse until the big chestnut stood still and stopped pawing the ground.

"Here, Alvin, get on," Teleo said.

Alvin stared helplessly at the stallion, who showed the whites of his eyes and tossed his head, breaking Teleo's grip. "It's just a horse," Teleo said, grabbing the bridle and patting his neck, speaking softly to calm him down. He held the bridle firmly while Alvin figured out how to manage the bundle of staves and hoist himself into the saddle. When Teleo was confident the young soldier wouldn't lose his seat, he let go of the fiery stallion. The red horse reared and backed away, but the soldier proved his worth by getting the chestnut under control without losing the flags.

"Follow me," Teleo said, mounting the palomino and trotting away from the toll road, white flag waving.

At the north side of the defensive perimeter, he found the next general, the bronze and boar-bristle helmet flashing in the sun.

The general was astride a pale gray gelding, well away from the clashing front lines, watching his men fight from a safe distance.

"*Lander!*" the general's soldiers alerted him, gesturing at Teleo. The tall, handsome general turned in his saddle and stared at the helmet crowning Teleo's surrender flag. "Whose is that?" he asked gruffly.

"Petros's," Teleo said.

"I thought you were dead," the man said warily, his mouth bunching up under thick black moustaches.

"You were mistaken. We are surrendering."

Lander harrumphed. "*You* are not *we*. You are a Verdant Valley interloper. And Petros was a fool. I am not."

"Even so," Teleo said, "Empress Larissa has taken power, and your army is surrendering to her Hill forces."

"I make the decisions here," Lander said scornfully. "The emperor was grooming me to follow in his footsteps."

Teleo laughed out loud. "Oh, yeah. I'm sure."

The diamonds flashed on Teleo's chest, catching the sun and Teleo's attention. He lifted his eyes away from their brilliance and met Lander's angry stare. If any soldier was going to take the emperor's place, it would be Teleo. *He* had killed the emperor. *He* had freed Larissa. *He* had killed the ministers. *He* had killed Raedwald. Well, technically, Sigrid had killed Raedwald the first time, but Teleo had killed him the second time and chopped his head off. But *he* was the one who had saved Jessum and discovered his heritage.

Teleo spat and challenged Lander with a contemptuous glare.

Lander said, "I was there when that witch killed Raedwald. You think you can kill me just because you're a Mage?" The general lifted his chin. "That witch saved your ass, but she's not here now."

"You're no Raedwald," Teleo said. "I could kill you before I ever became a Mage." Teleo had been going to offer to let the man live if he pledged fealty to Larissa, but he had no patience for disrespectful pricks. "You should have taken his sword," Teleo said, unsheathing Black Lightning with a satisfying ring.

Lander sneered at him and unsheathed his own sword—another Red Flag blade from the looks of it, but it did not shine white like a Mage's Blade.

He let the tall man make the first move. They sparred lightly from horseback. The general was very precise, with well-practiced technique. He knew how to swing a sword and was probably skilled with knives, judging by the single bandolier filled with small black throwing knives strapped across his chest. He also had a stave, because all soldiers practiced with staves. Axes, not so much. And hammers, rarely. Teleo steered the palomino alongside the general's gelding, pulled the axe from his belt, and swung it at the man's helmet. It glanced off Lander's sword and missed its mark. Teleo swung again, moved in, and switched to a blacksmith hammer. The general battered Teleo with his sword but Teleo was too close and his armor too sturdy. Teleo swung his hammer into the man's helmet, throwing the general off balance for a split second, which was all Teleo needed to plunge a dagger into Lander's armpit and another into his eye.

The general slowly slid from his saddle and hit the ground, his horse sidestepping away. Teleo dismounted and finished him off, using the axe to chop off his head. The conical helmet fell off and rolled around in the mud by the man's severed head and came to rest in a growing puddle of blood. The battlefield was silent around him, fighters from both sides watching in fascinated horror.

Teleo wiped off his blades and sheathed his weapons, then fished Lander's helmet from the muck and added it to the top of his staff. He then took three flags from Alvin and distributed them to three of Lander's foot soldiers, who accepted them wordlessly.

"Drake Bedon is coming," Teleo called out as he swung back

up into his saddle. "The battle is over. Fly those flags," he commanded, and the three men dutifully raised the white flags.

Teleo looked out over the front lines. Everyone was still
staring at him.

"You can stop fighting now," Teleo shouted, loudly enough
that his voice carried to the rebel side. "Help each other. Tend
the wounded."

Sapphire soldiers and Hill rebels regarded one another
uncertainly. Teleo waited until men from both sides lowered
their weapons and began tending to the injured. Archers on the
ramparts looked down, confused, their bowstrings slack.

"Drake Bedon is coming," Teleo called up to them. "Prepare
to welcome him."

Their faces were shadowed with doubt, but they squinted
at the glittering diamonds on Teleo's chest and sword pommel,
which flashed in the sun and sent shafts of light in every direction, and slowly lowered their bows.

Teleo turned away and rode westward, white flag flying, with his
assistant trailing on the stallion. Teleo noted with satisfaction that
white flags now draped the outer City Wall, in addition to the inner
Castle Wall. Bing and Philip had exceeded his expectations. Perhaps
they had used their heads and employed other soldiers to help them.

Word of the surrender had spread, and fighting in the west had
all but ceased. Men were milling about—some lost in confusion,
others gripped by frustration, and others showing mounting
excitement. Red-clad rebels walked through the lines, and the
blue-and-gray-uniformed soldiers let them pass. People glanced
curiously up at the palace and headed around the city's perimeter
to see the piked heads and get a glimpse of the empress.

Teleo didn't have to search for his next victim—the general
found him, riding straight at him in an angry canter, on a
Sapphire Empire white steed.

"General Ezios," Alvin told Teleo, his voice quavering.

"You there," Ezios called out, his bronze helmet shining in the midday sun and the black boar bristles pointing straight up. "Where did you get that flag?"

"Petros," Teleo said, just to mess with him.

Ezios's face contorted. "He always was a coward."

A light wind died and the flag settled, exposing the two helmets. Ezios stared at them.

"Larissa is Ruling Empress now," Teleo said. "Young Drake Bedon is coming. It's time to put down the sword."

Ezios swallowed and shifted his gaze to Teleo. "I always liked Larissa. She will make a good empress."

"So, you support her?" Teleo asked.

Ezios's gaze was fixed on Teleo's diamond amulet, and Teleo wondered if the general recognized it as the emperor's. Teleo glanced down. The gems were brilliant in the sun, the light dancing off them in multi-colored rays.

"Yes, yes," Ezios said. "I can help her. She will need support."

"Petros and Lander are dead," Teleo said.

Ezios lowered his eyebrows and stole another glance at the helmets. "Is that so? Then I will be humbled to be her Supreme Commander."

"No, I will be," Teleo said, his voice steely. He unsheathed Heart Fire and Black Lightning, gripping the saddle with his knees.

"You are a foreigner," Ezios said. "And a Mage. I saw you fight Raedwald. You lost."

"I am alive, and he is dead," Teleo said. "And I carry his sword." He twirled Black Lightning, and the diamonds flashed.

"Magic is outlawed. Punishable by death." Ezios smiled. "I can speak to Larissa so that she would grant you leniency."

"I don't need you to speak to Empress Larissa. I do her

bidding," Teleo said, and swung Heart Fire in a figure eight overhead, loosening his left arm.

"We can work something out," Ezios said, his smile faltering. "You're a good fighter. Losing to Raedwald and living to tell about it is no small feat. Perhaps I can make you a general over time. Once you've proven yourself."

"Once I've *proven* myself?" Teleo laughed derisively and considered how he would kill this man. Maybe he would toss the swords aside and strangle him, so that he could see the man's condescending eyes plead for his life.

Teleo went in for the strike, parrying Ezios's sword with Heart Fire and moving to the inside. The palomino was a smart horse and held her position tight against Ezios's mount. Teleo tossed his swords away along with his gauntlets, and Ezios reached for a knife. Teleo blocked the general's forearm before he could grab his weapon, then wrapped Ezios in a bear hug and wrestled him off his horse. They landed in the mud, hooves dancing nervously around them.

Men were rarely ready for hand-to-hand combat, Teleo reflected as he easily gained the upper position—they spent all their time drilling with the sword and thought battle was supposed to be polite and follow some sort of rules. He kneed Ezios in the groin and pounded the general's helmet against the ground as the man struggled. Ezios was not weak, however, and he'd done this before, it seemed. And he had many knives hidden on his body. The general punched him in the head while Teleo slid his hands up under Ezios's chainmail aventail and wrapped his bare hands around the general's throat.

Teleo had to release Ezios's neck several times to fend off more knives before he prevailed and got his wish. Ezios stared up at him, the realization dawning that he was going to lose his life. Like every man about to die, Ezios looked like a child, and Teleo was tempted to take pity. Then Ezios passed out. Teleo strangled him until he was dead, then climbed wearily to his feet.

Ezios's men were watching silently, and his white horse stood nearby, looking on. The horse stepped forward and lowered its head over the general's corpse.

Teleo went to its side and patted its neck. "It'll be okay," he said softly, and the horse blew dust from its nostrils and pawed the ground. It was a beautiful Sapphire Empire gelding, and would make a nice gift for Sigrid and companion for Star.

"Who's second in command here?" Teleo asked.

The soldiers looked around nervously, and a young man stepped through the ranks and marched slowly to Teleo, trying to look brave.

"Take the general's horse to the imperial stables and tell the head groom it is a gift from General Ezios to Princess Sigrid of Red Flag. Can you do that?"

The soldier nodded with relief. "Yes, sir."

"Good. Go on, then," he said, and the soldier took the gelding's bridle and headed towards the City Gate.

Teleo motioned for Alvin and took the three remaining flags, handing them randomly to three horsemen.

"Ride," he said, slapping a horse on its haunch. The three horsemen rode away, urging their mounts into a canter, with white flags flying.

To the rest of Ezios's men, he said, "Larissa is Ruling Empress now. Drake Bedon is coming from the southeast. Go welcome him."

A fog of confusion cleared from the men's faces as the meaning of his words sank in. One by one, then en masse, the Sapphire soldiers ran to welcome Jessum.

Teleo added Ezios's helmet to his collection and continued his counterclockwise circuit. He glanced over his shoulder. Behind him, Alvin trotted with a dozen cavalry. They were gazing at Teleo with bewildered awe. He let them follow and came upon the southwestern sector.

The fighting there had not stopped completely but carried on in muddled confusion, blues and reds mixing together. In some spots, groups of farmers bearing homemade weapons pushed through the fray and headed towards the city.

Teleo rode on, trotting towards the southern sector. There, the two sides still clashed across delineated lines, with several ranks of Sapphire infantry confronting a chaotic horde of rebels. Several small units of Sapphire cavalry were assembling behind the foot soldiers and appeared to be readying to cut through enemy lines. Teleo guessed their target was a pair of trebuchets being wheeled in their direction by a noisy band of rebels waving green flags and brandishing torches.

"Form ranks!" a voice bellowed. "Shields up!" A bronze helm glinted atop the bellowing man's head. "Cavalry, form your wedges!" Nearby, six mounted soldiers armed with crossbows formed a rough triangle, the horses jostling each other as they tried to position themselves behind an armored horse standing at the tip of the formation.

The bronze-helmed man could be no other than Vasilios, valiantly trying to stem the red tide that was slowly breaching the blue and gray. The general held a few hundred yards of the front line and rode back and forth on a black warhorse, whipping the haunches of his cavalrymen's mounts with a bullwhip, leaving bloody stripes on their hides as he struggled to move the agitated horses into formation—but his methods were only upsetting the horses more. Teleo spat on the ground.

"It's too late, Vasilios," Teleo yelled over the din as he rode up behind the general.

Vasilios turned his horse and glowered at Teleo.

"Who are you?" Vasilios demanded, then his eyes widened in recognition. "You?!" His gaze lifted to the three helmets dangling from atop Teleo's bloodied flag, and his mouth dropped open.

"You're the last one," Teleo taunted, reining in the palomino. "Cornwal and Raedwald are dead. The empress and the seven Hill Tribes have won, and you have lost. Drake Bedon has come."

Vasilios charged Teleo, his long bullwhip lashing out. Teleo met it with the flag, and the whip wrapped around the long wooden pole, tangling in the white linen. Teleo jerked the whip out of Vasilios's hand and tossed the flag aside. The next moment, a sword was in the general's hand and he bore down upon Teleo, hanging sideways from his saddle and slashing at the palomino's leg.

Teleo jerked the palomino aside and Vasilios's blade swished through empty air. The general's warhorse pivoted and reared, neighing loudly, front hooves waving in the air. Teleo backed the palomino away, unwilling to let the horses fight. He sneered at the general. Attacking Teleo was fair game, but no one attacked his horse and lived to tell about it.

The horses circled one another, several paces apart, and Teleo and the general stared each other down.

"What kind of crap sword is that?" Teleo asked. "Some sort of family heirloom?"

Vasilios scowled at Teleo and waved his bronze blade threateningly.

"Nobody carries bronze anymore," Teleo scoffed. "You don't fight much, do you? You just sit up there yelling orders and whipping other people's horses. Your men must hate you."

The general charged again, but this time Teleo was ready and vaulted from the mare, his Mage's Blades crossed above his head, glowing white. He sprang off the ground and met the general's blade with Heart Fire and Black Lightning, slashing the blades crosswise above his head with bursts of light, shattering Vasilios's bronze blade and sending chunks of metal hurtling through the air.

The general shuddered for a moment but recovered quickly, unsheathed an iron sword, and jabbed the long, heavy blade at Teleo. Teleo dodged and crouched. He took a breath and then spun with Heart Fire in the lead, severing Vasilios's sword hand with a blinding flash of the Mage's Blade. The hand and the iron sword fell in slow motion, turning end over end, blood spurting from the stub as Vasilios wailed. Teleo dragged the general from the saddle and tossed him to the ground, planted a boot on his chest, and with one hack of Black Lightning, beheaded the shrieking man. His scream cut off abruptly and silence emanated in waves over the gathering crowd. Vasilios's black warhorse snorted and reared, then lunged into the crowd, scattering everyone in its path.

Teleo staggered in a circle, hot with battle rage, his chest heaving with each breath. *He* was the master. *He* was the warrior who had freed the empire. *No one* could stand in his way. He searched the crowd for more bronze helmets, but there were no more.

It was done. Raedwald's generals were dead.

Teleo took in a shaking breath and retrieved Vasilios's helmet, fastened it to his flagstaff, and cut the whip into pieces, tossing the leather segments to the ground.

"Go, now!" Teleo yelled to the onlookers. "Drake Bedon comes. Go greet him. You, too," he said to Alvin, who was staring down at him, mesmerized by the glinting diamonds on Teleo's chest. "The stallion is yours now," Teleo said. "Treat him well."

Alvin started sputtering incoherent objections, but Teleo waved a bloody hand at him. The young soldier backed the horse away, then turned and trotted off with the dozen cavalry in the direction of the Sapphire City Gate.

33

VICTORY

Teleo did not actually know if Jessum was still alive or not. For now, it did not matter. The fighting had stopped and warriors from both sides were flocking to see Drake and Larissa. For the moment, the people were happy.

Teleo heeled the palomino and they loped across the muddy ground towards the City Gate. People were streaming in from all sides, and soon Teleo had to slow to a trot, and then a walk, wending his way through the noisy throng.

"*Bedon, Bedon,*" the crowd chanted, fists raised in the air, faces alight with joy. Sapphire soldiers, Hill rebels, field laborers, they were all mixing together now, some with arms around each other's shoulders, having already forgotten the bloody battle.

War was so foolish, Teleo mused. Why men constantly killed each other made no sense to him. Yet here he was, still practicing his chosen profession, even though he had tried to retire numerous times. It just kept coming back, as though the sword sought him out.

He rounded the bend of the southeastern corner of the City Wall where the crowd thickened, forcing the palomino to a slow walk as people pushed and shoved to get a look at the young Drake Bedon.

"There he is!" a man called out, his voice booming with excitement.

"Drake, Drake, Drake!"

Teleo's pulse quickened and he stood in his stirrups. He easily picked out Jessum and his party as the sea of people converged around him. Jessum was waving the scarlet pennant bearing his sigil, the gold griffin rising victorious over the slaughtered wolf. BlackJack reared and pivoted in a tight circle, the crowd cheering as the banner caught the wind and extended to its full length. Jessum's helmet was off, and one side of his head was freshly shaven and his scalp oiled, showing off his tattoo. The rest of his black hair hung down, blending in with the black-and-white falcon cloak that flowed from his shoulders. Underneath, the velvet brigandine stood out red as fresh blood.

"Drake, Drake, Drake!" The chant rose to a deafening roar. White flags flapped from both the City and Castle Walls, and soldiers on the ramparts cheered along with everyone else.

Teleo pushed the palomino through the crowd, drawing angry looks as everyone pressed forward, wanting to get closer to the young Drake.

Teleo prodded people aside with the butt of his flagstaff and kicked the palomino to move faster. A few mouths turned down in puzzlement at the helmets hanging from the top of his flag-staff, but most people were too intent on getting a glimpse of their new hero to notice.

Teleo spotted Kaspari, wearing her shimmering white cloak and astride his Daisy. He recognized men from Jessum's village and the band of brigands pushing their mounts through the throng and protecting the teenagers: Kegger, Gray, Mitchman, Jessum's great-uncle Bron—beaming with pride. Teleo should be by Jessum's side. *He* should be leading him forward. Frustration constricted Teleo's throat as he called out to Jessum, but his voice was lost in the hubbub.

Hunter was circling overhead, and Teleo searched the crowd for Dinsmora as he pushed forward. People cursed at him and pushed back, shoving the palomino. She tossed her head and obeyed Teleo, gaining a pace at a time. He slowly edged closer as Jessum's party moved towards the City Gate.

"Jessum!" Teleo called out.

Dinsmora's head appeared among the shifting crowd, and her eyes met his. Joyful recognition lit her eyes and then darkened to stunned confusion as her gaze dropped to the diamonds glinting on his chest. Her eyes lifted to meet his and her brow furrowed.

Anger twisted his face. Who was she to judge? Vengeful woman. She had always been critical of him, ever since they were children. Always challenging him, questioning his motives, telling him what to do. No more. *He* was in charge now. *He* had cleared the way for Jessum. *He* had killed the emperor and the ministers. *He* had unlocked the secrets of the Heliotrope. He unsheathed Black Lightning and waved it in angry triumph. The pommel's diamonds glittered and flashed, and Dinsmora's frown deepened.

Jessum and Kaspari looked his way and grinned as they caught sight of him. Jessum waved his arm at Teleo to join them. Teleo read his lips across the thunderous crowd. *"Teleo. Come on. Come with us."* But Jessum was swept forward by the crowd as people parted before the young hero to open a path to the City Gate.

Teleo pressed forward but was thwarted by the crush of bodies. He watched helplessly over the heads of the surging crowd and spotted several Red Flag blacksmiths following behind Jessum, riding the big Verdant Valley horses from Rickhart's gang and bearing red flags. Teleo caught a glimpse of Will and Waite. They too had joined Jessum, somehow, when Teleo had not. Star's bright white head appeared through a gap in the crowd. She tossed her long forelock, her eyes flashing. Teleo saw that the miller was riding her and his anger boiled over. Star was *his* horse. A gift from Queen Valona for killing Stone Guardian wolves. Teleo thrust Black Lightning into the air, and the diamonds sparked in a blazing fury.

This whole thing—this victory, this celebration, the cheering, the chanting—it was all because of Teleo. But here he was, again, forgotten in the crowd of common men. It was the endless nightmare of his life, and the unfairness stabbed at Teleo's heart. Always fighting for someone else. Always pushed into the shadows while others got the glory. *HE* should be riding into the castle bearing the flag of the champion. *HE* should be standing on the high castle overlooking the valley, next to the heads of the leaders whom *HE* had killed. But no, here he was, again—alone, carrying the white flag of surrender and being pushed aside.

He gripped the diamond amulet at his neck. Why did he stand aside and let this happen? He could kill Larissa with his eyes closed, and Jessum would be jelly under his fists. Teleo should rule this empire himself. He should step forward and take his rightful place as the strongest and wisest in all the land.

He kicked the palomino forward, mindless of the crowd barring their path. The mare reared, trying to avoid a man who had tripped in front of them. She stepped backwards on her hind legs into the people behind them and then staggered and lost her footing. Teleo sprang from the saddle to avoid being crushed as the big mare rolled to the ground and people scattered. Teleo tossed aside his flag and tumbled into two men who cursed him and backed away. The palomino struggled to her feet. Teleo got up and tried to grab her reins, but she was spooked and reared again. The crowd backed away, avoiding her flailing hooves.

The man who had tripped was down on his back in the mud, his hands up in the air, afraid of being trampled as the palomino whinnied and pranced in distress, people surging around them and spearing her haunches as she backed into them, kicking.

"You idiot!" Teleo yelled, bending over and backhanding the man upside the head with his steel gauntlet.

Blood blossomed on the man's cheekbone as he reached up and grabbed Teleo's forearms, trying to get to his feet. Teleo pushed the man away but he clawed at Teleo in desperation, grabbing the medicine bag that had swung free of Teleo's armor and breaking the leather lanyard as he fell back into the mud, the small bag clutched in his fist.

Teleo kicked him aside, snatched up his flagstaff of pillaged helmets, and scrambled to get control of the palomino. Teleo took hold of her mane and saddle and leapt onto her back. "Bitch of a horse," he growled, tugging viciously at the reins. She put her head down and bucked, scattering the crowd further. He kept his seat as the mare bucked in a circle until she finally stood on all fours, huffing and shaking.

He jerked angrily at the reins. She laid her ears back at him, her eyes rolling up in her head. Jessum's griffin pennant had drawn further away, his party approaching the City Gate. The crowd streamed past Teleo, chanting in crazed jubilation, *"Drake, Drake, Drake!"*

An insistent tugging on his cloak snapped the last thread of Teleo's patience, and he turned in a fit of rage. The man who had tripped was hanging onto his stirrup, blood trickling down his cheek. "You forgot this," the man yelled over the noise, the medicine bag dangling from his outstretched hand.

"I don't need that," Teleo said, tearing the bag from the man's hand and hurling it out over the sea of men. The bag contained naught but cold, Stone Guardian hematite magic—guttering his fire, taming his instincts, luring him into the icy clutches of a slow, insignificant death. The leather bag flew through the air in a high arc and began its descent, the thongs following like feathers of a bird plummeting to its death.

A white flash dove towards the little leather bag. Hunter grabbed it in her talons and rose, flapping slowly towards Teleo.

Teleo stared at the white and gray gyrfalcon, her wingspan nearly as wide as his own arm span. Her black eyes drilled into his as she landed with a flutter on his gauntlet, then she lowered her beak and pulled at the leather bag clutched in her yellow foot, tearing at it like a piece of flesh, and drew out the buckskin. Seven hematite beads winked up at Teleo.

Teleo drew in his breath in horror. He pulled the buckskin from the falcon's beak and pressed the cold beads against his cheek and lips, kissing them. The falcon held his eyes as the icy hematite doused the diamond fire ravaging his soul.

"Hunter," he cried, relief flooding through him. "Hunter," he repeated, stroking her smooth crown of feathers. "You saved me. You saved me from the evil diamond magic." Shame overwhelmed him as his jealous, psychotic rage faded, bringing to mind the crazed behavior of Queen Valona.

Teleo held the buckskin in his teeth, lifted his gauntleted forearm for Hunter to ride on, and with his other hand clutched the flagstaff and reins and navigated the palomino against the current away from the chanting masses.

"I'm sorry," he mumbled through his teeth to the mare, who had suffered unjustly under his fury. She did not seem angry with him, only glad to leave the crushing mob.

The crowd thinned out quickly. Teleo headed to the base

of the sun-drenched southern wall where a line of medic tents flapped white in the breeze. A few faithful men were helping their injured friends hobble across the ripped-up ground while everyone else rejoiced. Teleo found a tent that was not over-flowing with bodies. He tethered the palomino to a stake in the shadow of the tent wall, then took Hunter and his looted helmets with him inside the tent. Two medics glanced up from where they were performing surgery on a man's leg.

"If you're walking, you don't need us," one medic said, handing a suture to his partner.

"I'm not hurt, I just need some shade," Teleo said, holding the buckskin and flagstaff tightly in one hand while Hunter perched on the other.

The medic looked askance at the falcon and bloody helmets but did not object, and turned back to his patient.

Teleo found an empty corner behind a camp table and sat on a canvas tarp, laying the helmets down beside him. Hunter hopped off his hand onto the ground, pecking at the thong of the leather medicine bag, while Teleo opened his shaking fist and regarded the buckskin scrap. He was afraid to look at the diamonds on his chest, but he could not ignore them any longer and pretend he could withstand their malign magic. He pressed the beaded side of the buckskin against the glittering diamonds, shielding their glow, and unclasped the gold chain from around his neck.

He should get rid of the whole thing. Find a fire and destroy the diamonds. Bury the hematite beads in the gravel of a stream-bed where they would never be found. Could he live without walking through walls? He could, he admitted. But he didn't want to. Why should he? He gritted his teeth. Was that the diamonds talking? Or the Stone Guardian magic? He didn't know. All he knew was that he had revealed himself to be a terrible person. The lowest of the low. No better than Queen Valona, or Cornwal, Gerik, or Gerik's father, Henrik. He looked into Hunter's eyes, ashamed. Hunter gazed back at him. What a magnificent creature she was. Free and loyal. Wise and fearless. Strong and graceful.

Teleo never wanted to lay eyes on those diamonds ever again, as beautiful as they were, as exquisite were the carvings of the lions and eagles and rampant griffin.

He stood and asked the medics if he could use some suture. The same medic looked up and nodded, directing his gaze to a table of medical supplies. Teleo found spools of silk suture, white and black. He took one of each and a steel needle, then went back to his corner. The diamond amulet and scrap of hematite-beaded buckskin were roughly the same size, the buckskin slightly overhanging the edges of the amulet. It took him several tries with trembling fingers to thread the needle. He then painstakingly stitched the buckskin and amulet together, face to face. He sewed around the edges with black silk, passing the needle through gaps between the gold creatures of the emperor's pendant and pushing the needle through the buckskin with his calloused thumb. Diamonds pressed against hematite, leaving plain leather and gold facing out, the gold chain still hanging from the loop of the emperor's pendant. He tied the sutures off and then placed the combined talisman into the medicine bag. He cut off the thongs and gave them both to Hunter to play with. She immediately swallowed one, and Teleo returned to his task. With the power object safely hidden inside the medicine bag, Teleo sewed the bag closed all the way around the edges of the talisman and then trimmed away the excess leather, resulting in a leather disk filled with magic. He took a deep breath and regarded his work. He did not trust himself. He could still tear open the stitches in a fit of insanity.

Hunter was staring at him. Teleo wished Dinsmora were there to embroider her magic, but he could not wait any longer to seal the gems. He was a Mage Stone Master, after all; he had fashioned the falcon mosaic for Queen Valona's throne, with eyes that had grounded him back into reality.

He threaded the white silk suture and meticulously embroidered a falcon head on one side of the leather disk and then the other, wishing he'd had the presence of mind to lay the stitches before he'd sewn it closed. Hunter watched, following the needle as it passed through the tight but pliable leather. Teleo used the gyrfalcon as his model, working to imbue the life force of the falcon's spirit into the silk stitches.

Teleo's back was aching by the time he'd created the likeness of two falcon heads, back-to-back. Then he threaded black floss and added beaks and eyes. Deep, silken eyes gazed sternly up at him, admonishing him to leave the jewels encased in their protective shield where the two opposing elements balanced the powerful magic and tempered it into something useful, canceling out each other's harmful aspects.

Teleo took in a breath and held the finished work by its chain. He and Hunter watched his creation turn in a circle, one pair of embroidered eyes fastening on him until the other pair took over. It was the best he could do. If this did not work, the talisman would find the flames.

He put it around his neck, slipping it under his armor next to the Heliotrope pendant, and then stood and stretched. The tent was subdued in late afternoon shadow. The two medics had left and a different medic was tending to a man who lay on a cot, recovering from surgery.

Teleo found a burlap sack, untied the helmet straps from the flagstaff, dumped his plundered helmets into the bag, and left the staff and white flag behind. Hunter jumped onto his gloved fist, and Teleo left the tent. The palomino was where he had left her. She was probably thirsty and hungry. Teleo could not remember the last time he had drunk or eaten, himself.

He searched the corpses lined up under sheets against the tents until he found a full waterskin. He drained it, then went into a medic tent and found a tin bucket half-filled with clean water and brought it out for the horse.

"I'll find you more water later," Teleo promised, patting the horse's neck as she lifted her head from the empty bucket and gazed at him. "You deserve a name," Teleo said, taking her by the reins. She was a beauty, with her dark brown coat and long blond mane and tail. "How about Victory?" She nuzzled his hand and he patted her velvety nose.

Hunter had hopped from Teleo's fist to his shoulder and dug her talons into the hooded cloak and chainmail coif that draped over his shoulder armor. The gyrfalcon's small black eyes were level with Teleo's. Together, they surveyed the vast, bloody battlefield, still littered with bodies and exhausted medics. Small units of men carted the dead further out into the fields where they would set fire to them in huge, stinking bonfires.

The celebration inside the city was well underway, but the dirty business of war was not done—the cleanup could not wait. Vultures and crows were already gathered in large circles, fighting over the dead. The crows were noisy, and the vultures were quiet. It was always like that.

Teleo climbed into Victory's saddle and headed for the City Gate.

34

FAMILY

The City Gate stood unguarded, and sounds of revelry filled the air. He would talk to Larissa about restoring order later, but for now, let the people celebrate. Teleo dismounted and led Victory through the crowded streets. Pubs and inns were overflowing. Men and women staggered over the blue stone streets, and Sapphire soldiers and Hill rebels sang drunkenly with their arms around each other's shoulders. Festival mead stands had opened back up, and troupes of musicians played on street corners and on stages in the large square at the Castle Wall.

Teleo navigated through the crowd and approached the Castle Gate. It was guarded by two weary soldiers, who were sitting on their haunches and holding white surrender flags. Teleo approached one of them.

"Bing?" he asked.

Bing stood and smiled at Teleo, and Philip rose from the other side and joined them.

"We did it!" Philip said. "We did what you said, and look, it worked! You were right. Drake came!"

"Well done," Teleo said, chuckling and clapping them on the shoulders. "You are free to leave your post. Go have fun."

"Thank you, sir, thank you," Philip said, eyeing Hunter.

"Will you put in a good word for us with Drake?" Bing asked.

"Yes, of course I will. I'll find you later."

The soldiers set their flags aside and disappeared into the crowd. Teleo passed through the gate and made his way over the back streets to the imperial stables. The building was crowded, two horses to a stall. Some horses were wounded, and grooms and medics were doing what they could for them.

"Stable's full up," a groom called over to him.

"I'm just looking for some water and grooming brushes, if you don't mind," Teleo said.

The groom eyed Teleo's bronze helm and fine armor and the gyrfalcon on his shoulder, and nodded.

Hunter flew up into the rafters while Teleo drew a bucket of water from the stable well and let Victory drink. He then drew water for himself. Daisy's whinny led him down the long aisle where he found his beloved dapple gray sharing a large stall with Petunia. Next to them were Cinnamon and Nutmeg, then BlackJack in his own stall, Star in her own stall, and the new white gelding in a stall next to Star's. Teleo smiled, imagining Sigrid's delight upon receiving her gift. Across the aisle were Gerik's thugs' Verdant Valley warhorses, two to a stall.

He visited each of his horses, happy they had survived relatively unscathed. Unsurprisingly, BlackJack had the most wounds—most notably, a tear along his neck with twelve neat sutures, which looked to be Dinsmora's work.

"That there's Drake Bedon's horse," a medic said, coming up behind Teleo. "He's mean. Won't let strangers touch him. You might get bit if you're not careful."

"He knows me," Teleo said, reaching out and scratching the big black's ears.

"Hmph," the medic grunted. The man's gaze settled on Teleo's light-colored eyes. "How do you know the young Drake?" the man asked with a mixture of suspicion and envy.

"I'm his falconer," Teleo said, gesturing at Hunter, who was perched on a beam overhead, staring into a hayloft.

The medic's eyes darted from the majestic gyrfalcon to Teleo's Red Flag armor and swords, then back to BlackJack, who was nuzzling Teleo's palm, begging for treats. The man furrowed his brow, then nodded politely and turned his attention to Victory.

"Pretty filly," the medic said. "She's got some lacerations and a puncture wound," he said, examining her hindquarters. "Here's another one. Rough time out there, eh?" the medic asked.

"More than you can imagine," Teleo said, stepping over to examine Victory's wounds with the medic.

"Want me to help clean her up for you?" the man asked. "This one needs a few stitches," he said, examining a small but gaping wound on her lower thigh.

"I'd be much obliged," Teleo said, silently chastising himself for not noticing the wounds himself. He shook his head at the pernicious power of the diamonds. His hand went to Black Lightning where it hung at his side, and he wrapped his hand around the pommel, shielding the glint of the diamonds from his peripheral vision.

The medic tied Victory to a hitching rail and then cleaned and stitched her up while Teleo stood at her head and did his best to keep her calm. When the medic was finished, Teleo thanked him and put Victory in with Star, who shuffled aside so that Victory could get to the feeding rack.

Hunter had caught a mouse and was tearing it apart in a corner. When the falcon was done, Teleo whistled for her and grabbed the burlap sack of helmets. With the gyrfalcon perched on his forearm, he left the stable.

The Palace Gate was guarded by several men he recognized from Jessum's village and Red Flag. They recognized him and waved him through, cheering and slapping him on the back as he passed. Teleo walked around to the back of the palace and found an unlocked gate that led to the herb gardens. He climbed blue stone stairs that meandered through the terraced herb beds, then entered the kitchens. Cooks and servers were busy loading roasted fowl and pigs onto carts and wheeling them out towards the muted din of the feast hall. Others carried baskets of bread and trays of steaming vegetables and sauces. Curious glances settled briefly on his bronze, feathered helm, jeweled sword hilts, and the falcon on his arm, but the staff quickly returned to their tasks.

He inquired with a serving boy and learned that the banquet was for Empress Larissa and Drake Bedon. Teleo asked a friendly cook for a plate of food and took it out to the herb garden. He ate in the shelter of the stone gazebo, away from the boisterous festivities, while Hunter stood nearby on the bank of a small garden pond, eating a frog.

Teleo rested there until the sun disappeared behind the horizon, then took his empty plate to the kitchen. It sounded like the banquet was still in full swing, if not more so. Trays of cheeses and fruits were leaving the kitchen propped on servants' shoulders, and casks of ale and mead were being trundled out on cask barrows. Cooks were pulling pies from the ovens while others were ladling hot cream sauce into tureens next to platters of spice cakes.

Teleo found a likely servant. The young woman was bright-eyed and curious.

"Do you like birds?" he asked.

She regarded Hunter, asleep on his shoulder. "I had a pet chicken, growing up," she said.

"Good. Falcons are not so different from chickens. Here." He wrapped her hand and wrist in a towel and transferred the sleepy bird to her. "Take her out to Empress Larissa's table. She belongs to a female companion of Drake Bedon. She has red hair and freckles. You can't miss her. And give this to the empress," he said, handing her the sack of helmets.

The woman gaped at him.

"Go ahead. You'll be fine. My name is Tesserman. Tell them I'm okay and will see them soon."

The servant carefully carried Hunter away, with the burlap sack slung over her shoulder.

———◆———

Teleo made his way on foot back out to the killing fields. He spent the night helping load corpses onto wagons and out to the heaps of bodies to be burned. The moon was full and shone down on them, making torches largely unnecessary.

He carried a torch anyway and checked every corpse for his son's face. Whenever he came upon someone who was still alive, he staked the torch in the ground, called for help, and took the injured to the medic tents. He then returned to the torch to continue his methodical search. He asked everyone he encountered if they'd seen any Verdant Valley orphans, or one named Owen. They promised him they would look. He knew Oren could be in the mounds of dead bodies that were growing by the hour all across the valley, but he did what he could.

He finished loading up a wagon, and as it trundled off, he heard a man calling for help among some remaining bodies in a nearby field. Teleo lifted the torch and looked for him. The man was covered in mud and blood, and Teleo would have missed him had he not called out. Teleo knelt next to him. He was a Hill man, not more than thirty. One of the man's legs was badly mutilated and a tourniquet was tightened around his upper thigh.

"You tied this yourself?" Teleo asked, examining the tourniquet and trying to figure out how to carry the man with such a mangled leg.

"Yeah," the man grunted.

"Brave man," Teleo said. "You're going to lose this leg," he said, stating the obvious.

The man tried to laugh through the pain. "I'm a cobbler. I don't need two legs," he said.

"Keep talking," Teleo said as he looked around on the ground.

"But I have two kids and a wife, and they need me," the man said. "I'll make my own fake foot."

Teleo found a tattered red flag trampled in the mud. It would do. The man was going to lose his leg anyway. Teleo did not have the heart to take his axe to the pulpy mess himself. Let the medics do it. He cut the flagpole down to use as a splint while the man talked nonsense just to keep his mouth busy. Teleo wrapped the flesh and bone as best he could, to screams of agony, and lifted the man in his arms, propping up the splinted leg with his elbow and trying to keep it as still as possible. He hailed another man, and together, they carried the cobbler as smoothly as they could across the rough ground. Halfway to the tents, the man mercifully passed out. They brought the quiet but breathing body into a medic tent and laid him on a table. Two medics with black circles under their eyes came over, assessed the situation, and went to work.

Teleo headed back out on his own and continued looking for his son.

He spent the next day and night on corpse duty, napping briefly in a medic tent and eating food the castle kitchens brought out to the field. The following morning, a Sapphire soldier ran over to him.

"I found Owen the orphan," he said, gently grabbing Teleo's arm, the soldier's somber eyes telling him the boy's fate.

Teleo's heart jumped into his throat and he ran with him to the western field, across dried mud and sharp stubble of what had once been a hayfield. The soldier stepped back as Teleo knelt next to the corpse and carefully removed the Sapphire-issued helmet with trembling hands. The sun shone down on fair skin and light brown hair. The face was thin, and the long straight nose was off-center from an old break. He looked young, no more than sixteen. Teleo opened the dead boy's eyes. They were small, sky blue, and set close together. Oren had Bella-Mae's large and wide-set, storm-gray eyes, and these were not them. It was not his son. Teleo let out a sob of relief, laced with guilt and despair.

Teleo pulled the dead stranger into his arms and wept. He wept for the boy who had been taken from his parents. He wept for the boy who had been beaten up and his nose broken. He wept for the boy who had been raised to fight in the army that had kidnapped him. He wept for the parents who had been murdered or were still alive and hoping beyond hope that their son had survived and would someday be reunited with them. He wept until he had no more tears, and rocked the dead boy to the beat of his broken heart.

———————◆———————

Teleo spent the remainder of the morning scouring the fields and finding fewer and fewer fallen men who still lived, until all that remained were the dead. He ran his gaze across the vast and bloody field, where small groups hauled bodies to pyres all around the perimeter. If Oren was out there, he was either dead or healthy enough to carry the dead. If he was alive, Teleo would find him eventually—he'd started spreading the word to bring all Verdant Valley orphans to Drake Bedon.

Teleo tried to hang on to hope and made another tour of the medic tents and the large exhibition hall inside the Castle Ring, which had been converted into a makeshift hospital. He examined the faces of the wounded—Sapphire soldiers and Hill Tribe lads—lined up in row after row of cots, but he did not find his boy.

If Oren was dead, there was nothing Teleo could do about it. He abandoned his search and went back to the fields and helped clear bodies until there were no more. Later that day, the mounds of corpses were set on fire. Plumes of black smoke drifted skyward. He had no sadness left in him as he watched thousands of souls rise to the heavens.

Black Lightning hung at his side, its pommel wrapped in leather to hide the evil diamonds. He trudged across the fields to a metalsmith's shop he had discovered in a small village not far down the Emperor's Toll Road, and paid the man a Silver Bit to use his tools. It took him an hour—with the help of the metalsmith—to get the sword's pommel off without damaging the tang. Damn Jarnsmidt.

They had needed to unwrap the pommel to remove it. It had seven diamonds on each side, and the metalsmith ooh'd and ahh'd at their beauty. Teleo wrapped the apple-sized pommel with leather and tied it closed with a hemp cord and a firm knot, stuck it in his pocket, and then thanked the metalsmith and went back out to the nearest burning pyre.

Teleo bit his lip until it bled as he fought with himself over the necessity to destroy such a magnificent hunk of metal and jewels. He wished Hunter were still there with him.

He could not get himself to do it, and so he approached a burly man, Jonas, whom he had worked with side by side, piling brush and wood and the last of the corpses onto the pyre. Now, the massive blaze was raging, and men looked on from a safe distance as flames roared and climbed into the sky.

"Can you please throw this onto the fire for me?" Teleo asked Jonas. Teleo held the leather-wrapped ball out on his trembling palm.

"What is it?" Jonas asked, wrinkling his soot-streaked forehead.

"Just, uh ... something that belonged to ... someone who died in battle. I think it should ... burn with the fallen heroes."

"Ah, okay," Jonas said, raising an eyebrow. "You don't want to throw it yourself?"

Teleo forced himself to answer. "I do, but I have a bad shoulder. I want to make sure it lands right in the center."

"I'd be glad to," Jonas said, and reached for the ball.

Teleo's fingers closed around it and sweat dripped down his face. Jonas met his eyes.

"It's ...," Teleo faltered, "... sentimental."

It took all of Teleo's will to open his fingers and let Jonas take the diamond pommel away from him, as though it were not an evil talisman but the heart of his son whom he could not bear to say goodbye to.

Teleo held his breath and gripped his hands together as Jonas cocked his arm back, aimed, and launched the leather ball towards the fire.

Teleo wanted to chase after it but kept his boots planted in the dirt and watched it disappear into the flames.

He exhaled silently. He stood with Jonas and counted to himself as, one by one, the diamonds exploded. Jonas gave him a strange look after the third one, but Teleo stared into the blaze and kept counting all the way to fourteen.

He was drenched with sweat and out of breath by the last one. He wanted to fall to the ground in a pitiful heap, but he thanked Jonas and plodded towards the castle.

As he approached the walled city, he pulled the fox-and-hare cloak loose from the bundle he had tied to his back and draped it around himself. He didn't care if anyone saw him or didn't see him, but he was too despondent to walk through the gates and face the cheerful city dwellers or chat with any gate guards who might recognize him.

He had listened to the festivities the night before from the fields. The coronation of Empress Larissa had been followed by more revelry, and hordes of drunken people sang and chanted *Larissa, Larissa, Larissa,* alternating with chants of *Bedon, Bedon, Bedon,* and *Drake, Drake, Drake.* The trampled dirt surrounding the City Wall was littered with empty ale mugs and random items of clothing. Teleo kicked aside a soiled white wig and kept walking.

He made his way around to the city's western wall, which was relatively quiet, and walked through the thick, blue stone. His diamond-and-hematite falcon talisman worked, Teleo noted dully, as he traversed the stone barrier without effort or dizziness. He should have been happy, but the wall was just stone, and he was just a man. He navigated the narrow city streets, walked through the Castle Wall, then the Palace Wall, and finally through the stone wall surrounding the lower bailey. The battle yard was quiet and the Heliotrope was still marred with dried blood and muddy footprints. Teleo walked across the magical mosaic, through the gate, and around to the herb garden.

The sun was shining and the gardens were in full bloom. The round gazebo was shaded by a lapis lazuli tile roof, and its interior was encircled by a low argillite wall and ornately carved lapis lazuli benches. The floor of the gazebo was blue argillite polished to a watery sheen.

Teleo unstrapped his swords and other weapons and stashed them in a thicket of rosemary bushes. He had left his armor and helmet behind at some point—in a medic tent somewhere on the southeastern flank. If they should get stolen, it was only metal, he reflected, and he knew where to get more. He lay flat on his back in the center of the gazebo, draped the fox-and-hare cloak over himself like a blanket, and lifted the hood to cover his face. He folded his hands over his chest and closed his eyes.

The cold stone felt good against his back. He let himself slowly sink down into it, the minerals parting and closing around him. He sank until his body was completely submerged. He could still breathe inside the stone, but he did not know for how long, and he did not much care. The stone was still and silent and quieted his mind. He would let himself doze off, and if he awoke, so be it. If he did not ... well, he would not know the difference.

———◆———

Teleo led Thunder into the small field next to the house, removed his bridle, saddle, and heavy saddlebags, gave him a quick brushing, and left the big warhorse with an armful of hay and a bucket of fresh water. He tried to contain himself as he jogged out to the back orchard to look for his family. He wanted to surprise Bella-Mae, and had made Dinsmora promise not to send one of her birds to alert her.

He spotted them back amongst the trees, gathering apples from the ground and placing them in bushels. Oren saw him first, dropping his apples and running to him, hopping over bushels and rakes. Teleo ran to meet him and scooped him up in his arms. Oren had grown since he had last seen him but was still young enough for a great big bear hug. Teleo sank his face into his son's shirt, which smelled like Bella-Mae's lavender soap. Abigail ran up, braids flying and her cheeks red like ripe apples. Bella-Mae was not far behind, her eyes overflowing with love. He put Oren down and lifted Abigail in his arms, kissing her cheeks and looking into her big green eyes.

"I missed you, baby," he said, holding her tight and then setting her on his hip so that he could rest his hand on Oren's head, the soft, sandy-blond hair like silk under his rough soldier's hands. Bella-Mae wrapped her arms around him and their little girl, kissing his face all over.

"I miss him," the soft, male voice said.

"Me too," the girl's voice said.

"I hope he comes back," he said.

"What if he's dead?" she asked.

"He's not dead."

"How do you know?"

"I just know."

Silence.

Teleo sorted through the bleariness of half-sleep. He was in a dark chamber of sorts. He reached out and felt around, meeting the resistance of cold sand in water and the wool lining of his cloak. His eyes flew open. He remembered now—he was submerged in the stone slab of the gazebo. He had been dreaming of home but had been roused by Jessum and Kaspari talking above him. He stirred and then settled back into his stone vault and listened.

"I don't want to be Supreme Commander," Jessum said.

"Why not?" Kaspari asked. "That's the next most powerful post after Empress."

"I don't want power. I want to make swords."

"Can't you do both?" she asked.

"If Teleo would help me, then maybe I could. He could do the Commander part," Jessum said, chuckling. "He could make all the decisions and teach me how to fight like him. He's a great teacher."

"Yeah," she agreed. "He's the best."

Teleo breathed in and out, wiggling his toes. It was cold inside the stone.

Jessum continued, "That way, people can be united by my Drake Bedon blood and live in peace. In the meantime, I can forge steel."

Teleo could almost hear him smiling. Jessum loved fire and bending metal, and he was good at it.

Jessum continued, "Mostly I want him to help me so I can hang out with him more often. He's like a father to me. He's the only father I have."

"Me too. We're both lucky he found us," Kaspari said. "He's the only one who knew my parents and what my life was like ... before. He's the only person I can trust, besides Dinsmora. And you. You're like my brother. You grew up in my castle, but I think you and I lived in completely different worlds."

"Yeah," Jessum said wryly. "Totally different. You saw the best and I saw the worst. But yes, I know where you grew up. I always wanted a sister. I didn't think she'd be a princess, though," he said, teasing.

"I didn't think my brother would be from the ancient Bedon bloodline, our arch enemy."

They both laughed and then grew quiet.

Teleo sat up, the stone flowing away from him, and the fox-and-hare cloak sliding silently onto his lap. He closed his eyes against the daylight and then opened them again. Jessum and Kaspari were sitting on the low wall surrounding the gazebo, looking out over the garden pond with their backs to him. Teleo rose slowly on weak legs and stood on the solid slab, letting the cloak fall to the ground. He cleared his throat, and Jessum and Kaspari turned their heads at the sound.

"Teleo," Jessum said, swinging his legs over the wall.

The teenagers hopped over the bench and stepped forward hesitantly. Their faces were drawn and dark circles shadowed their eyes.

"Where have you been?" Kaspari asked, reaching out and touching his arm. "We've been worried sick. You look ... terrible. What happened?"

"We thought maybe you weren't coming back," Jessum said, his voice strained.

"Sigrid is very upset," Kaspari said. "Dinsmora, too. They were both crying."

"I know," Teleo mumbled. "I'm sorry."

"What's the matter, Teleo?" Jessum asked, peering at him.

He had tried to hide it, but he couldn't hold it back any longer. Tears pooled in his eyes. "I miss my family. My wife, Bella-Mae, and my son and daughter," he said, choking up. "I miss them so much, sometimes I can't live with the pain." Warm tears streamed down his face. "Oren and Abigail would have been your ages by now." A sudden sob shook him.

Kaspari and Jessum stepped forward and hugged him. The three of them stood together, their arms wrapped around each other and Teleo's head pressed between both of theirs.

"It's okay, Teleo," Jessum said soothingly, patting his back.

"You'll be okay," Kaspari said. "I know it's hard, but things will get better. You'll see."

He forced back his tears and squeezed the shoulders of these two magnificent human beings—acutely aware that he was complaining about missing his family to two orphans. Here they were, comforting him like he was the child and they were the adults.

"We'll be your family," Kaspari said. "We don't have anybody else. Don't you ever leave us."

"I won't," Teleo promised. "I will never leave you." Tears streamed shamelessly down his face, and he voiced what had been obvious all along: "You are my family now."

He hugged them and they cried, and laughed, and cried some more.

◆

"I saw those diamonds around your neck," Dinsmora said, confronting Teleo when they stood alone in Larissa's library. Her hands were on her hips and her eyes were blazing. "Where are they?" she asked. "Lying hypocrite."

"I hid them," Teleo said, raising his hands defensively. "I can explain. Diamonds are really dangerous," he said.

"Yeah," she said snidely. "They result in arrogant control freaks murdering your best friend."

Teleo gave her an abashed smile and nodded. "I can't argue with that. Look, Dinsmora. I was wrong. I'm sorry. I should not have killed Queen Valona. It was not her fault. She couldn't help it. Believe me, I know. Those diamonds were controlling her. I should have been patient and found a way to save her."

Dinsmora stood with her mouth hanging open, and Teleo instantly regretted admitting to the queen's murder.

Dinsmora tilted her head at him. "Did you just say you were wrong?" she asked.

Teleo threw back his head and laughed. "Yes. Is that so surprising?"

Dinsmora cocked an eyebrow. "I don't think I've ever heard those words uttered from your mouth before."

"Oh, come on," Teleo said.

"No, seriously," she said.

"Well, I was wrong," he repeated.

Dinsmora pursed her lips and folded her arms, inspecting him. "Why?"

"Because there's an antidote to the diamonds," he said. "A balancing stone. Hematite."

She knit her eyebrows together. "Hematite? How did you figure that out?"

"Because I have some from the Stone Guardian witch's cloak, and it works. It saved my life—or my sanity, at least. Hunter's the one who really saved me."

She looked sideways at him, puzzled.

He related how Sonderson had found the hematite-beaded scrap and how Teleo had hurled it out over the crowd and Hunter had grabbed it. "She's a wise bird," Teleo said.

"She is," Dinsmora agreed. A grin softened her face, showing her dimples.

"Anyway," he continued. "I cannot look at those diamonds ever again. I sewed them together with the hematite and sealed them with embroidery." He held up his falcon talisman and Dinsmora examined it, running her fingers over the falcon heads.

"Nice stitches, for a thick-fingered stonemason," she said.

"Thanks," he said, grinning.

"Seriously. They're really good," she said. "They have power stitched in with them. How did you learn to do that?" She squinted at him.

He shrugged. "I realized that I do that with stone, with my mosaics. I figured thread is not so different."

"Like Valona's falcon throne?" she asked.

Teleo nodded. "Yes. Like that. Plus, Hunter watched the whole time I was laying the stitches. She helped. She really is smart."

"Birds know things," she said, laughing, and handed him back the talisman. "You know," she said, her eyes deepening.

"I was furious and grief-stricken when you killed Valona. She was my friend. But I was just as hurt that you did not trust me enough to confide in me." Her voice was thin and high like it got when she was trying not to cry. "You felt you had to go around my back and do all that without telling me."

He lay his hands on her shoulders. "Dinsmora, you were under her spell. I tried to talk to you several times. Don't you remember?" He squeezed her shoulders. "But you wouldn't listen, no matter what I said or did. You just got mad at me. Plus, you were never around. You forgot about Nutmeg and neglected Hunter and the kids. That was not like you."

She started to argue but her voice trailed off. "Maybe you're right," she admitted.

"You're my family," he told her, holding her gaze. "I love you."

She started crying, and he hugged her.

"Can you ever forgive me?" he asked, suddenly needing her forgiveness more than anything.

"Yes, Teleo. I forgave you a long time ago." She sniffled and pulled away, wiping at her nose with the back of her hand.

"You did?"

"Yes. You're my cousin. My dearest friend from childhood. I love you. But I was still mad at you. You can both love someone and be angry with them at the same time, you know?"

"I suppose," he said.

"So the diamonds are inside that falcon talisman along with the hematite? Why do you need to keep them at all, if they cancel each other out?" she asked.

"Because the hematite allows me to walk through walls."

She stared at him. "Walk through walls?" Her face grew pale. "Like a Stone Guardian?"

He shrugged self-consciously. "Sort of. Yes."

"But ... but ...," she stammered.

"It comes in very handy," he said.

"You stole Valona's cloak!" she exclaimed. She shook her finger at him, her mouth pinching into a knot. "You sneaky, no good ..."

He twisted his face guiltily. "I needed to," he said. "Her diamond cloak had everybody enthralled. It made everyone love her. It made her young, and beautiful, and irresistible—no matter what atrocities she committed. But I forgot about her diamond tiara. Turns out I was under her spell, too."

Dinsmora squinted at him, her eyes roaming over his face. "I don't think that falcon embroidery and hematite are shielding your diamonds all the way. I think they're still working their magic," she said. "Casting a glamour over you. You look really good."

"Thanks ... I think," he replied dryly.

"No, really. Your scars are gone."

"That was the Heliotrope," he said.

"What Heliotrope?" she asked, wrinkling her brow.

He took in a deep breath and let it out slowly. "I have a lot to tell you."

EPILOGUE

35

<hr>

LINEAGE

One year later—one week before the Summer Solstice

Teleo sat in the purple overstuffed armchair in Empress Larissa's study and crossed one ankle over the other. His boots needed polishing, he observed idly as he waited for everyone else.

Larissa eventually bustled in, wearing a pale-blue brocade gown edged in ivory satin and seed pearls, with her cloak tossed back over her shoulders. Her hair was loose, falling in long black curls down her back. She refused to follow the fashion of powdered wigs, and ladies all over the Sapphire Empire were imitating her natural hairstyle. She sat behind her desk and grinned at Teleo.

"Early as always, eh, Teleo?"

He smiled back. The sun had already passed its zenith—she was late, as usual.

The other Ladies of the Empire came in after Larissa and took their seats near her desk, arranging their silk skirts and long curls. Sigrid had taken the role of First Advisor. Dinsmora was Special Counselor. Kaspari was being tutored by all three women in preparation for one day taking back the Verdant Valley throne. She was carrying a large bound volume and set it on her lap.

Jessum came in with Jarnsmidt, winked at Teleo, and they sat in wooden chairs against the wall. Jessum was the official Supreme Commander, although in reality he was Commander-in-Training, with Jarnsmidt and Teleo advising him and making day-to-day decisions while Jessum spent most of his time at the armory forging steel.

Jarnsmidt's primary responsibility was to serve as one of Empress Larissa's ministers. Each of the seven Hill Tribe monarchs had a seat at the Imperial Ministers' table, and each had a general who served under Jessum but trained their own troops in their own lands.

Teleo, in his role as Master of Arms, was in charge of the empress's security, as well as that of Sapphire City. As such, he oversaw the training of the Sapphire City troops and Palace Guard but let his captains do most of the work. When he wasn't busy with his official duties or with his betrothed, Sigrid, he stole what time he could with the Verdant Valley orphans who were under his care.

The edict to bring all Verdant Valley orphans to Drake Bedon had been sent out by the empress, and the seven kings had spread the word to their Hill Tribes. That had turned up two dozen war orphans. Teleo, Jessum, and Kaspari met with all of them. None were Oren. Either Teleo's son was dead, or he did not want to be found, or perhaps he had escaped to the mountain kingdoms. Teleo considered searching for him in the wild and treacherous Blue Mountains, but if Oren had escaped the Sapphire Empire, he was probably safe and would be nearly a full-grown man able to take care of himself by now. If Oren had escaped to Verdant Valley and was searching for Teleo there, well ... dwelling on that possibility drove Teleo crazy, and so he tried not to imagine that unlikely scenario. Or perhaps Teleo would turn around one day and his son would be standing there, having tracked him across the mountains and valleys. In the meantime, he forced himself to set aside his dream of finding Oren and devoted himself instead to his loved ones here, his responsibilities in the burgeoning empire, and his orphans.

Teleo had encountered a few of the orphans during his search years before, and he had carried guilt for not trying to rescue them at the time. They did not seem to recognize him or bear him any ill will. They were happy to meet him, a Verdant Valley man their fathers' age, as well as Kaspari, daughter of King Elke, but none of them wanted to go home. Many of the orphans had witnessed their parents being killed and did not want to return to Verdant Valley under King Henrik's reign. Those who were unsure of the fate of their parents did not want to risk searching for them now, given the Staggas' conscription of teenaged boys. Half of the orphans were content with their foster families and decided to stay with them. The rest moved into the Imperial Palace, and Empress Larissa arranged for castle apprenticeships in the trades of their choice. Teleo was in charge of their well-being. His latest effort was to teach them horsemanship. He had given each of them one of Gerik's thugs' eleven remaining warhorses to care for, and the twelfth orphan, Teleo's favorite because he reminded him of his uncle Brady, was responsible for Victory.

"So," Larissa said, interrupting Teleo's musings. "What have you all decided?"

They exchanged glances and nodded at Sigrid, who shared their plan with the empress.

"You will dance the solstice in your tower, Larissa," Sigrid said. "I will dance in my tower. My father will dance in your battle yard. Jessum will fold steel in the solstice light in the armory. Teleo will dance in his tower at Trillifort. And Dinsmora will dance in the sewing chamber at Trillifort."

Larissa said, "But I thought the sewing chamber is now the new king's chamber."

"We are betting that King Cutter will not rise before dawn, after a night of Solstice Eve festivities," Teleo answered. "Or, he will be outside watching the sunrise and sharing in the solstice morning mead. If he does show up, then Dinsmora will need to explain herself."

Dinsmora nodded, and Larissa glanced at Kaspari, who was scowling at the book in her lap.

"And what do you say, my young queen-in-exile?" Larissa asked Kaspari.

Kaspari raised her eyes. "I object, Your Highness."

Larissa lifted an eyebrow. "You object to what?"

"I object to being left out." Kaspari's lower lip jutted out in a sulky frown.

Larissa said gently, "I understand, my dear, but we have all read the ancient manuscript, and I quote," she said, looking down at a parchment on her desk as though having anticipated this moment. *"Standing in the light of the Summer Solstice in the Sun Circle of a Heliotrope is for a Mage the elixir that awakens the power of a thousand lifetimes. But beware. For if the soul holds not a drop of Mage blood, then you will find them dead upon the moon slab. For within the blood of a Mage flows the light of the stars. But for those who are of common blood, earth and metal are their primary elements, and the light of the solstice, like lightning, will strike them down."*

Kaspari sniffed haughtily and raised her chin. "I have a drop. I have many drops." She opened her book to a marked page, and read, *"And the Mage, Abaris, left his homeland south of the Blue Valley and crossed the mountains to the Green Valley, whereupon he fell in love with a peasant girl and made their descendants queens."* Kaspari looked up defiantly.

Teleo exchanged glances with Dinsmora, then returned his gaze to Kaspari and crossed his arms.

Kaspari closed the book and continued, "I have such an ancestor, named Abaris, who arrived from the Sapphire Valley, married a farmer's daughter, and defeated the Royal Mage at Verdant Castle and became Royal Mage himself. Their son, Abaris the Kind, went to war to defeat the Coastal Kingdoms. He later married a sea captain's daughter, and their daughter, Ribhanna, married a prince, who later bore a daughter, Irabella, whose great-granddaughter married King Elke the First."

She lifted her chin again and dared them with her eyes to challenge her.

Teleo uncrossed his arms and said, "How do you know all this about your ancestry, Kaspari, seeing as how magic has been outlawed? No royal family would admit to being descended from Mages, even if it were so many generations ago."

"Because my mother had a book that says so," Kaspari said. "She got it from my father's grandmother and hid it in her bedchamber in a stone box with a lock that only she could open. She read it to me many times and told me never to tell anyone. But that I should know, because Mages have certain powers that she wanted me to learn, if she could ever find me a teacher. She said her side also had Mage blood, but she could not prove it."

"Just because the names are the same, doesn't mean it was the same Abaris," Teleo said. Kaspari's answering glare reminded Teleo of her mother, Queen Eleanor, making him want to bow to her wishes, but he returned her stubborn gaze. "How do you know it's the same Abaris?"

Kaspari's confident scowl wavered and she sat up straighter. "Because I counted the generations in the book here, and they match."

"If we could see your mother's book, darling," Larissa said, "I would feel more comfortable. But to risk your life based on such a thin thread feels reckless and irresponsible."

"I agree with the empress," Sigrid said. "If you die, who will take back Verdant Valley from the Staggas? They're still encouraging criminals to kidnap children and smuggle them over the mountains to sell to the Staggas' slave trading network. They must be stopped. We must shut down that evil market for good, on both sides of the mountains."

"There's another way," Jessum said. They all turned to him. "Remember?" he asked. "It said that only Mages can travel from Heliotrope to Heliotrope. They used to test novices that way before letting them dance the sword during the solstice. If they were successful, they made them practice traveling in order to strengthen them. We can test her. If she can travel, then that means she's a Mage."

Kaspari nodded and cast her brother a grateful glance.

"The manuscript also said," Dinsmora cut in, "that some novices with very weak bloodlines disappeared during traveling, never to be seen again."

Teleo and Dinsmora traded concerned looks. They had argued with Kaspari about traveling many times over the past year. Dinsmora and Jessum—son of the Drake Bedon line, his veins thick with Mage blood—had been dancing the sword and practicing traveling between the Heliotropes at Red Flag and Sapphire Palace for just that purpose, in preparation for the solstice.

The previous summer, Teleo had traveled to the Third Tower in the dead of night, stolen into Trillifort's masonry, and chipped off enough Angel Wings marble and Down in the

Deep for several Heliotrope amulets. He had made one each for Dinsmora, Jessum, and Kaspari, but he had never given Kaspari hers. She had danced the sword with them but had not been allowed to travel, and often stormed off in a fury after reminding them that she had been dancing in a Heliotrope her entire life, and going on about how unfair it all was.

Everyone frowned at one another, except for Kaspari, who said, "I will prove them both at once. I will travel home to my Heliotrope in the Royal Garden at Verdant Palace and retrieve my mother's book." She stood up, placed the leather-bound volume on her chair, and marched over to Teleo. She stuck out her hand. "Please, Teleo, may I have my Heliotrope amulet?"

He pursed his lips at her. "No, Kaspari. We've discussed this."

"Then ... *you* go get the book for me. Please?" Her eyes glittered mischievously, and Teleo laughed out loud. She was a devious little schemer, setting him up like that. She was surely the descendant of a Royal Mage, who were reputed to have been manipulative politicians. She smiled sweetly at him, and despite his reputation as a hardened warrior, everyone knew she had him wrapped around her little finger.

"You want me to go back to Verdant Palace and get your book?" he asked. "In the middle of that nest of vipers?"

She nodded, her eyes darkening. "It could be dangerous," she said.

"Could be?" he asked, laughing again, and shook his head.

"You're right," Kaspari said. "I'd better go instead." She stuck her hand out again. "I'll be fine."

"You don't even know where that box is anymore," Teleo said, recalling the sounds of Gerik's men ransacking the palace on that fateful day. "Maybe they opened it and destroyed the book."

She shook her head. "No. Not possible. It was sealed by Stone Guardian magic. That's what my mother said."

"So your mother knew Stone Guardian magic?" Teleo asked, cocking an eyebrow.

"She said the Mages and Stone Guardians used to inter-marry, back when everyone got along. She said that the mix of the two magics was the most potent. She said the Staggas knew about our mixed bloodline, somehow, and if they could not intermarry with us, then they would want to destroy every last drop of Elke blood."

Teleo sighed. "That does not make me want to send you into their arms, Kaspari, if that's your argument."

But he knew her argument was intended to convince him to go to Verdant Palace and retrieve her precious book. Who was he to dispute the power of blended Mage and Stone Guardian magic? His falcon talisman burned hot and cold against his skin.

"How exactly do you intend to open that box, if it's sealed with Stone Guardian magic?" he asked.

She shrugged her shoulders and cast him a sly glance. "I know somebody who can hide themselves in stone gazebos," she said. "I've even heard that someone close to us knows how to walk through stone walls. It should be easy to stick one's hand through a simple stone box."

Teleo glanced around the room. Sigrid and Larissa returned his gaze with feigned innocence, Jarnsmidt busily worked at a hangnail with a tiny sleeve dagger, and Dinsmora snickered.

"Can a man have no secrets anymore?" he complained. "Okay, fine," he said, standing up. "I'll go. How big is this box? What kind of stone is it made of?"

She described the box—a rectangular gray stone box, big enough to hold a large bound volume like the one sitting on her chair, with a pattern of inlaid stones on one side. She then sketched a map of the interior layout of the residential palace, and he committed it to memory.

An hour later, he and his companions assembled in Larissa's Heliotrope chamber.

He wore his two Mage's Blades at his side—Black Lightning had a new pommel set with fourteen cabochons of black obsidian—plus his usual assortment of knives and hammers, and an axe for good measure. Jarnsmidt insisted he wear his plate armor, which he grudgingly donned, but he refused to carry the pike Jarnsmidt offered and the shepherd's crook Dinsmora held out for him.

"I can't hide those under my cloak. Don't you know anything about assassins?" he asked.

"Are you going to kill Gerik while you're there?" Kaspari asked hopefully.

"To be honest, I hope to avoid him," Teleo said. "Assassin was the wrong word. I meant thief."

"I hate Gerik," Kaspari said.

"Me too," Jessum said.

"As do I," Teleo said. "But you do want me to return, do you not?"

Kaspari frowned but did not press him further.

Teleo knelt and peered into the Sun Circle. It was dark, with only glimmers of light and shadow around the edges. He stood and stepped into the center.

"Good luck," everyone said in unison as they gathered around and watched him pull up his hood and fasten his fox-and-hare cloak.

Teleo closed his eyes and remembered sweeping the Royal Garden's Heliotrope for the first time, pruning away the overgrowth, and rolling aside the bronze urn.

The urn.

At the last moment, Teleo squatted and raised his hands, and found himself pushing against a cold ring of metal. He stepped aside and caught the tall urn as it toppled over in the center of the Royal Garden, catching it just before it hit the ground. He held his breath and silently rolled it back to the center, then crept into the shadows of the pear tree, disturbing a small flock of gray-and-white finches who fluttered from the branches and settled among the pink blossoms of a crape myrtle across the courtyard. A bright blue dragonfly darted and hummed in the open air of the sunlit courtyard above the Heliotrope, whose colored stones shimmered and rippled as though a light breeze were brushing across a pond.

The courtyard was immaculately manicured but unoccupied, and the palace's upper chambers, consisting of bedchambers, studies, and libraries, were silent. But the sounds of court life filled the ground-floor reception halls, and pots clattered from the kitchen. Teleo stood still and listened. The tinkling of a bell called for a servant. A door slammed. Faint male voices argued in the king's audience chamber behind him. He peered through the screen of branches into the audience chamber's windows, which stood several paces away under the dark portico, but the glass reflected the bright green garden back at him. The courtyard's north entry archway stood beyond fronds of fern trees, but no guards were in sight—they would be guarding the exterior, not expecting an attack from within.

The royal bedchambers on the second level of the western wing behind him all had balconies, but the studies and libraries in the southern wing above the dining room were sheer walls of stone and glass. The eastern wall housed guest chambers, crowned by the Focal Point window, and the northern wall held the garden gate archway and servants' quarters above. Everything was quiet.

Teleo pulled himself up into the V of the pear tree's trunk and climbed onto the thick branch where Kaspari used to hide behind its dense foliage. He edged across the branch, grimacing as it swayed and the small green fruit bobbed up and down. The branch overhung the former queen's balcony, and he stepped onto the white marble balustrade and dropped silently onto the terrace. His pear tree mosaic glimmered up at him—meticulously laid gold-leaf pears and seashell dragonflies, tiger-eye bark and jade leaves, slate finches with amber eyes catching the midday sun.

He took a moment to marvel at his masterpiece, then stalked across the terrace and tried the door handle. It was unlocked. He slowly pushed open the door, silent on well-oiled hinges, and stepped into the chamber. A curtained bed dominated one wall, facing a small marble fireplace. Wooden chests and armoires filled the available wall space. It was a man's room now, with dark green velvet curtains and a musky scent. A Stagga shield was mounted over the fireplace and swords hung from a rack on the wall next to the door.

Teleo knelt and looked under the bed where Kaspari had said her mother kept the stone box. He crept under the high-set bed frame and let his eyes adjust. Nothing but dust bunnies hid there. He stood up and carefully opened drawers and armoires, rifling through men's undergarments, silk and velvet pantaloons, brocade waistcoats and doublets, and fur-trimmed cloaks. He opened small inlaid boxes filled with gold brooches and found a hidden drawer filled with a collection of ornamental daggers. One large armoire held only armor—a polished steel cuirass with the Staggas' leaping stag sigil, spaulders, greaves, faulds, gauntlets, two helmets, mail, and gambesons. Polished boots stood in the corner next to a sheathed longsword propped against the wall. He believed this was now Gerik's bedchamber. The stone box was not there.

He pushed his head through the cold stone wall and peered

up and down the hallway. It was empty. He stepped through the wall and crept down the marble corridor, humble compared to Sapphire Palace's opulence, and tried the next door. It was locked. He stepped to the side and walked through the wall, emerging into a much larger bedchamber. This must have been King Elke's chamber, now taken over by King Henrik, Teleo assumed. A stag's head was mounted over the fireplace, its massive twelve-point antlers spreading out like branches of a tree. Teleo went through Henrik's belongings as he had Gerik's, trying to leave things as he'd found them. Clothing, weapons, jewels. Stacks of books and manuscripts on a large desk, which overlooked the courtyard. Henrik was a widower and there were no signs of a woman having been there. Neither was there a stone box the size of a large book.

Teleo inspected four smaller bedchambers, ghosting along the abandoned hallway and passing through stone walls, then moved on to the next wing. There were no young children in the Stagga household, and the room where Kaspari and her brothers had been tutored appeared to be unused. Wooden desks, tables, and chairs stood dusty and neglected. Shelves lined the walls and were filled with books and manuscripts, arranged haphazardly, as though someone had hastily returned them to the shelves after the palace had been ransacked and had not returned since. It occurred to Teleo that perhaps the stone box had been breached, and Kaspari's prized ancestral record was sitting on the shelves, mixed in with the other tomes. But she had said the box was sealed with magic.

The next room was perhaps the king's study. A massive oak desk was cluttered with ink wells, quills, and rolled manuscripts. Teleo quickly searched the drawers. One was locked but was too small to hold the box Kaspari had described. The next room was a proper library. Teleo browsed the shelves for a large book-shaped stone box but saw only leather-bound volumes and rolled parchments. He went to the next room, which held random pieces of furniture covered with muslin sheets.

The last room was locked. Teleo stepped through the cold marble wall. It was a storage room with one small window high in the wall facing the courtyard, letting in diffused light. Shelves and tables held a random assortment of items—chests, candelabra, books, and urns. Large metal statuettes of sea creatures filled one table—a great serpent, a leaping whale, a kraken clutching a ship, and a mermaid brandishing a trident in one hand and a closed clam shell in the other. Human skulls draped with cobwebs lined an upper shelf and looked down at Teleo as he prowled in the shadows. Helmets of various sorts lined the shelf below—perhaps belonging to the skulls which sat above on the macabre trophy wall. A few large wooden chests stood on the floor, and smaller chests sat on a table. Each chest was secured with a thick metal padlock.

Teleo reflected for a moment. He had never tested his Stone Guardian magic on metal. Was he able to penetrate metal like he could stone? He pressed forefinger to thumb around one of the lock hooks and closed his eyes. For a second, he thought he was bending it, but then the metal pushed back at him in a silent buzz. The harder he pressed, the stronger the vibration, until a burning sensation made him release his grip. He shook his hand until the pain subsided. He tried again, with the same result.

He gave up and looked around the room for a likely hiding place for the keys to the many chests. If they were on a key ring carried by Gerik or Henrik, Teleo pondered what his next move would be. He reached up to the dusty door lintel. No keys. He pushed aside books on the shelves, looked inside urns, and lifted the bases of the statuettes while the helmets and skulls watched.

He lifted one helmet and then the next. Teleo lifted the fourth helmet and jerked back.

A huddle of brown mice stared out at him from a nest in a shredded skullcap. One was the mother. The others were small but not babies anymore. As though on cue, they burst from the nest and ran in every direction. One jumped straight at Teleo and clawed its way up his chest. Teleo backed against a table, frantically flapping his cloak to get it off. It was at his collar, and he twisted and tried to brush it off, but the mouse ran up into his hood and around the chainmail coif at his neck. Teleo dropped the helmet, and his elbow caught the mermaid, sending the statuette teetering and toppling off the table. The helmet and mermaid hit the stone floor with a loud clatter as Teleo tore off his cloak and swatted at his neck. The mouse flew off and ran under a table, and Teleo dove at the helmet to stop it from noisily rocking back and forth on the stone floor.

Teleo winced at the racket he had made and grabbed the mermaid. The clamshell in her hand had popped open, disgorging a ring of small brass keys. Teleo snatched the keys and returned the helmet and mermaid to the shelf and table.

He pulled on his cloak and hurriedly tried the keys in the large chest at his feet until one slipped into the lock. He opened the chest. Mounds of gold coins, rings, and bracelets glinted and shone. He dug his hands through the gold, feeling for a stone box, but met only more gold. He locked the chest and went to the next one. This one held two desiccated human heads, the papery skin and hair still relatively intact. Teleo swallowed and locked the chest and then went to the next one. The third chest was empty, lined with red velvet and smelling of incense. He moved to the smaller chests on the table. In the first one, he found a stack of loose parchments with records of slave trades. In the second chest, he found a rectangular box of gray stone.

He stared at it, then lifted it from the plain wooden chest. A row of black and white inlaid stones decorated one side of the box, just as Kaspari had described. He shook it and felt something heavy shift back and forth inside. He set the stone box on the table, locked the chest, and returned the keys to the clamshell, snapping it shut.

The door handle rattled. Teleo turned and drew his fox-and-hare cloak about himself and pulled the hood down over his brow as the door swung open. A tall, lean form stood in the doorway. It took Teleo a moment to recognize Henrik. His gray hair had thinned, and his posture had grown more stooped since the last time Teleo had seen the elder Stagga.

Henrik stepped inside and peered around the dimly lit room. Teleo stood stone-still, his embroidered cloak the same dusky grays and browns as the shadowy storage room. Henrik's eyes narrowed and landed on Teleo.

"Stone Guardian!" Henrik bellowed over his shoulder out the open door. "Stone Guardian!"

Teleo grabbed the stone box and clambered over and around chests and tables, intent on escaping through the nearest wall before help arrived. Teleo dodged a small dart whizzing through the air from Henrik's hand, and then another. A third dart landed with a thunk in Teleo's shoulder armor. Teleo threw the stone box at Henrik, the corner of the box hitting the king in the forehead. Henrik stumbled backwards, landing against the door and slamming it shut. Teleo leapt onto the old man and grabbed his wrist as Henrik struggled to throw another dart clutched in his fingers. Teleo twisted Henrik's arm behind his back and threw his weight against him, pressing the wiry man against the wooden door and wrenching his arm until he dropped the dart.

Another dart appeared in Henrik's free hand—the dart's tip was stained a dark purple. Teleo tackled Henrik to the ground, kneeing him in the back as the king writhed and twisted, face down, trying to stab Teleo's leg with the poison dart. Teleo pulled the axe from his belt and with a single heavy blow, severed Henrik's hand. Henrik shrieked and the poison dart rolled to the floor and into a fresh pool of blood. Teleo dropped the axe and grabbed Henrik's head with one hand and his chin with the other, and with a knee between the old man's shoulder blades, wrenched Henrik's head in one swift motion, breaking his neck with a loud crunch. Henrik gave a final heave, then grew limp.

Footsteps pounded outside the door, and the handle rattled and turned. Teleo shoved the dead body against the door, grabbed the stone box and his axe, and then backed away. The door pushed open and Gerik squeezed through, with two large men shouldering their way in behind him and more mustering in the hallway.

Teleo took another step back. His hood had fallen away, and Gerik stared at him and then down at his dead father.

Teleo raised his axe to confront him, then thought better of it as a half-dozen armed men pushed into the room behind Gerik and his two henchmen. Gerik grimaced at Teleo as he and his men drew their swords and moved forward to pen Teleo in between the tables and the back wall. Teleo swept statuettes and candelabra off the tables, sending them to the floor between himself and Gerik. One of Gerik's men pelted Teleo with helmets and skulls from the shelves—bronze, steel, bone—bouncing off Teleo's axe and gauntlets as he ducked and backed away. Gerik raised his sword and roared in anger and grief, charging at Teleo.

Teleo turned and ran, crossing the room in two long strides, and launched himself at the back wall. The solid stone enveloped him with its cold embrace, muffling sound and slowing down time as he entered another realm. Then he was scrabbling, his limbs flailing, swimming through the air as he fell from the second story and landed in a roll onto the shimmering pattern of the Heliotrope. He ran at the urn, body-slammed it away from the center stone, and then jumped feet-first through the Sun Circle.

Teleo landed in a sprawled heap at the feet of Sigrid, Larissa, and Dinsmora, who stood around the Sun Circle of Larissa's Heliotrope, staring down at him. He lay there, stunned for a moment, then rose on shaky legs, holstering his axe and wiping sweat from his brow.

Kaspari, Jessum, and Jarnsmidt had been dancing the sword around the outer rings, and stopped, crossing the Heliotrope to join them in the center. Teleo gazed down at the glowing Sun Circle, panting and worrying that Gerik might chase him through the stone. But no, the likelihood of Gerik having ever set foot in Larissa's Heliotrope chamber was close to none.

Teleo knelt down and looked through the Angel Wings marble. The Royal Garden came into focus. The pear tree overhung the terrace, and the dragonfly had been joined by a second one. They flitted about, their sapphire-blue bodies and gossamer wings gleaming like jewels in the sunshine. The urn lay on its side at the edge of the Heliotrope. Gerik and his men came into view, running into the yard and circling about in confusion. Some began beating at the bushes with their swords while others ran towards the archway gate.

Teleo got to his feet and stepped away from the Sun Circle.

"Here you go, Your Highness," Teleo said, bowing and handing Kaspari the stone box.

"You found it!" she cried, taking the box and clutching it to her chest.

"What's this?" Dinsmora asked, putting her hand to his shoulder.

Lodged in his steel spaulder was a dart, having pierced his embroidered cloak through the eye of a fox.

"Careful," he said. "I think it's tipped in poison."

Dinsmora jiggled it free and smelled the purple tip. "Labridinium," she said. "Deadly."

"I was lucky, then, I guess," Teleo said, and smiled at Sigrid, who clutched his arm and gazed up at him with concern. "I'm fine," he said, kissing her forehead. "Thanks to your father's armor."

Jarnsmidt lifted his nose proudly. "Told you so," he said.

"Did you kill Gerik?" Kaspari asked.

"Yeah, Teleo," Jessum chimed in. "Did you kill Gerik?"

"No," Teleo said, shaking his head at the disappointed teenagers. "But I did kill Henrik."

"His father?" Jessum asked.

Teleo nodded.

"So, that means," Kaspari said, her face growing pale, "that Gerik is now king?"

Teleo's eyes locked onto hers, and his blood ran cold.

———————◆———————

They sat around the table in Larissa's library, trying to open the stone box.

"My mother used to press these black and white squares in a certain combination," Kaspari said, pressing her fingers against the side of the box.

"But what combination?" Teleo asked. There were five white squares alternating with five black squares. If multi-finger combinations were possible, then they would never crack the code.

They tried all evening, passing it around the table for everyone to try.

"Can't we just smash it?" Jessum asked.

"No," Kaspari said, shaking her head. "It's Stone Guardian magic. It cannot be broken."

The box made its way back to Kaspari and she handed it to Teleo. "It's up to you, Teleo. Do that stone trick of yours."

Teleo tightened his lips and hefted the box. He didn't know how to do it—but he hadn't known how to walk through walls, either.

He set the box on the table and pressed his hands against it. The stone was cold and solid. He closed his eyes and relaxed, willing his hands to melt into the gray stone, but nothing happened. He opened his eyes and struck the box with his fist. He hugged the box. He put it on the floor and jumped on it. He threw it against the wall. It bounced to the stone floor, landing on its side, the black and white squares facing up and mocking him.

He took the box and went by himself into Larissa's Heliotrope chamber. He sat cross-legged on the floor at the outer edge of the Heliotrope with the box in his lap and thought.

He held the falcon talisman between his fingers. The diamond and hematite beads were safely sealed inside. He thought back on the Stone Guardian crone who had formed a wall of stone before his eyes. He dug into his pants pocket and fished out the rock chip that he always carried around with him and turned it over in his palm. It was the same grayish-blue argillite as the box. She had been able to make the stone wall on the Falcon's Nest cliff appear and disappear. But how?

The crone had so much power in her cloak, covered in dozens of hematite beads swirling in a sea of spirals—but he had only seven beads in a single spiral. He needed to get more beads, but then he would need the same amount of diamonds to balance them out. Or maybe he could amplify the talisman's power somehow.

He set the box in the center of the Sun Circle, unclasped the gold chain from around his neck, and placed the falcon talisman on top of the box. Then he removed his boots, stepped bare-footed onto the shimmering Heliotrope mosaic, unsheathed his two Mage's Blades, and danced.

Heart Fire and Black Lightning flashed and cut through the air as Teleo leapt and turned. The floor turned with him, glowing with a pale silvery light and lifting him off his feet. He flipped backwards and forwards, filled with the familiar exhilarating rush. An untold amount of time passed until finally the turning Heliotrope slowed and Teleo landed softly on his feet, dizzy and elated.

Sitting in the center of the Sun Circle was a thick leather-bound book. He approached it on tiptoes, afraid of disturbing the magic. The leather cover was dry and cracked. Embossed in faded gold script were three simple words: *Royal Mage Lineage*. On the cover below the letters rested his falcon talisman. A pair of embroidered black eyes stared up at him, sending shivers up his spine. Teleo hung the talisman from his neck, picked up the heavy book, and gazed, transfixed, at the floor. A Heliotrope amulet sat on the Angel Wings marble, where it had been hidden by the thick tome, nestled on a coil of gold-link chain.

Teleo picked up the unexpected treasure with trembling fingers. The amulet was a perfect miniature mosaic of the mystical pattern. Its micro-tesserae were worn smooth with age, and Teleo imagined the years of use it must have seen, rubbed between Mages' fingers for generations, to have achieved such a soft sheen. He turned it over, and on the back, the gold setting was engraved with an exquisitely detailed image of an elk's head with branch-like antlers. Teleo swallowed and pocketed the amulet.

He returned to the library and plunked the book onto the table in front of Kaspari, sending up a small puff of dust.

"You did it!" she cried, placing her palm on the cover. "How did you open the box?"

"I don't quite know," he said sheepishly.

"Where is the box?" she asked.

He shrugged his shoulders. "I don't know that, either. I just hope it doesn't come back before you find what you need."

She knit her eyebrows together and opened the book.

It did not take her long to find the section detailing the lineage of Abaris. They set the two books side by side. The dates and names in the *Royal Mage Lineage* were almost identical to the information in the book from Larissa's library, showing a direct line of descent from the Royal Mage Abaris to Princess Kaspari Elke.

Kaspari stood up, smoothed her silk skirts, and pulled her seed pearl cloak around her shoulders. "So, now," she said, "I will prove to you that I can travel."

She turned to Teleo and held out her hand.

He sighed, took the Elke Heliotrope amulet from his pocket, and placed the family heirloom in her open palm. "This was in the box, too," he said.

Kaspari gaped at it, turning it over and examining the engraving. Tears pooled in her eyes. "It was?" she asked, turning her gaze to Teleo. Everyone else looked on curiously, and he nodded.

"Yes," he said, wondering silently if Queen Eleanor had known its purpose. "It's yours," he said gently. She hugged him, and he felt guilty for having prohibited her from traveling this entire year.

They followed Kaspari to Larissa's Heliotrope chamber, and Dinsmora lagged behind with Teleo.

"I'm still worried," Dinsmora said. "Are you sure we should let her try this?"

Teleo rested his hand on his cousin's shoulder. "We can't

shelter her forever," he said. "She needs to step into her power sooner or later. The books and the Heliotrope amulet are sure signs that she is descended from Mages."

"But what if she disappears and never comes back?" Dinsmora asked.

Unbidden, Bella-Mae's and his little Abigail's faces filled Teleo's vision. He wiped at his eye. "Life is short, Dinsmora. If she really is a Mage, she will need training. That might be her best chance at survival in this world. If she hides away as a pampered monarch, she might end up locked in a tower, like so many other royal women, while her husband takes the throne and forces her to bear his children."

Dinsmora's eyes grew round. "That would be horrible."

"Yes, it would be. Come on," he said, patting her hand, which had slipped into the crook of his elbow.

Kaspari was waiting with the others, standing on the Down in the Deep rays surrounding the Sun Circle, her amulet glimmering from where it hung on her bodice.

"I will travel to Larissa's battle yard," Kaspari announced.

"Wait for her there," Teleo said, gesturing at Jarnsmidt, Jessum, and Dinsmora.

Jarnsmidt went first, then Jessum, then Dinsmora, each entering the Sun Circle and disappearing.

"Take your shoes off," Sigrid suggested to Kaspari. "I always feel the connection more strongly that way."

Kaspari removed her pointed satin slippers and stepped barefooted onto the Sun Circle.

Teleo hugged her and then backed away. He joined Sigrid and Larissa, and they took up their swords and danced.

Within two circuits around the mosaic, the Heliotrope was spinning and glowing. Sigrid, Larissa, and Teleo were floating, and their swords were shafts of light. Next time Teleo looked, Kaspari was gone.

They settled onto the floor and knelt around the Sun Circle, peering through the Angel Wings marble into the battle yard.

Jessum, Dinsmora, and Jarnsmidt were standing around the Sun Circle on the other side, waiting.

Teleo, Sigrid, and Larissa exchanged alarmed glances, then leaned over and looked again.

"How long does it take?" Larissa asked.

They glanced at one another. They all knew it took no time at all to travel from one Heliotrope to another.

Teleo sat back on his heels. His heart was thundering and he was having trouble breathing. He stood up and paced around the Heliotrope, guilt and panic threatening to overwhelm him.

"We must keep dancing," Sigrid said.

She was right.

They danced again. The spinning, glowing Heliotrope lifted them off their feet and steadied Teleo's galloping pulse. He closed his eyes and danced, thinking of Kaspari's golden-brown eyes and teasing grin. Her stubborn chin and proud posture. Her inquiring mind and love of history. Her detailed sketches and the finch and dragonfly tiles she had made. How she rode Daisy better than he ever had and could hit an archery target across a windswept field. How she loved animals and cared for Jessum as though he were her brother. What would Abigail have been like if she had lived to be Kaspari's age? The love for Abigail he'd kept dammed up inside he had let flow for Kaspari. If she died, he was not sure he could withstand the grief. Tears streamed from his eyes as he flipped through the air, twisting and turning, not wanting to land.

After a few minutes, they stopped and rushed to the Sun Circle again. Dinsmora, Jessum, and Jarnsmidt were pacing nervously on the other side. Teleo knelt down and pressed his hands onto the polished Angel Wings marble, closed his eyes, and traveled to the battle yard.

He stood up and stepped off the Sun Circle in the open-air yard. "We've lost her," Teleo said, and pulled Dinsmora into his arms. "She left not long after you did, but she's not here."

Jessum joined them and they clung together.

"We had to let her try," Dinsmora said into his shoulder.

"We shouldn't have let her," Jessum said, his voice cracking.

"It's my fault," Teleo said. He should have known better than to let a young teenager make such a big decision. He held Jessum and Dinsmora, trying to be strong as they crumpled in his arms.

"We need to read the manuscript again," Sigrid said, appearing at his side, followed by Larissa.

"Yes, I'll go back and get it," Larissa said. "We must have read it wrong. There must be some mistake. Some explanation."

Larissa and Sigrid joined their group hug.

"We can't give up," Sigrid said.

"Kaspari!" Jarnsmidt said.

They broke their hug and turned.

Kaspari was kneeling on the Sun Circle, her head hanging down. She rose unsteadily to her feet and staggered off the center stone. Jarnsmidt caught her by the arm.

"What happened?" Sigrid cried, rushing to Kaspari and helping Jarnsmidt prop her up.

Teleo and the others hurried over as she slumped down and sat on the Heliotrope, holding her head.

"I got lost," she said, rubbing her skull. "I was thinking about how warm the stones were under my feet, just like when I used to sit around the table in Queen Valona's sewing chamber, and then suddenly I was there. Only, I hit my head on the table and it hurt and I was kind of dizzy. So I waited there for a little while."

Teleo sighed with relief. "Was Cutter there?"

"No. But it stank like sour ale."

Teleo burst out laughing, relief flooding through him.

"What took you so long?" Jessum asked.

"I was so tired and my head hurt, and I couldn't really dance around the Heliotrope because the big sewing table was there. It was too heavy to move. So finally, I just knelt underneath the table on the Sun Circle and thought of the battle yard, and here I am."

She lifted her hands and smiled. "See? I am a Mage."

Teleo, Dinsmora, and Sigrid exchanged concerned glances.

Sigrid furrowed her brow and said, "Okay. But you must be able to go where you want, not somewhere by mistake."

"Yeah," Teleo said. "What if you had thought about your garden at Verdant Palace and landed in Gerik's court? Remember that urn in the middle of the garden? I almost hit my head on that too. You could have been knocked out for Gerik to snatch you up."

Kaspari frowned. "I'll be more careful."

Teleo locked gazes with Dinsmora, who grimaced in a sort of painful surrender. The river of life had taken hold of Kaspari and would not let her go.

Teleo mirrored Dinsmora's helpless expression and turned to Kaspari. "Let's practice, then, young Mage," he said. "Meet me back in Larissa's chamber. I'll go first."

Kaspari nodded, and Teleo stepped onto the Sun Circle and immediately arrived in Larissa's tower. He stepped off the Angel Wings marble and folded his arms, staring at the translucent white circle.

A few too many seconds passed, setting his heart racing, but Kaspari appeared in the next breath, smiling proudly.

"See? I did it," she said.

"Well done," he said. "Now meet me in Sigrid's tower. Do you remember how that Sun Circle feels?"

"Of course I do," she said. "I'll go first."

Before he could object, Kaspari was gone.

He took in a deep breath, stepped onto the Sun Circle, and waited a few seconds for her to vacate the center stone—he hoped she remembered to move aside. He thought of Sigrid's tower, and then he was there, the amber and lemon verbena scent of Sigrid filling his head. Kaspari stood on a Down in the Deep ray, hopping up and down on her toes.

"I did it!" she said, grinning widely.

"Yes, you did. Good job." Teleo knelt and looked into the battle yard. Five faces stared back at him.

"Where are you?" Sigrid asked. "Oh, in my chamber. Is Kaspari there? Oh, there she is. Did she go there by mistake again?"

Kaspari knelt beside him, squinting down at the stone.

"No," Teleo said. "We came here on purpose."

"It's all blurry," Kaspari said, rubbing at the marble as though trying to wipe fog from a mirror. "And I don't hear anything. Are you talking to somebody?"

"Yes, I'm talking with Sigrid," he said. "You're just starting out, Kaspari. You'll be able to see and hear later."

Kaspari looked up at him, beaming, and said, "See, Teleo? I really am a Mage."

◆

They gathered in Larissa's Heliotrope chamber in the pre-dawn of the Summer Solstice. Everyone wore a cloak of one sort or another. Teleo was in his fox-and-hare cloak, Jessum in his falcon cloak, Kaspari in her ivory satin with seed pearls, and Dinsmora in Sonderson's homespun, which she had embroidered with owls and bats, mice and lizards, snails and snakes. Sigrid was in a cape of red velvet edged with ermine, Jarnsmidt was in the crimson minister's cloak Teleo had stolen and the old man quite fancied, and the empress wore her imperial mantle, a bold velvet patchwork of red, white, and gold griffins.

One by one, they left through the Sun Circle for their Heliotropes: Jessum to the armory, Sigrid to her tower, Kaspari to Larissa's battle yard, and Jarnsmidt to a Heliotrope in an abandoned tower he knew of at Green Flag fortress.

Teleo and Dinsmora prepared to travel to Trillifort. Dinsmora went first, then Teleo knelt and peered through the Angel Wings marble into Cutter's chamber. He saw Dinsmora on her knees underneath the table. When she moved aside, he joined her there and crawled out between chair legs, gray light leaking in through the windows. The table was littered with ale mugs and tobacco pipes, the sour stench lingering in the air. A suit of Cutter-sized armor gleamed softly in the corner.

Teleo and Dinsmora silently slid the bolts to lock the doors to the hallway and bedchamber, then moved the chairs and heavy table to the edges of the room. Teleo nodded at Dinsmora and then sat cross-legged on the Sun Circle. He closed his eyes and in the next breath, the squeak of bats and a cold draft welcomed him to the Third Tower.

Two bats swooped in as Teleo stood and pivoted slowly, surveying the dim room. He missed this place. The solitude. The exuberant sword dancing. The secret times with Sigrid. He took a candle from his pocket, lit it from his tinderbox, and placed it in the candleholder on the mantelpiece. He then quickly swept the mosaic, working his way outwards from the Angel Wings marble and rays of Down in the Deep, across the perfectly interlocking tesserae of triangles and diamonds and petals of every color.

Teleo set aside the broom and unsheathed Heart Fire and Black Lightning. He slowly paced counterclockwise around the flowing vortex, getting caught up in its waves and currents. Soon he was twirling and leaping, swords cutting through the cool mountain air. Sunlight flashed orange through the Focal Point window, and the golden beam of solstice sun hit the white stone wall, bright and round like a full moon. Teleo's pulse thrummed and he danced into the ray of light and let it warm his face, then stepped forward with it as it descended down the wall and crossed the floor.

Teleo stood in the center of the Sun Circle, arms and swords spread wide, when the sunbeam hit the center stone with a blinding burst, illuminating the entire Heliotrope chamber. Teleo's body was a torch, lit white and gold from within. He floated off the floor and danced in the shaft of light. Seconds stretched to infinity, and suddenly he was flying through the tower walls and past shimmering gems of water particles vibrating in the sky. He soared above the white towers of Trillifort and over the Blue Mountain peaks, still capped in snow and painted pink by the sunrise. He flew over the western foothills, pelted by the glittering essence of the Summer Solstice sun raining down like jewels and hail-fire. He rode a current to the waving banners of Red Flag and found Sigrid floating above her tower, gazing up at the heavens.

They recognized each other in their bodies turned to sunlight, dancing in the solar wind. They were formed of millions of dew-like diamond points reflecting every color of the rainbow, flowing into the shapes and pathways of skin and hair, bones and blood, heart and mind. They swirled and dove around each other, sparring with swords of light. Heart Fire and Black

Lightning clashed with Raven's Blood in a shower of sparks. Teleo danced with Sigrid until the beam of light returned him to Trillifort's Third Tower and dropped him gently onto the Angel Wings marble. He stepped forward with the golden sunray as it retreated across the shimmering Heliotrope and then finally disappeared.

Teleo staggered backwards against the tower wall, the air rushing from his lungs as a wave of dizziness took him to the floor. He collapsed onto his side and gazed across the glistening tesserae, the vibrating stones settling and quieting until the mosaic was still and its colors faded to shades of gray. More gray washed across his vision—an incoming tide, rising and drawing back, wiping smooth his mind. He succumbed to the waves, closed his eyes, and slept.

"Teleo. *Teleo.*" Sigrid's voice was soft and urgent.

Teleo cracked open his eyelids. "Hi," he murmured.

"Are you okay?" Sigrid asked, shaking his shoulder.

"Yeah, why?" He sat up and rubbed his eyes.

"I was afraid you died or something," she said, and moved into the circle of his arms.

"No," he said, smoothing her hair. "I must have fallen asleep. We danced together in the solstice sun. Do you remember?" he asked.

She lifted her head and wrinkled her forehead. "I think so. Were we in the sky? Flying like gyrfalcons?"

"Yes, indeed," he said, chuckling. "Like dragonflies. How long have I been passed out?"

"It's only been a few minutes," she said, kissing his cheek.

"Oh, no," he said, pushing himself to his feet and giving Sigrid a hand up. "I've got to go help Dinsmora. Meet me back at Larissa's tower." He grabbed his swords from the floor, blew out the candle, and strode over to the Sun Circle, sheathing his blades and dropping to his knees.

Teleo focused his mind on Cutter's Heliotrope chamber and looked through the stone circle. The murkiness cleared and the view widened until he could see Cutter's entire room as though it were a reflection inside an empty brass goblet. Dinsmora was still dancing around the outer rings of the Heliotrope in a swaying trance. He stood and waved to Sigrid as he left the Third Tower. Suddenly, he was in the room with Dinsmora. He held his breath and listened briefly—there were no sounds from Cutter's bedchamber or the hallway.

"Dinsmora," he hissed softly.

She stopped dancing and gazed across the room at him, her eyes dreamy. "That was amazing. Why didn't you tell me about this last year? I'm mad at you," she said quietly. A drunken, dimpled smile creased her freckled cheeks. "What do you think would happen if I laid embroidery stitches in the Summer Solstice sun?" she asked.

"A Mage's Shroud stitched in a Heliotrope's solstice sun could quite possibly render you completely invisible," he guessed. He returned her gaze, intrigued by the possibilities. "Come on, we should go," he whispered, and walked over to the table.

They arranged the furniture as they had found it, and Teleo arrayed Cutter's collection of pipes in a circle with the shanks and lips pointing outward like sunrays, just to mess with him. Dinsmora sat under the table in the Sun Circle and disappeared. Teleo crept to the two doors and quietly unbarred them, then crawled under the table and traveled to Larissa's battle yard.

Kaspari was still dancing around the Heliotrope, enraptured. She stopped dancing and rushed over to him, grinning. He hugged her, grateful to be holding her solid, living body.

They traveled to Sigrid's tower and then ran to the armory. Jessum was still hammering steel on an anvil next to a mobile forge they had wheeled onto the armory's Sun Circle. Jarnsmidt was already there, instructing him. Jessum became aware of them standing there and put aside the folded steel, wiping soot-black sweat from his brow.

"Hi, Kaspari—glad you survived, little sister," the young Drake Bedon said, his eyes bright. "Hey, Teleo. Guess what? The steel in my hand melted into a shaft of light."

"It did?" Teleo asked.

"You don't believe me?" Jessum asked, holstering his hammer.

"Oh, I believe you," Teleo assured him.

"Yeah, it was golden, like a ray of sunshine, and it was hot and cold at the same time," Jessum said, and continued describing it as they wheeled the forge to its normal spot.

Jessum and Jarnsmidt cleaned off the Sun Circle, setting aside Jessum's Mage's steel for later, and then they all took turns returning to Larissa's Heliotrope. Larissa was beaming, telling them how she had worn her gold circlet and it had shone like a halo. Jarnsmidt said he had felt strong as an ox in the shaft of light, like when he was twenty. He did look a bit younger, Teleo had to admit.

"Come," Larissa said, holding out her hands.

They stood around her Heliotrope's Sun Circle. Sigrid reached for Teleo's hand, and Dinsmora reached for his other one. Dinsmora held Kaspari's hand, who reached for Jessum's, who clasped Jarnsmidt's, who held Larissa's, who held Sigrid's. The moment their circle was complete, the Heliotrope ignited in a soft, incandescent glow.

"Ooooh," Kaspari said, and Jessum laughed.

His laughter was contagious, and soon they were all laughing. The harder they laughed, the brighter the magical circle glowed, sending them into a hysterical fit. Dinsmora's hand slipped from Teleo's, and the glow subsided. Their laughter cut off.

"What happened?" Kaspari asked.

Teleo and Dinsmora grabbed hands, closing the circle again, and the glow returned. They experimented and confirmed it glowed brightest when all seven were joined together.

"Sigrid makes it really glow when she dances," Teleo bragged.

"She certainly does," Dinsmora agreed. "Will you dance for us?"

They stepped aside, and Sigrid danced the sword. The more exuberantly she danced, the brighter the Sun Circle glowed. Dinsmora joined in, then Larissa, and soon, all seven were dancing and leaping. The Heliotrope turned and the entire mosaic shone with brilliant colors. Teleo floated above the undulating pattern with the others. A white and gold cloud swirled and rose around them, lifting them together in a luminescent orb. They twirled in the air, cloaks fluttering, swords flashing, flying in a slowly spinning globe of light.

RETURN OF THE MAGES

By Kaspari Elke, Verdant Valley's Queen-in-Exile,
The Second Year of Empress Larissa's Reign

Kingdoms may fall, but the blood of the Mages still flows
Through mountains, hills, and vales.

The Mages will rise from ancient thrones,
There will be seven, as in days of old.

First, a daughter who dances the sword amidst flame and forge,
And travels the realm in search of her brothers' bones.

Second, the father who turns stone into steel,
His crystalline blades of light transformed.

Third, wife of a slain ruler and wed to his slayer,
Who locks her in a tower where she plots his death.

Fourth, a young girl who dances with dragonflies,
Saved by her mother's pear tree and vowing revenge.

Fifth, a young blacksmith stolen from his home,
Whose red blood flows with the rivers of the lost lands.

Sixth, a woman who communes with animals and plants,
And weaves magic with her fingertips.

Seventh, a grieving soldier who learns the magic of stone,
And brings balance to forces that would kill him.

We may die, but the blood of the Mages still flows,
Through mountains, hills, and vales.

The Mages will rise from ancient thrones,
There will be seven, as in days of old.

ᴛʜᴇ ᴇɴᴅ

Also from Palmer Pickering

Moon Deeds

Star Children Saga: One

An award-winning adult science-fantasy adventure

Twins Cassidy and Torr must save Earth from a ruthless enemy at a time when the only force more powerful than alien technology is magic. Moon Deeds launches the siblings' journey across the galaxy, where they must learn their power as the Star Children, claim their shamanic heritage, and battle dark forces that threaten humankind.

"Intelligent, high science fiction at its finest."

-Asher Syed for Readers' Favorite

The Saga Continues

Light Fighters

Star Children Saga: Two

Sequel to *Moon Deeds*

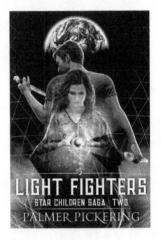

Cassidy and Torr are trying to survive on the moon while facing threats from all sides. As their shamanic heritage surfaces and they hone their magical skills, they are hunted for their power, escalating into a tension-filled game of cat and mouse.

"This is some high-level badassery."

-Shreya, Goodreads

CPSIA information can be obtained
at www.ICGtesting.com
Printed in the USA
JSHW022338150623
43254JS00005B/1